IT TAKES MORE THAN GOOD GRADES TO GRADUATE FROM CENTRAL ACADEMY . . .

Discover the chilling adventures that shadow the halls and stalk the students of
TERROR ACADEMY!

LIGHTS OUT

Mandy Roberts digs up the suspicious past of the new assistant principal. The man her widowed mother plans to marry . . .

STALKER

A tough punk comes back to Central with one requirement to complete: vengeance . . .

SIXTEEN CANDLES

Kelly Langdon discovers there's more to being popular than she thought—like staying alive . . .

SPRING BREAK

It's the vacation from hell. And it's up to Laura Hollister to save her family. And herself . . .

THE NEW KID

There's something about the new transfer student. He's got a deadly secret . . .

continued . . .

STUDENT BODY

No one's safe at Central—
when a killer roams the halls . . .

NIGHT SCHOOL

The most handsome teacher in school . . .
is a vampire!

SCIENCE PROJECT

There's a new formula for terror:
E = mc scared . . .

THE PROM

It's a party that could raise the dead . . .

THE IN CROWD

A group of misfits learn a deadly lesson:
if you don't fit in, you may be out—
for good!

This book also contains a preview of the next exciting book in the TERROR ACADEMY series by Nicholas Pine:
BREAKING UP

Dedicated To Donna Urey
and the Staff of Whitebirch Booksellers

SUMMER SCHOOL

ONE

On a warm day in May, Cara Richards sat in study hall, gazing out the window. Her dark green eyes peered out at the expanse of the Central Academy campus, most of which was visible from the cafeteria where the study hall was held. Cara sighed and ran a hand through her auburn hair. Her smooth, pretty face wore an expression of worry. She dreaded the task that lay ahead of her. It wasn't something that a girl wanted to do on a spring day, when spring fever and the promise of summer had gripped everyone.

Cara leaned on her hand, pressing her high cheekbone into her palm. Her full lips pouted and her posture slumped lazily in the chair. How was she going to do it? She had been thinking about it for two weeks but she hadn't found the courage.

Cara's eyes wandered over the campus again. Central Academy was a fairly new structure that had been built in the 1980s. She could see the pool dome in the distance, sitting in front of the football stadium. The rest of the school consisted of three classroom buildings, designated for sophomores, juniors and seniors. A huge library was attached to the sophomore building and the cafeteria where Cara attended study hall extended from the senior wing. As a senior, set for graduation in less than two months, Cara should have been concentrating on her English term paper. Instead, she could only dwell on her miseries—dire circumstances that came along with complications of romance.

Turning her attention away from the glorious May day, Cara glanced nervously at the clock on the wall. She would be free in thirty minutes. Free for what? she wondered. To do what she had to do, what had to be done.

Her stomach flipped and flopped as she anticipated the words she would say, that had to be said. There was no way around it. Not with summer so close. And the prom lay before her—that had to be considered. It was all so complex and disturbing; yet, she had to deal with it and the solution was all too simple.

Cara flinched when a tall woman stepped between her and the clock. Her green eyes gazed up at Mrs. Palmer, the study hall monitor. Mrs. Palmer was also her English teacher.

"Cara, are you all right?" Mrs. Palmer asked with a quizzical expression on her tight face.

Cara shrugged. "Yeah, I guess."

"You seem distracted today," Mrs. Palmer went on. "Like you're having trouble concentrating."

Cara sighed. "I'm fine."

Mrs. Palmer put her hands on her hips. "Need I remind you, Cara, that your English term paper is one half your final grade. A failure to turn it in could result in a failing score or summer school."

Cara held up her notes. "It's going to be done in time, Mrs. Palmer. I promise."

"I hope so, Cara. I hope so."

When Mrs. Palmer left to go back to the front of the room, Cara leaned on her hand and stared into space. Everyone had been on her case lately. Her teachers couldn't stop talking about the imminent graduation and her parents wouldn't stop harping about Cara going to college.

Cara sighed dejectedly. What difference did it make? Everything seemed so dark and hopeless.

"Psst!"

Cara glanced up to see Brenda Anderson on the other side of the table. Cara squinted at her as if to say, "What?" Brenda, who was a casual friend, shoved a note across the table.

After a quick look to Mrs. Palmer, who didn't

seem to notice, Cara grabbed the note and pulled it under her notebook. She felt a tightness in her chest. Who had written the note? Would it only complicate the task ahead of her?

"Psst!"

She looked at Brenda again.

Brenda gestured for her to open the note and read it.

Cara frowned. She pulled the communication from beneath her notebook and held it in her hand. After a deep breath, she unfolded the paper and scanned the large printing.

"Meet me after school at my locker. Chris."

Cara breathed easier. Chris Hall was a nice guy, her best friend in fact. She had been talking to him about what she had to do. Chris had been supportive. They had been friends since elementary school. Chris was the only one who knew about her problem, the only one she could turn to.

"Psst!"

Cara looked up at Brenda who slid another note across the table.

Cara read Brenda's writing: "Are you going to meet Chris at his locker after study hall?"

Cara focused on Brenda and nodded.

Brenda quickly scribbled something and slid it across the table.

"Do you think Chris likes me?" the note read.

Cara shrugged. Brenda was cute, button-nosed, slender. A lot of boys had asked her out but she hadn't gone steady with anyone since her sophomore year. Rumors around school had pegged Brenda as a prude who wouldn't give the boys what they wanted, a sentiment that evoked sympathy from Cara.

Brenda sent another folded paper in Cara's direction. "Would you see if you can get Chris to ask me to the prom?"

Cara blushed, feeling a bit jealous. Of course, she had no right to be jealous, since she and Chris were strictly platonic friends. Maybe her envy came with the foreknowledge that after Cara finished what she had to do, she might not have a date for the prom.

Brenda grimaced, begging with her eyes, asking, "Please!"

Cara nodded reluctantly, bringing a grin to Brenda's face. Chris was cute with his sandy hair and blue eyes. He had a kind face and a swimmer's build. He held the county record for swimming one hundred meters freestyle. Cara wondered why Chris wasn't going out with anyone. A lot of girls wanted to date him. Chris had gone steady with a few girls in his sophomore and junior years, but he had avoided dating in his senior year. Cara worried about him sometimes. When she asked Chris why he wouldn't go out with anyone, he just shrugged it off and said that the right girl hadn't come along.

"Psst."

Another note was forthcoming from Brenda.

"Thanks a lot, Cara. Chris is so cute. He's a nice guy too. Tell him I really want to go out with him."

Cara nodded, thinking that Chris *should* be with someone like Brenda. It was only natural. Somebody should be happy.

Cara sure wasn't happy.

She languished at the table, barely accomplishing anything on her term paper, despite sidelong stares of disapproval from Mrs. Palmer. Cara didn't really care about her term paper at this point. She had other things to worry about.

When the bell rang to end study hall, Cara froze.

She didn't want to do it.

But she had to. There was no way around it.

Chris Hall waited at his locker, glancing up and down the hall, looking for Cara. Chris wore jeans, a white T-shirt and a hooded sweatshirt from the swim team. His blue eyes met a longing gaze from Brenda Anderson, who strolled past his locker with a smile on her face.

Chris quickly looked away, brushing the sandy lock of hair from his forehead. He knew Brenda liked him, but he didn't care. Chris wasn't interested in Brenda.

"Hi, Chris," she called.

He just nodded and stared at the floor.

Chris had a wicked crush on Cara. He had

been in love with her for the better part of his life. In and out of love, really. They had always been friends. Sometimes he denied that he wanted to be with Cara, choosing to stay close to her as a friend.

He thought about her all the time, her reddish hair, those dark green eyes. She had a perfect face—smooth, white skin, pinkish cheeks, a thick mouth and a strong nose. Her picture graced the mirror in his room, tucked in the corner of the glass.

Chris shifted on his feet. Where was she? Had Brenda given Cara the note? He needed to see her. He needed a lot more but he wondered if it would ever come.

What would it be like to kiss her? Not as a friend, but as a *boyfriend!* Chris knew what was coming. Would this finally be his chance to go steady with Cara?

"Chris!"

His spirits soared when he heard her voice.

Cara strode toward him with a smile on her face. She looked great in her faded jeans, sneakers and the patchwork vest that she had made herself. He nearly dropped to the floor when she drew close to him and put her hand on his forearm.

"Hi," she said. "I got your note."

He smiled back, wishing he could wrap his arms around her. "How are you?"

"Not so good," she replied. "By the way,

Brenda Anderson wants to go to the prom with you."

"There's a surprise," Chris replied. "She's all over me."

Cara frowned. "Chris, I'm going to do it today."

"Really?"

Could this be true? Chris thought.

His heart pounded.

He could use this as an excuse to ask Cara to the prom.

"Have you seen him today?" Chris asked.

She sighed. "No, but he thinks we're going out tonight. He—"

"Hey, Cara! Over here."

Chris tensed. He recognized the voice.

Sean McGovern was walking toward them.

Chris held his breath. Sean was the cause of both their troubles.

And Chris wanted Sean out of the way.

TWO

Sean McGovern swaggered toward Cara and Chris with a confident grin on his handsome face. He was tall, six feet three inches, with black hair, brown eyes and an athletic build. During the basketball season Sean had led Central Academy to the state finals where they lost to Durham by a single point.

Sean stopped in front of them and put his hands on his hips, scowling at Chris. "Hey, look here. It's my girlfriend and her shadow, Chris Hall."

Chris blushed and looked away. "Hello, Sean."

Cara sighed. "Hi, Sean."

Sean kept glaring at Chris. "Hall, how come every time I find my girlfriend, you're with her?"

Chris tensed, focusing his eyes on Sean, glaring back. "We're just friends, Sean."

Cara stiffened, hoping they could avoid a fight. "Yes," she told Sean, "we're just friends."

Sean made a face. "Ooh, Chris is the kind of guy who likes to hang out with girls."

"Bite it, McGovern!" Chris snapped.

Sean raised a fist. "You want some of this, sister-boy?"

Chris started to move toward him. "Let's do it—"

Cara stepped in between them. "That's enough! Stop it. I don't want you fighting like a couple of apes!"

Chris eased back. "Whatever you say, Cara. But he started it. I was just—"

Sean pointed at him. "You couldn't take me the best day you lived, jerk-face!"

"Don't bet on it," Chris challenged.

"Hey, why don't you go for a swim in the pool?" Sean replied. "You're all wet anyway!"

"Enough!" Cara cried. "Both of you."

Sean and Chris just stood there for a moment, locked in a wide-eyed staring match.

Cara shook her head. "What is this, anyway? Raw meat day at the jungle cage?"

Chris grabbed her forearm. "Come on, Cara. Let's get out of here right now."

Sean snorted. "She's not going anywhere with you, loser-boy."

"Shut up!" Cara insisted. "You're both acting like cavemen!"

Chris drew back. "I'm outta here!"

He started off in the other direction, storming down the hall.

Cara called to him. "Wait, Chris!" She took a step toward Chris, but Sean pulled her back.

"Let him go, sweetcakes," Sean said. "You and I have to spend some time together. We have a lot of talking to do."

Cara wriggled to get out of his grip. "Let go of me!"

Sean held her tightly, pushing her against the wall of lockers. "What's wrong? Don't tell me you're falling for that swim-team sissy. He's a wimp!"

Cara glared at him with her angry green eyes. "I told you, he's just a friend."

Sean eased off a little, letting go of her. "That's more like it. I don't mind you hanging out with a guy who doesn't like girls. He's a—"

"It's not like that," Cara insisted. "We've been friends for a long time, Sean."

Sean chortled. "Yeah, I bet, played with dolls and everything since you were both little girls."

Cara shook her head, sighing. "You just don't have a clue, do you, Sean?"

His lip curled and his eyes grew narrow. "How about a kiss, sweetcakes? A little lippage for your man."

"Sean—"

But his face came toward her, imposing and expectant. Cara tried to turn her head away. Sean grabbed her chin, spinning her toward him. His lips pressed against her mouth. Cara resisted, squirming until he drew away.

"What's wrong?" Sean asked. "Didn't I put enough tongue in it?"

Cara grimaced. "Is that all you think about, Sean?"

He leaned forward, pinning her with his weight. "Hey, you know it's been coming. You want it too."

"No, Sean. We have to talk."

"Talk!" he said. "That's all you do is talk. When am I going to see a little action?"

"Please, Sean," she said in a soft voice. "Let's talk."

He stepped back, throwing out his hands. "Okay, talk away. Talk all you want."

"Not here," Cara replied. "Not in the hallway. Let's go into one of the classrooms."

Sean offered a leering smile, like he figured something good was going to happen. "In one of the rooms, eh? Okay, sure. I can get behind that."

They ducked into the first available classroom, which was the empty biology lab. Cara hadn't wanted to air her dirty laundry in the hallway. Some students stayed after school for extracurricular activities. Cara didn't want an audience when she finally got up the courage to break up with Sean. It had been a long time coming. She had to follow through now. There was no way she could stay with him, not with Sean pressuring her so much.

Make it quick and painless, Chris had told her. *Just tell him and get it over with.*

Cara leaned against a lab table, but Sean was right there, trapping her in his arms, pressing his body into her.

"Let's talk about this," Sean said, lowering his lips to kiss her.

Cara fought him. "No, Sean. Don't—"

"I thought you wanted it," he insisted. "I thought you wanted to be alone."

"To talk!" she cried. "Sean—"

He held her tightly. "No talk, baby. Play!"

He's making it easy for me, Cara thought. *Real easy!*

"Sean—"

"You know what I want, baby. It's been coming. You aren't going to tease me anymore."

Cara gave a hard push with her arms. "Sean, stop!"

He glared at her. "What!"

An angry expression covered her smooth face, igniting her green eyes. "You jerk! It's over, Sean. Finished. The lights are out, the party's over."

A dumb look cross his countenance. "Huh?"

When his body went slack, Cara moved away from him, slipping to the other side of the lab table. "I'm breaking up with you, Sean. You're a jerk and I don't want to hang out with you anymore, much less go steady with you."

His brow fretted and his mouth hung open a little. "Breaking up? Nah!" He shook his head.

Cara felt her courage growing. "We're finished, you knuckle-dragging dweeb. Over. Through."

Sean blushed. "You can't do this."

"Watch me."

His body began to tremble. "No way, you little tease. You've been leading me on all semester. You owe me!"

"Owe you? That's sick, Sean. I don't owe you anything!"

He shook his head slowly. "I can't believe it. I've wasted all this time with you."

Cara hesitated. "Wasted time?"

He laughed derisively. "You think I really cared about you, honey? I just wanted you because you have a great face and a tight body. You're good enough to be with me."

Cara exhaled. "Wow, how did I ever care about a shallow guy like you?"

"Shallow? What's that supposed to mean?"

"No depth, Sean. If you knew about the dictionary you could look it up yourself."

He shrugged. "Who cares about depth? I'm good-looking, I'm buff. I made the grades to get a basketball scholarship to State. You oughtta bow down and worship me, babe."

"Forget it, Sean. We're finished."

He said, "Not so fast, babe. I'm not letting you walk out on me like this."

"Watch me."

She started for the door of the biology lab.

Sean moved with catlike agility and quickness, leaping to catch her by the arms.

"Let go of me!" Cara cried.

"No way, you little tease. You're gonna give me what I want. What I've been waiting for."

He tried to kiss her.

Cara lifted her knee, trying to kick him in the groin.

Sean avoided the blow. "So, you like it rough, huh?"

"I'm going to scream!" Cara threatened.

"Go ahead," Sean told her. "Nobody is gonna hear you."

Cara opened her mouth.

Sean drew back, striking her with the flat of his hand. The blow stung Cara's cheek, preventing her from screaming. She staggered away from him.

Sean shouted at her, "Tease!"

"No, please—"

"You want some more of this?"

Cara shook her head. "No."

"Then get down on the floor and shut your mouth!"

"Please, don't—"

Sean balled up his fist. "I'll smash you, Cara! I'll beat you unless you do what I say."

A paralyzing fear swept over Cara. He was no longer an obnoxious ex-boyfriend. The gleam in Sean's eyes told her that he had become a monster.

And there didn't seem to be any way to escape him.

THREE

Cara started to inch backward toward the open window behind her. The warm breeze blew into the classroom, surrounding her in a pocket of balmy air. If she could dive out the window, she could run to safety. It was broad daylight. There'd be someone around to see Sean if he chased her.

Sean took a deep breath as he stalked his prey. "You know, I was almost ready to like you, Cara. When I'd see you out there on the basketball court, spinning around in your cheerleader uniform, I'd think that I could really care about you. But you've been a big disappointment to me."

"How have I been a disappointment to you?" Cara replied, stalling for time. "Go on, tell me."

Sean laughed. "Oh, you know, honey. You

know what I've been waiting for. And you know what's coming next. Don't you?"

The wall was only a couple of feet away. Cara felt the air on her skin as it flowed through the casement. It would have to be one quick movement. Her body might hit the ground with a hard thud, but it was better than facing Sean. After all, the drop was only from the first floor. It wouldn't kill her. But Sean might!

"What do you want from me?" she asked, shuffling her feet closer to the wall. "I never did anything bad to you, Sean. Why do you want to hurt me?"

Sean grinned at her. "It's not gonna hurt. It's gonna feel real good, honey. Now, you just—hey!"

Cara made her move. She darted toward the open window. Her head burst through the casement, emerging in the spring air. But before she could fall to safety, she felt Sean's hand on her ankle. He had caught her before she could escape.

"No!"

Sean pulled her back into the biology lab. As Cara's body fell, she caught herself with her hands. She still hit with a force that stunned her. When she tried to rise, she felt Sean's foot in her back. He pressed her down to the floor.

"No! Help!"

Sean sat on her back, his weight pinning her. Grabbing a handful of her hair, Sean pushed her face into the linoleum. Cara tasted the filth of the floor. She tried to scream but her cries were now muffled.

Sean's foul mouth touched her ear as he bent down to whisper. "Now, this can be real easy or it can be real rough. Which way do you want it?"

Cara was silent for the moment. She tensed, hoping that she could fight him when he let up on her. There had to be a way to get out of this.

Sean pulled her head back and then smashed her face into the floor. "How do you want it?"

"Easy," she muttered, blood streaking from her lip.

Her head spun in a dizzy whirlpool. The strength ebbed from her body. But her spirit wasn't dying. Somewhere inside her, Cara found the resolve not to give in. She imagined herself clawing at his eyes with her fingernails. She'd blind him if she had to.

Sean let go of her hair. "All right, then. I'm going to let you turn over. Then we're going to finish this. Okay?"

Cara lay motionless, petrified by the demon who had trapped her. She had to move, to act. But she couldn't do anything with his weight on her back.

"Okay?" he cried. "Answer me!"

"Okay."

The word barely escaped her lips as a whisper.

Sean nodded. "Yeah, that's my girl. Now, I'm gonna let up and you turn over."

His hands forced her to flip onto her back.

Cara gazed up at his hateful eyes. How could she have ever cared for this beast? She had never seen him clearly before this terrifying moment.

Sean smiled. "That's better. Now listen, when this is over, you're not going to tell anyone—"

Cara had swiped at his face with her hand. Sean caught her wrist. He caught the other one too when she took a second poke at him. Sean leaned forward, throwing her hands back, wriggling on top of her until his face was right over hers.

"You creep!" Cara muttered.

Sean's eyes narrowed and his lip curled again. "If you cause trouble, I'll kill you! I swear I will."

She tried to struggle but he was too strong.

Sean started to kiss her cheek. When she jerked her head to the side, his lips touched her neck. Cara gazed at the ceiling, ready to cry out again. But then she saw the face there, hovering above them. A brown-eyed boy was leaning through the open casement.

"Help!" she cried.

Sean lifted his own head. "I thought I told you to—"

"Hey, guys, what's doin'?"

The boy in the window had spoken.

Sean gazed back over his shoulder with a startled look of disbelief. They had been discovered. The intruder just hung there from outside, half in and half out of the classroom.

"Really bad technique there," the brown-eyed kid said. "You shouldn't have to hold her down."

Sean snarled at the intruder. "Get out of here and leave us alone, Jacobs."

Sean knew the boy.

Cara wondered if their guest would let Sean continue his assault. Sometimes boys did that if their friend was involved. And this kid looked rough.

"Go on," Sean insisted. "Beat it."

The boy shook his head, making a *tsking* noise with his thin lips. "You're something, Sean. Big basketball hero, huh?"

"Get your worthless carcass back to Pitney Docks where you belong, Eddie!"

Cara put the two names together. Eddie Jacobs. He was one of the local toughs from Pitney Docks, the worst area in Port City. Eddie wasn't the type of guy to rescue her. He might even *join* the horrid spectacle.

Yet, Eddie's tone seemed to be one of concern. "She doesn't look like she wants to play with you, McGovern."

"Help me," Cara moaned. "Please—"

Sean drew back his balled fist. "Shut up, you—"

Eddie Jacobs had grabbed Sean's wrist, stopping him from hitting her. Sean started to struggle himself. Somehow, Eddie rolled into the room, twisting Sean's arm, causing Sean to scream and fall to the side. When Eddie released his grip on Sean, he jumped to his feet and glared down at Cara and her attacker.

"Don't worry," Eddie said. "I'm not going to let him hurt you, Miss Cheerleader."

Sean reeled when he stood up. "You're going to get hurt, Jacobs."

Eddie shook his head, which was covered by short-cropped brown hair, a crew cut that had been allowed to grow out for a couple of months. "You can't lay a glove on me, Sean. I'm not a basketball. You can't slam dunk me."

Sean made a move toward Eddie. "You little—"

Eddie, who was a head shorter than Sean, reached into the zippered pocket of his leather jacket. Something clicked in his hand. Metal flashed in the fluorescent light of the biology lab.

"Come on," Eddie said. "Let's do it, pretty-boy!"

Sean's eyes focused on the long, glistening blade of the switchblade knife. "You wouldn't."

Eddie grinned, his eyes bulging. "Sure I would! I'd fillet you like a codfish, pretty-boy."

"That's murder!" Sean cried.

Eddie nodded toward Cara, who still lay on the floor, watching the confrontation. "What do you call that wild thing you were about to do to her? Huh, pretty-boy?"

Sean gestured to the knife. "I don't fight like that."

"No, you pick on girls," Eddie replied. "You force yourself on them."

Sean moved again. "You dirty—"

Eddie jabbed at Sean's stomach, almost catching his gut with the point of the knife.

Sean jumped backward. "I told you, I don't fight like that."

"Well, I do," the leather-jacketed kid said through clenched teeth. "Come on, jock-boy. I'll give you another smile in your gut. Let's party."

"It's murder," Sean insisted. "They'll put you away."

Eddie shook his head. "No way, man. I'll be saving this chick from you. Won't I, honey?"

Cara felt a jolt through her body. She leapt to her feet, staring at Eddie. He wanted to save her—but for what?

"You wouldn't turn me in, Cara!" Sean pleaded. "Would you?"

Eddie laughed. "Listen to him. Squawkin' like a chicken. Ain't he somethin', Miss Cheerleader?"

Cara turned her eyes on Sean, who now seemed pitiful. "Just go, Sean! Get out of here!"

Sean had suddenly grown penitent. "Hey, I didn't mean anything, Cara. Honest."

Eddie guffawed. "The worm has turned."

"You aren't going to turn me in, are you, Cara?" Sean asked.

Cara could barely stand on her wobbly legs. "Please, just go, Sean. Get out of here."

"Okay, okay."

When he started to move toward the door of the biology lab. Eddie jabbed at him with the knife. Sean shrieked and bolted into the hall. Cara heard his footsteps echoing in the corridor as he ran away.

Eddie shook his head. "I hate guys like that. Don't you?"

He turned to regard Cara.

But she did not reply.

Her green eyes were now focused on the weapon in Eddie's hand.

The blade shone in the light from the ceiling.

Cara leaned back against the wall, wondering what Eddie was going to do with the knife.

FOUR

Eddie used the knife to gesture in the direction in which Sean had fled. "Yeah, them Prescott pukes are all alike."

He was referring to Prescott Estates, the nicest neighborhood in the quaint Atlantic Seaboard town of Port City. Cara lived in Prescott Estates. Her father was president of Port City Savings Bank. She wondered if Eddie would resent her for that.

Eddie gazed at her with an expression that was hard to decipher. His eyes were hard, his face rugged. Everything about him was rough. Had Cara escaped the frying pan only to fall into the fire?

"Hey, I bet you live in Prescott Estates," Eddie said. "Is that right, gorgeous? You cheer for the ol' team spirit in your Prescott mansion?"

Cara shrugged. "It's not a mansion."

Eddie sighed. He still gripped the knife in his hand. Cara couldn't take her eyes off the flashing blade.

Eddie went on in a tired voice. "Yeah, you Prescott types are somethin'. The world just lays down for you. Good grades, good homes, college, a great job somewhere down the road."

Cara ignored the urge to defend herself by saying that she worked hard for her good grades, that her father worked hard to keep them in a nice house. She didn't want to enrage Eddie. And she owed him something for saving her from Sean—unless Eddie had a similar fate in mind.

Her lips trembled as she nodded toward the blade. "Maybe you should put that thing away."

"Huh?"

He didn't seem to understand what she was saying.

"The knife," Cara said. "I mean, Sean is gone. You don't need that anymore."

Eddie laughed. "I didn't need it to take care of him. I wanted to scare him. Those kind never have anybody on their case. They think they're gonna live forever."

Cara said, "Yeah."

Eddie stood there between Cara and the door. He didn't put the knife back in his pocket. Cara felt her stomach churning. What was this unpredictable savage going to do to her?

Eddie eased into a desk, reaching inside his jacket for a pack of cigarettes. He put a filtered butt in his mouth and lit the end with a silver Zippo lighter. The smoke filled the room making Cara even more nauseous.

Eddie caught her staring at him. "You want one?" he asked, offering her the pack.

Cara shook her head. "I don't smoke."

"No, I don't guess you would," Eddie replied.

He put the knife on the desk.

Cara took a step away from the wall. "I better be going."

Eddie shrugged. "Knock yourself out."

Something made her hesitate. She studied the rough-hewn boy, wondering what circumstances had led him to be like this. He wasn't ugly, but it appeared that he was deliberately trying to make himself appear that way.

"Thanks for helping me," Cara said. "I appreciate it."

Eddie reached for the knife. "Don't mention it."

Cara tensed. But then Eddie folded the blade into the handle and slipped the knife back into the zippered pocket. Cara let out the breath she had been holding.

Eddie scowled at her. "Man, did you think I was going to hurt you? Geez—"

"No, I—I'm just scared," Cara replied. "Sean almost—"

He waved her off. "Get out of here."

Tears swelled in Cara's eyes. "I—I'm afraid." She started to sob in front of him.

Eddie grimaced. "Don't turn on the faucet. Hey—"

He rose slowly, moving toward her, wrapping his arms around her. Cara embraced him, trembling. He smelled horribly but there was some comfort in his arms.

"Thank you," Cara said.

Eddie drew back quietly. "Hey, I ain't the Prince Charmin' type, okay? Why don't you just get out of here?"

Cara stepped toward the door, wiping her eyes. She stopped at the archway, turning back to Eddie. The cigarette dangled from his lips. She had seen him around school, but she had never really noticed him. Now she owed him—what?

"Eddie, if there's anything I can do for you—"

He chuckled. "Like what?"

"I—I don't know."

He shook his head. "Nah, just forget about it."

"Maybe I could help you study or something. Give you some money. If you need—"

Eddie seemed to grow impatient. "Okay, how about I come over to your house tonight for dinner? Sit down with the folks and feed my face on some lobster?"

Cara blushed. "I—"

She didn't know what to say. And what would her parents think if Eddie showed up? She would have to tell them about Sean. She wasn't sure she wanted to tell anyone about what had happened.

Eddie scoffed. "I thought so. Can't have me at the same table with Mom and Dad?"

"No!" Cara insisted. "It's just—well, tonight's not good. How about another night?"

Eddie seemed to soften a little. "You mean it?"

"Sure—if you want to come for dinner, that's okay."

He eyed her skeptically. "Sure. If you really mean it, then give me your phone number."

"All right."

Cara told him the number. She asked if he wanted to write it down. Eddie replied that he could remember it. He wasn't totally stupid, despite what everyone might think.

Cara smiled. "Thanks again."

Eddie said to her, "Look, don't get no ideas about goin' to the cops, okay? I don't like cops. Besides, they'd never take my word over that Sean kid. He's the one they'd believe."

Cara took a deep breath. "I understand. I think it's over anyway."

"Don't bet on it, honey. I saw the way he was looking at you. He'll be back."

"I hope not."

"I'll call you," Eddie said.

"Thanks."

Cara turned quickly and fled down the hallway. She felt sick inside. The entire incident had left her with a bad taste in her mouth. She just wanted to get to her car and go home.

The senior parking lot was almost empty. Cara approached her Toyota Camry, the blue compact car her parents had given Cara for her seventeenth birthday. When she opened the driver's side door, she jumped back and gasped. There was someone sitting in the passenger seat. Cara wanted to run until she heard the familiar voice from inside the car.

"Hey, it's me," Chris said.

Cara started to cry again.

Chris got out of the Toyota and ran to her side. "What's wrong? Hey, don't cry—"

Cara asked Chris to drive her home. They climbed into the car and rolled out of the parking lot. Cara told Chris to take the long way. She wanted to try to talk about it, at least to Chris.

Chris's eyes grew wide as she told him what Sean had tried to do to her.

"That bastard!" Chris cried. "I'll kill him!"

"He came pretty close to dying today."

Chris looked sideways at her. "What're you talking about?"

She recounted the tale of Eddie Jacobs coming to her rescue.

Chris shook his head. "Wow, Eddie Jacobs. I heard he killed a guy in junior high school."

"He smokes cigarettes," Cara replied. "And he had a knife. I think he would've killed Sean."

"That wouldn't have been a big loss to the world," Chris said. "Are you going to call the cops on Sean?"

She shook her head. "No."

"Cara! He tried to rape you!"

"Eddie doesn't like cops," Cara replied. "He won't back me up. Besides, it's all right. I think Sean is too scared to try anything else."

Chris grimaced and shook his head. "Wow. I should have stayed with you."

"I'm okay," Cara replied.

"Well, at least you broke it off with Sean."

Now I have a shot, Chris thought to himself.

Cara became silent as they rolled along River Drive. Her eyes peered out at the gulls that drifted lazily over the rippling waters of the Tide Gate River. Port City was a perfect New England seacoast community. Chris steered the car into town, through Market Square. They drove down Congress Street, passing North Church and Town Hall. It was a great spring afternoon, even if Cara wasn't in the mood to enjoy it.

Chris lived near Cara, so he could walk from her house. He turned onto Middle Road, heading for Prescott Estates. Chris tried to make small talk, but Cara wasn't able to listen. The horrible incident kept replaying in her mind. What if Eddie Jacobs *hadn't* come to her rescue?

She shivered and folded her arms.

"Are you okay?" Chris asked.

"Yes. I'll be all right."

They passed Old Cemetery. Cara shuddered, wondering how close she had come to ending up in a grave. Would Sean really have killed her?

As they entered Prescott Estates, Chris smiled at her. "Want me to come in with you?"

Cara shook her head. "No, I'll be fine. I just want to be alone for a little while."

"Will you call if you need me?" Chris asked.

She nodded. "Sure."

Chris pulled into the driveway of the white, two-story Victorian house. The structure was nearly a hundred years old. Cara's mother and father had completely remodeled the place. It was one of the nicest houses in Prescott Estates, which was a combination of old and recently built houses.

When they climbed out of the car, Chris made a big deal of coming around to embrace her for a moment. "If there's anything you need, Cara, call me."

She tried to smile. "Thanks, Chris."

He watched her walk into the house, disappointed that she had not invited him in. Would they ever get together the way he wanted to? Or would Cara move on to the next hateful guy who would dump all over her and leave her? Chris started off toward his own house, following the sidewalk past the lawns that were becoming greener with the warm spring weather.

He was in love with her, but it appeared that she would never feel the same way about him.

What did it matter? he told himself.

School would be out soon. They would both go off to college.

It didn't matter.

But he knew it did.

Cara was lying in her room, staring at the ceiling, when she heard the front door open and close. She sat up on the bed, wondering who had entered the house. She hadn't heard her mother's car. Her mother usually came home first from her job at the mall. Mrs. Richards worked part-time at the jewelry counter of a big department store. Cara held her breath. What if Sean had come after her? She hadn't thought to lock the front door.

She jumped off the bed, rushing to lock her bedroom door.

But before she could reach the doorway, her mother's voice echoed through the house. "Cara? Are you home, honey?"

She took a deep breath. "I'm up here, Mom. I'm doing my homework."

"Fine, honey. You keep at it."

Cara returned to her bed, lying back on the covers. She could not shake the dreary feeling that had overtaken her. Why had Sean acted like such a jerk? How could she face him in school tomorrow? The phone rang, startling

Cara from her dark daydream. Her parents had given her a private line next to her bed.

She picked up the receiver. "Hello?"

For a second, there was no voice from the other end.

"Hello?"

Cara could hear breathing.

"Who is this?" she asked.

"Hey, babe."

Her heart jumped. It was Sean. She could hear him laughing on the other end of the line.

"You've got some nerve calling me," Cara told him.

"You loved it," Sean replied. "You and me aren't through, babe. That punk may have rescued you today, but we have some unfinished business."

"Drop dead, Sean."

She slammed the receiver down.

The phone rang immediately.

Cara did not answer. Instead, she switched off the ringer. Lying back on her bed, she stared at the ceiling. Her body tingled with an electric intensity. What was she going to do about Sean?

She had to solve the problem quickly, before he tried to hurt her again.

But it would be solved . . . in a way that Cara never could've imagined.

FIVE

Cara sat at the dinner table with her mother and father, dabbing at a pile of mashed potatoes with her fork. She couldn't get Sean's hateful voice out of her head. In her thoughts she debated telling her parents about Sean. If she didn't tell, Sean would continue to bother her. If she told, it could get really complicated, especially if the police were brought into the situation.

Daniel Richards, a chubby, half-bald gentleman with a double chin, gazed across the table at his daughter. "You look sad tonight, Princess. Is everything okay?"

Cara shrugged without looking at him. "I'm okay."

Ann Richards, who resembled her daughter with green eyes and gray-streaked auburn hair, studied Cara with a concerned expression. "Are you sure everything is all right, Cara?"

She looked back and forth between their faces, wondering how to find the words. "I'm fine," she lied, trying to uphold the illusion of strength. "I'm just a little bit worried about graduation. And the prom."

Mrs. Richards smiled. "Oh, is that all? Well, you've got a perfect grade point average, honey. And I'm sure Sean will ask you to the prom."

Cara blushed. "I broke up with Sean."

Mr. Richards gave a fatherly nod. "Oh, I see. Well, honey, it's not the end of the world."

It is if Sean kills me! Cara thought.

Mrs. Richards reached over to pat her daughter's hand. "I'm glad you broke off with Sean, Cara. We both felt that he was getting too serious about you."

"Yes," her father added, "we wouldn't want you to make a mistake this early in life, something you might have to pay for later. I'm glad he's gone."

Not completely gone, Cara thought. *Not if that phone call this afternoon is any indication of what he still has in mind.*

"Sean didn't take it too well," Cara went on, edging around the truth. "He's angry."

"Tough," her father replied. "If that little jerk gives you any trouble—"

"Dan!" Mrs. Richards was glaring at her husband. "Please, take it easy."

But Cara took her father's cue. "Dad, he called me this afternoon. He's harassing me."

An angry look spread over Mr. Richard's round face. Despite his harmless appearance as a banker, Dan Richards had grown up in a tough section of Rochester, the next town over from Port City. He had worked his way through college, so he took pride in owing nothing to anyone. He pulled the napkin from his lap and threw it on the table, rising from his chair.

"What are you going to do?" Cara asked.

Mr. Richards started for the telephone. "Mac McGovern has a business loan with us. I'll make sure that little punk stays away from you."

"Dad!"

Mrs. Richards gave Cara a reassuring look. "It's okay, honey, your father will nip this in the bud."

Cara waited nervously at the table while her father made the phone call. She could hear his voice in the other room. Dan Richards's tone was firm without being too hostile. In a couple of minutes he was back at the table, replacing the napkin on his lap.

Cara was trembling. "What happened?"

"You don't have to worry about Sean McGovern," her father replied. "He'll leave you alone."

"Are—are you sure?" Cara asked.

Her father smiled. "You don't have anything

to worry about, honey. If he calls here, you let me talk to him."

Cara took a deep breath and exhaled, feeling a sense of relief. "Thanks, Dad."

"You're welcome, Princess."

They finished dinner, chatting about the upcoming prom and graduation. Cara had already finished her applications for two universities and Port City Community College, and had been accepted by all three. She wasn't sure where she wanted to attend college just yet.

After the meal, the three of them cleared the table. Cara's father washed the dishes, her mother dried and Cara put the dishes away. Cara was beginning to put the bad day behind her when the phone rang in the kitchen. She froze, thinking that Sean was calling on her parents' line.

Mr. Richards answered. "Hello? Cara, yes, she's here."

Cara bit her lip.

Mr. Richards smiled. "It's Chris, honey."

Cara breathed easier. "Hello?"

Chris sounded bummed. "I'm sorry to bother you, Cara, but I think you have my compass from math class."

"You're right," Cara replied. "I do have it."

Chris sighed. "Look, can you leave it on your front porch and I'll stop by to—"

"I'll bring it over," Cara told him.

Chris seemed to hesitate. "You will?"

"Sure."

"How is everything?" he asked.

"Fine," she replied. "Dad talked to Sean's father. Sean is going to leave me alone."

"Really? Did you tell your father about—"

"Not exactly. Listen, I'll tell you all about it when I see you."

Chris's mood took an upturn. "Cool. I'll be waiting."

"I'm on the way."

Cara hung up and turned to her parents. "I'm going over to Chris's," she told them. "I have to take him his compass for math."

Mr. Richards glanced at the clock. "It's a little late to be going out."

"It's only eight o'clock," Cara offered. "I'll be back by ten. Okay?"

Mrs. Richards sighed. "I think nine o'clock is better. Chris only lives up the street."

Cara shrugged. "Okay, nine. I'll drive so you won't have to worry about me."

"Nine it is," her father replied.

Cara hurried up to her room, finding the pointed instrument that Chris used to draw circles and plot graph points. It was too sharp to carry in her pocket, so she carried it down to her car, putting the compass on the dashboard. Darkness had fallen over Port City so Cara flashed the headlights on the Toyota. She started toward Chris's house with the radio blasting.

There was only one stop sign on the cross streets between her house and Chris's place. Cara braked at the sign to let another car pass. Her foot eased off the brake but she never pressed the accelerator. Something warm and moist touched the back of her neck. Cara slammed on the brake pedal.

"What—"

Someone rose up from the backseat. Cara saw the silhouette of a boy's head in the rear-view mirror. A hand closed on her neck.

"Don't move, you little tease."

Sean! He had been hiding in her car, slouched down in the backseat. His other hand clamped her neck. She could feel his hot breath, hear him as he sucked in the night air.

"You had your old man call my old man, Cara. You have to pay for that."

Her chest had grown tight. A burning sensation filled her lungs. She slammed the car into park so it wouldn't roll into the intersection.

"You can't get away with this, Sean," she said in a cracking voice. "You'll be in big trouble."

"No, I won't. You're not going to tell anyone. Now, put the car in gear and drive out of Prescott Estates."

"Sean—"

He tightened his grip on her neck. "Do it!"

Cara's hand moved toward the dashboard. "Sean—please—"

"Nobody's gonna come to your rescue this time. You're not gonna put me off."

"Sean, I'll tell the police. I swear—"

He leaned closer to her ear. "If you don't do what I say, I'll snap your neck right now."

"Okay, Sean. Just give me a second. Please, you're holding my neck too tight. Ease up, okay, and I'll do what you want."

Her hand was on the dashboard now, groping in the dark.

Sean laughed. "Now you're starting to understand. Take me to that alley off River Run Road. You know the place?"

Cara nodded. "Yes."

"Don't worry," Sean went on. "If you do what I say, I won't hurt you."

She felt the metal object under her fingertips. "That's fine, Sean. But you have to take it easy on my neck."

"Sure, sweetcakes, whatever you say."

Cara felt his hands leaving her neck. She gripped the compass in her right hand, bracing for the strike. In one quick movement, she stabbed the compass point deeply into Sean's palm.

Sean cried out, reaching for the sharp object that protruded from his hand. He cursed her as he pried the compass out of his palm. But it was too late for him to grab her. Cara had already opened the door and fled the front seat of the Toyota.

Her chest was on fire as she ran into the night.

Sean's voice followed her. "Come back here, you little—"

Cara somehow found the strength to run on wobbly legs. She had to get away. Chris's house wasn't far. She sprinted along the sidewalk, never thinking to cry out so someone would hear her.

Sean's footsteps echoed in the night as he chased her. Cara realized that she would never outrun him. She had to escape some other way. She saw the high fence in front of her. If she could just climb over the wooden barrier, she'd land in someone's backyard. She'd have time to knock on the back door to ask for help.

Cara hit the fence, scuffling to roll over the top. Sean was right behind her. He caught her ankle before she could escape into the backyard.

"Come on," Sean said. "You owe me big time now. You—"

Suddenly his grip went slack, releasing her foot. Cara fell to the other side of the fence. She expected Sean to follow. Jumping to her feet, she listened for a moment in the darkness. Everything had gotten quiet in a hurry.

Cara turned to look at the dark house behind her. She was trespassing in the yard. But she would gladly welcome a visit from the Port City police.

She started for the back door. A strange sound rose in the night to stop her in her tracks. She froze, listening as someone or something bumped the fence that she had just climbed. The commotion lasted for a few seconds and then died.

"I'm going to scream, Sean!" Cara called.

No reply.

Did she hear footsteps retreating into the night? Or was Sean coming after her? Cara hurried to the back door, knocking frantically. But no one was home.

She followed the fence until she found the gate. Luckily it was open. She eased through the portal, listening for Sean. If he came at her from the shadows, she would scream.

But Sean was nowhere to be seen or heard. Had he given up? Or was he lying in wait somewhere between the dark house and Chris's place?

Cara hit the sidewalk and started to run again. Her body ached by the time she reached Chris's house. He was waiting for her on the front stoop.

"What's wrong?" he asked as she tried to catch her breath.

Cara began to cry.

Chris wrapped his arms around her. He felt her trembling body close to him. He loved her even more now that she seemed to need him.

Cara gradually composed herself. She told

Chris about Sean's attempt to attack her. She sobbed as she described the way she had stabbed him with the compass.

"You did that?" Chris asked, his eyes wide.

She nodded. "I had to. I had to get away from him."

Chris stroked her hair. "Are you kidding? Don't feel sorry about stabbing that jerk. He had it coming."

Cara drew back away from him. "My car! It's still sitting at the intersection."

"Come on," Chris said, taking her hand. "We'll get it."

They walked back toward the street where Cara had left her Toyota. The car was still there, the motor running. They climbed in and Cara drove Chris back to his place. She parked the car in the driveway and they sat in the night shadows.

"You have to call the police," Chris said finally.

Cara shook her head. "No!"

"Why not?" Chris asked in dismay.

"I don't know."

He took her hand. "Cara, you have to stop this. Now!"

"I know."

"Then call the police!" he insisted.

She nodded. "All right. But not tonight. Tomorrow."

He breathed a sigh of relief. "That's better.

Come on, I'll ride home with you and then walk back."

On the way to Cara's house, Chris offered words of encouragement. Cara was stunned, silent. She felt numb inside. What would it take to stop Sean? Could the police really help her?

Chris walked her to the front door. They embraced for a moment, and Cara turned her head to let him kiss her cheek. Chris offered his support again before he left.

Cara entered her house to find that her parents were in the living room watching television. She considered telling them about Sean but she balked, choosing to wait until morning. She didn't want to face the police tonight and she knew her father would call them immediately if she told them. So she said good night and went upstairs to her room.

She worried that she would not be able to fall asleep, but fatigue overtook her and she dropped off into a restless slumber. She awakened the next morning to her mother's dreadful cries from downstairs. Mrs. Richards urged Cara to come down right away.

Cara put on her robe and joined her mother in the kitchen. Mr. Richards was also there. The television was blaring with the morning news.

A boy's body had been found floating in the river in the early hours. The corpse had been discovered by a tugboat captain who fished it from the Tide Gate with a boat hook. Cara shuddered when she heard the name from the newscaster.

The corpse had been identified as Sean McGovern.

Apparently he had committed suicide by jumping from the New Market Bridge.

Speculation by the Port City police had Sean plummeting to his death because he was distraught over breaking up with his girlfriend.

Cara just stood there, her mouth hanging open.

SIX

Classes were not canceled at Central Academy because of Sean McGovern's untimely death. The administration decided to keep the school open and hold a morning assembly for the entire student body. Assistant principal Harlan Kinsley addressed the students, expressing his own grief for the loss of Sean, as well as advising everyone that counselors would be available to anyone who wanted to talk about this tragedy. The administration at Central feared "copycat" behavior wherein other students might take their own lives like Sean had. They wanted to avoid any subsequent horrors of teen suicide.

Cara sat in the bleachers of the gym/auditorium, listening to the doleful speech. Chris was next to her, showing his friendly support. Cara's parents had told her that she could miss school if she needed some time to get over Sean's death, but Cara wanted to go to her classes. She felt badly about Sean, but after the way he had treated her, she wasn't going to let him upset her anymore. A vague sense of grief stirred inside her, though the weird circumstances of Sean's demise left her more numb than anything else.

Chris touched her arm. "Are you all right?"

She nodded slightly. It was hard to believe that Sean had taken his own life. Was he really that distraught over their breakup? He hadn't exactly seemed suicidal the night before. He had been murderous, hateful, but not suicidal.

When the assembly was over, Chris walked Cara to her first-period class. As they strode down the hall together, heads were bent to whisper and vicious comments filled the air. The sympathies of the student body were with the dead boy.

"There she is."

"He killed himself over *her*?"

"What a waste."

"You know he had a scholarship."

"It's all her fault."

"Hey, Cara, how does it feel to be a killer?"

Cara's face went slack when she heard the disparaging remarks. Why were they attacking her? She hadn't forced Sean to jump from the New Market Bridge. How was she going to tell them that Sean had been stalking her?

"Don't listen to them," Chris said.

"It's not my fault," Cara insisted.

Chris put his arm around her shoulders. "I know."

More taunts and insults came from the crowded hallway. By the time Cara reached the classroom, she was on the verge of tears. She left Chris, taking her seat in the back of the room. All eyes turned to look at her. Why couldn't they just leave her alone?

"What did you do to make him kill himself?" someone asked.

"Yeah, he seemed fine yesterday," another voice rejoined.

"I hope you're happy, Cara."

"Yeah, you really did it this time."

"Stop it!" Cara cried. "Just stop it! I didn't do anything to Sean."

"You must have done something."

"Yeah, he was okay before he started going with you."

"Killer!"

"Murderer!"

Cara put her face in her hands and began to cry.

"Hey, Cara, why don't *you* jump off the New Market Bridge!"

The classroom erupted in cruel laughter. Why were they doing this to her? Sean had been the monster. Cara hadn't done anything to deserve this.

"All right, that's enough!"

Their heads snapped forward. Mrs. Olivetti, their teacher, had entered the room. She glared at the smirking faces of Cara's tormentors. Cara looked up, wiping her eyes.

"Are you all right, Cara?" Mrs. Olivetti asked.

Cara nodded, sobbing, her face red.

Mrs. Olivetti gave the class another stern look. She was a graying, middle-aged woman who was almost ready to retire. She never put up with any nonsense in her history classes, much less the harassment of a student who was obviously in pain.

"We've suffered a horrible tragedy," she told them. "Sean's unfortunate death is not Cara's fault. Do you understand?"

They were silent, though some of the faces wore hateful smirks. Cara knew they wouldn't leave her alone. How could she convince everyone that Sean had assaulted her, that he had probably jumped from the bridge because he knew that she was going to turn him in to the police?

"Now," Mrs. Olivetti went on, "if you'll all turn to page one hundred thirty in your textbooks, we'll begin our lesson."

Cara opened her book, though she couldn't see the page through her tears. Everything had somehow been turned against her. And it didn't get any better when the loudspeaker blared in the classroom.

"Cara Richards, please report to the assistant principal's office immediately. Cara Richards, please report to the assistant principal's office."

Everyone looked at her again. Their faces were leering, cruel, expectant. Why did they enjoy her pain so much?

Mrs. Olivetti came toward her with a sympathetic expression on her countenance. "You'd better go, Cara."

Cara rose from her desk, taking her books with her. She was sort of relieved to flee the mocking stares of her classmates. But as she moved down the corridor, she realized what had happened. The assistant principal wanted to talk to her. And Cara knew he was going to ask her questions about Sean.

When she reached the assistant principal's office, she saw Mr. Kinsley standing in the reception area. He was a tall, severe-looking man with red hair and accusing eyes. Another man stood next to Kinsley. This man had sandy hair and a dark suit. Cara knew from newspaper pictures and television reports that the man was Victor Danridge, chief of the Port City police department.

"Hello, Cara," Mr. Kinsley said in a kind voice. "I'd like you to meet—"

"I know who he is," Cara said softly.

Danridge nodded at her. "Do you know why I'm here?"

"To talk about Sean," Cara replied.

Danridge sighed. "Yes."

Mr. Kinsley ushered them into his office, which was dark and dreary. The assistant principal sat behind his desk. Cara and Danridge took the wooden chairs on the other side. Cara's heart was pounding, even though she kept telling herself that she had nothing to hide. She wasn't afraid of the truth.

Mr. Kinsley spoke first. "Cara, you aren't in any trouble, but if you'd like to have your parents here, I can call them."

Cara shook her head. "No, I'll tell you anything you want to know. Anything."

"Chief Danridge," Kinsley said. "You may begin."

Danridge turned in the chair so he could look at Cara with steely eyes. "Cara, Sean was your boyfriend, wasn't he?"

"For a while," Cara replied.

"How long?"

She sighed and shrugged. "We started going together this semester. But I broke off with him before—"

Danridge made a note on a small pad. "I see. How close were you and Sean?"

Cara's face reddened, her expression changed into a scowl. "Not as close as Sean wanted it to be!"

"Take it easy," Danridge urged.

But anger had replaced Cara's sullen mood. "Sean and I never did anything to be ashamed of, Chief Danridge. I'm still a virgin, if that's what you're asking."

"I just want to find out why this boy would want to kill himself," Danridge offered. "Do you have any ideas?"

Cara took a deep breath, trying to compose herself. "Sean—Sean wanted more than I could give."

"And that's why he jumped from the bridge?"

She shook her head, looking at the floor. "No—he—he was stalking me."

Danridge's brow wrinkled. "Stalking you?"

She nodded. "Yes."

"Why didn't you report him?" Kinsley asked.

Cara glanced up. "It all happened so fast. Yesterday, I told him I didn't want to go steady anymore."

"How'd he take it?" Danridge inquired.

"He didn't like it," Cara went on. "He cornered me in the biology lab. He said that I owed him, that he had been waiting for a long time, that I had to give in or—"

"Or what?"

Tears formed in her eyes again. "Or he'd kill me."

Kinsley's face went slack. "Sean McGovern threatened to kill you?"

"Yes, but I managed to get away," Cara told them, stopping short of mentioning that Eddie Jacobs had saved her. "Last night, I told my father that Sean harassed me. He called Sean's father. Then I went over to my friend's house after dinner. Sean was waiting in my car. He threatened me again, but I got away from him."

Danridge gave her a skeptical look. "You got away from him twice?"

She nodded. "Yes. I climbed out the window the first time."

How could she tell them about Eddie when he wouldn't back up her story?

"Then, last night, when Sean was in my car, I stabbed his hand with a compass."

"He did have a wound on his hand," Danridge said. "You did that to him?"

"Yes, I had to!" Cara pleaded. "He kept threatening me. After I stabbed his hand, I ran away. He chased me for a while and then he gave up."

"He couldn't catch you?" Danridge asked. "An athlete like Sean? You outran him?"

"I—I climbed over a fence," Cara replied, sobbing. "He didn't follow me. I guess his hand was hurting. He left me alone after I went over the fence. Then, this morning, I heard about him on television."

"Did anyone see Sean and you together?" Danridge asked.

Cara hung her head. "No."

Danridge kept staring at her with those eerie police officer eyes. "If the McGovern boy was harassing you, why didn't you tell someone? Why didn't you report him?"

"I did tell my father," Cara replied. "He called Sean's father. Just ask them."

"I'll check on that," Danridge said, making a note on his pad. "I'd like to know why you didn't call the police last night after your encounter with Sean."

Cara wiped her eyes, drawing an uneven breath. "I was confused. My friend Chris wanted me to call you—"

Danridge squinted at her. "Chris? That's the first time I've heard this name."

Cara hesitated, wondering if Chris would get in trouble now. "Chris Hall," she said finally. "I ran to his house after I got away from Sean. Chris went back with me to get my car. I left it at the intersection when I ran from Sean."

Danridge wrote something on his pad. "Very well, I'll talk to Chris Hall too."

Kinsley was studying Cara. "Why didn't you call the police last night?" he asked.

"I wanted to wait," Cara replied. "I didn't want to go through this last night. I was going to tell my father in the morning and ask him what to do."

Danridge looked up from his pad. "So, Sean McGovern was threatening you, and you wanted to wait?"

Cara's expression grew hostile again. "Look, I didn't do anything! Sean tried to force himself on me, okay?"

Danridge glanced at Mr. Kinsley. "Had Sean been in trouble for anything like this before?"

Kinsley shook his head. "No."

"I want my parents here!" Cara blurted out. "Now!"

Danridge smiled at her. "It's all right, Cara. You aren't in any trouble. In fact, you can go now."

"I can?"

"Yes," Danridge replied. "And if I have to talk to you again, you can bring your parents and a lawyer if you like."

Her face slackened. "A lawyer?"

Danridge nodded. "Yes, it's only a matter of procedure. You do have rights. And I want to thank you for talking to me."

Cara glared at him. "I didn't do anything wrong, Mr. Danridge. Sean was trying to hurt *me*!"

Kinsley leaned forward. "That's enough, Cara. You can go."

She rose from the chair and fled from the office.

The rest of the day was unbearable. Everyone talked about her, whispering behind Cara's back in the halls. At lunchtime she sat with Chris, her only ally. Chris said that Kinsley and Danridge had talked to him. Cara asked if Chris had mentioned Eddie Jacobs. He told her that he hadn't.

Chris promised to stand beside Cara, but she

didn't seem to hear him. When the bell rang, Chris walked her to the fourth-period English class. Again, Cara was greeted by smirks and whispers. She hated all of them for torturing her. When would they understand?

After her fifth-period math class, Cara decided to skip study hall. She couldn't take it anymore. She just wanted to go home, to be alone in her room.

Slipping out of the corridor, she ran across the campus to the senior parking lot. When she arrived at her car, she saw someone standing there, leaning against the Toyota. It was Eddie Jacobs. He blew smoke between his lips and nodded to her.

"Eddie—what're you—"

He laughed. "Take it easy, gorgeous. I'm not going to bite you. What'd the cops say?"

She hung her head. "They wanted to know about Sean."

"You tell them about me?"

Cara glanced up. "No! I swear."

He dropped the cigarette on the ground and crushed it with the heel of his boot. "Good girl. So, what else did they say?"

"I—I don't know," Cara replied. "I think they believe I did something to Sean."

Eddie folded his arms and sighed. "Well, if you had, you'd have been doin' the world a favor."

"Why are they after *me*, Eddie?"

He chortled. "Hey, kid, you know how many things I've had pinned on me? Things I didn't do? They always go after the innocent people. Now you know how the system works."

"I guess I do," Cara replied sadly.

Eddie came off the car, dropping his arms to his sides. "Okay, Cara, I'm calling in my marker."

"What?"

"You owe me," Eddie went on. "Remember yesterday when I saved you from cheese-boy. You said I could come over for dinner."

Cara hesitated. "Yes, I—"

Eddie threw out his hands. "Okay, I'm coming over for dinner, just like you asked. You name the night, gorgeous, and I'm there!"

Cara was trapped. There was no way out. She *had* extended an invitation to Eddie after he had saved her from Sean the first time. What would Eddie do now if she put him off? Would he try to hurt her too? She couldn't take the chance.

"All right," she said in a halting voice. "How about tonight?"

"I'm there," Eddie replied.

"Seven o'clock," Cara told him.

As she gave him the address, Cara wondered how she was going to explain Eddie to her mother and father.

SEVEN

Cara looked at her reflection in the mirror on her vanity dresser. Her face was pale, her eyes bloodshot from crying so much. It had been a rough day—a rough two days. First Sean had gone after her, then the police. Why did they think she was the bad guy? She had been the victim in all of this.

Now she had to get through a dinner with Eddie Jacobs. Why had he suddenly accepted her invitation? She should have put him off instead of having him over for dinner tonight. Did it really matter? she thought. Could things get any worse?

The phone rang next to her bed, startling her. Maybe it was Eddie. Maybe he wanted to cancel. No, she couldn't be that lucky.

"Hello?"

"Cara, it's me, Chris."

She sighed. "Oh. Hi."

"You hanging in there?"

"I'm doing my best. Chris, I still can't believe that the police think I did something to Sean."

Chris grew angry again. "Man, I can't believe it either. He tried to rape you. Twice!"

"How am I going to get them to believe me, Chris?"

"I don't know. Unless that Jacobs kid will back you up."

Cara hesitated, wondering if she should tell Chris about her dinner guest. "I never should've stabbed him with that compass."

"Think of what he would've done if you hadn't stabbed him," Chris replied. "*You* might be the one who's getting buried."

A shudder played through her shoulders. "Chris, this is horrible. How am I going to convince Chief Danridge that I didn't do anything to Sean?"

"You shouldn't have to prove your innocence!" Chris cried. "Not after he tried to hurt you!"

"I know, I know."

Chris sighed. "This bites."

"What am I going to do?"

"Cara, why don't you come over and we can talk?"

She stiffened. "Uh, Chris, I can't, not tonight."

"It's Friday," he replied. "We don't have school tomorrow—"

"Uh, it's not that—I—I'm having company. Someone is coming over for dinner."

Chris's tone became defensive. "Who?"

She didn't know how to tell him, but it had to be done. "Uh, it's somebody you don't know very well."

"Who?" he demanded.

"Eddie Jacobs."

His voice rose dramatically. "Eddie Jacobs! Why are you—"

"Because he saved me from Sean," she replied. "I owe him something. He wanted to come over for dinner."

"Great!" Chris said sarcastically. "He'll probably kill your whole family and steal the silverware!"

"Look, I have to do it, all right? It won't be that bad. He'll just have dinner and go home. Then I won't owe him anymore."

"You know he could back you up on your Sean story," Chris offered, "but he won't."

"I'm going to talk to him tonight," she replied. "Maybe I can convince him to talk to the police."

"Let me come over too," Chris pleaded.

"No, it'll be fine. He'll eat and then leave. I don't need you to baby-sit for me, Chris."

"You need me more than you think," he railed. "I—"

Cara's anxiety turned to anger. "Just leave me alone, Chris!"

"Cara, please—"

"I don't need it, Chris. Leave me alone!"

She slammed the phone down. Cara fought the urge to cry. There had been enough tears. When she got through this horrible evening, it would be finished. The police couldn't do anything to her because she was innocent. And Sean would soon be in his grave.

Her red eyes glanced at the clock. It was almost time for Eddie to arrive. She looked back in the mirror. Cara had decided not to wear any makeup. She didn't want to look good for Eddie. It wasn't a date. She only owed him a dinner, nothing more.

Rising from the vanity, Cara dressed in faded jeans and a plain white sweatshirt. She slogged down the stairs to the living room where she plopped on the couch. A numbness set in almost immediately. She still could not believe that Sean had died. He hadn't seemed like the type who would kill himself.

"Honey?"

She looked up to see her mother standing at the entrance to the living room.

"Hi, Mom."

Mrs. Richards smiled. "Is your friend here yet?"

He's not my friend, Cara thought.

"It's past seven," Mrs. Richards offered. "I can serve dinner anytime."

"He's a little late," Cara said. "I'm sorry!"

A concerned expression crossed over her mother's face. "Honey, I know you've had a rough couple of days. But if there's anything that I can do to—"

The doorbell rang.

Cara tensed. Eddie had arrived. It was the last thing she needed today. She had been hoping that he wouldn't show up.

"Want me to get it?" her mother asked.

Cara sighed dejectedly. "No, I'll go."

She stumbled to the front door, wondering if Eddie had bathed for his big night out.

Her hand closed on the doorknob.

Here goes nothing, she thought.

When she opened the door, she saw a well-dressed boy standing on the stoop. He wore a dark suit, a white shirt and a red tie. His clean-shaven face had been scrubbed and the scent of his cologne filled the night air. Cara would not have recognized him if the shaggy haircut had not given him away.

"Eddie?"

He grimaced. "Duh."

"You look—nice!"

"What'd you expect? Hey, just because I come from Pitney Docks, it doesn't mean that I can't afford a suit."

Cara stepped aside. "Come in."

Eddie strode in with the surprising ease of an elegant gentleman. Everything about him seemed different. Cara suddenly felt badly that she hadn't taken the time to dress in better clothes.

Eddie looked her up and down. "Oh. I didn't know we were going casual tonight."

"I—I'm sorry," Cara replied. "I've had a bad day."

He smiled. "It's all right. I understand."

Was this the same knife-wielding hoodlum who had scared Sean away in the biology lab?

Cara stood there for a moment, not sure what to say.

Eddie shifted nervously on his feet, glancing around the fancy house. "Nice place."

"Thanks."

"Tough break about Sean," he said.

She sighed. "I guess so."

"It wasn't your fault," he assured her. "You shouldn't feel guilty, Cara."

"I know."

Mrs. Richards appeared in the foyer. "Hello, you must be Eddie. I'm so glad to meet you." She extended her hand.

Eddie shook hands politely. "Glad to meet you, Mrs. Richards."

"Well, don't you look nice. Cara, you should've worn a dress. Eddie's all dressed up."

Cara smiled slightly. "I could change."

"That's all right," Eddie replied. "You look lovely, Mrs. Richards. I want to thank you for having me."

Seeing this side of Eddie was baffling. How

had he changed so quickly? Maybe he wanted to associate with a better class of people. At least he was making an effort to be decent.

Mr. Richards appeared behind his wife. “Hello, is this Eddie?”

Eddie extended his hand. “Glad to meet you, Mr. Richards.”

“Well, he has a firm handshake,” Cara’s father remarked.

“Thanks for having me over,” Eddie replied.

“Shall we go in to dinner?” Cara’s mother said.

Cara followed them into the dining room. She sat next to Eddie, who remarked how nice the table looked. They began to eat. Eddie was full of compliments for Mrs. Richards and the meal.

Cara kept looking at Eddie, wondering if this was some sort of strange dream. The entire evening had taken on a surreal quality. Eddie was making a better impression on her parents than Sean or any of her past boyfriends. He really seemed to be trying.

When dinner was over, Mr. Richards leaned back and looked at Cara. “So, Princess, what do you kids have planned for tonight?”

Cara grimaced. “Uh, I don’t know.”

Eddie smiled at her father. “Well, there’s a new movie at the Majestic. We could catch the nine o’clock show.”

They were all looking at Cara. She was on the spot. She wanted to say no, but Eddie had been so nice. And if she went out with him, she might be able to talk him into corroborating her story about Sean. If Eddie would just talk to the police, everything might turn out okay.

Eddie picked up on her reluctance. "Hey, if you don't want to go, Cara—"

"No, I—"

The phone rang.

"I'll get it," Cara said, rising from the table.

She ran into the living room, grabbing the extension. "Hello?"

"How's it going?" Chris asked.

She sighed. "Fine. I'm sorry I hung up on you before."

"No, I'm sorry."

"Is Eddie there?" he asked.

"Yes. He's being pretty decent. He even wore a suit."

"Eddie Jacobs?"

Cara shrugged. "He's not that bad, Chris."

"Watch him, Cara. He's up to something."

"Yeah?" Her patience was wearing thin. "How do you know?"

"Cara, please, just get rid of him."

"You know, Chris, I can run my own life. I don't need you to tell me what to do."

"Are you going out with him?"

"I'll do whatever I want," Cara replied. "And if you don't like it, you can bite it!"

She slammed down the phone and returned to the dining room.

"Is everything all right?" her father asked.

"Fine," Cara replied. "That was just Chris."

Eddie smiled. "He seems like a nice guy."

"Sometimes," Cara replied.

Eddie looked at Mrs. Richards. "Would you like some help clearing the table?"

Mrs. Richards shook her head. "No, you kids go on to the movie. Just make sure Cara is back right after."

Eddie glanced at Cara. "Are you up for it?"

"Sure," Cara replied. "Let me get my coat."

It might do her some good to see a movie.

She followed Eddie out to his car, a beat-up green Dodge that had to be twenty years old.

Cara got in on the passenger side.

Eddie slid behind the wheel. "It ain't much, but it runs."

"I don't care," Cara replied.

Eddie put the car in gear and peeled rubber away from the house.

"What's the name of the movie?" Cara asked absently.

Eddie chortled as he ripped the tie from his neck. "We ain't goin' to any movie, babe. That was just a dodge to fool your parents."

"Eddie—"

Her heart started to beat faster.

"Just relax, babe, we're goin' to a party."

"A party?"

"Yeah, I want you to meet some of my friends."

Cara folded her arms and leaned back. She couldn't relax, however. Something inside told her that going out with Eddie had been a big mistake.

EIGHT

Eddie's beat-up Dodge roared out of Port City on the Northway Turnpike. The headlights cut through the darkness on the road, illuminating the pavement. A moonless sky hung overhead, an omen for this evening. Eddie stared into the beams with a strange gleam in his eyes.

Cara sat in the passenger seat, her hands gripping the musty upholstery. "Where are we going?" she asked.

Eddie laughed. "Relax, we blew off Mom and Pop. Hey, I really got 'em with the suit, didn't I?"

Cara's chest was so tight that she could barely breathe. Why had she gone with Eddie in the first place? The day had been so dark and confusing. She had bought into Eddie's good-boy routine. She should have listened to Chris.

"Eddie, I'd like you to take me home," Cara said haltingly.

Eddie glanced sideways at her. "What? I thought we were going to have some fun to-night."

"What about the movie?" she offered diplomatically.

He bristled behind the wheel. "Movie? Movies are for geeks and Sunday schoolers. We're goin' to a party."

"Eddie, I told my parents we were going to the movie. I don't like to lie to them—"

His face grew tense. "What's with you? A few minutes ago you were hot to trot. Now you're gonna chicken out on me."

Cara could feel his anger, his violence. He was no better than Sean. What would he do to her when they got to their destination? What kind of *party* did he have in mind? She had to play it cool, keep him happy until she got a chance to run.

"You know," Eddie went on, "you could stand to loosen up a little, babe. If you don't—"

"All right, all right," Cara replied quickly. "I'll go to your party with you!"

He grinned. "That's more like it."

Cara decided to cop an attitude so he wouldn't see that she was really scared. "You could at least tell me where we're going, Eddie. It won't kill you to tell me."

Eddie lit a cigarette and shrugged. "I got

some buddies who're havin' a party out at Thunder Lake. A big fire and some brewskis. We're gonna get down. You'll love it."

Cara wondered what Eddie meant by "get down," but she was too afraid to ask. She started to think of a way to coax Eddie into pulling off the turnpike. If they stopped in a public place, she could walk away from him, call her parents to come after her.

"Eddie, how much fun are we going to have tonight?" she asked. "I mean, is it going to get wild?"

"You never know, babe," he said, exhaling a cloud of foul smoke. "I've been known to act crazy."

"Maybe we should stop," Cara offered. "Pick up some party favors. If you know what I mean?"

She gave him a knowing wink.

Eddie laughed and nodded. "Yeah, now you're gettin' with it. My kinda party babe."

"So, I have some money," Cara persisted. "I could spring for a couple of six-packs and some other—well, you know."

"Nah, there'll be plenty of brew at the party. We're gonna have a good time."

Cara's spirits plummeted even further. Did he know what she was trying to do? Or was he just so calculating that he had the entire evening planned from the beginning?

They rolled on into the night, taking the exit

marked "Thunder Lake." Eddie steered the rickety green vehicle along a narrow, two-lane road that wound back into an area of dense forest. When the trees seemed to loom darkest overhead, Eddie turned onto a dirt road that took them between low branches that scratched the windows.

This is a nightmare, Cara thought.

Eddie peered into the headlight beams. "I hope I took the right road."

What are they going to do to me?

"See anything?" he asked.

Cara shook her head. "No. Let's go back to my place, Eddie. We can party in my room."

"Nah, we'll find 'em."

The car kept rolling until they emerged in a clearing. A huge bonfire roared in the middle of the opening in the woods. Several shady figures hung by the fire, lifting beer cans to their lips. It didn't take Cara long to figure out that she was going to be the only girl at the party.

Eddie got out of the car and yelled to his friends. "Hey, dudes, the entertainment is here!"

Cara was frozen in the passenger seat. She decided not to get out of the car. Eddie came around to open her door.

"Let's go, gorgeous."

Cara shook her head. "No."

"What's the matter?" Eddie asked. "I thought you wanted to party big time."

"I want to go home," Cara insisted.

"No, we've come too far for that," Eddie replied.

He reached for her.

Cara drew back. "You're no better than Sean."

Eddie laughed. "Didn't take you long to figure that out."

"Then why did you help me?" Cara asked. "Why did you stand up to Sean?"

"I hate jerks like him," Eddie told her. "Besides, I was saving you for a real party. Tonight, you're gonna get what you deserve. Come on!"

He pulled her out of the car. Cara fell to the ground. Her face hit the moist dirt. Eddie grabbed her hair, pulling her head back. He told her to get up.

Cara shook her head. "No!"

"Get up, dollface. You're gonna make me happy. Me and my friends."

Catcalls rose from around the fire. "Whatsamatter, Eddie?"

"Can't you make her do what you say?"

"I thought you were gonna bring the party to us!"

Eddie's voice turned into a raspy growl. "You better get up, slut! Or I'm gonna hurt you!"

I've got to hurt him! Cara thought.

"All right," she said. "Let go of me and I'll get up!"

Eddie released his grip on her hair. "That's more like it."

Cara struggled to get to her feet. She wasn't going down without a fight. As she rose, Eddie turned back to his friends, the black shapes around the fire. They were leaving the warmth of the flames to move toward him.

Eddie laughed. "She's ready for a good time, guys. Just like I promised you."

"Check out the merchandise," one of them called.

"I want a closer look."

"Where'd you get her, Eddie?"

Cara leaned back against the car. Eddie had turned toward his friends. It was her only chance. She had to get away.

Reaching around with her hands, Cara sunk her fingernails into Eddie's face. He cried out, grabbing his eyes. Cara broke away from the group, running along the narrow trail that they had taken into the woods. She had to get to the main road—if it was possible on her wobbly legs.

As she fled, she could hear them in the clearing.

"What'd she do to you, Ed?"

"My face," Eddie cried. "I'm bleeding."

"She can't do that!"

"Let's get her!"

Cara could hear their cries as they came after her. She had a head start. And her legs had thawed out, allowing her to run with a velocity born of fear. The tree branches lashed at her as she fled through the darkness.

I can't let them catch me!

The road had to be up ahead. Maybe she could flag down a car. Or find a good hiding place. She wanted to wake up from this horrid dream, roll over in her bed, see her mother's smiling face at the breakfast table. But the nightmare voices rose in the trees.

"Get her!"

"She can't go far!"

Eddie bellowed, "After all I did for her!"

"We'll find her!"

Cara ran into an overhanging limb that knocked her to the ground. As she struggled to her feet, a blinding light flashed in her eyes. She stared into the sudden glow of car headlights.

"No!"

It was a late party-goer, arriving to block her path to the main road.

Now they would catch her for sure.

Unless she ran into the woods.

Cara started to push into the trees.

"Cara, don't!"

The voice had come from the car ahead of her. It sounded so familiar. She hesitated at the edge of the forest.

"Cara, it's me!"

She squinted through the beams. "Chris?"

"Get in!" Chris cried. "Hurry!"

Cara could not believe it. Was this part of the bizarre dream? She ran toward the car, climbing in on the passenger side of the red Subaru Justy that belonged to Chris's parents.

"Where did you—"

Chris put the Justy in reverse. "I followed you. You didn't think I was going to let you go out with Eddie by yourself, did you?"

"Hurry," Cara told him. "They're coming!"

Chris glanced up to see the demonic party boys in the beams of the headlights.

"There they are!" Cara cried.

Chris stomped the accelerator, backing away from the onrushing gang. Eddie took a flying leap through the air and landed on the hood of the Justy. He grabbed the windshield wipers, hanging on as Chris backed onto the main road. The momentum of the sudden sharp turn tossed Eddie from the hood of the car. He landed with a thud on the pavement.

Slamming the car into Drive, Chris squealed tires as he pulled away from Eddie. "Fasten your seat belt," he told Cara.

She fixed the belt across her waist. "I didn't see you following us," she offered.

"I know," Chris replied. "I did a good job."

She touched his arm. "Thank you! God, thank you!"

They drove in silence for a few minutes. Chris kept looking in the rearview mirror as he explained how he had borrowed his parents' car so he could follow Cara and Eddie. He knew Eddie would be trouble, that Cara was making a terrible mistake by going out with him. Cara could not stop trembling as they rolled down the dark country road.

"How far are we from the turnpike?" Cara asked.

Chris nodded to the rearview mirror. "Not far enough."

A pair of headlights had appeared behind them. The pinpoint glow of the twin beams grew larger as the car came on. Was it Eddie and his friends?

"Go faster," Cara urged.

The demons weren't going to give up. They wanted revenge. They wanted to hurt Cara.

"I'm doing seventy already!" Chris replied. "This little car won't go any faster."

"Maybe it's not them!"

But it was. Eddie's green car roared up behind them, smashing into the rear of the Subaru. Cara screamed. Chris held tightly to the wheel.

The Dodge pulled around them, drawing even with the Subaru. Eddie hung out of the passenger side, holding a bottle. He threw the bottle, smashing it against the windshield of the Subaru. The glass splintered, sending spiderweb cracks through the plate to obscure Chris's vision.

"I can't see!"

Cara gripped the sides of the seat. "Faster!"

"They're going to kill us!" Chris cried.

Eddie shook his fist at them, screaming. He threw another bottle that missed the Subaru. But it didn't matter. The driver of the Dodge swerved, smashing into the side of the Subaru. The impact sent the smaller car barreling off the road.

"No!" was the last word from Cara's mouth before the Subaru hit the ditch.

The wreck seemed to happen in slow motion.

The red Subaru turned over and over, rolling through a low patch of brush.

Cara rattled around in the front seat, held in place by the safety belt.

Chris banged against the wheel, his body shaking like a toy action figure.

Cara lost consciousness before the car came to a halt.

And when she awoke again, she opened her eyes to a bright, glowing light that made her wonder if she had entered the realm of the afterlife.

NINE

There was movement all around Cara. The smell of alcohol hit her nostrils. She knew she had been hurt but she could not remember exactly how it had happened. Cara wanted to move, to get up off the table where she lay, but the pains shot through her body, immobilizing her. She lay back on the table, listening to the authoritative voices.

"Blood pressure?"

"One-twenty over sixty."

"This leg looks like a compound fracture."

"Have her parents been notified?"

"They're on the way."

"Good, we may have to operate."

In the painful haze, one thought kept speeding through Cara's mind: *I'm going to die.*

"How's the boy?" someone asked.

"About the same as her."

"The paramedics had a devil of a time getting them out of the wreck. It took more than an hour."

"Are they going to make it?"

Before the answer came, another voice said, "The girl's parents are here."

Mom and Dad!

Would she get to see them before she died?

"Make sure the parents sign the consent form before we operate. I'll take her upstairs."

"She may need blood."

"Get it from the parents."

"I'll have them tested for blood type."

Cara's eyes opened enough to see the ceiling rushing overhead. The lights seemed to whoosh past her face. She tried to speak, to tell them that she wanted to see her mother and father. But her lips could not move. She had no voice inside her.

The lights grew brighter when they wheeled her into the operating room. Cara wanted to ask if she would live. Or would she pass away, die with the incredible pain shooting through her?

Her lips parted slightly. "Help me," she moaned.

A kind face hovered over her for a moment. "Don't worry, honey, we'll do everything we can."

A needle pricked a vein in Cara's arm.

She closed her eyes.

When she opened them again, she was lying in a hospital bed in a private room. The bed was surrounded by flowers. Cara tried to sit up but she was weak and her right leg had been elevated in traction. She also wore a plaster cast from her hip to her toes.

Cara moaned, unable to stir except for a slight movement of her head. She still could not remember what had happened to her. A vague memory of tumbling over and over repeated in the whirlpool confusion of her thoughts.

She had enough perception left to figure out that she was in Port City Community Hospital. Had there been some kind of wreck? She seemed to recall a huge bonfire in the woods. Where had she been before all of this pain started? What had she been doing?

"Hello there. Wide awake, I see."

The kind face of a young man loomed over her bed. He had a chart in his hand. He had to be a doctor, though he looked more like a college kid.

"I'm Dr. Baker," the young man told her. "I'd ask you how you're feeling, but I think I know."

Cara stared at the ceiling. Her entire body ached with a dull, throbbing agony. At least she was alive. If only she could remember the circumstances that had brought her here. Had there been a red car? And a green car?

"I'm going to give you something for the pain, Cara. You're going to be all right. I had to put a couple of pins in your leg to hold the bone together. But you're going to be fine after physical therapy. Of course, you'll be in bed for a while, but you'll recover completely."

Cara's lips parted again. "Water," she said weakly.

Her mouth was dry.

Dr. Baker smiled. "Not just yet. But you can drink something a little later this afternoon."

Cara closed her eyes.

"I think you'd like to know that your friend is going to be okay," the doctor said. "His shoulder was a lot like your leg, but he's going to make it."

"Friend?" she asked without opening her eyes.

"Yes, Chris Hall. He was in the car with you. Do you remember anything about the accident?"

"No, not much."

Chris had been with her. Where had they been together? An image of dark woods appeared in her memory. Why did she suddenly have a feeling of dread about the woods?

Dr. Baker's voice distracted her from the gray recollections. "There's somebody here who'd like to see you, Cara."

"Where is she?"

Cara recognized her mother's worried tone.

"Thank God. Thank God she's all right."

Her father was there too.

They came next to the bed, looking down at

their daughter. Mrs. Richards took her daughter's hand. Both of them were crying. After a moment, Cara began to cry too.

"Come on, Cara," Chris Hall said. "You can do it. Come on, work those crutches for all they're worth."

Cara leaned on a pair of aluminum crutches, trying to walk for the first time since she had gotten out of bed. Her physical therapy had been scheduled for the same hour as Chris's rehabilitation. Chris's entire right shoulder and arm were immobilized in a thick plaster cast. They had both been confined to their rooms for more than a week, but the doctors decreed that it was time for them to get moving again.

A light layer of perspiration had broken on Cara's face as she struggled with the crutches. Her leg ached inside the cast but she had to try. The padded crutches hurt the soft spots under her arms. She almost fell when she tried to take the first step.

The physical therapist, an older woman with graying hair, caught Cara before she could hit the floor. "That's all right," the therapist said in a caring voice. "You're doing fine."

Cara sighed. "I'm a dweeb!"

"No, you're not," Chris offered. "Come on, you can do it."

Cara balanced herself on the crutches. A bead of sweat dripped off her nose. She hobbled for another step, stopping to make sure she didn't fall.

The therapist was right there. "One more, Cara. Come on, you can do it."

Cara exhaled. "I never knew walking on crutches could be so difficult."

"Just thank God you can walk," Chris offered. "We were lucky to get out of that car wreck with our lives."

Cara hesitated, flashing on the images that had been plaguing her thoughts and dreams. She remembered a green car smashing into the red Subaru. She saw a hateful face leering at her. Had it really happened? Or was her imagination running wild?

"Are you all right?" the therapist asked.

Cara nodded. "Yes. I want to try again."

She started forward on the crutches. Dragging the cast was cumbersome, but she did it, walking about ten yards before she had to stop again. A slight smile parted her lips.

Chris was also smiling. "Good job, Cara."

The therapist patted her on the shoulder. "Keep practicing. I'll be right back." She walked away from Cara and Chris.

Cara used the crutches to retrace her awkward steps. She made it back to Chris, who nodded approvingly. Cara leaned on the crutches, standing in front of him. They had not talked much about the accident while they had been in the hospital. Cara figured it was time to discuss the tragedy with him.

"Chris, what do you remember about the car wreck?"

The smile disappeared from his face. "Cara, I don't remember a thing. Nothing."

"What were we doing out there on that road in the middle of the night?" she wondered aloud.

He shook his head. "I wish I knew."

"I keep seeing this other car in my head," Cara went on. "It's an old jalopy. And there's a boy hanging out the window. Then the car smashed into us. Didn't it?"

For a moment there was a flash of recognition in Chris's eyes. But then he seemed to go blank. Cara's memories could not spark his own recollections. Amnesia had erased everything about the accident.

"I wish I could remember," Cara offered. "There's like this—I don't know—this black demon that's hovering in my head. Something bad came down out there on that road, Chris."

"Maybe it will come back to us in time," Chris replied. "I'll keep trying to remember. I—"

"There's my girl! Cara, look at you!"

Her mother had arrived. Mrs. Richards strode across the physical therapy room. Her outstretched arms embraced Cara who almost fell off-balance.

"I'm sorry," her mother said, steadying Cara.

"Look at you! The doctor says you'll be out of that cast in another six weeks."

Cara grimaced. "Six weeks?"

Mrs. Richards smiled at Chris. "How's the shoulder?"

"It hurts," Chris replied. "But I'm going to live."

Cara leaned on the crutches. "Mom, watch this."

She went back and forth on the floor, dragging the cast behind her. Mrs. Richards applauded. Tears formed in her mother's eyes.

"I'm so proud of you, Cara."

"Mom!"

Mrs. Richards embraced her again.

Chris blushed. "Uh, do you want me to leave you two alone?"

Mrs. Richards dabbed at her teary eyes. "No, it's all right. When I think of what could've happened to you two—"

"I know," Cara said, shivering.

Mrs. Richards regarded her daughter again. "Honey, now that you're better, maybe you can tell me what happened. I mean, you left the house with that Jacobs boy. You were going to the movies."

Cara's eyes narrowed. "Jacobs?"

"Yes, Eddie Jacobs," her mother replied. "He came for dinner. He seemed like such a nice boy. But no one knows how you and Chris ended up together out there on that road. Do you remember?"

Cara recalled Eddie Jacobs saving her from Sean, but that was it. She had no recollection of dinner or the rest of the evening, except for the sensation of tumbling and the obscure face that leered at her from the mysterious green car. Did the face belong to Eddie Jacobs? She just didn't know!

"I'm sorry, Mom, I can't remember."

Mrs. Richards turned to Chris. "How about you?"

He shook his head. "No. I'm sorry—"

"That's okay, kids. It may come back to you. In the meantime, I hate to bring it up, but we have to talk about school."

"Did you bring some homework for us?" Cara asked.

Mrs. Richards took a deep breath. "No. Honey, I've been talking to Mr. Kinsley and he thinks by the time you get out of the hospital that you'll have missed too much school to catch up before graduation."

A dire expression spread over Cara's face. "We won't get to graduate with everyone else?"

"I'm afraid not," her mother replied. "You'll have to miss the prom too."

Chris frowned. "No prom! What a bummer." He wanted to go with Cara.

"Oh no, Mom. What will we have to do to get our diplomas?"

Mrs. Richards braced herself to answer the question. "I'm afraid you'll have to go to summer school, Cara."

"Summer school!" Cara cried. "Why? I've got enough credits to graduate. Why can't they—"

"You can't make up everything you've missed," her mother went on. "If it was only one or two classes there wouldn't be a problem. But you can't make it back to school before the end of the semester. If you don't go to summer school, Cara, you'll have to repeat the fall semester next year and that means you can't go to college in September. I'm sorry, honey, especially about the prom."

"I guess I don't have any choice," Cara muttered.

Summer school! She had always thought that summer school was for geeks and dweebs and dumb kids who couldn't cut it during the regular school year. It would ruin everything. No beach, no sailing, no fun outdoors. Summer school.

"Don't look so sad," her mother replied. "It's not the end of the world."

Cara sighed. "I know, I know."

"At least we'll be able to go together," Chris offered. "We won't be alone."

Cara turned away, walking on her crutches again. She finished her therapy and then talked with her mother for a while. After Mrs. Richards left, Cara returned to her private room.

She ate the bland hospital food and watched television for an hour.

The nurse came in about nine o'clock to give her a sedative. Cara took the pill and went right to sleep. That night, she dreamed of the accident, replaying it in the darkness of her nightmare. And when she awoke, she could not be sure if the images were real or simply a product of her mind.

In the light of morning, the dream faded and reality set in.

The words formed on Cara's lips as she sat up in bed.

There was no way around it.

She had to do it.

"Summer school," she muttered to herself. "Summer school."

TEN

The alarm clock blasted next to Cara's bed, shaking her from a deep slumber. Reaching for her nightstand, she pressed the button that silenced the dreaded noise. Flopping back on her pillows, Cara gazed to her right, checking the calendar on the wall. It was indeed June 15, the first day of summer school.

Cara had been home from the hospital for almost a week. Her leg was still in the hip cast. According to her doctors, the bones were healing well, if somewhat slowly. She would have to endure the entire summer school session in the cast. Even after the cast came off they would have to operate again to remove the pins from her leg. Cara wondered how much longer the pain would last.

She took a deep breath of warm summer air. The first heat wave of the year had swept over

Port City. Already the sun had begun to beat down on the quaint village. A thin layer of perspiration formed on Cara's face and her skin began to itch inside the cast. She made a growling noise of frustration and started to scratch the hardened plaster.

"Summer school," she muttered to herself.

Was it worth all the hassle? Maybe she should just wait to graduate during the fall semester. No, she had been accepted at State and Port City Community College, pending her graduation from Central.

A rapping resounded on her door. "Honey, are you awake?"

"Yes, Mom."

But I don't want to do this, especially with my leg in a cast.

"Cara, do you need any help?"

She sighed. She was too old to have her mother helping her get ready for school. But with her leg immobilized, she didn't have much choice.

"Sure, Mom, whatever."

Mrs. Richards entered the bedroom, trying to be cheerful.

Cara struggled to get out of bed, rising on her crutches. She had slept in a long T-shirt the night before. Her mother helped her to the bathroom where she had to wear a plastic garbage bag over her cast so she could take a shower. It was embarrassing, humiliating, and ridiculous.

After she dried her hair, Cara returned to her room. Mrs. Richards had laid out a nice silk blouse and a special pair of jeans. One leg of the jeans had been cut off at the hip so Cara could get the pants over the cast. Of course, she would need only one sock and a single running shoe.

Mrs. Richards helped her into the outfit and stepped back to look at her daughter. "Well, you're as pretty as ever. Would you like to put on some makeup?"

Cara made a face and sighed. "What's the point? There won't be anyone there but me and a bunch of geeks."

"Chris will be there," her mother replied.

"Yes, I forgot. Chris. At least I won't be completely alone with the geek squad."

Mrs. Richards smiled. "Honey, if this is all too much, you can wait until the fall semester. Your father and I won't mind."

Cara shook her head. "No, it's all right. I'm getting kind of bored anyway."

"Let's go down to breakfast."

Maneuvering through the hall and down the stairs was a major task on the crutches. Her mother preceded Cara, helping her take each step with deliberate precision. They finally emerged in the kitchen where Mr. Richards sat with his morning paper.

He grinned at his daughter. "Well, the princess has arisen. How are you, honey?"

Cara's entire body was covered with sweat on this hot day. "I'm fine, Dad," she replied with no enthusiasm.

Mr. and Mrs. Richards exchanged a concerned look as Cara flopped into the chair. Her broken leg extended to the side. She grabbed a butter knife and tried to scratch inside the cast.

"Damn," she said with a huff. "This thing is going to itch for the rest of my life."

Mr. Richards gently reminded her that he didn't appreciate that sort of language from his daughter.

Cara apologized and picked up a piece of toast, nibbling at it with little appetite.

Mrs. Richards tried to be positive. "I was talking to your counselor, Miss Monica, and she told me that if you can pass a couple of tests at the end of the week, they might go ahead and give you enough credits for graduation."

Cara seemed to perk up with that bit of news. "Really?"

"Yes. Of course, there's your English term paper. That has to be finished."

Cara nodded, smiling. "It's almost finished. I just have to type it."

Mr. Richards shrugged. "Give it to me and I'll have my secretary take care of it for you."

"Would you, Dad? Thanks!"

One week in summer school! Cara could

endure that. And she had been caught up in all her courses before the accident. A little review and she would pass the tests in a hurry.

"You're the greatest!" Cara said. "I love you both, Mom and Dad. I really do!"

She returned to her breakfast, gobbling the eggs and toast with renewed gusto.

"Uh, Cara," her father started, "have you remembered anything more about the accident?"

Cara shook her head. "No. I keep having these dreams, but I can't be sure if they're real."

"What sort of dreams?" her mother asked.

Cara's brow fretted as she recalled the nightmares. She kept seeing a green car and a boy's twisted face. But that was it. She wasn't sure about the car or the boy's identity.

"Cara?"

She was staring blankly into space. "Sorry. No, I don't remember anything."

Her father sighed. "I'd still like to know how you and Chris came to be on that road in the middle of the night. Also what happened out there and why it happened."

"So would I," Cara replied. "So would I."

They were silent as Cara finished her breakfast.

Mr. Richards dabbed at his forehead with a napkin. "Gonna get up to ninety today. What a scorcher."

"Is your school air-conditioned?" her mother asked.

Cara shrugged. "I don't know."

Her father rose from the table. "Well, my office has an air conditioner so I'm on my way. Have a good day at summer school, Princess." He kissed her on the forehead.

Mrs. Richards smiled at her daughter. "We'd better get going too. We have to pick up Chris. I promised him a ride."

Cara balanced on the crutches again, making for the front door. "Cara Richards," she said humorously, "summer school dweeb!"

Mrs. Richards laughed. "It's good to see that you can chuckle at all this."

"I just want it to be over so I can go to college in the fall," Cara replied.

Getting to the car was an ordeal. They emerged in the hot sun that had already raised the temperature to a steamy eighty-five degrees. Cara bumped the cast down the front steps. Luckily, Mrs. Richards drove a big, roomy Cadillac, but Cara still had to twist like a contortionist to sit down in the front seat. When she was finally settled, she drew a deep breath and exhaled, wiping the sweat from her face with a tissue.

Her mother climbed in on the driver's side. "Are you all right, honey?"

Cara nodded. "I'm sweating like a pig. Even though pigs don't have sweat glands."

"Well, I just had the air-conditioning system charged so this car will be cool in no time."

As they rolled toward Chris's house, cold air began to flow from the vents on the dashboard. Cara lowered her face into the stream of frigid air. At least she'd be comfortable on the way to summer school.

Summer school!

She still couldn't believe it.

Chris was waiting for them by the curb. His cast had been removed, but he still wore his arm in a sling. He climbed awkwardly into the backseat.

"Hi, Cara. Hi, Mrs. R. Wow, air-conditioning. Cool! Hey, Cara, ready for summer school?"

"Yeah, when monkeys fly out of my nose!"

They all laughed.

Mrs. Richards hit the accelerator and they roared off toward Central Academy.

The school looked empty as they approached.

"Where should I let you off?" Mrs. Richards asked.

Chris pointed to the sophomore building. "My notice said that classes were being held over there."

Mrs. Richards steered the Cadillac into the sophomore parking lot. Sure enough, there was a sign with an arrow pointing the way to "Summer Classes." A few cars had been parked in a temporary lot.

"Bye, Mom." Cara kissed her mother on the cheek. "See you at three o'clock."

"I'll pick you up right here," Mrs. Richards replied.

Chris was already out of the car, opening Cara's door with his good hand. "Here, I'll help you."

Cara struggled until she was back in the hot air, balancing on the crutches. She watched her mother leave. It was great to have the support of her parents.

Chris took her arm. "Let's get it over with."

As Cara turned toward the door of the classroom building, her eyes caught a flash of green. She stopped, staring at the green Dodge that had been parked in the temporary lot. It was the same car in her dreams. Or was it?

"Cara?"

"Huh?"

"We have to go in."

She nodded. "Sure. Chris? Do you see that green car?"

"Yeah. So?"

"Does it look familiar?" Cara asked.

"No, not really. Cara, come on, we have to go."

She was transfixed by the image of the green Dodge in her nightmares. Could this be the same car? Or was it simply a coincidence? It couldn't be the same.

"Cara—"

"Okay, okay!"

Cara propelled herself forward on the crutches. The heat immediately drew moisture from her skin. Her heart had begun to pound. The sight of the green car had shaken her.

"Are you okay?" Chris asked.

"Yeah."

But she wasn't.

They entered the cool air of the hallway.

"Room Four-eighteen," Chris said. "There."

It took her a few extra seconds to reach the classroom. She felt weak, hot, short of breath. She had to stop for a moment to compose herself.

"Are you sure you're okay?" Chris asked.

She nodded. "I think I need to sit down."

Chris opened the classroom door.

Cara entered, stopping when she heard the wicked voice.

It came from the back of the room, as haunting as her nightmares. "Well, well, look who's here!"

Cara's bones turned to ice. She lifted her eyes to see Eddie Jacobs sitting with a gang of rough-looking boys in the last row of desks. The sight of his face and his hateful voice brought it all back in one rush of memory.

Suddenly Cara remembered everything about the accident and the horrible evening that had preceded the car wreck.

ELEVEN

Eddie Jacobs leaned forward on the desk, glaring at Cara. "Hey, Miss Cheerleader. Headin' for summer school or what?"

Cara's body trembled as she replayed the night of terror in her mind. She remembered now leaving with Eddie, thinking that they were going to a movie. The woods surrounded her, the bonfire reflected in her eyes. She had fled for the main road, then Chris was there. Eddie's hateful face hung out of the green car's window. The Dodge smashed into the red Subaru, sending them off the road.

She could see the expectation in Eddie's glassy eyes. Why hadn't she turned him in yet? Why hadn't she gone to the cops to tell them about his dirty work?

Chris leaned closer to Cara, whispering,

"Let's pass our tests so we can get away from these scum puppies."

Cara nodded, but she wasn't sure what Chris had said. She knew what she had to do. But she couldn't leave just yet. She had to wait until the class was finished at three o'clock.

"We better sit down," Chris told her.

Cara settled into a desk, extending her broken leg. Chris sat next to her, watching Cara, wondering why she had suddenly become so nervous and distracted. Why was the sweat soaking through her silk blouse?

"Cara—"

"I'm all right," she replied quickly. "We can talk later."

"Talk about what?"

She turned to glare at him with narrow eyes. "Chris—"

One of the hateful voices rose from the back row. "Hey, Red, what'd you do to your leg?"

"Yeah," Eddie rejoined, "you in a' accident or somethin'?"

Cara turned bright red. She flicked the ball of sweat that hung from the end of her nose. Did Eddie realize that she had remembered everything? What would he do if she went to the police now?

"Hey, gorgeous, how about me and you after school? We could—"

"All right, all right. Enough!"

Cara's eyes lifted to the doorway of the classroom. Coach McCarron stood there with his briefcase in hand. He would be their teacher for the summer school sessions. Coach McCarron had a rough manner and a tough disposition. His beady brown eyes had focused on the troublemakers in the back row.

He walked to the desk and threw his briefcase down. "Now, you clowns in the back row better shape up pronto, otherwise you'll get bounced from here in a hurry."

Eddie's contrite voice rose again. "Uh, sorry, Coach. You won't have any trouble out of us."

Cara cringed at the good-guy act. She had fallen for it once before at dinner. She had believed Eddie's routine and it had almost gotten her killed.

A few more summer students came in just before the bell rang. Coach McCarron went into his speech, telling them how their summer studies were going to be self-motivated, self-directed. He winked at Cara once, as if to say, "Don't worry, you'll be out of here soon."

I hope so, Cara thought.

After the speech, Coach McCarron passed out workbooks to everyone. Cara's workbook consisted of math problems. Chris got the one for history. Cara opened the book, but she couldn't concentrate, not with Eddie sitting behind her.

Coach McCarron stepped between Chris and Cara. "Hi, kids. Look, I know what happened to you two and I'm sorry. Just do the workbooks this week and we'll test you on Friday. All you have to do is pass and you'll get to go home. Okay?"

Chris breathed easier. "Thanks, Coach."

"You're welcome. Hall, is that wing gonna be okay for the swimming team at State?"

"I hope so, Coach."

He looked at Cara. "You okay, Cara?"

She nodded, wondering if she should tell Coach McCarron about Eddie. No, she'd wait. There was no need to confess now.

For the remainder of the morning, Cara did problems in the workbook. At lunchtime, she hung out with Chris in the plaza courtyard in the middle of the campus. Eddie and his friends sat nearby, watching them. What would he do when Cara told her story to the police? Hopefully, they would take him into custody immediately.

When they came back from lunch, Coach McCarron launched into another speech. "All right, listen up, you geniuses. Just for the record, summer school is confined to the sophomore building. The other buildings are locked up tight, even the library. So don't go wandering, otherwise you might get locked in. Okay? Now, how many of you finished your workbooks this morning?"

Chris and Cara were the only ones who raised their hands. Cara thought she heard snickering in the back of the room. She hoped to put an end to their laughter.

That afternoon, she filled in the pages of a science workbook. Her eyes kept watching the clock on the wall. When the bell rang at three, Chris helped her to the parking lot outside. Her mother waited in the Cadillac.

"Hi, dear," Mrs. Richards said. "How was it?"

Cara's eyes were focused on the green car where Eddie and his friends stood smoking their cigarettes. "Take Chris home first," Cara replied. "Then take me to the police station."

Her mother frowned. "What?"

"Just do it," Cara replied. "I remember what happened. And I want to tell Chief Danridge everything."

Chief Danridge leaned back in his chair and folded his hands over his chest. "Now, let me see if I have this straight, Cara. You left your house with Eddie Jacobs. He said you were going to a movie, but once you were on the road, he took you to some kind of party at Thunder Lake."

Cara nodded. She sat on the other side of Danridge's huge desk. Mrs. Richards stood beside her daughter, watching nervously as Cara told her story.

"But then things went sour?" Danridge asked.

Cara took a deep breath, bracing herself. "Yes, like I said, they were threatening me."

"How?" Danridge challenged.

Cara shifted in the seat, her aching leg extended at an angle to the wooden chair. "Threatening!"

"What did they say?"

"I—I can't remember exactly," Cara said. "But I had to run away. Then Chris was there. He had followed us."

Danridge leaned forward. "Why?"

"He didn't want me to go out with Eddie," she replied.

"But you did anyway?"

Sweat started to ooze from Cara's pores. "Yes, I was confused. Sean had just died. I thought—it seemed okay."

Why did Danridge refuse to believe her?

"Okay," he went on, "you ran away from the party. Chris was there. You left with him?"

"Yes," Cara said, "and they followed us. Eddie and his friends. They smashed into us with his car. They forced us off the road. That's why we had the accident."

"I see."

Mrs. Richards glared at Danridge. "My daughter isn't a liar! If she says it happened that way, then it did!"

Danridge held up his hands. "Take it easy. I just want to get all of the facts straight before we go accusing anyone."

"I'm telling the truth," Cara insisted.

Danridge's steely eyes peered right through

her. "Then why did you wait until now to tell me?"

Cara fought her anger, trying not to lose her temper in front of Danridge. "I didn't remember until I saw Eddie's car at school," she replied. "It all came back to me."

"Okay," Danridge said, "I'll look into it and call you later tonight."

"You will?" Cara asked skeptically.

He nodded. "Yes. You've raised some questions that have to be answered. I'll investigate."

"Thank you."

Cara walked out of the police station on crutches. Her mother helped her into the Cadillac. They drove through the narrow streets, heading back to Prescott Estates.

"I hope he believed me," Cara said.

Mrs. Richards sighed. "Honey, are you sure about all of this? I mean, you have been very confused lately."

"I'm sure," Cara replied. "Mom, you have to believe me!"

"I do, honey. I do."

When they reached the house, Cara went into the living room and plopped down on the couch. What a lousy summer, she thought. And it would only get worse.

The phone rang, but it was Chris instead of Chief Danridge.

"How'd it go?" he asked.

"They're investigating," Cara replied. "I should hear from them soon."

"How are you doing?"

Cara sighed. "Okay. I'll feel better after I hear something."

"Want me to come over?" Chris offered.

"Sure. Come for dinner. We can study."

"See ya."

She hung up.

Her eyes wandered to the picture window that looked out onto the street. For a moment a flash of green filled her view. An old car roared past her house. Cara's chest tightened. Was Eddie coming after her again?

The phone rang, startling her.

Cara picked up to hear her mother talking to Chief Danridge. It was bad news. There was no way to check Cara's story. The red Subaru had been shipped to a junkyard upstate, where it was destroyed in a crusher. Eddie had been called in for questioning, but according to his story, everything had been amicable. Chris had arrived at the party and Cara had gone home of her own free will. There hadn't been any fight, no hard feelings, no car chase.

"That's a lie!" Cara cried. "Check Eddie's car."

"We did," Danridge replied. "And there has been some recent body work. But that car is covered with body work. And he has four friends to back him up, Cara. I'm sorry, there's nothing I can do. Nothing at all."

Cara slammed the phone down. "What a jerk!"

She had told the truth, but it hadn't done her any good.

After a moment Mrs. Richards appeared at the archway of the living room. "I'm sorry, honey."

"Mom, I'm not lying. I swear."

"Honey, can't you put it all behind you? You're alive and well, that's all that matters."

"What if Eddie tries something?"

A worried expression flashed on her mother's face. "I—I don't think he will, Cara. Maybe your father can talk to him if—"

"No! You're right, Mom. I have to put it behind me. There's nothing else to do."

"It'll be all right, honey."

Cara nodded. "Yeah, I guess. I invited Chris for dinner."

"That's fine, dear."

She left Cara alone in the living room.

Cara opened her notebook, gazing at the pages of an English workbook that had to be completed. She tried to work on the lesson but she was too upset. Finally the doorbell rang and her mother answered to let Chris into the house.

"Hi," he said. "What happened?"

Cara told him the entire maddening story.

Chris shook his head. "Wow. I wish I could remember something. I wish I could help."

"So do I," Cara replied. "So do I."

But nothing could be done.

Like it or not, they had to attend summer school with Eddie Jacobs and his gang of idiots.

The next day Cara and Chris approached their summer class with a sense of caution. Eddie's green Dodge sat in the parking lot, a reminder of Cara's nightmares. Would the dreams ever go away now that she remembered the reality?

Mrs. Richards had suggested that Cara forget summer school and pursue her diploma in the fall. But Cara had refused, saying that she could not let Eddie win. She would not give in to the fear, no matter how much it had gripped her.

When Cara and Chris entered the classroom, Coach McCarron was already sitting at his desk. Cara's heart hopped as she lifted her eyes to the back of the classroom. Eddie and his cohorts were in place, though every one of them avoided looking at her. They were diligently at work, pretending to ignore her.

Coach McCarron smiled at Cara. "Don't worry, you're not late. Take a seat. I need to talk to you."

Cara feared the worst but it was only good news for her and Chris. Coach McCarron praised their efforts on the workbooks, saying that they could be tested on Friday in all their subjects, providing that the rest of the workbooks were completed. If they passed the tests, they'd get their diplomas and summer school would be completed.

Cara breathed easier. In a few short days, she'd be finished with Eddie Jacobs and his ilk. College awaited her and Chris. They could get on with their lives, putting all this misery behind them.

"Are you okay?" the coach asked.

Cara nodded. "Yes. It's just—those boys, the ones in the back of the room. I've had trouble with Eddie before and I don't want to—"

Coach McCarron waved his hand. "Don't worry about it. I won't let those jerks bother you. You just concentrate on your work and make sure you get that term paper in for your English teacher."

Cara tried to smile. "I'll have it for you soon. It's being typed."

Coach McCarron patted her hand. "Good. Now, you guys go to it until lunch. I'm counting on you."

Chris nodded. "Thanks, Coach."

McCarron pointed a finger at him. "You know, Hall, you would've made a good wide receiver on the football team. Too bad you liked swimming more."

"Sorry, Coach."

For the rest of the morning, they worked on history and English. Eddie and the others were well behaved, keeping quiet and ignoring Cara. Was it over? Cara wondered. Or was Eddie biding his time, waiting to retaliate?

Her answer came at lunchtime when Eddie approached her and Chris in the outdoor plaza. Chris stood up, facing Eddie, though there was little Chris could do with his arm in a sling. Cara stiffened, pulling the crutches in front of her.

Eddie had a hangdog expression on his rough face. "Uh, hey, what's doin'?"

"What do you want, Eddie?" Chris asked.

Eddie looked at Cara. "I wanted to say I'm sorry for all the trouble. I didn't mean to—"

Cara's eyes flashed and her nostrils flared. "Sorry? Sorry for almost killing us?"

A slight smirk spread across Eddie's thin mouth. "Hey, nobody proved nothin'."

"You were lucky I didn't remember sooner," Cara replied. "Otherwise, you'd be in jail."

Eddie pointed a finger at her. "I wasn't drivin' that car when it smashed into you!"

"It doesn't matter," Cara told him. "You and those 'friends' of yours were going to hurt me."

Eddie's anger, his true self, boiled up to turn his face red. "You came to that party of your own free will!"

"We were supposed to go to the movies!" Cara shot back. "I asked you to take me home, but you refused. You wanted to do something horrible to me but I got away. Then you tried to kill us, Eddie! I can't forgive you for that. Never!"

Eddie had begun to tremble with anger. "You ain't seen the last of me, Miss Cheerleader. You hear that?" He stormed away to join his hoodlum friends for a cigarette break.

"That guy's got some nerve," Chris offered.

Cara drew a jerky breath, hoping that she hadn't doomed herself to a horrid fate. "We have to stay away from him, Chris. Just get through it. We'll be okay."

"I hope you're right, Cara. I really do."

That afternoon Mrs. Richards picked up Cara right on time. She dropped Chris off and returned home where Cara studied until her father arrived. Mr. Richards had Cara's finished, typewritten English term paper.

Cara began to cry. She told her parents that she would be through with summer school on Friday if she passed all her tests. Then she confessed that Eddie had threatened her.

"I'll take that little punk apart!" Mr. Richards replied.

Cara's mother restrained him. "Don't! It will pass if you leave it alone. The police know all about this boy, so I don't think he'll try anything."

"I'll call his father!" Mr. Richards insisted.

"I don't think he has a father," Cara interjected. "He's a creep, Dad. I just want to stay away from him. And Coach McCarron says he'll protect me."

Mr. Richards deflated a little. "Well, if that kid tries anything else, I'll personally kill him."

Cara assured her father that wouldn't be necessary.

The next morning Cara handed in her English term paper and worked on her Latin and civics credits. Eddie Jacobs shot her a couple of hostile looks, but he left her alone. Chris and Cara ate lunch in the classroom to make sure Eddie didn't bother them. Mrs. Richards arrived at three to take them home, putting an end to a less stressful day of summer school.

Thursday came and went quickly, with Chris and Cara brushing up for their exams on Friday. Eddie and the last-row bullies kept their distance. Cara still didn't venture into the courtyard for lunch. When she climbed into her mother's car later that day, Cara figured it would be finished the following afternoon.

But she was wrong.

The trouble wasn't over.

It was just beginning.

TWELVE

On Friday morning Cara and Chris began the battery of tests that could free them from the twelfth grade and Central Academy. At first, Cara was happy to get under way with the process that would send her on to college. But as the morning wore on, she started to feel a bit nostalgic and melancholy. This was her last day at Central. No more would she trod the corridors, never to cheer again. She had missed the prom and graduation. It was sort of sad for everything to wind up like this, but it had to be.

Just pass the tests and get on with it, she told herself.

At the lunch break, she talked with Chris, who seemed confident that he was acing the tests. He talked about the colleges they had applied to and had been accepted at. His enthusiasm was not catching, for Cara kept watching

Eddie Jacobs and his friends from the corner of her eye. Would she really be free of them at the end of the day?

They returned to the classroom after lunch to find that Coach McCarron had already graded their tests from the morning session. Both Chris and Cara had done well, which meant that they would be receiving A's in those subjects. They still had to take two more exams and then they would be free.

As Cara eased into her desk, she heard Eddie and his cohorts snickering and whispering behind her. She cringed, wondering what lies Eddie was telling them. She'd be rid of him after three o'clock, but Cara had to wonder if the nightmares would ever end.

Coach McCarron gave them the next tests and they started to work. Cara found herself ripping through the exam questions. While she was breezing along, the classroom door opened and her English teacher, Mrs. Palmer, walked in to talk to Coach McCarron. Mrs. Palmer handed the coach a large manila envelope and then turned to look at Cara before she left.

This could be more trouble, Cara thought.

By the time she finished the last exam, it was almost three o'clock. Coach McCarron told her to wait while he graded the papers. Chris waited with her. It didn't take long for the coach to tell them that they had both passed with flying colors.

Cara exhaled. "Thank God."

Chris grinned. "Yes!"

Coach McCarron was not smiling. "There's just one thing, Cara—"

Her face turned white. "What?"

The bell rang to end the session officially.

"Wait a minute," Coach McCarron told them. "Okay, everybody else, turn in your workbooks and hit the bricks!"

One by one, the rest of the class filed by the coach's desk, dropping their papers and workbooks.

Cara could smell the cigarette stench of Eddie and his gang as they passed her. She did not look up. Cara never wanted to see Eddie's face again.

"Make sure you're in here on Monday!" the coach called after them. "Boy, I wish all of my summer school students were like you, Cara. You too, Hall."

Cara's dark green eyes focused nervously on Coach McCarron. "What's wrong?"

Coach McCarron sighed as he removed Cara's term paper from the manila envelope. "Uh, I'm afraid Mrs. Palmer wasn't exactly thrilled with your paper."

That witch! Cara thought.

"She gave you an incomplete," the coach went on. "Seems you didn't have all your sources footnoted and your bibliography was incomplete."

Cara took a deep breath. "Great. So I failed English?"

Coach McCarron smiled. "No! Mrs. Palmer isn't that bad. She's going to let you correct it. Look."

He unfolded the paper, showing her the red marks from Mrs. Palmer's correction pencil.

"It's nothing, Cara. All you have to do is rework your footnote page and do another bibliography."

She studied the work that had been savaged by her English teacher. She had included all of the footnotes and sources in her handwritten draft of the paper. Her father's secretary must've screwed up when she typed the manuscript.

"How can I fix this?" Cara said aloud. "My notes are all in the garbage. And the library is closed."

Chris patted her shoulder. "You can go to the public library."

"No," she replied. "I couldn't find those books at the public library. Most of them aren't there."

Coach McCarron tried to be sympathetic. "Uh, Cara, it's not all that bad. I'll see if I can get special permission from the assistant principal so you can spend Monday in the library."

Tears were forming in Cara's green eyes. "Monday! That's no good, Coach. I'll have to come back and see those idiots. Eddie and his gang. Couldn't I go today?"

"I don't know, Cara—"

Chris pleaded for her. "You've got keys to every door in the school, Coach. You could let us in. We won't trash the place. We could do our stuff and get out of there."

"We?" the coach challenged.

"Sure," Chris replied, wanting desperately to be with Cara every moment, "I could help her. I mean, she's on crutches. It's not like she can find all the books and everything like that."

Coach McCarron seemed to be waiting, but he hung tough for another minute. "I don't know, kids. I could get in a lot of trouble. I don't think I'm authorized to let you use the library."

Cara wanted the summer school session to end this day. "I promise we won't cause any trouble. I'll just find my sources and get out of there. Please, Coach. I don't want to come back Monday. I mean, if I hadn't hurt my leg, I'd already be out of here. I'd have graduated with everyone else."

He was starting to feel sorry for her. "You have had a bunch of lousy breaks."

"Please, Coach!"

He sighed. "What about your mother? Isn't she waiting for you outside?"

Chris stood up. "I'll go tell her to come back later."

Coach McCarron wavered for a moment, but then he saw the pitiful expression on Cara's face. "Okay. But you two better shoot in and out of there in a hurry. And if you get caught, I don't know anything about it. You got that?"

"Great," Chris replied. "I'll go tell Mrs. Richards!"

Cara smiled warmly. "Thanks."

Coach McCarron pointed a finger at her. "The only reason I'm doing this is because you're such a good kid!"

"I really appreciate it."

"And—you're the best cheerleader we ever had at Central."

Chris ran back into the room. "Okay, it's all set. I told your mom that we'd get a ride from my mom when we're finished. You can come for supper too—if you want to."

"Can you type the stuff on your computer?" Cara asked.

Chris shrugged. "Sure, why not?"

The coach rose from his desk, dangling the huge ring of keys. "All right, let's do it. But remember, I never let you in."

"Cool," Cara said.

They followed Coach McCarron to the end of the hall where he unlocked the first door. "Now, you can get out of here, because I'm going to prop this door open. And the door at the other end of the hall will be open too. Make sure you close it when you leave."

"Great," Cara rejoined.

Coach McCarron grimaced. "We're not finished yet. Come on, we have to navigate a few more doors."

At the end of the adjoining corridor, Coach McCarron unlocked a padlock that secured a chair through the handles of the double doors. "Make sure you lock this back up when you leave."

"No problem," Chris told him.

"Hey! I don't want you two getting locked in. You got me?"

"Don't worry," Cara assured him. "We won't."

Cara ambulated on the crutches until they reached a side door that led into the library.

Coach McCarron unlocked the door with a master key. "Now, on this one, there's a lock inside on the doorknob. Make sure it's closed and locked when you leave. Don't leave it open. There's no maintenance workers in the summer. If you leave it open and the librarian finds out—just don't leave it open, okay?"

"Thanks, Coach," Cara told him, giving him a peck on the cheek. "I won't forget you."

"Just make sure you lock up! And turn that paper in on time. I don't want to see you back here in the fall."

"You're awesome, Coach."

Cara and Chris entered the library, switching on a few lights. The sunlight still streaked in the windows, allowing them to see the book stacks clearly. Cara hobbled to the center of the main room and sat at a table.

"What books do you need?" Chris asked, removing his arm from the sling.

"I'll have to figure it out from my paper," Cara replied. "I can't believe Mrs. Palmer. I mean, does she sleep under a rock or what?"

She told Chris the title of the first book that she needed. After he had fetched it from the stacks, Cara wrote down all the information. Chris took the book back to the stacks and got the next one.

"This is going to be easy," Chris offered. "My shoulder feels great."

Cara grimaced. "I'm glad. Hey, I used some magazines, too. I don't know if we can get into the periodical room."

"Give me the magazines' titles and I'll take a look."

When Chris had gone, Cara sat by herself in the library. Outside, the summer day was starting to grow dark. Cara flinched when she heard the dull rumble of thunder in the distance. A storm was blowing in from the Atlantic. Summer boomers could be scary in Port City. Sometimes the power would go out for hours.

Chris did not return right away. Cara started to become anxious. Lightning cracked overhead and the rain began to pelt the windows of the library building.

"Chris!" she called.

No answer.

Suddenly the library was filled with horrid

screeching and the sounds of static. A weird sound came out of the loudspeakers on the walls. Something had activated the public address system used for the morning announcements.

"Chris!"

The speakers went dead. It had to be the results of the storm. Cara no longer cared about her term paper or the incomplete grade. She simply wanted to get out of the school and go home. Everything else could wait until Monday.

"Chris!"

"I'm right here, Cara."

He bolted from the long shadows between the high metal book stacks.

"Let's go," she told him.

Chris nodded. "Good idea. I can't get into the periodical room anyway. And this storm has got me spooked."

They gathered up the papers and started for the hallway.

"Hey," Chris said, "there's a phone in the office. I'll call my mom from here. She'll be glad to hear I can take my arm out of the sling."

Cara waited, listening to the thunder. She hated storms. She wanted to be home in her room, safe and secure.

Chris came back, frowning. "The line's dead. Must be the storm."

"Come on, Chris, let's get out of here."

They emerged in the hall, locking the door

behind them. Cara moved as fast as she could on the crutches. They reached the next door, the one that had been secured with a chain and padlock.

Chris frowned. "Look, the chain and lock are gone."

"I don't care," Cara replied. "Let's just go."

"But the coach said—"

Cara started for the end of the hallway. "I don't care. I'm getting the hell out of here."

Chris fell in behind her. "I hope we don't get in trouble."

When they reached the end of the hallway, their mouths fell open. Someone had been here. But who?

"It's locked," Chris said. "How'd that happen?"

The chain and padlock had been used to close the door that the coach had left open. Chris pulled at the lock but it was fixed tight.

"We're locked in," Cara said, her face turning white.

Somewhere in the recesses of the building, the loudspeaker crackled to life, bringing with it Eddie Jacobs's hateful voice.

"Attention, shoppers," the loudspeaker blared, "this is Mr. Ed. You're locked in, Cara. It's all over for you, Miss Cheerleader. Welcome, children. Welcome to *Hell*!"

THIRTEEN

Cara stumbled, falling back against the wall, balancing herself on one of the crutches. The other crutch fell to the floor, sending a metallic echo through the corridor. Chris reached out with his right hand, grabbing Cara's arm.

Eddie's voice reverberated in every corner of the school. "Miss Cheerleader and Mr. Swim Team. Trapped like rats. Let's see you get out of this one, you losers!"

Cara's lips trembled and her body shook. "My God!"

Chris shook her. "Stop it."

"Don't you see," Cara muttered. "He's going to kill us, Chris. He won't be happy until we're dead!"

Thunder rumbled over Port City.

Chris's face came closer to Cara. "You've got

to keep it together, Cara. Please. We can get out of this."

"We're locked in!"

A jagged bolt of lightning seared the heavens.

"Cara—"

Eddie's voice filled the hallway. "You Prescott pukes are all alike. Sucking up to the coach. By the way, I've got his keys. So I can follow you anywhere you want to go."

"No!" Cara cried.

Chris scowled her. "Don't lose it!"

But her nerves were frayed, jangled by days of anxiety, worn thin by the ordeal that had begun with Sean's attempted rape. "I can't make it, Chris. He's going to kill me!"

"No! He's not going to get us. Now come on, let's see if we can book out of here."

Cara froze against the wall. "I can't move, Chris. I'm—"

Eddie was there again, piercing their ears with his hateful dialogue. "Hell is for Prescott pukes! You should've stayed at the party, Cara. It would have been fun. You could've had a great time with the guys. But now you have to pay. You went to the cops. And I don't like cops. Now it's your turn to die. You should've died in that car wreck. I wish you had. It would've been so great. I could've stood there at your funeral, the same way I went to Sean's funeral. I loved it when they buried that puke!"

"Sean," Cara whispered.

"You don't think Sean really committed suicide, do you?" Eddie went on. "No way. I was watching you that night Sean hid in your car. I chased him. I pulled him off that fence. I knew he'd come back for more, so I took care of him. And you didn't even seem to appreciate it, Cara. You wouldn't even party-down with me and my friends. Now we're going to have a different kind of party. And you're the guest of honor."

"No! Leave me alone!" Cara cried.

Chris hated to do it but he slapped Cara's cheek, stinging her back to reality. "Snap out of it!"

Cara stared wide-eyed at him. "He's going to kill us!"

"No, he's not," Chris replied. "Now come on, let's try to get out of here."

He picked up the fallen crutch, putting it under Cara's arm. When Cara wouldn't come off the wall, Chris pulled her, making her stand on the crutches. He felt horrible about being so rough with her, but he had to force Cara to move.

"Come on!"

With a sharp jerk, Chris propelled Cara forward. She had to use the crutches again. As soon as she was moving, she seemed to gain strength. Chris helped her flee toward the door at the other end of the corridor. He kept thanking Heaven that both his arms were working.

"I hope this one didn't lock," Chris said under his breath.

When they reached the door, he pushed on the handle. The door flew open. Chris helped Cara through the archway.

"We can't get out this way!" Cara said.

Chris took her hand. "Maybe we can. Come on, we have to try."

As they headed back to the library, Eddie made another demonic announcement. "You won't escape. The school is locked up tight. And my boys are everywhere. Even if you find an open hole, you'll still be trapped little mice! Or should that be little rats!"

How many friends from Hell did Eddie have? Cara wondered. She had counted five of them, including Eddie, in the back row. Would they all be with Eddie? Maybe he had brought more thugs from outside the school.

"We have to lock ourselves in the library," Chris offered. "We can hide in there."

But when they reached the door that they had entered before, it was locked from the inside.

Sweat poured from their faces. Cara leaned against the door, trembling. Chris's eyes scanned the shaded corridor as thunder rolled across the sky again.

"There's got to be a way!"

Cara closed her eyes. "I hate him. I wish he were dead!"

Eddie would not let up. “Little rats? Have you found the cheese? No one can help you. No one!”

Chris pointed toward a door in a dark corner. “There!”

Cara opened her eyes. “What?”

Chris helped her again. “Come on, maybe we can hide.”

Cara struggled on the crutches. Her leg ached inside the cast. Why had she stayed after school? She didn’t want to die.

The door was open. Chris had expected to find a closet or a janitorial storage room. Instead, he saw a set of stairs leading upward. Was this a way out?

“I’ll bet they go to the roof,” Chris said.

Cara grimaced. “I don’t know.”

“We have to try. Come on, can you make it?”

Cara had to forgo the crutches in order to step sideways up the narrow stairwell. Chris came behind her, making sure she didn’t fall. They could still hear Eddie’s incessant tirade, but they could no longer make out the words.

“If we can get to the roof, we can climb down the fire escape,” Chris told her. “Once we’re on the ground, we can get to a phone.”

Cara felt her spirits soaring all of a sudden. “Yes! The fire escape. Why didn’t I think of that?”

“Because you’re scared,” Chris replied. “And so am I.”

As they neared the top of the stairs, they

heard something rattling and clicking. The door that led to the roof was open and flapping in the wind. Had someone been there before them?

Cara hesitated. "Chris, why is the door open?"

He urged her toward the roof. "I don't know, let's just get out of here."

They emerged onto the flat roof of the library. A stiff wind from the storm almost knocked them over. Chris took Cara's arm, helping her toward the fire escape in the rain.

Cara's eyes lifted to see a male figure standing at the edge of the parapet. "No!"

Chris glanced at one of the punks who had been sitting in the back row with Eddie. "Oh no."

A knife flashed in the punk's hand. "You!" He gestured at Chris. "You can go. Hit the bricks."

Chris glanced toward the metallic railing of the fire escape. "He wants me to leave."

"It's me they're after," Cara said with trembling lips.

Chris shook his head. "I'm not leaving without you."

"Go!" the punk insisted. "Or I'll cut you."

"Save yourself," Cara urged. "Chris—"

"No! I'm not leaving you to them. It's a trick, Cara!"

The punk's voice rose as lightning streaked the sky. "Get out of here, you little wuss! Or I'll kill you!" He took a step in their direction.

Chris emitted a harsh cry. He grabbed one of

Cara's crutches, pulling it from beneath her right arm. Cara fell to the roof, landing on her side. She looked up to watch Chris as he charged the knife-wielding creep.

The punk hadn't been expecting the attack. He tried to step aside, but he wasn't quick enough. The flat end of the crutch caught him squarely in the chest. The punk's body flew through the air, smashing into the iron grating of the fire escape.

Suddenly sparks flew up around the body of the twitching punk. He tried to roll off the grating but he was caught in a current of electricity. His body jerked and convulsed as the mega-voltage surged through his body. His eyes were wide in shock and surprise as smoke seeped from his shirt and pants, filling the air with the sickening aroma of cooking flesh. The juice bit him until his smoking body was still.

Chris gaped at the dead boy. "My God! They electrified the fire escape. That's why he wanted me to step on it."

"Help me!" Cara moaned.

Chris lifted her up. "I'm sorry I knocked you down."

Cara gazed toward the scorched body. "It's all right."

"We can't take the fire escape. They put an electric charge into it. We have to go back down the stairs."

Lightning flashed overhead. They made their way to the staircase and back into the hall. As soon as they entered the shadowed corridor, Eddie's voice rang in their ears again.

FOURTEEN

Eddie didn't sound so confident this time. "What's going on out there?" he said over the loudspeaker. "Turk, where are you? What happened? Did you get them?"

Cara stood in the hallway, listening to her tormentor. "He doesn't know we're alive!"

Chris nodded. "Maybe we're off the hook for a while."

"What's going on? What—huh?"

They could hear someone else talking in the background.

Eddie returned after a moment. "So, you got Turk! You're tougher than I thought, swimmer boy. Or maybe you're just lucky. Well, your luck has run out. They're back in the hall, guys. Let's get 'em. Go for it."

Cara shook from the soles of her feet. "My God, how many of them does he have?"

A shiver played through Chris's body. "I don't know."

They were wet from the rain on the roof. Where would they go now? They had to find a way out. There had to be an escape exit somewhere.

Cara's eyes grew wide. "Chris, look!" She pointed toward the brick wall.

"What—"

"The fire alarm," she said. "If we pull it down, the fire department and the police will come."

Chris lunged toward the wall, grabbing the handle for the alarm switch. For a couple of seconds the alarm blared. But then it stopped abruptly.

"What happened?" Cara said.

Chris shook his head. "I don't—"

"Nice try," Eddie told them. "But I'm in command central, students. Central Academy command to dead meat preppies. No alarm, no cops, no way. You're dead. They're still by the library, boys. You know what to do!"

Cara's face contorted in rage. "Eddie! You bastard! Come out and look us in the eye!"

But the loudspeaker was silent.

Chris touched her shoulder. "Come on."

"There's no way out," Cara replied.

"We don't know that yet. Come on."

They started away from the library, retracing their steps down the hall. Chris kept moving from door to door, trying the knobs. All the doors were locked tight, however.

When they reached the end of the hallway, they pushed through the opening into the adjacent corridor.

Chris kept trying doors as Cara limped along behind him.

They both stopped dead when a door creaked open. It was only a janitor's closet, not an exit. Chris peered into the shadows where the maintenance and custodial equipment were kept.

"What's in there?" Cara asked.

Chris switched on a light. "Mops, brooms—hey, check it out. A pry bar." He grabbed the heavy piece of steel that served as a lever to pry things apart.

"Anything else?" Cara asked.

"A hammer, a screwdriver. Maybe we can use these to get through that lock and chain," Chris offered.

For a moment they were hopeful.

But then Eddie's voice pealed through the corridor. "We're getting closer, students. Can you hear us coming? We can hear you. We're right around the corner."

Cara drew in a deep breath. "I'm really starting to *hate* him."

"Come on," Chris said, "let's see if we can break through that lock."

They moved as quickly as they could to the end of the hallway. Chris held the pry bar in his hand. The hammer was tucked in his belt. Cara carried the screwdriver in her back pocket.

"Do you think we can break the lock?" Cara asked.

Chris didn't sound confident in his reply. "I doubt it. But we have to try."

However, when they reached the door, the lock and chain dangled loosely from one side of the aluminum handle. Someone had opened the padlock. But why? And who was on the other side of the door?

"We can get out!" Cara said.

Chris stood there, staring at the door, sweat dripping from his face. "Somebody wants us to go through that door."

"What?"

"Why else would they open it?" Chris offered.

Cara inched closer to the portal. "But we have to do it."

Chris shook his head. "No. We're going back the other way. We can use these tools on another door."

Cara pushed past him on the crutches. "I don't care what you say, I'm going to—"

"No, Cara!"

As soon as she pressed against the door, someone lurched at her. A leather-clad arm wrapped around Cara's neck, trying to pull her into the opposite corridor. Cara screamed, lifting a crutch sideways to keep the intruder from dragging her through the opening.

Chris swung the steel bar, smashing the arm. He heard bone cracking beneath the blow. The intruder cried out, momentarily releasing his grip on Cara.

Cara fell out of the doorway, tumbling to the ground. The attacker jumped through the door, his injured arm hanging limply at his side. Chris lifted the bar again, squaring off with the punk.

A knife clicked open in the intruder's good hand. "You can't do that to me, you little freak!"

Chris took a stand with his weapon. "Stay off me, creep!"

"I'm gonna slice you up. Then we're gonna have some fun with your little friend!"

"No!" Cara cried.

Chris swung the bar, missing his stalker. "Stay away from her. I swear, I'll kill you!"

"You ain't got it in you, sweet-boy!"

The punk made a move at Chris. Chris swung the pry bar, missing him. When Chris fell off-balance, the punk kicked at him, hitting Chris in the stomach.

Chris grunted and fell back against the wall. The punk lunged again, coming hard with the knife. Chris managed to roll to the side, but it didn't help. Another swift kick sent Chris sprawling on the floor.

The punk was all over him, kicking Chris in the ribs with the pointed toe of a leather boot. Chris cried out with each painful strike. His attacker cursed him. He was going to kill Chris before he went after Cara.

Cara struggled to sit up, listening as Chris begged for help. She couldn't let him die. She just couldn't! But how would she stand up to the monster with a knife?

The punk quit kicking Chris. He hovered over the fallen boy, holding the knife in his hand. Chris looked up, begging for mercy.

"Please, don't—"

The punk laughed. "Ha! Beggin' like a little girl. You're dead meat, sister-boy!"

"No—"

Chris felt the boy's weight on top of him. The punk kneeled on his chest, pinning Chris to the floor. He grabbed Chris's hair, jerking his head back.

"I never killed a guy before," the punk whispered. "You're gonna be my first."

"No, don't—"

"I love it when you beg. So long, sucker."

Chris felt the point of the knife against his throat. He struggled desperately but he could not move. He flashed on the thought of what it would be like to die.

"All I have to do is nip you right there," the killer told him. "There's gonna be a lot of blood!"

"No—"

"Yes! It's all—arrr—"

Suddenly the punk was screaming like a banshee. He reached for his own back, forgetting about Chris. Chris pushed hard, knocking the punk off him. He scrambled to his feet as the punk wrestled himself on the floor.

Cara stood over the brute, her hands covering her mouth. "I—I had to—"

Chris gazed down at the dying boy. Cara had stabbed him under the left shoulder blade. The screwdriver that she had carried in her pocket now protruded from the boy's back.

"I had to," Cara repeated. "He was going to kill you."

Chris put his arm around her shoulders. "It's all right. You saved me. You did the right thing."

Cara turned away from the body, sobbing.

"Two down," Chris muttered. "But how many more of them are in here?"

The boy on the floor gave a last gasp as the life flowed from his body.

Chris turned toward the door. "We have to go through here. Maybe there's a way out."

Cara nodded. "Please, get me home, Chris."

"Okay, baby, come on."

But as soon as they opened the door, they heard footsteps coming toward them. Someone ran down the corridor. Chris could see the silhouette barreling through the shadows.

"Oh no!" Cara cried.

Chris pulled her back. "Quick, lock the door."

His hands fumbled with the chain and padlock. The onrushing intruder drew closer as Chris threaded the lock through the thick links.

A body crashed against the door on the other side of the archway. Chris snapped the lock shut. But the door opened enough for the attacker to thrust his arm through the crack. A strong hand grabbed the front of Chris's shirt.

"No!" Cara cried.

Chris jerked the hammer from his belt, smashing the arm that held him. The intruder cried out and released his grip. Chris fell back, touching Cara's shoulder.

"You little freak!" the assailant cried. "I'm gonna kill you!"

"You have to catch me first," Chris replied. "Come on, Cara. We're going back to the library."

"You won't get away!" the voice threatened. "We'll get you and your girlfriend. You hear me!"

Chris urged Cara away from the door. They started slowly along the corridor. Chris didn't feel as helpless now. They had killed two of the punks. They had weapons. They were going to fight back. Eddie wasn't going to take them without a battle.

"Maybe they'll leave us alone now," Chris offered.

When they reached the library again, Chris used the hammer and the pry bar to break open the door.

Cara chortled. "You did it."

"Maybe there's another door inside that we can break open to get out of this place."

They entered the shadows of the library, searching for a route to escape. But the library was secure. The wooden doors that opened to the outside were too thick to surrender to the pry bar and the deadbolt locks wouldn't give way. Chris even tried breaking one of the windows, but the thick glass had been reinforced for security and the windows weren't the type that would open in the climate-controlled atmosphere that was used to protect the books.

"Damn it!" Chris said. "Nobody can break in and we can't break out."

Cara shuddered. "Irony."

"What?"

"They built the library this strong to keep guys like Eddie from breaking in to trash the place. Now he has us right where he wants us. Ironic."

Chris started to reply, but the loudspeaker crackled to life again. "Oh, no—"

Eddie's voice sounded angry. "You think you're so smart, you Prescott punks! You killed two of my friends. But we know where you are, Cara. And we're coming to get you. When we find you, Miss Cheerleader, we're gonna make you wish you were dead."

Chris shook his head. "Man, that guy is wicked sick."

"What are we going to do?" Cara said.

Chris sighed. "I don't know."

His eyes lifted to the dull luster of the windows. The storm raged in the sky, promising an early nightfall. Chris went into the library office. He tried the phone again, but it was dead. Either the storm had killed it, or Eddie had disabled the line.

Chris returned to Cara's side, taking her arm, leading her to a wooden chair beside one of the library tables.

"We're dead," Cara offered.

Chris shook his head. "No, we're not."

"What are we going to do then?" Cara asked.

Chris's eyes roamed the library, studying everything that he could see. "We found some weapons. We can find some more."

Cara sighed. "I'm in pain. My leg is killing me."

"Don't worry," Chris replied. "I'm gonna protect you."

He had to think like Eddie. He had to find ways to fight. Eddie and his gang weren't so tough. Chris and Cara had already proven they weren't invulnerable.

"We can do it," Chris told her. "You and me, Cara."

She gazed into his eyes. "Yes, we can. But how?"

Chris glanced at the darkening glass of the library windows. "We wait."

"For what?" Cara asked.

"We wait for them to come to us," Chris replied.

"Then what?"

He took a deep breath. "Then we stand up to them."

Cara nodded slowly. "Yes," she said softly. "We stand up to them."

There was no other way out.

Thunder sounded overhead as Chris left the chair, moving through the library to look for more weapons.

He saw the flag stand with the Stars and Stripes and the state flag hanging from the pointed poles.

It was going to be all right, he told himself.

And even if it wasn't all right, he wasn't going to die without defending himself first.

FIFTEEN

Shortly after dark, the storm subsided, though Cara could still hear the rumble of thunder in the distance. She sat with Chris, hiding behind the tables that they had turned over to act as shields from Eddie and his pals. Their makeshift fortress rested in a far corner of the library, where they could be assured that no one would attack from the rear.

Cara leaned against the wall, her cast extending in front of her. It had been several hours since they had heard anything from Eddie. He was out there somewhere in the school, advancing slowly, biding his time. Eddie had all weekend. Unless someone finally noticed that Cara and Chris were missing. Maybe their parents would come looking for them. Of course, they would eventually come looking or at least call the police—but when?

Cara took a deep breath and exhaled dejectedly.

Chris looked up from his task. "How're you doing?"

She shrugged. "Not good. I keep wondering when they'll finally come after us."

"Maybe they won't."

"I hope so. Could I have some more of that water?"

Chris handed her the decorative pitcher that he had found on the librarian's desk. He had filled it from a water fountain in the hallway. Cara drank and handed the pitcher back to Chris.

Chris sipped from the container and returned to his task. Cara watched as he sharpened the ends of the wooden flagpoles by carving them with a razor blade he had found in the librarian's supply cabinet. He kept studying the sharp point, trying to get it perfect.

"Chris?"

"Yeah?"

She sighed. "You saved me. Thanks."

He glanced at her smiling slightly. "You saved me too. So we're even."

He looked at the spear point again.

"Chris?"

"Yeah?"

She couldn't take her eyes off him. Strange thoughts had filled her head. Why hadn't she realized it before? Why had it just now occurred to her?

Chris glanced at Cara. "What?"

"Chris—how—how do you feel about me?"

His face blanched, turning ashen. "What do you mean?"

Her eyes became moist. "I—we—I mean, we may not survive this. And I just want to know why you've been such a good friend to me all this time."

He looked away, focusing on his handiwork. "We're friends, Cara. You've got to stand behind your friends."

"Chris—look at me!"

His eyes focused on her face again. "Cara—"

Tears rolled down her cheeks. "My God," she said, sobbing. "Why didn't I see it before? You're in love with me. Aren't you?"

Chris hung his head. "Yes."

"Why didn't you tell me?"

"Because you seemed to be in love with everyone else," Chris replied. "I thought you'd blow me off if you knew."

"Chris, you should've been honest with me. That's much better than—what—Chris, look!"

Chris lifted his gaze to see a pair of headlight beams flashing through the darkness, spilling into the library. Two circles of radiance swelled on the window glass. A car had entered the faculty parking lot next to the library.

"Go!" Cara cried. "Make them see you!"

Chris jumped to his feet, streaking toward the window. He leapt up on a shelf, banging on the glass. He could see the police car as it circled the parking lot. But the officers could not see Chris. Instead, the cruiser completed the circle and rolled back out into the street.

"Damn!" Chris cried.

He jumped down, rushing back to the sanctuary of their fortress.

"What happened?" Cara asked.

"They didn't see me," Chris replied. "I've got to find some kind of light to swing when they come back."

"Do you think they'll come back?" Cara asked, her spirits taking an upturn.

"I don't know, Cara. Maybe."

They were quiet again. Chris kept honing the spear. Cara listened in the shadows as the North Church clock tolled nine o'clock. They had already considered finding the right switch so they could flash the library lights to attract attention. But most of the power in their wing had been cut off. Only the dim emergency lights, which were battery operated, glowed dully over two doors. Even if they flashed the security lights a hundred times no one would notice.

Thunder boomed again in the distance. Rain started to splatter the windows, coming down harder. More lightning illuminated the cloudy night sky.

"Do you think Eddie turned out the power?" Cara asked.

Chris sighed. "Probably."

"I wonder if they're still out there? Maybe they gave up. It's been a long time."

"We'll wait till morning, unless somebody comes."

Cara touched her cast. "My leg is aching. I wish I had an aspirin. Our parents are going to notice that we're missing, Chris. Somebody will come."

Chris stopped sharpening the crude lance. "Cara?"

"Yes?"

"Did you ever think about you and me—you know?"

Cara shook her head. "Honestly—no."

Chris felt a pain in his chest. "Well, what do you think—I mean, now that you know how I feel about you—what do you think?"

"I care about you, Chris. I don't know if I'm in love with you, though. I—"

He lifted his hand, showing her his palm. "Don't say another word."

"But, Chris—"

"Please. Just leave it alone. Forget I even said anything."

Cara felt badly, but she couldn't bring herself to lie to Chris. Maybe she cared about him more than she knew. If she wanted to love him, would it happen? Her mother had often told her that sometimes true love grew out of friendship.

She was about to say something else when an atomic burst of lightning seared the air. The thunderclap was deafening. There seemed to be an explosion in the distance.

"What was that?" Chris muttered.

Cara listened. "Sirens. I—Chris, get up, maybe you can see what's happening through the window."

Chris ran to the window, jumping up on the shelf again. In the distance, he could see flames leaping up over the roofs of Port City. But then something else struck a note. Except for the fire the entire town had grown dark. No lights. He hopped down and ran back to Cara.

"What is it?" she asked.

"A fire. But the lights are out all over town."

Cara's brow wrinkled. "What does that mean?"

"The electricity is off here at Central, Cara. The fire escape isn't charged anymore. If we can get to the roof, we can climb down now."

Cara reached up. "Help me to my feet."

Chris lifted Cara, putting the crutches under her arms. "Once we're down, we move as fast as we can to the street. We flag the first car we see. If we don't see a car, we run to the first house. Got it?"

Cara nodded. "Chris?"

"Yeah?"

She leaned toward him, pressing her lips against his mouth.

Chris kissed her for a moment. He managed a smile. "Later, Cara. We have to go."

They took a couple of steps before they heard the slamming door. The noise stopped them cold. They listened as someone—more than one person—moved into the library.

"They're here!" Cara whispered. "What are we going to do now?"

Chris reached back for his makeshift spear. "Shh."

The murmur of conspiratorial voices rose in the dank air.

More movement in the shadows.

Eddie's voice rose in the darkness, but this time he wasn't on the loudspeaker, he was live.

His tone chilled Cara's flesh.

"Hello, children," Eddie called. "Daddy's home. And he's ready to settle the score!"

"What are we going to do?" Cara repeated.

"Kill him" was Chris's only reply.

They had no choice. They had to kill Eddie.

Before he killed them.

SIXTEEN

Cara and Chris listened as the intruders began to stalk them. How many thugs had Eddie brought with him? Two? Three? How were they going to fight superior numbers?

Chris touched Cara's arm and pointed toward the book stacks. Cara understood. Chris wanted to hide in the rows of metal shelves. Cara tried to step quietly, but it was hard on the crutches. And the pain in her chest was growing sharper.

Eddie's voice haunted them again. "I know you're in here, Miss Cheerleader. You and your Prescott petunia won't escape. Give it up and make it easy on yourself. We won't dispose of the bodies. And we'll leave enough for your mommy and daddy to have a good cry at the funeral."

He was trying to goad them into revealing their position, Cara thought.

She slipped between the shelves with Chris next to her. They stood silently at the end of the aisle, listening as Eddie and the others stalked in the shadows.

Chris tapped her on the shoulder. When Cara looked at him, he held up two fingers, as if to say, "There's two of them." Cara wasn't so sure. She thought she heard three or four voices whispering in the darkness.

What if they had guns? With the police at the fire, there'd be no one to receive a report of gunshots. How could Chris and Cara stand up to guys who were carrying firearms?

"See 'em?" Eddie called.

"No, man. I don't think they're in here."

Two voices.

And one of them was really close.

Chris nodded to Cara. He had an idea. She grimaced as he plucked a book from the shelf.

Chris tossed the book toward one of the other aisles. They held their breaths, listening as one of the intruders came in the direction of the falling book. He had to be less than ten feet away from them.

Suddenly Chris bolted down the aisle, leaving Cara alone behind the shelves. Cara fought the urge to call out. Why had Chris left her? Had he abandoned her, or simply lost it?

Cara heard another noise resounding in the dark stacks. More books hit the floor. Was it Chris? Or one of the other punks?

"Hey, I heard something!"

Eddie called out again. "What'd you hear?"

"I don't know, I think it's the preps!"

"Get 'em!"

The punk ducked into the aisle just ahead of Cara. She could see him through the opening above the rows of books. Someone bumped against her. She started but Chris put his hand over her mouth before she could gasp.

"I hear 'em! I know they're here!"

"Dust 'em!" Eddie cried.

"I can't see 'em!"

Chris put his good shoulder against the bookshelf. He began to push, trying to push the shelf over. Cara caught on quickly, using her own shoulder. She couldn't push hard with the cast on her leg, but she had to help Chris.

"I hear somethin'," the punk called.

"Do it," Eddie urged. "Hurt 'em!"

The shelf started to shake. Cara wondered if they were strong enough. Chris was huffing, giving it his all.

The punk stopped in the aisle. "Hey, somethin's happenin', Eddie. I think—uh oh! I'm gettin' outta here!"

He turned to run but it was too late.

The shelf gave way. Chris and Cara pushed it over. The heavy structure fell, landing on the opposite row, causing a chain reaction that sent five more shelves crashing to the ground. The punk cried out as the falling shelf trapped him.

"Help!" he cried. "Help me!"

Cara peered into the wreckage. The punk lay there, his head sticking up. One of his arms had been snapped into several pieces. It hung limply through the shelves.

Chris pulled at Cara's arm. "Come on, let's get out of here."

Cara tripped as she started forward. As she staggered, Chris caught her. He lifted her again, helping her until she had regained her balance.

"We have to get to the roof!" Chris whispered.

Cara nodded, unsure if she had the strength to make it. But she followed him. At least until they reached the far wall. Eddie and his cohorts had chained the door shut. Chris and Cara could not leave without the key.

"Damn," Chris whispered.

"What are we going to do?" Cara asked in a low voice.

Chris pointed toward a low table. "Get under there."

"What?"

"Just do it!"

With Chris's help, Cara managed to duck under the table. It was an awkward fit and the plaster cast extended beyond the tabletop. She heard Chris bolt off into the darkness. Where was he going? What did he think he could do against Eddie?

It seemed like forever before she heard movement near the table. Was it Eddie? She wondered if there were more of Eddie's pals in the shadows. Or had Chris finished them?

Footsteps shuffled across the carpet, coming closer to the table where she hid. The cast extruded, visible to anyone who simply glanced down. Cara held her breath. Had Chris returned finally? Or had Eddie found her?

Leather boots stopped just short of the plaster-encased leg. "Well, well, look what we have here."

Suddenly the table flew back. The punk had tipped it over, revealing Cara's hiding place. He bent down to look at her.

"Yeah," he said in a smooth voice. "Eddie said you wasn't half-bad lookin', but you're a fox."

Cara trembled on the floor, wishing there was some way to reason with this brute. "Please, we haven't done anything to you. Why are you doing this?"

The punk laughed. "We don't need a reason. We just don't like your kind."

"Please," Cara said, her voice trailing off. "Don't."

The punk turned his head to call to his leader. His lips parted but he didn't utter a word. Eddie was still trying to free his fallen comrade from the shelves.

The punk's head turned back and his face glowered at Cara. "Ain't no need to call him just yet."

"What?"

"Nah, me and you, we could have some fun."

Cara tried to inch backward, scooting on the floor. She wanted to call to Chris, but she didn't want them to know that Chris was still in the library. Maybe he could escape and get help before they killed her. Or did something worse.

"Where you think you're goin'?" he asked.

"Stay away from me," Cara muttered.

"No way, babe. Not the way you look. I ain't never had a shot at a Prescott girl like you. But now it appears you and me got a date, honey."

"No, not here. You can't."

He nodded. "Good thinking! We can find a private spot. I knew I could count on you."

He reached for her, grabbing Cara's auburn hair. The pain was excruciating as he dragged her across the carpet. His boot kicked open the door to the librarian's office.

"Yeah, this oughtta be fine," he told her. "You ready to party, babe?"

He pulled her into the office and let go of her hair. Cara's head hit the floor. The punk took off his jacket and stretched out next to her.

"Hi there, gorgeous—hey!"

Cara struck at his face.

He caught her wrist, twisting her arm, forcing her to cry out in pain. "Listen to me, you little tease. This has been comin'. So you just relax. Otherwise I'll hurt you!"

Cara began to whimper. "Don't do this. Please."

"Like I said, baby, just relax. I ain't gonna take long."

His face hovered over her. She felt the stubble of his beard as his chin raked across her cheek. He smelled of liquor and cigarettes. Cara's entire body tensed with revulsion.

"No," she said. "Please—"

He raised up. "I'm gonna have to hurt you, ain't I?" He lifted his hand to slap her.

Cara closed her eyes, anticipating the sting of the blow. But she never felt the flat of his hand. Instead, the punk made a grunting noise. His body lurched, went limp, and then he collapsed on top of her.

"What the—"

Suddenly his body rolled off her, landing next to Cara with a dull thump.

Cara gazed up at a silhouetted figure. "Who—"

Chris knelt down next to her, the bloody pry bar clutched in his right hand. "Are you okay?"

Cara sat up. "Yeah. Where did you go?"

"I had to get the bar so we can break the lock. Come on, get up. Where are your crutches?"

"Back in the library. Cave-boy didn't let me bring them."

Chris helped Cara to her feet. "Here, lean on me. And use this to steady yourself."

He handed her the sharpened flagpole.

"Chris—"

"Watch the point," he told her.

They hobbled to the door that had been secured by the chain. Chris put the bar in the padlock and twisted it until the lock gave way. The chain fell to the floor, freeing them.

But Eddie's voice wasn't far away. "Who's there? Rex? Mikey? Who's there?"

"Hurry," Chris said.

"I can't walk any faster!"

They moved into the hallway, stepping to the door that led to the roof. Eddie hadn't locked this door. The stairs were tough with Cara's leg. They had to take the steps one at a time, clumping on each riser. Eddie cried out behind them, getting closer.

"We aren't going to make it," Cara said.

Chris pulled her onto the next step. "Don't give up!"

Cara's leg throbbed inside the cast. Sweat poured from her face. Chris dragged her through the open door onto the roof. Lightning flashed in the sky, illuminating Port City for a moment.

Cara gazed toward Congress Street. "Look, everything is dark. The electricity is still off."

"We can make it," Chris replied. "Come on, before Eddie catches up to us!"

Rain pelted their faces as they hobbled across the roof. Cara's cast thumped on the tar and gravel surface. She tried to use the sharpened pole to steady herself, but she didn't find it to be a very good walking stick.

They had almost reached the fire escape when the sparks started to crackle in front of them. The dead body still lay on the iron grating, twitching and smoking as the current ran through it. Chris glanced up to see that the lights had come on all over the city.

"Damn it!" he cried.

Cara shook her head. "No! Please, God, no!"

Chris took a deep breath and exhaled. He knew what he had to do. There was no other option.

He guided Cara away from the deadly fire escape. "Sit down," he told her.

Cara grabbed him, clinging tightly. "What are you going to—"

"Just sit," Chris replied. "And give me that pole."

"Chris, you—"

"Cara! I have to face Eddie. Alone."

"But he's dangerous!"

Chris sighed. "I don't care. You wait here. I'll be back to get you when I'm finished."

"Chris—"

But he took the pole from her grasp and ran over the roof, disappearing in the darkness. A bolt of lightning illuminated his entrance back into the stairwell. Then he was gone.

Cara turned away from the wind, shouting, screaming for help. But no one heard her over the din of the storm. Her body trembled in the cool air. She felt like she could not stand up for another minute. Slumping to the roof, she sat down in the rain and leaned back against the parapet, closing her eyes.

"Please, God, protect Chris."

It seemed like an eternity before she heard the door open and close.

Cara gazed in the direction of the footsteps that shuffled across the roof.

A burst of lightning illuminated the male figure moving toward her.

"Chris?"

The figure stopped in front of her. "No, Miss Cheerleader, it ain't Chris."

The spectral light from the sky revealed Eddie's hateful face.

"No!" Cara cried.

Eddie nodded. "Oh yes, Miss Cheerleader."

Cara heard the clicking of a switchblade knife.

"You've had this coming for a long time," Eddie told her. "Now, get up. We're going inside to have a little fun."

Chris was dead. Cara knew it. Eddie had murdered him with the knife. There was no one to save her now.

Eddie kicked her cast. "Get up!"

The pain shot through her shin into her hip.

"Get up, you witch!"

Cara scowled at him. "Screw you, Eddie! If you're going to kill me, then do it now!"

"Whatever you say, honey!"

Cara anticipated the sharp bite of the knife blade. She closed her eyes, awaiting death. How would it feel to die?

A guttural cry came out of Eddie's mouth. Was this the last sound she would ever hear? Eddie made a gurgling noise and then started to choke.

Cara opened her eyes to see Eddie's horrid expression reflected in the lightning flash. He dropped the knife. His body began to quiver violently. Eddie staggered backward away from her. In the next wash of heavenly light, Cara saw the point of the wooden flagpole protruding from Eddie's chest.

Eddie turned to look at Chris, who had stuck him from behind with the crude lance. He reached out, trying to grab Chris. But Chris easily avoided the zombie movements of the dying boy.

Eddie did not give up the ghost easily. He staggered around, reaching back, trying to pull the spear from his body. Finally, he lurched forward, falling on the fire escape. His body twitched and sputtered, frying in a hail of sparks. A death rattle escaped from Eddie's lungs.

Chris looked at Cara. "I couldn't find him. So I came back for you. Lucky, huh?"

Cara had begun to sob. "Yeah, lucky."

Chris walked away again. He came back five minutes later, telling Cara that he had found a phone in the front office. The police were on the way.

Cara thought their troubles were over, but when the police arrived, things went sour again. They arrested Chris and Cara for trespassing and suspicion of manslaughter. They were hauled away in a police van that took them to juvenile detention.

Cara kept pleading with them that she hadn't done anything. But they wouldn't listen. Instead, they locked her in a small cubicle that stank of prior inhabitants.

Cara asked for something to relieve the pain, but the guard ignored her.

Later, she was strip-searched by a matron in a gray uniform.

Someone said her parents were on the way.

It had to be a dream, Cara thought.

They couldn't blame her and Chris for defending themselves against Eddie and his gang.

Or could they?

This had been a nightmare all the way.

Would she ever wake up to a bright morning?

Or would the bad dream go on forever?

EPILOGUE

The radio alarm clock went off, blasting Cara from a dreamless slumber. She sat up in her bed, gazing at the bright sunshine on the window. It was a warm August morning. And Cara, who was now a graduate of Central Academy, intended to enjoy it.

Every day had been better since her release from the detention cell at the County Juvenile Authority. They had held her overnight, until the facts had been sorted out about the incident at the school. Luckily, the boy who had been trapped under the falling bookshelves had lived. His testimony had totally exonerated Chris and Cara. The boy told the police everything about Eddie's vendetta against the two kids from summer school.

Chief Danridge had been so embarrassed about arresting Chris and Cara that he never pressed the issue of their trespassing on school grounds after classes were over. Cara's father had asked the family lawyer about suing the police department for false arrest. But Cara had urged her father not to take the case to court. It was over. That was all that mattered.

Cara eased her injured leg over the side of the bed. The pins had been removed from the bone in a second surgical procedure. She had been wearing a soft cast that could be taken off at night. More and more, she was getting around without the use of the crutches. The doctor had told her that she would have no trouble attending college in September.

When she stood up, Cara tested the leg. There was some pain, but it wasn't sharp. She felt like she was sore from running or playing softball. Forgoing her cast and crutches, she walked into the upstairs bathroom, showering and blow drying her hair.

Her mother was surprised to see her walking into the kitchen without the crutches. "Well, you look like you're feeling well."

Cara shrugged. "Not bad."

Her father came in with his newspaper. "Whoa, the Princess is on two legs now."

"Dad!"

"How's the leg?" he asked, repeating a question that Cara had heard a thousand times since the accident.

"Good."

Mrs. Richards turned away from the stove with a platter in her hands. "Anyone for French toast?"

"Oui, oui," Mr. Richards replied. "Ooo-la-la."

Cara grimaced. "Geez, Dad, you're so geeky!"

They ate the French toast with real butter and maple syrup. Mr. Richards talked about the stories in his newspaper. Mrs. Richards and Cara made comments and offered their insights about local and regional affairs.

Mr. Richards reached a story about State University and the rising cost of education. "You know, Princess, you have to decide where you're going this fall."

Cara sighed. "I know."

"Any ideas?" her mother replied.

In addition to being accepted by State University and Port City Community College, Cara had also been accepted by two Ivy League schools.

Cara hesitated. "Uh—I—I've been thinking—"

The doorbell rang, putting off her decision for the moment.

"That's Chris," Cara said. "We're going to the beach today."

"I'll get it," Mr. Richards replied.

After a moment Chris joined them at the breakfast table. "Hi, Cara. It's gonna be sunny today."

Mr. Richards looked at Chris. "Cara was just

talking about which school she's going to next month."

Chris frowned, as if he feared Cara's decision.

"Uh, how about you, Chris?" Mrs. Richards asked.

He looked into his plate of French toast. "Uh, after everything that's happened, I think I'm going to Port City Community." He glanced at Cara, anticipating her reply.

Cara smiled. "Really? Hey, that's just what I was thinking. P.C.C. Mom, Dad, would you mind if I stayed here for a couple of years. I mean—"

Her father grinned. "Mind? I was hoping you'd stay home for at least your first year."

Mrs. Richards touched her daughter's hand. "I'm so delighted, honey. We'll go shopping for new clothes next week."

Chris wore the biggest smile of all. "Wow. It'll be great, Cara. You and me."

"Let's hit the beach," Cara offered. "Before all the good sun is gone."

In the car, on the way to Hampton Way Beach, Chris glanced sideways at her. "How are the nightmares coming?"

"Almost gone," she replied, shivering. "I don't think they'll ever leave completely."

Chris sighed. "Neither do I."

"Chris?"

"Yeah?"

"I think I'm in love with you," Cara said.

"Really?"

She sighed. "Yes. But let's take it slow, okay?"

"Sure," Chris replied. "Whatever you say."

He was grinning, unable to contain his joy.

They rolled on toward the beach, trying to put the horrid memories behind them. The little dreams of Eddie would never go away. But the big nightmare had ended on the roof of Central Academy.

WELCOME
TO CENTRAL ACADEMY . . .

It's like any other high school on the outside.
But inside, fear stalks the halls—
and terror is in a class by itself.

Please turn the page for a sneak preview of the next
TERROR ACADEMY book—
don't miss BREAKING UP!

Robin Anderson shut her locker door and turned to walk down the hall to her English class. In the crowded corridor of the senior building, Robin stood out boldly—a blond, statuesque senior who just happened to be going steady with the cocaptain of the Central Academy hockey team. As Robin glided between the other groups of students, most of the boys stole sidelong looks at the gorgeous-enough-to-be-a-model girl who belonged to Skip Chesterton. Of course, if any of them tried to make a move on Robin, Skip would pound them into little pieces, a fact that had thrilled Robin as a junior.

Robin nodded to one of her classmates, Candy Reed, who played on the girls' varsity field hockey team with Robin. Field hockey season had been over for a couple of months. It was

January, the beginning of a new semester. Time for Skip to shine on the ice.

Skip had made All-State as a center on the hockey squad. He was the star, and that had drawn Robin to him as a junior. Now she wasn't quite sure how she felt about Skip's fame. Not that she was jealous or anything. After all, Robin had been the captain of the girls' soccer team that had gone to the state finals last spring to beat Dover for the championship. Soccer was Robin's best sport and she liked it a lot more than field hockey.

Candy fell in beside Robin, trying to match the blond girl's healthy stride. "Hey. What's up?"

Robin shrugged and pushed a hand through her thick hair. "Just getting used to the old schedule again," she replied blankly.

"Are you going to the game tonight?" Candy asked.

Robin gave a sigh. "I guess."

Candy grimaced. "You guess?"

"I'll be there," Robin insisted testily. "Okay?"

"Well, Skip is starting," Candy replied, shaking her short-cropped auburn hair.

Candy had a major crush on Skip and Robin knew it. Candy wasn't as gorgeous as Robin, but she was still attractive. Blue eyes, dimpled chin, a freckly complexion that made her look wholesome. At one time, Robin had been jealous of Candy's attraction to Skip. But now she wasn't sure that it bothered her. Something had changed over Christmas break.

"Let's sit behind the bench so we can be close to Skip," Candy said. "If we—"

Robin glared at her. "Hey, why don't you just sit *on* the bench, Candy!"

Candy's face turned bright red. "But I—"

"Better yet—sit on Skip! I'm sure you'd love that."

Robin stormed away from a gaping Candy. She had never unloaded like that on Candy before. And she really wasn't angry at Candy for having a crush on Skip.

So why was she so quick to explode?

Rounding the corner, Robin stopped for a second, leaning back against the wall, closing her eyes. What was wrong with her? Why had she come back from Christmas vacation so sensitive and temperamental? After all, Skip had given her that ring, the one he called a pre-engagement symbol. Her parents had been so happy.

I'm a senior, she thought. *Going with the greatest guy in school, a guy who loves me. And I should love him. But do I?*

The ring had done it. Robin had been forced to look at the relationship with a serious eye. It wasn't like she didn't care about Skip. What was it?

A little voice in the back of her head offered one simple word: *BOREDOM!*

Robin shook her head, trying to clear the cobwebs. Her hair flew for a moment in several directions. She had to brush the long tresses from her face.

"Whoa, do that again, you hot babe. Owww!"

Robin gazed across the corridor in the direction of the male voice. Her blue eyes focused on one of the long-hairs from Pitney Docks. He actually looked sort of cute in the leather jacket but Robin couldn't let him get away with this harassment.

"How 'bout me and you tonight?" the long-hair said.

Wow, was he ever cute! A slender face, cool hazel eyes. But Robin wouldn't tolerate his attitude.

"Sorry," she said, grimacing. "I don't date outside my species, chimp-boy. I—"

Someone stepped next to the long-hair, another boy who wore a black overcoat and combat boots. "Hey, is he botherin' you, Miss Anderson? Huh?"

Robin immediately recognized the interloper. He was Danny Kovack from her English class. Danny was cool, attractive and forceful, but he had a reputation for being a delinquent. Robin had caught herself studying him more than once in class. Everyone knew Danny rode a Harley, even in the winter, and he went steady with a girl who had already graduated.

The long-haired boy started to retreat. "Hey, Dan, I wasn't botherin' her—"

Danny, who was bigger than the other boy, grabbed him and put him in a headlock. "Now don't you bother this girl. Okay? She's something special!"

"Awright, Danny! Awright!"

He let go of the boy's head. "Now, say you're sorry."

"I'm sorry!"

The long-haired boy ran off down the hall.

Danny glanced back at her with his dark brown eyes. "A thousand pardons, *mademoiselle!*"

Robin found herself smiling at him. "Hi, Danny."

"Did you do your English homework?" Danny asked.

Robin nodded. "Yes."

Danny made a face and shrugged. "I blew it off completely. What a jerk, huh?"

Robin wasn't sure how to reply. She couldn't take her eyes off Danny. He wasn't really cuter than Skip. In fact, Skip had it all over Danny. Except that Danny was rugged-looking and his personality was so different. If he dressed better, he might even give Skip a run for his money.

"Are you okay, Countess?" Danny asked.

Robin was about to reply when a hand fell on her shoulder.

"I was looking for you," Skip said, gazing into her eyes. "Is everything all right?"

Robin nodded absently, blushing as if she had been caught doing something wrong. "Oh, Skip . . ."

Skip turned to regard Danny Kovack, who still smiled in their direction. Robin studied Skip's handsome face. He had black hair and green eyes, a combination that had slayed Robin as a junior.

But now I'm a senior, she thought.

"Kovack, what are you doing to my girl?" Skip asked.

Danny shrugged. "Nothing. Some geek was hitting on her and I sent him skating."

Skip glanced back at her. "He helped you?"

Robin nodded. "He's in my English class."

Skip's half-scowl did not go away. "I'm not sure I want him—" He turned to glower at Danny, but the boy was gone.

Robin felt badly. "Skip!"

"That guy is a hound," Skip insisted. "He's a biker. You can't trust guys like that."

"He's not so bad," Robin replied. "He's kind of nice."

"Well, you just stay away from him." Skip grabbed her hand. "This ring means that you belong to me, Robin."

Well, maybe I should give it back, she thought.

What would the student body say about the most popular couple at Central breaking up?

Skip smiled warmly, a once charming trait that was no longer that appealing. "Where are you gonna sit at the game tonight?"

Robin shrugged. "I don't know."

He frowned again. "What's wrong with you?"

"Skip . . ."

She didn't want to hurt him. He had been so sweet. Robin didn't blame him for being impatient.

"I'm going to sit behind the bench," she told him. "Candy and some of the other girls will be there too."

It was the easiest way to get rid of him.

Skip smiled again. "Great. You got a kiss for me?"

Their lips brushed lightly. Robin remembered deeper kisses, passionate embraces. But it all seemed so cold now. Had she simply lost it? Was that how the magic vanished in relationships?

Skip winked at her and headed in the direction of his sociology class. Robin moved again in the corridor, aware that the bell was going to ring at any moment. As she crossed through the doorway of her English class, the tardy signal pealed down the hall.

Easing into her desk, Robin lifted her eyes to see Mrs. Traxler glaring at her. She wasn't really late. But Mrs. Traxler was wound so tightly that she'd give a student a hard time for a close call.

"Glad you could make it, Miss Anderson."

Robin smiled weakly, thinking, *Bite it, you old geek*.

Mrs. Traxler fixed her eyes on Robin and started some lecture about punctuality.

Robin looked away, gazing out the window. As Mrs. Traxler droned on, Robin felt something on her face. It was almost like a hot spot was forming on her skin.

Her eyes wandered back into the room, focusing on the face of Danny Kovack, who was grinning. He had just sent a note in Robin's direction. It was coming across the desks to her, a dispatch between rows.

Robin felt her heart pounding. Why would Danny send her a note? Moreover, why would she want to read it?

She *did* want to read it!

Maybe he was inviting her to take a ride on his motorcycle.

She glanced quickly at Mrs. Traxler, who had turned toward the chalkboard. The note landed on her desk. Robin opened it quickly.

"Sorry about that punk bothering you," Danny had written. "If he keeps bugging you, let me know and I'll dust him for you. Your pal, Danny."

She looked at him again, her body tingling with a strange sensation. Why did he quicken her pulse? Why did she want to wrap her arms around him and ride on the Harley through the streets of Port City? Good girls weren't supposed to want guys like Danny Kovack.

"Miss Anderson, excuse me? Miss Anderson?"

Robin gazed back at Mrs. Traxler, who was gawking at her. "Uh, yes?" Robin offered weakly.

Mrs. Traxler, a stout, gray-haired matron, looked down her long nose, staring through thick glasses. "Is there something you'd like to share with us, Miss Anderson?"

Robin, who hated being in trouble, shook her head. "No, I—"

Danny Kovack stood up quickly. "Uh, Ms. Trax, I was just asking Robin if she could help me with my homework. I've been having some trouble in your class."

Mrs. Traxler smiled, though it wasn't a sunny proposition. "I see. Well, you could certainly use a tutor, Mr. Kovack. Would you like to volunteer?" she asked Robin.

Robin sat up straight. "Sure, why not?"

There was a gasp from almost everyone in the room.

Was Robin, one of the most popular girls at Central—*the* most popular girl!—really volunteering to help a ne'er-do-well? Robin came from Prescott Estates, the best section of Port City. Danny lived over by the waterfront in Pitney Docks. She swam at the country club, he rode a Harley that he had rebuilt in shop class.

They weren't even supposed to talk to each other, much less study together.

Mrs. Traxler grinned sadistically, thinking she had embarrassed Robin. "Very well, then it's settled. You'll tutor Danny, Robin."

She lifted her pretty chin, glaring right back at the instructor. "Fine!"

Danny shook his head. "Wow."

Robin didn't care what everyone thought.

She was going to tutor Danny in English.

Robin wanted to tutor him.

She just didn't know *why*!

Some of the other girls were whispering together.

Robin heard, "What will Skip say?"

What *would* Skip say? Robin thought.

She didn't care.

Whether Skip liked it or not, Robin was going to spend time with Danny Kovack!

Contemporary Research in Behavioral Pharmacology

Contemporary Research in Behavioral Pharmacology

Edited by

D. E. Blackman

and

D. J. Sanger

University College, Cardiff, Wales

PLENUM PRESS · NEW YORK AND LONDON

Library of Congress Cataloging in Publication Data

Main entry under title:

Contemporary research in behavioral pharmacology.

Includes bibliographies and index.
1. Psychopharmacology. 2. Behavior modification. I. Blackman, D. E. II. Sanger, D. J. [DNLM: 1. Behavior–Drug effects. 2. Psychopharmacology. QV77 C761]
BF207.C66 615'.78 77-16206
ISBN 0-306-31061-9

A Division of Plenum Publishing Corporation
227 West 17th Street, New York, N.Y. 10011

Printed in the United States of America

Contributors

James E. Barrett • Department of Psychology, University of Maryland, College Park, Maryland 20742

D. E. Blackman • Department of Psychology, University College, Cardiff CF1 1XL, Wales, U.K.

P. K. Corfield-Sumner • Department of Psychology, University of Birmingham, Birmingham B15 2TT, England, U.K.

Hugh L. Evans • Environmental Health Sciences Center, Department of Radiation Biology and Biophysics, School of Medicine and Dentistry, University of Rochester, Rochester, New York. Present address: Institute of Environmental Medicine, New York University Medical Center, New York, New York 10016

R. M. Gilbert • Addiction Research Foundation, Toronto, Ontario, Canada

Vincent P. Houser • CNS Disease Therapy Section, Lederle Laboratories, Pearl River, New York. Present address: Department of Pharmacology, Schering Corporation, Bloomfield, New Jersey 07003

Chris E. Johanson • Department of Psychiatry, Pritzker School of Medicine, The University of Chicago, Chicago, Illinois 60637

James W. McKearney • Worcester Foundation for Experimental Biology, Shrewsbury, Massachusetts 01545

D. J. Sanger • Department of Psychology, University College, Cardiff CF1 1XL, Wales, U.K.

I. P. Stolerman • MRC Neuropharmacology Unit, The Medical School, Birmingham B15 2TJ, England, U.K.

Donald M. Thompson • Department of Pharmacology, Georgetown University, Washington, D.C. 20007

Bernard Weiss • Environmental Health Sciences Center, Department of Radiation Biology and Biophysics, School of Medicine and Dentistry, University of Rochester, Rochester, New York 14642

J. C. Winter • Department of Pharmacology and Therapeutics, School of Medicine, State University of New York at Buffalo, Buffalo, New York 14214

Preface

The effects of drugs on behavior are of inherent interest and psychopharmacology has provided a focus for research activity for many years. Until recently, however, it could be claimed that the contribution of pharmacology was more obvious than that of psychology in the development of what should surely prove to be a matter for interdisciplinary endeavor. Pharmacological analyses of drug action have frequently been expressed in terms of dose–response functions, for example, with the dependent variable taking the form of patterns of behavior whose controlling influences were but poorly understood. The introduction of operant conditioning techniques has transformed psychopharmacology in this respect. Operant analyses have traditionally emphasized the environmental determinants of behavior and have explored the behavioral outcomes of many different experimental arrangements. These different behavioral repertoires have quickly proved to be of great importance in influencing the behavioral effects of drugs, and so psychologists have begun to play a role which better balances that of the pharmacologist in experimental psychopharmacology.

To reflect the development of these interdisciplinary studies, several excellent books have been published in recent years. These have included introductory texts,[1] collections of important experimental reports which had appeared in learned journals,[2] and authoritative handbooks which survey the current scene.[3] We felt, however, that there was a need for a compilation which fitted none of these categories directly, one which would display the impact of operant approaches to behavioral pharmacology but which allowed chosen contributors to be more evaluative of research in their own areas of special competence. Such a book would select a number of broad themes, and the evaluative reviews would be of interest to other specialists, to graduate programs

[1] S. D. Glick and J. Goldfarb, eds., 1976, *Behavioral Pharmacology,* C. V. Mosby, St. Louis. S. D. Iversen and L. L. Iversen, 1975, *Behavioral Pharmacology,* Oxford University Press, New York. T. Thompson and C. R. Schuster, 1968, *Behavioral Pharmacology,* Prentice-Hall, Englewood Cliffs, N.J.

[2] J. A. Harvey, ed., 1971, *Behavioral Analysis of Drug Action,* Scott, Foresman, Glenview, Ill. T. Thompson, R. Pickens, and R. A. Meisch, eds., 1970, *Readings in Behavioral Pharmacology,* Appleton-Century-Crofts, New York.

[3] L. L. Iversen, S. D. Iversen, and S. H. Snyder, eds., 1975–1977, *Handbook of Psychopharmacology* (14 vols.). Plenum Press, New York.

in behavioral pharmacology, and to the still limited senior undergraduate courses on this topic.

We have had the excitement of coordinating a most enthusiastic team, and this book has suffered few of the delays which often affect edited anthologies. Such commitment from our contributors emphasizes their belief that the book has a useful role to play. We are also very conscious that we have been given the greatest possible support by our contributors, and thank them for their cooperation.

We wish to acknowledge our appreciation for other forms of support. Marjorie Sanger has given particularly valuable secretarial assistance whenever we have asked for it. We also thank Professor P. L. Broadhurst of the Department of Psychology at the University of Birmingham. The bulk of the work on this book was completed while we were both members of his department, and we are happy to thank him for his personal and departmental support.

D. E. Blackman
D. J. Sanger

Contents

4 • Drug-Induced Stimulus Control

J. C. Winter

5 • The Effects of Drugs on Adjunctive Behavior

D. J. Sanger and D. E. Blackman

6 • Schedule-Induced Self-Administration of Drugs

R. M. Gilbert

8 • Behavioral Tolerance

P. K. Corfield-Sumner and I. P. Stolerman

9 • Behavioral Toxicology

Hugh L. Evans and Bernard Weiss

Schedule-Controlled Behavior and the Effects of Drugs 1

James W. McKearney and James E. Barrett

1. Introduction

For living organisms, behavior of some kind is ubiquitous. We are constantly either reacting to, or interacting with, our environments. In technical language, certain behaviors seem to be reactions *to* the environment and are classified as reflexive (though many important reactive behaviors are clearly not reflexive), and these can be modified beyond genetically determined bounds through the conditioning process first systematically investigated by Pavlov (1927). Though reflex behaviors, either left alone or brought under environmental control through Pavlovian (respondent) conditioning, are clearly important parts of both human and animal behavior, they account for a relatively small portion of what we normally consider to be complex, acquired behavior. Another important class of behavior is not under the direct control of stimuli that can reliably elicit it, as is the case with reflex behaviors. For such "emitted" behaviors, there appears to be no clear environmental event or stimulus that reliably precedes or "causes" them. This is not to say that they are capricious or undetermined, only that the variables responsible for their occurrence are different. For example, general patterns of locomotor activity—sometimes described as "exploratory"—are said to be emitted, since nothing easily identifiable seems responsible for their occurrence. Just as initially elicited behaviors are brought under new control through Pavlovian conditioning,

James W. McKearney • Worcester Foundation for Experimental Biology, Shrewsbury, Massachusetts 01545 **James E. Barrett** • Department of Psychology, University of Maryland, College Park, Maryland 20742

emitted behaviors can be brought under control of antecedent and consequent changes in the environment through a process called operant conditioning (Skinner, 1938). In this process, emitted behaviors are changed through their effects on the environment; operant behaviors, in short, are behaviors controlled by their consequences. While reflex or Pavlovian-conditioned responses are essentially reactions *to* the external environment, operant behaviors reflect *inter*actions *with* the environment. Although Pavlovian conditioning is restricted to behaviors for which there is originally an eliciting or reflex stimulus, the range of behaviors that can be changed through operant conditioning is far less limited.

In the study of behavior, formal distinctions between procedures or event classes may become blurred in actual practice. For example, while there are clear differences in the procedures involved in respondent as opposed to operant conditioning, it must be emphasized that, practically speaking, the two types of conditioning rarely exist in isolation. Since most consequent events that maintain or suppress operant behavior are also capable of directly eliciting certain behaviors, this leaves open the likelihood that respondent conditioning of some kind will also take place; on the other hand, behaviors initially engendered through the procedures of respondent conditioning can clearly be modified by their consequences. Indeed, most complex behaviors no doubt reflect changes brought about through both respondent and operant conditioning. Similarly, although a clear distinction is frequently drawn between antecedents and consequences in the study of operant behavior, the distinction may not always be clear. What is seen as an "antecedent" and as a "consequence" may depend less on any necessary properties of stimuli or their formal relation to behavior than on the vantage point from which we observe. One behavior's consequences may be another behavior's antecedents.

2. Schedule-Controlled Behavior

Whatever its other determining factors, all behavior is nonetheless profoundly influenced by the nature of its relation to environmental antecedents and consequences. Effective response consequences may be either reinforcing or punishing, depending on whether similar responses are subsequently increased or decreased. The class of similar responses that is changed is defined in terms of a common effect on the environment, and is referred to as an "operant" (Skinner, 1938).

Behavior is shaped and controlled not only by the nature of its consequences, but also by the way in which these consequences are related to particular behaviors (the schedule). The concept of schedule control implies an emerging or ongoing behavior that is modulated and maintained through constant dynamic relations with its setting factors and with its effects on the environment. Schedule control is most obvious when existing behaviors are modified or when new behaviors emerge from earlier forms. In both instances, behavior assumes distinctive features characteristic of the prevailing schedules. The concept of schedule control encompasses the diverse effects that environmental events can have, both when these events depend on behavior and when they do not, and when the events are presented or are terminated. Indeed, the fundamental behavioral processes of reinforcement and punishment cannot be separated from consideration of the schedules involved. When one deals with the consequences of behavior it is necessary to consider how, when, and under what circumstances those consequences are presented (Morse, 1966). Reinforcers and punishers are *always* scheduled.

The relevance of schedules of reinforcement to behavioral research is inestimable. The use of schedules has also had substantial influence on the developing course of behavioral pharmacology. Traditional assumptions about the effects of drugs on behavior have been modified considerably, and entirely new viewpoints have emerged. Although the benefits from schedule concepts that have accrued to the field of behavioral pharmacology have been substantial, analysis of the effects of drugs on behavior likewise has had considerable impact on experimental psychology. Many cherished psychological concepts have been radically revised or discarded as a result of findings in behavioral pharmacology, and schedules of reinforcement have been of critical importance in this development.

This chapter will discuss the processes of reinforcement and punishment as basic determinants of behavior and as determinants of the effects of experimental interventions such as the administration of drugs. We will focus on a variety of related factors that can influence both the effects of new environmental events and the effects of drugs on behavior. These include:

1. Characteristics of presently ongoing behavior (its rate, temporal pattern, physical topography).

2. That behavior's antecedents and consequences (control by eliciting and discriminative stimuli; the type and parameter value of the schedule; the types of maintaining and suppressing events).

3. The individual's prior experience (with both the drug or other intervention, and prior behaviors themselves).

4. The total environmental context in which behavior occurs (characteristics of other behaviors in the repertoire; existence of stimuli or events with multiple functions).

Ongoing behavior is the product of continuing dynamic interplay between the organism and the environment, and the effects of drugs on behavior can be understood only when the many factors that influence the development and maintenance of behaviors are understood as well. Since most, if not all, of the variables that determine the effects of changes in environmental conditions are also important in determining the effects of drugs on behavior, there is a natural complementarity between the experimental analysis of behavior and behavioral pharmacology. Both emphasize changes in behavior as the primary datum. Since an understanding of behavior is prerequisite to understanding the behavioral effects of drugs, this chapter will begin with a discussion of selected factors that determine the control of behavior by its consequences. The first section is devoted to examination of reinforcement and punishment as the basic processes through which behavior is maintained and changed.

2.1. Processes of Reinforcement and Punishment

When an event is presented or terminated consequent on some behavior, and that behavior subsequently increases in frequency, this outcome exemplifies the process of reinforcement and the event is identified as a reinforcer. Conversely, if the presentation or termination of an event results in the subsequent decrease in frequency of the behavior that produced it, the process of punishment is implicated, and the event is identified as a punisher. It is important to note that the only defining characteristic of reinforcers and punishers is that they produce, respectively, increases and decreases in behavior. Environmental events cannot justifiably be referred to as reinforcers and punishers without explicit knowledge of their effects on behavior in particular situations. Though there have been many theoretical speculations about why particular events may serve as reinforcers and punishers, none of these explanations can predict with accuracy when, how, and in what situations these events will change behavior. Reinforcement and punishment are empirical behavioral processes that cannot be isolated from the particular situations in which they occur (see Morse and Kelleher, 1977).

A given stimulus may affect behavior in a variety of ways (Skinner, 1938). Under certain conditions the presentation of a stimulus may elicit stereotyped patterns of behavior, but under other circumstances the same event may serve as a discriminative stimulus, setting the occasion for the occurrence or nonoccurrence of a behavior. Under some conditions ongoing behavior is suppressed by the presentation of a stimulus (punishment), and under other conditions responding can be enhanced and maintained by the presentation of a stimulus (reinforcement). One of these functions may be most obvious under one set of conditions, while another may dominate when the circumstances are changed. The effects of all environmental events depend on the conditions under which they are imposed or experienced. For example, a loud noise will elicit a startle reaction in a naive subject, but will do so to a lesser extent, or not at all, in a subject exposed repeatedly to the noise. If this same stimulus is frequently paired with the occurrence of another event, for example, the delayed presentation of food, presentation of the noise may occasion a quite different behavior—in this case, approaching the food source. If the noise is sufficiently loud, its presentation following the occurrence of some response may reduce the future probability of occurrence of that response. Under conditions of sensory deprivation, however, responding might be enhanced by response-dependent noise presentation. Thus, depending on the circumstances under which it occurs, the same physical event could directly elicit behavior, could serve as a discriminative stimulus, or could serve as a reinforcer or punisher.

Among the factors that determine the behavioral effects of consequent events is whether these events are presented or withdrawn. In many circumstances, certain events are reinforcing when presented, while other events are reinforcing through their termination or postponement. This difference is the basis for the distinction frequently drawn between positive and negative reinforcement. For a variety of reasons, however, this may not be a particularly helpful distinction. For one thing, this distinction tends to obscure the fact that the sole defining feature—an increase in behavior—is the same in both cases (see Morse and Kelleher, 1970). Also, there has been an unfortunate tendency to equate "negative" with "unpleasant" or "aversive," and "positive" with "pleasant" or "attractive," even though all that is technically meant by the terms is that something is either presented (positive) or removed (negative). Thus, the terms themselves have connotations that go beyond mere definition. Further, a variety of experiments have shown that the same event can serve as either a positive or a negative reinforcer depending on factors other than its physical characteristics; thus, classifying events into positive and negative categories again does not seem useful. As Morse and Kelleher (1977) have pointed out, there is little reason to make use of the terms positive and negative reinforcement if all that is meant is that events are either presented or terminated.

Though the terms "positive reinforcement" and "negative reinforcement" themselves may not be especially useful, there can be differences in performances maintained by event presentation as opposed to event termination that may be important because of differences in the ways events are scheduled. For example, consider behaviors maintained either by food presentation or by termination or postponement of an intense electric shock. Behavior controlled by one or another of these events may be very preemptive in certain circumstances. Under conditions of moderate food deprivation, for example, termination of an intense electric shock may be a much more compelling contingency than the possibility of receiving a food pellet. Further, the prevailing state of deprivation may be important in the case of food-maintained responding, but for responding maintained by shock termination no prior deprivation is necessary since continued responding is ensured by the recurring presence of electric shock. There are also differences between the two situations in the consequences of not responding (as might result from a high dose of drug). In the case of food presentation, not responding results in a lack of food presentation, whereas in the other case cessation of responding results in repeated exposure to electric shocks. Depending on the exact circumstances, forgoing a food pellet and receiving electric shock may not be comparable consequences. Other differences between control by presentation or termination of events (e.g., in resistance to extinction, in shaping and response differentiation, and in the role of elicited behaviors) could be important in many situations.

Though it has often been proposed that reinforcers should have effects that are "transituational" (e.g., Hilgard and Marquis, 1940; Meehl, 1950), the effects of most events that change behavior actually depend to a great extent on the circumstances under which they occur. This is sometimes not appreciated because there has been a tendency to focus on a few consequent events (e.g., food and water presentation), whose effects have been thoroughly studied in fairly standardized situations, and then to assume that the conditions critical for optimizing the reinforcing efficacy of these events will be the same as those necessary for other events. However, the conditions that optimize the tendency of one event to serve as a reinforcer may be very different from those that are critical for another event. While palatability and appropriate deprivation may be very important for food delivery to serve as a reinforcer, these may be less important in the case of stimuli that impinge more directly on the organism and need not be consumed (e.g., shock presentation, brain stimulation, drug infusion).

Generations of textbooks and popular belief alike would have it that certain classes of response-consequent events strengthen or reinforce behavior, while different classes of events instead weaken or punish. The focus is thus on the supposed invariant properties of particular events themselves, without consideration of the conditions under which they are experienced. However, these assumptions clearly violate both common experience and experimental findings that attest to widespread variations in the effects of a given consequent event. Information about the physical nature of a consequent event, or even knowledge of its effects in other situations, may be of very little help in predicting its effects on behavior in another individual or even in the same individual under different circumstances. The same consequent event may have no effect on, may increase, or may decrease behavior, depending on factors such as the characteristics of present behavior, the individual's prior experience and current deprivation state, the schedule under which the new event is presented or terminated, and the total environmental context in which behavior occurs.

That consequent events do not have invariant properties is elegantly illustrated by the work of Premack, showing that particular consequences can have either reinforcing or punishing effects. For example, in one experiment (Premack, 1971), the relative probabilities of drinking and running in rats were manipulated by restricting access to either a running wheel or a water bottle. When rats were deprived of running, otherwise improbable drinking was increased (reinforced) when it resulted in access to the wheel. On the other hand, when rats were water-deprived but allowed free access to the running wheel, water drinking was suppressed (punished) when it resulted in forced running in the motorized wheel. Thus, the same event—running—could serve as either a reinforcer or a punisher. The capacity to reinforce or to punish is not something that particular events "have" or "do not have." For every event that can serve as a reinforcer under particular conditions, there are other conditions under which this effect will be absent; often there are circumstances in which the event will have the opposite effect. For example, in experimental animals food presentation may very generally serve as a reinforcer, but there are conditions in which it maintains behavior poorly, if at all, and there are conditions under which behavior can be maintained by food postponement rather than presentation (Clark and Smith, 1977). Other experiments have shown that electrical stimulation of the brain will maintain behavior when it is response-produced, but that the same rats will terminate identical levels of stimulation presented independently of responding (Steiner *et al.*, 1969). Similarly, the consequent adminstration of amphetamine can either increase or decrease subsequent behavior depending on the conditions of its presentation (e.g., Cappell and LeBlanc, 1971). The multiple behavioral effects of stimuli have been further demonstrated in experiments showing that morphine-dependent monkeys will terminate an infusion of an antagonist that precipitates withdrawal, but that there are conditions under which responding in the same monkeys can be maintained when it produces such infusions (Goldberg *et al.*, 1971). Further, a variety of experiments discussed later in this chapter show that response-dependent presentation of electric shock can either support or suppress behavior depending on the exact conditions that prevail. Clearly, there is much more to the processes of reinforcement and punishment than the simple existence of particular classes of events.

2.2. Schedules and Other Determinants of Reinforcement and Punishment

The schedule, as a precise description of the relation of a behavior to its consequences, is implicit in and inseparable from the concepts of reinforcement and punishment. Wherever there is a consequence, there is a schedule. As Morse (1966) and others have pointed out, intermittency of reinforcement inevitably occurs in the development of complex behaviors. Further, it is only under conditions of intermittency that dynamic interrelations between behavior and environmental stimuli are fully manifested (Morse, 1966; Morse and Kelleher, 1977).

Exhaustive discussion of the prodigious amount of information now available on schedule-controlled behavior is beyond the scope of this chapter and would duplicate several excellent discussions already available (e.g., Morse and Kelleher, 1977; Zeiler, 1977; Dews and DeWeese, 1977). Therefore, our discussion will focus selectively on aspects of schedule control that are important in the analysis of the behavioral effects of drugs, and on interactions of schedule conditions with other important determinants of behavior.

Though there are many different schedules of reinforcement, most are variations of procedures under which the delivery of the consequent event depends either on the quantity of behavior emitted (ratio schedules) or on a behavior that occurs in relation to the passage of a period of time (interval schedules). Under ratio schedules, reinforcement depends on the emission of a particular number of responses. Under a fixed-ratio schedule, there is a fixed relation between the number of responses required and the delivery of the reinforcer. Under a variable-ratio schedule, on the other hand, the number of responses required varies about some average value. Under interval schedules, reinforcement depends on the passage of some minimum period of time, and then on the occurrence of a single response. Under fixed-interval schedules, a fixed period of time must pass before a response will be followed by the reinforcer. Under another type of interval schedule, the variable-interval, reinforcement also depends on the passage of time and then a single response, but the times between reinforcer availabilities are variable rather than fixed.

Each reinforcement schedule generates a characteristic pattern of responding (i.e., a unique distribution of responses in time). For example, Figure 1 shows cumulative records of responding under several different schedules. Under fixed-ratio schedules, a brief pause is typically followed by rapid and sustained responding. Performance under fixed-interval schedules is characterized by a period of little or no responding and then an increase in responding as time elapses; though the schedule only specifies the necessity of a single response, many more than this are characteristically emitted. Under variable-interval and variable-ratio schedules, pauses are minimized and responding tends to occur at a uniform rate over time. Discrete schedules of reinforcement can also be combined and studied in the same subject during an experimental session. For example, Figure 1 illustrates responding under a multiple fixed-interval fixed-ratio schedule of food presentation. In the presence of a red light, the first response after 3 min resulted in food delivery, whereas in the presence of blue light, 30 responses were necessary for food presentation. Red and blue lights alternated throughout the experimental session, and responding was typical of that observed under the associated fixed-interval and fixed-ratio schedules. Similar multiple schedules have found wide use in behav-

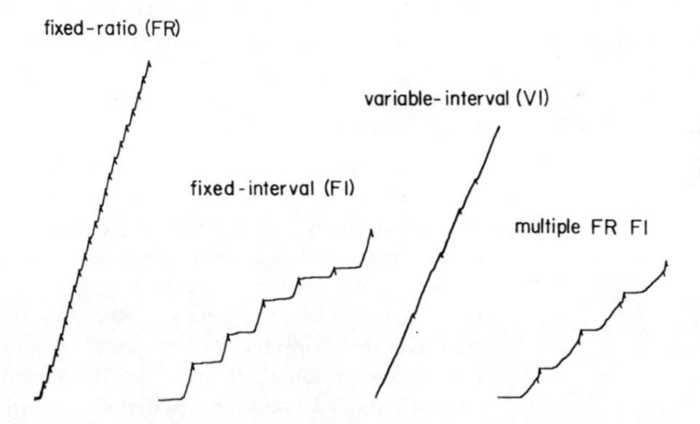

Figure 1. Cumulative records of responding under different reinforcement schedules. Ordinate: cumulated responses. Abscissa: time. Diagonal strokes indicate the presentation of the reinforcer. Records are segments taken from longer experimental sessions. FR: 50-response food presentation (pigeon). FI: 3-min shock (10 mA) presentation (squirrel monkey). VI: 3-min food presentation (squirrel monkey). FR FI: 30-response, 3-min food presentation (pigeon).

ioral pharmacology since they permit simultaneous assessment of the effects of drugs on very different rates and patterns of responding.

There are several important features of schedule-controlled responding, in both its initial generation and its continued maintenance, that warrant emphasis here. First, most schedules maintain large quantities of behavior and orderly patterns of responding with relatively few reinforcer presentations. A second, and related, point is that behavior that has been maintained under an intermittent schedule will generally persist much longer after reinforcement is discontinued (extinction) than will behavior that has been reinforced each time it occurred. Third, stable and schedule-characteristic performances such as those illustrated in Figure 1 will develop only when an individual has been exposed to the conditions for some time, and the eventual development of these performances may also depend on the subject's experience at intermediate parameter values of the schedule. For example, if a subject who will eventually respond under a 100-response fixed-ratio schedule is not given sufficient exposure to schedules with gradually escalating response-number requirements, responding may be poorly maintained, if at all, under the 100-response schedule. Finally, there may be a considerable difference between the behavior that a schedule requires and the actual performance that the subject characteristically emits. For example, only a single response is actually required under fixed-interval schedules, yet many more than this are usually made.

Performances under each of the various reinforcement schedules are very similar across a wide variety of conditions, including species of subject, different occasions in the same subject, types of responses, and types of reinforcers. This constancy of response pattern, irrespective of the details of the situation, points out how powerful reinforcement

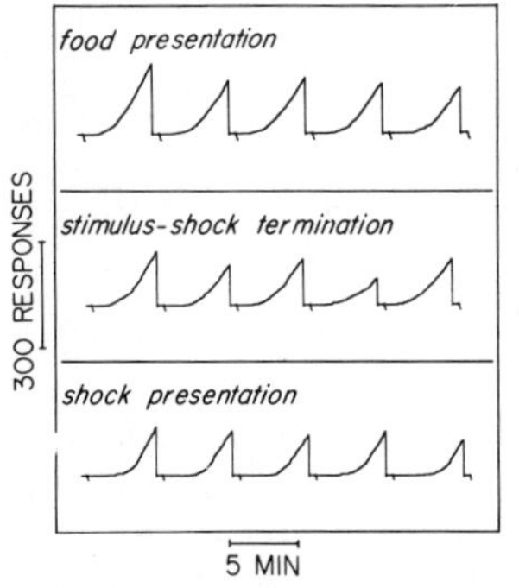

Figure 2. Similar patterns of responding maintained by different events under 5-min fixed-interval schedules in squirrel monkeys. The recording pen was reset at the end of each cycle. A 30-sec time-out period separated successive fixed-interval cycles. Diagonal strokes denote the end of time-out periods. Records are segments selected from longer experimental sessions. Upper: food presentation (250 mg). Middle: termination of a stimulus-shock complex (schedule complex); brief electric shocks (10 mA) were scheduled to occur every 5 sec after 5 min had elapsed in the presence of a stimulus. A response occurring after 5 min terminated the stimulus and instituted the time-out period. Lower: shock presentation (5 mA). Note the comparable patterns of positively accelerated responding regardless of the type of maintenance event. [From Morse *et al.* (1977).]

schedules are in determining behavior. For example, Figure 2 shows cumulative records of responding of squirrel monkeys under three different 5-min fixed-interval schedules. The consequence that maintained responding was either a food pellet (upper), termination of a visual stimulus associated with shock delivery (middle), or presentation of electric shock (lower) (the conditions under which response-produced shock will maintain responding are discussed in a subsequent section). Even though the maintaining events were very different, characteristic fixed-interval patterns of responding, a pause and then a gradual increase, were maintained. Essentially identical performances could have been illustrated for fixed-interval schedules in which responding is maintained by electrical brain stimulation (Pliskoff *et al.*, 1965), by infusions of cocaine (Goldberg and Kelleher, 1976), or by a variety of other consequent events. Quite clearly, the schedule itself can determine the pattern of responding independently of the specific characteristics of the maintaining consequence.

The importance of schedule control goes far beyond the fact that orderly and reproducible patterns of behavior are engendered and maintained. The influence of how consequences are scheduled, and other details of the relation between behavior and the environment, are probably responsible for much that is traditionally attributed to processes such as "motivation" or "perception" (Skinner, 1938, 1974). We have already briefly illustrated how similar scheduling can produce behaviors that are identical in appearance even though they are maintained by events as dissimilar as food and electric shock; in this case, any presumed "motivation" or "emotion" would be different in the two situations, yet the schedule-controlled performances are the same. Observation of subjects performing under ratio and interval schedules of food presentation would reveal to the uninitiated eye that one subject seemed to work constantly while the other seemed to respond more sporadically and rarely at a high sustained rate. Though the former subject might be described as being more highly motivated, both performances are in fact characteristic of the prevailing schedule. The appearance of hard work as opposed to sporadic performance is related to the prevailing schedules rather than to the subjects' industriousness or eagerness to be fed.

As mentioned earlier, current behaviors and changes in them as a result of new conditions are determined not only by (1) the exact relation (schedule) between the emission of behaviors and the occurrence of critical environmental events (reinforcing, punishing, discriminative), but also by (2) the individual's prior experience, and by (3) characteristics of currently ongoing behaviors in the individual's repertoire. Though there is sometimes a tendency to focus attention on one or another of these determinants, it seems likely that an overemphasis on one to the exclusion of others may lead to limited conclusions that do not recognize the multidetermined character of behavior (McKearney, 1975; see also Kantor, 1959). Consideration of the experimental history of the subject is important, for example, but not to the exclusion of an examination of the influence of current environmental circumstances. Similarly, concentration on current schedule conditions, influential as these may be, may limit conclusions if previous experience is overlooked. Finally, there must be an appreciation, even when history and current schedule conditions are held constant, that the effects of new experimental interventions (including pharmacological ones) can be profoundly influenced by characteristics of the full range of behaviors currently in the individual's repertoire; that is, by the context in which the behavior occurs. In the sections that follow we will illustrate how these factors (current behavior, schedule conditions, past experience, and context) interact to determine behavior in a variety of ways.

2.3. Control of Behavior by Noxious Stimuli

Since noxious stimuli, such as electric shock, can have effects that exemplify a variety of behavioral processes, they have been used extensively both in the experimental analysis of behavior and in studies of the behavioral effects of drugs. In this section we will illustrate a number of general points about the processes of reinforcement and punishment by reference to experiments in which behavior is controlled by noxious stimuli.

Though response-produced presentation of noxious stimuli such as electric shock can suppress behavior in many situations, there are conditions under which the opposite effect is observed; rather than suppressing behavior, response-produced electric shock can maintain typical schedule-controlled performances. Morse and Kelleher were first to systematically investigate performances maintained by shock, and they have summarized the experimental literature and some of its implications (Morse and Kelleher, 1970, 1977). We will here review one set of experiments to illustrate these performances and to call attention to their implications.

In these experiments (McKearney, 1968), squirrel monkeys first responded under a continuous avoidance schedule (Sidman, 1953) in which each response postponed the delivery of shock for 30 sec; a steady rate of responding developed, and few shocks were delivered (Figure 3A). Then, in addition to the avoidance schedule, the first response to occur after 10 min produced a shock. The addition of this

10-min fixed-interval schedule increased responding somewhat. Subsequently, when the avoidance schedule was removed and only the 10-min fixed-interval schedule was in effect, a pattern of responding similar to that observed under other fixed-interval schedules gradually developed (Figure 3B–E). There was little or no responding just after shock, and then a gradual increase in responding until the next shock was presented. Figure 3 (F and G) also shows the terminal performance of two other monkeys under the fixed-interval schedule. Performances under the fixed-interval schedule of shock presentation were the same as those observed under comparable schedules of food presentation or of stimulus-shock termination (Figure 2). Similar performances under fixed-interval schedules of shock presentation were also obtained in the squirrel monkey by Kelleher and Morse (1968a, 1969; see also Morse and Kelleher, 1970) and by Stretch *et al.* (1968) and in the cat (Byrd, 1969).

In subsequent experiments (McKearney, 1969), further comparisons with typical fixed-interval performances were made. When shocks were no longer presented (extinction), responding decreased to near-zero levels. When shocks were again presented under the 10-min fixed-interval schedule, the previous pattern of responding quickly redeveloped; over a 0.3- to 5.6-mA range, the rate of responding was directly related to the intensity of the shock. Response-dependent shocks were then presented under fixed-interval schedules of different durations (1, 3, 5, and 10 min); over this tenfold range of parameter values, the characteristic pattern of positively accelerated responding persisted. Further, the rate of responding was inversely related to the duration of the fixed interval, but the pattern of responding remained unchanged, just as with fixed-interval schedules of food or water presentation. Characteristic patterns of responding are also maintained by response-produced shock under multiple fixed-interval fixed-ratio (McKearney, 1970a), variable-interval (Barrett, 1975; McKearney, 1972, 1974), and second-order fixed-interval (Byrd, 1972) schedules.

These experiments clearly demonstrate that there are conditions under which intense electric shocks can maintain characteristic schedule-controlled performances indistinguishable from those observed under comparable schedules of food presentation or of termination of stimuli associated with shock delivery. Performances maintained by shock presentation dramatically illustrate the importance of experimental history, characteristics of ongoing behavior, and of the schedule under which an event is presented in determining the effects of that event on behavior. For example, it is likely that naive animals exposed immediately to the terminal conditions of these experiments would

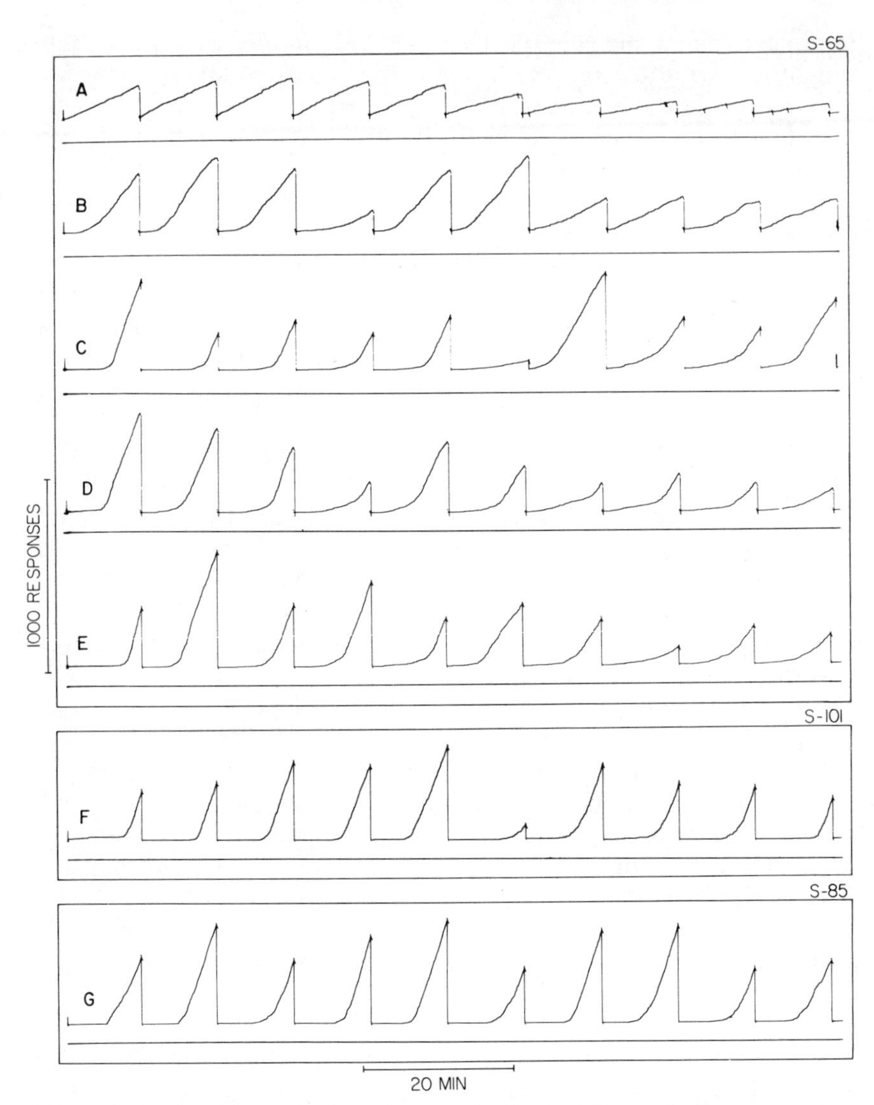

Figure 3. Responding maintained by electric shock delivery. Ordinate: cumulative number of responses per 10-min fixed interval. Abscissa: time. The recording pen was reset to the base line at the termination of each fixed interval. (A) Schedule of shock-postponement and 10-min fixed-interval (FI 10) schedule of shock presentation programmed concurrently (tenth session after introduction of FI 10, monkey S-65). (B) FI 10 shock presentation only (twenty-first session after elimination of shock-postponement schedule, monkey S-65). (C) FI 10 shock presentation, 30-sec time-out period after each shock (fourteenth session after introduction of time out, monkey S-65). (D) FI 10 shock presentation, no time-out period (sixteenth session after removal of time-out period, monkey S-65). (E) FI 10 shock presentation, 30-sec time-out period reinstated (fourth session after reinstatement of time out, sixty-third session after elimination of shock-postponement

have no lasting tendency to respond. One factor that seems to be important for engendering performances such as these is that the subject comes to the situation with a preexisting tendency to respond, that is, that some level of behavior already exists to be modulated by the schedule of shock presentation. In the experiments just described, subjects initially responded under a continuous avoidance schedule, and while it may be tempting to attribute the eventual maintenance of responding to this experience under the avoidance schedule, the same schedule-appropriate performances have been developed in subjects with no such history. For example, Kelleher and Morse (1968a) reported the maintenance of responding under fixed-interval schedules of shock presentation with monkeys whose responding was initially engendered under a schedule of food presentation. Morse *et al.* (1967) maintained responding under a fixed-interval schedule in which responding (leash pulling) was initially elicited by shock delivery. In unpublished experiments we have successfully maintained responding under fixed-interval schedules of shock presentation in monkeys who initially demonstrated some tendency to press the response key before any consequences were scheduled. Thus, while it seems important that some level of responding exist before the schedule of shock presentation is introduced, the critical features of already ongoing behavior and past experiences remain to be identified experimentally.

That the schedule under which electric shock is presented is critically important in determining its effects is illustrated by experiments in which electric shock has both maintained and suppressed responding in the same subjects during the same experimental session. In experiments by Kelleher and Morse (1968a), squirrel monkeys initially trained under a variable-interval schedule of food presentation also received an electric shock for the first response after 10 min. Later, the food schedule was eliminated and a pattern of positively accelerated responding was maintained under the fixed-interval schedule of shock presentation. In one phase of these experiments, each 10-min fixed-interval cycle was followed by a 1-min period in which each response produced a shock. Under this two-component schedule, responding was maintained under the fixed-interval schedule but was markedly

---

schedule, monkey S-65). (F) Terminal performance of monkey S-101 under the FI 10 schedule of shock presentation with a 30-sec time out after shock (fifty-seventh session after elimination of shock-postponement schedule). (G) Terminal performance of monkey S-85 under the FI 10 schedule of shock presentation with a 30-sec time out after shock (sixty-seventh session after elimination of shock-postponement schedule). The variation in numbers of responses in successive intervals within a session is typical of fixed-interval schedules in general. [From McKearney (1968); © 1968 by the American Association for the Advancement of Science.]

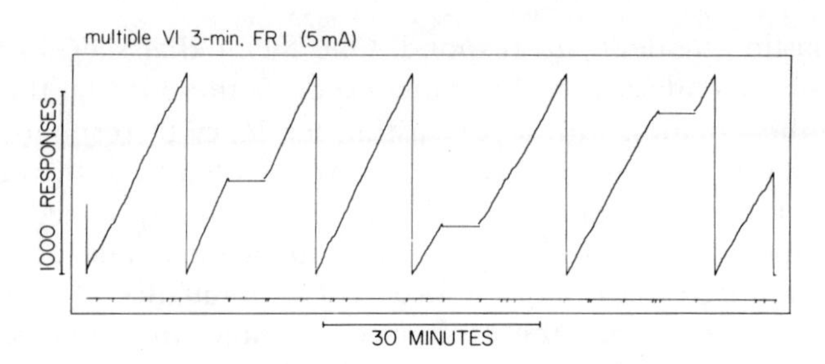

Figure 4. Maintenance and suppression of responding under a multiple schedule of electric shock presentation (monkey S-221). During the 3-min variable-interval component a response-produced shock (5 mA) was delivered on the average of once per 3 min. During minutes 21–25, 51–55, and 81–85 of each experimental session, the color of the lights in the chamber changed and each response produced a 5-mA shock (one-response fixed-ratio schedule). Electric shocks are denoted by diagonal marks on the event record. During fixed-ratio components, the response pen was offset. This monkey had previous exposure to a shock postponement schedule and exposure to a variety of schedules of shock presentation. Note that responding was well maintained during variable-interval components, but was suppressed during one-response fixed-ratio components. [From McKearney (1975 © 1975, the Williams and Wilkins Co., Baltimore]

suppressed under the one-response fixed-ratio schedule during the eleventh minute. Thus, whether shock maintained or suppressed responding depended on the schedule under which it was presented. In another experiment, McKearney (1972) demonstrated both maintenance and suppression of responding under a multiple schedule of shock presentation. In squirrel monkeys with prior training under an avoidance schedule, responding was maintained under a 3-min variable-interval schedule of shock presentation. In addition, during certain segments of each experimental session the color of the lights in the chamber was different and shocks were delivered under a one-response fixed-ratio schedule. Figure 4 illustrates the patterns of responding observed under this multiple schedule of shock presentation. Responding was well maintained under the variable-interval schedule but was suppressed during the one-response fixed-ratio schedule. In both of these experiments, identical electric shocks either maintained or suppressed responding depending on the schedule of presentation. The schedule thus determined whether the effects of electric shock exemplified the process of reinforcement or of punishment.

Barrett and Glowa (1977) have recently demonstrated both maintenance and suppression of responding with electric shock in a different situation. Squirrel monkeys with prior training under an avoidance schedule responded under 5-min fixed-interval schedules; in the presence of different visual stimuli, responding was maintained by either the presentation of shock or the presentation of food. Characteristic patterns of positively accelerated responding were maintained in both schedule components. Then, during food presentation components, every thirtieth response resulted in the delivery of a shock. When responding was maintained by either food or shock presentation, characteristic fixed-interval patterns of responding were maintained (Figure 5A). When every thirtieth response during food-presentation components also resulted in shock, however, responding during food-presentation components was suppressed (Figure 5B). Thus, responding was both maintained by shock in the fixed-interval shock-presentation components and suppressed by shock during food-presentation components. Clearly, the effects of response-produced shock differed depending on the schedule under which it was presented and on the characteristics of the behavior on which it was superimposed. Again, electric shock could be shown to have either reinforcing or punishing effects on behavior.

There are many other situations in which electric shock can either maintain or suppress responding depending on the schedule under which it is presented or terminated. For example, under appropriate conditions, characteristic fixed-interval performances are maintained when responding terminates a visual stimulus associated with shock delivery (Morse and Kelleher, 1966; see also Figure 2). In recent experiments (McKearney, 1976) we studied the effects of delivering response-produced shocks under this schedule. Squirrel monkeys responded under a 5-min fixed-interval schedule in which the first response after 5 min terminated a visual stimulus associated with shock delivery; in the absence of responding, shocks were delivered every few seconds after the 5-min interval elapsed. A pattern of positively accelerated responding was maintained under this schedule, as has been reported previously (Morse and Kelleher, 1966). Then, in addition to the fixed-interval schedule, every thirtieth response resulted in the delivery of a

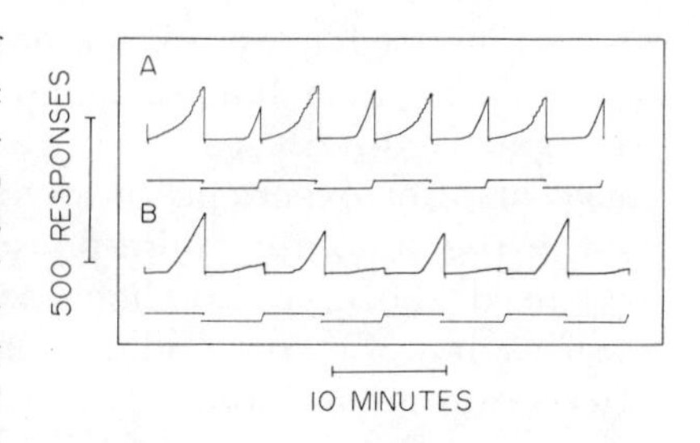

Figure 5. Maintenance and suppression of responding by response-produced electric shock. In panel A a multiple 5-min fixed-interval schedule of food or shock (10mA) presentation was in effect. Responding was maintained at approximately equal rates by both food and shock. Panel B shows the suppression of food-maintained responding when each thirtieth response during the fixed-interval food-presentation component also produced a 10-mA shock. The event pen was displaced during the food-presentation schedule and the pens were reset after each component. [Adapted from Barrett and Glowa (1977).]

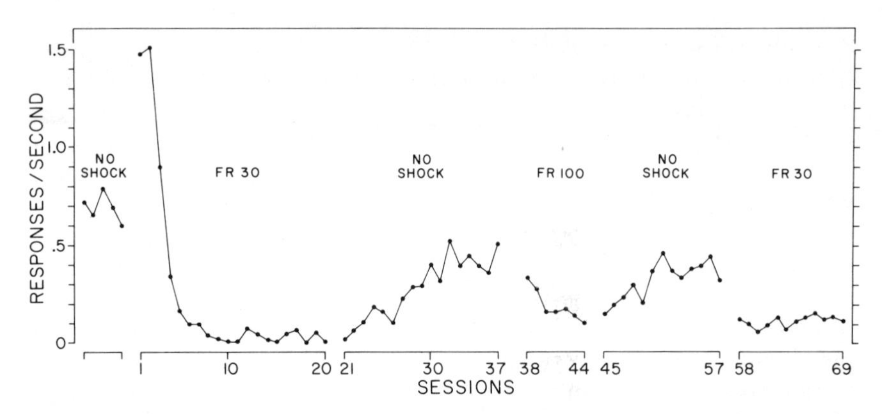

Figure 6. Effects of response-produced shock on responding under a 5-min fixed-interval schedule of stimulus-shock termination (monkey S-538). Response-produced shock was delivered after every thirtieth response (sessions 1–20, 58–69) or every one-hundredth response (sessions 38–44). Note that responding initially increased (sessions 1–3) and was then suppressed. Responding recovered when response-produced shocks were no longer presented (sessions 21–37, 45–57), and was immediately suppressed when response-produced shocks were again delivered. [Adapted from McKearney (1976).]

shock. Figure 6 summarizes the results of this procedure in one monkey (S-538). In the absence of response-produced shock, a response rate of about 0.7 per second was maintained under the schedule of stimulus-shock termination. The initial introduction of response-produced shock under the 30-response fixed-ratio schedule markedly increased responding during the first few experimental sessions, but then responding was suppressed to 0.1 response/sec or less. Responding recovered when response-produced shocks were eliminated, but was immediately suppressed when shocks were again presented under 30- or 100-response fixed-ratio schedules. Several features of these results are relevant to the present discussion. The results demonstrate clearly another situation in which responding can be both maintained and suppressed by shock; responding was maintained by stimulus-shock termination but was suppressed when shocks were presented under a fixed-ratio schedule. These results also illustrate the importance of prior experience in determining the effects of shock. When first exposed to the 30-response fixed-ratio schedule of response-produced shock, responding markedly increased; during later exposures, however, responding was immediately suppressed. The initial effects of response-produced shock depended on the fact that responding was maintained by stimulus-shock termination, since response-produced shock does not generally produce these transient increases in responding when responding is instead maintained by food presentation. The difference in the effects during later exposures to the same schedule, however, depended on the earlier experience.

Recent experiments have studied other situations in which electric shock can have different effects depending on how it is scheduled. In one experiment (Barrett and Spealman, 1977) squirrel monkeys with prior training under an avoidance schedule were studied under a concurrent schedule in a restraining chair containing two response levers. During one phase of this experiment, responding on the right-hand lever resulted in the delivery of a 7-mA shock on the average of once every 3 min (3-min variable-interval schedule of shock presentation); concurrently, responding on the left-hand lever was maintained under a 3-min fixed-interval schedule in which the first response after 3 min terminated all lights in the chamber, resulting in a 60-sec period during which no shocks were delivered and responding had no consequences. Thus, responding on one lever produced shock, while responding on the other lever terminated shock availability and the shock-associated stimulus. Figure 7 illustrates performances under this concurrent schedule in two monkeys. Characteristic patterns of responding were maintained under both component schedules. Under the variable-interval schedule of shock presentation there was a steady rate of re-

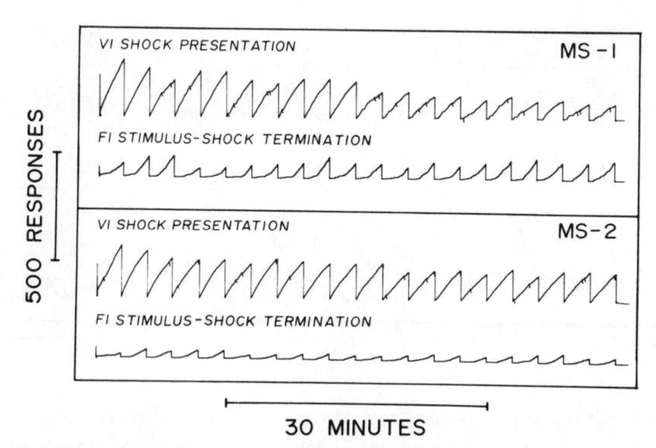

Figure 7. Cumulative records of responding maintained under a concurrent schedule of shock presentation and stimulus-shock termination. Two levers were simultaneously available. Presses on the right-hand lever produced a 7-mA electric shock on the average of every 3 min (variable-interval 3-min shock-presentation schedule). A press on the left-hand lever after 3 min turned off the houselights in the chamber for 1 min, during which responding had no scheduled consequences (3-min fixed-interval stimulus-shock termination schedule). Shock presentation is indicated by diagonal marks; the pens returned to base line at the end of each time-out period. Responding by these monkeys was maintained by both the presentation of shock (top record of each pair) and by the termination of shock and shock-correlated stimuli (bottom record of each pair). [From Barrett and Spealman (1977). © 1977 by the Society for the Experimental Analysis of Behavior.]

sponding typical of this schedule, while under the fixed-interval schedule of stimulus-shock termination there was a pause and then a gradual increase in responding. Thus, responding was concurrently maintained by the presentation of shock (variable-interval) and by termination of shock-associated stimuli (fixed-interval).

There are many instances in which prior experience can exert a profound influence on a subject's reaction to present schedule conditions. For example, Figure 8 illustrates the effects of response-produced shock under three different conditions. Squirrel monkeys were studied under 5-min fixed-interval schedules in which responding was maintained by food presentation or by termination of a shock-associated stimulus, and then response-produced shock was also pre-

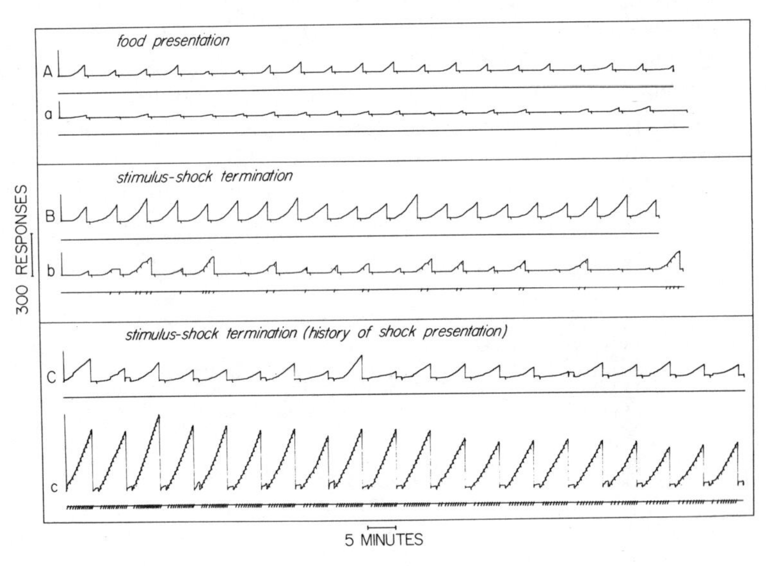

Figure 8. Effects of response-produced shock under different response-maintenance conditions. Ordinate: cumulative responses. Abscissa: time. The response pen reset at the end of each interval. A 30-sec (A and B) or 60-sec (C) time-out period separated successive FI cycles; the end of time out is signified by the first diagonal stroke on the response record. *A*: 5-min FI schedule of food presentation. *B*: 5-min FI schedule of stimulus-shock termination (10-mA shocks occurred every 5 sec after 5 min had elapsed, and the first response initiated time-out). *C*: as in *B*, except that time out was 60 sec, in a subject with prior experience of response maintenance with electric shock. Records *a*, *b*, and *c* are taken from the tenth session, in which every thirtieth response produced a shock (3 mA in *a*, 10 mA in *b* and *c*). Response-produced shocks are indicated by diagonal strokes on both the response and event lines (*b* and *c*) or only on the event line (*a*). Note that responding was suppressed under the schedule of food presentation and of stimulus-shock termination, but enhanced under the schedule of stimulus-shock termination in a subject with a history of response maintenance by electric shock.

sented under a 30-response fixed-ratio schedule. Response-produced shock eventually suppressed responding maintained by food presentation (Figure 8, A and a) or by stimulus-shock presentation (Figure 8, B and b) in the two subjects illustrated. A third subject, also responding under the fixed-interval schedule of stimulus-shock termination, had previously responded under a fixed-interval schedule of shock presentation as described earlier (i.e., responding had once been maintained by shock delivery). In this monkey, responding under the schedule of stimulus-shock termination was comparable to that observed in the monkey without the history of shock-maintained responding (compare Figure 8, B and C), but when the 30-response fixed-ratio schedule of shock presentation was added, there was a dramatic and sustained increase in responding. Even though that monkey's behavior just prior to introduction of response-produced shock was similar to the other subject's, the effects of shock were opposite. Clearly, the effects of response-produced shock in this situation depended more on the monkey's prior experience than on current maintenance conditions.

2.4. Nature and Significance of Schedule-Controlled Behavior

The continued maintenance of more or less stable behaviors, their transient modulation in the face of momentary changes in circumstances, as well as the production of more pronounced and durable changes in behavior all depend on constant interplay between behavior and its consequences. In the preceding sections we have illustrated some of the many ways in which the effects of consequent events depend on factors other than their physical nature. Particular events themselves, divorced from the exact circumstances under which they are experienced, do not have specifiable effects. Of necessity, events occur in context and indeed take on their major properties through being embedded in particular contexts. Food presentation, shock termination, drug infusion, the landing of a lucrative account, or the culmination of a long-sought sexual conquest can be very effective consequences of behavior, but only under the right circumstances. The efficacy of the consequences of behavior cannot be assessed *in vacuo*. Past experiences, the totality of our present situation, and the characteristics of new conditions that impinge on us interact to determine ongoing and emerging behaviors.

The ways in which environmental events affect behavior are *in*completely predictable from expectations based on the physical nature of the events or knowledge of their effects in other situations. The interplay between behavior and its consequences is an evolving, dynamic one. As Morse and Kelleher (1970) point out, when behavior is changed by its consequences, the consequences that further affect behavior also may change. A corollary is that the conditions optimal for initially engendering a behavior may not be the same as the conditions that ensure its continued maintenance.

Current behaviors, and changes in them as a result of new conditions, are the product of multiple factors, including (1) the history of the individual; (2) currently ongoing behaviors, including not only those of direct experimental interest, but also other behaviors in the individual's repertoire; and (3) the relation (schedule) between the emission of behaviors and the occurrence of critical environmental events (reinforcing, punishing, discriminative). In the analysis of ongoing and newly emerging behaviors these factors initially must be assumed to be of equal importance.

Though the ways in which consequences can change behaviors are often dichotomized and treated as separate entities (reinforcement and punishment) the implication that basically different processes are involved can be misleading. One result of such a separation of reinforcement and punishment is that there is then a tendency to classify events as *either* reinforcers *or* punishers. But the appropriateness both of conceptualizing reinforcement and punishment as separate processes and of classifying events as reinforcers or punishers is called into question by results summarized here and elsewhere, indicating that events can have totally different effects depending on the conditions of their presentation. As Morse and Kelleher (1977) have pointed out, describing reinforcement as presentation of a "thing" called a reinforcer puts undue emphasis on this "thing" at the expense of other important determinants of behavior change. Since characteristic changes in a behavior's rate or temporal pattern depend on a variety of factors other than the simple existence of particular consequent events, there seems to be little point in categorizing events and giving them names (Morse and Kelleher, 1977). Reinforcement and punishment are the names we have given to the processes or relations through which behavior is changed, and the processes encompass behaviors themselves, their setting factors and consequences, and particular behavioral effects. Rather than being basically different processes, reinforcement and punishment are simply the opposite extremes on a continuum along which behavior can be changed.

The conceptualization of reinforcement and punishment, and maintenance and suppression of behavior, as extremes along a continuum of behavior change is in line both with observations in the laboratory and with analysis of natural environments. A given event that in one situation may clearly engender and maintain behavior may do so to a lesser extent under other conditions, and be ineffective or even have graded suppressing effects under yet other circumstances. At what point does an event cease to be a reinforcer and become either a "neutral stimulus" or a punisher? In complex situations with constantly fluctuating conditions this can be such a difficult question that it becomes practically meaningless.

The control of behavior by the environment is as exquisitely complex as experience tells us it must be. Though complex patterns of responding do result from what in isolation appear to be specifiable and simple relations between a behavior and its consequences, the eventual patterns of responding that evolve may not be simply predictable from even exhaustive knowledge of these isolated determinants. As we have emphasized, behavior is determined not only by current conditions, but also by factors such as the individual's prior experience, the past and present contexts in which behavior occurs, and assuredly by a host of other factors. Knowing all there is to know about only one of these classes of determinants is not sufficient for accurate prediction and control.

Though the primary focus of this chapter is on the effects of drugs, we have first emphasized some of the complexities of behavior itself, for it is only with full realization of these complexities that we can hope to make any sense whatever of the varied effects that drugs can have. Understanding of the behavioral effects of drugs must be predicated on a full appreciation of the complexities of behavior itself. We have explored some of these complexities here, and others will appear in subsequent discussions of the effects of drugs.

3. Effects of Drugs on Schedule-Controlled Behavior

Behavior is changed not only by interactions with antecedent and consequent events, but also by a variety of factors or interventions that impinge in a nonconsequential way. Drug administration is an important and widely studied intervention of this type.

Psychological theories often emphasize explanatory mechanisms that go well beyond the observation of overt behavior, but these "explanations" often involve little more than restatement of phenomena in different words. Thus, even a behavior as simple as eating may be attributed, not to the fact that the organism has been deprived of food, but to the operation of a hypothetical "hunger drive." Similarly, responding maintained by postponement or termination of electric shock, or behavior suppressed by shock presentation, is often attributed to the effects of "fear" or "anxiety" rather than to a more direct operation of the environmental events leading to these behaviors. In keeping with this predilection to interpret and explain behavior in terms of hypothetical intervening processes (motivational and emotional), early interpretations of the behavioral effects of drugs often appealed to the drug's supposed effects on these intervening states. Thus, a particular drug did not simply increase punished responding, but it reduced "fear" and thereby changed behavior. Though explanations like this have waned noticeably over the years, they have by no means disappeared entirely. One latter-day variation on the same theme makes use of hypothetical chemical or physiological mediators in the nervous system (e.g., "go" and "stop" mechanisms, "reward" systems and pathways), but these are often little more than the same motivational constructs couched in new terminology.

Efforts to systematically relate the effects of drugs to hypothetical intervening mechanisms, whether conceptual or quasi-neurological, have generally not been supported by experimental evidence; instead, there has been a growing recognition that the effects of drugs depend overwhelmingly on specifiable features of behavior itself and the situation in which it occurs. Among the determinants of the behavioral effects of drugs known to be important are (1) the rate and temporal pattern of ongoing behavior and the nature of its control by antecedent and consequent stimuli, (2) the types of controlling events and whether these maintain or suppress behavior, (3) the individual's prior experience, and (4) the total environmental context in which behavior occurs. The remainder of the chapter will be devoted to discussion of the importance of these and other factors in determining the effects of drugs on maintained and suppressed behavior.

3.1. Response Rate as a Determinant of the Behavioral Effects of Drugs

Though it has long been recognized that the effects of interventions or new conditions on living tissue can be influenced by its quantitative "state" at the time of the intervention, application of similar thinking to analysis of the behavioral effects of drugs dates more recently from an initial statement by Dews (1958a). His suggestion was that the behavioral effects of many drugs seemed rather accurately predictable from the frequency of occurrence of the behavior in the absence of drug. Though the perspective of time may make this assertion seem somewhat self-evident and straightforward, it was not then so apparent.

The suggestion that there were readily observable characteristics of behavior that could, with reasonable generality, predict the effects of drugs was offered to behavioral pharmacology at a time when it was very ripe for development of general principles. In the years that followed there has been a remarkably focused effort to determine the conditions under which this dependence is applicable. In this section we will discuss some of the conditions and drugs for which control response rate is reasonably predictive of the effects of drugs, the similarities and differences in the dependency on control rate for several drug classes, and certain factors that modify such a dependence on response rate. We have no intention of exhaustively covering what is by now a substantial literature on this topic, as several comprehensive reviews are available (e.g., Dews and DeWeese, 1977; Sanger and Blackman, 1976; Weiss and Laties, 1969). Further, we will focus only on the effect of a few representative drug classes (amphetamines, barbiturates, and phenothiazines) to illustrate the kinds of rate-dependent effects that can be obtained with many other drugs.

3.1.1. Generality of a Dependence of the Effects of Drugs on Control Response Rate

In the first published experiment to clearly demonstrate a dependence of the effects of drugs on different patterns of schedule-controlled responding, Dews (1955) studied keypecking of pigeons under either fixed-interval or fixed-ratio schedules of food presentation. Low overall rates of responding (about 0.4 response/sec) were maintained under the fixed-interval schedule, and much higher rates (about 1.7 response/sec) were maintained under fixed-ratio schedules. The effects of pentobarbital differed depending on the schedule of reinforcement and resultant rate of responding. Certain doses of pentobarbital markedly suppressed fixed-interval responding but either had less effect on or actually increased responding under fixed-ratio schedules. The same difference in the effects of pentobarbital and other barbiturates on different rates of responding under fixed-interval and fixed-ratio schedules has been found in a number of other experiments, and is also observed when the two schedules are alternately present during the same experimental session (e.g., Morse and Herrnstein, 1956).

In a later experiment, Dews (1958a) studied the effects of methamphetamine on responding by pigeons under several different schedules of food presentation. When food was presented for each fiftieth keypeck (fixed-ratio schedule) or for a response on the average of once per minute (variable-interval schedule), control rates of responding were rather high (in excess of one response per second); when food was presented for the first response every 15 min (fixed-interval schedule) or under a 900-response fixed-ratio schedule, however, control rates of responding were much lower (0.1–0.2 response/sec). Dews found that the effects of methamphetamine seemed to depend on the control response rate engendered under these schedules. When control rates were high, methamphetamine had little effect at lower doses and decreased responding at higher doses; when control rates were lower, however, methamphetamine markedly increased responding at low and intermediate doses and decreased responding only at the highest doses. Thus, the same dose of methamphetamine could either increase or decrease responding, depending on the control response rate. Dews first discussed this dependency in terms of relatively long and short interresponse times engendered under the two sets of schedules (Dews, 1958a), and later he (1958b) and others (e.g., Dews and Morse, 1961; Kelleher and Morse, 1968b) generally spoke of a dependency on response rate rather than on interresponse times. It is important to note that neither in its initial statement nor in its later elaboration by Dews or his colleagues was this any more than a description of the effects of certain drugs, and as a factor that might predict drug effects in certain situations. It did not, and indeed it does not, directly "explain" the effects of drugs. It is still a descriptive statement, not a "theory" or a "hypothesis," and its generality and biological significance, rather than truth or falsity, are what should be elaborated experimentally.

A recent experiment by Heffner *et al.* (1974) illustrates the dependence of the effects of *d*-amphetamine on control rates of responding under several different schedule types and parameter values. Rats responded under either 90-sec variable-interval, 120-sec fixed-interval, or fixed-ratio schedules requiring either 1, 2, 5, 10, or 20 responses, and these schedules engendered a broad range of control response rates (from 0.35 to 3.59 responses/sec). The effects of *d*-amphetamine (0.3–3.0 mg/kg) were different depending on the control rate of responding; when control rate was relatively low (as under the 90-sec variable-interval or the one-response fixed-ratio schedules), *d*-amphetamine increased responding, but when control rate was higher (e.g., under the 20-response fixed-ratio schedules), only decreases in responding were observed. In general, there was an inverse relation between control rate and the magnitude of increase produced by *d*-amphetamine, whereas there was a direct relation between control rate and decreases produced by amphetamine.

The rate-dependent effects of drugs first described by Dews have since been confirmed by many other investigators using diverse species, types of responses, and types of reinforcement schedules (see reviews by Kelleher and Morse, 1968b, and by Sanger and Blackman, 1976), and have been extended to many classes of drugs, including sympathomimetic amines (McMillan, 1968a,b), barbiturates (Dews, 1955; Waller and Morse, 1963; McKearney, 1970b), benzodiazepines and related drugs (Cook and Kelleher, 1962; Cook and Catania, 1964; Wuttke and Kelleher, 1970), phenothiazines and tricyclic compounds (Marr, 1970; Smith, 1964), and many others. Further, a general dependence of the effects of drugs on control rates of responding has been shown to apply not only across different schedule types in the same or different subjects, but also within patterns of responding maintained by a single schedule.

In analyzing the influence of control response rate in determining the effects of drugs, responding under fixed-interval schedules is particularly useful since a wide variety of rates is available for study. Responding under fixed-interval schedules is characterized by increases in rate as time elapses; response rates may change from near zero at the beginning to one or more responses per second at the end. In analyzing local rates it is common to separately record responding in successive temporal segments of the interval, cumulated over all fixed-interval cycles that comprise an experimental session.

Figure 9 summarizes rates of responding during 10 1-min segments of a 10-min fixed-interval schedule and illustrates three different methods of examining the effects of a drug on this performance. As shown in the left panel, there is an orderly progression in response rate over the 10-min fixed interval, ranging from a little over 0.03 response/sec in the first segment to over 2 per second in the final segment. This figure also compares different ways of examining changes in local response rate (during individual tenths of the interval) after a peak rate-increasing dose of *d*-amphetamine. In the left panel the distribution of absolute response rates over the interval under control conditions (concave line) is compared with the rates observed under *d*-amphetamine. It can easily be seen that the effect of this dose was to increase low local rates and either to have no effect on or to decrease higher rates. Though the plot in the left panel makes clear that relative changes in rate seem greatest when rate is normally lowest, this is more easily assessed by directly plotting changes in rate relative to rates occurring under control conditions (Figure 9, right panel). Here, analysis of relative changes as a function of ordinal fixed-interval segments reveals that responding in early segments was increased over 20-fold, whereas responding in later segments was either increased less or even slightly decreased. The orderliness of the relation between the magnitude of changes in local rates of responding after *d*-amphetamine relative to rates occurring in the absence of drug is perhaps best seen when plotted on logarithmic coordinates as in the lower panel of Figure 9. Plotted in this manner, the effects of this dose of *d*-amphetamine are an inverse linear function of control rate. Though the data summarized in Figure 9 are from a squirrel monkey responding under a

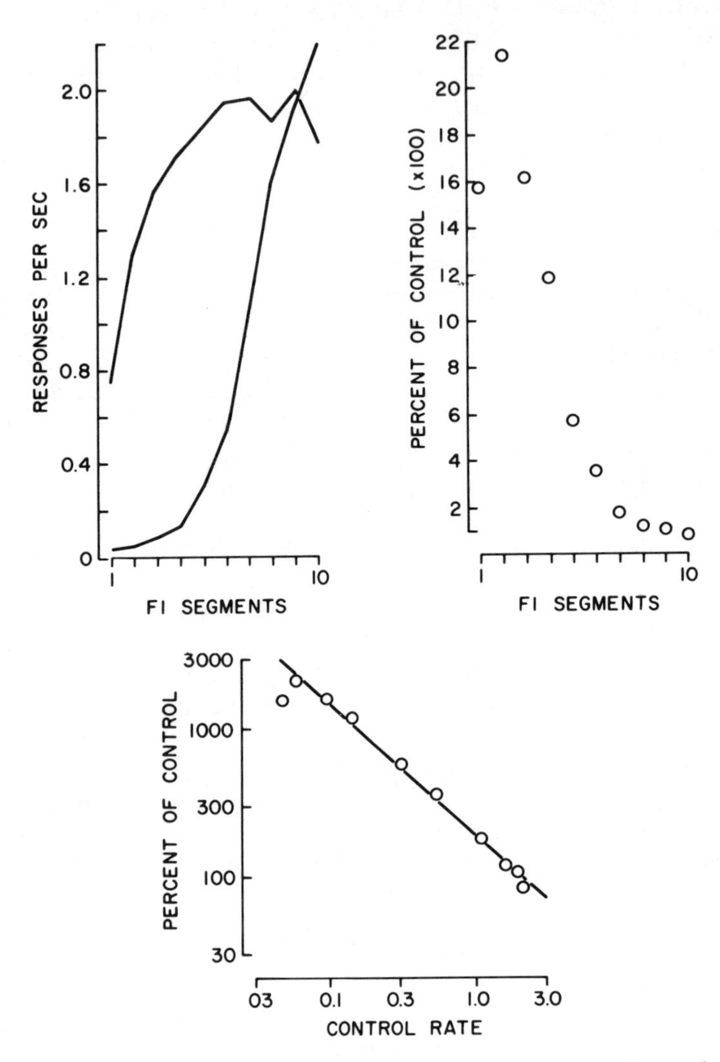

Figure 9. Effects of 0.3 mg/kg *d*-amphetamine on local rates of responding under a 10-min fixed-interval schedule of shock (5.6 mA) presentation (monkey S-101). Rates of responding were separately recorded during individual 1-min segments of each 10-min interval (cumulated over 10 FI cycles). Left: response rate in successive 1-min segments; line with positive acceleration is from control sessions, and convex line is from a single drug session. Right: changes in responding during successive 1-min segments, expressed as percentage of rate during control sessions. Lower: relative changes in rate plotted against control rates in individual 1-min segments (logarithmic coordinates). Identical data are plotted in all graphs.

10-min fixed-interval schedule of shock presentation, essentially the same effects of amphetamine have been shown in other species with responding maintained by events such as food or water presentation (e.g., McMillan, 1968a; Heffner *et al.*, 1974) or termination of shock or associated stimuli (Cook and Catania, 1964; Kelleher and Morse, 1964, 1968b). The rate-dependent effects of amphetamines apply very generally across a wide variety of experimental conditions, as described below.

Though the effects of many different drugs have been shown to be related in an orderly way to control rates of responding, the exact nature of the dependence on rate may differ somewhat for different drug classes. For example, under certain conditions amphetamines and barbiturates have very similar effects; at low and intermediate doses under a fixed-interval schedule both may increase low local rates of responding to a proportionally greater extent than higher local rates. At higher doses, and under procedures in which much higher control rates of responding are also sampled (e.g., a multiple fixed-interval fixed-ratio schedule), however, there are clear differences in the effects of the two drug classes. Amphetamines tend to increase normally low rate responding (e.g., in a fixed interval) over a relatively wide dose range, while higher control rates (e.g., in a fixed ratio) begin to decrease at relatively low doses. In contrast, barbiturates generally either have little effect on or increase high rates of responding over a wide dose range, while normally lower rates tend to decrease at intermediate and upper doses. Thus, at certain doses the two drugs have opposite effects on high and low rates of responding under ratio and interval schedules. Figure 10 illustrates the differences that can be observed under a multiple fixed-interval fixed-ratio schedule of food presentation. Under the conditions studied, *d*-amphetamine increased responding during the fixed-interval component but completely suppressed responding under the fixed-ratio schedule, whereas pentobarbital severely suppressed fixed-interval responding but left fixed-ratio responding relatively unaffected. Thus, while amphetamines and barbiturates both tend to increase low rates of responding at appropriate doses, amphetamines tend to decrease higher rates at these same doses whereas barbiturates have a much lesser tendency to decrease high response rates.

3.1.2. Factors Modifying the Rate-Dependent Effects of Drugs

Though the control rate of responding is a very influential determinant of the behavioral effects of drugs, it is not, of course, the sole determinant of these effects. In this section we will discuss a number of

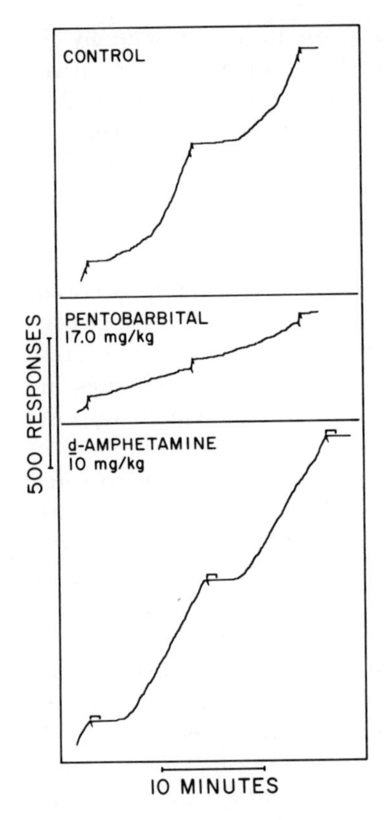

Figure 10. Effects of pentobarbital and amphetamine on responding under a multiple fixed-interval (10-min) fixed-ratio (31-response) schedule of food presentation (pigeon 288). FI and FR components alternated throughout experimental sessions, each correlated with a different color keylight. If no response was made within 60 sec of the end of the FI, or if 31 responses were not emitted within 60 sec during the FR, the alternate schedule component was presented (60-sec limited hold). All records are segments selected from longer experimental sessions. Upper: control performance. Middle: performance at about 2.5 hr after i.m. injection of 17 mg/kg pentobarbital sodium. Lower: about 4 hr after 10 mg/kg *d*-amphetamine. Note that pentobarbital markedly decreased FI responding but had little or no effect on FR responding. *d*-Amphetamine increased FI responding, but completely abolished responding during FR segments (portion under brackets).

factors that have been shown to alter the nature of a dependence on control rate.

Although amphetamines and similar drugs generally tend to increase low rates of responding, there are some situations in which *very* low rates of responding may not be increased as much as would be predicted. For example, Verhave (1958) has shown that normally effective doses of methamphetamine do not increase responding when control rates are very low either because responding has no consequences or because responding was as yet poorly developed. McMillan (1968a) and others have also observed that amphetamine may not increase very low control rates of responding that occur in the initial portion of fixed-interval schedules.

Responding that is well controlled by discriminative stimuli may not be affected by drugs in the same way as responding not under such control. For example, Laties and Weiss (1966) compared the effects of several drugs on responding under two different conditions in pigeons responding under 5-min fixed-interval schedules of food presentation. Under one condition, stimuli remained constant throughout each 5-min period. Under the other condition ("added clock") a different symbol was projected on the response key during each minute of the fixed interval. Under the first condition the usual pattern of positively accelerated responding prevailed, but under the "clock" condition, responding was largely confined to the last minute of the fixed interval. Even though control rates of responding during the early portion of the fixed interval under the clock condition were very low, the rate-increasing effects of *d*-amphetamine, scopolamine, and pentobarbital were less marked here than on the somewhat higher rates occurring during early segments of the simple fixed-interval schedule. Thus, the "clock" stimuli exerted sufficient control over responding so that these low rates were not increased by these drugs.

Another experiment (McKearney, 1970b) also demonstrated that the degree of stimulus control can modify the rate-dependent effects of drugs. Responding by pigeons under a fixed-interval schedule of food presentation was lower in the presence of a periodically recurring visual stimulus uncorrelated with food delivery (S^{Δ}) than during a stimulus that was present during food delivery (S^{D}). When differences between S^{D} and S^{Δ} were relatively great, as when the keylight color was changed or when overall illumination in the chamber was changed markedly, changes in responding after amobarbital were inversely related to control rates during individual S^{D} and S^{Δ} periods, but the relative magnitude of change during S^{Δ} was considerably less than expected on the basis of changes during S^{D} periods. When plotted against control rates (Figure 11), data points for S^{Δ} periods (filled circles) fell considerably below the regression line fitted to S^{D} points. In unpublished experiments, essentially the same results were obtained with *d*-amphetamine, imipramine, and chlorpromazine. Changes in S^{Δ} responding were limited, presumably, by differences in discriminative stimuli. This was further shown in experiments with varying intensities of the S^{Δ} stimulus (general illumination of the chamber). As the intensity of S^{Δ} was decreased, control rates of responding did not change appreciably, but amobarbital produced greater relative increases in S^{Δ} responding. At certain S^{Δ} intensities, data points for S^{D} and S^{Δ} periods fell along a common regression line. Thus, the effects of amobarbital on local rates of S^{D} and S^{Δ} responding could be changed by varying the intensity of the stimuli.

Taken together, the results of the experiments by Laties and Weiss (1966) and by McKearney (1970b) show that the rate-dependent effects of drugs can be modified in situations in which behavior is well controlled by discriminative stimuli.

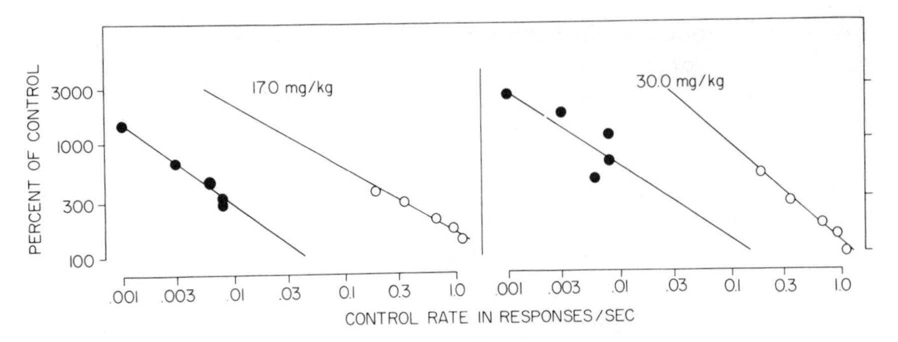

Figure 11. Effect of amobarbital on responding during individual 1-min segments of a 10-min fixed-interval schedule with multiple S^{Δ} periods. Ordinate: rate after amobarbital, expressed as percent of control. Abscissa: control rate during individual 1-min segments of the FI. Ordinate and abscissa are logarithmic. Open circles: S^{D} (red keylight). Closed circles: S^{Δ} (green keylight). Control rates are means of 15 nondrug sessions, and each point is the mean of two injections in each of three birds. Regression lines were fitted by the method of least squares. [From McKearney (1970b); © 1970 by the Society for the Experimental Analysis of Behavior.]

Since rates of responding and frequency of reinforcer presentation are frequently directly related, it is possible that differences in reinforcement density rather than differences in response rate could determine the effects of drugs. Several recent experiments have examined this question, and the results generally support the conclusion that drug effects are determined more by differences in response rate than by differences in reinforcement density. For example, MacPhail and Gollub (1975) and Sanger and Blackman (1975) compared the effects of drugs on responding under variable-interval schedules of food presentation in which response rate and frequency of food presentation were varied independently by requiring that the food-producing response be separated from the previous response by some minimum time period. The effects of *d*-amphetamine, scopolamine, and chlordiazepoxide depended more on overall control response rates than on associated food-presentation frequencies. Stitzer and McKearney (1977) compared the influence of response rate and reinforcement density by using different response-spacing requirements under a procedure that also made it possible to analyze the effects of drugs on local as well as overall rates of responding. Pigeons responded under multiple 3-min fixed-interval schedules in which either a long (4- to 6-sec) or short (40-msec) interresponse time was necessary for food presentation. Long-pause and short-pause schedules engendered different overall rates of responding (0.22 and 0.95 response/sec) with similar food-presentation frequencies. Pentobarbital markedly increased low rates under the long-pause schedule, and either increased less or decreased higher rates under the short-pause schedule. *d*-Amphetamine, however, did not increase the low overall rates under the long-pause schedule at any dose. Analysis of responding within fixed-interval components showed that increases in local rates of responding were inversely related to control rates under both schedules for both drugs. However, pentobarbital had quantitatively similar effects on comparable local rates under the two schedules, whereas *d*-amphetamine generally increased a given rate less if that rate came from the schedule with the long-pause requirement.

The experiments by MacPhail and Gollub (1975), Sanger and Blackman (1975), and Stitzer and McKearney (1977) indicate that the effects of certain drugs depend more on control response rate than on the frequency of food presentation. In all three experiments, response-spacing requirements were used to vary response rate independently of reinforcement density. In the former two experiments, only a limited range of overall rates of responding was studied, whereas in the Stitzer and McKearney (1977) experiment a wider range of local response rates was also analyzed. In the latter experiment, the effects of *d*-amphetamine on comparable local rates of responding were different depending on whether the schedule required a long or a short pause for food presentation. Thus, it appears that response-spacing requirements, independently of control rate or of reinforcement density, can impose constraints on the effects of drugs. These experiments clearly indicate that reinforcement density is a less important determinant of the effects of drugs than is control response rate. Further experiments will be necessary to delineate more precisely the role of response-spacing requirements in procedures such as these.

The extent to which the effects of drugs are determined by control response rates can also be influenced by such factors as (1) characteristics of the schedule and its parameter values, (2) whether a given response rate is maintained or suppressed, and (3) the effects of drug-produced changes in responding. For example, comparable local rates of responding under different parameter values of fixed-interval schedules have been reported to be changed to different extents (MacPhail, 1971). Also, Thompson and Corr (1974) observed that low control rates of responding are not increased by *d*-amphetamine if these rates are maintained by response-independent food presentation, or under a schedule in which a discriminative stimulus is correlated with food availability. This failure to observe rate increases with *d*-amphetamine in low response rates may be related to the previously reported absence of increases in very low rates of responding (Verhave,

1958; McMillan, 1968a) or to the previously mentioned differences in drug effects on responding well controlled by discriminative stimuli (Laties and Weiss, 1966; McKearney, 1970b).

Figure 12 illustrates another condition under which control response rate alone does not predict the direction or magnitude of drug effects. Here, virtually identical response rates were maintained in squirrel monkeys under two different shock-titration schedules. Under escape titration, each response decreases in intensity by one step an electric shock that is otherwise incremented every few seconds. Under punishment titration, each response maintained under a variable-interval schedule of food presentation also increases by one step an electric shock that would otherwise decrease every few seconds. Under escape titration responding is *maintained* by shock reduction, whereas under punishment titration, food-maintained responding is *suppressed* by shock increments. By appropriate adjustments in parameter values, comparable rates of responding can be engendered under both schedules. Despite this comparability in control rates, however, *d*-amphetamine has different effects that depend on the consequences of responding rather than simply its rate of occurrence (Figure 12). Responding under escape titration is increased by *d*-amphetamine, but responding under punishment titration is only decreased. Other drugs [e.g., chlordiazepoxide (not shown)] increase responding only under the punishment-titration schedule. Again, the effects of drugs depend not only on control response rates, but also on the consequences of responding.

Other factors that can alter the nature of a dependency of drug effects on control rates of responding will be discussed more fully in subsequent sections. For example, as discussed earlier, amphetamines have a widespread tendency to increase normally low response rates but generally do not increase food-maintained responding that has been suppressed with response-produced electric shock (punished responding); barbiturates, however, tend to increase low response rates whether responding is punished or not. Also, under schedules in which periods of no responding are necessary for food presentation, amphetamines and barbiturates may increase responding (and thus decrease food presentations) when first administered but not on subsequent occasions (Section 3.3.3). This is an instance in which a subject's prior experience can influence the effects of drugs.

In conclusion, although the rate-dependent effects of drugs can be modified by factors discussed in this section, the ubiquity with which rate-dependent effects are observed is most remarkable. This seems clearly to be a case in which exceptions highlight the generality of the

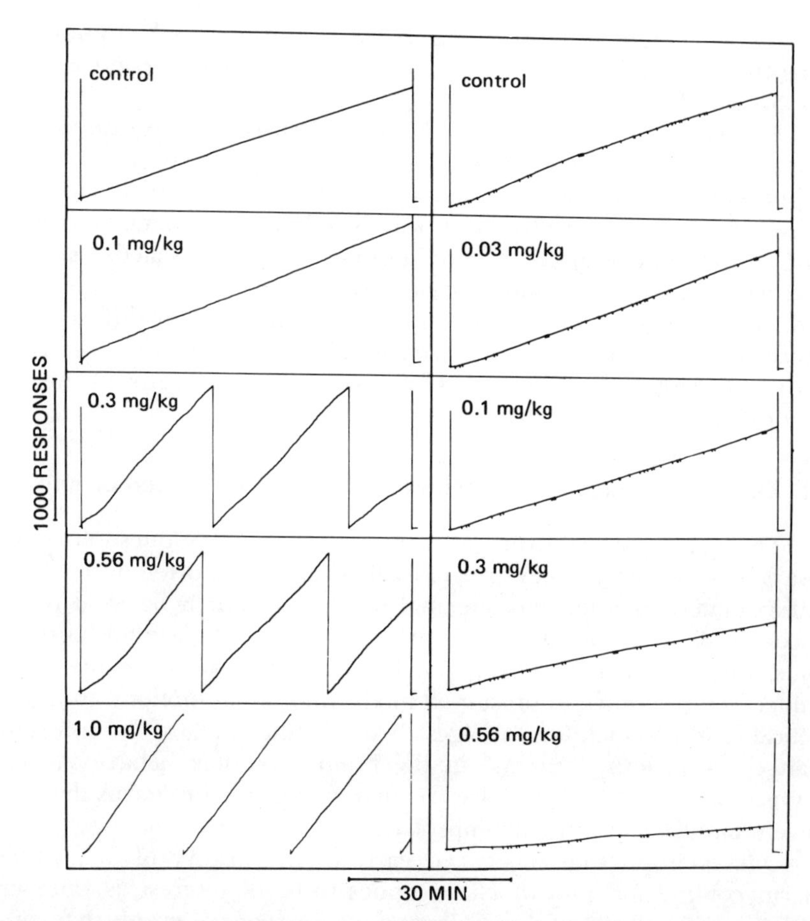

Figure 12. Effects of *d*-amphetamine on responding under escape- and punishment-titration schedules. Left (Monkey S-519): escape titration. Right (Monkey S-522): punishment titration. See the text for details of both schedules. Diagonal marks denote presentation of food. Note that comparable control rates of responding were maintained under both schedules, and that amphetamine increased responding under escape titration but only decreased responding under punishment titration. [Adapted from Smith *et al.* (1977).]

rule. Even when a factor such as stimulus control or the presence of punishment may change certain features of the rate-dependent relationship, an underlying dependence on rate is still very much apparent. For example, though comparable local rates of punished and unpunished responding may not be similarly affected by drugs in many situations, changes in responding in both punished and unpunished performances are nevertheless systematically related to control rates (see Section 3.3).

Although the evidence is most comprehensive in the case of amphetamines, dependence of the effects of drugs on control rates of responding is seen with most commonly studied drugs that affect behavior. Further, these effects appear whether one examines overall rates in the same subjects responding under different schedules, local rates within a schedule-controlled performance, or diverse control rates in different subjects responding under either the same or different reinforcement schedules. In the absence of other information, the control rate of responding seems to be the single best predictor of the behavioral effects of many drugs.

3.2. Effects of Drugs on Behaviors Maintained by Different Events

Though simple and categoric answers to complex questions have always been attractive, they are generally elusive, and often misleading. Unfortunately, neither experimental psychology nor behavioral pharmacology have totally avoided the seduction of the simple answer. Thus, the effects of the drugs on behavior are still sometimes "explained" by reference to presumed motivations and emotions, to hypothetical entities such as "analgesia" or "addiction," or to inferred changes in various "systems" in the brain. Complex behaviors, and changes produced by drugs, are frequently explained in terms that are naively simplistic and highly improbable.

One question that was asked early in the history of behavioral pharmacology, and one which continues to be of interest, is whether the behavioral effects of drugs depend on the types of events that control behavior. Though this question at first appears to be relatively simple and straightforward, no correspondingly simple answers have been forthcoming. To some extent, asking whether the effects of drugs depend on the types of events that control behavior is analogous to asking about *the* effects of a drug, or *the* effects of a particular consequent event such as electric shock. In all these cases, there are no definitive and encompassing answers. The effects of a drug may differ markedly over its effective dose range, and generally depend on details of the situation in which it is administered, just as the same consequent event can have many different effects depending on a variety of factors other than its physical nature. Similarly, the effects of drugs on behaviors controlled by different events depend on many things other than the simple physical nature of the events.

Early beliefs that drugs have differential effects depending on the type of maintaining event were based on an assumed correspondence between the nature of an event controlling behavior and a presumptive underlying motivational state. According to this view, drugs affect behavior by operating on motivational mechanisms which, in turn, then change behavior. However, experimental results generally did not support interpretations in terms of motivational states, and it was not long before behavior itself, and the variables directly affecting it, became more prominent in analysis of the behavioral effects of drugs. In retrospect, one difficulty during the initial phases of research in this area was the failure to fully appreciate the important difference between the nature of an event and its effects on behavior. The tacit assumption was that a given event induced the same motivational state regardless of the way it was scheduled and of the way it changed behavior. It was but a minor extension to adopt the view that the effects of drugs on behavior could be understood in terms of the events that occurred, with little regard to other factors.

As Dews and Morse (1961) pointed out, the importance of any relationship of motivational factors to differential effects of drugs has been questionable from the outset. Evidence then existing clearly indicated that highly differential drug effects could easily be obtained when different rates and patterns of schedule-controlled responding were maintained by the same event even in individual subjects during the same experimental session (see Section 3.1). Because the control rate and pattern of responding can have important influences even when the maintaining event is the same, comparisons of the effects of drugs on behavior controlled by different events are best made when comparable schedules and resulting patterns of responding are studied over a wide range of values. Even then, there may be difficulties with functionally equating the effects of very different events. Predictably, early studies that did not take this into account had widely inconsistent results.

The extent to which the behavioral effects of drugs might depend on the type of event maintaining responding, independently of the schedule-controlled response rate, was directly investigated in a number of experiments conducted over 10 years ago. These studies generally indicated that, with comparable schedule-controlled rates of responding, the effects of a variety of drugs were independent of the type of consequent event that maintained responding (Cook and Catania, 1964; Kelleher and Morse, 1964, 1968b; Waller and Waller, 1962; Weiss and Laties, 1963).

In 1964, both Kelleher and Morse, and Cook and Catania, reported results of experiments comparing the effects of drugs on comparable patterns of schedule-controlled responding maintained by different events. Kelleher and Morse studied responding in squirrel monkeys under a multiple fixed-interval fixed-ratio schedule of food presentation, and under a similar multiple schedule in which responding was maintained instead by termination of a visual stimulus associated with electric shock delivery. Similar control patterns of responding were maintained regardless of which event maintained behavior, but there were, of course, marked differences in the patterns of responding engendered under the fixed-interval and fixed-ratio schedule components. Under both fixed-interval schedules there was a pause and then a gradual increase in responding, whereas under the fixed-ratio schedules there was a higher, sustained rate of responding. The experiments by Kelleher and Morse (1964) showed that the effects of *d*-amphetamine and chlorpromazine depended more on differences in rates and patterns of responding under the fixed-interval and fixed-ratio component schedules than on the types of consequent events. At intermediate doses, *d*-amphetamine increased responding under both fixed-interval schedules but only decreased responding under the fixed-ratio schedules; chlorpromazine decreased responding under all schedules, but the lower doses had less effect on responding under the fixed-ratio schedules than under the fixed-interval schedules. Thus, the effects of these drugs depended on the schedule and resultant pattern of responding, not on whether responding was maintained by food presentation or by stimulus-shock termination. In the experiments by Cook and Catania (1964), comparable patterns of responding were maintained under fixed-interval schedules in which responding was maintained either by food presentation or by termination of a continuously present electric shock. The effects of a variety of drugs (chlorpromazine, imipramine, meprobamate, and chlordiazepoxide) were similar regardless of whether responding was maintained by food presentation or by shock termination. Thus, under the conditions studied in these experiments, the effects of a variety of drugs seemed to depend more on schedule-controlled rates and patterns of responding than on differences in maintaining events.

Technical and theoretical advances in the study of behavior have resulted not only in greater understanding of the factors controlling behavior, but also have had substantial impact on the analysis of the effects of drugs. The development of conditions under which responding could be maintained by the presentation of electric shock (discussed earlier in this chapter) extended the range of consequent events that could be used to engender comparable schedule-controlled performances and also offered some distinct advantages for study of the behavioral effects of drugs. In the experiments just discussed, the effects of drugs on responding maintained by food presentation were compared with effects on responding that terminated shock or a stimulus associated with shock. Though the patterns of responding maintained by these different events were formally comparable, many potentially important differences still existed. As pointed out earlier, decreases in responding have different consequences under schedules of food presentation or stimulus-shock termination. With decreases in food-maintained responding, food delivery is delayed or eliminated, whereas decreases in responding under the termination schedule result in marked increases in the number of shocks delivered. When responding is maintained by shock presentation, however, decreases in or cessation of responding have the same effect as under schedules of food presentation.

McKearney (1974) and Barrett (1976) have recently studied the effects of several drugs on comparable patterns of responding under fixed-interval schedules of food presentation or of shock presentation. *d*-Amphetamine produced comparable increases in responding under both schedules (McKearney, 1974), supporting and extending the conclusion that the effects of amphetamines depend more on ongoing rates and patterns of responding than on the nature of the maintaining event (Dews, 1958a; Kelleher and Morse, 1964, 1968b; Smith, 1964). Likewise, cocaine had similar rate-increasing effects under both schedules (Barrett, 1976), extending the conditions under which its effects have also been shown to depend on ongoing rates and patterns of responding (Smith, 1964; McMillan *et al.,* 1975). Chlorpromazine generally decreased responding under both schedules (McKearney, 1974), although decreases in shock-maintained responding were proportionally greater at a given dose than those observed under the food-presentation schedule.

In contrast to the generally similar effects of amphetamine, cocaine, and chlorpromazine on responding maintained by food and shock presentation, morphine increased responding maintained by shock at doses that decreased food-maintained responding (McKearney, 1974). Figure 13 illustrates the effects of *d*-amphetamine and morphine in one monkey responding under a multiple schedule of food or shock presentation. While *d*-amphetamine had similar effects during both schedule components, morphine increased shock-maintained responding at doses that either decreased or did not affect responding under the food-presentation schedule. In more recent experiments (McKearney, 1975) it was shown that certain doses of morphine, methadone, nalorphine, and naloxone increase responding under fixed-interval schedules of either shock presentation or of stimulus-shock termination, whereas these drugs only decrease responding under comparable schedules of food presentation.

Alcohol, chlordiazepoxide, and pentobarbital also had different effects on responding maintained by food or shock presentation, but the selectivity was different from that of morphine. These drugs all decreased responding maintained by shock presentation at doses that markedly increased food-maintained responding (Barrett, 1976). Further, the selective increases in food-maintained responding with chlordiazepoxide were similar regardless of whether the control rate of responding in the food component was lower than, equal to, or higher than that prevailing in the shock-presentation components (see Figure 14).

In the experiments by McKearney (1974) and Barrett (1976), the effects of several drugs on comparable patterns of responding were different depending on whether responding was maintained by food or shock presentation. On the other hand, under the conditions studied by Kelleher and Morse (1964) and by Cook and Catania (1964), the effects of several other drugs were the same regardless of whether responding was maintained by food delivery or by termination of shock or an associated visual stimulus. Similar performances maintained by different events may be similarly affected by drugs, but they need not be similarly affected under all conditions. Though differences in the effects of drugs on similar patterns of responding maintained by food and by shock presentation may reflect a basic dependence on the nature of the consequent event itself, other factors may contribute to the differences in the effects of drugs. For example, food and shock pre-

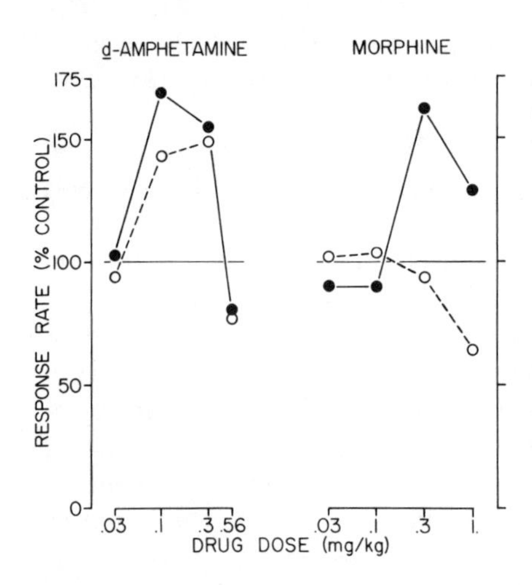

Figure 13. Effects of *d*-amphetamine sulfate (left) and morphine sulfate (right) on responding under a multiple 5-min fixed-interval (food presentation) 5-min fixed-interval (5-mA shock presentation) (monkey S-511). Open circles: food presentation. Filled circles: shock presentation. All points are the mean of at least two observations. Food-presentation and shock-presentation components were correlated with different colored lights and were alternately present, separated by 30-sec time-out periods, for 100-min experimental sessions. Note that *d*-amphetamine had similar effects on responding under both schedule components, but that morphine increased responding under shock presentation at doses that either decreased or did not affect responding under food presentation. [Adapted from McKearney (1974) and reprinted from Morse *et al.* (1977).]

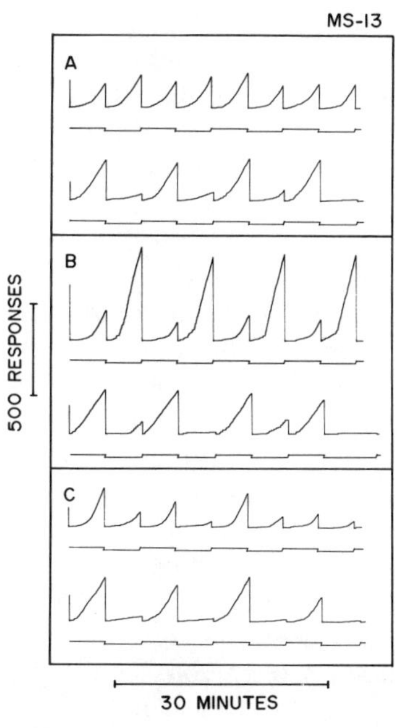

Figure 14. Effects of chlordiazepoxide on different control rates of responding under schedules of food presentation and electric shock presentation. Responding was maintained under a multiple 5-min fixed-interval schedule of food or shock presentation. The event pen was deflected downward during the shock-presentation component. The top record of each pair represents the control performance and the lower record the effects of chlordiazepoxide. Panel A: top record shows comparable rates of responding maintained under the food and shock components of the schedule; the lower record shows the effects of 5.6 mg/kg chlordiazepoxide. Panel B: top record shows substantially higher control rates of shock-maintained responding, and the lower record the effects of 17.0 mg/kg chlordiazepoxide; shock intensity was 4 mA in panels A and B. Panel C: control response rates maintained by food were higher than those maintained by a 1-mA shock; the lower record shows changes in performance with 17.0 mg/kg chlordiazepoxide. Although control rates of responding maintained by shock differed widely throughout the various phases of this experiment, chlordiazepoxide consistently decreased shock-maintained responding, while responding maintained by food was only increased. [From Barrett (1976); © 1976 by The Williams & Wilkins Company, Baltimore.]

sentation have very different durations, and engender different types and intensities of elicited behaviors (McKearney, 1974). Since food and electric shock are so different in many respects, complete functional comparability may not be possible; valid information may then only come from systematic comparison of the events under a broad range of experimental conditions (Morse *et al.*, 1977).

That the type of maintaining event may determine changes in the effects of drugs under certain conditions is undoubtedly relevant to a more complete understanding of the effects of drugs on behavior, but conclusions more general than this will require exhaustive parametric analysis. Unfortunately, we know very little about the generality of either the similar or different effects of drugs that have been reported for comparable patterns of responding controlled by different events. Just as it is impossible to characterize the effects of a drug or to compare one drug with another by studying only a narrow dose range, it is also unreasonable to compare behaviors controlled by different events by studying only a limited range of schedules and parameter values (see Morse *et al.*, 1977).

The experiments by Kelleher and Morse (1964) and by Cook and Catania (1964) did establish that the effects of certain drugs can be independent of maintenance events as long as comparable schedule-controlled patterns of responding are studied. However, the number of drugs studied and the range of conditions under which these comparable effects were established were limited. With other drugs and schedule conditions, there are circumstances under which different effects are observed (McKearney, 1974; Barrett, 1976). In the absence of parametric information, any of a variety of conditions could determine whether differential effects of drugs are observed. The importance of parametric analysis is illustrated by the Cook and Catania (1964) experiments described earlier. Chlorpromazine and imipramine consistently decreased responding under fixed-interval schedules of either food presentation or shock termination, while *d*-amphetamine increased responding under both conditions. However, chlordiazepoxide and meprobamate either increased or decreased responding under the shock termination schedule, depending on the intensity of electric shock and the resultant control rate of responding. Though increases in responding maintained by food presentation were consistently observed with both of these drugs, it is likely that differences in their effects could have been observed if the control rate of responding had been manipulated under this schedule as well. Further, it is even possible that the uniform rate increases with amphetamine and rate decreases with chlorpromazine and imipramine could have been changed by appropriate manipulations in schedule parameters. Although certain conditions responsible for performances maintained by shock presentation are known, little is known about the effects of drugs on these performances. It seems probable that manipulation of shock duration or intensity, or of the type and parameter value of the schedule, would modify what appear to be selective effects of drugs. To the extent that changes in schedule or in the characteristics of the consequent event may change patterns of ongoing behavior, the effects of drugs should be expected to change as well.

The effects of events that control behavior are very complexly determined, and it is as erroneous to assume that the effects of a drug will depend on the nature of an event, exclusive of the effects that event actually has on behavior, as it is to assume that behavior will be uniformly affected by a given event. The nature of events is less important than the way they change behavior. Demonstrations of differences in drug effects that seem to depend on the type of maintenance event are fraught with the same difficulties as demonstrations of a lack of such differences. Since the extent of our information is so limited, conclusions cannot justifiably go beyond the particular conditions and parameter values employed. Instances in which the nature of events appear to determine specific drug effects may not necessarily reflect differences in the inherent properties of these events. Any consistent relation between schedule type and type of maintaining consequence could make it appear that the event rather than correlated differences in the controlling schedules might determine differential effects of drugs. For example, natural environments could most often associate noxious events with certain types of schedules and nonnoxious events with different schedules; in this case, differential effects of drugs would not be surprising, but these could be due to either event or schedule differences. While the two factors can be separated in experimental settings, this may not be practical or feasible in the natural environment. Experimental demonstration of similar performances under comparable schedules with different maintaining consequences *does* emphasize the power of schedules, but the usefulness of this for predicting the clinical effects of drugs may be limited if dissimilar events in the natural environment are rarely scheduled identically.

To ask whether the effects of drugs depend on the types of consequent events that maintain behavior may not only be a difficult question, it may have limited practical significance as well. We have already discussed the many difficulties inherent in comparisons of the effects of drugs on performances maintained by different events. In addition, there are also practical considerations about the likely relevance of comparisons between any two or three arbitrarily chosen events. Comparisons of the effects of drugs on behaviors maintained by food presentation or by shock termination are often carried out under the tacit assumption that these two events are representative of "appetitive" and noxious events, and that results obtained with them may apply equally to other consequent events in the environment; however, there is little direct support for assuming this degree of generality. It is possible, for example, that if reliable differences in the effects of drugs on behaviors controlled by food as opposed to electric shock were demonstrated, these might be matched by equally marked differences in the effects of drugs on behaviors maintained by different kinds of foods. Since the types of consequent events that can maintain behavior may change markedly from moment to moment, from individual to individual, or from situation to situation, the task of cataloguing drug effects in terms of types of maintenance events would not only be impossibly involved, it would also appear to be theoretically questionable and of doubtful practical significance. Rather than focusing on consequent events, it would appear more advisable to concentrate on factors that come into play regardless of the nature of particular consequent events. As discussed earlier, patterns of responding under different schedules are important determinants of the behavioral effects of drugs, regardless of the particular events involved. As Morse *et al.* (1977, p. 168) have pointed out, "Since patterns of schedule-controlled responding can transcend particular maintaining events, description of drug effects in these basic quantitative terms will be of greater generality than descriptions restricted to particular consequent events."

3.3. Effects of Drugs on Punished Responding

Although the effects of drugs on responding maintained by food or shock presentation, or by the termination of visual stimuli correlated with shock, have been emphasized thus far, many studies in behavioral pharmacology have been concerned instead with the effects of drugs on responding suppressed by the presentation of electric shock. In most experiments on punished behavior, responding is established and maintained under a schedule of food delivery, and then suppressed by presentation of response-produced electric shock. The degree of suppression produced by shock depends on a host of variables such as shock frequency, intensity, duration, and, importantly, on the schedule under which responding is maintained (see reviews by Azrin and Holz, 1966; Fantino, 1973; Morse and Kelleher, 1977). These variables are also among those that modify the effects of drugs on punished responding (McMillan, 1975; Morse *et al.,* 1977).

The effects of a number of drugs on punished responding were examined by Geller and his associates in early studies in which punished and nonpunished responding occurred in separate components of a multiple schedule (Geller and Seifter, 1960; Geller *et al.,* 1962, 1963). Responding was maintained under a variable-interval schedule of food delivery and, periodically, a tone sounded during which each response produced both food and shock (punishment component). Suppressed responding during the punishment component was increased by meprobamate, phenobarbital, pentobarbital, and chlordiazepoxide, but other drugs such as amphetamines, phenothiazines, and morphine, only further decreased punished responding. These effects have been confirmed repeatedly under a wide variety of conditions, with different species, and using different schedules of food and shock presentation (e.g., Cook and Davidson, 1973; Cook and Sepinwall, 1975; McMillan, 1975; Morse, 1964; see Chapter 2).

At least some of the earlier research on the effects of drugs on punished responding was guided in part by theoretical beliefs not unlike those discussed in the preceding section. The punishment procedure appeared to have a certain amount of face validity for producing "conflict," and it was believed that this might be changed by drugs affecting anxiety. Early research findings seemed congruent with this view, since the drugs that were most effective in increasing punished responding were also clinically effective minor tranquilizers. Further, it seemed that the effects of drugs on punished responding were easily characterized, since certain drug classes seemed to increase responding while others did not. However, more recent work suggests that the effects of drugs on punished responding are not so simple, but are every bit as complexly determined as the effects of drugs on any behavior. Just as it is not meaningful to speak of the "behavioral" effects of a drug, or the effects of a drug on "reinforced behavior" without specifying a great deal more than this, it appears that the same is true of "punished behavior." The remainder of this section focuses on some of the determinants of the effects of drugs on punished responding, and on certain complexities and exceptions that seem to preclude broad generalizations about the effects of drugs on punished responding.

3.3.1. Rate-Dependent Effects of Drugs on Punished Responding

As Kelleher and Morse (1968b) suggested, the effects of drugs on responding suppressed by punishment must be separated from any general tendency of drugs to increase low control rates regardless of how those rates are engendered. As with comparisons of the effects of drugs on responding maintained by different events, the determination of any specificity of a drug's effects on punished responding requires the study of comparable rates and patterns of both punished and unpunished behavior.

In one experiment, Cook and Catania (1964) developed comparable overall rates of punished and unpunished responding in squirrel monkeys. Responding was maintained under either a 6-min or a 2-min variable-interval schedule of food presentation, depending on which of two colored lights was illuminated. Food-maintained responding under the 2-min schedule also produced shock under an independent variable-interval 2-min schedule. Responses on a second lever changed the color of the lights and which of the two schedules was in effect at any given time. Shock intensity was adjusted to produce comparable rates of punished and unpunished responding. Under these conditions, both chlordiazepoxide and meprobamate produced greater relative increases in punished responding than in responding that was not punished.

Several experiments on the effects of drugs on punished responding have employed fixed-interval schedules which, as mentioned earlier, engender graded increases in responding as the interval progresses. The characteristic reproducible patterns of responding under fixed-interval schedules have proven to be very sensitive to the behavioral effects of many drugs (Morse, 1975). Further, the wide range of rates occurring in different portions of this schedule permits comparison of punished and unpunished behaviors occurring at comparable rates. Using an analysis of this type, Wuttke and Kelleher (1970) maintained responding of pigeons under fixed-interval schedules of food delivery. For one group, every thirtieth response produced shock, and this suppressed the overall rate without changing the pattern of positively accelerated responding. Chlordiazepoxide, diazepam, and nitrazepam all increased comparable local control rates of both punished and unpunished responding to an equivalent degree. Low control rates of responding, regardless of whether responding was punished or not, were increased proportionally more than were higher rates of responding. These results suggested that the benzodiazepines do not selectively affect punished responding but tend to increase low response rates regardless of how these rates are engendered.

A similar analysis was performed with squirrel monkeys responding under multiple fixed-interval schedules of food presentation (Glowa and Barrett, 1976). During one component responding was punished when every thirtieth response produced shock; responding during the other component was not punished. Ethanol increased overall rates of punished responding but decreased overall rates of unpunished responding. When comparable local response rates occurring in different segments of the two fixed intervals were compared, however, changes in both punished and unpunished responding with ethanol were remarkably similar and depended on the control rates at which these behaviors occurred.

In contrast to the generally similar effects of drugs on comparable rates of punished and unpunished responding in the experiments by Wuttke and Kelleher (1970) and by Glowa and Barrett (1976), McMillan (1973) has reported differences in the effects of certain doses of benzodiazepines and pentobarbital on comparable local rates of punished and unpunished responding during a multiple schedule. It is difficult at this time to draw conclusions about the comparative effects of drugs on local rates of punished and unpunished responding because of the differences in both behavioral procedures and methods of response-rate analysis that have been used. Many studies have relied on differences or similarities in regression lines relating local control rates to changes in rate after drug administration to assess the relative effects of drugs on punished and unpunished responding. When a reasonable range of relatively comparable control rates under both conditions is available, and when these comparable rates seem to be similarly changed by a drug, conclusions can be relatively unambiguous and straightforward. However, when control rates are similar over only a very restricted range, if at all, and when the conditions under which the punished and unpunished behaviors occur are otherwise different, conclusions are more difficult to reach. Changes in local rates of responding under fixed-interval schedules can differ substantially depending on a variety of factors, and this possibility must be considered when using this as a method of assessing differences in the effects of drugs on punished and unpunished responding. For example, comparable local rates of responding maintained by the same event but under different parameter values of the same schedule have been shown to be differently affected by *d*-amphetamine (MacPhail, 1971). Also, drugs can have different effects on comparable local rates of responding when behavior is controlled by different discriminative stimuli (McKearney, 1970b), when response-spacing requirements are in effect (Stitzer and McKearney, 1977), or when responding occurs on two different response keys (Barrett, 1974), and can be different depending on whether or not a brief auditory stimulus follows each response (Byrd, 1974). Additional problems arise when punished and unpunished responding are compared by examining changes in local rates under different fixed-interval schedules, since rates of punished and unpunished responding are frequently drawn from very different segments of the fixed interval. A control response rate occurring, for example, in the second minute of a 5-min fixed-interval schedule in which responding is not punished might be most similar to responding in the final minute of a similar schedule in which responding is punished. Though there is no direct evidence, it is possible that the effects of a drug on a given local rate of responding could be very different depending on the ordinal position of that rate in a response sequence. Quantitatively different changes in similar local rates of punished and unpunished responding might also depend on factors such as the schedule of punishment, and on whether the punished and unpunished responding are studied separately or in the same situation as components of a multiple schedule. In all these cases, differential changes in local rates of responding may depend on factors other than the simple presence or absence of punishment.

Though it is clear that the quantitative effects of drugs on punished responding are systematically related to control rates, in that lower control rates are increased relatively more than normally higher rates, it is also clear that other factors determine the effects of drugs. For example, Figure 15 shows that pentobarbital can have different effects when responding is punished at two different shock intensities (Witkin and Barrett, 1976). In this experiment, pigeons responded under a 5-min fixed-interval schedule of food presentation in which

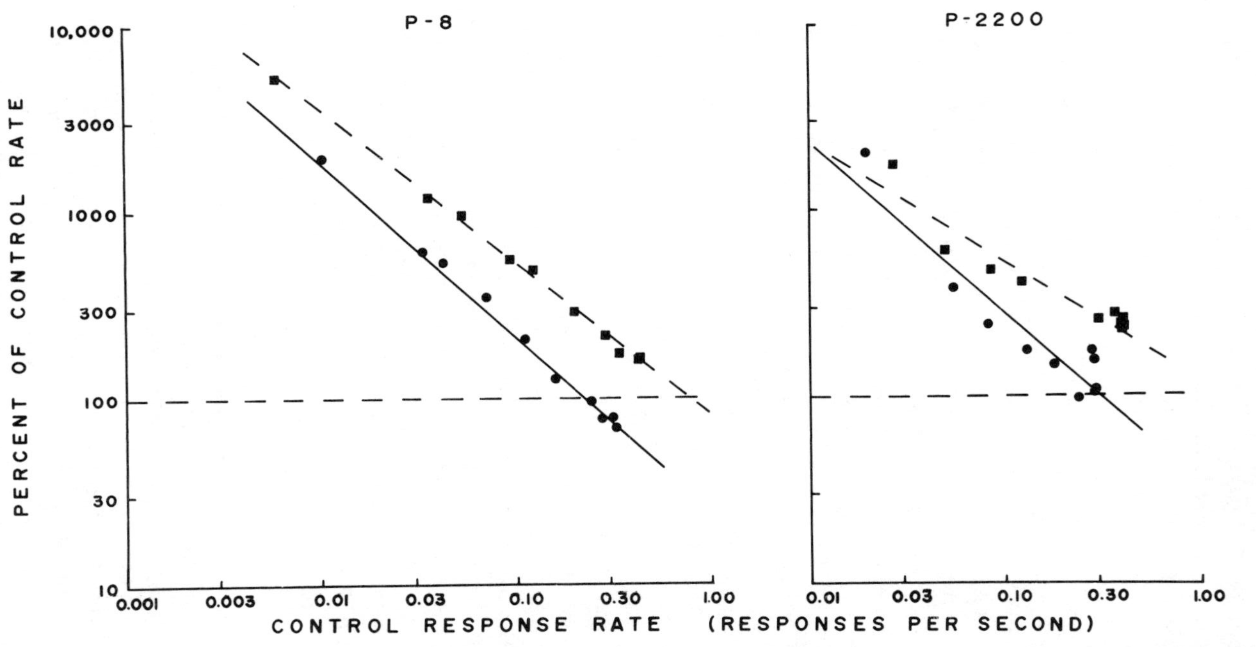

Figure 15. Effects of 10.0 mg/kg pentobarbital on local response rates when responding was punished at two different shock intensities. Keypecking by pigeons was maintained under a 5-min fixed-interval schedule of food presentation; every thirtieth response also produced either a 2- or 4-mA electric shock. Abscissa: average control rate of responding obtained during individual 30-sec segments of the 5-min fixed-interval schedule. Ordinate: response rate after drug as a percentage of the control rate of responding. Squares represent local response rates at the 2-mA intensity, circles at the 4-mA intensity. Although overall control rates of punished responding, differed little under the different shock intensities, pentobarbital produced substantially larger increases in both overall and local rates of punished responding at the lower intensity. Both abscissa and ordinate are log scales. Regression lines were fitted by the method of least squares. [From Witkin and Barrett (1976).]

every fiftieth response also produced an electric shock. Although overall control rates of punished responding differed little (<0.025 response/sec) when shock intensity was 2 mA as compared with 4 mA, the effects of this dose of pentobarbital (10 mg/kg) were different under the two intensities. Increases in local rates of punished responding were inversely related to control rates at both intensities, but comparable rates under the higher intensity were uniformly increased less than under the lower intensity. Thus, local rates of responding alone were not as important as shock intensity. At present, conclusions about differences in the effects of drugs on punished and unpunished responding seem to require much more information about the conditions under which changes in punished behavior occur (McMillan, 1975).

While drugs that increase punished responding also tend to rather generally increase low rates of responding under many other conditions, not all drugs that increase low rates of responding will increase punished responding. For example, while amphetamines increase low rates of responding in many situations, they do not generally increase low rates of food-maintained responding that have been suppressed by response-produced shock (Geller and Seifter, 1962; Hanson *et al.*, 1967; Kelleher and Morse, 1968b). Although moderate increases in very low local rates of punished responding occurring early in a fixed interval have been reported when shock intensity is low and response suppression is moderate (McMillan, 1973; Foree *et al.*, 1973), these increases are slight compared with those obtained with drugs such as the benzodiazepines or barbiturates. Thus, while amphetamines increase low rates of responding *maintained* by shock presentation or by stimulus-shock termination (McKearney, 1974; Kelleher and Morse, 1964), they generally do not increase responding that is instead *suppressed* by shock. Differences in the effects of drugs depending on the way behavior is controlled by the same event have also been found with other drugs. For example, although morphine, like amphetamine, does not usually increase responding suppressed by the presentation of electric shock (Geller *et al.*, 1963; Kelleher and Morse, 1964), responding maintained by shock presentation or by the termination of shock can be increased by morphine (McKearney, 1974, 1975). Alcohol, chlordiazepoxide, and pentobarbital all increase responding suppressed by shock presentation (Cook and Davidson, 1973; Glowa and Barrett, 1976), but only decrease behavior maintained by response-produced shock (Barrett, 1976). These differences emphasize the fact, mentioned earlier, that it is not particular events themselves, but rather the types of effects these events have on behavior that determine the effects of drugs.

Despite the apparent orderliness of the effects of various drugs on punished responding, many factors can modify the "typical" findings described above. Some of these are discussed in subsequent sections. When the effects of these other factors are considered, the question of whether rate-dependent effects of drugs can alone account for changes in punished and nonpunished responding seems less relevant than previously. The effects of drugs on punished responding are sufficiently complex to defy the more general characterizations that once seemed possible.

3.3.2. Environmental Context and the Effects of Drugs on Punished Responding

A description of the effects of drugs on punished responding, or on any other behavior, is not possible apart from a consideration of the precise conditions under which that behavior occurs. It is as wrong to view punished responding as an unchanging, unitary phenomenon as it is to assume that the behavioral effects of environmental events will be the same across all circumstances. It is reasonable to expect that the effects of drugs on behavior are as complex and as different as the determinants of the behavior itself. In addition to variables of most obvious importance in determining the effects of drugs on punished responding (such as the intensity and frequency of the noxious event, and the schedule under which the reference behavior is maintained), several other factors are important in determining both the direction and magnitude of drug effects. For example, the individual's prior experience, characteristics of other behaviors in the repertoire, and any aspect of the total environmental situation in which a behavior occurs can potentially influence the effects of drugs. Certain of these factors will be discussed in this and the following section.

Changes in behavior not only inevitably occur as a function of the immediate consequences of responding, but also derive from more remote influences. Events that have occurred in the past, as well as more immediate and ongoing influences under other conditions, can affect behavior in a given situation. In attempting to understand behavior and those factors which might account for behavior change, the greatest emphasis typically has been placed on relatively isolated events in the immediate environmental setting. Although there is little question that the immediate consequences of behavior are of great importance, there is also convincing evidence that behavior in a given situation can be profoundly modified by events occurring in temporally more remote situations. These factors also play an important role in determining the behavioral effects of drugs.

A recent experiment by McKearney and Barrett (1975) illustrates how the context in which punished behavior occurs can influence the effects of a drug. Responding by squirrel monkeys was maintained under a 10-min fixed-interval schedule of food presentation and suppressed by presenting electric shock following every thirtieth response. When this schedule alternated with a 10-min period during which a different discriminative stimulus was present and responding had no scheduled consequences (extinction), *d*-amphetamine either had no effect on or further decreased punished responding as expected from previous experiments. Subsequently, however, when a shock-postponement (avoidance) schedule was introduced in place of the extinction component, *d*-amphetamine (0.01–0.56 mg/kg) substantially increased punished responding (Figure 16). Although the control rate of punished responding was similar under the two conditions of this experiment, the effects of *d*-amphetamine on punished responding differed depending on whether responding in another schedule component also postponed shock. These results suggest that features of the environment not actually present at the time a behavior is occurring can still critically influence the effects of drugs.

In a related experiment, food-maintained punished responding was studied in a context in which responding was also maintained by shock presentation (Barrett, 1977a). Squirrel monkeys initially responded under a multiple 10-min fixed-interval schedule of food presentation or a schedule of shock postponement. A 10-min fixed-interval schedule of shock delivery was subsequently arranged concurrently with the avoidance schedule. Later, when the avoidance schedule was removed, responding was maintained by shock under one component,

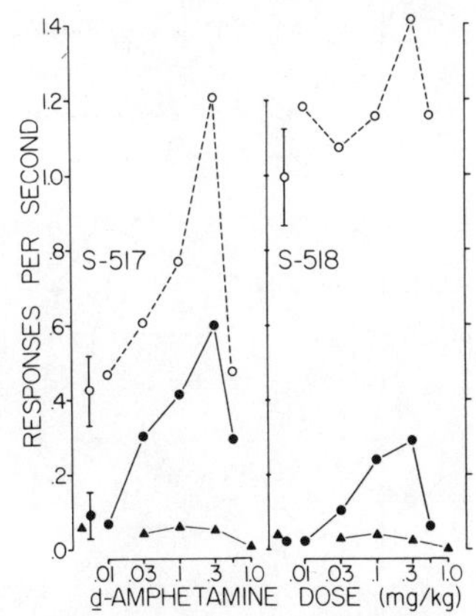

Figure 16. *d*-Amphetamine sulfate effects on responding under the multiple avoidance-punishment schedule. Ordinate: responses per second. Abscissa: log dose. Unconnected points with brackets indicate mean control rates of responding ± one standard deviation; where there are no brackets, these fall within the area covered by the data point. With the exception of 0.03, 0.1, and 1.0 mg/kg under the multiple punishment-extinction schedule (triangles), each point is the average of two observations. Control values are based on at least five sessions. Triangles refer to punished responding during the multiple punishment-extinction schedule (no avoidance). Filled circles refer to punished responding (avoidance present), and open circles to avoidance responding, during the multiple punishment-avoidance schedule. Note that *d*-amphetamine increased punished responding only when the avoidance schedule was in effect during the other component. [From McKearney and Barrett (1975).]

while food presentation maintained responding during the other component. The introduction of shock following each thirtieth response during the food schedule reduced these response rates by approximately 55%. Thus, food-maintained responding was suppressed by shock during one component, while responding during the alternate component was maintained by presentation of the same shock (10 mA). Development of performance under these conditions was illustrated earlier for different monkeys (Figure 5). Figure 17 shows the effects of *d*-amphetamine on responding that was alternately suppressed and maintained by shock presentation under this schedule. *d*-Amphetamine produced marked increases in punished responding, as well as in responding maintained by shock presentation. Interestingly, at a dose of 0.56 mg/kg, punished responding was still increased, whereas shock-maintained responding was decreased considerably.

In the experiments by McKearney and Barrett (1975) and by Barrett (1977a), amphetamine increased punished responding maintained by food presentation when responding in another schedule component was maintained either by shock postponement or by shock presentation. Other experiments have shown similar effects when punished behavior itself is maintained by shock presentation or by the termination of a shock-associated stimulus. In one experiment (McKearney, 1973), responding by squirrel monkeys with previous histories of shock postponement was maintained under a 3-min variable-interval schedule of shock presentation. During a second component of this multiple sched-

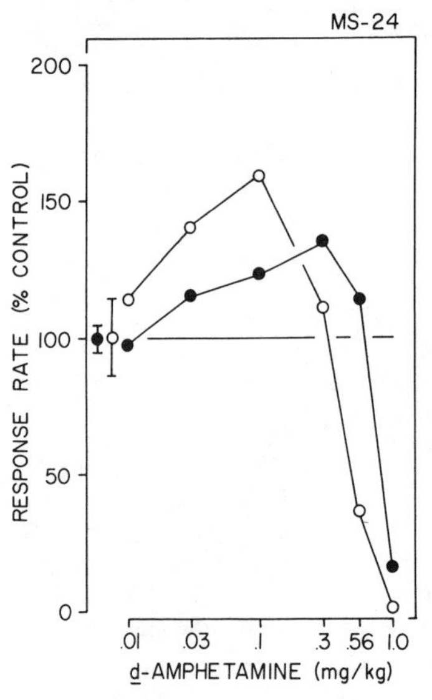

Figure 17. Effects of *d*-amphetamine on responding maintained and suppressed by the presentation of electric shock under a multiple schedule. Responding was maintained under 10-min fixed-interval schedules of either food or shock (10 mA) presentation (average rates were 0.683 and 1.734 response/sec, respectively). Every thirtieth response during the food-presentation component also produced shock; responding was suppressed by shock during this component (0.305 response/sec) but was maintained by shock under the fixed-interval schedule (1,353 response/sec). *d*-Amphetamine increased responding that was both suppressed (i.e., punished) and maintained by shock. Filled circles refer to shock suppressed, and open circles to shock maintained. [From Barrett (1977a).]

ule, shock followed every tenth response. Response rates of one monkey were very low under the 10-response fixed-ratio schedule but were maintained at a high constant rate during the variable-interval component. Though responding was suppressed under the fixed-ratio schedule, it was markedly increased by methamphetamine. Thus, methamphetamine increased responding suppressed by shock in this situation in which responding was also maintained by shock presentation.

Another experiment compared the effects of *d*-amphetamine and pentobarbital on punished responding maintained either by food presentation or by stimulus-shock termination. Comparable patterns of responding were maintained under 5-min fixed-interval schedules in which the first response after 5 min either produced a food pellet or terminated a visual stimulus associated with periodic shock delivery. Then, responding under both schedules was suppressed by presenting an electric shock after every thirtieth response. Thus, responding was suppressed under both conditions, but the events maintaining responding were different. Figure 18 illustrates the effects of *d*-amphetamine and pentobarbital on punished responding under these different maintenance conditions. As previously shown in a variety of situations, responding maintained by food presentation and suppressed by response-produced shock was increased by pentobarbital but was only further decreased by *d*-amphetamine (S-525). In contrast, when punished responding was maintained by stimulus-shock termination (S-532), the effect of both drugs were exactly opposite: *d*-amphetamine increased, and pentobarbital only decreased punished responding. The effects of both drugs on punished responding were different depending on the event that maintained behavior (McKearney, 1976).

In the experiments discussed in this section, responding was both maintained and suppressed by the same event, and the effects of certain drugs on punished responding were different from those generally observed. Taken together, these results provide compelling evidence that the effects of drugs on punished responding depend on the prevailing environmental context and on the event maintaining responding.

Though it goes without saying that particular behaviors never exist in isolation, this is frequently not recognized in designing experiments or in generalizing from experimental findings. Virtually all that is known about maintenance of behavior and suppression of behavior by noxious events, and about the effects of drugs on these behaviors, has come from experiments in which each of these processes is studied in isolation. Yet, natural environments may not often impose one of these conditions in the complete absence of the other. The effects of drugs on punished responding seem very different when studied in isolation

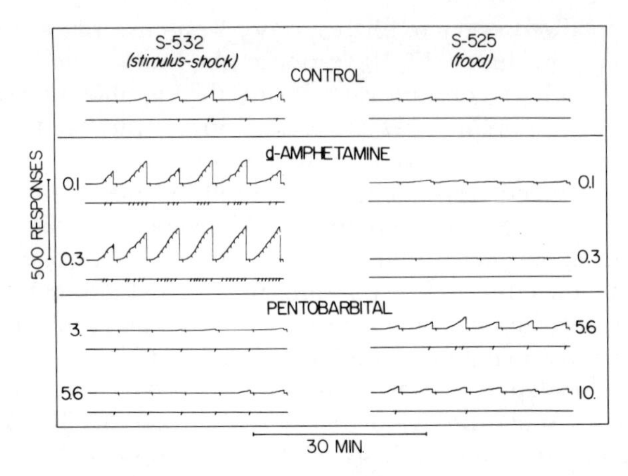

Figure 18. Cumulative records of punished responding under 5-min fixed-interval (FI) schedules of (left) stimulus-shock termination (S-532) or (right) food presentation (S-525). Ordinate: cumulative responses. Abscissa: time. The response pen reset at the termination of each FI. The end of 30-sec time-out periods is indicated by the first diagonal stroke on the response record. Shocks delivered under the punishment schedule (30-response fixed-ratio) are indicated by diagonal strokes on the event record (S-525) or on both the response and event records (S-532). Shocks delivered under the schedule of stimulus-shock termination are indicated by diagonal strokes on the event record only. With the exception of S-525 at 0.3 mg/kg *d*-amphetamine, all records represent the first six cycles of longer experimental sessions. Numbers next to each record refer to drug dose in mg/kg. Note that *d*-amphetamine increased punished responding only under the schedule of stimulus-shock termination, and that pentobarbital increased punished responding only under the schedule of food presentation. [From McKearney (1976); © 1976 by the Society for the Experimental Analysis of Behavior.]

as opposed to occurring in a context in which behavior is also maintained by noxious events. To the extent that behaviors maintained and suppressed by noxious events may significantly interact, information derived from studying either process in isolation may be of limited applicability (McKearney, 1976).

Since the effects of drugs on punished responding are different depending on certain immediate and more remote features of the environment, punishment cannot be conceptualized as a unitary phenomenon. Ongoing behavior, even though apparently well controlled by the immediate setting, is still subject to multiple environmental influences. Significantly, the contribution of certain of these factors is made evident by the administration of drugs. As discussed in the next section, these influences encompass not only factors existing at the time, but also experiences that occurred in the past.

3.3.3. Influence of Prior Experience on the Effects of Drugs on Punished Responding

That existing behaviors, and changes in them as a result of new conditions, are critically determined by prior experience needs little or no documentation here. The conditions under which an individual is first exposed to particular events can profoundly influence the later effects of those events on behavior. For example, pigeons will normally begin pecking a lighted disk when its illumination regularly precedes food presentation ("autoshaping"; Brown and Jenkins, 1968). However, if pigeons are first exposed to randomly related presentations of food and illumination of the light, later development of keypecking through light–food pairings is markedly retarded (Gamzu and Williams, 1973). Other experiments have shown that subjects exposed to repeated response-independent electric shocks later take much longer to acquire an avoidance or escape response than subjects without this experience (Seligman and Maier, 1967). With regard to punishment, responding may persist in the face of rather intense noxious stimuli if the subject has had experience at gradually increasing intensities (Masserman, 1946; Azrin, 1960; Sandler, 1964; Appel and Peterson, 1965); on the other hand, very intense noxious stimuli can have suppressing effects that persist long after the noxious stimulus has been reduced in intensity or completely eliminated (Azrin and Holz, 1966). Further, while response-independent shock usually suppresses ongoing behavior, it may instead enhance responding in subjects previously exposed to shock postponement schedules (Sidman *et al.*, 1957; Kelleher *et al.*, 1963; Waller and Waller, 1963), and response-produced shock may even engender and maintain responding in subjects with the same experimental history (Morse and Kelleher, 1970; McKearney, 1968). Both common experience and experimental findings amply attest to the profound importance of prior experience as a determinant of current and emerging behaviors.

While the importance of prior experience in the maintenance of behavior itself is generally acknowledged, its role in determining the effects of drugs on behavior is not as widely appreciated. A notable exception, of course, is the importance of experience in the development of tolerance to the behavioral effects of chronically administered drugs (see Chapter 8). In this section we will discuss several other situations in which the effects of drugs are different depending on the subject's prior experience.

One experiment (Barrett, 1977b) examined the role of prior experience with shock postponement and shock presentation in determining the later effects of amphetamine on punished responding maintained by food presentation. In squirrel monkeys with prior training under a shock-postponement schedule, similar patterns of responding were engendered under a multiple schedule (5-min fixed-interval) in which responding was maintained either with food or electric shock presentation. After approximately 1 year under this multiple schedule, the shock-presentation component was eliminated and responding under the fixed-interval schedule of food presentation was suppressed when every thirtieth response produced a shock. In these monkeys, *d*-amphetamine markedly increased punished responding (Figure 19, left panel). Though amphetamine does not generally increase punished food-maintained responding, particularly when this behavior is studied in isolation (see right panel of Figure 19, and Figure 18, S-525), it did so in these monkeys whose responding had earlier been maintained by the presentation of shock. Significantly, chlordiazepoxide also increased punished responding with these monkeys. Since chlordiazepox-

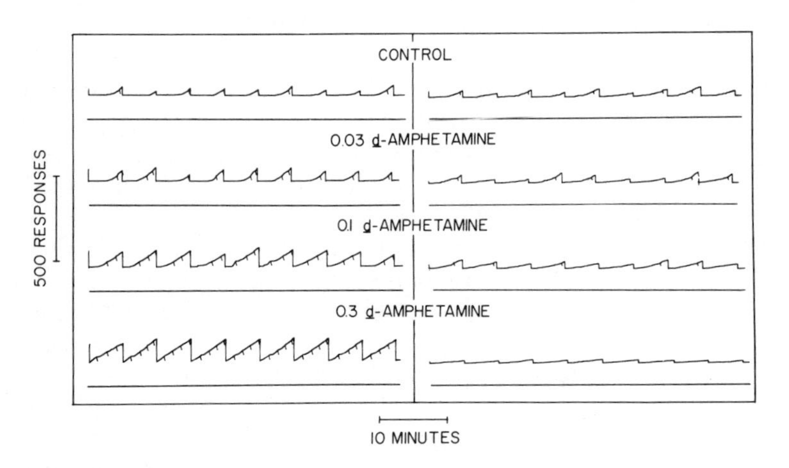

Figure 19. Dependence of the effects of *d*-amphetamine on behavioral history. Squirrel monkeys responded under a 5-min FI schedule of food presentation. Responding was suppressed by the delivery of a 5-mA shock following each thirtieth response (punishment). Subject MS-12 (left panel) had responded previously under shock-postponement and shock-presentation schedules, whereas MS-21 (right panel) had no prior history with shock. *d*-Amphetamine increased punished responding only with those monkeys having previous experience with shock. Ordinate: cumulative responses. Abscissa: time. The response pens reset following the delivery of food at the end of each FI. Shocks are indicated by diagonal strokes on the response record. Doses of *d*-amphetamine are in mg/kg. Note that amphetamine substantially increased punished responding in MS-12, the monkey with the preceding shock history, whereas responding was only further decreased in MS-21, the monkey without prior exposure to conditions under which responding was maintained by the postponement or presentation of shock. [From Barrett (1977b); © 1977 by the American Association for the Advancement of Science.]

ide increases food-maintained responding that has been suppressed by punishment in a variety of situations, this seems to indicate that, in contrast to amphetamine, the effects of chlordiazepoxide in this situation were not changed by the monkeys' prior experience.

In the experiment just described, prior experience with responding maintained by shock postponement and shock presentation changed the later effects of amphetamine on food-maintained punished responding. In view of these results, a related and somewhat opposite question may be asked: would prior experience with punishment alter the later effects of drugs on behavior maintained by shock? A recent experiment by Smith *et al.* (1977) examined this question. Responding in squirrel monkeys was maintained under two different shock-titration schedules described in an earlier section of this chapter. Under escape titration (Weiss and Laties, 1959), responding is maintained when it produces a decrement in an otherwise periodically increasing shock intensity, whereas under punishment titration (Rachlin, 1972) food-maintained responding is suppressed, since each response also increases by one step an electric shock that otherwise decreases every few seconds. As described earlier (Figure 12), *d*-amphetamine produces dose-related increases in escape responding but only decreases punished responding. Subjects who had earlier received amphetamine while responding under the punishment schedule were then studied under the escape-titration schedule, and the effects of amphetamine were redetermined. In these subjects, amphetamine did not increase responding under the escape schedule. Further experiments established that the different effects of amphetamine on escape responding were related to the subjects' earlier exposure to amphetamine-produced momentary increases in responding and in shock intensity under the punishment-titration schedule (see below).

Though it is clear that amphetamines do not increase punished responding in many situations, it is not clear whether this is due to some influence of the basic punishment process itself, or if this effect instead develops from a dynamic interaction between behavior and its consequences in the presence of the drug. That is, does the effect of amphetamine depend in any way on the subject's experience with increases in shock frequency (or intensity) as a result of amphetamine-produced increases in responding? This question has been examined in further experiments by Smith *et al.* (1977) and by Smith and McKearney (1977).

As part of the experiments described earlier, Smith *et al.* (1977) analyzed the role of response-produced increments in shock intensity in determining the effects of *d*-amphetamine on responding under a punishment-titration schedule. In this situation, where increases in food-maintained responding also resulted in increments in shock intensity, shock increments were first eliminated during sessions in which drugs were administered. Under this condition, *d*-amphetamine increased "punished" responding even though responding under predrug conditions had been suppressed by shock increments. Thus, there appears to be nothing about the punishment process itself that renders suppressed responding insensitive to amphetamine's rate-increasing effects. When shock increments were allowed to occur in subsequent sessions, *d*-amphetamine no longer increased punished responding. Thus, the actual occurrence of increased shock intensity seemed critical for the effects of amphetamine.

In related experiments (Smith and McKearney, 1977) pigeons responded under a 10-min fixed-interval schedule of food presentation in which every one-hundredth response also produced an electric shock. Responding was suppressed under this schedule of shock delivery, and when shock was removed on certain days and saline was injected, responding remained suppressed. When the schedule of shock delivery was removed for single sessions and *d*-amphetamine was injected, responding was substantially increased (Figure 20). However, when amphetamine was given during sessions with the shock schedule in effect, responding did not increase. In the same experiments, pentobarbital increased responding regardless of whether or not shock was present during experimental sessions, but the magnitude of increase was greater during sessions when shock was not present. Thus, the lack of increases in punished responding with amphetamine seem to depend on the occurrence of response-produced shock during drug ses-

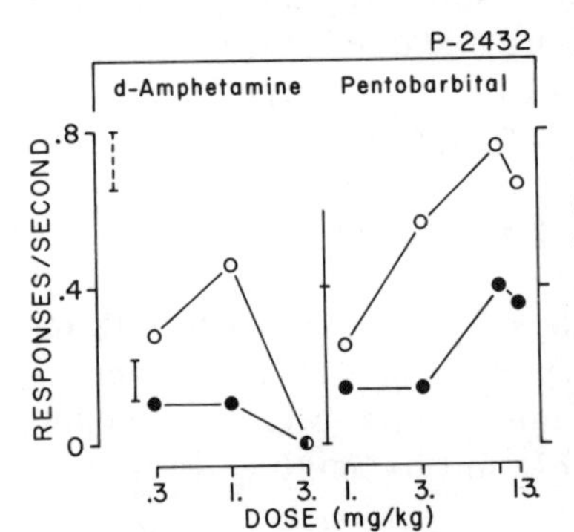

Figure 20. Effects of *d*-amphetamine (left) and pentobarbital (right) on punished responding. Responding was maintained under a 10-min fixed-interval schedule of food presentation and suppressed by presenting electric shock for every one-hundredth response. The dashed bracket represents the range of response rates before punishment, and the solid bracket is the range of response rates during the punishment condition. For individual drug sessions, shock was either present (filled circles) or absent (open circles). When shocks were removed for single sessions and either saline (not shown) or low drug doses were given, responding remained suppressed. *d*-Amphetamine increased responding only when shocks were removed during drug sessions, whereas pentobarbital increased responding without regard to the presence or absence of shock. Each point is the mean of at least three observations in this pigeon. [Adapted from Smith and McKearney (1977).]

sions. An important question not addressed by either of these experiments is whether having experienced amphetamine-produced increases in shock would later attenuate or eliminate increases in responding after amphetamine during sessions when shock is absent.

The experiments by Smith *et al.* (1977) and by Smith and McKearney (1977) show that the usual effects of amphetamine on punished food-maintained responding depend on interactions between responding and the occurrence of shock in the presence of the drug. Smith and McKearney (1977) also showed that amphetamine's effects on responding maintained by food presentation can change as a result of amphetamine-produced changes in response consequences. A low rate of responding was maintained in pigeons responding under a schedule in which a single response had to be followed by a 30-sec period without responding in order for food to be presented (Figure 21A). Increases in responding under this schedule could result in decreases in the frequency of food presentation. When *d*-amphetamine was first administered there were marked increases in responding and decreases in food presentation (Figure 21B); however, the next administration of the same dose had a markedly smaller effect (Figure 21C), and the third and fourth injections of this dose had little detectable effect (Figure 21D and E). Essentially the same changes in effects were observed for doses of pentobarbital that initially increased responding (not shown). Thus, experience with drug-produced increases in responding that resulted in decreased food presentation changed the subsequent effects of amphetamine and pentobarbital. In later experiments, the 30-sec delay requirement was removed during sessions when drugs were administered, and increases in responding with *d*-amphetamine and pentobarbital persisted over successive drug sessions. When the delay requirement was reinstated, these increases were eliminated. These experiments show that the effects of drugs can depend not only on characteristics of behavior prior to drug administration, but also on the consequences of behavior when the drug is present (see Chapter 8).

Experiments discussed in the preceding sections make it clear that the effects of drugs on punished responding are by no means as simply determined as was once thought. Although ongoing response rate is very important, it cannot alone account for the effects of drugs on punished responding in all situations. In this respect, punished behavior is like other behavior controlled by its consequences. The importance of schedule-controlled patterns of responding to an understanding of the effects of drugs on maintained behavior is now generally acknowledged; different schedules, or changes in the parameter values of the same schedule, can dramatically alter the effects of drugs. Though it is now generally recognized that there is no such thing as a "typical" reinforced behavior, it is much less widely appreciated that the same is true of punished behavior. Recent results, some of which are summarized here, show clearly that punished behavior and the ways it is affected by drugs are as complexly determined as with any other behavior. Although it has been known for some time that the quantitative effects of drugs on punished responding are influenced by factors such as the control rate of responding and the intensity and

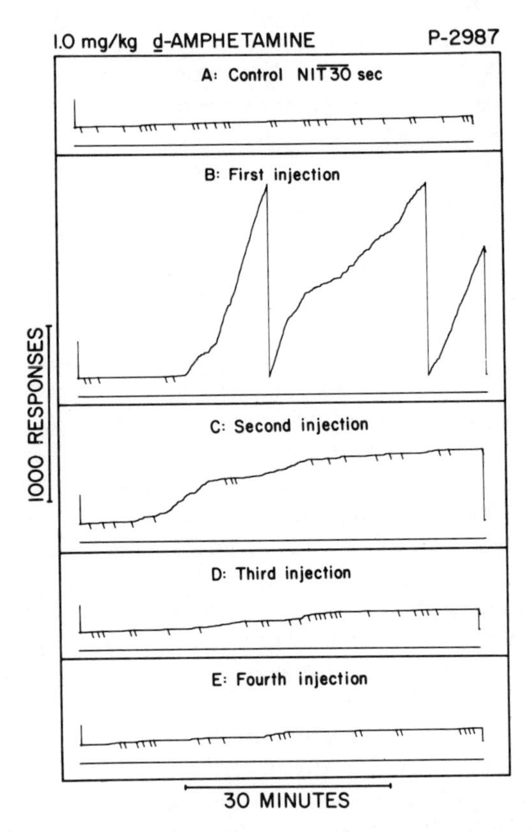

Figure 21. Effects of successive administrations of *d*-amphetamine on responding under a food-presentation schedule with a pause requirement. Food was presented (diagonal mark) whenever a response was followed by a 30-sec period without a response. Four experimental sessions intervened between injections 1–2 and 3–4, and nine sessions between injections 2 and 3. Other doses of *d*-amphetamine were given on the third session after injection one (3.0 mg/kg), on the third (0.1 mg/kg) and seventh (0.3 mg/kg) session after injection two, and on the second session after injection three (0.1 mg/kg). Note that there were marked increases in responding during the first drug session (B) and that these decreased and were eliminated with succeeding administrations (C–E). [Adapted from Smith and McKearney (1977).]

frequency of the punishing stimulus, recent work suggests that the magnitude and even the direction of change in punished responding by drugs can depend also on a variety of factors apart from these most obvious ones. The effects of drugs on punished responding can be completely different depending on the environmental context in which the punished behavior is studied, the type of event maintaining responding, and the individual's prior experience. Because of this complexity, it is inappropriate to think of "punished behavior" as a unitary phenomenon, and it is unreasonable to expect that the effects of particular drugs on punished responding will be the same in all situations.

4. Summary and Conclusions

Events that control behavior are necessarily presented or withdrawn according to a schedule, and the exact nature of this relation between behavior and its consequences is of inestimable importance in determining both ongoing behavior itself and the behavioral effects of drugs. Indeed, the processes of reinforcement and punishment cannot be conceptualized independently of considerations related to the scheduling of consequent events.

The study of schedule-controlled behavior has had tremendous influence on the field of behavioral pharmacology. Schedules produce remarkably uniform and reproducible patterns and rates of responding that are determined by both previous and current consequences. Significantly, a greater emphasis on schedules of reinforcement in controlling behavior has allowed other important features, such as prior experience and environmental context, to become evident as influential determinants of the behavioral effects of drugs. As Morse (1975) has pointed out, schedules of reinforcement have "fundamental as opposed to a practical significance for drug action" (p. 1869).

In addition to prevailing and emerging schedule factors, current behaviors and changes produced by drugs are also determined by the individual's past experiences and by characteristics of the total environmental context in which behavior occurs. In fact, the ways in which behavior is changed by particular consequent events or by a given drug may depend less on the physical nature of the event or the chemical structure of the drug than on the nature of the currently ongoing behavior, the individual's prior experience, and the context in which behavior occurs. Effective environmental events do not have invariant effects on behavior, and the effects of drugs on behavior are no less complex than the determinants of that behavior itself.

Though there have been attempts to understand the behavioral effects of drugs by appeal to traditional motivational and emotional constructs, this approach has not been useful in interpreting experimental findings, in suggesting new directions for research, or in developing principles generally useful in predicting the effects of drugs on behavior. Rather, as with the maintenance and modification of behavior itself, the effects of drugs seem more directly determined by characteristics of ongoing behavior and the ways behavior is controlled by antecedent and consequent environmental events. The effects of drugs are more clearly related to specifiable features of behaviors themselves than to presumed or inferred factors that occur at other levels of analysis.

Under a wide variety of conditions, the behavioral effects of drugs are determined by the rate and pattern of schedule-controlled responding in the absence of drug. This dependence on control rate has been an important unifying principle. At present, the rate and pattern of schedule-controlled responding seems to be the best general predictor of the behavioral effects of drugs in many different situations. Continued research is necessary to further delineate the conditions under which control rate is important, to identify other significant factors that modulate or change rate-dependent effects, and to elucidate the possibly broader biological significance of such a dependency. As the contribution of control rate becomes better understood, this will permit more thorough assessment of the role of other significant factors that determine the effects of drugs.

Though there has long been interest in whether the effects of drugs are determined by the quality of the environmental events that control behavior, categorical and encompassing answers to this question are not likely to be forthcoming. Since environmental events themselves can have so many different effects on behavior, it is unreasonable to suppose that the effects of drugs will bear any necessary or consistent relation to the physical characteristics of particular controlling events. Overemphasis on particular consequent events can impede both the experimental analysis of behavior and analysis of the effects of drugs by diverting attention away from other important factors. Though there appear to be situations in which the behavioral effects of certain drugs can differ depending on which event maintains behavior, comparisons have been made under very restricted conditions, and there is insufficient systematic information available to warrant general conclusions. For certain drugs it is clear that the nature of the maintaining event is far less important than the pattern of schedule-controlled responding that prevails. The behavioral effects of drugs are very generally determined by characteristics of schedule-controlled responding. Since these patterns of responding can be independent of particular consequent events, and since the events that control behavior are diverse and changing, descriptions of drug effects in terms of quantitative aspects of schedule-controlled responding are likely to be more generally applicable than descriptions based on events themselves (see Morse *et al.*, 1977).

As with maintained behavior, the effects of drugs on punished responding are by no means simply determined. Though it once seemed that certain drugs either did or did not increase punished responding, experiments were generally performed under restricted conditions. For example, when food-maintained responding is suppressed by response-dependent electric shock, many studies have shown that barbiturates and related drugs increase punished responding, whereas amphetamines do not. However, more recent experiments have shown that when punished responding is instead maintained by stimulus-shock termination, pentobarbital and amphetamine have directly opposite effects on punished responding. Further, amphetamines may increase punished responding when studied in a context in which behavior is also maintained by shock postponement or shock presentation, or when studied in subjects with prior experience under schedules in which responding was maintained by shock. Clearly, punished behavior is no more a cohesive and unitary phenomenon than is maintained behavior, and it is not uniformly affected by drugs.

General statements about the effects of drugs on behavior must be made with caution. The eager search for general principles must proceed with a corresponding regard for the complex and multiple ways in which behavior is determined. Findings on the effects of drugs on punished responding, for example, convincingly illustrate the necessity for considering broader aspects of the environmental situation for an adequate understanding of the effects of drugs. There is little predictive utility in specifying simply that responding is "punished" if historical and contextual details are inadequately specified.

The necessity for more fully specifying relevant aspects of the organism's history and of the prevailing features of the environmental setting may appear to unduly complicate attempts to understand the behavioral effects of drugs. To do otherwise, however, ignores the spectrum of different effects behavioral consequences can have, which are, in turn, significant determinants of drug effects. Ongoing behavior is an exceedingly complex product of a variety of dynamically interacting factors, and it is erroneous to expect that the effects of drugs on behavior are any less complexly determined. Schedule factors are of tremendous importance, but not to the exclusion of the profound influence of the total environmental context and of the individual's past experiences. Full appreciation of these complexities is a necessary prerequisite to meaningful understanding of either the environmental control of behavior or of the behavioral effects of drugs.

ACKNOWLEDGMENTS

Preparation supported in part by grants MH-18421, DA-01015, and AA-02104 from the U.S. Public Health Service. We thank A. V. Bacotti, L. R. Gollub, J. L. Katz, W. H. Morse, J. B. Smith, and D. M. Thompson for helpful comments, and E. Anderson and N. Gehman for help in preparation of the manuscript.

5. References

Appel, J. B., and Peterson, N. J., 1965, Punishment: effects of shock intensity on response suppression, *Psychol. Rep.* **16:**721–730.

Azrin, N. H., 1960, Effects of punishment intensity during variable-interval reinforcement, *J. Exp. Anal. Behav.* **3:**123–142.

Azrin, N. H., and Holz, W. C., 1966, Punishment, *in: Operant Behavior: Areas of Research and Application* (W. K. Honig, ed.), pp. 380–447, Appleton-Century-Crofts, New York.

Barrett, J. E., 1974, Conjunctive schedules of reinforcement. I. rate-dependent effects of pentobarbital and *d*-amphetamine, *J. Exp. Anal. Behav.* **22:**561–573.

Barrett, J. E., 1975, The Estes–Skinner procedure: inadequacy of traditional interpretations, *Psychol. Rec.* **25:**167–172.

Barrett, J. E., 1976, Effects of alcohol, chlordiazepoxide, cocaine and pentobarbital on responding maintained under fixed-interval schedules of food or shock presentation, *J. Pharmacol. Exp. Ther.* **196:**605–615.

Barrett, J. E., 1977a (in press), Effects of *d*-amphetamine on responding simultaneously maintained and punished by presentation of electric shock, *Psychopharmacology*.

Barrett, J. E., 1977b (in press), Behavioral history as a determinant of the effects of *d*-amphetamine on punished responding, *Science*.

Barrett, J. E., and Glowa, J. R., 1977, Reinforcement and punishment of behavior by the same consequent event, *Psychol. Rep.* **40:**1015–1021.

Barrett, J. E., and Spealman, R. D., 1977 (in press), Behavior simultaneously maintained by both presentation and termination of noxious stimuli, *J. Exp. Anal. Behav.*

Brown, P. L., and Jenkins, H. M., 1968, Auto-shaping of the pigeon's key-peck, *J. Exp. Anal. Behav.* **11:**1–8.

Byrd, L. D., 1969, Responding in the cat maintained under response-independent electric shock and response-produced electric shock, *J. Exp. Anal. Behav.* **12:**1–10.

Byrd, L. D., 1972, Responding in the squirrel monkey under second-order schedules of shock delivery, *J. Exp. Anal. Behav.* **18:**155–167.

Byrd, L. D., 1974, Modification of the effects of chlorpromazine on behavior in the chimpanzee, *J. Pharmacol. Exp. Ther.* **189:**24–32.

Cappell, H., and LeBlanc, A. E., 1971, Conditioned aversion to saccharin by single administrations of mescaline and *d*-amphetamine, *Psychopharmacologia* **22:**352–356.

Clark, F. C., and Smith, J. B., 1977 (in press), Schedules of food postponement. II. Maintenance of behavior by food postponement and effects of the schedule parameter, *J. Exp. Anal. Behav.*

Cook, L., and Catania, A. C., 1964, Effects of drugs on avoidance and escape behavior, *Fed. Proc.* **23:**818–835.

Cook, L., and Davidson, A. B., 1973, Effects of behaviorally active drugs in a conflict-punishment procedure in rats, *in: The Benzodiazepines* (S. Garattini, E. Mussini, and L. O. Randall, eds.), pp. 327–345, Raven Press, New York.

Cook, L., and Kelleher, R. T., 1962, Drug effects on the behavior of animals, *Ann. N.Y. Acad. Sci.* **96:**315–335.

Cook, L., and Sepinwall, J., 1975, Reinforcement schedules and extrapolations to humans from animals in behavioral pharmacology, *Fed. Proc.* **34:**1889–1897.

Dews, P. B., 1955, Studies on behavior. I. Differential sensitivity to pentobarbital of pecking performance in pigeons depending on the schedule of reward, *J. Pharmacol. Exp. Ther.* **113:**393–401.

Dews, P. B., 1958a, Studies on behavior. IV. Stimulant actions of methamphetamine, *J. Pharmacol. Exp. Ther.* **122:**137–147.

Dews, P. B., 1958b, Analysis of effects of psychopharmacological agents in behavioral terms, *Fed. Proc.* **17:**1024–1030.

Dews, P. B., and DeWeese, J., 1977, Schedules of reinforcement, *in: Handbook of Psychopharmacology—Principles of Behavioral Pharmacology* (L. L. Iversen, S. D. Iversen, and S. H. Snyder, eds.), Vol. 7, pp. 107–150, Plenum Press, New York.

Dews, P. B., and Morse, W. H., 1961, Behavioral pharmacology, *Ann. Rev. Pharmacol.* **1:**145–174.

Fantino, E., 1973, Aversive control, *in: The Study of Behavior—Learning, Motivation, Emotion, and Instinct* (J. A. Nevin and G. S. Reynolds, eds.), pp. 239–279, Scott, Foresman, Glenview, Ill.

Foree, D. D., Moretz, F. H., and McMillan, D. E., 1973, Drugs and punished responding. II. *d*-Amphetamine-induced increases in punished responding, *J. Exp. Anal. Behav.* **20:**291–300.

Gamzu, E. R., and Williams, D. R., 1973, Associative factors underlying the pigeon's key pecking in auto-shaping procedures, *J. Exp. Anal. Behav.* **19:**225–232.

Geller, I., and Seifter, J., 1960, The effects of meprobamate, barbiturates, *d*-amphetamine, and promazine on experimentally induced conflict in the rat, *Psychopharmacologia* **1:**482–492.

Geller, I., and Seifter, J., 1962, The effects of monourethans, di-urethans, and barbiturates on a punishment discrimination, *J. Pharmacol. Exp. Ther.* **136:**284–288.

Geller, I., Kulak, J. T., Jr., and Seifter, J., 1962, The effects of chlordiazepoxide and chlorpromazine on a punishment discrimination, *Psychopharmacologia* **3:**374–385.

Geller, I., Bachman, E., and Seifter, J., 1963, Effects of reserpine and morphine on behavior suppressed by punishment, *Life Sci.* **4:**226–231.

Glowa, J. R., and Barrett, J. E., 1976, Effects of alcohol on punished and unpunished responding of squirrel monkeys, *Pharmacol. Biochem. Behav.* **4:**169–173.

Goldberg, S. R., and Kelleher, R. T., 1976, Behavior controlled by schedules of cocaine injection in squirrel and rhesus monkeys, *J. Exp. Anal. Behav.* **25:**93–104.

Goldberg, S. R., Hoffmeister, F., Schlichting, U. U., and Wuttke, W., 1971, Aversive properties of nalorphine and naloxone in morphine-dependent rhesus monkeys, *J. Pharmacol. Exp. Ther.* **179:**268–276.

Hanson, H. M., Witoslawski, J. J., and Campbell, E. H., 1967, Drug effects in squirrel monkeys trained on a multiple schedule with a punishment contingency, *J. Exp. Anal. Behav.* **10:**565–569.

Heffner, T. G., Drawbaugh, R. B., and Zigmond, M. J., 1974, Amphetamine and operant behavior in rats: relationship between drug effect and control response rate, *J. Comp. Physiol. Psychol.* **86:**1031–1043.

Hilgard, E. R., and Marquis, D. G., 1940, *Conditioning and Learning,* Appleton-Century, New York.

Kantor, J. P., 1959, *Interbehavioral Psychology,* Principia Press, Chicago.

Kelleher, R. T., and Morse, W. H., 1964, Escape behavior and punished behavior, *Fed. Proc.* **23:**808–817.

Kelleher, R. T., and Morse, W. H., 1968a, Schedules using noxious stimuli. III. Responding maintained with response-produced electric shocks, *J. Exp. Anal. Behav.* **11:**819–838.

Kelleher, R. T., and Morse, W. H., 1968b, Determinants of the specificity of the behavioral effects of drugs, *Ergeb. Physiol. Biol. Chem. Exp. Pharmakol.* **60:**1–56.

Kelleher, R. T., and Morse, W. H., 1969, Schedules using noxious stimuli. IV. An interlocking shock-postponement schedule in the squirrel monkey, *J. Exp. Anal. Behav.* **12:**1063–1079.

Kelleher, R. T., Riddle, W. C., and Cook, L., 1963, Persistent behavior maintained by unavoidable shocks, *J. Exp. Anal. Behav.* **6:**507–517.

Laties, V. G., and Weiss, B., 1966, Influence of drugs on behavior controlled by internal and external stimuli, *J. Pharmacol. Exp. Ther.* **152:**388–396.

MacPhail, R. C., 1971, Rate-dependent effects of amphetamine are also schedule dependent, *Proceedings, 79th Annual Convention, APA,* pp. 755–756.

MacPhail, R. C., and Gollub, L. R., 1975, Separating the effects of response rate and reinforcement frequency in the rate-dependent effects of amphetamine and scopolamine on the schedule-controlled performance of rats and pigeons, *J. Pharmacol. Exp. Ther.* **194:**332–342.

Marr, M. J., 1970, Effects of chlorpromazine in the pigeon under a second-order schedule of food presentation, *J. Exp. Anal. Behav.* **13:**291–299.

Masserman, J. H., 1946, *Principles of Dynamic Psychiatry,* W. B. Saunders, Philadelphia.

McKearney, J. W., 1968, Maintenance of responding under a fixed-interval schedule of electric shock presentation, *Science* **160:**1249–1251.

McKearney, J. W., 1969, Fixed-interval schedules of electric shock presentation: extinction and recovery of performance under different shock intensities and fixed-interval durations, *J. Exp. Anal. Behav.* **12:**301–313.

McKearney, J. W., 1970a, Responding under fixed-ratio and multiple fixed-interval fixed-ratio schedules of electric shock presentation, *J. Exp. Anal. Behav.* **14:**1–6.

McKearney, J. W., 1970b, Rate-dependent effects of drugs: modification by discriminative stimuli of the effects of amobarbital on schedule-controlled behavior, *J. Exp. Anal. Behav.* **14:**167–175.

McKearney, J. W., 1972, Maintenance and suppression of responding under schedules of electric shock presentation, *J. Exp. Anal. Behav.* **17:**425–432.

McKearney, J. W., 1973, Methamphetamine effects on responding under a multiple schedule of shock presentation, *Pharmacol. Biochem. Behav.* **1:**547–550.

McKearney, J. W., 1974, Effects of *d*-amphetamine, morphine, and chlorpromazine on responding under fixed-interval schedules of food presentation or electric shock presentation, *J. Pharmacol. Exp. Ther.* **190:**141–153.

McKearney, J. W., 1975, Effects of morphine, methadone, nalorphine, and naloxone on responding under fixed-interval (FI) schedules in the squirrel monkey, *Fed. Proc.* **34:**766.

McKearney, J. W., 1976, Punishment of responding under schedules of stimulus-shock termination: effects of *d*-amphetamine and pentobarbital, *J. Exp. Anal. Behav.* **26:**281–287.

McKearney, J. W., and Barrett, J. E., 1975, Punished behavior: increases in responding after *d*-amphetamine, *Psychopharmacologia* **41:**23–26.

McMillan, D. E., 1968a, The effects of sympathomimetic amines on schedule-controlled behavior in the pigeon, *J. Pharmacol. Exp. Ther.* **160:**315–325.

McMillan, D. E., 1968b, Some interactions between sympathomimetic amines and amine-depleting agents on the schedule-controlled behavior of the pigeon and the squirrel monkey, *J. Pharmacol. Exp. Ther.* **163:**172–187.

McMillan, D. E., 1973, Drugs and punished responding. I. Rate-dependent effects under multiple schedules, *J. Exp. Anal. Behav.* **19:**133–145.

McMillan, D. E., 1975, Determinants of drug effects on punished responding, *Fed. Proc.* **34:**1870–1879.

McMillan, D. E., Dearstyne, M. R., and Engstrom, T. G., 1975, Some effects of local anesthetics on schedule-controlled behavior, *Pharmacol. Ther. Dentistry* **2:**57–64.

Meehl, P. E., 1950, On the circularity of the law of effect, *Psychol. Bull.* **47:**52–75.

Morse, W. H., 1964, Effect of amobarbital and chlorpromazine on punished behavior in the pigeon, *Psychopharmacologia* **6:**286–294.

Morse, W. H., 1966, Intermittent reinforcement, *in: Operant Behavior: Areas of Research and Application* (W. K. Honig, ed.), pp. 52–108, Appleton-Century-Crofts, New York.

Morse, W. H., 1975, Schedule controlled behaviors as determinants of drug response, *Fed. Proc.* **34:**1868–1869.

Morse, W. H., and Herrnstein, R. J., 1956, Effects of drugs on characteristics of behavior maintained by complex schedules of intermittent positive reinforcement, *Ann. N.Y. Acad. Sci.* **65:**303–317.

Morse, W. H., and Kelleher, R. T., 1966, Schedules using noxious stimuli. I. Multiple fixed-ratio and fixed-interval termination of schedule complexes, *J. Exp. Anal. Behav.* **9:**267–290.

Morse, W. H., and Kelleher, R. T., 1970, Schedules as fundamental determinants of behavior, *in: The Theory of Reinforcement Schedules* (W. N. Schoenfeld, ed.), pp. 139–185, Appleton-Century-Crofts, New York.

Morse, W. H., and Kelleher, R. T., 1977, Determinants of reinforcement and punishment, *in: Handbook of Operant Behavior* (W. K. Honig and J. E. R. Staddon, eds.), pp. 174–200, Prentice-Hall, Englewood Cliffs, N.J.

Morse, W. H., Mead, R. N., and Kelleher, R. T., 1967, Modulation of elicited behavior by a fixed-interval schedule of electric shock presentation, *Science* **157:**215–217.

Morse, W. H., McKearney, J. W., and Kelleher, R. T., 1977, Control of behavior by noxious stimuli, *in: Handbook of Psychopharmacology—Principles of Behavioral Pharmacology* (L. L. Iversen, S. D. Iversen, and S. H. Snyder, eds.), Vol. 7, pp. 151–180, Plenum Press, New York.

Pavlov, I. P., 1927, *Conditioned Reflexes,* Dover Publications, New York.

Pliskoff, S. S., Wright, J. E., and Hawkins, T. D., 1965, Brain stimulation as a reinforcer: intermittent schedules, *J. Exp. Anal. Behav.* **8:**75–88.

Premack, D., 1971, Catching up with common sense or two sides of a generalization: reinforcement and punishment, *in: The Nature of Reinforcement* (R. Glaser, ed.), pp. 121–150, Academic Press, New York.

Rachlin, H., 1972, Response control with titration of punishment, *J. Exp. Anal. Behav.* **17:**147–157.

Sandler, J., 1964, Masochism: an empirical analysis, *Psychol. Bull.* **62:**197–204.

Sanger, D. J., and Blackman, D. E., 1975, Rate-dependent effects of drugs on the variable-interval behavior of rats, *J. Pharmacol. Exp. Ther.* **194:**343–350.

Sanger, D. J., and Blackman, D. E., 1976, Rate-dependent effects of drugs: a review of the literature, *Pharmacol. Biochem. Behav.* **4:**73–83.

Seligman, M. E. P., and Maier, S. F., 1967, Failure to escape traumatic shock, *J. Exp. Psychol.* **74:**1–9.

Sidman, M., 1953, Avoidance conditioning with brief shock and no exteroceptive warning signal, *Science* **118:**157–158.

Sidman, M., Herrnstein, R. J., and Conrad, D. R., 1957, Maintenance of avoidance behavior by unavoidable shocks, *J. Comp. Physiol. Psychol.* **50:**553–557.

Skinner, B. F., 1938, *The Behavior of Organisms,* Appleton-Century, New York.

Skinner, B. F., 1974, *About Behaviorism,* Alfred A. Knopf, New York.

Smith, C. B., 1964, Effects of *d*-amphetamine upon operant behavior of pigeons: enhancement by reserpine, *J. Pharmacol. Exp. Ther.* **146:**167–174.

Smith, J. B., and McKearney, J. W., 1977, Changes in the rate-increasing effects of *d*-amphetamine and pentobarbital by response consequences, *Psychopharmacology* **53:** 151–157.

Smith, J. B., Branch, M. N., and McKearney, J. W., 1977, unpublished manuscript.

Steiner, S. S., Beer, B., and Shaffer, M. M., 1969, Escape from self-produced rates of brain stimulation, *Science* **163:**90–91.

Stitzer, M., and McKearney, J. W., 1977, Modification of drug effects by pause requirements for food presentation, *J. Exp. Anal. Behav.* **27:**51–59.

Stretch, R., Orloff, E. R., and Dalrymple, S. D., 1968, Maintenance of responding by fixed-interval schedule of electric shock presentation in squirrel monkeys, *Science* **162:**583–586.

Thompson, D. M., and Corr, P. B., 1974, Behavioral parameters of drug action: signalled and response-independent reinforcement, *J. Exp. Anal. Behav.* **21:**151–158.

Verhave, T., 1958, The effect of methamphetamine on operant level and avoidance behavior, *J. Exp. Anal. Behav.* **1:**207–219.

Waller, M. B., and Morse, W. H., 1963, Effects of pentobarbital on fixed-ratio reinforcement, *J. Exp. Anal. Behav.* **6:**125–130.

Waller, M. B., and Waller, P. F., 1962, Effects of chlorpromazine on appetitive and aversive components of a multiple schedule, *J. Exp. Anal. Behav.* **5:**259–264.

Waller, M. B., and Waller, P. F., 1963, The effects of unavoidable shocks on a multiple schedule having an avoidance component, *J. Exp. Anal. Behav.* **6:**29–37.

Weiss, B., and Laties, V. G., 1959, Titration behavior on various fractional escape programs, *J. Exp. Anal. Behav.* **2:**227–248.

Weiss, B., and Laties, V. G., 1963, Characteristics of aversive thresholds measured by a titration schedule, *J. Exp. Anal. Behav.* **6:**563–572.

Weiss, B., and Laties, V. G., 1969, Behavioral pharmacology and toxicology, *Ann. Rev. Pharmacol.* **9:**297–326.

Witkin, J. M., and Barrett, J. E., 1976, Effects of pentobarbital on punished behavior at different shock intensities, *Pharmacol. Biochem. Behav.* **5:**535–538.

Wuttke, W., and Kelleher, R. T., 1970, Effects of some benzodiazepines on punished and unpunished behavior in the pigeon, *J. Pharmacol. Exp. Ther.* **172:**397–405.

Zeiler, M. D., 1977, Schedules of reinforcement: the controlling variables, *in: Handbook of Operant Behavior* (W. K. Honig and J. E. R. Staddon, eds.), pp. 201–232, Prentice-Hall, Englewood Cliffs, N.J.,

The Effects of Drugs on Behavior Controlled by Aversive Stimuli

2

Vincent P. Houser

1. Introduction

The present chapter will review the effects that various drugs exert upon behavior that is under aversive control. Since it would be impossible to present an exhaustive review of all the pertinent literature within the present context, selected topics have been chosen as representative examples of the type of research being conducted in this area. Care has been taken to analyze critically the work cited under each topic and to summarize, whenever possible, the principles that govern drug–behavior interactions. The principal topics to be discussed include the effects of drugs on behavior controlled by the following three operant procedures: (1) conflict–punishment schedules, (2) Sidman avoidance, and (3) the conditioned emotional response procedure (CER). The types of compounds that have been studied with these procedures include representatives of the following clinical classes of drugs: neuroleptics, anxiolytics, antidepressants, narcotics, hallucinogens, and other psychoactive agents (alcohol, Δ^9-THC). Whenever possible, attempts will be made to identify the specific behavioral effects of individual classes of drugs that are observed under the various operant procedures. In addition to the clinically active classes of drugs listed above, brief mention will be made of the behavioral effects of compounds that

---

Vincent P. Houser • CNS Disease Therapy Section, Lederle Laboratories, Pearl River, New York. Present address: Department of Pharmacology, Schering Corporation, Bloomfield, New Jersey 07003

are known to alter synaptic function within the central nervous system. These agents have recently generated much interest within the scientific community because of their utility in evaluating the role that various biochemical mechanisms may play in controlling specific behaviors. Although much of the work concerning the effects of these drugs upon behavior under aversive control is still in its infancy, several interesting hypotheses have been offered which will undoubtedly inspire further research. An evaluation of this work will thus be included in the present chapter.

Before turning to our review of the drug literature, however, the term "aversive stimuli" should be carefully defined to indicate how behavior can be controlled by schedules that utilize these stimuli. In addition, a brief description of the methodological issues surrounding the use of aversive stimuli will be included to provide the reader with enough information to properly evaluate the data to be reviewed below.

The term "aversive stimulus" may be defined as an environmental event which an animal will seek to escape from or avoid whenever it is made available. Behavior may be maintained or controlled by the presentation of aversive stimuli if the occurrence of these events is made contingent upon the presence or absence of specific responses. Thus, animals will press a lever to postpone the delivery of a shock (avoidance) or fail to press a lever which delivers a food pellet if this response also produces a painful shock (punishment). There are, of course, many types of aversive stimuli that animals will seek to avoid. These include such noxious events as intense cold or heat, loud noise, bitter taste, aversive brain stimulation, time out from positive reinforcement, and electric shock. Although all these aversive stimuli can be and have been used in experimental settings to maintain various patterns of behavior, electric shock is by far the most popular choice, for a variety of reasons. This aversive stimulus is quantifiable, produces no lasting tissue damage, and is easy to deliver to free-moving animals. Thus, electric shock can be delivered to animals on a recurring basis over varying time intervals. Finally, the presentation of electric shock as an aversive stimulus has a certain "face validity" associated with its use. Since the administration of electric shock produces the aversive sensation of pain, it seems reasonable to assume that the actual or threatened presentation of electric shock would generate a state of fear or anxiety in animal subjects. This particular aversive stimulus has thus provided the basis for the experimental techniques that have been used in studying the effects of various drugs upon the development of fear or anxiety. Since electric shock has been the most popular aversive stimulus used by psychopharmacologists over the past two decades, the present chapter will focus only on those studies that employ this particular aversive event.

1.1. Methodological Issues Surrounding the Use of Electric Shock

One of the most difficult problems associated with the use of electric shock concerns the need to apply constant intensities of shock through a grid floor to freely moving animals. The electrical resistance of animals varies widely (i.e., from several thousand to several million ohms) as they move about on a grid floor. This alteration in resistance, in turn, causes proportional variations in current flow, voltage drop, or power dissipation, depending on what type of shock source is employed. Thus, grid shock is by its very nature a variable stimulus. Several different types of shock sources have been developed to reduce the variability associated with grid shock. Of these various sources, the constant-current shock generator appears to offer the greatest advantages and has thus enjoyed wide use in the drug literature. By placing a large resistance in series with the animal subject, this type of generator reduces the variability in current intensity associated with large changes in animal resistance. This design is limited, however, by the fact that very large series resistances require the use of high source voltages. These voltages, in turn, can produce painful current arcs from the grid to the animal's body. Thus, constant-current generators are useful only within a limited range of source voltages. As such, they provide only relative control of the variability in shock intensity associated with changes in animal resistance (Campbell and Masterson, 1969). The other widely used shock sources (fixed impedance) have similar limitations and thus do not supply a constant electrical stimulus to freely moving animals.

The variability associated with electric shock can be considerably reduced if this stimulus is delivered via fixed electrodes rather than through a grid floor. This is the case simply because fixed electrodes (held firmly on the skin of the animal subject) provide relatively constant resistance values, owing to the fact that the electrode never loses contact with the animal's tissue. The greater control over shock intensity is offset, however, by the reduced mobility that is caused by the use of such electrodes. Thus, many operant procedures that call for the use of unrestrained animal subjects cannot make use of fixed electrodes.

Finally, animal resistance can be altered by factors other than movement across a grid floor. It has been demonstrated that tissue resistance can be significantly modified as a function of shock intensity, local humidity conditions, the type of cage in which the animal is housed (Campbell and Masterson, 1969), or the administration of a drug (Glick *et al.*, 1973). Thus, tissue resistance, which can influence shock intensity dramatically, as noted above, can be altered by numerous factors, including drug administration. This suggests that a drug may influence behavior under the control of electric shock indirectly by altering tissue resistance, which, in turn, may modify the intensity of shock delivered to the animal subject.

The preceding discussion thus clearly suggests that electric shock is an extremely difficult stimulus to control accurately when it is applied to a living organism. Many variables can influence the physical characteristics of the shock stimulus. These factors must be kept in mind when studies which use electric shock are evaluated. In general, experimental designs which attempt to control for fluctuations in shock intensity are to be preferred over those that make no attempt at such control. Some of the techniques mentioned above that can be used to enhance control of the shock stimulus include the use of fixed electrodes and the selection of the proper shock source (either fixed impedance or constant current). As a general rule, most operant studies that use pigeons or restrained primates make use of fixed electrodes. If shock must be applied through a grid floor, attempts should be made to control local humidity conditions (Houser and Paré, 1972) and to ensure that fecal material and urine cannot cause electrical shorts within the grid system (Houser and Paré, 1973). Even in drug studies that incorporate such controls, however, it is possible that the administration of the drug, by itself, may significantly alter tissue resistance, thus modifying the physical characteristics of the aversive stimulus.

1.2. Problems Associated with Operant Schedules That Utilize Electric Shock

The methodological issues that surround the use of aversive schedules of reinforcement to evaluate the behavioral effects of drugs can be classified under two separate categories: pharmacological and behavioral. The major pharmacological problems that one encounters when exploring the effects of drugs on behavior under aversive control are identical to those noted whenever drugs are administered to living organisms. Such variables as the route of administration, species utilized, differential rates of metabolism, chronic versus acute dosing, as well as the development of tolerance are often influential in determining the degree to which a specific drug will affect behavior. Many of the variables listed above can interact with each other to produce significant behavioral effects. Thus, a particular animal species may metabolize a given compound in an atypical fashion, producing novel metabolites in sufficient quantities to directly affect aversively controlled behavior.

Other species, however, may not produce these metabolites and thus demonstrate a different behavioral effect to the same drug. A final variable that is often overlooked in psychopharmacological research concerns the fact that behavioral testing should take place during the peak time of drug activity. If a drug produces its major behavioral effects 4 hr after oral administration, testing that takes place 1–2 hr after the compound has been given may not detect any significant drug effects. Thus, the elapsed time between drug administration and testing is often a critical variable which determines whether a behavioral effect of a drug will be detected by operant procedures. It is advisable, therefore, to make peak-time determinations for every compound that is to be tested in a specific behavioral procedure.

In addition to the pharmacological problems mentioned above, there exist many behavioral factors that can influence the type of effect that a drug will exert. One of the most important of these factors is the control rate of responding. It has been well established that many different classes of drugs will elevate low rates of responding and decrease high rates, irrespective of the type of operant schedule that maintains the ongoing behavior. This finding, as we shall see in our discussion of conflict behavior, often makes it difficult to determine if a specific class of drugs has a differential effect upon behavior under aversive control not shared by other types of compounds. The discovery of rate-dependent effects complicates the interpretation of drug studies simply because it is such a pervasive phenomenon that can be used to describe the behavioral effects of a wide range of compounds. It is thus essential that the proper controls be available whenever attempts are made to explain the behavioral effects of drugs without recourse to the rate-dependence hypothesis. Other behavioral factors that may influence drug activity include alterations in learning or motivation. If, for example, a drug directly affects the learning process (e.g., produces memory deficits), behavior under the control of operant schedules can be directly affected. Likewise, if a compound produces anorexia or enhances appetitive motivation as do some of the anxiolytic drugs, behavior under the control of schedules that use food reward may be directly altered. Finally, the production of drug-induced analgesia would be expected to alter dramatically any behavior that was maintained through the use of electric shock. Thus, whenever a drug alters behavior under the control of operant schedules of reinforcement, it is possible that these effects merely reflect changes in learning or motivational processes.

Before turning to our review of the drug literature, some mention should be made of the "motivational" hypothesis that has been used to explain how aversive stimuli maintain behavior. It has been assumed that aversive stimuli control behavior by generating a generalized state of fear or anxiety, and that drugs can modify this behavior by altering these underlying emotional states. The strength of this hypothesis lies in its generality. Explanations of drug effects in terms of fear or anxiety reduction have been applied to behavior under the control of punishment, avoidance, and CER paradigms. An important goal of the present chapter is to explore the value of this motivational analysis to see if this general hypothesis is sufficient to explain the behavioral effects of one or more classes of drugs across a number of aversive schedules of reinforcement. It should be kept in mind that a similar attempt has been made to apply motivational interpretations to the effects of drugs upon behavior maintained by appetitive schedules of reinforcement. Changes in behavior after drug administration have been explained in terms of hunger, thirst, etc., but experiments expressly designed to evaluate the effects of alterations in motivational states demonstrate that these interpretations are inadequate. As we shall see below, the "motivational" hypothesis which assumes that some classes of drugs alter behavior under aversive control by altering the level of fear or anxiety is not able to account adequately for much of the data which bear on this issue. The manner in which drugs affect behavior under aversive control is a complex process that may not lend itself to unitary explanations. The reasons for this conclusion should become apparent during our review of the drug literature.

2. Drug–Behavior Interactions in Conflict–Punishment Procedures

2.1. Geller Conflict Schedule

One of the first and most widely used techniques to investigate the effects of drugs on punished behavior was introduced by Geller and Seifter (1960). Although many variations of this procedure have been developed since that time, the basic experimental paradigm has provided valuable insights into how specific classes of drugs affect punished behavior. Since this technique has enjoyed such wide appeal, we will describe it in detail before summarizing the rather extensive literature that surrounds this topic.

Basically, the Geller conflict procedure consists of a multiple schedule that alternates periods of food-maintained behavior with discriminated periods in which this behavior is suppressed with response-contingent shock. In the typical situation, animals (usually rats) are deprived of food and then trained to press a lever to obtain a liquid food reward on a variable-interval 2-min schedule of reinforcement. After this behavior has stabilized, a 3-min tone is introduced every 15 min to act as the discriminative cue for the second component of the multiple schedule. During this period animals are placed on a continuous reinforcement schedule for both food and shock. Thus, during the 3-min tone periods, animals are simultaneously rewarded with food and punished with shock for every lever-press response that is emitted. Since the rate of responding during the tone is inversely related to the intensity of shock (Cook and Kelleher, 1963), the degree of response suppression during this period can be easily controlled for each animal by individually adjusting shock levels (0.35–0.75 mA). In order for this technique to detect both increases and decreases in punished responding, it is essential that the response rate during the tone be only partially suppressed (e.g., 50% of that generated during the variable interval portions of the multiple schedule). Since one cannot always predict in advance in which direction a drug will affect punished responding, it is usually advisable to test unknown compounds initially under a moderate shock level. If the drug elevates punished responding, further testing can be carried out using a higher shock level, while the effects of lower shock levels can be investigated if the opposite effect is noted upon initial screening. Geller and Seifter (1960) suggest that titrating shock levels in the preceding manner tends to minimize both ceiling and floor effects and thus allows one to explore a wider portion of the dose–effect curve.

Initially, Geller and his associates explored the effects of a variety of psychoactive drugs upon the degree of response suppression generated by this conflict procedure. Figure 1 is taken from one of Geller's initial reports, which summarized the effects of meprobamate (an anxiolytic with sedative properties) upon punished behavior. The cumulative records in this figure indicate that 120 mg/kg of meprobamate significantly elevated the number of punished responses that this animal emitted during the tone under a high shock condition. Moreover, it should be noted that the elevation in punished responding occurred instantaneously upon the presentation of the first tone period. Thus, the drug effects noted in Figure 1 were immediate and did not require several punishment periods to reach maximum effect. This point is of some importance, as we shall see later when the mechanisms of drug action are discussed.

The response rates during the variable-interval portion of the schedule in Figure 1 were also considerably elevated in this animal after drug administration. The effects of meprobamate upon the number of punished responses emitted during the tone period was consistent across a group of nine rats, but the increase in variable-inter-

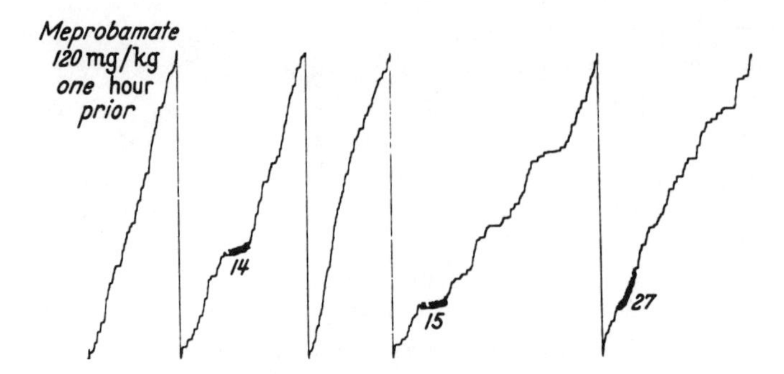

Figure 1. Effect of 120 mg/kg of meprobamate upon conflict behavior maintained by high shock (0.60–0.75 mA). Pen offsets indicate conflict trials; upward pips of the pen represent responses that were simultaneously rewarded with food and punished with shock. [From Geller and Seifter (1960).]

val response rates was not. The authors suggested that performance on the variable-interval schedule between conflict trials could be utilized as an index of ataxia or other undesirable drug effects. Thus, the multiple schedule could be used to assess the primary conflict-reducing properties of a drug as well as determining the degree of side-effect liability of various compounds (Geller and Seifter, 1960). Using such reasoning meprobamate would thus be classified as a drug which effectively reduces experimentally induced conflict (i.e., increases punished responding) without producing significant undesirable side effects (i.e., consistently altering variable-interval base-line performance). Other investigators (Cook and Kelleher, 1963), however, take exception to the preceding conclusions, noting that it is probably unwise to assume that alterations, especially decrements, in variable-interval response rates are direct indications of the degree of debilitating side effects produced by a drug. This is the case since various side effects, such as observable signs of ataxia or sedation, can occur without producing decreased response rates on appetitive schedules of reinforcement (Cook and Kelleher, 1961, 1962). Thus, the use of the conflict procedure to assess both primary and secondary drug effects is a relatively controversial issue. Until more direct evidence is advanced indicating that alterations in variable-interval rates are reflections of side-effect liability, it would seem inappropriate to assume that this relationship does indeed exist.

After the initial demonstration that the conflict procedure was sensitive to the sedative anxiolytic meprobamate, many other drugs were tested using the Geller conflict procedure. Compounds that were similar to meprobamate in elevating punished responding at doses that did not affect variable-interval performance included the barbiturates phenobarbital and pentobarbital (Geller and Seifter, 1960, 1962; Cook and Kelleher, 1963; Blum, 1970); the hypnotics urethan and hedonal; the sedative anxiolytic emylacamate (Cook and Kelleher, 1963); the minor tranquilizers of the benzodiazepine series, chlordiazepoxide, diazepam, and oxazepam (Geller *et al.,* 1962; Geller, 1964; Blum, 1970); and the major tranquilizer reserpine (Geller *et al.,* 1963). Inactive compounds that either produced no change in the level of punished responding or actually decreased it included the narcotic analgesic morphine (Geller *et al.,* 1963); the stimulant *d*-amphetamine (Geller and Seifter, 1960); and the neuroleptics chlorpromazine (Geller *et al.,* 1962), promazine (Geller and Seifter, 1960), and trifluoperazine (Geller and Seifter, 1960). The Geller conflict procedure thus appeared to be sensitive to drugs which had depressant anticonvulsant properties and/or significant clinical utility as anxiolytic agents. The fact that a CNS stimulant (*d*-amphetamine) that is known to elevate operant response rates (Dews, 1958) did not enhance punished responding suggested that the positive effects noted with other drugs were probably not the result of nonspecific behavioral stimulation. Furthermore, the negative results observed with respect to morphine strongly indicated that activity in the Geller conflict procedure could not be accounted for in terms of drug-induced analgesia. The sensitivity of the conflict procedure to agents which were clinically useful in the treatment of anxiety disorders, along with the assumption (Geller and Seifter, 1960) that changes in variable-interval response rate could be used to measure side-effect liability, led some authors (Blum, 1970) to suggest that this technique might be a useful tool in predicting the therapeutic index of a variety of anxiolytic drugs.

Before continuing our review of the effects of drugs on punished responding, we should mention several points concerning the early work accomplished by Geller and his associates. First, as was mentioned above, it was common practice to screen drugs using both a high and low shock base line to determine if drugs would enhance or retard punished responding. When the anxiolytic chlordiazepoxide was initially screened in this procedure (Geller *et al.,* 1962), it failed to elevate punished responding under a low shock base line, while dramatic increments were noted under high shock conditions. Thus, even in the earlier literature, there were signs that drug effects in the conflict procedure might be affected by a number of schedule parameters, thus reducing the generality of the results obtained. Second, there were early reports which were at variance with the results summarized above concerning the effects of chlorpromazine upon punished responding. For example, Dinsmoor and Lyon (1961) reported that chlorpromazine produced reliable increments in punished responding under high shock conditions rather than the decrements noted by Geller *et al.* (1962). Thus, although the initial work concerning the conflict procedure did indicate that sedative anxiolytics were able to disinhibit punished behavior, there were indications that this selectivity might be a function of the schedule parameters as well as the type of drug tested.

2.2. Effects of Drugs on Other Punishment Schedules and Species

Since the initial work of Geller and his associates, there has been a proliferation of modified conflict–punishment procedures that have been used to evaluate a variety of drugs in many different species. These studies indicate that, within limits, variations in schedule parameters across a wide variety of conflict–punishment procedures do not generally alter the type of drug effect noted in various species. A review of these results will thus provide evidence which suggests that these procedures can be used as powerful tools in evaluating the effects of drugs upon behavior under aversive control.

In a modification of the traditional conflict–punishment paradigm, McMillan and Leander (1975) tested the effects of drugs upon pigeons who were trained to peck a response key under a fixed-interval 5-min schedule of food reinforcement. A punishment contingency was then superimposed on this schedule. Each response by one pigeon produced electric shock (response-dependent shock) to that pigeon, as well as identical amounts of shock (response-independent shock) to another (i.e., yoked) bird working under an identical schedule of food reward. Thus, half the birds received shock for every response emitted under the schedule, while the other half received shocks during the schedule that were not contingent upon their behavior. Both response-dependent and response-independent shock partially suppressed behavior. Pentobarbital, chlordiazepoxide, and ethanol increased responding suppressed by response-dependent shock, but only pentobarbital increased responding suppressed by response-independent shock. *d*-Amphetamine and chlorpromazine, as well as two analgesics, morphine and pentazocine, either had no effect or enhanced the suppression of responding under both conditions. These results indicate that drugs with possible anxiolytic properties appear to selectively disinhibit behavior that is suppressed by response-dependent shock. Behavior that is suppressed by noncontingent shock is more resistant to the disinhibitory properties of anxiolytic drugs. This fact will become more apparent when the CER paradigm is discussed at the end of this chapter.

Other investigators (Miczek, 1973a; Vogel *et al.*, 1971) have resorted to the more traditional punishment paradigms to investigate the disinhibitory effects of a number of drugs. Miczek (1973) explored the effects of scopolamine, amphetamine, and chlordiazepoxide on a variety of punishment procedures in rats and monkeys. In one experiment, rats were subjected to a typical conflict procedure in which behavior was maintained by a variable-interval 30-sec schedule of food reinforcement. One-minute periods of continuous reinforcement with food pellets and shock occurred every 10 min throughout the experimental sessions. Scopolamine produced significant decrements in punished responding, chlordiazepoxide enhanced this behavior, while amphetamine had no effect. In a second experiment, rats were subjected to two concurrent schedules of reinforcement, a variable-interval 30-sec schedule for food pellets and a fixed-ratio 12 schedule for shock. As with the Geller conflict procedure, chlordiazepoxide significantly elevated punished responding while scopolamine decreased it. *d*-Amphetamine, on the other hand, produced a biphasic dose-dependent effect on responding suppressed by intermittent shock. Lower doses tended to increase and higher doses tended to decrease punished responding. In a final experiment, Miczek (1973a) trained water-deprived squirrel monkeys to drink an 8% dextrose solution from metal water spouts. The punishment contingency consisted of shocking animals every time they touched the spout. Under this continuous punishment procedure, scopolamine had a slight facilitatory effect and enhanced punished dextrose solution intake at low doses while decreasing intake at the higher doses. As was the case with behavior suppressed by intermittent shock, *d*-amphetamine had a dose-dependent biphasic effect with low doses enhancing consumption and high doses decreasing intake. Chlordiazepoxide consistently enhanced punished licking behavior. These results support the previous work cited above, which utilized the Geller conflict technique. Chlordiazepoxide, but not amphetamine, consistently elevated response rates that were punished by a continuous reinforcement schedule. These data do indicate, however, that when other punishment contingencies are utilized, *d*-amphetamine can produce both increases and decreases in punished responding, depending on the dose that is administered. In a similar study, Vogel *et al.* (1971) reported that various anxiolytic drugs (meprobamate, pentobarbital, diazepam, oxazepam) were able to reliably elevate punished responding in thirsty rats which were shocked for licking metal water spouts. Unlike Miczek (1973a), however, these authors saw no changes in punished responding after the administration of various stimulants (*d*-amphetamine and magnesium pemoline) or scopolamine hydrobromide. It is possible that differences in shock intensity and species may account for these divergent results.

Most of the reports mentioned above that have studied conflict behavior have employed multiple schedules that maintain base-line behavior by means of variable-interval schedules of reinforcement. Some investigators, however, have explored the effects of drugs upon punished behavior maintained by fixed-ratio schedules of reinforcement. Hill (1974) trained rats on a fixed-ratio 50 schedule of liquid food reinforcement. During the pauses that normally occur after each reinforcement, a clicker sounded signaling "conflict" periods. A shock was then delivered upon the first response that terminated the pause and initiated the next response period. The effect of this punishment procedure was to lengthen the duration of conflict pauses. Drugs that were able to reliably decrease conflict pauses at low doses included chlordiazepoxide, diazepam, phenobarbital, and meprobamate. Agents that reliably increased pause duration included *d*-amphetamine and imipramine. Standard neuroleptics were essentially inactive in altering pause duration, although they did appreciably reduce overall response rates. In contrast to Hill's use of a simple schedule, Hanson *et al.* (1967) utilized a multiple schedule to analyze various drug effects on fixed-ratio behavior. In the first component, behavior was maintained by a variable-interval 1-min schedule of liquid food reinforcement. The second component presented a concurrent schedule in which every tenth response was reinforced by food while every fifteenth response on average was followed by shock. The third component presented a neutral stimulus in the presence of which responses were neither reinforced nor shocked. Pentobarbital, chlordiazepoxide, and meprobamate increased responding in all three components. Chlorpromazine, *d*-amphetamine, and scopolamine decreased variable-interval performance but had little effect upon punished responding. Thus, typical anxiolytic agents are able to disinhibit punished behavior that is maintained by fixed-ratio schedules as well as behavior maintained by variable-interval and continuous reinforcement schedules.

Although most of the studies that have explored the effects of anxiolytic drugs upon punished behavior have used rats and pigeons, several reports in the literature suggest that the disinhibiting effects of these compounds can be generalized to other species. Dantzer and Baldwin (1974) and Dantzer and Roca (1974) have noted that pigs subjected to a modified Geller conflict procedure demonstrated enhanced punished response rates after the administration of chlordiazepoxide or diazepam. Although both these drugs were active, diazepam appeared to be much more potent in elevating punished responding than was chlordiazepoxide (Dantzer and Roca, 1974). Thus, anxiolytic drugs are capable of disinhibiting behavior that has been suppressed by punishment in a variety of animal species.

Since the typical conflict–punishment procedures appear to be especially sensitive to drugs that have been classified as anxiolytics because of their activity in clinical settings, several laboratories have attempted to use these techniques to identify new anxiolytic drugs. The β-adrenergic blocking agent, propranolol, drew interest recently as one such possible compound because of preliminary clinical data (Suzmann, 1971; Wheatley, 1969), which suggested that this drug might have anxiolytic properties. Several investigators (Sepinwall *et al.*, 1973; Robichaud *et al.*, 1973; McMillan, 1973b) thus decided to explore propranolol's effects on punished behavior and compare it with the standard anxiolytics to see if the behavioral profiles of these drugs were similar. In one report (Robichaud *et al.*, 1973) a typical Geller conflict procedure was used. Chlordiazepoxide, as expected, elevated the level of both punished and unpunished responding, while propranolol had no effect on either component. Similar negative effects were noted when propranolol was tested in rats subjected to a multiple variable-interval 30-sec, fixed-ratio 10 (food and shock) schedule of reinforcement (Sepinwall *et al.*, 1973), or pigeons subjected to a multiple fixed-ratio 30, fixed-interval 5-min (with every response punished) schedule (McMillan, 1973b). It thus appears that propranolol is not able to increase the level of punished responding generated by a variety of punishment schedules. Another compound that has stirred interest recently because of its possible anxiolytic properties is Δ^9-tetrahydrocannabinol (Δ^9-THC), the active constituent of marijuana (Kubena and Barry, 1970). McMillan (1973a) studied the effects of both Δ^9-THC and Δ^8-THC upon the behavior of pigeons subjected to a multiple fixed-interval 5-min, fixed-interval 5-min schedule in which all responses in one component were punished with electric shocks. Both compounds produced only decreased rates of responding under both punishment and nonpunishment components, suggesting a behavioral profile that is distinctly different from standard anxiolytic drugs (McMillan, 1973a).

Other compounds that have been tested in conflict–punishment paradigms include the antidepressant imipramine, and the cholinergic stimulant nicotine. Wuttke and Kelleher (1970) investigated the effects of imipramine with two separate groups of pigeons responding under either a fixed-interval 5-min schedule or a fixed-interval 5-min schedule of food reinforcement in which every thirtieth response was shocked. The benzodiazepines chlordiazepoxide, diazepam, and nitrazepam greatly enhanced response rates under the punishment schedule, while elevating rates only slightly in the unpunished group. Imipramine (0.3–5.6 mg/kg), on the other hand, increased rates of responding in the unpunished schedule while decreasing rates in the punished group. Similar results were reported by Morse (1964), who utilized a multiple variable-interval schedule with pigeons. During one component of the multiple schedule, animals received shock after every response that was emitted. Under these conditions, imipramine (0.3–10 mg) decreased the rates of punished responding under all doses while reducing unpunished behavior only under the higher dosages. In agreement with these results, Hill (1974) has noted that imipramine increased the length of conflict pauses, recorded during a punished fixed-ratio schedule of reinforcement. Nicotine produced effects that were similar, in direction, to that of imipramine when tested in a typical Geller conflict paradigm. Nicotine and *d*-amphetamine enhanced the suppression of response rate produced by punishment, while chlordiazepoxide had opposite effects (Morrison, 1969). It thus appears that both imipramine and nicotine tend to enhance the suppressive effects of shock-induced punishment.

Much of the drug data reviewed above concerning the conflict–punishment procedure is consistent in showing that compounds with sedative, anticonvulsant, and/or anxiolytic activity enhance behavior suppressed by punishment. The data concerning compounds that are inactive, however, are not as clear-cut. Although some reports indicate that stimulants such as amphetamine (Geller and Seifter, 1960; McMillan and Leander, 1975; Hill, 1974; Morrison, 1969; Vogel *et al.*, 1971) and magnesium pemoline (Vogel *et al.*, 1971) do not enhance punished responding, other reports indicate that under certain conditions *d*-amphetamine (Miczek, 1973a; Foree *et al.*, 1973; McKearney and Barrett, 1975) and caffeine (Morrison, 1969) can reliably increase the rate of punished responding. Furthermore, conflicting results are reported with regard to the effects of various neuroleptics on punished responding. Both chlorpromazine (Geller *et al.*, 1962; McMillan and Leander, 1975; Morse, 1964; Hill, 1974; Hanson *et al.*, 1967) and trifluoperazine (Geller and Seifter, 1960) have been reported to be ineffective in releasing behavior suppressed by punishment. Two separate studies, however, indicate that chlorpromazine (Dinsmoor and Lyon, 1961) and trifluoperazine (Cook and Davidson, 1973) can significantly elevate punished responding in a Geller conflict or multiple variable-interval 30-sec fixed-ratio 10 punishment schedule. Thus, even a rather cursory review of the pertinent literature indicates that punished behavior may not be an unitary phenomenon upon which drugs can exert similar effects regardless of the experimental conditions under which the behavior was generated.

2.3. Review of Drug Effects upon a Standard Conflict–Punishment Paradigm

It is generally accepted that conflicting drug results can often be accounted for by differences in schedule parameters, training procedures, environmental variables, and the species employed. It is thus extremely valuable when one laboratory standardizes experimental procedures and evaluates a large number of compounds using the same behavioral schedule. For those interested in the effects of behavior suppressed by punishment, it is indeed fortunate that Cook and Davidson (1973) have presented data on a wide variety of compounds utilizing a standardized punishment paradigm. These authors trained rats to lever-press for food pellets on a multiple variable-interval 30-sec fixed-ratio 10 schedule of reinforcement. The variable-interval schedule was in force for 5 min followed by the fixed-ratio component for 2 min. Daily experimental sessions consisted of seven periods of the interval component and six periods of the ratio component. After stable base-line performance was obtained, a punishment contingency was added to the fixed-ratio schedule so that animals received a shock as well as a food pellet after every tenth response. A discriminative stimulus was available during each component of the multiple schedule to indicate to the animal that the reinforcement contingencies had been altered. A continuously illuminated stimulus light was presented during the variable-interval component, while a flashing light was presented during the fixed-ratio punishment component of the multiple schedule. This punishment contingency (shock ranging from 0.8 to 2.5 mA) did not substantially affect variable-interval rates, but did significantly suppress response rates during the fixed-ratio component of the schedule.

Figure 2 shows the effects of the punishment contingency on behavior generated in both components of the multiple schedule. The rats normally responded at a fairly high rate during the variable-interval 30-sec schedule, and at even higher rates during the fixed-ratio 10 component when shock was not presented (first panel of Figure 2). The introduction of grid shock, however, in the fixed-ratio component severely reduced the level of fixed-ratio responding, as seen in the second panel of Figure 2, without substantially altering variable-interval rates. The final panel in Figure 2 represents the effects of 2.2 mg/kg of chlordiazepoxide upon behavior generated under this multiple schedule. As the data indicate, chlordiazepoxide significantly elevated fixed-ratio rates in the punishment component of the schedule without altering variable-interval rates. Thus, animals continued to respond during

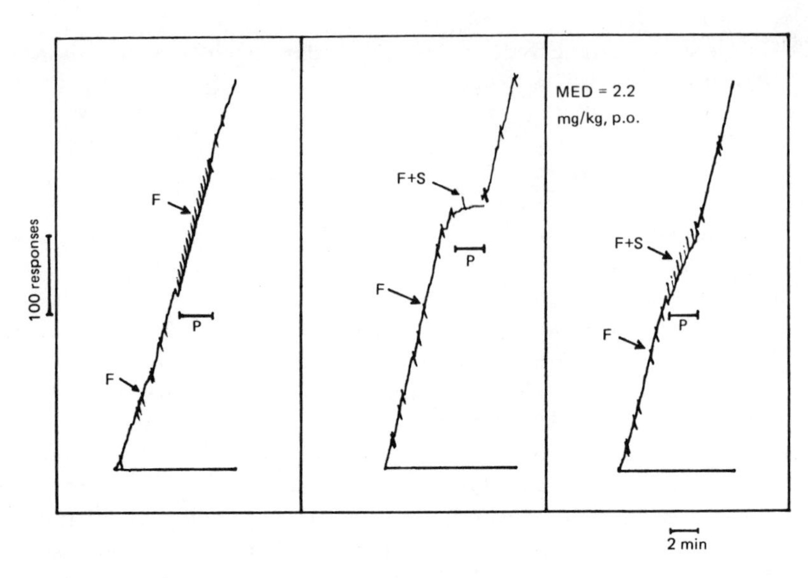

Figure 2. Segments of cumulative response records illustrating response patterns in punished FR 10 component (P) and nonpunished VI 30-sec component. Left panel: high response rate in P before introduction of shock; center panel: suppressed responding in P after introduction of concurrent food and punishing shock (F + S) in absence of drug; right panel: increased responding in P after treatment with chlordiazepoxide. Pen deflections indicate delivery of food (F) in VI 30-sec component and of concurrent F + S in FR 10 component. F = food only, F + S = food and shock, and P = punishment period. [From Cook and Davidson (1973).]

the fixed-ratio component at high rates even though they were receiving substantial numbers of shocks.

Many different drugs were tested using the behavioral schedule above to determine which class of drugs would be most effective in disinhibiting behavior suppressed by punishment. Table I summarizes the results of this work. Effective drugs were those that produced significant enhancement of the suppressed behavior at more than one dose. Ineffective agents included those that did not alter suppressed behavior or did so at only one dose. The effective compounds include the benzodiazepines, which were rank-ordered according to potency as follows: diazepam > oxazepam > chlordiazepoxide. It should be noted that this rank order is identical to the one reported by Geller (1964). In addition to these agents, other compounds that have been used as anxiolytics in a clinical setting were effective in elevating punished responding. The only neuroleptic found to be effective in this procedure was trifluoperazine. Inactive compounds included the stimulant *d*-amphetamine, the neuroleptics chlorpromazine and haloperidol, the narcotic analgesic morphine, and the antidepressant imipramine. Since this work is the only summary available that compared various drugs over a wide dose range in an identical punishment schedule in the same species, it probably provides the best data base upon which various drugs can be compared with respect to their ability to disinhibit punished behavior. Thus, the results in Table I strongly suggest that compounds with anxiolytic, sedative, or anticonvulsant properties selectively release behavior suppressed by response-dependent electric shock. Stimulants such as *d*-amphetamine and the neuroleptics chlorpromazine and haloperidol do not have such selective activity.

In support of the conclusions above, Babbini *et al.* (1975) have correlated the results obtained with the Geller conflict procedure with

Table I. Activity of Behaviorally Active Compounds[a]

Compound	Punishment M.E.D. (mg/kg, P.O.)	Relative potency
Effective compounds		
Chlordiazepoxide	2.2	1
Oxazepam	1.25	1.8
Diazepam	0.625	3.5
Tybamate	80	0.03
Meprobamate	62.5	0.04
Amobarbital	5	0.4
Phenobarbital	4.5	0.5
Methaqualone	10	0.2
Ethanol	1000	—
Phencyclidine	4.4	0.5
Benactyzine	4.5	0.5
Trifluoperazine	0.165	13.0
	Range of doses tested (mg/kg, P.O.)	
Ineffective compounds		
Iproniazide	20–120	
Imipramine	0.55–17.7	
Morphine	0.24– 7.5 (i.p.)	
Haloperidol	0.03– 0.48	
Diphenhydramine	0.55–17.5	
d-Amphetamine	0.18– 1.5	
Chlorpromazine	0.27–17.9	

[a]M.E.D. indicates lowest dose tested which significantly ($p<0.05$) attenuated effects of punishment. Potency was calculated relative to chlordiazepoxide. Within the range of doses shown for ineffective compounds, no consistent attenuation of the effects of punishment was measured. Doses are expressed as free base.
Source: Cook and Davidson (1973).

Table II. Comparison of Clinical Potency with Rat Test Results[a]

	Rat conflict			Clinical psychoneurotics		
Compound	M.E.D. (mg/kg, P.O.)	Relative potency	Rank order	Average daily dose (mg), oral	Comparative studies, relative potency	Rank order
Diazepam	0.63	3.5	1	20	2	1
Chlordiazepoxide	2.2	1.0	3	40	1	2
Oxazepam	1.25	1.8	2	49	0.8	3
Phenobarbital	4.5	0.5	4	115	0.3	4
Amobarbital	5.0	0.4	5	175	0.17	5
Meprobamate	62.5	0.04	6	1410	0.03	6

[a] M.E.D. indicates lowest dose tested which significantly ($p < 0.05$) attenuated effects of punishment. Average daily dose (clinical) obtained from 74 published clinical reports. Complete list of references can be obtained from the authors. Relative potency (clinical) based on studies in which drugs were compared directly to chlordiazepoxide.
Source: Cook and Davidson (1973).

other pharmacological tests (motor activity, inhibition of metrazol-induced seizures, electroencephalographic studies) used to detect anxiolytic activity. They conclude that the conflict procedure correlates very well with these other tests, indicating that the technique can be used as a specific test for the detection of anxiolytic activity.

Although the data above are quite convincing, the best evidence to support the specificity of a pharmacological procedure is how well its results correlate with clinical activity in man (Hill and Tedeschi, 1971). Cook and Davidson (1973) have provided such information comparing the relative drug potencies obtained in their conflict–punishment procedure with clinical potencies in man. Table II presents these comparisons. As is clearly evident from this table, the rat punishment procedure is able to reliably predict clinical potency in man. These correlations, along with all the behavioral data reviewed above, strongly suggest that the conflict–punishment procedure may be sensitive to the anxiolytic properties of drugs. This conclusion, in turn, provides evidence for the motivational hypothesis mentioned in the introduction of this chapter. If punishment does indeed enhance levels of anxiety, reductions in the levels of motivation should release behavior that has been suppressed by aversive events. Unfortunately, this rather simplistic analysis is complicated by the fact that explanations other than a drug-induced reduction in motivation can often account for a compound's effects on punished behavior. In addition, several drugs which are not clinically active as anxiolytics are able to reliably disinhibit punished behavior. It is to these problems that we will now turn our attention.

2.4. Analysis of the Mechanisms by Which Drugs May Affect Punished Responding

There have been a number of mechanisms proposed by various investigators which could account for a drug's effects upon the conflict–punishment paradigm. We will review each possibility citing the pertinent drug literature that bears upon each issue.

2.4.1. Weakening of the Behavioral Control of the Stimulus Associated with Punishment

If a drug was able to impair the effectiveness of the discriminative stimulus which signals onset of the punishment component of the multiple schedule, animals might continue to respond as if they were still performing under the nonpunished portion of the conflict schedule. Thus, a drug might appear to enhance responding suppressed by punishment by merely removing the effectiveness of the discriminative stimulus. To explore whether or not this was the mechanism by which active compounds enhanced punished responding, Cook and Davidson (1973) turned off the stimulus light which acted as the discriminative stimulus for the two components of the multiple conflict–punishment schedule. Figure 3 presents a cumulative record of the behavior that was generated when an animal was subjected to this schedule without the presence of a discriminative stimulus to differentiate the two separate components. Without an external signal, this animal continued to respond during the first fixed-ratio punishment component as if it were still under the variable-interval 30-sec schedule. After the emission of the first 10 responses and subsequent shock (A), however, this animal abruptly ceased responding for a period of time, followed by a brief probe (emission of a few responses, B), and an even longer pause that extended beyond the fixed-ratio component. The next response occurred in the variable-interval component and produced a food pellet (C) which was unaccompanied by shock. This reinforcement produced a progressive return to base-line variable-interval rates until the next shock occurred in the subsequent fixed-ratio component (D). Similar effects were noted throughout the remainder of the session. Response probes were emitted to determine which component the animal was in, followed by pauses if shock was delivered, or more vigorous responding if shock did not accompany the delivery of food pellets (E). After

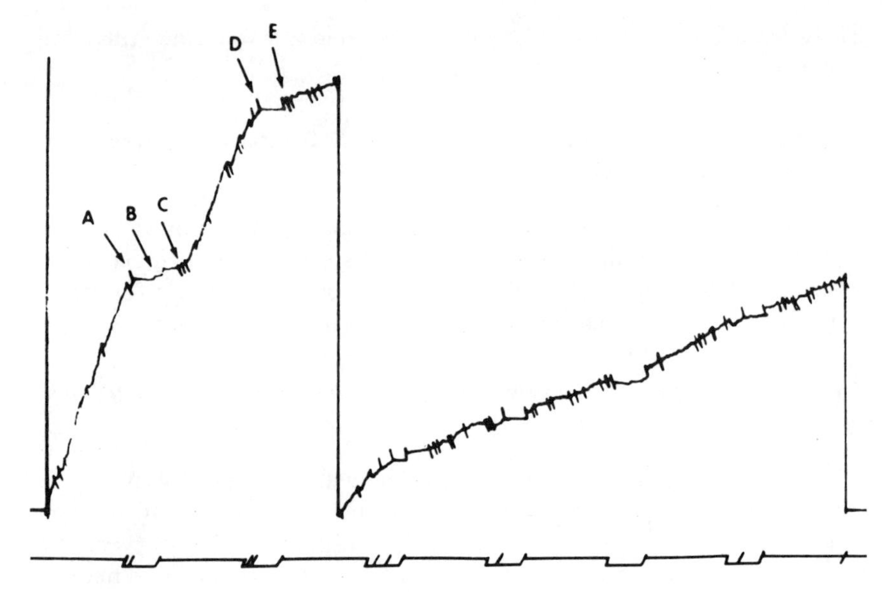

Figure 3. Cumulative response recording of complete session in the absence of the discriminative stimuli used to differentiate punishment and nonpunishment components. On the upper (response) tracing, and on the bottom (event) tracing, punishment components are shown by the pen offset downward and concurrent deliveries of food and shock by brief upward deflections. Delivery of food only (during nonpunished components) is shown by brief downward deflections on response tracing; response tracing automatically resets after cumulation of 500 responses. [From Cook and Davidson (1973).]

the second fixed-ratio component, the unpredictability of the situation led to rather severe decrements in variable-interval responding (beginning at E in Figure 3). The data in Figure 3 clearly indicate that the removal of the discriminative stimulus produces a pattern of behavior that is distinctly different from that seen when an active compound such as chlordiazepoxide (e.g., Figure 2) is administered to rats. Chlordiazepoxide produced consistent responding during the fixed-ratio component of the multiple schedule without substantially affecting variable-interval performance. Thus, it would appear that active compounds do not produce their effects by removing behavior from the control of a discriminative stimulus. Support for this conclusion is also available from the work of Morse (1964), who noted that amobarbital was able to enhance punished responding as effectively in a simple one-component schedule (with no discriminative stimulus) as in a two-component schedule that utilized such a stimulus.

2.4.2. *Increased Hunger or Thirst Motivation*

Another possible mechanism through which drugs might affect punished behavior is by influencing the level of appetitive motivation that energizes the ongoing operant response. Thus, if an animal is more hungry or thirsty under drug conditions, it might be more likely to accept greater levels of punishment (i.e., shocks) in order to gain access to food or water rewards. In an attempt to explore this possibility, several investigators have systematically increased the levels of deprivation for water (Margules and Stein, 1967) and food (Margules and Stein, 1967; Cook and Davidson, 1973) to see how this manipulation affects punished responding. In both cases increasing the level of deprivation had only slight facilitatory effects upon punished response rates. In neither case did the elevations in punished responding after increased deprivation approach that seen when anxiolytic drugs (oxazepam or chlordiazepoxide) were administered. It thus appears that compounds that are active in the conflict–punishment paradigm are probably not producing their effects by enhancing levels of appetitive motivation.

2.4.3. *Drug-Induced Analgesia*

Whenever a drug modifies behavior that is associated with the presentation of electric shock, one must entertain the possibility that the drug has indirectly affected behavior by modifying the aversive qualities of the shock. In the present case, it is possible that active compounds in the conflict procedure are able to elevate punished responding by producing analgesia. Geller *et al.* (1963) have suggested that since their data indicate that morphine does not elevate punished responding in the conflict procedure, drug-induced analgesia cannot account for the positive results noted with other drugs. Conflicting evidence, however, with regard to morphine's effects on punished responding has been reported by other laboratories. Leaf and Muller (1965) have noted that morphine increased the number of shock-punished licking responses made by rats. Furthermore, McMillan (1973a) has indicated that morphine was able to elevate the number of punished responses emitted by pigeons subjected to a multiple fixed-interval 5-min fixed-interval 5-min schedule in which all responses were punished in one component.

Since the data with regard to morphine's effects on punished behavior are unclear at the present time, they cannot be used as evidence in determining whether drug-induced analgesia is a mechanism whereby active compounds release behavior suppressed by punishment. More definitive evidence has been obtained by various investigators, who have compared behavior after drug administration with that generated when animals perform under a conflict–punishment paradigm in which all shocks are omitted. Cook and Davidson (1973) trained animals to respond under a multiple variable-interval 30-sec fixed-ratio 10 punishment schedule and then turned off the shock generator to see what effect this manipulation would have on behavior. Figure 4 presents the results of this experiment. Responding during the fixed-ratio punishment component of the schedule gradually increased over a period of six sessions, where it remained for the entire 19 sessions. Upon reinstatement of the shock contingency punished responding fell to control levels. It should be noted that fixed-ratio rates during the first day of shock removal were only about 50% of that noted after chlordiazepoxide administration in animals who were receiving shock. Thus, the total elimination of shock was only half as effective as chlordiazepoxide in elevating the level of punished responding. Another full day of experience without shock was necessary to

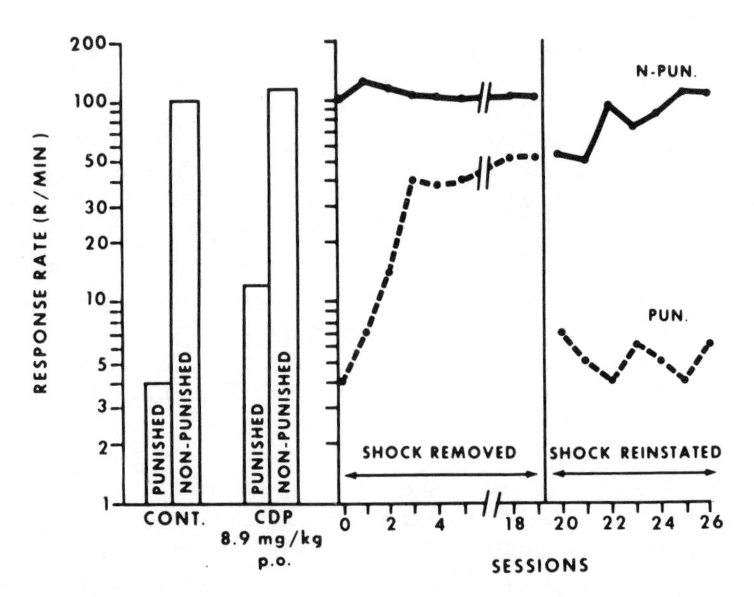

Figure 4. Representative effect of discontinuation of shock punishment. Response rate shown on ordinate; control (cont.) rates and rates after chlordiazepoxide (CDP) treatment shown in histograms on left. Effects of shock removal for 19 consecutive sessions and of reinstatement of shock before the twentieth session shown in right panels (broken line, punished responding; solid line, nonpunished responding). [From Cook and Davidson (1973).]

produce comparable fixed-ratio rates. The fact that the immediate and total removal of the shock contingency fails to mimic the intensity of drug effects during the first session has led Cook and Davidson (1973) to conclude that active compounds probably do not elevate punished responding by an analgesic action. Similar conclusions were reached by Margules and Stein (1967) and Kelleher and Morse (1964), who likewise noted that the removal of shock from conflict procedures elevates punished responding in a gradual fashion, while active drugs do so immediately. Thus, even if a drug produced total analgesia so that the shock was not perceived, it should elevate suppressed response rates only gradually. The consistency of the results above obtained from various laboratories strongly indicates that compounds that elevate punished responding probably do not produce this effect through an analgesic mechanism of action.

2.4.4. *Effects of Shock Intensity and Frequency*

Up to this point, we have discussed possible explanations as to how drugs may act to elevate punished responding and have found them unconvincing. Apparently, drugs that are active in the conflict procedure do not reduce the effectiveness of the discriminative stimuli, increase appetitive motivation, or produce analgesia. There is rather compelling evidence, however, that altering various schedule parameters, including shock intensity and frequency, may substantially affect the manner in which drugs alter punished responding.

McMillan and his colleagues (McMillan, 1973c; Foree *et al.,* 1973) have conducted a series of experiments which analyzed the effects of shock intensity as a determinant of drug effects. These investigators trained pigeons to peck at a response key to obtain food reward under a multiple fixed-interval 5-min fixed-ratio 30 schedule of reinforcement. After behavior was stabilized under this schedule, the punishment contingency was introduced so that all responses under both components produced electric shocks. The general procedure was to punish all responding at a given shock intensity until behavior was stabilized; then several drug dosages were administered to ascertain the effects of various drugs upon behavior suppressed by a particular shock intensity. Subsequent to these tests the shock intensity was changed, behavior stabilized, and the same drugs were retested. In this manner an accurate assessment of drug effects on behavior suppressed by different shock intensities could be determined. The drugs assayed in this procedure included diazepam, pentobarbital, morphine, chlorpromazine, and *d*-amphetamine. As would be expected, the degree of behavioral suppression noted under this punishment schedule was directly related to shock intensity with the lower intensity (2.5 mA) producing less suppression than the higher ones (4.3, 5.2 mA). Diazepam had little effect on overall rate of punished responding when behavior was punished with 2.5 mA of shock. When responding was more markedly suppressed with the two higher intensities, however, diazepam greatly enhanced punished response rates. In addition, this compound increased responding suppressed by 4.3 mA considerably more than rates suppressed by 5.2 mA. Similar results were noted with various doses of pentobarbital. The relatively high control rates of punished responding under the low shock intensity were not affected by small doses of pentobarbital (3 and 10 mg/kg), while a larger dose (17.5 mg/kg) reduced rates. Pentobarbital, however, did increase punished responding when behavior was suppressed by the two higher shock intensities. Morphine, on the other hand, did not increase the rate of punished responding under any of the shock intensities or doses (0.03, 1.0, 3.0 mg/kg) that were utilized. Chlorpromazine increased punished responding only when the shock intensity suppressed responding greatly and when the dose of the drug was high (30 mg/kg). Finally, *d*-amphetamine did not elevate punished responding under either schedule component at any dose or shock intensity. These results thus confirm earlier reports cited above (Geller and Seifter, 1960; Hanson *et al.*, 1967; Morrison, 1969), which indicate that amphetamine does not enhance punished responding. An analysis of local rates of responding, however, indicated that although overall rates were unaffected, *d*-amphetamine enhanced punished responding during the initial segments of the fixed interval when rates were low under the low shock intensity. The data above thus clearly indicate that changes in shock intensity can affect the manner in which drugs affect punished responding.

In a separate experiment, Foree *et al.* (1973) indicated that shock frequency is also an important variable in determining drug effects. Pigeons were trained to respond under a multiple fixed-interval 5-min fixed-interval 5-min schedule in which two different punishment contingencies were in effect. During one component of the schedule, animals were punished (2.5 mA) for every response, while in the other component every thirtieth response was punished (2.5 mA). Responding was suppressed to a greater degree under the continuous-reinforcement component than under the fixed-ratio schedule. *d*-Amphetamine generally decreased overall fixed-interval rates in a dose-dependent manner in both punishment components of the multiple schedule. Analysis of local rates, however, again indicated that *d*-amphetamine was able to increase punished responding when rates were low and when shock was presented intermittently. Thus, shock frequency as well as intensity can modify the manner in which a drug will affect punished responding.

The results above are important in that they allow one to reconcile some of the conflicting data, reviewed above, on the effects of drugs upon punished responding. Several experiments previously mentioned (Geller and Seifter, 1960; Hanson *et al.,* 1967; Morrison, 1969) have demonstrated that amphetamine was not able to elevate punished responding. Both Geller and Seifter (1960) and Hanson *et al.* (1967) used relatively severe levels of punishment that greatly suppressed responding. Under these conditions amphetamine's rate-increasing effects would not be evident. Morrison (1969), on the other hand, used both mild and severe shock intensities for various animals subjected to a Geller conflict procedure. Interestingly enough, a careful analysis of Morrison's data indicates that animals who were administered amphetamine (0.4 mg/kg) under low shock conditions showed increases in punished responding, while the same dose decreased rates at higher intensities. Since most of Morrison's (1969) rats were subjected to high shock intensities, the majority of the animals demonstrated reductions in punished responding after amphetamine administration. Finally, the fact that McMillan (1973c) demonstrated that chlorpromazine could elevate punished responding under certain conditions helps to explain the divergent results of Dinsmoor and Lyon (1961). As we noted in our review of the punishment literature, most reports indicate that chlorpromazine does not elevate punished responding (Cook and Davidson, 1973; Geller *et al.,* 1962; McMillan and Leander, 1975; Morse, 1964; Hanson *et al.,* 1967; Margules and Stein, 1967). The one exception to this finding was noted by Dinsmoor and Lyon (1961), who reported increases in punished responding after the administration of chlorpromazine in rats. These authors noted this facilitatory effect, however, only when severe intensities of shock were employed and when high doses (2.0–4.0 mg/kg) were tested. These findings were replicated by McMillan (1973c) and thus support the notion that shock intensity can determine the manner in which a drug will affect punished responding.

It may appear somewhat surprising that drug-induced analgesia cannot account for drug effects on punished behavior, while shock intensity and frequency can influence this behavior. This apparent inconsistency can be more clearly understood when it is remembered that shock intensity and frequency determine the degree to which punished behavior is suppressed. Control rates of punished responding, in turn, are an important variable in determining the effect that a drug will exert on behavior suppressed by punishment. It is to this variable that we will now turn our attention.

2.4.5. Effects of Predrug Control Rate

Dews (1958) was one of the first to note that an animal's base-line control rate of responding was an important determinant of a drug's effect upon behavior. He noted that appropriate doses of amphetamine increase low rates and decrease high rates of responding generated under different schedules of reinforcement. Since that time many other studies have corroborated this finding with regard to the amphetamines (McMillan, 1968, 1969; Clark and Steele, 1966; Smith, 1964), as well as other drugs, including the barbiturates (Rutledge and Kelleher, 1965; Dews, 1955, 1964), meprobamate (Cook and Kelleher, 1962; Kelleher *et al.*, 1961; Cook and Catania, 1964), and the benzodiazepines (Richelle *et al.*, 1962; Cook and Kelleher, 1962; Cook and Catania, 1964). Since all the conflict–punishment procedures by their very nature produce low base-line rates, it is possible that the increased rates noted after the administration of active compounds merely represent a further demonstration of the rate-dependency principle.

In an attempt to further explore the possibility described above, several investigators have equated base-line control rates under both punished and unpunished schedules of reinforcement to see if various drugs specifically disinhibit punished responding or merely produce a generalized elevation of low base-line rates irrespective of how they are generated. A detailed discussion of this work is presented in Chapter 1. For the present purposes we can simply summarize by saying that both factors appear to be involved when various drugs are administered to animals subjected to conflict–punishment procedures. Evidence supplied by Wuttke and Kelleher (1970) suggested that the benzodiazepines produced equivalent elevations in both punished and unpunished response rates. On the other hand, Cook and Catania (1964) reported that the anxiolytic drugs meprobamate and chlordiazepoxide increased response rate to a greater degree under a punishment component than under an unpunished component of a multiple schedule. These conflicting results have been brought into perspective by McMillan (1973a), however, who demonstrated that rate-dependent drug effects are noted in punishment procedures but that these effects are accompanied by specific drug-related activity. This author noted that many different types of drugs produce rate-dependent effects by increasing low rates of both punished and unpunished responding, while increasing higher rates less or decreasing them. Anxiolytic drugs such as pentobarbital, diazepam, and chlordiazepoxide, however, increased low rates of punished responding to a greater degree than matched rates of unpunished responding. Thus, these data seem to indicate that the effects of specific classes of drugs upon punished responding cannot be accounted for solely in terms of a rate-dependent hypothesis. Anxiolytic drugs appear to increase low rates of punished behavior to a greater extent than comparable rates of unpunished behavior. It should be clear from the analysis above, however, that the rate-dependency hypothesis does appear to account for a portion of the drug effects noted in punishment paradigms and thus should be considered as an important contributing factor in determining how a drug will affect behavior under aversive control.

2.4.6. Effects of Other Experimental Variables

There are several other experimental variables not previously mentioned that can influence the manner in which a drug will alter punished responding (see Chapter 1 for a more detailed discussion of these variables). These factors include the schedule of positive reinforcement utilized, the dose of the drug administered, the behavioral context in which the punished response occurs, as well as the type of event that maintains ongoing behavior. McMillan and his colleagues (McMillan, 1973c; Foree *et al.,* 1973) have demonstrated that both pentobarbital and *d*-amphetamine affect the rate of punished responding differently, depending on whether the behavior was maintained on a fixed-ratio or fixed-interval schedule of reinforcement. Therefore, it appears that the schedule of positive reinforcement can influence the effects that drugs will exert on punished responding. Likewise, the dose can also alter the intensity of a drug's effect on punished responding (Foree *et al.,* 1973) or even alter the direction of the behavioral effect (Miczek, 1973a). Thus, amphetamine can increase or decrease punished responding, depending on the dose administered (Miczek, 1973). In addition to the above-mentioned factors, McKearney and Barrett (1975) have provided evidence which indicates that the effects of drugs on punished responding can be dramatically altered by the behavioral context in which the punished behavior occurs.

Finally, in another report, McKearney (1976) has demonstrated that the type of reinforcement that maintains ongoing behavior can alter the way in which a drug affects punished behavior. This author noted that under a typical fixed-interval punishment schedule which utilized food reward, punished responding was significantly elevated by pentobarbital but not by amphetamine. Under a fixed-interval avoidance schedule, however, completely opposite results were noted. Amphetamine elevated punished responding while pentobarbital only decreased responding. Thus, the effects of drugs upon punished responding can be quite different, depending upon whether the behavior is maintained by appetitive or aversive events.

2.4.7. Delayed Development of Anxiolytic Profile

Cook and Sepinwall (1975) have provided evidence which suggests that the benzodiazepines may not produce their anxiolytic effects during initial exposure to the drug. In agreement with the work of Margules and Stein (1968), these authors noted that the benzodiazepines produced increases in punished responding only after the drug had been administered on several occasions. The initial drug experience in both rats and squirrel monkeys produced decrements in unpunished responding with relatively little change noted in punished behavior. Behavioral effects after three separate drug treatments, however, were quite different. Drug-experienced animals demonstrated large increases in punished behavior, while unpunished responding returned to predrug levels. This delayed anxiolytic profile takes place even if the drug treatments are spaced at weekly rather than daily intervals (Cook and Sepinwall, 1975). Furthermore, this process can take place if the drug is administered in the home cage after the conflict-punishment paradigm is completed, provided that the drug is given in sufficiently high doses. If chlordiazepoxide, for example, is administered once in the home cage (160 mg/kg), rats will demonstrate drug-experienced profiles when tested 27 days later in the conflict–punishment paradigm under the drug state (10 mg/kg). This immediate display of the drug-sophisticated profile during the first test session makes it highly unlikely that a drug–behavior interaction is involved in producing the delayed development of the antianxiety effects of the benzodiazepines. These results thus suggest that some sort of physiologic or metabolic change must be occurring in response to drug administration (Cook and Sepinwall, 1975) which influences the type of behavioral effect animals will display during subsequent exposure to the drug.

2.4.8. Conclusions Concerning Mechanisms by Which Drugs May Affect Punished Responding

McMillan (1973a) has pointed out that it may be inappropriate to make the generalization that a particular class of drugs affects all punished responding in a certain way, just as it has been shown to be incorrect to make the generalization that a drug increases the rate of food-reinforced behavior. Such generalizations are inappropriate simply because they fail to take into account the multitude of variables, some of which have been discussed above, that can influence the manner in which a drug will affect punished behavior. Whenever attempts are made to summarize how drugs affect punished responding, care must be taken to delineate the specific conditions under which the behavior is being observed.

With the preceding consideration in mind, several conclusions can be made with respect to the effects of drugs upon conflict–punishment paradigms. Of the many variables discussed above, it would appear that shock intensity, control rate of responding, the type of reinforcer, and the behavioral context in which punishment occurs are the most critical factors that can affect the manner in which a drug will alter punished behavior. The latter two factors are generally of little consequence when the typical Geller conflict or multiple-punishment schedules are used. This is the case since only appetitive reinforcers are used to maintain the ongoing behavior, and the behavioral context remains constant. Thus, if the standard punishment schedules are utilized, similar drug effects will be noted across a wide variety of dose ranges, species, and experimental procedures. The major stumbling block to obtaining consistent results appears to be differences in the level of shock employed and variability in the control rates of responding. Even with these difficulties in mind, however, there appears to be a remarkable consistency in the results obtained from various laboratories concerning the effects of drugs upon punished behavior generated under a variety of multiple schedules. There is general agreement that drugs which possess clinical anxiolytic activity are effective in releasing behavior that has been suppressed by punishment. Other compounds, including antidepressants, stimulants, and most neuroleptics, lack this activity. Furthermore, the ability of anxiolytic drugs to release punished behavior cannot be accounted for solely in terms of a rate-dependent effect (McMillan, 1973a; Cook and Catania, 1964). Thus, anxiolytic drugs appear to exert significant disinhibitory effects on behavior generated under the typical conflict–punishment paradigm.

This disinhibitory effect on punished behavior can also be demonstrated in operant situations that do not use electric shock. For example, Margules and Stein (1967) have demonstrated that the benzodiazepines can disinhibit behavior suppressed by nonreinforcement, aversive brain stimulation, bitter taste, or satiety. Thus, the ability to release behavior that has been suppressed by a variety of aversive events appears to be a general characteristic of anxiolytic compounds. This disinhibition, however, does appear to be relatively specific to behavior suppressed by aversive events and not to behavior suppressed by positive reinforcement. This conclusion rests upon the work of Tang and Kirch (1973), who studied the effects of diazepam on behavior suppressed by food reward in rhesus monkeys. In this study animals were trained to avoid shock on a Sidman avoidance schedule. Alternating with every 8 min of this schedule was a 2-min period signaled by a tone in which every unavoided shock in the Sidman schedule was accompanied by a food pellet. The deprived monkeys suppressed responding during the tone and they therefore obtained free food pellets (though they were accompanied by shock). Diazepam (1, 2, 4 mg/kg) had little effect in restoring the suppressed responding in the majority of animals tested. Thus, the disinhibition of response output produced by anxiolytic drugs can be generalized to behavior suppressed by a variety of aversive events, but not to behavior suppressed by positive reinforcement.

The fact that the conflict–punishment paradigm is sensitive to the anxiolytic properties of drugs makes it an ideal tool with which to explore the mechanism by which these drugs may exert their activity on the brain. Many investigators (Margules and Stein, 1967; Stein *et al.*, 1973; Margules, 1971; Blakely and Parker, 1973; Robichaud and Sledge, 1969; Geller and Hartmann, 1973) have utilized various punishment procedures to evaluate the anxiolytic activity of a variety of compounds that alter synaptic activity within the brain. Since this type of work demonstrates how the conflict–punishment paradigm can be used as a research tool to gather information on how drugs affect behavior, we will briefly summarize some of the literature in this area.

2.5. Effects of Drugs That Alter Synaptic Activity upon Punished Behavior

2.5.1. *Acetylcholine*

Many of the drugs that alter synaptic activity have the distinct disadvantage for the purposes of research of not readily passing through the blood–brain barrier. Thus, if these agents are given systemically, they do not gain access to the central nervous system in sufficient quantity to affect either brain chemistry or behavior. Therefore, it has become standard practice to administer these drugs directly to various brain sites via indwelling cannulae. Since anxiolytic drugs of the benzodiazepine series were known to increase food intake in satiated animals, Margules and Stein (1967) concluded that these compounds may produce their disinhibitory effects on punished behavior through a direct action on the "satiety center" of the hypothalamus (i.e., the ventromedial nucleus). They therefore implanted cannulae into the ventromedial nucleus of rats who had been trained to respond under a Geller conflict procedure, and proceeded to test the effects of various cholinergic drugs. Direct application of carbachol, a cholinergic stimulant, physostigmine, an anticholinesterase, or acetylcholine plus physostigmine to the ventromedial nucleus generally enhanced the suppressive effects of punishment in the conflict procedure (Margules and Stein, 1967). Contrasting effects were noted when the anticholinergic atropine methyl nitrate was administered to the same site. Application of this compound had a strong disinhibitory effect upon punished responding. Evidence linking the activity of anxiolytic drugs to the effects above was obtained when it was noted that systemic administration of oxazepam could block the suppressant effects of carbachol and physostigmine upon punished responding. Thus, the evidence above was used to suggest that the ventromedial nucleus exerts an inhibitory influence over punished responding as measured in the Geller conflict procedure (Margules and Stein, 1967). Furthermore, this inhibitory control appeared to be mediated through a cholinergic mechanism, since cholinergic stimulation suppressed punished responding, while cholinergic blockade induced by anticholinergics or lesions released behavior suppressed by punishment. Finally, it was suggested that the benzodiazepines might produce their anxiolytic activity by blocking the normal function of this inhibitory cholinergic system.

Evidence which supports the conclusions above has been provided by Sepinwall and Grodsky (1969). They trained rats to respond on two levers under a discrete-trial conflict procedure. During this schedule animals were reinforced with a food pellet for responding on the right lever during one tone and on the other lever during a second tone. The punishment contingency consisted of punishing 10% of the correct responses made on one of the levers. In agreement with Margules and Stein (1967), application of atropine methyl nitrate to the ventromedial nucleus of the hypothalamus produced significant elevations in punished responding. Carbachol, on the other hand, decreased both punished and unpunished response rates when administered to the ventromedial nucleus, but released punished behavior when injected into the lateral hypothalamus. The general inhibitory effect on all behavior produced when carbachol was given to the ventromedial nucleus casts some doubt upon the assumption that cholinergic stimulation of the ventromedial nucleus produces specific anxiolytic activity. Finally, systemic administration of the anticholinergic, atropine sulfate, only reduced unpunished response rates, while the systemic administration of the cholinergic stimulants pilocarpine and physostigmine produced suppression of both punished and unpunished responding. These results indicate that although cholinergic manipulations do influence the level of punished responding, they do so differentially, depending upon the site to which they are administered.

Finally, in a rather extensive report, Miczek and Grossman (1972) explored the effects of cholinergic drugs upon punished behavior generated under a variety of schedules. They noted that methyl atropine applied to the ventromedial nucleus of monkeys produced increases in both punished and unpunished responding under a Geller conflict procedure. Methyl atropine and neostigmine, an anticholinesterase agent, also enhanced or reduced punished responding, respectively, in a multiple variable-interval 45-sec fixed-ratio 12 punishment schedule, but these effects were much smaller than those noted during the Geller conflict procedure. These results indicate that the effects of cholinergic compounds applied to the ventromedial nucleus may not directly affect punished behavior and may, in fact, produce effects that are situation-specific. As further evidence of this lack of specificity, atropine methyl nitrate applied to the ventromedial nucleus of monkeys led to reliable decreases in drinking that was punished by electric shock (Miczek and Grossman, 1972). The data above thus strongly suggest that cholinergic compounds given either systemically or intracranially do not appear to specificially affect punished responding in a variety of behavioral test situations. Finally, the fact that both atropine methyl nitrate and carbachol administered to the ventromedial nucleus are known to reduce unpunished food and water intake in the monkey may account, at least in part, for some of the behavioral effects noted when these drugs are studied in the conflict procedure.

2.5.2. Norepinephrine

Most of the work to be reviewed concerning the effects of drugs that affect adrenergic (i.e., norepinephrine—NE) activity has been carried out by Stein and his associates (Stein *et al.*, 1973). These authors administered various adrenergic drugs intraventricularly to rats who were trained to respond under a Geller conflict procedure. They noted that the administration of an α-noradrenergic antagonist, phentolamine, or a β-antagonist, propranolol, produced no reliable elevation in the rate of punished responding emitted during the conflict test. *l*-Norepinephrine, on the other hand, caused large increases in the rate of punished behavior when it was given alone or in conjunction with systemically administered oxazepam. *d*-Norepinephrine and dopamine produced negligible effects. Thus, Stein *et al.* (1973) concluded that anxiolytic drugs probably do not release punished behavior by blocking adrenergic systems in the brain.

Margules (1968, 1971), however, has presented somewhat different results. Direct bilateral placement of *l*-norepinephrine into the amygdala abolished the suppressant effects of punishment in rats responding under a Geller conflict procedure (Margules, 1968). This effect was blocked, however, by pretreating the amygdala bilaterally with the α-antagonist, phentolamine, before the administration of *l*-

norepinephrine. *dl*-Isoproterenol, a β-agonist, on the other hand, intensified the suppressive effects of punishment when it was administered to sites within the amygdala. These results indicated that there are two functionally separate adrenergic systems within the amygdala which modulate punished behavior: α-receptors when activated reduce the suppressive effects of punishment, while β-receptors when stimulated enhance the effects of punishment.

The results reviewed above demonstrate that various adrenergic drugs produce differential effects, depending on where they are administered (i.e., intraventricularly or directly into the amygdala). It is impossible with the limited data that are available to indicate whether adrenergic mechanisms are involved in mediating the suppressive effects of punishment. More information will have to be collected concerning the effects of adrenergic drugs administered to other brain sites upon behavior suppressed by punishment in a number of behavioral paradigms before any definitive conclusions can be drawn.

2.5.3. Serotonin

The final amine system to be reviewed with respect to its relationship with punished responding will be that of 5-hydroxytryptamine, or serotonin. Studies in this area have involved the administration of drugs either systemically or intraventricularly. Several investigators (Geller and Blum, 1970; Robichaud and Sledge, 1969; Geller and Hartmann, 1973) have reported that systemic administration of drugs which block serotonergic activity produced an attenuation of the suppressive effects of punishment. Geller and Blum (1970) reported that para-chlorophenylalanine (PCPA), a drug which depletes endogenous levels of brain serotonin, reliably enhanced the rate of punished responding in rats trained to respond under a Geller conflict procedure. The administration of 5-hydroxytryptophan (5-HTP), a precursor of serotonin, reversed the effects of PCPA and reinstated the typical suppression of response rate noted during punishment. Robichaud and Sledge (1969) obtained similar results with PCPA, noting that punished responding was dramatically elevated at doses which did not affect rates of unpunished responding. Another serotonin antagonist, cinanserin, has also been reported to be effective in attenuating the suppressive effects of punishment as measured in a Geller conflict situation (Geller and Hartmann, 1973) or a multiple-schedule punishment procedure (Cook and Sepinwall, 1975). As is generally the case, however, some negative results are available. Blakely and Parker (1973) have noted that they failed to obtain changes in the rate of punished responding 3 days after the administration of PCPA in rats subjected to a modified Geller conflict paradigm. These negative results are of interest because unlike the studies mentioned above, a measure of brain serotonin levels was obtained for the animals who were administered PCPA. This (Blakely and Parker, 1973) indicated that serotonin levels in the brain were significantly decreased even though no behavioral effects upon punished responding were detected. Thus, it is possible that the behavioral effects noted after the administration of PCPA may be caused by factors other than the depletion of serotonin.

Studies utilizing other types of punishment procedures have also been used to explore the effects of serotonergic drugs upon behavior suppressed by electric shock. Graeff and Schoenfeld (1970) trained pigeons to respond under a multiple schedule which contained fixed-interval 5-min and fixed-ratio 30 food-reinforced components as well as a fixed-interval 5-min schedule for food with a concurrent fixed-ratio 30 schedule for shock. Relatively large increases in punished and unpunished responding were noted after the intramuscular administration of low doses of two serotonin antagonists, methysergide and 2-bromo-D-lysergic acid (BDL). The serotonin agonist, α-methyltryptamine, on the other hand, decreased the level of both punished and unpunished responding. Similar facilitatory effects have been noted with methysergide in rats subjected to a Geller conflict procedure (Stein *et al.,* 1973). The fact that the serotonin antagonists enhance both punished and unpunished response rates suggests that reductions in serotonergic activity may not selectively disinhibit behavior suppressed by punishment. It is possible that the increases seen by various investigators (Geller and Blum, 1970; Geller and Hartmann, 1973; Robichaud and Sledge, 1969; Graeff and Shoenfeld, 1970) in the rates of punished responding may represent a general facilitatory effect on all behaviors. As Blakely and Parker (1973) have pointed out, it is important in studies of this type to compare changes in both unpunished and punished responding (e.g., by means of suppression ratios) to ensure that any elevations in the rate of punished responding are not merely a reflection of a generalized facilitation in all responding.

Direct application of serotonin to the brain via intraventricular cannulae produces a complex triphasic effect upon the behavior of rats in a Geller conflict procedure (Stein and Wise, 1974; Stein *et al.,* 1973). At doses of 5 to 200 μg, an initial phase of intense behavioral suppression lasting approximately 10 min is followed by several hours of normal or facilitatory responding, during which punished behavior is often increased. This period is then followed by an extended interval (i.e., 1–2 days) of behavioral suppression. In an attempt to determine if the anxiolytic oxazepam disinhibited punished behavior by altering serotonergic mechanisms, Stein *et al.* (1973) attempted to block the activity of oxazepam by intraventricular administration of serotonin. In the majority of cases, serotonin was able to block the disinhibiting effects of oxazepam in the Geller conflict procedure when measurements were taken during the initial phase of serotonin's activity (during the first 10 min after administration). In the same animals, intraventricular injection of *l*-norepinephrine increased the antianxiety effect of oxazepam. These results, along with the other data reviewed above, indicate that drugs which alter serotonergic activity can affect the degree of punished responding generated under conflict–punishment paradigms. It is still not clear, however, whether these changes are specific to behavior suppressed by punishment or merely reflect a generalized facilitation of all responding.

2.6. Summary

It is clear that many types of experimental variables can directly influence the manner in which drugs affect punished behavior. If these experimental variables are kept relatively constant, however, as in those studies that have used the Geller conflict procedure, consistent drug results can be obtained. It appears that certain anxiolytic drugs such as meprobamate, the barbiturates, and the benzodiazepines are able to selectively elevate punished responding. Such selective effects may, therefore, allow this behavioral technique to be successfully used as a research tool in exploring the mechanisms by which drugs may produce their anxiolytic effects. To date, several synaptic transmitter systems have been studied to see if alterations in their activity would produce anxiolytic effects in the conflict procedure. Although the data are by no means conclusive, it appears possible that changes in serotonergic activity may alter the suppressive effects of punishment. In any case, the conflict–punishment paradigm does appear to provide a reasonable method for evaluating the anxiolytic properties of drugs.

3. Continuous Avoidance Procedures

One of the most popular tests which incorporates operant technology into the repeated measures design is known as the continuous or Sidman avoidance procedure. Under this schedule, animals are trained to make some type of response (bar press, wheel turn, etc.) which postpones the onset of an electric shock (Sidman, 1953). The period of time between the response and onset of shock is called the response–shock (R–S) interval, while the delay between shocks is known as the shock–shock (S–S) interval. Animals are thus required to make at least one response during the R–S interval to avoid the presentation of the aversive stimulus. If no response occurs, a brief shock is presented at specific intervals (the S–S interval) until the animal emits a response. Behavioral measures taken during this procedure include the number of responses recorded in R–S and S–S intervals, number of shocks received, latency to first response after shock, and response distributions during the R–S interval. The continuous or Sidman avoidance schedule can be subdivided into two distinct categories: nondiscriminated and discriminated avoidance procedures. The nondiscriminated avoidance schedule does not present a discriminative cue to indicate the passage of time, whereas the discriminated procedure does. Animals subjected to a discriminated avoidance schedule are usually presented with a visual or auditory signal to warn them of impending shock. A response during this period terminates the signal and recycles the interval clock to the beginning of the R–S period. Thus, under a discriminated avoidance schedule, any R–S interval consists of a nonsignaled period followed by a signaled period that continues up to and during the presentation of electric shock. In addition to the behavioral measures listed above, the discriminated avoidance procedure allows one to classify avoidance responses made during the R–S interval into those emitted before (i.e., nondiscriminated) or during (i.e., discriminated) the warning stimulus. Furthermore, the latency to first response after onset of the warning stimulus can also be determined. Thus, Sidman avoidance schedules provide several behavioral measures which can be used to detect drug effects.

The avoidance procedures described above have been used extensively to evaluate the behavioral effects of a wide variety of chemical agents. The data from these studies indicate that avoidance techniques have several advantages over other procedures in detecting drug effects. These advantages include stability, sensitivity, and versatility (Heise and Boff, 1962). Variability, especially intrasubject variability, of the Sidman avoidance base line is very low for most species under nodrug conditions. Thus, repeated measures may be taken on a small number of subjects, each animal acting as its own control. This stability in base-line behavior, in turn, ensures that drugs need only to alter avoidance rates slightly to produce significant effects. Thus, continuous avoidance behavior tends to be extremely sensitive to low doses of various drugs. This sensitivity is evident when it is noted that the minimum effective dose of chlorpromazine or *d*-amphetamine necessary to alter Sidman avoidance behavior is generally lower than that required to alter spontaneous motor activity (Heise and Boff, 1962). In addition to stability and sensitivity, these procedures are also versatile in that they allow one to determine peak time, duration of action, dose–

response relationships, and drug interactions, all in the same subject. Finally, as we shall see in our review of the drug literature, continuous avoidance procedures are able to differentiate various classes of drugs according to their behavioral profiles. Thus, as was the case with the conflict–punishment paradigm, avoidance procedures may provide psychopharmacologists with reliable and sensitive techniques that can be used to detect specific drug effects. Before we begin our review of the pertinent drug literature, a brief review of the methodological issues surrounding the use of continuous avoidance procedures is in order.

3.1. Methodological Problems Associated with Continuous Avoidance Procedures

3.1.1. Drug-Induced Analgesia

As was mentioned earlier, drug-induced analgesia is a process that can conceivably influence behavior that is under the control of electric shock. In this regard it has been reported that as shock intensity was augmented under continuous avoidance schedules, escape latency as well as the number of shocks received was decreased, while avoidance rates and resistance to extinction was increased (Boren *et al.,* 1959). These findings suggest that the performance of a continuous avoidance task is enhanced as a function of shock intensity. Furthermore, evidence exists which indicates that drugs can interact with shock intensity to decrease avoidance behavior to varying degrees. Chlorpromazine, for example, produced greater decrements in responding under a discriminated avoidance schedule (Nigro, 1967) when the shock intensity was low (0.5 mA) than when it was more intense (4.0 mA). It therefore seems reasonable to suggest that drugs which decrease shock intensity (via analgesia) might produce decrements in Sidman avoidance performance.

3.1.2. Acquisition of Continuous Avoidance

It is common knowledge among investigators who utilize continuous avoidance procedures that rats are notoriously difficult to train in the bar-press avoidance situation (Paré and Houser, 1973; Bignami and De Acetis, 1973; Bignami and Gatti, 1972; Latz *et al.,* 1969; Myers, 1962; Hoffman *et al.,* 1961; Beaton *et al.,* 1974; Lipper and Kornetsky, 1971). In a typical experiment (Hoffman *et al.,* 1961) up to 45% of the animals tested failed to reach an acceptable behavioral criterion by avoiding 90% of all programmed shocks within 24 1-hr sessions. Many factors have been suggested to account for this low rate of acquisition in the rat, some of which are known to interact with drug effects. One such factor involves the development of "crouching or freezing" behavior after shock administration, which often interferes with the execution of the lever-press response. During training, rats tend to hold the lever in the depressed position for long periods of time, ensuring that a shock will be delivered while the avoidance response is being made. Shock administration, in turn, promotes the development of "freezing" behavior on the lever, which interferes with the rapid acquisition of the lever-press (i.e., a depression and release) response. If another response, such as wheel turning, is substituted for lever pressing, rats generally show enhanced rates of acquisition and performance (Latz *et al.,* 1969; Bravo and Appel, 1967). The introduction of the wheel apparatus which rotates upon contact makes a holding response difficult to execute, thus ensuring that shock will not be delivered when the animal is making the avoidance response. "Freezing" behavior near the wheel is therefore diminished, increasing the probability that the proper behavioral response will be emitted.

The discussion above indicates that the type of behavioral response required by the avoidance schedule can dramatically influence the level of acquisition and performance demonstrated by laboratory rats. Of more importance, however, is the fact that drugs exert differential effects on avoidance behavior generated by schedules that control these different types of responses. Thus, chlorpromazine produces fewer decremental effects on the behavior of rats trained to high levels of performance in a wheel-turning apparatus than in animals trained under the same schedule to avoid shock by pressing a lever (Latz *et al.,* 1969). Thus, at least in rats, the type of avoidance response that is required may influence the degree of drug effect recorded, either directly or by some other means (e.g., by producing different levels of base-line performance).

Other factors known to influence the rate at which rats acquire a continuous avoidance lever-press response include the presence or absence of a response-contingent feedback stimulus, the relative duration of R–S and S–S intervals, and the type of discriminative stimulus presented prior to shock delivery. It has been noted that rats will demonstrate higher avoidance rates and lower shock rates when a feedback light stimulus is presented to indicate the execution of an effective avoidance response (Paré and Houser, 1973). The presence of such a stimulus has been found to affect the degree to which nicotine will affect avoidance behavior (Morrison, 1974a). In addition, continuous avoidance schedules that combine the presence of relatively long (i.e., 20–30 sec) equivalent R–S, S–S intervals with intense shock generally produce low levels of avoidance performance in the rat (Bignami and

De Acetis, 1973; Bignami and Gatti, 1972). Finally, several studies (Latz *et al.*, 1969; Myers, 1962) have indicated that in a discriminated Sidman avoidance procedure, the type of conditioned stimulus that is used can influence the rate of acquisition and performance demonstrated by laboratory rats. A buzzer stimulus produces better avoidance performance than a tone CS even when they are matched for loudness (Myers, 1962).

3.1.3. Good vs. Poor Performance

As we noted earlier in this chapter, base-line rate of response is often an important variable which can influence the type of effect that a drug will exert upon behavior under aversive control. Several studies have reported that rate-dependent drug effects can be demonstrated in rats performing a continuous avoidance response (Takaori *et al.*, 1969; Stone, 1965; Weissman, 1962, 1963). Anxiolytic drugs, for example, decrease the response rate and increase the shock rate of rats which demonstrate good performance base lines (i.e., high response and low shock rates). Animals with poor performance histories, however, show enhanced avoidance behavior after the administration of anxiolytic drugs (Takaori *et al.*, 1969). Neuroleptic agents, on the other hand, produce avoidance decrements in both well and poorly performing rats, while stimulants such as amphetamine and scopolamine produce the opposite effect (Takaori *et al.*, 1969; Stone, 1965). Thus, as is the case with other types of behavior under aversive control, the base-line rate of continuous avoidance responding is a critical factor in determining the type of effect various classes of drugs will produce.

3.1.4. Warm-Up Effect

It has been well documented that rats demonstrate a "warm-up" effect when they are performing a Sidman avoidance task (Morrison, 1974b; Hoffman *et al.*, 1961; Owen and Rathbun, 1967; Paré and Houser, 1973). This effect is characterized by poor avoidance performance early in the session, followed by better performance throughout the latter half of the experimental period. The base-line rate of responding is, therefore, not consistent across a given session even within the same animal. In addition, there is evidence which suggests that poor avoiders demonstrate a greater warm-up effect than good avoiders (Hoffman *et al.*, 1961). Since base-line rate of response (i.e., good vs. poor responders) has been shown to influence the type of effect a drug will exert upon continuous avoidance behavior, it is possible that the warm-up phenomenon could produce differential drug effects within a given session. A particular drug might elevate responding early in the session while decreasing rates in the final segments of the experimental period when control rates are usually high. This tendency to produce differential drug effects might appear to be greater in animals with poor performance histories, since it is these animals that show the greatest degree of warm-up.

3.1.5. Schedule Parameters

Morrison (1974a,b) has provided evidence which suggests that changes in certain schedule parameters can influence the degree to which drugs will affect avoidance behavior. For example, the performance of rats receiving nicotine during training and testing was disrupted when saline was substituted for the drug. When the avoidance schedule contained a discriminative stimulus that preceded each shock, or a feedback signal that followed every response, however, rats trained under nicotine and tested under saline showed no such deficits (Morrison, 1974b). In agreement with these results, Dobrin and Rhyne (1969) have noted that chlorpromazine produces avoidance decrements in animals performing a nondiscriminated Sidman avoidance task in doses that did not affect behavior under the control of a discriminated schedule. Thus, it would appear that avoidance behavior under the control of discriminative stimuli is more resistant to the effects of drugs than behavior that is not controlled by such stimuli. Other changes in schedule parameters, however, do not appear to alter the effects of drugs on avoidance behavior. For example, altering the duration of the warning signal in a discriminated Sidman avoidance schedule does not appear to affect avoidance performance (i.e., response rate or percentage of shocks avoided) nor to alter the effects of chlorpromazine upon behavior (Lipper and Kornetsky, 1971).

3.1.6. Behavioral Context

As was the case with the conflict–punishment paradigm, the effects of drugs upon avoidance responding can be influenced by the context in which the behavior occurs. For example, Fielding and his colleagues (Fielding *et al.*, 1971) have noted that imipramine produced stimulant effects upon the avoidance responding of squirrel monkeys when this behavior was generated by a multiple schedule that contained a fixed-ratio, a punishment, and an avoidance component. When the behavior was generated by a single-component avoidance schedule, however, imipramine produced the opposite results and depressed response rates.

It should be clear from the discussion above that many different methodological problems exist when one attempts to use continuous avoidance procedures to evaluate the behavioral effects of drugs. These problems are particularly noticeable when rats are selected as the experimental subjects. This species is difficult to train and often demonstrates wide intersubject variability as well as intrasubject variability. This differential performance, in turn, establishes a wide range of base-line response rates which can influence the type of effect a drug will exert on behavior. Some of these difficulties can be partially eliminated by various training procedures, which include: providing a feedback cue (Morrison, 1974a; Paré and Houser, 1973), reducing lever holding by disabling the lever during and 0.5 sec after shock (Paré and Houser, 1973), replacing the lever with a wheel manipulandum (Lipper and Kornetsky, 1971), or selecting for drug testing only those animals that reach an acceptable behavioral criterion. Although these procedures are useful in eliminating low rates of performance, wide variability in base-line rates can still occur. Thus, it is often advisable to use other species, such as guinea pigs (Beaton *et al.*, 1974), dogs (Houser and Paré, 1974a,b; Houser *et al.*, 1976), or monkeys (Fielding *et al.*, 1971; Houser, 1976; Houser and Cash, 1975), which tend to acquire the avoidance response more readily than rats. As we review the drug literature to determine how various classes of drugs affect continuous avoidance behavior, the above species-related factors should be kept in mind so that various studies can be evaluated with the proper perspective.

3.2. Analysis of Continuous Avoidance Behavior in Terms of Motivational Processes

Before turning to our review of the literature, some attempt should be made to frame the motivational hypothesis mentioned in the introduction of this chapter in the context of conditioned avoidance. Anger (1963) has proposed that reinforcement in the nondiscriminated avoidance procedure consists of the resetting of an internal clock which he labeled "a conditioned aversive temporal stimulus." The internal temporal stimulus becomes increasingly more aversive as the time interval from the last lever-press response is lengthened, thus enhancing the reinforcing properties of the next response. Since the aversiveness of the temporal stimulus is based upon its association with electric shock presentation, it seems reasonable to assume that this stimulus generates fear or anxiety in animal subjects. Lever-pressing behavior is positively reinforced by resetting the internal clock, thus reducing the level of anxiety engendered by the "conditioned aversive temporal stimulus." According to this hypothesis, then, drugs which possess anxiolytic activity should selectively reduce the anxiety level generated by the internal clock, thus reducing the motivation that underlies the avoidance response. Anxiolytic drugs would therefore be expected to produce decrements in nondiscriminated avoidance performance. Similar theoretical accounts have been offered to explain the maintenance of behavior under the control of a discriminated avoidance schedule. According to these formulations (Dinsmoor *et al.*, 1971) a signal paired with shock should elicit a state of fear or anxiety in an experimental subject which is analogous to clinical anxiety in man. Termination of this signal by a response is assumed to be reinforcing because it relieves the anxiety associated with the aversive stimuli. If these assumptions are valid, it is tempting to conclude that the reasons various compounds affect discriminated avoidance behavior is that they alter the level of motivation (i.e., anxiety) that underlies the avoidance response. We will now review the pertinent literature to determine which classes of drugs reliably alter nondiscriminated and discriminated continuous avoidance behavior. One of the goals of this review is to see if the motivational hypotheses outlined above are able to account for some or all of the data that have been collected on this topic. Prime interest in this regard will center on the effects of clinically active anxiolytic compounds, which should selectively attenuate avoidance behavior if the assumptions of the motivational hypotheses are valid.

3.3. Review of the Drug Literature

3.3.1. Neuroleptics

It has been known for some time that neuroleptic drugs cause a selective depression of discrete shuttlebox avoidance behavior at doses that do not retard escape responding (Cook and Weidley, 1957). Verhave and his colleagues (Verhave *et al.*, 1958) have demonstrated similar effects using a continuous discriminated avoidance procedure in which rats were required to turn a wheel manipulandum to avoid shock. Chlorpromazine (1.6, 2.0, 4.0 mg/kg) was able to selectively depress avoidance behavior in a dose-dependent manner without blocking the execution of the escape response. Similar avoidance deficits have been noted after chlorpromazine administration by other investigators (Lipper and Kornetsky, 1971; Bravo and Appel, 1967), who studied a wheel-turning response in rats. In comparing the effects of chlorpromazine on discriminated avoidance behavior in situations that required the execution of various responses (wheel turning, hurdle jumping, or lever pressing), Latz *et al.* (1969) noted that drug-induced decrements in performance were a function of acquisition history. The fastest learners (wheel turners) were the least affected, while the slower learners (hurdle jumpers and lever pressers) demonstrated greater avoidance decrements in response to chlorpromazine administration. Thus, base-line rate of response appears to influence the magnitude of the drug's effect on avoidance behavior. Chronic administration of chlorpromazine (1.5–2.0 mg/kg) to rats has been reported to produce decremental effects in a discriminated avoidance procedure that are similar to those noted after acute administration (Levison and Freedman, 1967). Complete recovery of the avoidance base line after 10 days of chronic administration occurs within 24 hr. Finally, the decremental effects of chlorpromazine upon the acquisition of a discriminated avoidance response have been replicated in mice (Sansone *et al.*, 1972). Various doses of the drug (1, 2, 3 mg/kg) reliably decreased both discriminated avoidance responding and the high rates of unreinforced intertrial lever pressing that are emitted by this species of animal.

The effect of chlorpromazine upon avoidance responding is similar whether the behavior is under the control of discriminated or nondiscriminated continuous avoidance schedules. Nondiscriminated avoidance behavior, however, does appear to be more sensitive to the effects of neuroleptic agents than discriminated avoidance (Dobrin and Rhyne, 1969). Thus, chlorpromazine in low doses produces avoidance decrements in rats without affecting escape behavior only in nondiscriminated procedures. Higher doses lead to decrements in avoidance performance under both schedules, but escape behavior is reduced only under the nondiscriminated procedure (Dobrin and Rhyne, 1969). Thus, the dose–response curve for chlorpromazine is shifted to the left under nondiscriminated schedules, producing decrements in avoidance and escape behavior at lower doses than that seen under discriminated avoidance procedures. Further evidence for the sensitivity of nondiscriminated techniques has been provided by Stone (1964), who noted that rats demonstrated avoidance decrements in response to chlorpromazine administration across a wide range of doses (2.0–8.0 mg/kg). In agreement with other reports (Sansone *et al.*, 1972), unreinforced responding during extinction periods was also reduced after chlorpromazine administration. Similar dose–response effects have been noted by other researchers (Heise and Boff, 1962; Niemegeers *et al.*, 1969b), some of whom have demonstrated chlorpromazine-induced avoidance decrements in rats at doses as low as 1.0 mg/kg s.c.

In addition, it has been reported that other species, including dogs and squirrel monkeys, have demonstrated nondiscriminated avoidance decrements in response to very low doses of chlorpromazine (Houser *et al.*, 1976; Houser, 1976). In fact, the minimum effective oral dose of chlorpromazine in the squirrel monkey has been computed to be 1.3 mg/kg (Buser *et al.*, 1970). As was the case with discriminated procedures, the base-line rate of responding is an important factor in determining the degree to which chlorpromazine will affect nondiscriminated avoidance behavior. In contrast to the work cited above with reference to discriminated procedures (Latz *et al.*, 1969), however, evidence exists which indicates that slow learners and/or animals who demonstrate low base-line rates of nondiscriminated avoidance behavior are least affected by chlorpromazine administration (Stone, 1965). Thus, chlorpromazine appears to interact with base-line performance differentially, depending on whether the behavior is under the control of discriminated or nondiscriminated avoidance schedules.

Other neuroleptic drugs are also active in continuous avoidance procedures. Reserpine, for example, produces large avoidance deficits in rats subjected to either a discriminated (Levison and Freedman, 1967) or a nondiscriminated (Heise and Boff, 1962) avoidance schedule. A dose of 1.0 mg/kg i.p. administered acutely to rats dramatically reduced response rates in a discriminated avoidance task (Levison and Freedman, 1967). Recovery from one injection of this compound extended over a 12-day period. On the other hand, acute administration of 0.1 mg/kg of reserpine to rats subjected to a nondiscriminated avoidance procedure produced no discernible behavioral effects (Heise and Boff, 1962). Chronic dosing (0.1 mg/kg day) over a 10-day period, however, produced a complete block of the avoidance response by the seventh day of administration. These decrements persisted to some degree for a period of 6 days after the final drug treatment (Heise and Boff, 1962). Another neuroleptic drug, trifluoperazine (0.1–1.0 mg/kg), produced dose-related avoidance decrements in rats trained to turn a wheel under a discriminated avoidance procedure (Owen and Rathbun, 1967). Escape responding was also retarded, especially under the higher dose. Similar effects have been reported by Heise and Boff (1962), who noted that the minimum effective dose (MED) of trifluoperazine necessary to produce decrements in nondiscriminated avoidance was 0.02 mg/kg in the rat. The MED required to produce elevations in shock rate was 0.03 mg/kg, while the MED to block escape was 0.05 mg/kg. Thus, the dose of trifluoperazine required to produce reliable decrements in ongoing avoidance behavior is relatively small, suggesting that this compound is reasonably potent. Sulpiride, a new psychotropic drug which may possess neuroleptic properties (Fontaine *et al.*, 1974), has also been tested in rats subjected to a nondiscriminated avoidance procedure. Unlike other neuroleptic agents, however, sulpiride (1.0–80.0 mg/kg) did not disrupt avoidance behavior. In fact, shock rates fell slightly and response rates were elevated. These two measures, however, did not appear to be correlated (Fontaine *et al.*, 1974). Thus, sulpiride remains one of the few neuroleptic compounds that fails to produce decrements in continuous avoidance procedures.

Niemegeers *et al.* (1969a,b) have evaluated the effects of 20 neuroleptic drugs in rats subjected to a lever-press nondiscriminated avoidance procedure. Since these studies have held all the experimental and schedule parameters constant, this work provides one of the few examples where the effects of many different compounds can be directly compared. All 20 neuroleptic drugs inhibited avoidance rates and elevated shock rates at very low doses. The order of drug potency was as follows: benperidol = spiroperidol > trifluperidol > droperidol = spiramide > clofluperol = fluphenazine = haloperidol = spirilene > moperone > perphenazine > amiperone > fluanisone = trifluoperazine > pimozide > thioperazine > chlorpromazine > pipamperone = thioridazine > promazine. The nondiscriminated procedure can thus be used as a means of determining the relative potency of various neuroleptic drugs. The ability to predict relative potency, however, becomes valuable only when a test procedure can rank-order compounds according to a particular type of activity. In this regard Niemegeers *et al.* (1969a) have correlated the ED_{50} values (i.e., the dose at which 50% of the animals tested showed a behavioral response) of various neuroleptic compounds computed from the Sidman avoidance procedure and from the antiamphetamine test in rats. Nearly all neuroleptic drugs are relatively specific inhibitors of amphetamine induced stereotyped movements and nonstereotyped motor excitation in rats (Janssen and Lenaerts, 1967). Thus, the antiamphetamine test represents one of the most sensitive methods of detecting neuroleptic activity. Figure 5 presents the correlation between these two test procedures with respect to the 20 neuroleptic drugs listed above. As this figure clearly indicates, the ED_{50} values from the nondiscriminated avoidance procedure correlates extremely well with the results of the antiamphetamine test. This similarity thus suggests that the nondiscriminated Sidman avoidance procedure may be useful in providing a relatively specific and sensitive method for evaluating the potency of neuroleptic drugs. Niemegeers and his associates (Niemegeers *et al.*, 1969b) have suggested that the sensitivity of the continuous avoidance procedure can be enhanced by introducing extinction periods throughout the experimental sessions. Response rate during these extinction periods appears to be more sensitive to the effects of neuroleptic drugs than behavior generated during the avoidance components (R–S = S–S = 20 sec) of the multiple schedule. In addition, an analysis of the temporal distribution of interresponse times (IRTs) suggested that IRTs of 0–5 sec and 6–15 sec were more sensitive to neuroleptic compounds

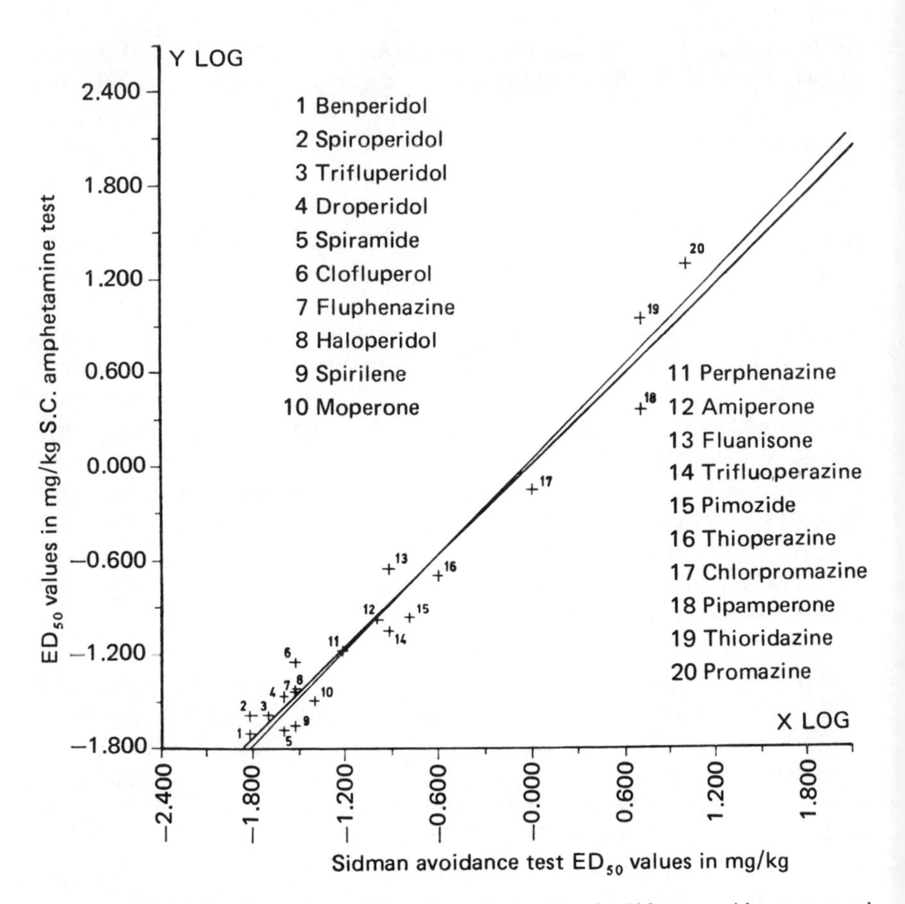

Figure 5. Correlation between the ED_{50} values obtained in the Sidman avoidance test and ED_{50} values of the same compounds in the antiamphetamine test in rats. [From Niemegeers *et al.* (1969a).]

than IRTs from 16–20 sec. The introduction of extinction periods to the Sidman avoidance procedure along with an analysis of IRT distributions has allowed this technique to become one of the most sensitive tests currently available to evaluate the potency of neuroleptic agents in rats.

Although the nondiscriminated avoidance procedure is useful in determining the relative potencies of neuroleptic drugs, it is not as useful in making qualitative distinctions between compounds. In an attempt to rectify this deficiency, Niemegeers *et al.* (1970) have used discriminated avoidance behavior to evaluate the ability of neuroleptics to antagonize the effects of amphetamine. The administration of amphetamine (0.63 mg/kg) to rats performing a discriminated avoidance task

(R–S = S–S = 20 sec with a 5-sec warning stimulus) produced an increase in avoidance responding (R) and decreases in warning stimuli (W), responses during the warning stimulus (WR), and shocks (S). Low doses of selected neuroleptics were able to antagonize the amphetamine-induced changes in avoidance behavior. By establishing the dose of the various neuroleptics that was required to restore base-line avoidance responding (i.e., $R.ED_{100}$), these investigators were able to compute a ratio for the W, WR, and S measures which represented the increase in these measures over control rates when each neuroleptic was administered prior to amphetamine at the $R.ED_{100}$. All the neuroleptics tested restored the S, W, and WR measures at lower doses than those required to reestablish base-line avoidance response rate. It was suggested that the S ratios (i.e., number of shocks obtained at the $R.ED_{100}$/number of shocks received under no-drug conditions) could be used to predict the therapeutic potency of neuroleptic compounds (Niegemeers *et al.*, 1970). The ratio was assumed to be directly related to neuroleptic efficacy, with higher ratios reflecting greater therapeutic potency (i.e., haloperidol $\geqslant$ pimozide > chlorpromazine > pipamperone). The difference between the S and WR ratios, on the other hand, was suggested to reflect the neurological side effects of these compounds. Again, a direct relationship was assumed with larger differences representing greater potency (i.e., haloperidol > chlorpromazine > pimozide > pipamperone). Clinical data cited by Niemegeers *et al.* (1970) concurred with the above findings in that pimozide was the most specific antipsychotic agent known, closely related to haloperidol with respect to therapeutic potency, but possessing less side-effect liability. Thus, the work of Niemegeers and his associates suggests that the nondiscriminated avoidance procedure is the more specific test for determining the relative potency of neuroleptic compounds, while discriminated avoidance is more useful in evaluating the various activities of this class of drugs.

Finally, no discussion of neuroleptic compounds would be complete without mentioning the fact that anticholinergic drugs are able to reverse the decremental effects of these drugs upon continuous avoidance behavior. Hanson and his associates (Hanson *et al.*, 1970) have summarized the effects of several anticholinergics upon the nondiscriminated avoidance decrements produced by a large number of neuroleptic drugs in squirrel monkeys. These authors noted that pretreatment with anticholinergic drugs reliably reduced the antiavoidance activity of all neuroleptic drugs tested, but did not attenuate the decrements produced by chlordiazepoxide, pentobarbital, meprobamate, chloral hydrate, or paraldehyde. These results are in agreement with other pharmacological procedures, such as reversal of neuroleptic-induced catalepsy by anticholinergics (Morpurgo, 1962), that have been used to detect antipsychotic activity. Thus, the use of anticholinergics to block the antiavoidance effects of neuroleptic drugs provides another relatively specific technique for detecting antipsychotic activity.

3.3.2. Anxiolytics

The effects of anxiolytic drugs on continuous avoidance behavior vary as a function of the type of schedule employed, dose of the drug administered, and species that is tested. Bignami and his colleagues (Bignami and De Acetis, 1973; Bignami and Gatti, 1972) have reported that chlordiazepoxide produces differential effects in rats performing a discriminated avoidance task depending on the type of warning signal that is presented. If the signal consisted of turning the houselight off and was present in the S–S interval, chlordiazepoxide produced significant facilitation of avoidance responding. If, however, the signal consisted of turning the houselight on and was terminated during the S–S interval, chlordiazepoxide administration produced slight or even opposite effects (Bignami and De Acetis, 1973). Acquisition of the discriminated avoidance response did not appear to be affected by drug administration (Bignami and Gatti, 1972). In contrast, Sansone *et al.* (1972) noted that chlordiazepoxide did affect the acquisition of discriminated avoidance in mice, but this effect was dose-related. Acquisition was enhanced by 5.0 mg/kg, not affected by 10.0 mg/kg, and retarded by 15.0 mg/kg. In addition, an analysis of intertrial responding indicated that chlordiazepoxide at all doses tested reliably reduced the relatively high rates of such responding normally shown by this species. Thus, various experimental variables can influence the manner in which chlordiazepoxide will affect discriminated avoidance behavior.

The minor tranquilizers produce similar differential effects on nondiscriminated avoidance behavior. For example, diazepam, nitrazepam, and chlordiazepoxide produce consistent decrements in the avoidance rates of rats which demonstrate high levels of base-line performance. Animals with low control rates, however, generally demonstrate increased response rates with a decrease in the frequency of escape failures (Takaori *et al.*, 1969). Thus, control rate of responding is another factor which influences the effects of anxiolytic drugs upon continuous avoidance behavior.

In a rather extensive summary of the effects of many drugs upon behavior under the control of a nondiscriminated avoidance schedule (R–S = 40 sec, S–S = 20 sec), Heise and Boff (1962) have noted that anxiolytic drugs normally depress the avoidance performance of rats. They have computed the minimum effective dose necessary to depress avoidance rates, elevate shock rates, and increase escape failures for a number

Table III. Minimum Effective Doses for Various Anxiolytic Drugs

Compound	Route	*N*	Shock rate increase MED (mg/kg)	Avoidance rate decrease MED (mg/kg)	Escape failure MED (mg/kg)	Avoidance rate increase (mg/kg)
Chlordiazepoxide	i.p.	5	4.2	13	18	
Diazepam	i.p.	6	10	13	67	2–10 (3/6 rats)
Meprobamate	i.p.	4	103	112	105	
Pentobarbital	s.c.	5	12	7.6	18	
Phenobarbital	s.c.	4	30	33	61	
Hexobarbital	s.c.	4	42	45	75	
Chlormezanone	i.p.	3	62	61	70	
Hydroxyzine	s.c.	3	21	16	25	
Emylacamate	i.p.	4	56	73	78	

Source: Heise and Boff (1962).

of anxiolytic compounds. These results are summarized in Table III. As can be seen from these data, the MED values for shock-rate increases are generally lower than those noted for the other two measures. Thus, anxiolytic drugs tend to elevate the number of shocks received before avoidance rates or escape failures are altered. In agreement with other reports (e.g., Dallemagne, 1970), meprobamate was ineffective in altering avoidance behavior until it was administered in doses which produced severe motor deficits. Diazepam was the only compound that produced stimulation of avoidance response rates at low doses. Thus, it would appear that the predominant effect of anxiolytic compounds on nondiscriminated avoidance behavior is to produce response-rate decrements and elevations in shock rate. High doses of these drugs also block the emission of the escape response. Since neuroleptic drugs produce qualitatively similar effects, Heise and Boff (1961) have concluded that nondiscriminated avoidance procedures cannot be used to differentiate the major and minor tranquilizers. It is only when pretreatment procedures (i.e., reversal of drug activity by anticholinergics) are used in conjunction with continuous avoidance schedules that these techniques are able to distinguish neuroleptic from anxiolytic activity.

3.3.3. Stimulants

Of the stimulant drugs, *d*-amphetamine has been by far the most popular compound investigated for its effects on continuous avoidance behavior in various species. Verhave (1958) was one of the first to report that administration of amphetamine (0.65 mg/kg) produced large increases in the nondiscriminated avoidance rates of rats during acquisition. Higher test doses (1.0 mg/kg), however, produced some depression in response rates, while even larger doses (2.0–4.0 mg/kg) totally eliminated all responding. These drug-induced changes were apparently dependent upon an individual animal's dose sensitivity and control rate of responding, since each animal reacted to drug treatment somewhat differently. Animals with low base-line rates had a greater tendency to demonstrate response increments, while the opposite was true for animals with high control rates of responding. Milner (1974) has extended the work of Verhave to note that certain test doses of amphetamine (0.3, 1.0 mg/kg) can produce significant increases in shock avoidance during acquisition without radically altering response rate. In addition, Milner (1974) reported that a test dose (1.0 mg/kg) which produced the fewest shocks elevated the number of well-timed responses (i.e., those during seconds 12–20 of a 20-sec R–S interval) without significantly enhancing the number of poorly timed or "burst" responses (i.e., interresponse times less than 2.0 sec). Thus, amphetamine improved the acquisition of a nondiscriminated avoidance response by mechanisms other than a generalized enhancement of response output. These data suggested that amphetamine did not produce its effects by simply increasing motor activity (Milner, 1974).

Other investigators (Stone, 1964; Heise and Boff, 1962) have replicated the basic findings reported above using nondiscriminated avoidance procedures. Stone (1964), for example, has reported that rats performing a nondiscriminated avoidance task demonstrate clear dose–response effects after amphetamine administration. Doses of 1.0–2.0 mg/kg generated moderate to severe increments in response rate and lowered the number of shocks received, while higher doses (4.0–8.0 mg/kg) completely blocked the execution of the avoidance response. In addition, response rates during unreinforced components of a multiple schedule were also elevated in response to drug administration (Stone, 1964). Finally, in partial support of a rate-dependent effect, Stone (1965) has noted that animals with high base-line shock rates (i.e., poor avoiders) demonstrated a greater susceptibility to the avoidance-enhancing effects of amphetamine than subjects with low shock rates. There was, however, no relationship between control rate of responding and change in response rate noted under amphetamine (Stone, 1965). Thus, it appears clear that amphetamine administration produces alterations in nondiscriminated avoidance behavior that can be best described as reflecting a dose-dependent effect. Low to moderate doses facilitate responding and lower shock rates, while high doses completely block the execution of the avoidance response in rats. These effects are somewhat rate-dependent, in that animals who demonstrate low shock avoidance performance often show the greatest facilitation in response to amphetamine administration.

As might be expected, behavior under the control of discriminated avoidance procedures is affected by amphetamine in a similar fashion. For example, Kulkarni (1972) has shown that some doses (0.5, 1.0 mg/kg) of methamphetamine administered to rats increased the number of avoidance responses during acquisition of a discrete two-lever discriminated avoidance procedure. This increase, however, was not associated with an elevation in extra responses (on the avoidance lever) or wrong responses (made on the second lever). These data, therefore, add support to the conclusion that enhanced levels of avoidance responding produced by the amphetamines are not a direct consequence of an increase in all responding. It would appear that these stimulant drugs may have a specific facilitative influence on the acquisition of continuous avoidance behavior. Rate-dependent effects have also been reported with respect to amphetamine's activity on discriminated avoidance behavior (Latz *et al.*, 1965; Sansone *et al.*, 1974). Latz *et al.* (1965) noted that *d*-amphetamine (0.5, 1.0, 2.0 mg/kg) enhanced the performance of poor avoiders tested under a discrete-trial discriminated avoidance procedure. Rats with high base-line avoidance histories, however, did not demonstrate any alterations in performance in response to amphetamine administration. Moreover, these results could not be accounted for merely in terms of increased response output, since changes in the percent avoidance and the total number of responses emitted were not correlated. These basic findings have also been replicated in another species, the golden hamster, which normally demonstrates low levels of base-line avoidance performance (Sansone *et al.*, 1974).

Finally, it should be noted that the net effect of interactions between various doses of stimulant and neuroleptic drugs upon discriminated avoidance behavior is often a facilitation of performance. Del Río (1971) has reported that if animals are pretreated with chlorpromazine (1.0 mg/kg) 30 min before amphetamine administration (0.5, 1.0 mg/kg), discriminated avoidance behavior is enhanced to a greater degree than if amphetamine is administered alone. Thus, chlorpromazine, instead of antagonizing the effects of amphetamine on continuous avoidance behavior, actually potentiates the facilitatory effects of this compound. This potentiation, however, may simply reflect the fact that chlorpromazine retards the metabolism of amphetamine (Sulser and Dingell, 1968), thus elevating blood levels of the drug.

To summarize, it appears that the amphetamines enhance both the acquisition and performance of continuous avoidance behavior in a dose-dependent fashion. Low to moderate doses elevate responding while high doses interfere with the execution of the avoidance response. In addition, a rate-dependent effect is evident, animals with poor performance histories demonstrating greater facilitation than animals with high base-line rates of shock avoidance.

Nicotine is another representative of the stimulant class of drugs which enhances the performance of a continuous avoidance task. Rats trained under nicotine demonstrated higher response rates (Balfour and Morrison, 1975) and received fewer shocks (Morrison, 1974b) in a nondiscriminated avoidance procedure than saline-treated controls. Similar results have been noted in rats trained under a discriminated avoidance schedule (Erickson, 1971). The doses of nicotine which facilitated avoidance (0.1, 0.4 mg/kg) actually depressed motor activity as measured in photocell cages, suggesting that elevated levels of activity were not responsible for this enhanced performance.

The anticholinergics scopolamine and atropine represent compounds that have both stimulant and depressant activity on continuous avoidance behavior. Heise and Boff (1962) have reported that the MED of scopolamine required to produce enhanced nondiscriminated avoidance rates in rats was 0.18 mg/kg s.c., while the MED of atropine was listed at 8.0 mg/kg i.p. Decrements in response rate, however, were produced by these two compounds when the dose was increased (i.e., 2.0 mg/kg s.c. and 40 mg/kg i.p., respectively). The effects above are complicated by the fact that increases in response rate produced by anticholinergics are often correlated with enhanced shock rates (Stone, 1964, 1965). Stone (1965) has noted that doses of scopolamine that decrease shock avoidance produce a paradoxical increase in response rates primarily by elevating the number of "burst" responses (i.e., responses with short interresponse times) emitted by rats. It was suggested that anticholinergics may produce these effects by disinhibiting unreinforced responses (Stone, 1965). This disinhibition would thus tend to elevate the number of lever presses with short interresponse times since it is these responses that are typically unreinforced in a Sidman avoidance schedule. Finally, the decremental effects of scopolamine upon nondiscriminated avoidance schedules have been replicated in other species, including the squirrel monkey (Houser and Houser, 1973) and the dog (Houser and Paré, 1974a).

Other stimulant drugs which enhance the performance of continuous avoidance behavior include cocaine and pipradol. Cocaine has been reported to stimulate nondiscriminated avoidance response rates at doses as low as 10 mg/kg in the rat (Heise and Boff, 1962). Similar effects were noted in a discriminated procedure when either cocaine (10 mg/kg) or pipradol (5 mg/kg) were administered to rats (Pearl *et al.*,

1968). Thus, it would appear that with the exception of the anticholinergics, stimulant drugs consistently act to elevate continuous avoidance response rates across a wide range of doses and generally produce reductions in the number of shocks received by experimental subjects.

3.3.4. Analgesics

Drugs which possess analgesic activity can be subdivided into two categories: the narcotic and nonnarcotic analgesics. Of the narcotic agents, morphine and codeine have been the most widely studied with respect to their effects on avoidance behavior. Morphine sulfate has been reported to generate a dose-response curve similar to the standard stimulant drugs when tested in nontolerant rats subjected to a nondiscriminated avoidance procedure that employed strong shock (1.0 mA for a duration of 3 sec). Low doses (0.3–3.0 mg/kg) of morphine produced graded increments in response rate, while higher doses (10 mg/kg) disrupted the efficient performance of the avoidance response (Holtzman, 1974a). The 10 mg/kg dose altered the temporal pattern of responding, which led to a fourfold increase in the mean number of shocks received. The stimulant effects of the lower doses of morphine were attenuated by 3 days of chronic drug treatment, as were the disruptive effects of the highest dose administered (Holtzman, 1974a). Other investigators, however, have reported only decrements in response rate after the administration of low doses of morphine to rats (Heise and Boff, 1962) or squirrel monkeys (Houser and Cash, 1975) performing a nondiscriminated avoidance task. Codeine, on the other hand, appears to produce a clear-cut facilitation of nondiscriminated avoidance behavior in rats when administered in a dose of 10 mg/kg (Heise and Boff, 1962).

Of the nonnarcotic analgesics, the narcotic antagonists have been the most widely studied for their ability to stimulate continuous avoidance behavior in rats. Pentazocine (Holtzman, 1974a), cyclazocine (Holtzman and Jewett, 1973), levallorphan (Steinert *et al.,* 1973), and nalorphine (Holtzman, 1974b) have all been reported to produce dose-related increments in nondiscriminated avoidance-response rates. Furthermore, naloxone, a potent narcotic antagonist with little agonistic activity, has been reported to block the stimulation of avoidance responding produced by the above-mentioned narcotic antagonists. As with morphine, however, narcotic antagonists such as pentazocine given in high doses disrupt the performance of a nondiscriminated avoidance task (Holtzman, 1974a). Finally, other nonnarcotic analgesics, such as sodium salicylate, given in doses up to 200 mg/kg were ineffective in altering continuous avoidance behavior in the rat (Heise and Boff, 1962). Thus, both the narcotic and narcotic antagonistic analgesics are effective in elevating response rates under the control of continuous avoidance schedules when these drugs are administered in low to moderate doses. As with stimulants, however, high doses of these analgesic compounds produce a decrement in avoidance performance.

3.3.5. Miscellaneous Compounds

The data concerning the effects of antidepressants upon continuous avoidance are somewhat conflicting. Heise and Boff (1962) have reported that imipramine in doses up to 40 mg/kg produced no alterations in the performance of a nondiscriminated avoidance task in rats. Other investigators (Fielding *et al.,* 1971), however, have indicated that imipramine (5–20 mg/kg) was able to produce both facilitation and decrements in the avoidance performance of squirrel monkeys, depending upon the context in which the behavior occurred. If imipramine was administered to animals who were exposed to a three-component multiple schedule with fixed-ratio, conflict–punishment, and avoidance components, the drug facilitated shock avoidance. If, however, this antidepressant was tested in a one-component avoidance schedule, the opposite effect was noted; response rates were decreased producing elevations in the number of shocks received. Thus, diametrically opposed results could be obtained, depending upon the context in which the avoidance behavior appeared. In a similarly complex report, Owen and Rathbun (1966) indicated that another antidepressant, nortriptyline, caused a general depression in the nondiscriminated avoidance behavior of rats. This depression was marked by a lowering of response rates with an increase in the frequency of shock occurrence. When animals were chronically dosed over a 10-day period and exposed to the avoidance schedule, the depressed response rates persisted for a 40-day postdrug period. If, however, nortriptyline was administered chronically for a 10-day period to animals who were not simultaneously exposed to the avoidance procedure, their postdrug performance was unaltered. Thus, the sustained (i.e., postdrug) lower response rates observed in the first instance were related to the interaction of the behavioral situation and drug rather than to the drug alone. If the drug itself, by reason of accumulations or toxicity, was responsible for the postdrug effects, both groups should have shown lowered response rates after drug administration was discontinued. Thus, if a drug alters the temporal pattern or frequency of a particular behavior, it is possible that this new pattern will perpetuate itself long after the drug has been withdrawn (Owen and Rathbun, 1966). This long-term change in behavior may therefore form the basis for the beneficial therapeutic effects of drug administration.

Other drugs which have been evaluated for their effects on avoidance behaviors include alcohol and Δ^9-THC. Alcohol depressed the response rates of rats subjected to a nondiscriminated avoidance schedule at doses in excess of 1.3 g/kg (Heise and Boff, 1962). The effects of Δ^9-THC were somewhat variable in rats. Some animals showed elevations in shock rate; others demonstrated decrements while they were under the control of a Sidman nondiscriminated avoidance schedule (Manning, 1974). Squirrel monkeys, on the other hand, showed consistent decrements in response rate and elevations in the number of shocks received after the oral administration of 12 mg/kg of Δ^9-THC (Houser, 1975). Thus, alcohol acted primarily to depress performance while Δ^9-THC had mixed effects on behavior under the control of a nondiscriminated avoidance procedure.

3.4. Classification of Drugs by Bovet–Gatti Profiles

Up to this point, we have attempted to review the drug literature to determine if specific classes of drugs differentially affect continuous avoidance behavior. This review suggested that neuroleptics and anxiolytics act to depress performance while stimulants and analgesics generally produce biphasic effects, with low to moderate doses elevating response rates while high doses lead to reductions in avoidance performance. In an attempt to provide a more specific method of classifying particular drugs according to their avoidance profiles, Bovet and Gatti (1964) have summarized the effects of various drugs upon the behavior of rats under the control of a discriminated avoidance schedule. In this type of schedule an animal may postpone signal onset by responding during the response–signal interval (premature responding); it may respond during the signal–shock interval (efficient responding); or it may respond during the shock–shock interval (late responding). By analyzing the effects of different compounds upon the temporal pattern of avoidance responses, these investigators have compiled specific behavior profiles for several classes of drugs. Stimulants such as amphetamine have been reported to increase premature responding and decrease efficient and late responding; neuroleptics decrease premature and increase late responding; while hallucinogens increase both premature and late responding. The construction of behavioral profiles is an important contribution, for it may provide a method of classifying newly synthesized compounds which may then be directly compared to various standard drugs with known therapeutic activity. These types of profiles may thus make it possible to predict drug activity in humans from data obtained from subhuman species.

To date, the data concerning the construction of behavioral profiles is somewhat incomplete and inconsistent. Beaton *et al.* (1974) trained rats and guinea pigs to respond to a discriminated avoidance schedule that had a response–signal interval of 20 sec and a signal–shock and shock–shock interval of 10 sec. *d*-Amphetamine produced similar Bovet–Gatti profiles in both species, in that there was an increase in premature responding with a related decrease in efficient and late responding. In addition, the drug produced a shift in the interresponse time distribution toward shorter IRTs. As an indication of this shift, the number of "burst" responses (responses with IRTs less than 3.0 sec) was significantly elevated in both species after amphetamine administration (Beaton *et al.*, 1974).

Webster and his colleagues (Webster *et al.*, 1971, 1973; Willinsky *et al.*, 1974) have evaluated the effects of THC on the performance of a discriminated avoidance task in rats. This compound has been reported to possess hallucinogenic properties in man (Hollister *et al.*, 1968) and thus would be expected to demonstrate an hallucinogenic profile in the continuous avoidance procedure. In an early report, Webster *et al.* (1971) noted that, in the majority of animals tested, THC produced profiles which conformed to those generated by other hallucinogens. This compound thus enhanced both premature and late responding with a consequent decrease in efficient responding. In a later report, however, Willinsky *et al.* (1974) noted that over a wide range of doses (1.5–96.0 mg/kg) THC produced reliable increases in both premature and late responding in only 33 of 54 cases. The fact that a substantial number of animals failed to show simultaneous increments in both measures led the authors to conclude that THC demonstrated only weak hallucinogenic properties according to the Bovet–Gatti profiles. Since there is little doubt that THC does possess hallucinogenic properties in man, it was suggested that the profile method may not provide a completely accurate way to identify hallucinogens.

Thus, the use of continuous avoidance procedures to construct the behavioral profiles of various classes of drugs is not without its difficulties. The response profiles of a variety of drugs will have to be evaluated in several different species before any definitive classifications are attempted. This methodology, however, does offer promise to those interested in predicting the therapeutic efficacy of newly synthesized compounds in man.

3.5. Effects of Drugs That Alter Synaptic Activity on Continuous Avoidance Behavior

The administration of various drugs which influence synaptic activity in the central nervous system has been reported to reliably alter behavior under the control of continuous avoidance schedules. In general, drugs which enhance serotonergic or adrenergic activity elevate avoidance responding while agents that reduce this activity produce the opposite effect. For example, the administration of reserpine or tetrabenazine, drugs which are known to deplete endogeneous levels of norepinephrine and serotonin, has been reported to produce consistent decrements in the performance of a discriminated avoidance task in rats (Levison and Freedman, 1967). Acute administration of reserpine (1.0 mg/kg) produced severe reductions in shock avoidance followed by prolonged gradual recoveries requiring up to 12 days to return to base-line levels. Tetrabenazine, on the other hand, produced similar decrements but recoveries were rapid; base-line performance was usually attained within 48 hr after drug treatment. These differential periods of recovery parallel the amine repletion rates noted after the administration of these two drugs. Thus, agents that deplete endogeneous levels of norepinephrine and serotonin for long periods (e.g., reserpine) produce prolonged decrements in avoidance behavior while short-acting depletors decrease performance only briefly.

Tetrabenazine acts to deplete levels of norepinephrine and serotonin by releasing these amines from their storage sites, where they can then be metabolized by monoamine oxidase. By pretreating animals with drugs which inhibit monoamine oxidase (MAO inhibitors) before the administration of tetrabenazine, one can explore the effects of enhanced amine activity. Pretreatment with harmaline (Bocknik *et al.*, 1968) or iproniazid (Aprison *et al.*, 1975), both MAO inhibitors, before the administration of tetrabenazine to rats has been reported to produce elevations in nondiscriminated avoidance responding. The fact that these elevations are relatively brief and do not correlate with the time course for MAO inhibition has led to the suggestion that other synaptic systems may be involved in mediating these behavioral effects (Bocknik *et al.*, 1968).

To investigate this possibility, Aprison *et al.* (1975) studied the effects of atropine on iproniazid–tetrabenazine treated rats subjected to a nondiscriminated avoidance procedure. A dose of atropine (0.8 mg/kg) was reported to block completely the enhanced avoidance rates normally seen after treatment with the two compounds. Equal molar doses of methyl atropine, which lacks central nervous system activity, did not block this excitation, suggesting that the effects of atropine are mediated centrally. It thus appears that cholinergic systems may be involved in producing the enhanced levels of avoidance responding noted after iproniazid–tetrabenazine administration.

The evidence thus far reviewed suggests that alterations in adrenergic activity may produce changes in continuous avoidance behavior. Support for this correlation has been provided by Scheckel and Boff (1964), who noted that the antidepressant imipramine produced no effects on nondiscriminated avoidance behavior when given alone, but did consistently produce stimulation when combined with nondepressant doses of tetrabenazine. Since it is known that imipramine prevents the reuptake of norepinephrine into presynaptic sites (Axelrod *et al.*, 1962), it seems reasonable to conclude that this drug increases the reactivity of CNS mechanisms to the stimulant effects of norepinephrine released by tetrabenazine (Scheckel and Boff, 1964). More direct evidence bearing on the role of adrenergic systems in continuous avoidance behavior has been supplied by Miller *et al.* (1970a). These authors have noted that pretreatment with nondepressive doses of α-methyl-*p*-tyrosine (α-MPT), a drug which blocks the synthesis of norepinephrine, had little effect on the stimulation of nondiscriminated avoidance responding produced by *p*-chloroamphetamine or *p*-chloro-*N*-methylamphetamine. In contrast, pretreatment with α-MPT converted the stimulation of avoidance responding after amphetamine administration into a marked depression in performance. These data thus suggest that the facilitation in avoidance produced by the *p*-chloroamphetamines is probably not mediated through adrenergic mechanisms. Amphetamine-induced stimulation, on the other hand, is apparently mediated through the release of norepinephrine (Miller *et al.*, 1970). In support of these conclusions, Miller *et al.* (1970b) have reported that the *p*-chloroamphetamines selectively lower brain serotonin levels, with no depleting effects on norepinephrine.

This brief review of the literature indicates that alterations in either serotonergic or adrenergic activity can influence behavior under the control of continuous avoidance schedules. Modulation of these amine systems, in turn, may influence other biochemical systems (e.g., acetylcholine, dopamine) in the brain which could directly alter the performance of an avoidance response. At present, the data concerning these complex interrelationships are still incomplete and thus no firm conclusions can be drawn.

3.6. Conclusions Concerning the Effects of Drugs upon Continuous Avoidance Behavior

It should be clear from the review above that the motivational hypothesis is incapable of accounting for the multitude of effects which drugs exert upon continuous avoidance behavior. Although anxiolytic drugs do produce decrements in avoidance behavior (with some notable exceptions, however), this effect is not exclusive to this class of compounds. The neuroleptics produce qualitatively similar results often at lower doses than the anxiolytics. Potent analgesic drugs, which should relieve the fear or anxiety associated with shock by reducing the painful qualities of this stimulus, instead of decreasing avoidance rates, actually produce facilitation in most cases. Thus, it would appear that drugs do not affect continuous avoidance behavior by simply altering the level of fear or anxiety that is assumed to motivate the avoidance response.

The use of continuous avoidance procedures, however, does appear to provide useful information concerning the behavioral effects of drugs. Avoidance paradigms are particularly sensitive to the neuroleptic properties of drugs, thus providing a method for assessing the relative potencies of selected compounds. These qualities may therefore make continuous avoidance procedures useful tools in predicting the therapeutic efficacy of newly synthesized compounds. The construction of Bovet–Gatti profiles, along with other modifications, such as interaction with amphetamine and anticholinergics, has enhanced the predictive value of these procedures in determining the neuroleptic, hallucinogenic, and stimulant activity of drugs. Further research will be necessary to determine if these procedures can successfully continue to predict therapeutic activity.

4. The Conditioned Emotional Response

Up to this point, we have discussed experimental procedures that have made the presentation of aversive stimuli contingent upon the behavior of the animal subject. This contingent relationship between behavior and the aversive event has been viewed by Millenson and Leslie (1974) as representing the major reason why both punishment and avoidance procedures have proved to be inadequate as experimental models for clinical anxiety. These authors note that "anxiety does not appear to be an appropriate label for what we do when we run to escape from a shower of rain, nor is a patient classified as anxious for refusing to go out into that rain" (Millenson and Leslie, 1974, p. 2).

Thus, experience indicates that aversive events that are controlled by our own behavior rarely generate an emotional state of anxiety. In contrast, a warning signal (e.g., smoke) that precedes an unavoidable aversive event (e.g., fire) often leads to an emotional state that more closely resembles clinical anxiety. This reasoning thus suggests that experimental procedures that use unavoidable aversive events might be more useful in constructing animal models of clinical anxiety than procedures that make the aversive event contingent upon behavior. The following discussion will present a summary of one such model, which has become known as the conditioned emotional response (CER) procedure. After describing the procedure and some of the methodological problems surrounding its use, we will review the pertinent drug literature to see if the CER can be used successfully to evaluate the various properties (e.g., anxiolytic) of pharmaceutical agents.

The CER procedure was first described by Estes and Skinner (1941). Animals are usually trained to press a lever on a schedule of intermittent food or water reinforcement (frequently a variable-interval schedule). When the animal has attained a stable response rate, the CER procedure is superimposed on the lever-pressing response. Specifically, a tone or clicking noise (conditioned stimulus—CS) is introduced, which lasts for several minutes. At the end of this period, the CS is terminated with an electric shock (the unconditioned stimulus—UCS). After only a few of these pairings, the animal will exhibit a set of symptoms (the CER) whenever the CS occurs. These symptoms have been most widely studied in the rat and include a suppression of lever pressing, immobility, crouching, defecation, and piloerection. Behavioral results from the procedure above are generally reported by means of a suppression ratio which reflects the interaction of response rates just before and during the presentation of the CS. Since the degree of suppression of the lever-press response during the CS is directly related to the intensity of the unavoidable shock (Annau and Kamin, 1961), the suppression ratio measure has been used to infer the intensity of the emotional response (i.e., fear or anxiety) produced by the CS. Drugs can then be administered to animals who have acquired the CER to see if this treatment can attenuate or intensify the suppression of ongoing behavior produced by the aversive CS.

Beyond the obvious analogy with clinical anxiety, the CER technique possesses many of the empirical advantages of other operant procedures. For example, the CER procedure may be presented to animals over long intervals so that the peak time and duration of action of various classes of drugs can be ascertained. Furthermore, since the degree of behavioral suppression can be titrated by selecting appropriate shock levels, an intermediate level of suppression can usually be generated in each animal. Thus, increases as well as decreases in behavioral suppression can be measured in response to drug administration. Finally, the CER procedure is basically a mixed schedule consisting of both CS and non-CS segments. Comparison of behavior in the non-CS segments before and after drug treatment may provide a within-subject control for side effects on sensory-motor function and appetitive motivation (Millenson and Leslie, 1974). Before turning to a review of the effects of drugs upon behavior generated by the CER procedure, a brief analysis of the methodological problems surrounding the use of this technique will be presented.

4.1. Methodological Problems Associated with the CER Technique

4.1.1. Motivational Variables

The CER procedure uses two distinct motivational processes to control behavior. First, animals are deprived of either food or water to provide the motivational substrate which energizes the ongoing behavior (usually lever pressing). Second, animals are subjected to electric shock, which introduces another motivational process (fear or anxiety) into the test situation. Alterations of either motivational process can conceivably alter the degree of behavioral suppression generated by the CER procedure. Thus, a drug which enhances hunger can elevate suppressed responding during the CS, while an anorexigenic agent may have the opposite effect (Houser, 1972a). As is the case with any behavioral paradigm that utilizes electric shock, drug-induced changes in pain sensitivity can alter the degree of behavioral suppression noted during an aversive CS. It has been well documented that the amount of suppression during the CS is a function of shock intensity (Annau and Kamin, 1961; Henton and Jordan, 1970). Relatively intensive shock produces a complete suppression of behavior that is insensitive to most drug manipulations, while low shock intensities generate a mild suppression that is more likely to be affected by drug treatment. Several reports have noted that some drugs attenuate conditioned suppression only when the shock intensity is relatively weak, suggesting that alterations in pain sensitivity may be the mechanism by which these drugs affect this behavior (Hill *et al.*, 1967; Appel, 1963). Thus, whenever a drug alters the degree of behavioral suppression generated by an aversive CS, one must entertain the possibility that it may produce this effect by altering either pain sensitivity or the degree of appetitive motivation.

4.1.2. Schedule Parameters

The maintenance of a stable behavioral base line is an essential prerequisite for testing drugs in the CER procedure. Aperiodic schedules have been successfully utilized for this purpose, but they have the disadvantage of requiring animals to be subjected to long training periods. Some investigators have attempted to reduce training time by utilizing continuous reinforcement or fixed-ratio schedules to maintain the ongoing behavior. Brady and Hunt (1955), however, have noted that if the initial lever-pressing behavior was maintained by a continuous reinforcement schedule or by ratio reinforcement, the CER is more difficult to condition than if lever pressing was under the control of a variable-interval schedule for primary reinforcement. Furthermore, Brady and Hunt (1955) noted that the CER extinguished more rapidly when lever pressing was maintained on ratio reinforcement than when any of the interval schedules were used. Thus, variable-interval schedules would appear to be the preferred method of generating stable behavioral base lines that allow for the rapid acquisition of a CER which demonstrates a reasonable degree of resistance to extinction.

The acquisition of the CER itself proceeds in several phases, each of which may interact with drugs to produce differential behavioral effects. Millenson and Dent (1971) have reported that the first occurrence of a variable-duration CS followed by a mild shock produced an intense suppression of lever pressing in subsequent CS and non-CS segments of the schedule. Over the next 20 sessions, non-CS responding gradually recovered to its preshock level. CS rates, however, remained suppressed, reaching a maximum level of 50% of the preshock rate. Furthermore, other studies (Henton and Jordan, 1970) have shown that the acquisition of the CER was dependent upon the shock intensity used. Very mild shock may produce a CER that totally habituates over time, while intense shock may produce maximum suppression that fails to habituate. The effects of drug administration on these various phases are highly complex, and it is doubtful that the effects seen during acquisition will necessarily be the same as those noted when the drug is tested on a stable CER.

4.1.3. Use of Conditioned Stimuli of Fixed Duration

Most of the drug studies to be reviewed below use CSs that are presented for a fixed period of time. Such schedules, however, foster the development of temporal discriminations that can conceivably influence the manner in which a drug will affect behavior (Millenson and Leslie, 1974). If the CS is relatively long, animals will soon learn that the initial portion of the CS interval represents a "safe" period during which shock is never made available. Suppression during this period will thus be minimal followed by greater reductions in lever pressing as the end of the CS interval approaches signaling the occurrence of electric shock. Thus, the use of fixed-duration CSs generally leads to differential response rates being generated throughout the CS interval. As we have seen earlier, many drugs produce rate-dependent effects upon behavior, irrespective of how these rates were generated. Thus, a drug that elevated the low rates normally seen at the end of the CS, without significantly altering the high rates at the beginning of the interval, would appear to be relieving anxiety when, in fact, it was merely producing a rate-dependent effect. Evidence of such an interaction has been reported by Sanger and Blackman (1976) with regard to amphetamine's effects on behavior generated during an aversive CS.

Probably the best example of the difficulties one can encounter in interpreting drug results using fixed-duration CSs occurred with data reported by Brady (1956). This author subjected rats and monkeys to a CER procedure that involved 3-min CSs programmed to occur at 7-min intervals. Administration of reserpine (0.2 mg/kg) led to a significant decrease in base-line responding, while response rates during the CS were elevated. Amphetamine (2.0 mg/kg), on the other hand, produced the opposite effect, elevating base-line rates while decreasing the number of lever-pressing responses emitted during the aversive CS. Brady (1956) suggested that these data indicated that reserpine may have reduced anxiety since the degree of suppression during the CS was alleviated even though base-line rates were depressed. A report by Blackman (1968), however, casts doubt upon this conclusion by applying a rate-dependent analysis to Brady's data. In Blackman's study, rats were subjected to a standard CER procedure, behavior being maintained by means of a variable-interval 60-sec reinforcement schedule. Then in one condition, reinforcement became available only if the animal responded at a high rate, while the opposite was true in another condition, reinforcement occurring only if the animal responded at a low rate. These changes in base-line rate altered the degree of suppression generated in the CS segments of the schedule in a fashion similar to that seen after reserpine and amphetamine administration in Brady's experiment (1956). Thus, when the animals were required to exhibit low base-line rates they demonstrated less suppression during the CS than under control conditions, but when demonstrating high base-line rates they exhibited greater suppression during the CS. These results clearly indicate that manipulations which alter response rates during one segment of the CER procedure may influence rates in other segments. Furthermore, these alterations in rate do not necessarily reflect changes in the motivational states that underlie the CER procedure. Thus, drugs may produce rate-dependent effects upon behavior in the CS and/or non-CS segments of the CER paradigm that appear to alter the degree of conditioned suppression without influencing any anxiety generated by the technique. Although there is no adequate method for controlling for all rate-dependent effects since response rates during the CS will always be suppressed in relation to base-line rates, one can abolish differential rates during the CS by presenting these stimuli for varying durations. If the CS is presented for relatively short random durations, consistent suppression will occur throughout the CS (Lauener, 1963), ensuring that drugs will not exert differential rate-dependent effects within the CS interval. Unfortunately, most of the CER literature to date has used fixed-duration CSs, thus making any interpretation of drug results exceedingly difficult.

4.1.4. Rate Measures

As mentioned in the description of the CER procedure, behavioral results are usually reported by means of a suppression ratio, which compares the relative response rate during the CS with that obtained during base-line periods of comparable duration. As Ray (1964) has wisely pointed out, however, the use of such ratios is often misleading, since it is possible to get a relative increase in responding during the CS merely through an absolute decrease in responding during the non-CS control period. Unfortunately, in many studies this ratio is the only measure that is presented, and thus no detailed information is available concerning how drugs affect both base-line and CS rates. Thus, since it is clear that changes in base-line rate can affect conditioned suppression, it is always advisable to present detailed information on the behavioral effects of drugs during both CS and non-CS segments of the CER schedule.

4.1.5. Diurnal Cycles

Probably one of the most overlooked experimental variables in psychopharmacological research concerns the time of day that drugs are administered to various animal species. Drugs can exert substantially different effects on behavior, depending on which portion of the diurnal cycle the compound is administered in. For example, Evans and Patton (1970) have noted that changes from saline to drug (scopolamine hydrobromide) conditions were more apt to block the acquisition of conditioned suppression if testing took place during the dark portion of the daily light/dark cycle than if testing took place during the light period. These data highlight the fact that rodents are nocturnal animals and thus should be tested during the dark portion of their cycle. If testing must be conducted during the daytime, rats should be placed on a reverse day/night cycle to ensure that drugs will be administered during the active or nonsleeping portion of the diurnal cycle. Unfortunately, many drug studies that have employed the CER procedure have not controlled for the effects of diurnal cycles, and thus direct comparisons between data from different species (e.g., rats and monkeys) are difficult to make.

The preceding discussion underscores some of the difficulties inherent in attempting to evaluate the data obtained from CER studies. Drugs can conceivably alter conditioned suppression by interacting with motivational variables, schedule parameters, response rates, and diurnal cycles. Since the proper controls for these variables are rarely present, definitive statements concerning the mechanism whereby drugs affect the CER are difficult to formulate. Nevertheless, if enough information can be summarized concerning the effects of a variety of drugs in many different types of CER procedure using numerous animal species, some general statements concerning the effects of drugs upon conditioned suppression can be made. In an attempt to formulate such generalizations, we will now review the pertinent drug literature to see how the various classes of chemical agents affect conditioned suppression in the CER paradigm.

4.2. Review of Drug Effects upon the CER

4.2.1. Anxiolytics

If one views the CER paradigm in terms of motivational processes, the onset of the aversive CS produces a negative increment in drive that summates with all other drive conditions to produce a decrease in the appetitive motivation that energizes the operant response. This reduction in motivation is reflected by a decrease in response rate. Any variable that attenuates the CER, according to this analysis, could either be augmenting the appetitive drive (i.e., hunger or thirst) or attenuating the negative drive (i.e., fear or anxiety) associated with the CS (Millenson and Leslie, 1974). Anxiolytic drugs would thus be expected to reduce the intensity of the negative drive, producing a decrease in the degree of conditioned suppression generated by the aversive CS. Unfortunately, as will be seen below, clinically active anxiolytic drugs do not consistently attenuate conditioned suppression. Furthermore, the results that have been obtained are open to various interpretations, since many of the anxiolytics have been reported to produce increments in appetitive motivation.

The benzodiazepines have been widely studied in different types of CER procedures with varying results. Cicala and Hartley (1967) reported that chlordiazepoxide significantly attenuated the conditioned suppression of lever pressing for food under a variable-ratio 6 schedule of reinforcement when the drug was administered after the CER was established. Administration of the drug during acquisition, however, failed to significantly attenuate the CER. Similar results concerning the effects of chlordiazepoxide upon the performance of a CER have been noted by Miczek (1973b). Tenen (1967), using a somewhat different CER procedure in which CS-shock pairings were superimposed upon ongoing licking behavior, produced similar results. This author reported that several benzodiazepines (chlordiazepoxide, diazepam, and nitrazepam) administered to rats produced faster recovery times (i.e., time required to accumulate 3 sec of drinking after CS presentation) than saline-treated controls. Furthermore, control experiments ruled out the possibility that chlordiazepoxide produced these effects as a result of state-dependent (dissociated) learning processes or through an increase in thirst motivation. In contrast, Scobie and Garske (1970) have noted that chlordiazepoxide (12 mg/kg) reduced the suppressive effects of an aversive CS in a dose-related manner if the drug was given during acquisition, but the drug had no effect upon the performance of this learned response. The attenuating effects of chlordiazepoxide upon acquisition were evident if the ongoing behavior was either lever pressing for food reward or milk licking from a metal tube. In support of these findings, Berger *et al.* (1967) have reported that another benzodiazepine, oxazepam, primarily affected CER learning and not performance.

Lauener (1963), in a well-controlled study, investigated the effects of a number of clinically active anxiolytic agents upon the acquisition and performance of the CER. In this procedure thirsty rats were reinforced with water for making a lever-press response at intervals of not less than 5 sec. Aversive CSs of variable duration (10–60 sec) were then presented, followed by unavoidable shocks. Temporal discriminations based on CS duration could not be made, and thus conditioned suppression was consistent and quite pronounced throughout the CS interval. Chlordiazepoxide reliably attenuated the acquisition and performance of conditioned suppression and at a dose of 20 mg/kg completely abolished the CER. Animals tested 24 hr after drug treatment demonstrated complete recovery of conditioned suppression. Unfortunately, chlordiazepoxide also reliably elevated response rates during the non-CS segments of the schedule, suggesting that the drug might be producing its effects through nonspecific behavioral activation, possibly by enhancing appetitive motivation. Evidence does exist which suggests that the benzodiazepines can enhance hunger motivation in both deprived (Soubrié *et al.*, 1975; Wedeking, 1974) and satiated rats (Wise and Dawson, 1974). Thus, the enhanced response rates during the aversive CS (i.e., attenuated conditioned suppression) may merely have been the result of enhanced appetitive motivation rather than a reflection of the anxiolytic properties of this drug.

The data above thus clearly suggest that the benzodiazepines can affect either the acquisition or the performance of a CER by attenuating the degree of conditioned suppression generated during the aversive CS. Stein and Berger (1969), however, have supplied conflicting evidence which demonstrated that the administration of oxazepam to rats produced a paradoxical increase in the degree of suppression noted during the CER procedure. Rats were trained to drink a milk solution from glass drinking spouts located in the test chamber. Once animals had reached a criterion of 100 licks within 50 sec, they were subjected to a single fear-conditioning trial (1-mA shock for 1 sec) in the test chamber with the drinking tube removed. Seven days after fear conditioning the rats were tested for conditioned suppression of drinking by measuring the amount of time required to make 100 licks in the test chamber. Chronic administration of oxazepam (20 mg/kg) 30 min before this retention test significantly elevated this latency measure, suggesting that the drug had intensified the CER. Chronic administration of diazepam also produced increased mean latencies, but they were not statistically greater than the control measures. Acute administration of chlordiazepoxide (15, 20 mg/kg) produced no reliable differences. Thus, minor tranquilizers of the benzodiazepine series produced either no effect or actually enhanced the performance of a learned CER.

Although this study represents a clear-cut example of the failure of the CER paradigm to detect the anxiolytic properties of drugs, it has been criticized for departing from typical procedures (Millenson and Leslie, 1974). Stein and Berger's (1969) design was unusual in that only a single aversive conditioning trial was presented without the use of a discrete CS, aside from the test chamber itself, and the test trial in which drug effects were measured occurred a week after aversive conditioning. Thus, it has been suggested that these differences indicate that Stein and Berger's (1969) study may have been measuring the effects of anxiolytic drugs upon the memory of a single traumatic event rather than upon the expression of a well-learned anxiety state (Millenson and Leslie, 1974). Even with these criticisms in mind, however, this study does suggest that the benzodiazepines can exert a wide variety of effects upon behavior that has been suppressed by the presentation of unavoidable shock.

Other clinically active anxiolytic drugs, including meprobamate and the barbiturates, have also been tested in the CER paradigm. Tenen (1967), for example, has reported that rats subjected to amobarbital administration demonstrated faster recovery of a suppressed drinking response than saline-treated controls. Lauener (1963), on the other hand, tested several other barbiturates, including phenobarbital, methylphenobarbital, barbital, aprobarbital, and amobarbital, and noted that all these agents significantly elevated the suppressed lever-pressing rates for water reinforcement emitted by rats during an aversive CS. Similar but less pronounced effects were noted after meprobamate administration. Other investigators, however, have reported negative results with regard to these same drugs. Ray (1964) noted that meprobamate (80–180 mg/kg) was ineffective in altering the level of conditioned suppression generated by a typical CER procedure. In this study thirsty rats were required to lever-press for liquid reward on a variable-interval 1-min schedule. Three-minute CSs followed by brief 1.0-mA unavoidable shocks were then superimposed upon this ongoing behavior to ensure the rapid acquisition of a CER. In addition to meprobamate, chlorpromazine was also inactive in this particular CER procedure. Finally, similar negative effects were noted in regard to amobarbital administration by Stein and Berger (1969) in a study that has been summarized above. These authors noted that amobarbital elevated the amount of time required to emit 100 licks in a test chamber in which the rats had previously been shocked. These results were similar to those noted with diazepam and suggest that amobarbital, at least under these conditions, seemed to enhance the expression of the CER.

Thus, it appears that the barbiturates and meprobamate are similar to the benzodiazepines in that these compounds can produce differential effects on conditioned suppression, depending on the experimental procedures that are employed. Furthermore, interpretation of the results above is made even more difficult when it is noted that both meprobamate and the barbiturate phenobarbital have been reported to increase food consumption (Kumar *et al.,* 1970), while the barbiturates stimulate water intake (Millenson and Leslie, 1974). Thus, the attenuating effects of the barbiturates upon conditioned suppression noted in Tenen's (1967) and Lauener's (1963) work may simply have been a reflection of the enhanced appetitive motivation produced by these compounds. In a review of the effects of anxiolytic drugs upon the CER, Millenson and Leslie (1974) have noted that out of 19 published examples, 12 demonstrated positive results (i.e., reduction in conditioned suppression), six demonstrated no effect, while one study showed a paradoxical increase in the CER in response to these agents. These mixed results strongly suggest that the effects of anxiolytic compounds upon the CER are extremely complex and as yet poorly understood. In any event, it seems clear that the data do not support the conclusion that the CER paradigm can be used successfully as a research tool in determining the anxiolytic properties of drugs.

4.2.2. Neuroleptics

Chlorpromazine and reserpine are the two neuroleptic drugs that have received the most attention with regard to their effects upon the CER paradigm. As with the anxiolytics, the results are mixed. Cicala and Hartley (1967) reported that chlorpromazine retarded the acquisition, but not the performance of the CER in a typical lever-pressing procedure. Appel (1963), on the other hand, has shown that chlorpromazine (1.5 mg/kg) attenuated the performance of a CER (i.e., conditioned suppression of lever pressing for liquid food reinforcement) when the drug was administered chronically for a 5-day period. Conflicting results, however, have been reported by Lauener (1963), who noted that various doses of chlorpromazine (1.5–6.0 mg/kg) had no reliable effect or lowered the lever-pressing rate for water reinforcement during both CS and non-CS segments of the CER procedure. None of the drug doses, however, significantly elevated the suppressed response rates noted during the aversive CS. In agreement with these results, Tenen (1967) has demonstrated that chlorpromazine (3.16 mg/kg) produced no reliable effects upon drinking latency in animals subjected to the CER procedure. A similar lack of effect has been reported by Ray (1964) and Kinnard *et al.* (1962) when chlorpromazine was administered to thirsty rats subjected to a typical CER procedure. Thus, the data appear to suggest that chlorpromazine may alter the CER differentially, depending on the type of experimental procedure that is selected.

The second neuroleptic compound to be widely studied in the CER procedure is reserpine. As with chlorpromazine, this compound produces differential effects, depending on the type of procedure used. Appel (1963), for example, noted that chronic administration of reserpine (0.2 mg/kg) over a 5-day period produced a reduction in conditioned suppression of a lever-press response for liquid food reinforcement if the shock intensity was low (0.8 mA). Use of higher intensities (1.0 mA), however, produced equivocal results. Similar reductions in conditioned suppression were noted by Ray (1964) when reserpine

(0.5, 1.0 mg/kg) was administered for 4 days to rats. In agreement with Brady's (1956) results, reviewed above, Ray reported that the drug also significantly reduced base-line response rate. To explore whether the changes in conditioned suppression might be due to alterations in base-line response rate, Ray tested the effects of reserpine in a discrete-trial CER paradigm. In this procedure CS-shock pairings were superimposed upon lever-pressing behavior that was maintained by a discriminated continuous reinforcement schedule for liquid reinforcement. Reserpine administration (0.25–1.0 mg/kg) reliably reduced response latency during the aversive CS when compared to control conditions (i.e., a reduction in the CER) without altering behavior during the non-CS segments of the discrete-trial schedule. These data suggest that reserpine may produce a specific attenuating effect on conditioned suppression during the aversive CS without producing concomitant effects on base-line or non-CS response rates.

Conflicting data concerning reserpine's effects on the CER, however, have been reported by Kinnard *et al.* (1962). These authors noted that reserpine (0.25–0.6 mg/kg) did not reliably alter the CER, as measured by a suppression ratio, when the drug was administered acutely. A similar lack of effect was also reported by Yamahiro *et al.* (1961), who indicated that 18 days of reserpine treatment (0.4, 0.8 mg/kg) failed to significantly alter the suppression ratios obtained from rats subjected to a typical CER procedure. It should be noted, however, that these negative effects were based solely on an analysis of the suppression ratio data. No data were presented with regard to the drug's direct effect on base-line or CS response rates. Thus, the drug may have altered absolute rates of responding during both CS and non-CS segments of the schedule. Finally, Valenstein (1959) has reported that reserpine (0.003, 0.004 mg/kg), administered acutely, enhanced the degree of conditioned suppression of lever pressing generated by an aversive CS in guinea pigs while concomitantly reducing base-line response rate.

The data above indicate that neuroleptic drugs are capable of enhancing, reducing, or not affecting the acquisition and/or performance of a CER, depending on the experimental procedures that are used as well as the species that is employed. These conflicting results thus suggest that the critical experimental variables that influence the manner in which neuroleptic drugs affect the CER have yet to be identified.

4.2.3. Analgesics

Many different studies have explored the effects of the narcotic analgesic morphine sulfate on the performance of a CER in rats. Hill *et al.* (1957) published one of the first reports on this topic, noting that morphine (1.0–11.0 mg/kg) reliably reduced base-line lever-pressing rates while elevating response rates during an aversive CS in a dose-dependent manner. This result is difficult to evaluate because of the possibility of a simple and nonspecific rate-dependent effect of the drug on behavior. In a more recent study, Hill *et al.* (1967) reported that morphine (5, 7, 9 mg/kg) produced similar effects even under conditions that normally produced almost complete suppression of responding during the aversive CS. Similar results have been reported by Babbini *et al.* (1973) who demonstrated that morphine (5, 10, 20 mg/kg) attenuated in a dose-dependent manner the conditioned suppression of locomotor activity demonstrated by animals who had previously received shock in the test apparatus. Contrasting results, however, have been published by Lauener (1963), who demonstrated that morphine (2, 4, 8 mg/kg), although lowering the overall response rate at the highest dose tested, did not attenuate the degree of conditioned suppression of lever pressing during an aversive CS. Finally, in a similar vein, Holtzman and Villarreal (1969) have shown that administration of morphine (0.5–6.0 mg/kg) to rhesus monkeys produced dose-related decrements in overall response rate without restoring the suppressed rates generated during a preshock CS. Thus, the literature with regard to morphine's effects on the CER is similar to the findings reviewed above concerning anxiolytic and neuroleptic compounds. No consistent pattern of results emerges, suggesting that the CER procedure is not specifically sensitive to this narcotic analgesic.

4.2.4. Miscellaneous Drugs

Tenen (1967) has shown that *d*-amphetamine (1.0 mg/kg) administered to rats did not influence the amount of recovery time required to execute 3 sec of licking behavior in the presence of a CS previously associated with shock. Similar results were reported by Lauener (1963), who indicated that amphetamine sulfate (1, 5 mg/kg) produced both increments and decrements in overall lever-press rate, but did not reliably alter the suppressed rates noted during the aversive CS. Thus, amphetamine does not appear to reliably alter the performance of an established CER.

Vogel *et al.* (1967) have presented evidence which suggests that the anticholinergics scopolamine and atropine do not block the acquisition of a CER. These authors noted that undrugged rats demonstrate conditioned suppression of drinking during a preshock CS when fear conditioning had taken place under drug conditions. Contrasting results have been reported by Evans and Patton (1970). Acquisition of conditioned suppression of drinking was impaired by scopolamine when conditioning and testing occurred under different states (i.e., drug vs. saline) and when testing took place during the dark period of the rat's daily light/dark cycle. Finally, Miczek (1973b) has reported that both scopolamine methyl nitrate and scopolamine hydrobromide do not affect the performance of a learned CER in rats. Anticholinergics, therefore, do not appear to consistently alter conditioned suppression.

The administration of alcohol to various animal species has consistently been reported not to affect the performance of a CER. Goldman and Docter (1966), for example, have noted that cats subjected to a modified CER procedure demonstrated reliable elevations in response rate during both non-CS and CS segments of the schedule after oral administration of alcohol (1 ml/kg). Thus, suppressed response rates during the aversive CS were not differentially affected. A control experiment in which no shock was administered indicated that alcohol enhanced the emission of the operant lever-press response under conditions that could not generate fear or anxiety. These results suggested that the elevations seen in the CER experiment in both segments of the schedule could not have been the result of an overall reduction in fear or anxiety that had generalized to the entire experimental procedure. Similar negative results have been obtained in the rat (Lauener, 1963; Cicala and Hartley, 1967). Thus, in contrast to results from the conflict–punishment paradigm, alcohol does not appear to attenuate the degree of conditioned suppression noted during an aversive CS in the CER procedure.

Numerous reports have indicated that marijuana compounds do not affect behavior under the control of a CER procedure in a consistent manner. For example, Boyd *et al.* (1963) have noted that dimethylheptyltetrahydrocannabinol enhances the conditioned suppression of bar-pressing behavior in rats. Similar results were obtained with Δ^9-THC, which produced longer drinking latencies (i.e., greater conditioned suppression) in rats shocked and retested under the drug (Robichaud *et al.*, 1973). Contrasting results, however, were reported by Gonzalez *et al.* (1972), who noted that rats treated acutely with marijuana extract demonstrated a reduction in the conditioned suppression of drinking behavior noted in the presence of a stimulus previously associated with electric shock. Furthermore, these authors noted that the rats treated with marijuana extract demonstrated decreased defecation during the CS when compared to control animals. These results were interpreted to suggest that marijuana compounds may retard the acquisition and retention of the CER by reducing the level of fear, thus facilitating the emission of ongoing behavior. Similar results were obtained by Abel (1969), who demonstrated that pyrahexyl, a marijuana homologue, partially blocked the suppressive effects of a CS previously paired with electric shock in a CER paradigm. Thus, marijuana compounds appear to produce differential effects on the CER, depending on the type of experimental procedures that are utilized.

Finally, Hartmann and Geller (1971) have provided evidence which suggests that modulation of serotonergic activity can influence the expression of a CER in rats. These authors used a standard CER procedure where hungry rats were trained to lever-press for liquid food reinforcement under a variable-interval 2-min schedule. Three-minute CSs followed by shock were then superimposed upon the ongoing operant behavior. *p*-Chlorophenylalanine attenuated the degree of conditioned suppression noted during the CS. Pretreatment with 5-hydroxytryptophan, a precursor of serotonin, reversed the attenuation produced by *p*-chlorophenylalanine in the majority of rats tested. It should be pointed out, however, that as in many CER studies, only group suppression ratios were reported and thus no detailed information was made available concerning changes in base-line and CS response rates. Nevertheless, these data are similar to other reports that have studied the conflict–punishment paradigm and which suggested that reduced serotonergic activity attenuated conditioned suppression generated during an aversive CS.

4.3. Conclusions Concerning the Effects of Drugs upon the CER

The literature reviewed above makes it abundantly clear that a wide variety of drugs produce differential effects upon the acquisition and expression of the CER. Unlike the data concerning the conflict–punishment or continuous avoidance procedures, however, these results do not allow one to conclude that the CER is consistently affected by one or more classes of drugs. The motivational hypothesis predicts that since conditioned suppression is a reflection of fear or anxiety, clinically potent anxiolytic agents should disinhibit behavior during the aversive CS. In their review of the CER literature, however, Millenson and Leslie (1974) have indicated that none of the major or minor tranquilizing drugs reliably affect the CER in a consistent manner. Although some of the variance in these results may be due to chronic versus acute drug administration (Millenson and Leslie, 1974), enough conflicting evidence remains to suggest that the CER procedure, as outlined above, cannot at present be successfully used to delineate the pharmacological properties of various classes of drugs.

4.4. Continuous Avoidance and the CER

One of the difficulties with the traditional CER procedure is that two distinct motivational processes are involved in the experimental procedure. Thus, certain classes of drugs (e.g., the anxiolytics) may produce equivocal behavioral results by exerting opposing effects upon these two motivational processes. The minor tranquilizers may reduce anxiety during the CS, producing an attenuation of conditioned suppression, but this effect may be masked by an overall increment in response rate throughout the schedule produced by an increase in appetitive motivation. In an attempt to reduce the complexity of the CER paradigm, several investigators have modified the typical procedure to superimpose CS-unavoidable shock pairings upon ongoing behavior maintained by a continuous avoidance schedule. Under this procedure only one motivational process is involved, and thus drug-induced changes in appetitive motivation would be less likely to interfere with the behavioral expression of the CER.

The introduction of CS-unavoidable shock presentation to animals performing a continuous avoidance response produces a change in lever-press rate that is different from that seen in typical CER procedures. Most reports (Rescorla, 1967; Sidman, 1958; Herrnstein and Sidman, 1958; Sidman *et al.*, 1957) have noted that under this type of schedule, avoidance rates are elevated in the presence of the CS. This enhancement of rate during the CS is maintained even when base-line avoidable shocks are not presented during the CS (Houser, 1972a, 1973), or when the avoidance behavior has been extinguished (Waller and Waller, 1963). This evidence has been cited as support for the two-process learning theories, which assume that Pavlovian conditioned responses motivate instrumental responses (Maier *et al.*, 1969). Thus, since both the instrumental avoidance response and the Pavlovian conditioned response are motivated by fear, combining the two responses in one behavioral schedule increases the level of fear during the aversive CS, as indicated by the enhanced instrumental response rates.

The preceding hypothesis is interesting since it suggests that the degree of response enhancement or facilitation during the aversive CS is a direct reflection of the level of fear generated by the preshock stimulus. Unfortunately, numerous investigators (Pomerleau, 1970; Scobie, 1972; Houser and Houser, 1973; Houser and Cash, 1975; Houser, 1976) have provided evidence that does not substantiate the earlier work cited above. This information indicates that under certain conditions both rats and monkeys will demonstrate suppressed nondiscriminated avoidance rates in the presence of an aversive preshock stimulus. Pomerleau (1970) suggested that this effect was the result of the temporal parameters of the avoidance schedule. He concluded that if the CS is relatively long and the R–S interval relatively short, suppressed rates will produce base-line shock during the CS and thus force the avoidance rates up. If, however, the CS is brief and the R–S interval relatively long, animals can suppress their avoidance rates without receiving base-line shock (Pomerleau, 1970). This analysis, however, cannot account for the results presented by Houser and his associates (Houser and Houser, 1973; Houser and Cash, 1975; Houser, 1976), who reported that squirrel monkeys demonstrated suppressed avoidance rates when the R–S interval was relatively short (20 sec) and the CS was relatively long (3 min). This discrepancy may be accounted for, however, when it is noted that squirrel monkeys often have high base-line avoidance rates (up to 180 responses/min) which make it possible for suppression to occur during the aversive CS without producing an elevation in base-line shock. Thus, Pomerleau may be correct in suggesting that schedule parameters may affect the development of response facilitation if these variables affect the amount of base-line shock that is received during the aversive CS. This conclusion is supported by behavioral data collected in the dog, a species which emits relatively low base-line operant avoidance rates (Houser and Paré, 1974a,b; Houser *et al.*, 1975; Houser, 1976). When the R–S interval is short and the CS interval is long, response facilitation is always noted during the preshock stimulus.

In addition to these schedule parameters, evidence exists which suggests that shock intensity can influence the avoidance rates of rats during an aversive CS (Scobie, 1972). According to this information, avoidance rates were increased during the CS only if the preshock stimulus had been paired with a relatively weak shock. Strong shocks led to suppression of rates during the CS (Scobie, 1972). This effect, however, may be species-specific, since Houser and Houser (1973) have noted that squirrel monkeys demonstrated both suppression and facilitation of response rates during an aversive CS that was associated with strong shock. In any case, Scobie (1972) has attempted to acccount for his findings in the rat by modifying the hypothesis of Maier *et al.* (1969) to suggest that the relationship between changes in avoidance response rate and fear elicited by the CS can best be described as an inverted U-shaped function. Weak to moderate unavoidable shocks lead to enhanced avoidance rates during the aversive CS, while strong shocks produced avoidance decrements during the CS due to the rat's propensity to "freeze" when fear motivation is intense. Although the work of Scobie (1972) and others complicates both the theoretical and empirical basis of the two-process explanations advanced by Maier *et al.* (1969), it is still compatible with the underlying assumption that the relative changes in avoidance rate during a preshock stimulus are motivated by fear. Thus, the degree of facilitation or suppression of avoidance responding during the aversive CS may provide a behavioral index of the intensity of fear motivation. This assumption is reinforced by the fact that various physiological measures, including elevations in heart rate and urinary cortisol, which have been used as indices of enhanced fear motivation, are correlated with elevated avoidance rates during an aversive CS (Houser and Paré, 1974a,b). Thus, the degree of behavioral facilitation or suppression could conceivably be used to measure the anxiolytic properties of a number of pharmacological agents. As we shall see, however, the motivational hypothesis as applied to the modified CER procedure is no more capable of accounting for drug effects than when it was applied to the traditional CER procedure.

4.4.1 Review of Drug Effects on the Modified CER Avoidance Procedure

To date, the use of continuous avoidance and the CER to evaluate the behavioral effects of drugs has been relatively limited. The preliminary data, however, do appear to correspond to the mixed results obtained with the more traditional CER techniques. The potent narcotic analgesic morphine sulfate has been reported to significantly attenuate the facilitation of avoidance response rates noted during an aversive CS in squirrel monkeys (Houser and Cash, 1975). In addition, one animal which normally suppressed its rates during the CS demonstrated facilitation under 1 and 3 mg/kg of morphine. Base-line avoidance rates were decreased while shock rates were augmented in a dose-dependent manner. General motor activity was decreased, especially under the higher doses (3, 4 mg/kg). Thus, morphine affected response rates during the aversive CS differentially, augmenting suppressed rates or decreasing the degree of response facilitation.

These results could be explained in one of two ways. First, the data could be used to suggest that a potent analgesic was able to reduce the level of fear motivation generated by an avoidance schedule whose aversive properties are the result of painful electric shock presentation. If the assumptions of two-process learning theory (Maier *et al.*, 1969) are accepted, reducing the level of fear motivation should produce substantial avoidance decrements in both segments of the behavioral schedule. The grouped results presented by Houser and Cash (1975) were in agreement with this analysis, but individual data demonstrated considerable variability, suggesting that complex and as yet unknown processes may be involved. A second explanation, however, which does not rely on a fear-reduction hypothesis, is also possible. The grouped data could be assumed to reflect a rate-dependent effect, in that the high rates of those animals who demonstrated facilitation were decreased, while the low rates of the suppressor were augmented. Thus, since various explanations are available, the morphine data cannot be cited as definitive support for the motivational hypothesis.

Similar effects to those noted for morphine have been reported with Δ^9-THC, when it was administered orally to squirrel monkeys subjected to the modified CER procedure. All doses of the drug tested (4, 8, 12 mg/kg) significantly lowered the degree of facilitation of avoidance rates noted during the aversive CS (Houser, 1975), while only the highest dose reliably reduced base-line response rate and elevated the number of shocks received. General motor activity was also substantially reduced with all doses of the drug. As with the morphine data, these results could be interpreted as reflecting a decrease in fear motivation that is demonstrated by a reduction in the normally high rate of avoidance responding generated during the aversive CS.

When drugs that interact with synaptic processes are administered to animals subjected to the modified CER procedure (R–S = S–S = 20 sec with a 3-min CS), mixed results are obtained. Drugs which modulate adrenergic activity in different directions (amphetamine and α-methyl-*p*-tyrosine) have no consistent effects upon the facilitation of response rate noted during an aversive CS in squirrel monkeys (Houser, 1973). Drugs which decrease cholinergic activity, on the other hand, do reliably affect the differential avoidance rates generated throughout the CS. The anticholinergic scopolamine hydrobromide dramatically reduced the facilitation of avoidance rate noted during the CS in squirrel monkeys (Houser and Houser, 1973) and dogs (Houser and Paré, 1974a). Furthermore, as with morphine, scopolamine hydrobromide consistently elevated the avoidance rates of those monkeys who normally demonstrated response suppression during the aversive CS. The peripheral acting anticholinergic scopolamine methylbromide had no reliable effects upon behavior in either the dog or monkey, while the cholinomimetic pilocarpine had no behavioral effects when administered to squirrel monkeys. Thus, only the central-acting anticholinergic was able to alter the pattern of avoidance behavior during the preshock stimulus. This effect was correlated with increments in the heart rate and urinary cortisol measures obtained in the dog (Houser and Paré, 1974a). The fact that response facilitation during the CS was reduced under drug conditions might indicate that scopolamine effectively reduced the level of fear or anxiety generated by the aversive CS. The relatively efficient modes of responding exhibited by the dogs during non-CS segments of the schedule under low doses of the drug, however, suggested that fear motivation was probably not severely reduced. It appeared more likely that the dramatic reductions in avoidance rate that occurred primarily during the CS probably represented an alteration in cognitive (possibly memory) processes. Thus, animals reacted as if they had not been previously exposed to the aversive CS (Houser and Paré, 1974a). This finding, combined with the fact that pilocarpine produced no reliable effects on avoidance behavior during the CS, suggested that cholinergic mechanisms did not appear to directly influence the level of response facilitation noted during an aversive CS.

Finally, the most direct pharmacological evidence currently available concerning the validity of the motivational hypothesis as it relates to the modified CER procedure has been supplied by evaluating the effects of the anxiolytic chlordiazepoxide. This drug given in a wide dosage range (45, 100, 200 mg) to dogs failed to affect the facilitation of avoidance-response, heart, and activity rates normally generated during the aversive CS. These doses were sufficient, however, to significantly lower base-line avoidance rate and to reliably reduce the amount of the adrenal hormone, cortisol, excreted in the urine (Houser *et al.*, 1975). These data strongly suggest that reductions in fear motivation produced by clinically active anxiolytic drugs do not affect the facilitated avoidance rates generated during a preshock stimulus. This, in turn, suggests that the assumptions of the motivational hypothesis may not be valid and/or that anxiolytic agents are not potent enough in the species tested to affect the level of motivation engendered by the experimental procedure. In any case, it is clear that the modified CER procedure which utilizes continuous avoidance is not sensitive to the anxiolytic properties of chlordiazepoxide. The fact that the neuroleptic chlorpromazine was also ineffective in reducing the facilitation of avoidance rates in the monkey (Houser, 1976) and dog (Houser *et al.*, 1976) indicates that this procedure is relatively insensitive to clinically active tranquilizing drugs. As such, this procedure does not appear to offer significant promise as a behavioral test that will be useful for delineating the various properties of pharmaceutical agents.

5. General Summary and Conclusions

The purpose of the present chapter was to summarize the effects of several classes of clinically active drugs upon behavior controlled by four distinct types of schedules of reinforcement that involve the presentation of electric shock. In two of these procedures (punishment and avoidance), the aversive event was made contingent upon the presence or absence of a specific behavior, while in the other two schedules (CER with appetitive or avoidance base lines) the shock was unavoidable and thus not contingent upon the emission of a specific response. Table IV summarizes the general effects of four classes of drugs on the behavior maintained by these schedules of reinforcement.

Although conflicting evidence is available concerning many of the findings in Table IV, the conclusions listed in this table are representative of the majority of data reported in the drug literature. Anxiolytic drugs specifically affect behavior under those schedules of reinforcement that make shock presentation contingent upon behavior. These compounds decrease avoidance responding and elevate punished responding under conflict schedules. The conflict–punishment technique is the only procedure that appears to be specifically sensitive to the anxiolytic properties of drugs. Neuroleptics, on the other hand, depress avoidance responding and appear not to exert a consistent effect on behavior under the control of any of the other schedules. The continuous avoidance procedure is not, by itself, able to distinguish anxiolytic from neuroleptic activity. The procedure must be modified by performing drug-interaction studies (e.g., pretreatment with anticholinergics) before continuous avoidance procedures can be employed as specific measures of neuroleptic potency. Finally, analgesics and stimulants enhance avoidance responding in a dose-dependent manner, while producing equivocal results in the other procedures. Thus, the present aversive schedules provide no means of distinguishing between analgesic or stimulant drugs.

The summary above thus suggests that the conflict–punishment procedure is particularly useful in assaying the anxiolytic properties of drugs, while continuous avoidance procedures can be used to evaluate

Table IV. Effects of Various Classes of Drugs upon Three Types of Aversive Schedules of Reinforcement

Compounds	Continuous avoidance	Appetitive CER	Avoidance CER	Conflict
Anxiolytics	Decreases avoidance responding	Mixed effects	No effect	Increases shock-paired responses
Neuroleptics	Decreases avoidance responding	Mixed effects	No effect	No effect
Analgesics	Increases avoidance responding	Mixed effects	Decreases facilitated responding during aversive CS	Mixed effects

neuroleptic activity. The CER procedures, on the other hand, do not appear to be useful in detecting the specific properties of any class of clinically active drugs.

The data summarized in the present chapter highlight the fact that relatively subtle changes in experimental variables can produce patterns of behavior that are differentially sensitive to various classes of drugs. The relationship of the aversive event to the behavior in question (i.e., unavoidable shock, response-contingent shock, or avoidable shock) is a critical determinant of the type of effect a particular drug will exert. In addition, other factors, such as base-line rate of responding, schedule parameters, shock intensity, the context in which the behavior occurs, diurnal cycles, and species employed, can dramatically influence the type and degree of drug-induced behavioral effect. As Cook and Catania (1964) have pointed out, such variables are *not* trivial. They have a profound influence upon drug–behavior interactions. As such, these variables deserve critical study and must be taken into account when psychopharmacological research is evaluated.

Finally, the present chapter presented evidence which clearly suggested that the motivational hypothesis is unable to account for the complex effects that various classes of drugs exert upon behavior under the control of aversive schedules of reinforcement. The major attraction of the motivational hypothesis lies in its plausible generality. It can be used to account for any type of drug effect that occurs on behavior under aversive control. Since this explanation assumes that both the suppression and maintenance of behavior by shock presentation is controlled by fear or anxiety, it can account for both increases and decreases in response rate within the framework of a single concept (Kelleher and Morse, 1964). Unfortunately, as has been noted above, drugs often produce differential effects upon behavior under the control of avoidance and punishment schedules of reinforcement. Thus, it appears unlikely that a unitary psychological concept will be able to account for the multitude of effects that various drugs exert upon the different behaviors that are generated by aversive schedules of reinforcement. The discipline of psychopharmacology must turn away from simplistic explanations of drug–behavior interactions and dedicate itself to the study of the complex interrelationships among experimental variables, drugs, and behavior. This approach should provide a more fruitful method for understanding the behavioral effects that are produced by the administration of various drugs.

ACKNOWLEDGMENT

The author wishes to express his appreciation to Sybella Halliday, Kathleen Monahan, and Dr. Johanna E. Dimitrov for their assistance in conducting the literature search that formed the basis for this chapter. I am also indebted to Frances L. Houser for her editorial assistance and for typing the manuscript.

6. References

Abel, E. L., 1969, Effects of the marihuana homologue, pyrahexyl, on a conditioned emotional response, *Psychon. Sci.* **16:** 44.

Anger, D., 1963, The role of temporal discrimination in the reinforcement of Sidman avoidance behavior, *J. Exp. Anal. Behav.* **3:**477–506.

Annau, Z., and Kamin, L. J., 1961, The conditioned emotional response as a function of intensity of the US, *J. Comp. Physiol. Psychol.* **54:**428–432.

Appel, J. B., 1963, Drugs, shock intensity, and the CER, *Psychopharmacologia* **4:**148–153.

Aprison, M. H., Hingtgen, J. N., and McBride, W. J., 1975, Serotonergic and cholinergic mechanisms during disruption of approach and avoidance behavior, *Fed. Proc.* **34:**1813–1822.

Axelrod, J. G., Hertting, A., and Potter, L., 1962, Effects of drugs on the uptake and release of ^{3}H-norepinephrine in the rat heart, *Nature* **194:**297–299.

Babbini, M., Gaiardi, M., and Bartoletti, M., 1973, Effects of morphine on a quickly learned conditioned suppression in rats, *Psychopharmacologia* **33:**329–332.

Babbini, M., Gaiardi, M., Bartoletti, M., Torrielli, M. V., and DeMarchi, F., 1975, The conflict behavior in rats for the evaluation of a homogeneous series of 3-hydroxybenzodiazepines: structure–activity relationships, *Pharmacol. Res. Comm.* **7:**337–346.

Balfour, D. J. K., and Morrison, C. F., 1975, A possible role for the pituitary–adrenal system in the effects of nicotine on avoidance behaviour, *Pharmacol. Biochem. Behav.* **3:**349–354.

Beaton, J. M., LeBlanc, A. E.,and Webster, C. D., 1974, The effects of *d*-amphetamine on the inter-response times of rats and guinea-pigs on a modified Sidman discriminated avoidance schedule, *Psychopharmacologia* **37:**199–203.

Berger, B. D., Margules, D. L., and Stein, L., 1967, Prevention of learning of a fear response by oxazepam and scopolamine, *Amer. Psychol.* **27:**492 (abstract).

Bignami, G., and De Acetis, L., 1973, An investigation on the nature of continuous avoidance deficits: differential response to chlordiazepoxide treatment, *Pharmacol. Biochem. Behav.* **1:**277–283.

Bignami, G., and Gatti, G. L., 1972, Acquisition and performance effects of chlordiazepoxide (CDZ) in several continuous avoidance situations, *Psychopharmacologia* **26:**53.

Blackman, D., 1968, Effects of drugs on conditioned "anxiety," *Nature* **217:**769–770.

Blakely, T. A., and Parker, L. F., 1973, The effects of parachlorophenylalanine on experimentally induced conflict behavior, *Pharmacol. Biochem. Behav.* **1:**609–613.

Blum, K., 1970, Effects of chlordiazepoxide and pentobarbital on conflict behavior in rats, *Psychopharmacologia* **17:**391–398.

Bocknik, S. E., Hingtgen, J. N., Hughes, F. W., and Forney, R. B., 1968, Harmaline effects on tetrabenazine depression of avoidance responding in rats, *Life Sci.* **7:**1189–1201.

Boren, J. J., Sidman, M., and Herrnstein, R. J., 1959, Avoidance, escape, and extinction as functions of shock intensity, *J. Comp. Physiol. Psychol* **52:**420–425.

Bovet, D., and Gatti, G. L., 1964, Pharmacology of instrumental avoidance conditioning, *in: Proceedings of the Second International Pharmacological Meeting* (Prague), pp. 75–89, Pergamon Press, Elmsford, N.Y.

Boyd, E. S., Hutchinson, E. D., Gardner, L. C., and Meritt, D. A., 1963, Effects of tetrahydrocannabinols and other drugs on operant behavior in rats, *Arch. Int. Pharmacodyn.* **144:**533–554.

Brady, J. V., 1956, Assessment of drug effects on emotional behavior, *Science* **123:**1033–1034.

Brady, J. V., and Hunt, H. F., 1955, An experimental approach to the analysis of emotional behavior, *J. Psychol.* **40:**313–324.

Bravo, L., and Appel, J. B., 1967, Effects of chlorpromazine on the acquisition of a wheel-turning avoidance response, *Arch. Int. Pharmacodyn.* **165:**451–458.

Buser, P., Cook, L., Giurgea, C., Jacobsen, E., Ray, O. S., Richelle, M., Silverman, A. P., Stein, L., and Votava, Z., 1970, The neuroleptics, *Mod. Probl. Pharmacopsyhiat.* **5:** 85–108.

Campbell, B. A., and Masterson, F. A., 1969, Psychophysics of punishment, in: *Punishment and Aversive Behavior* (B. A. Campbell and R. M. Church, eds.), pp. 3–42, Appleton-Century-Crofts, New York.

Cicala, G. A., and Hartley, D. L., 1967, Drugs and the learning and performance of fear, *J. Comp. Physiol. Psychol.* **64:**175–178.

Clark, F. C., and Steele, B. J., 1966, Effects of *d*-amphetamine on performance under a multiple schedule in the rat, *Psychopharmacologia* **9:**157–169.

Cook, L., and Catania, A. C., 1964, Effects of drugs on avoidance and escape behavior, *Fed. Proc.* **23:**818–835.

Cook, L., and Davidson, A. B., 1973, Effects of behaviorally active drugs in a conflict–punishment procedure in rats, *in: The Benzodiazepines* (S. Garattini, E. Mussini, and L. O. Randall, eds.), pp. 327–345, Raven Press, New York.

Cook, L., and Kelleher, R. T., 1961, The interaction of drugs and behavior, *Neuropsychopharmacology* **2:**77–92.

Cook, L., and Kelleher, R. T., 1962, Drug effects on the behavior of animals, *Ann. N.Y. Acad. Sci.* **96:**315–335.

Cook, L., and Kelleher, R. T., 1963, Effects of drugs on behavior, *Ann. Rev. Pharmacol.* **3:**205–222.

Cook, L., and Sepinwall, J., 1975, Behavioral analysis of the effects and mechanisms of action of benzodiazepines, *in: Mechanism of Action of Benzodiazepines* (E. Costa and P. Greengard, eds.), pp. 1–28, Raven Press, New York.

Cook, L., and Weidley, E., 1957, Behavioral effects of some psychopharmacological agents, *Ann. N.Y. Acad. Sci.* **66:**740–752.

Dallemagne, Gh., 1970, Action of chlorpromazine, meprobamate, and amphetamine on 3 situations conditioned under aversive control, *Arch. Int. Pharmacodyn.* **183:**46–59.

Dantzer, R., and Baldwin, B. A., 1974, Effects of chlordiazepoxide on heart rate and behavioural suppression in pigs subjected to operant conditioning procedures, *Psychopharmacologia* **37:**169–177.

Dantzer, R., and Roca, M., 1974, Tranquilizing effects of diazepam in pigs subjected to a punishment procedure, *Psychopharmacologia* **40:**235–240.

Del Rio, J., 1971, Facilitating effects of some chlorpromazine-*d*-amphetamine mixtures on avoidance learning, *Psychopharmacologia* **21:**39–48.

Dews, P. B., 1955, Studies on behavior. I. Differential sensitivity to pentobarbital of pecking performance in pigeons depending on the schedule of reward, *J. Pharmacol. Exp. Ther.* **113:**393–401.

Dews, P. B., 1958, Studies on behavior. IV. Stimulant actions of methamphetamine, *J. Pharmacol. Exp. Ther.* **122:**137–147.

Dews, P. B., 1964, A behavioral effect of amobarbital, *Archs. Exp. Pathol. Pharmakol.* **248:**296–307.

Dinsmoor, J. A., and Lyon, D. O., 1961, The selective action of chlorpromazine on behavior suppressed by punishment, *Psychopharmacologia* **2:**456–460.

Dinsmoor, J. A., Bonbright, J. C., Jr., and Lilie, D. R., 1971, A controlled comparison of drug effects on escape from conditioned aversive stimulation ("anxiety") and from continuous shock, *Psychopharmacologia* **22:**323–332.

Dobrin, P. B., and Rhyne, R. L., 1969, Effects of chlorpromazine on two types of conditioned avoidance behavior, *Arch. Int. Pharmacodyn.* **178:**351–356.

Erickson, C. K., 1971, Studies on the mechanism of avoidance facilitation by nicotine, *Psychopharmacologia* **22:**357–368.

Estes, W. K., and Skinner, B. F., 1941, Some quantitative properties of anxiety, *J. Exp. Psychol.* **29:**390–400.

Evans, H. L., and Patton, R. A., 1970, Scopolamine effects on conditioned suppression: influence of diurnal cycle and transitions betwen normal and drugged states, *Psychopharmacologia* **17:**1–13.

Fielding, S., McGreevy, T., Outwater, B., Cornfeldt, M., and Pacifico, L., 1971, The effects of imipramine on two tests involving shock avoidance behavior in squirrel monkeys, *Pharmacologist* **13:**206.

Fontaine, O., Libon, Ph., and Richelle, M., 1974, Action of a new psychotropic drug (sulpiride) on avoidance behavior in rats, *Psychopharmacologia* **39:**309–314.

Foree, D. D., Moretz, F. H., and McMillan, D. E., 1973, Drugs and punished responding. II. *d*-Amphetamine-induced increases in punished responding, *J. Exp. Anal. Behav.* **20:**291–300.

Geller, I., 1964, Relative potencies of benzodiazepines as measured by their effects on conflict behavior, *Arch. Int. Pharmacodyn.* **149:**243–247.

Geller, I., and Blum, K., 1970, The effects of 5-HTP on parachlorophenylalanine (*p*-CPA) attenuation of "conflict" behavior, *Eur. J. Pharmacol.* **9:**319–324.

Geller, I., and Hartmann, R., 1973, Attenuation of "conflict" behavior with cinanserin [2′-(3-dimethylaminopropylthio)cinnamanilide hydrochloride] a serotonin antagonist: reversal of the effect with 5-hydroxytryptophan (5-HTP) and α-methyl-tryptamine, *Fed. Proc.* **32:**817.

Geller, I., and Seifter, J., 1960, The effects of meprobamate, barbiturates, *d*-amphetamine and promazine on experimentally induced conflict in the rat, *Psychopharmacologia* **1:**482–492.

Geller, I., and Seifter, J., 1962, The effects of mono-urethans, di-urethans, and barbiturates on a punishment discrimination, *J. Pharmacol. Exp. Ther.* **136:**284–288.

Geller, I., Kulak, J. T., Jr., and Seifter, J., 1962, The effects of chlordiazepoxide and chlorpromazine on a punishment discrimination, *Psychopharmacologia* **3:**374–385.

Geller, I., Bachman, E., and Seifter, J., 1963, Effects of reserpine and morphine on behavior suppressed by punishment, *Life Sci.* **4:**226–231.

Glick, S. D., Greenstein, S., and Goldfarb, J., 1973, Increased electrical impedance of mice following administration of scopolamine, *Behav. Biol.* **9:**771–775.

Goldman, P. S., and Docter, R. F., 1966, Facilitation of bar pressing and "suppression" of conditioned suppression in cats as a function of alcohol, *Psychoharmacologia* **9:**64–72.

Gonzalez, S. C., Karniol, I. G., and Carlini, E. A., 1972, Effects of *Cannabis sativa* extract on conditioned fear, *Behav. Biol.* **7:**83–94.

Graeff, F. G., and Schoenfeld, R. I., 1970, Tryptaminergic mechanisms in punished and nonpunished behavior, *J. Pharmacol. Exp. Ther.* **173:**277–283.

Hanson, H. M., Witoslawski, J. J., and Campbell, E. H., 1967, Drug effects in squirrel monkeys trained on a multiple schedule with a punishment contingency, *J. Exp. Anal. Behav.* **10:**565–569.

Hanson, H. M., Stone, C. A., and Witoslawski, J. J., 1970, Antagonism of the antiavoidance effects of various agents by anticholinergic drugs, *J. Pharmacol. Exp. Ther.* **173:**117–124.

Hartmann, R. J., and Geller, I., 1971, *p*-Chlorophenylalanine effects on a conditioned emotional response in rats, *Life Sci.* **10:**927–933.

Heise, G. A., and Boff, E., 1962, Continuous avoidance as a baseline for measuring behavioral effects of drugs, *Psychopharmacologia* **3:**264–282.

Henton, W. W., and Jordan, J. J., 1970, Differential conditioned suppression during preshock stimuli as a function of shock intensity, *Psychol. Rec.* **20:**9–16.

Herrnstein, R. J., and Sidman, M., 1958, Avoidance conditioning as a factor in the effects of unavoidable shocks on food-reinforced behavior, *J. Comp. Physiol. Psychol.* **51:**380–385.

Hill, R. T., 1974, Fixed ratio conflict: a sensitive procedure for the detection and evaluation of anxiolytic drug activity in rats, *J. Pharmacol.* **5:**43.

Hill, R. T., and Tedeschi, D. H., 1971, Animal testing and screening procedures in evaluating psychotropic drugs, *in: An Introduction to Psychopharmacology* (R. H. Rech and K. E. Moore, eds.), pp. 237–288, Raven Press, New York.

Hill, H. E., Pescor, F. T., Belleville, R. E., and Wikler, A., 1957, Use of differential bar-pressing rates of rats for screening analgesic drugs. I. Techniques and effects of morphine, *J. Pharmacol. Exp. Ther.* **120:**388–397.

Hill, H. E., Bell, E. C., and Wikler, A., 1967, Reduction of conditioned suppression: actions of morphine compared with those of amphetamine, pentobarbital, nalorphine, cocaine, LSD-25, and chlorpromazine, *Arch. Int. Pharmacodyn.* **165:**212–226.

Hoffman, H. S., Fleshler, M., and Chorny, H., 1961, Discriminated bar-press avoidance, *J. Exp. Anal. Behav.* **4:**309–316.

Hollister, L., Richards, R., and Gillespie, H., 1968, Comparison of tetrahydrocannabinol and synhexyl in man, *Clin. Pharmacol. Ther.* **9:**783–791.

Holtzman, S. G., 1974a, Tolerance to the stimulant effects of morphine and pentazocine on avoidance responding in the rat, *Psychopharmacologia* **39:**23–37.

Holtzman, S. G., 1974b, Effects of nalorphine on avoidance behavior and locomotor activity in the rat, *Arch. Int. Pharmacodyn.* **212:**199–204.

Holtzman, S. G., and Jewett, R. E., 1973, Stimulation of behavior in the rat by cyclazocine: effects of naloxone, *J. Pharmacol. Exp. Ther.* **187:**380–390.

Holtzman, S. G., and Villarreal, J. E., 1969, The effects of morphine on conditioned suppression in rhesus monkeys, *Psychon. Sci.* **17:**161.

Houser, V. P., 1972a, The effects of drugs upon a modified Sidman avoidance schedule that employs response independent shock. A preliminary report on cholinergic agents, *Edgewood Arsenal Tech. Rept.* **4463:**1–25.

Houser, V. P., 1973, Modulation of avoidance behavior in squirrel monkeys after chronic administration and withdrawal of *d*-amphetamine or α-methyl-*p*-tyrosine, *Psychopharmacologia* **28:**213–234.

Houser, V. P., 1975, The effects of Δ^9-tetrahydrocannabinol upon fear-motivated behavior in squirrel monkeys, *Physiol. Psychol.* **3:**157–161.

Houser, V. P., 1976, The effects of chlorpromazine upon fear-motivated behavior in the squirrel monkey, *Physiol. Psychol.* **4:**189–194.

Houser, V. P., and Cash, R. J., 1975, The effects of chronic morphine administration upon a Sidman avoidance schedule that utilized response-independent shock, *Psychopharmacologia* **41:**255–262.

Houser, V. P., and Houser, F. L., 1973, The effects of agents that modify muscarinic tone upon behavior controlled by an avoidance schedule that employs signaled unavoidable shock, *Psychopharmacologia* **32:**133–150.

Houser, V. P., and Paré, W. P., 1972, A method for determining the aversive threshold in the rat using repeated measures: tests with morphine sulfate, *Behav. Res. Methods Instrum.* **4:**135–137.

Houser, V. P., and Paré, W. P., 1973, Measurement of analgesia using a spatial preference test in the rat, *Physiol. Behav.* **10:**535–538.

Houser, V. P., and Paré, W. P., 1974a, Anticholinergics: their effects on fear-motivated behavior, urinary 11-hydroxycorticosteroids, urinary volume, and heart rate in the dog, *Psychol. Rep.* **34:**183–197.

Houser, V. P., and Paré, W. P., 1974b, Long-term conditioned fear modification in the dog as measured by changes in urinary 11-hydroxycorticosteroids, heart rate, and behavior, *Pavlov. J. Biol. Sci.* **9:**85–96.

Houser, V. P., Rothfeld, B., and Varady, A., Jr., 1975, Effects of chlordiazepoxide upon fear-motivated behavior in the dog, *Psychol. Rep.* **36:**987–998.

Houser, V. P., Rothfeld, B., and Varady, A., Jr., 1976, Effects of chlorpromazine on fear-motivated behavior, urinary cortisol, urinary volume, and heart rate in the dog, *Psychol. Rep.* **38:**299–308.

Janssen, P. A. J., and Lenaerts, F., 1967, Is it possible to predict the clinical effects of neuroleptic drugs (major tranquillizers) from animal data? IV: An improved experimental design for measuring the inhibitory effects of neuroleptic drugs on amphetamine or apomorphine-induced "chewing" and "agitation" in rats, *Arzneimittel-Forsch.* **17:**841–854.

Kelleher, R. T., and Morse, W. H., 1964, Escape behavior and punished behavior, *Fed. Proc.* **23:**808–817.

Kelleher, R. T., Fry, W., Deegan, J., and Cook, L., 1961, Effects of meprobamate on operant behavior in rats, *J. Pharmacol. Exp. Ther.* **133:**271–280.

Kinnard, W. J., Aceto, M. D. G., and Buckley, J. P., 1962, The effects of certain psychotropic agents on the conditioned emotional response behavior of the albino rat, *Psychopharmacologia* **3:**227–230.

Kubena, R. K., and Barry, H., III, 1970, Interactions of Δ^1-tetrahydrocannabinol with barbiturates and amphetamine, *J. Pharmacol. Exp. Ther.* **173:**94–100.

Kulkarni, A. S., 1972, Selective increase in avoidance responding by methamphetamine in naive rats, *Psychopharmacologia* **24:**449–455.

Kumar, R., Stolerman, I. P., and Steinberg, H., 1970, Psychopharmacology, *Ann. Rev. Psychol.* **21:**595–628.

Latz, A., Kornetsky, C., and Bain, G., 1965, The effects of *d*-amphetamine on discrete avoidance as a function of the predrug level of performance, *Fed. Proc.* **24:**197.

Latz, A., Bain, G. T., and Kornetsky, C., 1969, Attenuated effect of chlorpromazine on conditioned avoidance as a function of rapid acquisition, *Psychopharmacologia* **14:**23–32.

Lauener, H., 1963, Conditioned supression in rats and the effect of pharmacological agents thereon, *Psychopharmacologia* **4:**311–325.

Leaf, R. C., and Muller, S. A., 1965, Effects of shock intensity, deprivation, and morphine in a simple approach-avoidance conflict situation, *Psychol. Rep.* **17:**819–823.

Lepore, F., Ptito, M., Freibergs, V., and Guillemot, J-P., 1974, Effects of low doses of chlorpromazine on a conditioned emotional response in the rat, *Psychol. Rep.* **34:**231–237.

Levison, P. K., and Freedman, D. X., 1967, Recovery of a discriminated lever-press avoidance performance from the effects of reserpine, chlorpromazine, and tetrabenazine, *Arch. Int. Pharmacodyn.* **170:**31–38.

Lipper, S., and Kornetsky, C., 1971, Effect of chlorpromazine on conditioned avoidance as a function of CS–US interval length, *Psychopharmacologia* **22:**144–150.

Maier, S. M., Seligman, M., and Solomon, R., 1969, Pavlovian fear conditioning and learned helplessness: effects on escape and avoidance behavior of (a) the CS–US contingency and (b) the independence of the US and voluntary responding, *in: Punishment and Aversive Behavior* (B. Campbell and R. Church, eds.), pp. 299–342, Appleton-Century-Crofts, New York.

Manning, F. J., 1974, Tolerance to effects of Δ^9-tetrahydrocannabinol (THC) on free-operant shock avoidance, *Fed. Proc.* **33:**481.

Margules, D. L., 1968, Noradrenergic basis of inhibition between reward and punishment in amygdala, *J. Comp. Physiol. Psychol.* **66:**329–334.

Margules, D. L., 1971, Alpha and beta adrenergic receptors in amygdala: reciprocal inhibitors and facilitators of punished operant behavior, *Eur. J. Pharmacol.* **16:**21–26.

Margules, D. L., and Stein, L., 1967, Neuroleptics vs. tranquilizers: evidence from animal behavior studies of mode and site of action, *in: Neuro-Psycho-Pharmacology* (H. Brill, ed.), pp. 108–120, Excerpta Medica Foundation, Amsterdam.

Margules, D. L., and Stein, L., 1968, Increase of "antianxiety" activity and tolerance of behavioral depression during chronic administration of oxazepam, *Psychopharmacologia* **13:**74–80.

McKearney, J. W., 1976, Punishment of responding under fixed-interval (FI) schedules of food presentation or shock termination in squirrel monkeys: effects of *d*-amphetamine and pentobarbital; paper presented at Eastern Psychological Association, New York, April, 1976.

McKearney, J. W., and Barrett, J. E., 1975, Punished behavior: increases in responding after *d*-amphetamine, *Psychopharmacologia* **41:**23–26.

McMillan, D. E., 1968, The effects of sympathomimetic amines on schedule-controlled behavior in the pigeon, *J. Pharmocol. Exp. Ther.* **160:**315–325.

McMillan, D. E., 1969, Effects of *d*-amphetamine on performance under several parameters of multiple fixed-ratio, fixed-interval schedules, *J. Pharmacol. Exp. Ther.* **167:**26–33.

McMillan, D. E., 1973a, Drugs and punished responding. I. Rate-dependent effects under multiple schedules, *J. Exp. Anal. Behav.* **19:**133–145.

McMillan, D. E., 1973b, Drugs and punished responding. IV. Effects of propranolol, ethchlorvynol, and chloral hydrate, *Res. Commun. Chem. Pathol. Pharmacol.* **6:**167–174.

McMillan, D. E., 1973c, Drugs and punished responding. III. Punishment intensity as a determinant of drug effect, *Psychopharmacologia* **30:**61–74.

McMillan, D. E., and Leander, J. D., 1975, Drugs and punished responding. V. Effects of drugs on responding suppressed by response-dependent and response-independent electric shock, *Arch. Int. Pharmacodyn.* **213:**22–27.

Miczek, K. A., 1973a, Effects of scopolamine, amphetamine, and chlordiazepoxide on punishment, *Psychopharmacologia* **28:**373–389.

Miczek, K. A., 1973b, Effects of scopolamine, amphetamine, and benzodiazepines on conditioned suppression, *Pharmacol. Biochem. Behav.* **1:**401–411.

Miczek, K. A., and Grossman, S. P., 1972, Punished and unpunished operant behavior after atropine administration to the VMH of squirrel monkeys, *J. Comp. Physiol. Psychol.* **81:**318–330.

Millenson, J. R., and Dent, J. G., 1971, Habituation of conditioned suppression, *Quart. J. Exp. Psychol.* **23:**126–134.

Millenson, J. R., and Leslie, J., 1974, The conditioned emotional response (CER) as a baseline for the study of anti-anxiety drugs, *Neuropharmacology* **13:**1–9.

Miller, F. P., Cox, R. H., Jr., and Maickel, R. P., 1970a, The effects of altered brain norepinephrine levels on continuous avoidance responding and the action of amphetamines, *Neuropharmacology* **9:**511–517.

Miller, F. P., Cox, R. H., Snodgrass, W. R., and Maickel, R. P., 1970b, Comparative effects of *p*-chlorophenylalanine, *p*-chloroamphetamine, and *p*-chloro-*N*-methylamphetamine on rat brain norepinephrine, serotonin, and 5-hydroxy-indole-3-acetic acid, *Biochem. Pharmacol.* **19:**435–442.

Milner, J. S., 1974, Effects of *d*-amphetamine on acquisition of leverpress Sidman avoidance in rats, *Physiol. Psychol.* **2:**392–396.

Morpurgo, C., 1962, Effects of antiparkinson drugs on a phenothiazine-induced catatonic reaction, *Arch. Int. Pharmacodyn.* **137:**84–90.

Morrison, C. F., 1969, The effects of nicotine on punished behavior, *Psychopharmacologia* **14:**221–232.

Morrison, C. F., 1974a, Effects of nicotine on the observed behavior of rats during signalled and unsignalled avoidance experiments, *Psychopharmacologia* **38:**37–46.

Morrison, C. F., 1974b, Effects of nicotine and its withdrawal on the performance of rats on signalled and unsignalled avoidance schedules, *Psychopharmacologia* **38:**25–35.

Morse, W. H., 1964, Effect of amobarbital and chlorpromazine on punished behavior in the pigeon, *Psychopharmacologia* **6:**286–294.

Myers, A. K., 1962, Effects of CS intensity and quality in avoidance conditioning, *J. Comp. Physiol. Psychol.* **55:**57–61.

Niemegeers, C. J. E., Verbruggen, F. J., and Janssen, P. A. J., 1969a, The influence of various neuroleptic drugs on shock avoidance responding in rats. I. Nondiscriminated Sidman avoidance procedure, *Psychopharmacologia* **16:**161–174.

Niemegeers, C. J. E., Verbruggen, F. J., and Janssen, P. A. J., 1969b, The influence of various neuroleptic drugs on shock avoidance responding in rats. II. Nondiscriminated Sidman avoidance procedure with alternate reinforcement and extinction periods and analysis of the interresponse times (IRT's), *Psychopharmacologia* **16:**175–182.

Niemegeers, C. J. E., Verbruggen, F. J., and Janssen, P. A. J., 1970, The influence of various neuroleptic drugs on shock avoidance responding in rats. III. Amphetamine antagonism in the discriminated Sidman avoidance procedure, *Psychopharmacologia* **17:**151–159.

Nigro, M. R., 1967, Chlorpromazine-induced suppression in appetitive and avoidance responding as a function of shock intensity, *Psychol. Rep.* **21:**61–69.

Owen, J. E., Jr., and Rathbun, R. C., 1966, Sustained changes of avoidance behavior after chronic nortriptyline administration, *Psychopharmacologia* **9:**137–145.

Owen, J. E., Jr., and Rathbun, R. C., 1967, Effects of long, intermittent schedules on phenothiazine-induced avoidance loss, *Psychopharmacologia* **12:**24–33.

Paré, W. P., and Houser, V. P., 1973, Rapid acquisition of a Sidman avoidance response, *Behav. Res. Methods Instrum.* **5:**287–289.

Pearl, J., Aceto, M. D., and Fitzgerald, J. J., 1968, Stimulant drugs and temporary increases in avoidance responding, *J. Comp. Physiol. Psychol.* **65:**50–54.

Pomerleau, O. F., 1970, The effects of stimuli followed by response-independent shock on shock avoidance behavior, *J. Exp. Anal. Behav.* **14:**11–21.

Ray, O. S., 1964, Tranquilizer effects on conditioned suppression, *Psychopharmacologia* **5:**136–146.

Rescorla, R. A., 1967, Inhibition of delay in Pavlovian fear conditioning, *J. Comp. Physiol. Psychol.* **64:**114–120.

Richelle, M., Xhenseval, B., Fontaine, O., and Thone, L., 1962, Action of chlordiazepoxide on two types of temporal conditioning in rats, *Int. J. Neuropharmacol.* **1:**381–391.

Robichaud, R. C., and Sledge, K. L., 1969, The effects of *p*-chlorophenylalanine on experimentally induced conflict in the rat, *Life Sci.* **8:**965–969.

Robichaud, R. C., Sledge, K. L., Hefner, M. A., and Goldberg, M. E., 1963, Propranolol and chlordiazepoxide on experimentally induced conflict and shuttle box performance in rodents, *Psychopharmacologia* **32:**157–160.
Robichaud, R. C., Hefner, M. A., Anderson, J. E., and Goldberg, M. E., 1973, Effects of Δ^9-tetrahydrocannabinol (THC) on several rodent learning paradigms, *Pharmacology* **10:**1–11.
Rutledge, C. O., and Kelleher, R. T., 1965, Interactions between the effects of methamphetamine and pentobarbital on operant behavior in the pigeon, *Psychopharmacologia* **7:**400–408.
Sanger, D. J., and Blackman, D. E., 1976, The effects of *d*-amphetamine on the temporal control of operant responding in rats during a pre-shock stimulus, *J. Exp. Anal. Behav.* **26:**369–378.
Sansone, M., Renzi, P., and Amposta, B., 1972, Effects of chlorpromazine and chlordiazepoxide on discriminated lever-press avoidance behavior and intertrial responding in mice, *Psychopharmacologia* **27:**313–318.
Sansone, M., Renzi, P., and Castellano, C., 1974, Effect of methamphetamine on discriminated lever-press avoidance behaviour in hamsters, *Pharmacol. Res. Commun.* **6:**187–192.
Scheckel, C. L., and Boff, E., 1964, Behavioral effects of interacting imipramine and other drugs with *d*-amphetamine, cocaine, and tetrabenazine, *Psychopharmacologia* **5:**198–208.
Scobie, S. R., 1972, Interaction of an aversive Pavlovian conditional stimulus with aversively and appetitively motivated operants in rats, *J. Comp. Physiol. Psychol.* **79:**171–188.
Scobie, S. R., and Garske, G., 1970, Chlordiazepoxide and conditioned suppression, *Psychopharmacologia* **16:**272–280.
Sepinwall, J., and Grodsky, F. S., 1969, Effects of cholinergic stimulation or blockade of the rat hypothalamus on discrete-trial conflict behavior, *Life Sci.* **8:**45–52.
Sepinwall, J., Grodsky, F. S., Sullivan, J. W., and Cook, L., 1973, Effects of propranolol and chlordiazepoxide on conflict behavior in rats, *Psychopharmacologia* **31:**375–382.
Sidman, M., 1953, Avoidance conditioning with brief shock and no exteroceptive warning signal, *Science* **118:**157–158.
Sidman, M., 1958, By-products of aversive control, *J. Exp. Anal. Behav.* **1:**265–280.
Sidman, M., Herrnstein, R. J., and Conrad, D., 1957, Maintenance of avoidance behavior by unavoidable shocks, *J. Comp. Physiol. Psychol.* **50:**533–557.
Smith, C. B., 1964, Effects of d-amphetamine upon operant behavior of pigeons: enhancement by reserpine, *J. Pharmacol. Exp. Ther.* **146:**167–174.
Soubrié, P. S., Kulkarni, S., Simon, P., and Boissier, J. R., 1975, Effects of antianxiety drugs on the food intake in trained and untrained rats and mice, *Psychopharmacologia* **45:**203–210.
Stein, L., and Berger, B. D., 1969, Paradoxical fear-increasing effects of tranquilizers: evidence of repression of memory in the rat, *Science* **166:**253–256.
Stein, L., and Wise, C. D., 1974, Serotonin and behavioral inhibition, *Advan. Biochem. Psychopharmacol.* **11:**281–291.
Stein, L., Wise, C. D., and Berger, B. D., 1973, Antianxiety action of benzodiazepines: decrease in activity of serotonin neurons in the punishment system, *in: The Benzodiazepines* (S. Garattini, E. Mussini, and L. O. Randall, eds.), pp. 299–326, Raven Press, New York.
Steinert, H. R., Holtzman, S. G., and Jewett, R. E., 1973, Some agonistic actions of the morphine antagonist levallorphan on behavior and brain monoamines in the rat, *Psychopharmacologia* **31:**35–48.
Stone, G. C., 1964, Effects of drugs on nondiscriminated avoidance behavior. I. Individual differences in dose–response relationships, *Psychopharmacologia* **6:**245–255.

Stone, G. C., 1965, Effects of drugs on avoidance behavior. II. Individual differences in susceptibilities, *Psychopharmacologia* **7:**283–302.

Sulser, F., and Dingell, J. V., 1968, Potentiation and blockade of the central actions of amphetamine by chlorpromazine, *Biochem. Pharmacol.* **17:**634–636.

Suzmann, M. M., 1971, The use of beta-adrenergic blockade with propranolol in anxiety syndromes, *Postgrad. Med. J.* **47:**104–108.

Takaori, S., Yada, N., and Mori, G., 1969, Effects of psychotropic agents on Sidman avoidance response in good- and poor-performed rats, *Jap. J. Pharmacol.* **19:**587–596.

Tang, A. H., and Kirch, J. D., 1973, The effects of diazepam on a conflict procedure in rhesus monkeys based on suppression of avoidance responding, *Pharmacologist* **15:**182.

Tenen, S. S., 1967, Recovery time as a measure of CER strength: effects of benzodiazepines, amobarbital, chlorpromazine, and amphetamine, *Psychopharmacologia* **12:**1–17.

Valenstein, E. S., 1959, The effect of reserpine on the conditioned emotional response in the guinea pig, *J. Exp. Anal. Behav.* **2:**219–225.

Verhave, T., 1958, The effect of methamphetamine on operant level and avoidance behavior, *J. Exp. Anal. Behav.* **1:**207–219.

Verhave, T., Owen, J. E., Jr., and Robbins, E. B., 1958, Effects of chlorpromazine and secobarbital on avoidance and escape behavior, *Arch. Int. Pharmacodyn.* **116:**45–53.

Vogel, J. R., Hughes, R. A., and Carlton, P. L., 1967, Scopolamine, atropine, and conditioned fear, *Psychopharmacologia* **10:**409–416.

Vogel, J. R., Beer, B., and Clody, D. E., 1971, A simple and reliable conflict procedure for testing anti-anxiety agents, *Psychopharmacologia* **21:**1–7.

Waller, M. B., and Waller, P. S., 1963, The effects of unavoidable shocks on a multiple schedule having an avoidance component, *J. Exp. Anal. Behav.* **6:**29–37.

Webster, C. D., Willinsky, M. D. Herring, B. S., and Walters, G. C., 1971, Effects of l-Δ^1-THC on temporally spaced responding and discriminated Sidman avoidance behavior in rats, *Nature* **232:**497–501.

Webster, C. D., LeBlanc, A. E., Marshman, J. A., and Beaton, J. M., 1973, Acquisition and loss of tolerance to 1-Δ^9-tetrahydrocannabinol in rats on an avoidance schedule, *Psychopharmacologia* **30:**217–226.

Wedeking, P. W., 1974, Schedule-dependent differences among antianxiety drugs, *Pharmacol. Biochem. Behav.* **2:**465–472.

Weissman, A., 1962, Nondiscriminated avoidance behavior in a large sample of rats, *Psychol. Rep.* **10:**591–600.

Weissman, A., 1963, Correlation between baseline nondiscriminated avoidance behavior in rats and amphetamine-induced stimulation, *Psychopharmacologia* **4:**294–297.

Wheatley, D., 1969, Comparative effects of propranolol and chlordiazepoxide in anxiety states, *Brit. J. Psychiat.* **115:**1411–1412.

Willinsky, M. D., Webster, C. D., and Herring, B. S., 1974, Effects of Δ^1-tetrahydrocannabinol on Sidman discriminated avoidance behavior in rats, *Activitas Nervosa Super.* **16:**34–38.

Wise, R. A., and Dawson, V., 1974, Diazepam-induced eating and lever pressing for food in sated rats, *J. Comp. Physiol. Psychol.* **86:**930–941.

Wuttke, W., and Kelleher, R. T., 1970, Effects of some benzodiazepines on punished and unpunished behavior in the pigeon, *J. Pharmacol. Exp. Ther.* **172:**397–405.

Yamahiro, R. S., Bell, E. C., and Hill, H. E., 1961, The effects of reserpine on a strongly conditioned emotional response, *Psychopharmacologia* **2:**197–202.

Stimulus Control and Drug Effects

3

Donald M. Thompson

1. Introduction

In general, stimulus control refers to differential responding in the presence of different stimuli. The specific type of differential responding depends on the specific stimulus-control procedure used. For example, in an S^D–S^Δ multiple schedule, responding may be reinforced on a variable-interval schedule in the presence of one discriminative stimulus (the S^D) but is extinguished (not reinforced) in the presence of another discriminative stimulus (the S^Δ). Ideally, the result would be a perfect S^D–S^Δ discrimination or a "go, no-go" situation. In other words, stimulus control would be evident if the subject responded in the presence of the S^D but did not respond in the presence of the S^Δ. The same result can be obtained by presenting the S^D and S^Δ sequentially in discrete trials.

An S^D–S^Δ multiple schedule may also be used to establish a gradient of stimulus control. In this case, instead of having only one S^Δ, there may be a number of S^Δs that vary along the same physical continuum (e.g., light intensity) as the S^D. Ideally, the result would be a "stimulus generalization gradient"; that is, S^Δ responding would decrease progressively as the difference between the S^D and S^Δ increased. The slope of the gradient can be used to quantify the degree of stimulus control established; the steeper the slope, the greater the stimulus control (see Blough, 1966; Nevin, 1973; Terrace, 1966). Although it has traditionally been assumed that the slope also indicates the "dis-

Donald M. Thompson • Department of Pharmacology, Georgetown University, Washington, D.C. 20007

criminability" of the stimuli, this assumption has more recently been questioned by "signal detection" analysis (to be discussed later).

Another type of differential responding can be established by using what might be called an "S^D–S^D" multiple schedule. For example, responding may be reinforced on a fixed-ratio schedule in the presence of one S^D but be reinforced on a fixed-interval schedule in the presence of a second S^D. Ideally, the result would be an S^D–S^D discrimination or a "go_1, go_2" situation. In other words, stimulus control would be evident if the subject responded one way (e.g., a "break-run" pattern) in the presence of the S^D associated with the fixed-ratio schedule but responded in a different way (e.g., a "scallop" pattern) in the presence of the S^D associated with the fixed-interval schedule. A related S^D–S^D procedure involves two response keys; for example, when one S^D is presented, responding on the left key is reinforced, and when the second S^D is presented, responding on the right key is reinforced.

An S^D–S^D discrimination can also be established by using a chained schedule of reinforcement. For example, responding on a fixed-ratio schedule in the presence of one S^D produces the second S^D, in whose presence responding is reinforced on a fixed-interval schedule. A related procedure, signaled fixed-consecutive number, involves two response keys. In this case, responding on one key in the presence of one S^D produces the second S^D, in whose presence responding on the second key is reinforced. Another related procedure is matching to sample. Here, responding on one key (an "observing response") in the presence of one S^D (the sample) produces the second S^D (a stimulus that matches the sample), in whose presence responding on a second key is reinforced. In a more complicated procedure, repeated acquisition of behavioral chains, a specified sequence of four responses on three keys is required for reinforcement; the sequence is changed from day to day.

The present chapter will review drug studies that have been conducted in the stimulus-control situations outlined above. These studies have raised several issues that are relevant to the concept of stimulus control. For example, while it is generally agreed that well-established performance on a multiple fixed-ratio fixed-interval schedule is under stimulus control, there has been some disagreement over whether drug effects on such performance should be interpreted in terms of stimulus control. An alternative interpretation is that the drug is simply producing a "rate-dependent" effect, that is, an effect that depends on the predrug rate of responding. Another issue concerns the "modulation" of drug effects by stimulus control. There is currently some question about which drug effects can be modified by the manipulation of discriminative stimuli. A related issue is whether a history of S^Δ responding provides the necessary and sufficient conditions for obtaining certain drug effects. Signal detection analysis of drug effects has pinpointed still another issue: does a drug effect on behavior under stimulus control reflect a change in "perceptual sensitivity" or a change in "response bias"? The development of these and other issues will be traced in the course of this chapter.

As to the scope and organization of the chapter, the review focuses primarily on studies that have established stimulus control through differential food presentation. Following the operant tradition, the emphasis will be on research in which each subject "served as his own control" and the data for individual subjects were presented separately. Within this restricted scope, representative studies will be examined in some depth. The chapter is organized in terms of stimulus-control procedures rather than drug classes. The drug studies using a particular type of procedure are reviewed more or less in chronological order.

2. Multiple Schedules and Related Procedures

2.1. S^D–S^Δ Multiple Schedules

The use of S^D–S^Δ multiple schedules has been the traditional way of establishing stimulus control over operant behavior (Skinner, 1938; Keller and Schoenfeld, 1950). In a pioneering study of stimulus control and drug effects, Dews (1955) used a multiple variable-interval 1-min extinction schedule of food presentation to establish "simple" and "conditional" S^D–S^Δ discriminations in pigeons. The procedure is summarized in Figure 1. Note that in the simple discrimination, the S^D and S^Δ were differentiated by the key color alone, whereas in the conditional discrimination, they were differentiated by both the key color and the houselight. The type of base-line performance generated by this procedure is illustrated in the left part of Figure 2. Note that there were a few "trickles" of S^Δ responses during the conditional discrimination (B and R+), whereas the S^Δ rate was virtually zero during the simple discrimination (W+). This could be interpreted to mean that the behavior in the latter situation was under stronger stimulus control.

The right part of Figure 2 shows what happened after 3 mg of pentobarbital was administered intramuscularly. The drug clearly increased S^Δ responding during the conditional discrimination but had no effect on the simple discrimination. Dews (1955) also found this type of differential drug effect with other doses of pentobarbital (1 and 5.2 mg) and with methamphetamine (0.3–1 mg). He cautioned, however, that further research was required since the constant sequence of stimuli in the multiple schedule meant that the differential drug effect

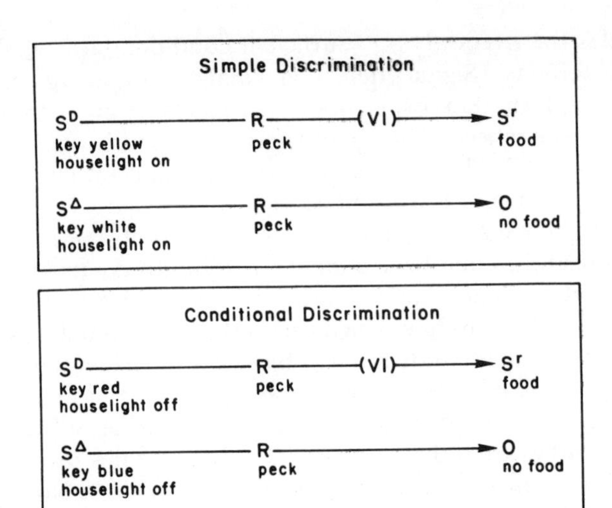

Figure 1. S^D–S^Δ multiple-schedule procedure: simple and conditional discriminations.

was confounded with time after drug. Nevertheless, the results are important because they were among the first to suggest that behavior under strong stimulus control is less readily disrupted by drugs than behavior under weak stimulus control.

A few years later, Dews (1963) reported a study in which a multiple fixed-ratio 25 extinction schedule of food presentation was used to establish an S^D–S^Δ discrimination in a pigeon. The S^D and S^Δ were differentiated by key color alone, as in the "simple" discrimination in the Dews (1955) study. After the discrimination had been established, responding occurred at a high rate during the S^D periods but did not occur at all during the S^Δ periods. A 10 mg (27 mg/kg) dose of chlorpromazine was then administered intramuscularly 2 hr presession. Although this large dose disrupted the S^D responding somewhat, it did not lead to any S^Δ responding. This indicated to Dews that there was no interference with "discriminatory behavior." Dews' (1963) finding with chlorpromazine is thus similar to his (1955) finding with pentobarbital and methamphetamine, in that none of these drugs induced S^Δ responding when the predrug S^Δ rate was zero.

A recent study by Wiltz *et al.* (1974) has confirmed Dews' (1963) finding in a somewhat different situation. These investigators used a multiple variable-interval 1-min extinction schedule of food presentation to establish an S^D–S^Δ discrimination in pigeons. The S^D and S^Δ were differentiated by a green light (on or off) above the unlit response key. After the discrimination had been established, responding occurred at moderate rates (about 40–90 response/min) during the S^D periods but did not occur at all during the S^Δ periods. Increasing doses of chlorpromazine (10–30 mg, administered orally 1 hr presession) produced progressive decreases in the rate of S^D responding but did not lead to any S^Δ responding. The failure of chlorpromazine to induce S^Δ responding was attributed to the maintenance of strong stimulus control.

Unlike the studies above, Terrace (1963) used a conventional discrete-trials procedure to establish an S^D–S^Δ discrimination in pigeons. The procedure was similar to a multiple fixed-ratio 1 extinction schedule of food presentation. The S^D and S^Δ were differentiated by the angular orientation of a line (vertical or horizontal) projected on the response key. After the discrimination had been established, the total

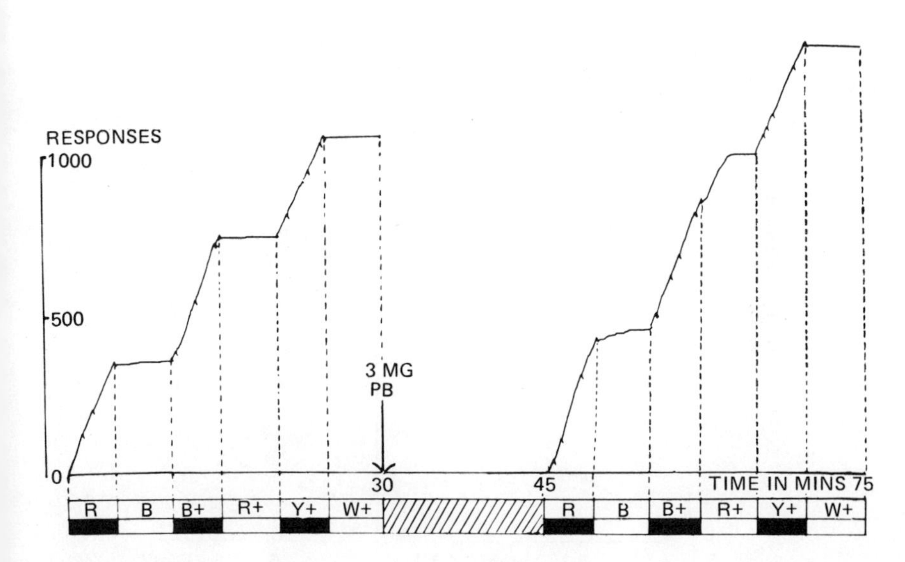

Figure 2. Cumulative records of a pigeon's performance on a multiple VI extinction schedule before (left) and after (right) 3 mg of pentobarbital was administered. Reinforcements are indicated by the momentary downward deflection of the response pen. The letters below the records indicate the key colors (red, blue, yellow, white) and the + indicates when the houselight was on. [From Dews (1955); © 1955 The Williams & Wilkins Company, Baltimore.]

S^D responses per session were at the maximum (one response per S^D trial) and the total S^Δ responses ("errors") per session were near zero. Figure 3 shows the effects of varying doses of imipramine and chlorpromazine (administered intramuscularly 30 min presession) on the total errors per session for two pigeons. As can be seen, errors increased as a function of dose for both drugs, and the error-increasing effect was greater with imipramine than with chlorpromazine. Neither drug affected the frequency of S^D responses (not shown), although the latency of these responses was lengthened as the dose of each drug was increased.

Terrace (1963) also used a "fading" discrete-trials procedure to establish an *errorless* S^D–S^Δ discrimination in pigeons. Training began with an "easy" red–green discrimination and shifted progressively to the "more difficult" vertical–horizontal discrimination. Following this training history, neither chlorpromazine nor imipramine led to any errors at any of the doses tested (1–17 mg). Terrace concluded that the drugs disrupt performance on the vertical–horizontal discrimination only if the discrimination was learned with errors. Wiltz *et al.* (1974) suggested that Terrace's observation that chlorpromazine disrupted stimulus control in subjects with a history of S^Δ responding may have depended upon the continuation of bursts of such responding after the discrimi-

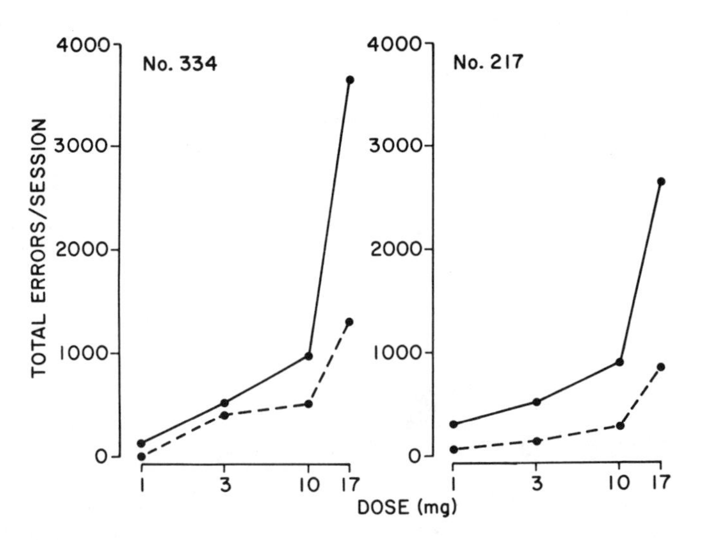

Figure 3. Dose effects of imipramine and chlorpromazine on the total errors (S^Δ responses) per session for two pigeons with a history of S^Δ responding. ●—●, imipramine; ●---●, chlorpromazine. [The figure has been constructed from data given in Terrace (1963), Table 1, first determinations.]

nation was established. In the Wiltz *et al.* study, chlorpromazine did not induce S^{Δ} responding in subjects with a history of such responding; in this study, however, the predrug S^{Δ} rate was zero. In short, a history of S^{Δ} responding seems to be a necessary but not a sufficient condition for obtaining the drug effect.

The final study to be discussed in this section (Hearst, 1964) stands apart from the others in that a *gradient of stimulus control* was obtained. Hearst used a multiple continuous-avoidance extinction schedule of shock presentation with rhesus monkeys to establish what could be considered an S^D–S^{Δ}–S^{Δ}–S^{Δ}–S^{Δ}–S^{Δ}–S^{Δ}–S^{Δ} discrimination. The discriminative stimuli were eight intensities of the houselight. The light intensities, "approximately equally spaced along a logarithmic scale," ranged from "very bright" (5.8 foot-candle) to "very dim" (0.003 foot-candle). The S^D, which Hearst referred to as the "critical stimulus" (CS), was either the brightest intensity (for two monkeys) or the dimmest intensity (for one monkey). In the presence of the S^D, the monkeys could avoid a brief electric shock (5 mA) by pressing a lever; the response–shock and shock–shock intervals were both 10 sec. The avoidance contingency was not in effect (no shocks) during any of the seven S^{Δ}s, which were presented in a mixed order. Nevertheless, even after extended base-line training, there was still responding during the seven "safe" intensities. The responding occurred more often during the S^{Δ}s that were more similar to the S^D than during the S^{Δ}s that were very different. In short, the responding showed a "gradient of stimulus generalization." Such gradients are shown in Figure 4 (see control and placebo sessions). The gradients are plotted in two ways. "Relative generalization" (left) was derived from response frequency (right) by assigning the value of 1.0 to the peak of each gradient; the other values are expressed as decimal fractions of this maximum value.

Figure 4 also shows the effects of two doses of *d*-amphetamine (administered intramuscularly "less than a minute" presession). Despite individual differences in the drug's effect on CS response frequency, the responding in the presence of the other intensities was increased in all three monkeys, thereby flattening the relative generalization gradients. Such flattening, which may be interpreted as a disruption of stimulus control, cannot be attributed to an increase in shock frequency, since the monkeys rarely received more than one shock per day during either the drug or nondrug sessions. Hearst (1964) also found that scopolamine (0.01–0.1 mg/kg) and caffeine (10–80 mg/kg) flattened the relative generalization gradients, although the effects were not as pronounced as with *d*-amphetamine. He concluded that the parametric manipulation of discriminative stimuli to yield a gradient of stimulus control serves ". . . as a useful tool for analyzing the relative sensitivity

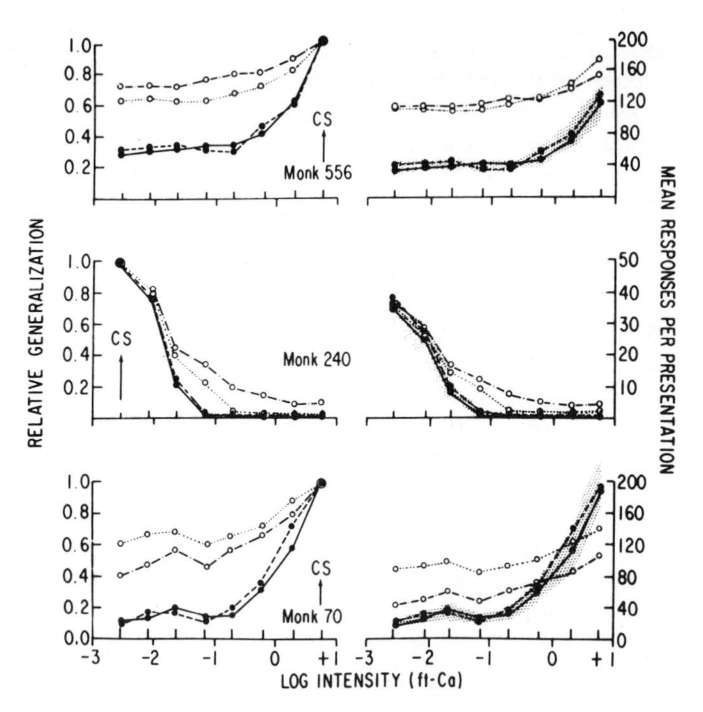

Figure 4. Effects of two doses of *d*-amphetamine on the absolute and relative "generalization gradients" for three monkeys. The shaded areas indicate the control ranges. The "critical stimulus" or CS (i.e., the S^D for avoidance responding) is shown for each monkey. ●—●, control (no injection); ●---●, placebo; ○ · · · · ○, *d*-amphetamine (1 mg/kg); ○-··-○, *d*-amphetamine (2 mg/kg). [From Hearst (1964).]

of normal and drugged animals to changes in their external environment" (Hearst, 1964, p. 57). It is surprising that Hearst's technique has not been used more in behavioral pharmacology.

2.2. S^D–S^D Multiple Schedules

Although operant "discrimination" was traditionally defined by differential responding in the presence of an S^D and an S^Δ, a more common form of discrimination studied in contemporary operant research involves two S^Ds. Such a discrimination can be established by using an S^D–S^D multiple schedule in which two different component schedules of reinforcement operate sequentially, each in the presence of a different stimulus. Stimulus control is evident when ". . . the performance appropriate to one or the other schedule occurs only in the presence of the corresponding stimulus" (Catania, 1968, p. 122).

One of the first studies of drug effects on an S^D–S^D discrimination was reported by Dews (1958). A multiple fixed-ratio 50 fixed-interval 15-min schedule of food presentation was used with pigeons. This procedure is summarized in Figure 5. The type of base-line performance generated by this procedure is illustrated in the top part of Figure 6. It is clear that different rates and patterns of responding occurred in the presence of the different colors (i.e., stimulus control was evident). The middle part of Figure 6 shows what happened after 3 mg of chlorpromazine was given (the route of administration and presession time were unspecified). Dews (1958) described and interpreted the drug effect as follows: ". . . the difference between the performances in the presence of the two stimuli became less; it was as though the stimuli had become less different" (p. 1028). As a way of validating the interpretation, an attempt was then made to mimic the drug effect by changing the multiple schedule to a mixed schedule. In the mixed schedule, the fixed-ratio and fixed-interval components occurred in the same sequence as in the multiple schedule, but the red and blue lights did not differentiate the components; both lights were on throughout the session. The first session under the mixed schedule ("no stimuli") is shown in the bottom part of Figure 6. Because Dews (1958) saw ". . . a clear resemblance of the performance on this day to the performance after chlorpromazine" (p. 1028), he considered the results to support the interpretation that the drug had weakened stimulus control.

Incidentally, despite laboratory lore to the contrary, Dews' (1958) finding that operant behavior (fixed-interval responding) can be increased by chlorpromazine, a "major tranquilizer," is not an effect peculiar to pigeons. The same type of effect has recently been obtained with chimpanzees, working on a multiple fixed-ratio fixed-interval schedule (Byrd, 1974), and with humans, working on a differential reinforcement of low rate schedule (Angle, 1973).

Another indication of weakened stimulus control in multiple fixed-ratio fixed-interval schedules can perhaps best be described as a brief

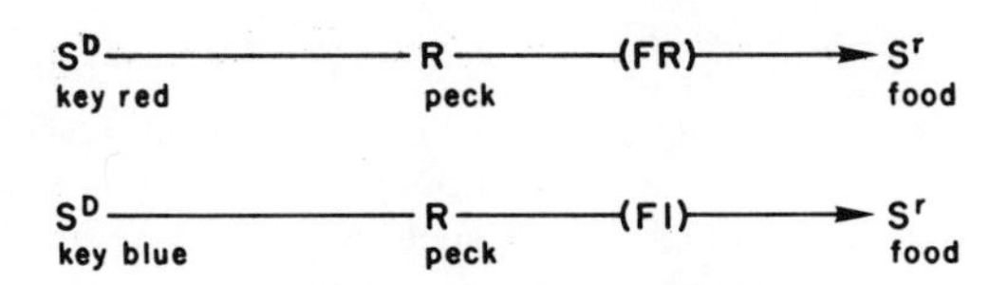

Figure 5. S^D–S^D multiple-schedule procedure.

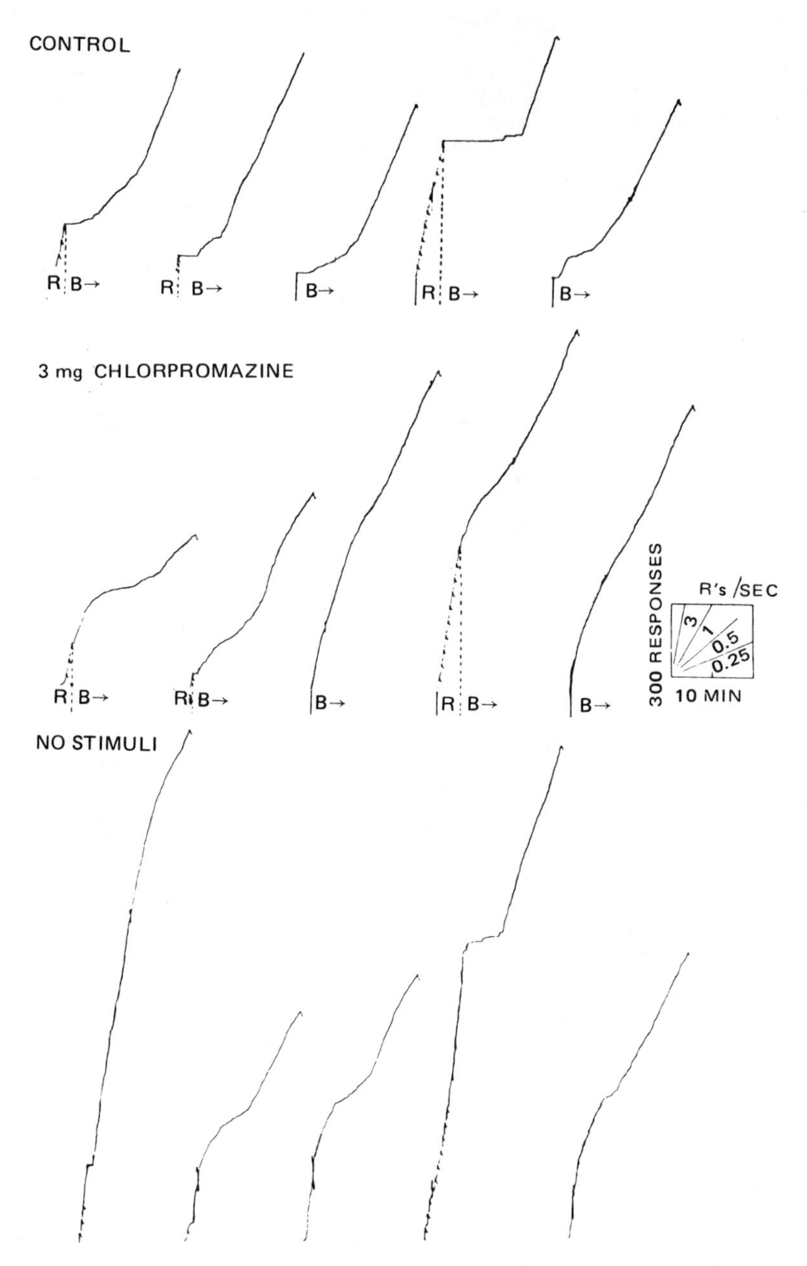

Figure 6. Cumulative records of a pigeon's performance on a multiple FR FI schedule, before (top) and after (middle) 3 mg of chlorpromazine was administered, and on a mixed FR FI schedule (bottom). Reinforcements are indicated by the momentary downward deflection of the response pen. The letters below the records indicate the key colors (red, blue). [From Dews (1958); reproduced from *Federation Proceedings* **17:**1024–1030.]

intrusion of fixed-ratio-like responding during the fixed-interval component. Such intrusions have been noted in several drug studies, e.g., Cook and Kelleher (1962), Verhave (1959), and Waller (1961).

In the study by Verhave (1959), a multiple fixed-ratio 40 fixed-interval 2-min schedule of water presentation was used to establish an S^D–S^D discrimination in rhesus monkeys. The discriminative stimuli were green and red lights above the response key. Verhave found that secobarbital (30 mg/kg administered subcutaneously immediately before the session) produced "groups of responses at high rates" during the fixed-interval component. It was suggested that this effect ". . . may represent a failure of discrimination" (Verhave, 1959, p. 119).

Cook and Kelleher (1962) reported a study in which a multiple fixed-ratio 30 fixed-interval 10-min schedule of food presentation was used to establish an "S^D–S^D discrimination" in squirrel monkeys. (Actually, an S^D–S^D–S^Δ discrimination was established since the fixed-ratio and fixed-interval components were separated by a time-out, an S^Δ.) The type of discriminative stimuli used was not specified. Cook and Kelleher found that 100 mg/kg of meprobamate (administered orally, presession time unspecified) produced bursts of responding in the fixed-interval component (see Figure 7 at *f, g,* and *h*). Kelleher (1965), in referring to the same data, suggested that these bursts ". . . indicate that stimulus control in the fixed-interval and fixed-ratio components had been disrupted" (p. 229). He also noted that the disruption of stimulus control was selective since meprobamate did not produce bursts of responding during the time-out (S^Δ) component, where the predrug rate was virtually zero.

Waller (1961) reported a simple way of validating the interpretation that intrusions of fixed-ratio-like responding during the fixed-interval component of a multiple schedule represent weakened stimulus control. Waller used a multiple fixed-ratio 50 fixed-interval 3-min extinction schedule of food presentation to establish an S^D–S^D–S^Δ discrimination in a dog. The discriminative stimuli were three lights above the response key. High doses of chlorpromazine (12–24 mg/kg, administered orally 2 hr presession) were found to produce short bursts of responding in the fixed-interval component. These bursts disappeared, however, when the fixed-ratio component was removed. Waller (1961) thus concluded: "the responding observed after the high doses with the fixed-ratio component intact is probably a function of induction, i.e., loss of stimulus control" (p. 355).

In all the experiments reviewed so far, the effects of drugs on multiple-schedule performance have been interpreted in terms of stimulus control. A drug was said to disrupt stimulus control if the difference in responding in the presence of different stimuli was reduced by the

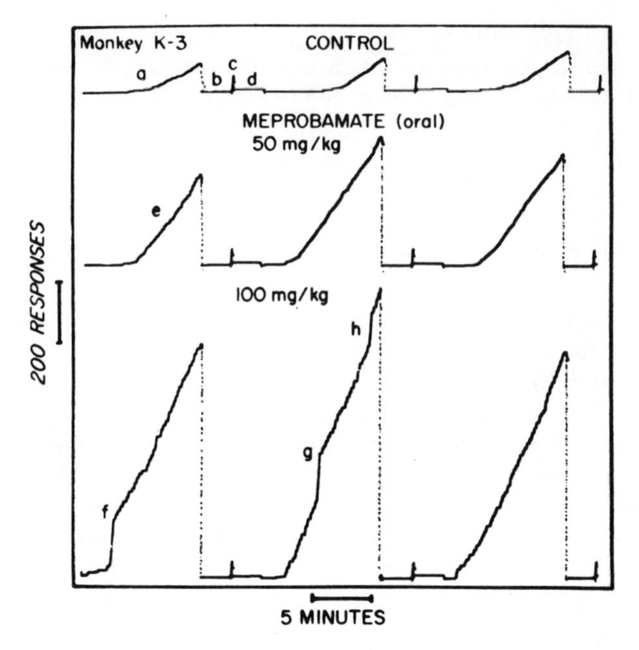

Figure 7. Cumulative records of a monkey's performance on a multiple FR FI schedule before (top) and after 50 mg/kg (middle) and 100 mg/kg (bottom) of meprobamate were administered. The FI (e.g., see *a*) and FR (e.g., see *c*) components were separated by a 2.5-min time-out (e.g., see *b* and *d*). The response pen reset when reinforcement occurred. [From Cook and Kelleher (1962).]

drug. Kelleher and Morse (1964) reported an experiment, however, that points to a problem with this seemingly straightforward interpretation. These investigators established an S^D–S^D discrimination in a pigeon by using a multiple schedule with punishment and nonpunishment components. In the nonpunishment component, a fixed-ratio 30 schedule of food presentation was in effect in the presence of an orange light. In the punishment component, each of the first 10 responses of the fixed-ratio 30 produced a brief electric shock (6 mA) in the presence of a white light. The type of base-line performance generated by this procedure is illustrated in Figure 8 (top left). There is clearly a difference in responding in the presence of the two discriminative stimuli. After 10 mg/kg of pentobarbital (administered intramuscularly 15 min presession), the difference in responding was almost entirely eliminated (see Figure 8, top right). One interpretation of this finding is that stimulus control was disrupted by the drug; it was as though the pigeon had become "confused" as to which S^D was present.

To check on this possibility, Kelleher and Morse (1964) also studied the punishment procedure in isolation. The procedure was in effect throughout the session in the presence of a white light. Figure 8 (bottom) shows the results. Pentobarbital again increased punished responding. In this case, however, it would be difficult to argue that the pigeon was "confused." A simpler conclusion would be that pentobarbital increased punished responding, regardless of whether the punishment procedure was a component of a multiple schedule or was studied in isolation (see Chapter 2).

Clark and Steele (1966) used a similar type of argument to question a stimulus-control interpretation of drug effects on multiple-schedule performance. In their experiment, a multiple fixed-ratio 25 fixed-interval 4-min extinction schedule of food presentation was used to establish an S^D–S^D–S^Δ discrimination in rats. The houselight and a red light above the lever were both on during the fixed-ratio compo-

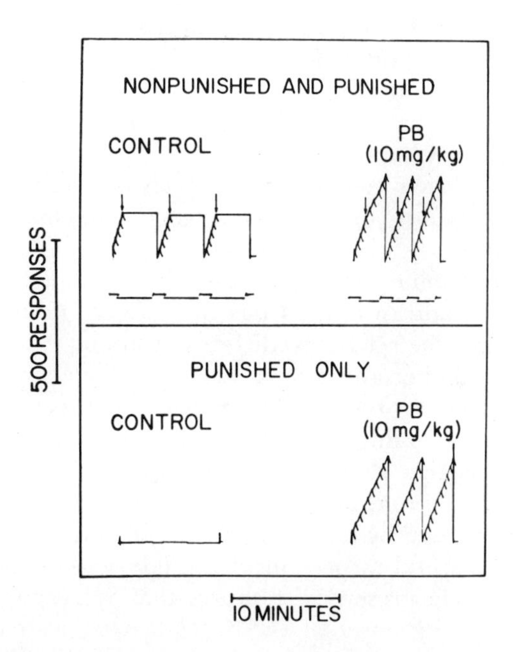

Figure 8. Top: cumulative records of a pigeon's performance on a multiple FR FR + punishment schedule before (left) and after (right) 10 mg/kg of pentobarbital was administered. The arrows indicate the beginning of each punishment component; at the end of this component, the response pen reset. Reinforcements are indicated by the momentary downward deflection of the response pen. Bottom: the punishment procedure was in effect throughout each session. [From Kelleher and Morse (1964); reproduced from *Federation Proceedings* **23:**808–817.]

nent, the houselight alone was on during the fixed-interval component, and both lights were off during the extinction component. Under baseline conditions, three different rates of responding occurred: high (fixed-ratio), intermediate (fixed-interval), and low (extinction). It was found that with increasing doses of *d*-amphetamine (0.5–4 mg/kg, administered intramuscularly 5 min presession), the fixed-ratio rate decreased progressively and the S^{Δ} rate increased progressively. The fixed-interval rate increased as the dose was increased to 1 mg/kg, but did not increase further with higher doses. In short, the rates in the three components tended to converge as the dose was increased.

In discussing their results, Clark and Steele (1966) argued that it was superfluous to interpret the convergence of rates in terms of a loss of stimulus control. Their reasoning was based primarily on previous research showing that ". . . the rate changes in each component can be individually described as interactions with the control rate of responding" (Clark and Steele, 1966, p. 167). In other words, amphetamine tends to decrease high rates of responding while increasing low rates, regardless of whether the responding is controlled by a component of a multiple schedule or is studied in isolation. Such rate-dependent effects have been found not only with amphetamine, but also with a number of other drugs (see reviews by Kelleher and Morse, 1968; Sanger and Blackman, 1976; see Chapter 1).

With regard to the rate-dependent effects of amphetamine in situations involving stimulus control, it is instructive to compare the Clark and Steele (1966) study with the Dews (1955) study. Recall that Dews found that amphetamine did not increase S^{Δ} responding in a "simple" S^{D}–S^{Δ} situation, in contrast to the Clark and Steele finding. The apparent discrepancy may be related to different training procedures in the two studies (see Kelleher and Morse, 1968). In the training procedure used by Dews, each S^{Δ} response reset the timer controlling the S^{Δ} period. This delay contingency, which prevented adventitious reinforcement (Herrnstein, 1966; Morse, 1955) of S^{Δ} responses by the onset of the S^{D}, produced an S^{Δ} rate that was virtually zero. In the training procedure used by Clark and Steele, S^{Δ} responses did not reset the S^{Δ} period. A careful inspection of the control cumulative records that Clark and Steele presented indicates that S^{Δ} responses often occurred just before the onset of the S^{D} associated with fixed-interval food reinforcement.

It appears that if the training procedure produces "trickles" of S^{Δ} responding, as in the Clark and Steele (1966) study, then amphetamine will increase such low-rate responding. On the other hand, if the predrug S^{Δ} rate is virtually zero, as in the Dews (1955) study, then amphetamine will not have this rate-dependent effect. The requirement of a certain minimum tendency to respond (Sanger and Blackman, 1976) may also apply to other drugs. For example, recall that such a tendency was present in Terrace's (1963) study in cases where chlorpromazine increased S^{Δ} responding, but was absent in the studies by Dews (1963) and Wiltz *et al.* (1974), where chlorpromazine did not have this effect.

The Clark and Steele (1966) experiment made it apparent that there is a basic problem in using multiple schedules to study drug effects *on* stimulus control unless rate-dependent effects can be ruled out as an alternative interpretation. An alternative approach has been to use multiple schedules to determine the extent to which drug effects can be modulated *by* stimulus control. For example, in a study by Laties and Weiss (1966), stimulus control was manipulated by using a multiple fixed-interval 5-min fixed-interval 5-min + "clock" schedule of food presentation in pigeons. The response key was red throughout the fixed-interval component but was illuminated by a series of five symbols, one per minute, during the fixed-interval + clock component. The type of base-line performance generated by this procedure is illustrated in Figure 9. As can be seen, the distribution of responding was clearly different in the two components. In the fixed-interval component, responding occurred at the start of the interval and the rate increased as the interval elapsed, whereas in the fixed-interval + clock component, virtually no responding occurred until the fifth stimulus

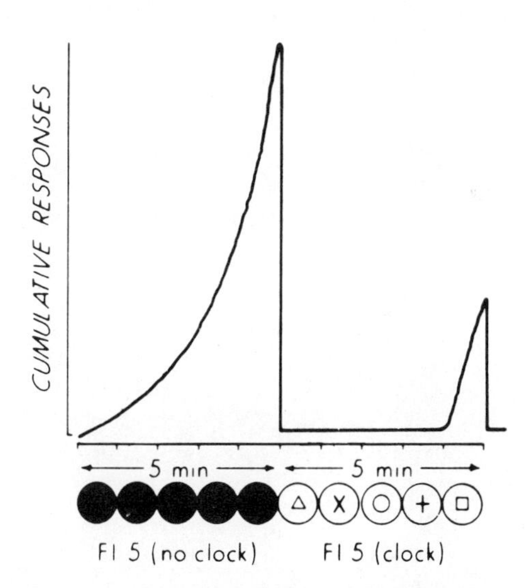

Figure 9. Cumulative record showing "typical" base-line performance on a multiple FI FI + clock schedule in pigeons. The response pen reset when reinforcement occurred. [From Weiss and Laties (1964); reproduced from *Federation Proceedings* **23**:801–807.]

appeared. Laties and Weiss found that amphetamine (0.5–4 mg/kg), scopolamine (0.02–0.08 mg/kg), or pentobarbital (2–8 mg/kg), administered intramuscularly immediately before the session, produced much greater changes in the response distribution during the fixed-interval component than during the fixed-interval + clock component. In other words, the effect of these drugs was modulated by stimulus control. Such modulation was not found, however, with chlorpromazine (1.5–12 mg/kg) or promazine (6–24 mg/kg). With these drugs, the response distribution changed markedly in both components.

In a recent study conducted in the author's laboratory, we (Thompson and Corr, 1974) manipulated stimulus control in much the same way as was done in the Laties and Weiss (1966) study. More specifically, we used a multiple variable-interval 1-min variable-interval 1-min + "signal" schedule of food presentation with pigeons. During the variable-interval component, the response key was red and the houselight was always on. During the variable-interval + signal component, the response key was green and the houselight was turned off whenever the reinforcer was available. Under base-line conditions, the response rate during the variable-interval + signal component was very low (about one response per reinforcement), whereas the response rate during the variable-interval component was relatively high (see Figure 10, brackets). Figure 10 also shows the effects of varying doses of *d*-amphetamine (administered intramuscularly 5 min presession). As can be seen, the response rate in the variable-interval component increased and then decreased as the dose was increased from 0.5 to 4 mg/kg, but the response rate in the variable-interval + signal component only decreased at the largest dose. One would have expected the low rate (variable-interval + signal) to be increased by *d*-amphetamine if the drug simply produced a rate-dependent effect. The failure of *d*-amphetamine to increase the low rate can be attributed to the strong stimulus control produced by the signal. Our results are thus consistent with the amphetamine data obtained in the Laties and Weiss (1966) study.

In another study of modulation of drug effects by stimulus control, Leander and McMillan (1974) used a multiple fixed-ratio 30 fixed-interval 10-min schedule of food presentation to establish an S^D–S^D discrimination in pigeons. The discriminative stimuli were differentiated on the basis of key color (red or blue). It was found that chlorpromazine (3–100 mg/kg, administered intramuscularly 10 min presession) produced a rate-dependent effect during the fixed-interval component; that is, the drug increased low rates at the beginning of the component while decreasing high rates at the end (see Figure 11, open circles). Chlorpromazine was also tested under a mixed fixed-ratio 30

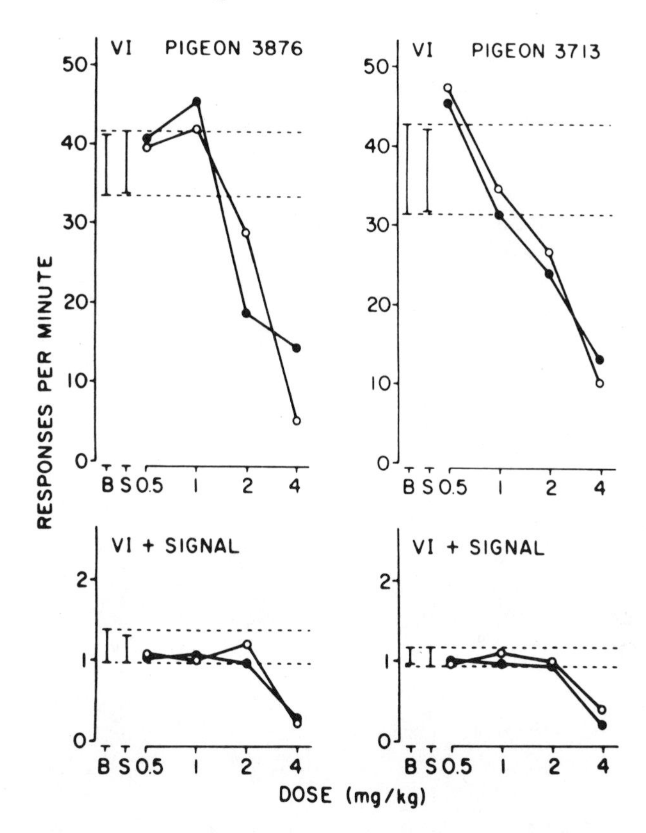

Figure 10. Dose effects of *d*-amphetamine on VI and VI + signal response rates. There were two determinations for each dose with each pigeon. The brackets and dashed horizontal lines indicate the ranges for the base-line (B) and saline (S) sessions. [Abstracted from Figure 2 in Thompson and Corr (1974).]

fixed-interval 10-min schedule, where the response key was white throughout both components. During the fixed-interval component of the mixed schedule, chlorpromazine again produced a rate-dependent effect, but the responding tended to be more suppressed than similar rates under the multiple schedule (see Figure 11, filled circles). The rate-dependent effect of chlorpromazine was thus modulated by stimulus control. Figure 11 also shows that responding during the fixed-ratio component of the mixed schedule (filled triangles) was more suppressed than similar rates under the multiple schedule (open triangles). In other words, behavior under stimulus control (multiple schedule) was less readily disrupted by chlorpromazine than behavior not under

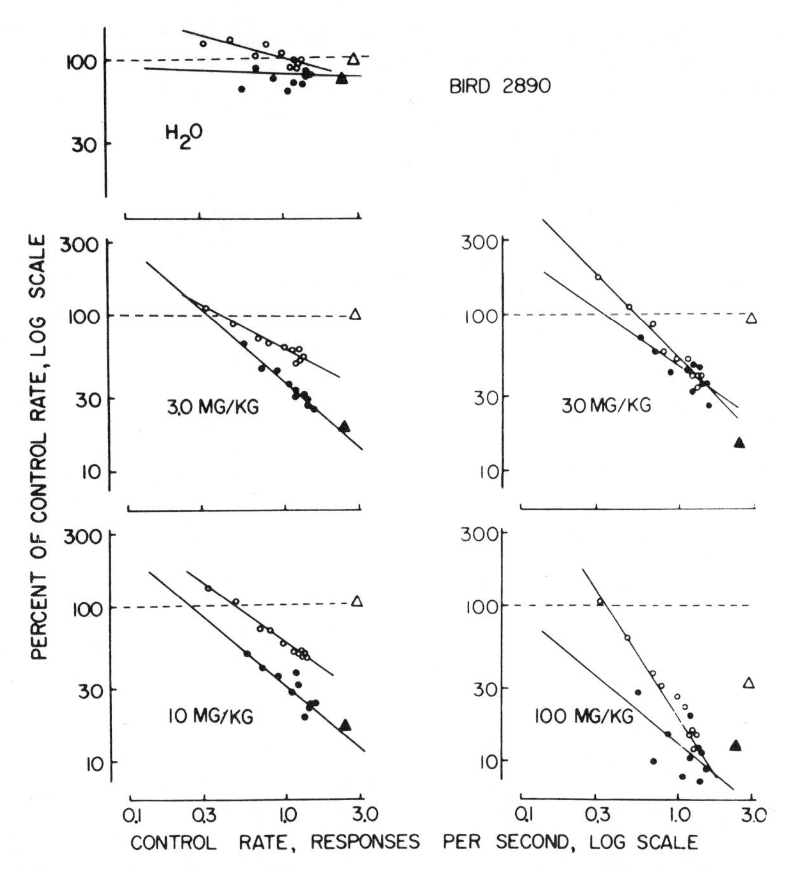

Figure 11. Rate-dependent effects of varying doses of chlorpromazine under a multiple FR–FI schedule (open symbols) and under a mixed FR–FI schedule (filled symbols). The response rate after drug administration, expressed as a percentage of the control rate, is plotted against the control rate during the FR component (triangles) and during the 10 1-min segments of the FI component (circles). The data points below the dashed horizontal lines represent drug-induced decreases in response rate; the points above these lines represent increases. Linear regression lines were fitted to the FI data by the method of least squares. [From Leander and McMillan (1974); © 1974 The Williams & Wilkins Company, Baltimore.]

such control (mixed schedule). Leander and McMillan also found that *d*-amphetamine (0.3–10 mg/kg) and pentobarbital (1–17.5 mg/kg) produced rate-dependent effects (not shown). However, unlike chlorpromazine, the effects of these drugs did not seem to be modulated by stimulus control. The apparent discrepancies between the results of this study and those of related studies (Laties and Weiss, 1966; Thompson and Corr, 1974), in terms of which drugs produced effects that were modulated by stimulus control, may be related to the different modulation techniques used (multiple vs. mixed schedule or multiple-schedule components with and without added stimuli).

2.3. S^D–S^D Two-Key Procedures

In each of the experiments reviewed so far, a single response key was used. There have also been several studies of drug effects on S^D–S^D discriminations involving two response keys, e.g., Blough (1956), Hearst (1959), and Nigro *et al.* (1967).

In the study by Blough (1956), a pigeon faced two semicircular keys that were separated by a vertical partition or bar. The procedure is summarized in Figure 12. Because the discriminative stimuli (bar lighted or dark) were presented sequentially, the procedure is similar to a multiple schedule. Unlike an S^D–S^D multiple schedule, however, each S^D in Blough's procedure also served as an S^Δ; that is, the lighted bar was an S^Δ for pecking the lighted key and the dark bar was an S^Δ for pecking the dark key. Figure 13 shows the effects of ethyl alcohol (1.6 g/kg) and pentobarbital (10 mg/kg), administered orally, on total response output and accuracy (percent correct) for three pigeons. Both drugs initially increased total responses but decreased accuracy. The initial effects on both measures were generally greater with pentobarbital than with alcohol at the doses tested.

Blough (1956) suggested that an S^D–S^D two-key procedure provides ". . . a more sensitive measure of discriminative behavior" than an S^D–S^Δ (single-key) multiple schedule. To illustrate his point, a "crude" but convincing example was given. Suppose that responding stopped because a drug produced a period of vomiting. If this happened in the single-key situation during the S^D presentation, the percent of correct responses would decrease. If it happened in the two-key situation, however, the percent of correct responses would remain unchanged. In other words, with the two-key procedure, the effects of a drug on stimulus control can be better isolated from its other effects.

Hearst (1959) used a two-lever procedure involving water reinforcement to establish an S^D–S^D discrimination in rats. When a clicking

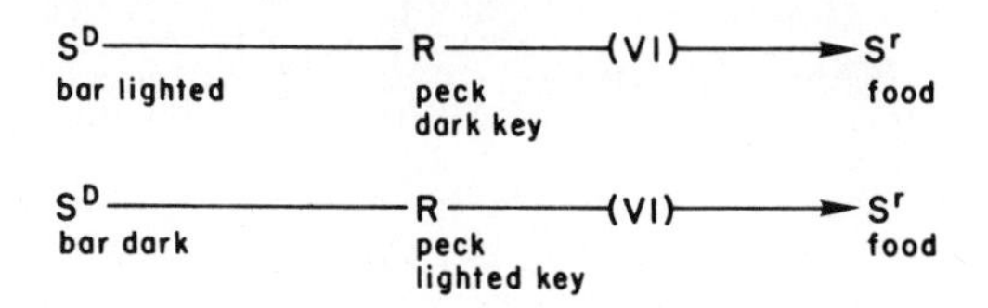

Figure 12. S^D–S^D two-key procedure.

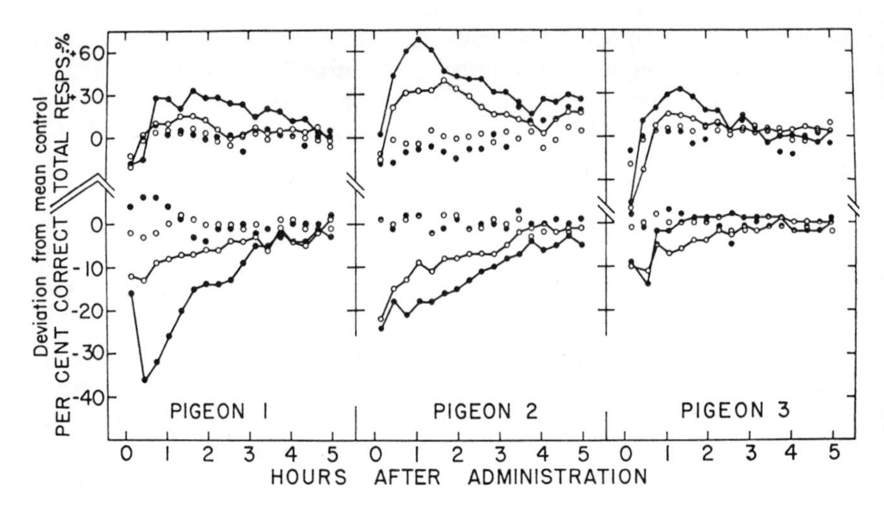

Figure 13. Effects of alcohol (1.6 g/kg) (○—○; control, ○ ○) and pentobarbital (10 mg/kg) (●—●; control, ● ●) on total responses and percent correct for three pigeons during 5-hr sessions. [From Blough (1956).]

noise was presented, a response on one lever was reinforced, and when a tone was presented, a response on the other lever was reinforced. It was found that scopolamine (0.2–1 mg/kg, administered intraperitoneally 10 min presession) increased the frequency of incorrect responding and produced ". . . an increased tendency for subjects to make successive responses on the same lever rather than to alternate responses between the two levers" (Hearst, 1959, p. 357). The increase in incorrect responding would usually be interpreted as a disruption of stimulus control. However, the second finding indicates a "response bias" that could account for the impaired accuracy.

Nigro *et al.* (1967) used a two-lever procedure involving food reinforcement to establish an S^D–S^D discrimination in rats. The discriminative stimuli were two intensities of a light located above and midway between the levers. When the light was brightly illuminated, a response on the right lever was reinforced, and when the light was dimly illuminated, a response on the left lever was reinforced. Accuracy of performance was measured in terms of a discrimination ratio (percent correct responses). It was found that accuracy decreased progressively with increasing doses of chlorpromazine (0.25–4 mg/kg, administered intramuscularly 30 min presession). The larger doses also produced long periods of pausing. Nigro *et al.* (1967) suggested that the effects they obtained ". . . may contribute to the understanding of the unresponsiveness to environmental stimuli exhibited by many psychiatric patients treated with chlorpromazine" (p. 745).

An intriguing extension of the three studies just reviewed was reported by Siegel (1969). In Siegel's procedure, a pigeon worked for food in a chamber containing three response keys. A trial began when the center key was illuminated with either a white triangle, another form (e.g., square, circle, rectangle, cross), or a color (e.g., red, blue, green, yellow). If the triangle appeared, responses on the center key were correct; if another form appeared, responses on the left key (white) were correct; if a color appeared, responses on the right key (white) were correct. In all cases, correct responding was reinforced on a fixed-ratio 10 schedule and errors had no consequences. After extended training on this complex discrimination, the overall accuracy ranged between 80 and 90% correct. In terms of the distribution of errors, they occurred about equally often on the two side keys and rarely occurred on the center key.

Siegel (1969) found that lysergic acid diethylamide or LSD (0.5–0.75 mg/kg, administered intraperitoneally 1 hr presession) decreased overall accuracy and increased "color errors" (i.e., responses on the right key when either the triangle or another form appeared on the center key). Siegel suggested that the pigeons were "reporting perceptual events." He cautioned, however, that "because of the procedure employed for scoring errors in this study, it remains possible that color errors may have resulted from failures to detect forms and not from 'color hallucinations' " (Siegel, 1969, p. 8). An alternative interpretation is that LSD produced a "position bias" toward right-key responding.

Siegel's (1969) study raises a fundamental question of whether a drug affects perceptual sensitivity, response bias, or both. One way to answer this question is through *signal detection* analysis. This relatively new approach was used in an experiment by Dykstra and Appel (1974). These investigators were interested in determining whether LSD affects auditory "perception." A two-lever procedure involving food reinforcement was used to establish S^D–S^D discriminations in rats. The discriminative stimuli were three pairs of tones of different frequencies (2000 vs. 5000 Hz, 3000 vs. 4000 Hz, and 3300 vs. 3800 Hz). In a given pair, when the higher tone (the "signal") was presented, a response on the left lever (a "hit") was reinforced, and when the lower tone (the "noise") was presented, a response on the right lever (a "correct rejection") was reinforced. Each S^D also served as an S^Δ; that is, the lower tone was an S^Δ for pressing the left lever (a "false alarm") and the higher tone was an S^Δ for pressing the right lever (a "miss"). Data were obtained for each tone discrimination under three reinforcement conditions. For example, under the "left 10 vs. right 2" condition, every tenth correct response on the left lever produced food and every second correct response on the right lever produced food. The other two reinforcement conditions were "left 10 vs. right 10" and "left 2 vs. right 10." In all cases, each correct response produced what was presumed to be a conditioned reinforcer (a flash of the lights that accompanied food presentation).

The type of base-line performance generated by the signal detection procedure is illustrated in Figure 14. For each pair of tones, there is a "receiver operating characteristic" (ROC) curve, which relates the probability of making a hit to the probability of making a false alarm. According to signal detection theory, "sensitivity" can be measured by the area under each ROC curve, and "bias" can be measured by the position of the data points along each curve, relative to the negative diagonal. As can be seen, sensitivity increased as the difference between the tones increased, whereas bias (lever preference) changed as a function of the reinforcement conditions.

Dykstra and Appel (1974) found that LSD (0.08 and 0.16 mg/kg, administered intraperitoneally immediately presession) produced changes in response bias that were similar to those produced by manipulating the reinforcement contingencies on the two levers. The same doses, however, had no effect on sensitivity. Thus, at least in this signal detection situation, "LSD seems to alter the way in which environmental contingencies control perceptual behavior . . ." (Dykstra and Appel, 1974, p. 306).

It would seem that all S^D–S^D two-key situations in behavioral pharmacology research should be subjected to a signal-detection type of analysis. This would permit an assessment of the extent to which a drug effect reflects a change in sensitivity (discriminability) and/or re-

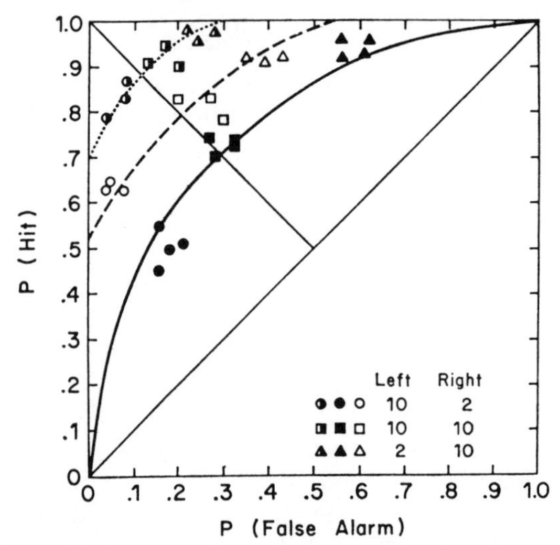

Figure 14. Three ROC curves for one rat under base-line conditions. (----), 2000–5000Hz; (– – –), 3000–4000Hz; (——), 3300–3800Hz. See the text for details. [From Dykstra and Appel (1974).]

S^D —	R —(FR)→	S^D —	R —(FR)→	S^D —	R —(FR)→	S^r
key red	peck	key white	peck	key green	peck	food

Figure 15. Chained-schedule procedure.

sponse bias. Although such an analysis can be used with rate of responding, it is simpler if the procedure involves discrete trials (see Green and Swets, 1966). As a matter of fact, if one considers no response as a behavioral event, then S^D–S^Δ single-key situations could also benefit from a signal detection analysis.

3. Chained Schedules and Related Procedures

A chained schedule has been defined as "a compound schedule in which reinforcement depends on the successive completion, in a particular order, of the requirements of two or more component schedules, each of which operates in the presence of a different stimulus" (Catania, 1968, p. 329). In conventional usage, a chained schedule, like a multiple schedule, involves one response key. As was the case with multiple schedules, stimulus control in a chained schedule is evident when there is differential responding in the presence of the different stimuli. The next three sections will review some studies of drug effects on *performance* maintained by a chained schedule or related procedures (signaled fixed-consecutive number and matching to sample). The final section will review some of my own research, which has focused on the repeated *acquisition* of behavioral chains as a base line for studying drug effects.

3.1. Chained Schedules

Thomas (1966) used a chained schedule of food presentation having three fixed-ratio 60 components to establish an S^D–S^D–S^D discrimination in pigeons. The procedure is summarized in Figure 15. For comparison, Thomas also studied a tandem fixed-ratio 60 fixed-ratio 60 fixed-ratio 60 schedule, where the keylight was yellow throughout all three components. The chained and tandem schedules were combined to form a multiple schedule. The type of base-line performance generated by this complex procedure is illustrated in the top part of Figure 16. There was clearly differential responding in the presence of the different discriminative stimuli in terms of the amount of pausing that occurred at the start of each fixed ratio. During the chained schedule (event pen up), long pauses occurred at the start of the first component, brief pauses occurred at the start of the second component, and virtually no pausing occurred at the start of the third component. During the tandem schedule (event pen down), there was no noticeable pausing during any of the three components.

Figure 16 also shows the effects of varying doses of chlorpromazine (administered intramuscularly 30 min presession). The most apparent effect at all doses was the elimination of long pausing during the first component of the chained schedule; the tandem performance remained relatively intact. The latter was also found with trifluoperazine (0.25–2.5 mg/kg), although this drug increased the amount of pausing during the first component of the chained schedule (not shown). In short, chlorpromazine and trifluoperazine had greater, albeit different, effects on chained performance than on tandem performance.

On the basis of Thomas' (1966) data, one might conclude that behavior under stimulus control (chained performance) is more readily affected by drugs than behavior not under such control (tandem performance). This conclusion is clearly at odds with other research on the modulation of drug effects by stimulus control. For example, recall that Leander and McMillan (1974) found that fixed-ratio performance in a multiple schedule was less readily disrupted by chlorpromazine than fixed-ratio performance in a mixed schedule. Although the divergent results may be related to the different modulation techniques used, Leander (1975) has suggested an alternative interpretation: ". . . chlorpromazine has a marked tendency to increase low rates of responding, such as those early in chained schedules, while trifluoperazine has no such tendency to increase low rates of responding" (p. 698). Thomas (1966) suggested still another interpretation that is difficult to rule out. It is well established that an S^D in a chained schedule may also function as a conditioned reinforcer for responding in the component that precedes it (Kelleher and Gollub, 1962). The drug effects could thus be accounted for by an increase (with chlorpromazine) or a decrease (with trifluoperazine) in the conditioned reinforcing efficacy of the discriminative stimuli in the chained schedule. More drug studies with chained schedules are sorely needed to determine which of the various interpretations is the best one.

3.2. Signaled Fixed Consecutive Number

Laties (1972) used a signaled fixed-consecutive-number (FCN) schedule of food presentation to establish an S^D–S^D discrimination in pigeons. This two-key chain procedure is summarized in Figure 17. At least eight consecutive responses on the left key were required before a response on the right key was reinforced. If the pigeon switched to the

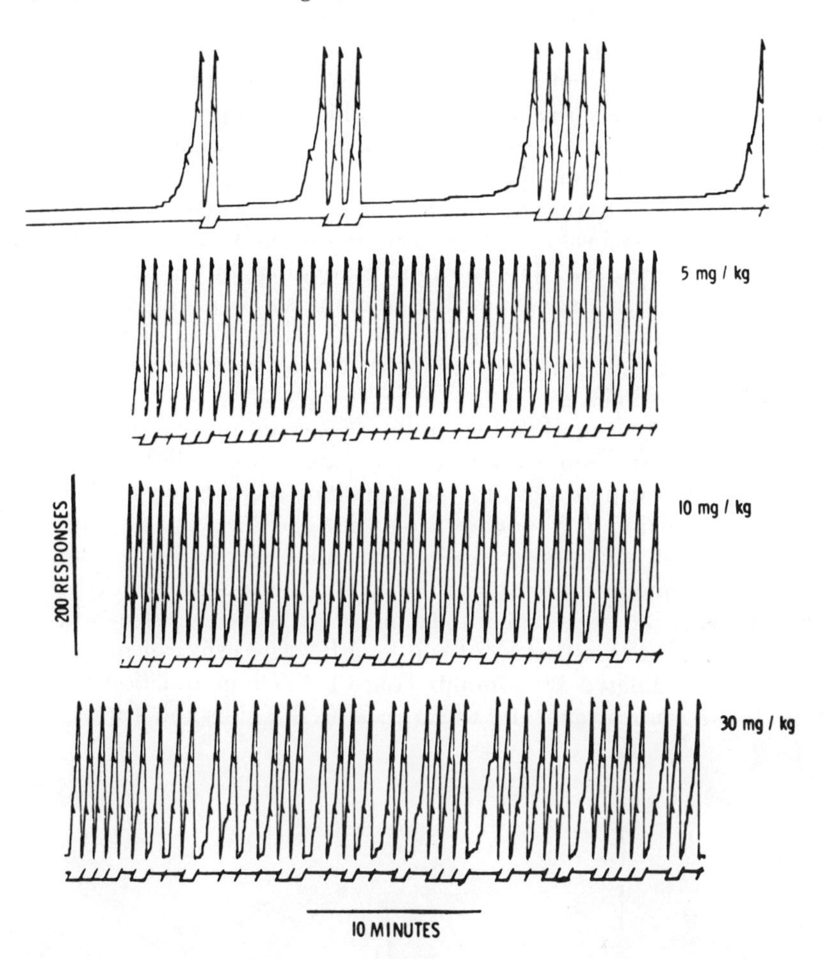

Figure 16. Cumulative records of a pigeon's performance on a chained FR–FR–FR schedule and on a tandem FR–FR–FR schedule before (top) and after varying doses of chlorpromazine were administered. The event pen below each record was up during the chained schedule and down during the tandem schedule. The response pen deflected downward at the completion of each FR and reset when food reinforcement occurred. [Modified from Thomas (1966).]

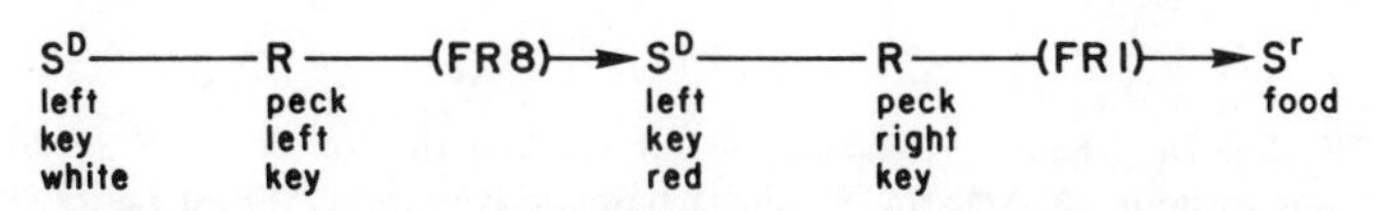

Figure 17. Signaled fixed-consecutive-number procedure.

right key before the count of eight, the run of responses had to be started again. For comparison, Laties also studied the FCN schedule without the red S^D; the left key was white throughout the response sequence. The type of base-line performance generated by the FCN schedule with and without the S^D is illustrated in Figure 18. With the S^D present, the distribution of run lengths showed a marked peak at the minimum required value of eight, whereas without the S^D, the distribution was relatively flat. The rates of responding during the runs with and without the S^D were about the same (not shown). This is important because it ensured that a differential drug effect on run length under the two conditions could not be attributed to rate differences in the base-line performance.

Laties (1972) found that when the S^D was not present, the distribution of run lengths tended to shift progressively to the left (shorter values) with increasing doses of *d*-amphetamine (0.12–8 mg/kg), scopolamine (0.003–0.6 mg/kg), or chlorpromazine (1–81 mg/kg), administered intramuscularly 30 min presession. In other words, these drugs increased the amount of premature switching to the right key. When the S^D was present, however, *d*-amphetamine and scopolamine had little or no effect on the distribution of run lengths. The effect of these drugs was thus modulated by stimulus control. Such modulation was not found with chlorpromazine, which produced a substantial increase in

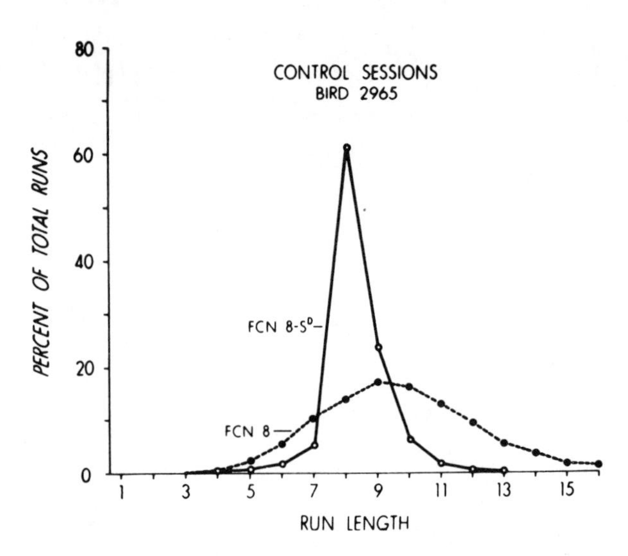

Figure 18. Relative frequency distributions of run lengths for the FCN schedule with (○—○) and without (●---●) the S^D under baseline conditions [From Laties (1972), © 1972 The Williams & Wilkins Company, Baltimore.]

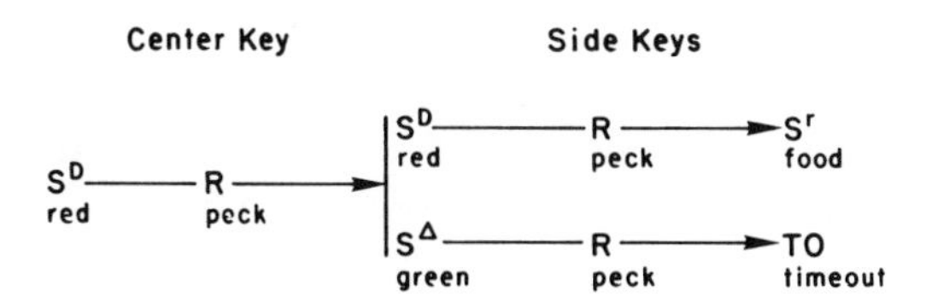

Figure 19. Matching to sample procedure.

the amount of premature switching even when the S^D was present. These results are consistent with those obtained by Laties and Weiss (1966), who studied the same three drugs under "clock vs. no clock" conditions. Laties (1972) also studied haloperidol (0.012–1.6 mg/kg). Although this drug, like the other three, produced a dose-related decrease in the response rate during the runs, it had relatively little effect on switching behavior, regardless of whether the S^D was present or absent. This seemingly unique characteristic of haloperidol deserves further study.

3.3. Matching to Sample

Berryman *et al.* (1962) used a matching-to-sample procedure to establish a conditional discrimination in pigeons. The procedure involved three keys and a chain of two responses; a typical trial is summarized in Figure 19. A trial was started by illuminating the center key with one of three colors (red, green, or blue) as the sample. When the pigeon pecked this key (an observing response), both side keys were illuminated, one with a color matching that on the center key, the other with one of the two nonmatching colors. A response on the matching side key (a correct response) was reinforced with food presentation, whereas a response on the nonmatching side key (an error) produced a brief timeout, during which the chamber was dark. After either event, there was an intertrial interval, during which the keylights were off and the houselight was on. The color of the center key and the position of the matching side key (left or right) varied randomly from trial to trial; correctness was thus conditional on the color of the sample. Berryman *et al.* found that overall accuracy (percent correct) was decreased markedly by pentobarbital (10 mg/kg), but was generally unaffected by LSD (0.05–0.3 mg/kg), administered intramuscularly 10 min presession. On the other hand, pentobarbital had no effect on trial time, whereas LSD initially produced long periods of pausing.

The disruptive effect of pentobarbital on matching accuracy is consistent with Blough's (1956) data. Recall that Blough found a decrease in accuracy when pentobarbital (10 mg/kg) was administered to pigeons working in an S^D–S^D two-key situation. The Berryman *et al.* finding that LSD did not affect matching accuracy may simply mean that the doses were too small. Recall that Siegel (1969) found that LSD, at larger doses (0.5–0.75 mg/kg), decreased the accuracy of pigeons working in a three-key discrimination situation.

An interesting extension of the Berryman *et al.* (1962) study was reported by Nevin and Liebold (1966). A pigeon was first trained to a high level of matching-to-sample accuracy under conditions that were basically the same as those in the Berryman *et al.* study, except that two key colors (red and green) were used instead of three. An "oddity" procedure was then introduced. For example, if the colors of the left, center, and right keys were green, green, and red, respectively, then a response on the nonmatching or odd side key (red) was reinforced. The oddity and matching contingencies alternated in blocks of trials during each session and were cued by the presence or absence of a yellow light above the center key. In this complex procedure, the yellow light may be thought of as a higher-order S^D that exerts control over a set of two conditional discriminations. At the end of base-line training, ". . . the bird was performing consistently between 86 and 99 percent correct on both matching and oddity" (Nevin and Liebold, 1966, p. 351).

Nevin and Liebold (1966) found that the accuracy of both performances decreased with increasing doses of pentobarbital (2–6 mg, administered intramuscularly 10 min presession). There was, however, a differential drug effect (Figure 20). Note that, ". . . with a single exception, accuracies under drug are higher for oddity than for matching, indicated by the fact that the data points appear above the 45° locus of equal accuracy" (Nevin and Liebold, 1966, p. 351). Although this finding provides another example of modulating a drug effect by stimulus-control procedures, it is difficult to explain why the modulation occurred. The predrug accuracies for matching and oddity were both high, which would indicate that strong stimulus control had been established in both cases. One possibility is that the differential drug effect is related to different histories of S^Δ responding under the matching and oddity contingencies (see Terrace, 1963).

Cook and Davidson (1968) reported a matching-to-sample study that was unusual in that a drug-induced *enhancement* of accuracy was obtained. These investigators used a delayed-matching procedure with squirrel monkeys. After an observing response to the sample on the center key, there was a 4-sec delay, during which all three keys were dark, before the onset of the "comparison stimuli" (red, three dots, and three vertical lines). The position of the matching key (left, center, or

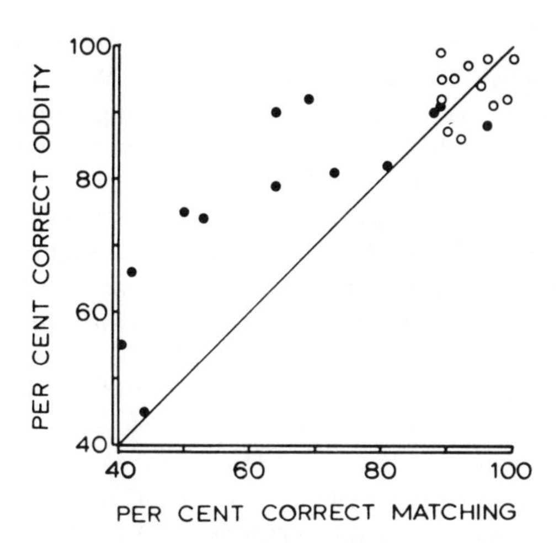

Figure 20. Pigeon's oddity accuracy plotted against matching accuracy for base-line sessions (open circles) and pentobarbital sessions (filled circles). The 45° line represents the locus of equal accuracy. [From Nevin and Liebold (1966).]

right) varied randomly. A food reinforcer was presented after two successive correct responses (matches); an error (mismatch) produced a brief time-out.

The type of base-line performance generated by the delayed matching procedure is illustrated in the left part of Figure 21. Note that there were never more than 20 consecutive correct responses during the session. The right part of Figure 21 shows the first hour of testing after 0.25 mg/kg of strychnine was administered orally. The drug clearly enhanced accuracy, as indicated by the longer runs of consecutive correct responses, as many as 40 in one instance. Interestingly, a similar effect was found on the day following drug administration (not shown). Cook and Davidson (1968) suggested that "this second day effect appears to be due to a residual effect of the interaction of drug and behavior on the day of treatment" (p. 946).

Although it is unlikely that the drug-induced enhancement of accuracy obtained by Cook and Davidson (1968) will have much practical application (strychnine can readily cause convulsions and is used as a rat poison), their procedure would seem to be a good matching-to-sample base line to use for studying other drugs. It seems likely that delayed matching accuracy would be less than simultaneous (no delay) matching accuracy under otherwise identical base-line conditions. If so, the delayed matching procedure, with its weaker stimulus control, should be more sensitive to drug effects. It should be especially sensitive to enhancement effects, since there would be more room for improvement than with simultaneous matching. With the latter procedure, the base-line accuracy levels may be so high that the only drug effect measurable would be a decrease (see Nevin and Liebold, 1966).

A more complicated delayed matching procedure was used in an excellent but infrequently cited drug study by Scheckel (1963). Rhesus monkeys worked individually in a chamber containing three levers. Above each lever was a disk that could be illuminated with red, green, or white light. Every two minutes, a trial began with the presentation of the sample (red or green, randomly varied) above the center lever. A response on this lever turned off the sample and started a delay interval. After the delay, the lights above the side levers came on (red and green, position randomly varied). If the monkey pressed the lever under the light that was the same color as the sample had been, food was presented and the trial was terminated. An error (mismatch) simply terminated the trial. During the intertrial interval, all three discs were illuminated with white light.

The feature of Scheckel's procedure that made it relatively complex involved the delay between the sample and the comparison stimuli. The delay was variable rather than fixed; the length of the delay depended on the monkey's performance. More specifically, if the monkey responded correctly (matched the sample) on two consecutive trials at a given delay, then the delay during the next trial was increased one step in a predetermined sequence (1, 3, 7.5, 15, 30, 50, 70, 90, and 105 sec). If an error occurred, or if the monkey did not respond to the sample within 10 sec (response failure), the delay during the next trial was decreased one step. In short, with this "titrating" delayed matching procedure, the delay increased progressively during each session until a limit was reached.

Figure 22 shows the average limit of delay under control (C) and drug conditions for one monkey. As can be seen, the limit of delay tended to decrease with increasing doses of chlorpromazine (adminis-

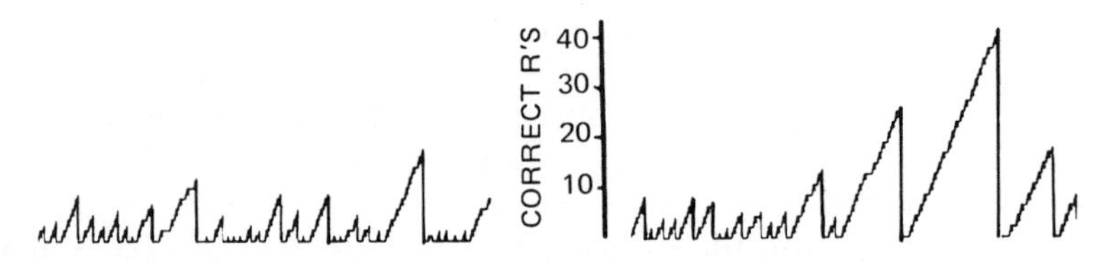

Figure 21. Cumulative records of a monkey's delayed matching performance before (left) and after (right) 0.25 mg/kg of strychnine was administered. The recording pen stepped upward with each correct response and reset when an error was made. [Abstracted from Figure 15 in Cook and Davidson (1968).]

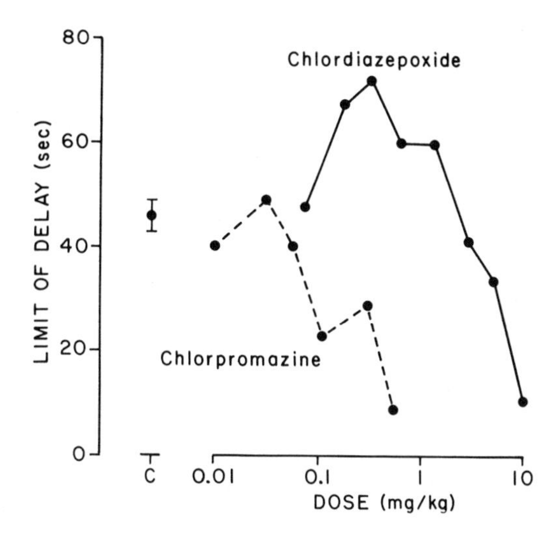

Figure 22. Dose effects of chlordiazepoxide and chlorpromazine on a monkey's limit of delay. The bracket indicates one standard error on either side of the mean for the control (C) sessions. [The figure has been constructed from data given in Scheckel (1963), Table 2.]

tered subcutaneously 15 min presession). In contrast, with chlordiazepoxide (administered orally 15 min presession), the limit of delay increased as the dose was increased to 0.3 mg/kg and then decreased at larger doses. The decrease in the limit of delay at the larger doses of both drugs was accompanied by an increase in response failures (not shown). The more interesting effect, that is, the increased limit of delay produced by the smaller doses of chlordiazepoxide, was ". . . considered to be due to increased attentiveness to the sample stimulus, and/or a decrease in distractability of the subjects during the delay interval" (Scheckel, 1963, p. 81). The problem with this interpretation is that it is untestable unless "attentiveness" and "distractability" can be measured.

In a follow-up study, Scheckel *et al.* (1968) used basically the same titrating delayed matching procedure to assess the effects of varying doses of *dl*-Δ^9-tetrahydrocannabinol (THC) in rhesus monkeys. It was found that the limit of delay decreased and the response failures increased progressively with increasing doses of THC (0.25–4 mg/kg, administered intraperitoneally 15 min presession). The duration of action of the largest dose was remarkably long; the performance did not return to base-line levels until 9 days after the injection. It might be worthwhile to determine whether the drug effects obtained with this procedure could be modulated by manipulating variables such as the step size in the progression of delay intervals.

3.4. Repeated Acquisition of Behavioral Chains

A few years ago, I became interested in studying the effects of drugs on learning. In virtually all previous studies of this problem (see reviews by Essman, 1971; Jarvik, 1972; McGaugh and Petrinovich, 1965), the critical comparisons were made between groups of subjects (drug vs. nondrug controls), usually over a relatively short period of time. When reliable effects were reported in these studies (usually interference, sometimes facilitation), they were generally small in magnitude and of little practical significance. It seemed to me that this failure to find convincing evidence that drugs affected learning could be related simply to the fact that there are large individual differences in rates of learning.

The problem of intersubject variability could be eliminated, of course, by using each subject as his own control. However, it has generally been assumed that this approach would be inappropriate for the study of acquisition phenomena (McGaugh and Petrinovich, 1965). The main reason stems from the well-established finding that if a subject is confronted with the same or an equivalent task after initial learning, he relearns it at a faster rate. Because of this sequential effect of "learning to learn" (Harlow, 1949), it has been argued that a subject's initial learning cannot serve as a base line for later learning under drug conditions.

I dealt with the problem of "learning to learn" by using a repeated-acquisition technique that was similar to one developed by Boren (1963). Briefly, the learning situation was as follows. A pigeon worked for food in a chamber containing three response keys. All three keys were illuminated at the same time by one of four colors. The pigeon's task was to learn a four-response chain by pecking the correct key in the presence of each color (e.g., see Figure 23). When the pigeon pecked an incorrect key (a key not included in the four-response chain), the error was followed by a 5-sec time-out. During the time-out, the keylights were off and a response had no effect. An error did not reset the chain; that is, the keylights after the time-out were the same color as before the time-out. The four-response chain (in this case, left–right–center–right or LRCR) was changed from session to session. The chains were carefully selected to be equivalent in several ways and their

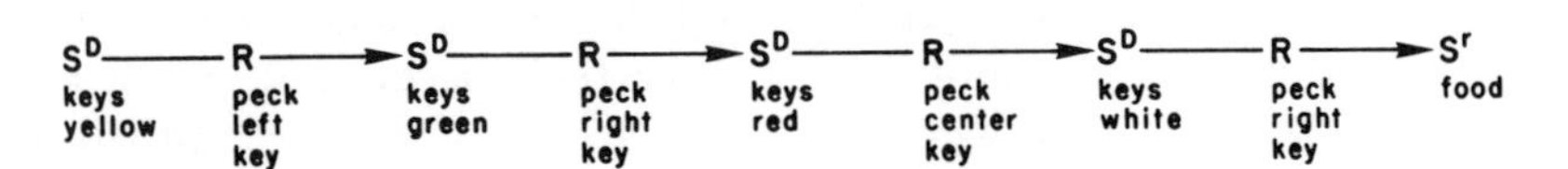

Figure 23. Four-response chain in a repeated acquisition procedure.

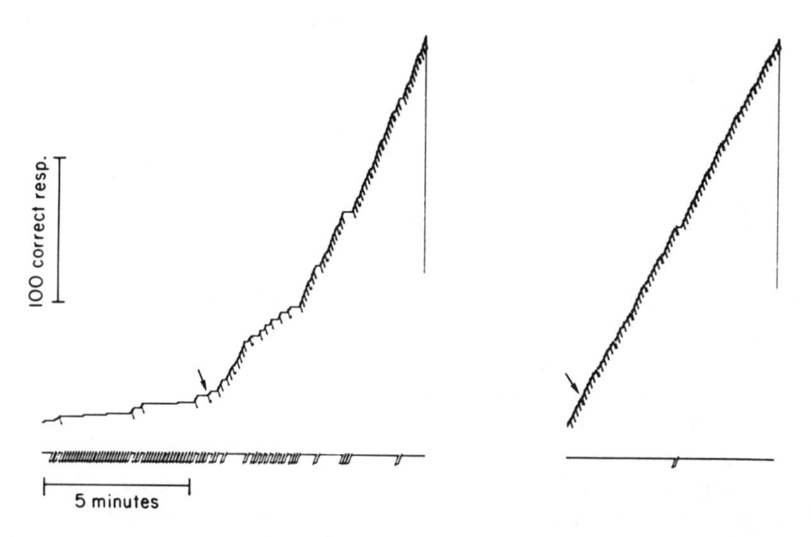

Figure 24. Cumulative records of a pigeon's correct responding under base-line conditions involving learning (left) and performance (right). The response pen deflected downward when the food magazine was presented (5-sec presentation for every fifth completion of the four-response chain; 0.5-sec presentation, presumably a conditioned reinforcer, for all other completions). The arrows indicate the first food reinforcement in each session. Errors are indicated by the event pen (bottom), which was held down during each time-out.

ordering was restricted across sessions (see Thompson, 1973). An example of a typical set of six chains is as follows: LRCR, CLRL, LRLC, RCRL, CLCR, RCLC; the order of the associated colors was always the same: yellow, green, red, white (food). After extended training under these conditions, each subject reached a steady state in terms of stable within-session error reduction. In short, a steady state of transition states (Sidman, 1960) was obtained. The steady state was also characterized by stable levels of overall accuracy, as measured by total errors per session (the number of correct responses per session was held constant).

That learning was produced by the repeated-acquisition procedure is illustrated in Figure 24 (left side), which shows the first part of a session for one pigeon at steady state. Note that errors decreased in frequency and the rate of completions of the chain increased as the session progressed. In other words, there was an improvement of performance as a function of reinforced practice, which is an accepted behavioral definition of learning (Kimble, 1967). Note also that toward the end of the learning curve, there is an instance of nearly 80 consecutive correct responses. Since three keys were involved, the "chance" probability of this happening would be incredibly low—about $(1/3)^{80}$. Under base-line conditions at steady state, essentially the same curve was obtained with each new chain this pigeon learned.

For comparison, I have also studied a performance condition, in which the four-response chain was the same from session to session. In contrast to the learning condition, the performance condition generated an error rate that was relatively constant (near zero) during the session. This is illustrated in Figure 24 (right side), which shows the first part of a performance session at steady state (the two records are from the same pigeon during different blocks of sessions).

To study the interaction between stimulus control and drug effects, the chain-learning and chain-performance conditions were compared with the corresponding tandem conditions. Under the tandem-learning and tandem-performance conditions, different-colored keylights were not associated with the four-response sequence; when the keylights were on, they were always white. (Lights were momentarily dimmed when the sequence advanced.) In all other aspects, the tandem-learning and tandem-performance conditions were identical to the chain-learning and chain-performance conditions, respectively.

Figure 25 shows the effects of varying doses of chlordiazepoxide and phenobarbital (administered intramuscularly 30 min presession) on the total errors per session under the four conditions for two pigeons. The brackets indicate the ranges of variability for the base-line (B) and saline (S) sessions. A drug was considered to have an effect on overall accuracy to the extent that the dose data fell outside both ranges. As can be seen, overall accuracy was impaired by the largest dose of each drug under all four base-line conditions, with chlordiazepoxide having a greater error-increasing effect than phenobarbital. At the smaller doses, however, there was differential base-line sensitivity to the error-increasing effect of the drugs. Whereas the smaller doses of both drugs had no effect on overall accuracy under the tandem-learning condition, errors increased slightly at 20 mg/kg of chlordiazepoxide under the tandem-performance and chain-performance conditions. The chain-learning condition was the most sensitive base line, in that an error-increasing effect was found at 20 mg/kg of phenobarbital with pigeon 6173 and at 10 and 20 mg/kg of chlordiazepoxide with both pigeons.

Figure 26 illustrates the within-session effects on accuracy obtained with the largest doses of phenobarbital and chlordiazepoxide. Each completion of the response sequence was considered a trial. The errors are plotted cumulatively so that the rate of errors during a given part of a session can be estimated easily from the slope of the curve. The curves for the drug sessions should be compared to the saline (min)

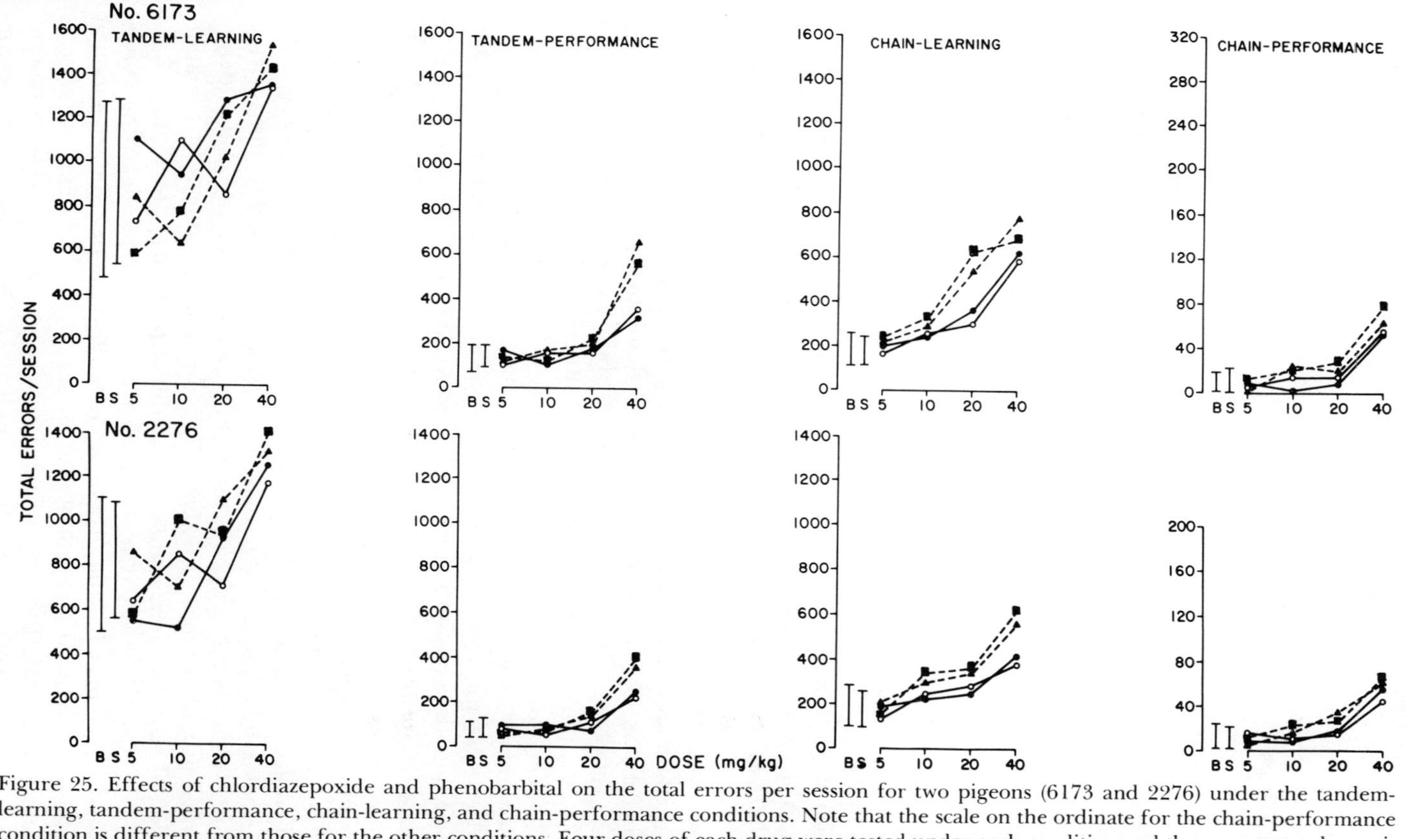

Figure 25. Effects of chlordiazepoxide and phenobarbital on the total errors per session for two pigeons (6173 and 2276) under the tandem-learning, tandem-performance, chain-learning, and chain-performance conditions. Note that the scale on the ordinate for the chain-performance condition is different from those for the other conditions. Four doses of each drug were tested under each condition and there were two determinations for each dose with each pigeon. ▲, chlordiazepoxide, first determination; ■, chlordiazepoxide, second determination; ●, phenobarbital, first determination; ○, phenobarbital, second determination. [From Thompson (1975); © 1975 by the Society for the Experimental Analysis of Behavior.]

and saline (max) sessions. Changes in error rate within a session were quantified by computing the index of curvature (see Fry *et al.,* 1960; Thompson, 1973). The index can range from −0.900 (maximum negative acceleration of error rate) to 0.900 (maximum positive acceleration), since each session was divided into tenths.

Figure 26 indicates that under both learning conditions, error rate decreased across trials within each session, but the degree of negative acceleration was less (smaller index values) in the drug sessions than in the saline sessions. Note also that the degree of negative acceleration was less during a given session under the tandem-learning condition than during the corresponding session under the chain-learning condition. In short, under the two learning conditions, the degree of negative acceleration generally decreased as total errors per session increased. Under the two performance conditions, however, the index values were not consistently related to total errors per session. In the saline and drug sessions under the performance conditions, there was either slight positive acceleration of error rate or less negative acceleration than that found under the corresponding learning condition. In short, error rate under the performance conditions was relatively constant across trials, but was higher in the drug sessions than in the saline sessions.

The finding that the chain-learning base line was more sensitive to the effects of phenobarbital and chlordiazepoxide than the tandem-learning base line (Figure 25) deserves some discussion with regard to the literature that has been reviewed. Recall that similar results were obtained with other drugs in a related performance situation, where two phenothiazines (chlorpromazine and trifluoperazine) had greater effects on the response rate of pigeons under a chained fixed-ratio schedule than under a tandem fixed-ratio schedule (Thomas, 1966). In a variety of other performance situations, however, it has been found that behavior under the control of external discriminative stimuli is *less* readily disrupted by drugs than behavior not under such control (Laties, 1972; Laties and Weiss, 1966; Leander and McMillan, 1974; Thompson and Corr, 1974). In discussing this apparent discrepancy, Laties (1972) pointed out that ". . . framing an explanation of how drug action is modified by stimulus control may require one to determine just what types of behavioral changes are produced by the addition of particular environmental stimuli at particular times" (p. 12).

Figure 25 shows that switching from the tandem-learning condition to the chain-learning condition (i.e., the addition of environmental stimuli) produced a decrease in total errors and less base-line variability. Either or both of these behavioral changes may be responsible for the greater sensitivity of the chain-learning base line to the error-increasing effects of phenobarbital and chlordiazepoxide. Detection of

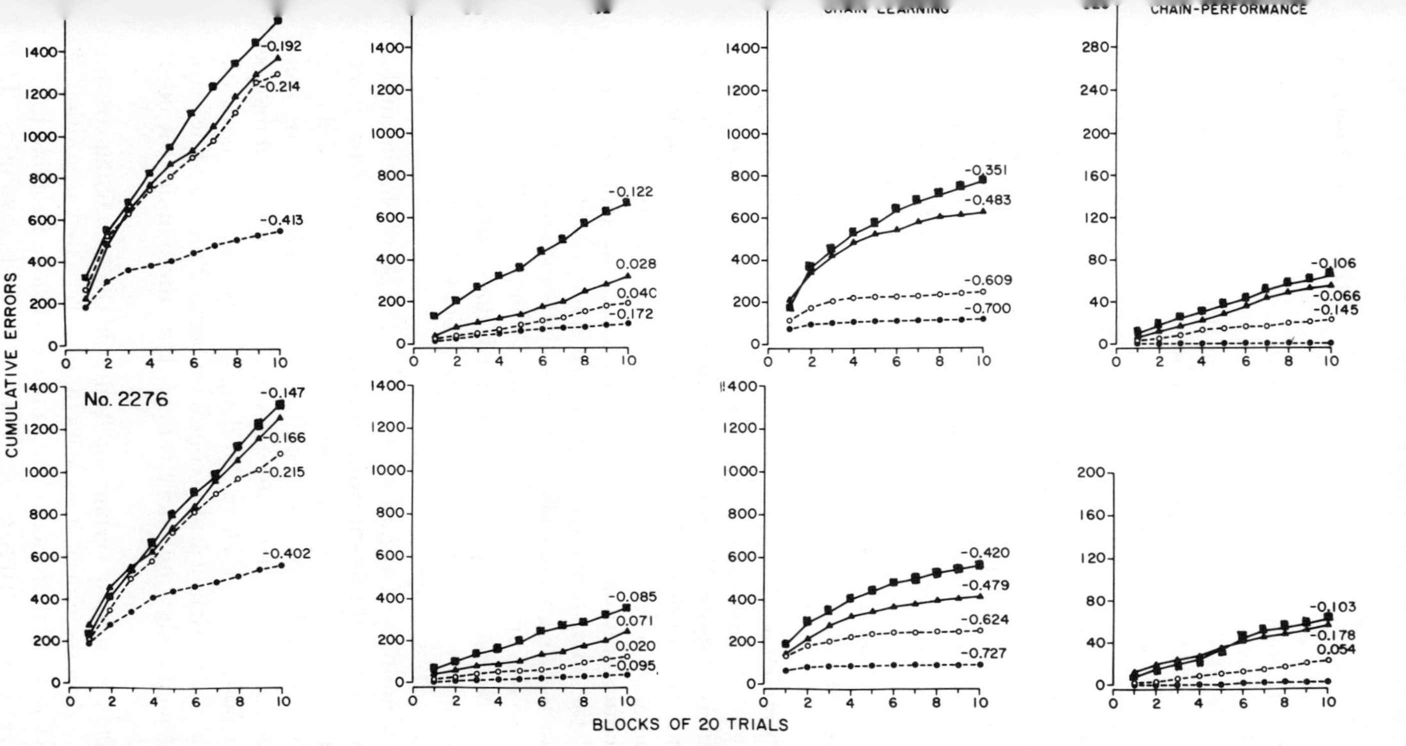

Figure 26. Within-session effects on accuracy obtained with the largest doses of phenobarbital and chlordiazepoxide (first determinations) for two pigeons (6173 and 2276) under the tandem-learning, tandem-performance, chain-learning, and chain-performance conditions. Note that the scale on the ordinate for the chain-performance condition is different from those for the other conditions. The saline (min) and saline (max) sessions were the sessions with the minimum and maximum total errors of all the saline sessions. The index of curvature value is shown for each session, except for the saline (min) session under the chain-performance condition, where virtually no errors were made. If all the errors in a session occurred during the first 20 trials, the index would take on its maximum negative value of -0.900; if the error rate were constant during the session, the index would equal 0. ●, saline (min); ○, saline (max); ▲, phenobarbital 40 mg/kg; ■, chlordiazepoxide 40 mg/kg. [From Thompson (1975); © 1975 by the Society for the Experimental Analysis of Behavior.]

a drug effect is obviously less difficult as the base-line variability decreases and, according to the "law of initial value" (Wilder, 1967), it should be easier to detect an error-increasing effect of a drug when the base-line error levels are relatively low. Although these types of behavioral changes may also explain why the tandem-performance and chain-performance base lines were slightly more sensitive than the tandem-learning base line (see Figure 25: chlordiazepoxide, 20 mg/kg), they cannot explain why the two performance base lines were less sensitive than the chain-learning base-line. For example, with pigeon 6173, total errors and amount of base-line variability were quite similar under the tandem-performance and chain-learning conditions; however, an error-increasing effect was found at 20 mg/kg of phenobarbital and at 10 mg/kg of chlordiazepoxide only under the chain-learning condition.

The finding that the chain-learning base line was more sensitive to drug effects than the chain-performance base line is consistent with the widely held view that "difficult tasks" are more susceptible to drug effects than "simple tasks." The fact that the base-line error levels under the learning condition were much greater than those under the performance condition (Figure 25) indicates that learning was a more difficult task. The two conditions may also be considered as representing strong vs. weak stimulus control (see Dews, 1955). In the performance condition, the stimulus–response sequence remains constant from session to session and the animals are highly practiced. One would assume that this behavior is strongly controlled by the stimuli and would therefore be resistant to disruption by drugs. In the learning condition, where the stimulus–response sequence is changed daily, stimulus control would be relatively weak and the behavior would therefore be more readily disrupted by drugs.

By the same type of argument, one would expect behavior under the tandem-learning condition ("difficult task," weak control by "internal" stimuli) to be more readily disrupted by drugs than behavior under the tandem-performance condition ("simple task," strong control by "internal" stimuli). That this was not the case (Figure 25) may be related to a point made earlier: the drug effects may have been obscured under the tandem-learning condition because the base-line error levels were much higher and more variable than those under the other conditions.

In conclusion, despite certain similarities in the data obtained with chain and tandem sequences, it appears that the repeated acquisition of behavioral chains is a more stable and a more sensitive base line for assessing the effects of drugs on learning in individual subjects. The same conclusion was also drawn from a similar experiment with *d*-amphetamine and chlorpromazine (Thompson, 1974b).

In another study with pigeons, I assessed the effects of varying doses of imipramine and methylphenidate (administered intramuscularly 30 min presession) under the chain-learning and chain-performance conditions. Figure 27 shows that (1) both drugs increased the total errors per session as a function of dose under both the learning and performance conditions, (2) the error-increasing effect of a given dose was greater with imipramine than with methylphenidate under both conditions, and (3) the error-increasing effect was detected at lower doses of both drugs under the learning condition than under the performance condition. In general, the greater the total errors, the slower the rate of learning, as measured by the degree of within-session error reduction (see Figure 28).

I have recently conducted a drug study that demonstrates the selectivity of the chain-learning base line. Representative data are presented in Figure 29 (left side), which compares the dose effects of *d*-amphetamine, cocaine, and fenfluramine (administered intramuscularly 5 min presession) on total errors per session. Both cocaine and *d*-amphetamine increased errors as a function of dose, the only difference being that cocaine was somewhat less potent on a mg/kg basis. In contrast, fenfluramine, which is structurally similar to *d*-amphetamine and used clinically as an appetite suppressant, had no effect on accuracy at any of the doses tested. That fenfluramine was tested within an effective dose range is shown by its effect on total trial time (Figure 29, right side). Total trial time (i.e., the total number of minutes that the keylights were on during a session) indicates the amount of pausing that occurred. At the highest doses, the pause-increasing effect of fenfluramine was similar to that of cocaine but less than that of *d*-amphetamine. It can also be noted that the error-increasing effect of *d*-amphetamine and cocaine occurred at doses (1 and 3 mg/kg) that had no effect on pausing. The finding that accuracy was impaired by cocaine and *d*-amphetamine but not by fenfluramine would seem to indicate a base-line selectivity for abused vs. nonabused drugs. It is well established that cocaine and *d*-amphetamine can serve as reinforcers to maintain self-administration behavior in monkeys, whereas fenfluramine is ineffective in this animal model of drug abuse (Woods and Tessel, 1974).

The steady state of repeated acquisition also provides a convenient means for assessing the effects of *chronic* administration of drugs on learning. For example, Figure 30 shows the effects obtained during a 30-day period in which 10 mg/kg of imipramine was administered (intramuscularly 30 min presession) for 15 sessions followed by 20 mg/kg for 15 sessions. Perhaps the most interesting aspect of the data is the relationship between the extent of tolerance development and the behavioral measure. Either complete or partial tolerance developed to the drug-induced increase in errors and trial time (except with pigeon 7

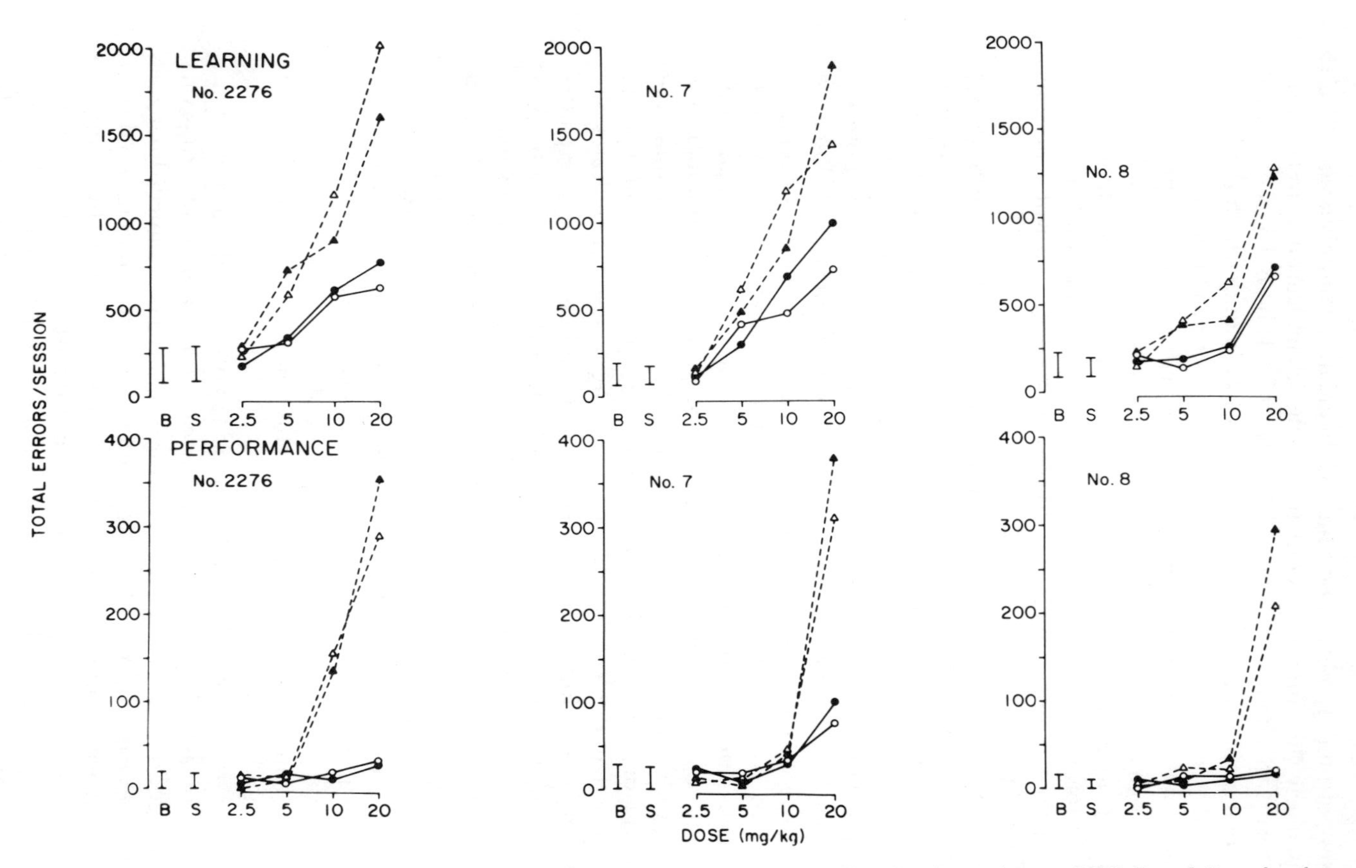

Figure 27. Dose effects of imipramine and methylphenidate on the total errors per session for three pigeons (2276, 7, and 8) under the chain-learning and chain-performance conditions. The brackets indicate the ranges for the base-line (B) and saline (S) sessions. ▲, imip- [illegible] methylphenidate, first determination; ○, methylphenidate, second

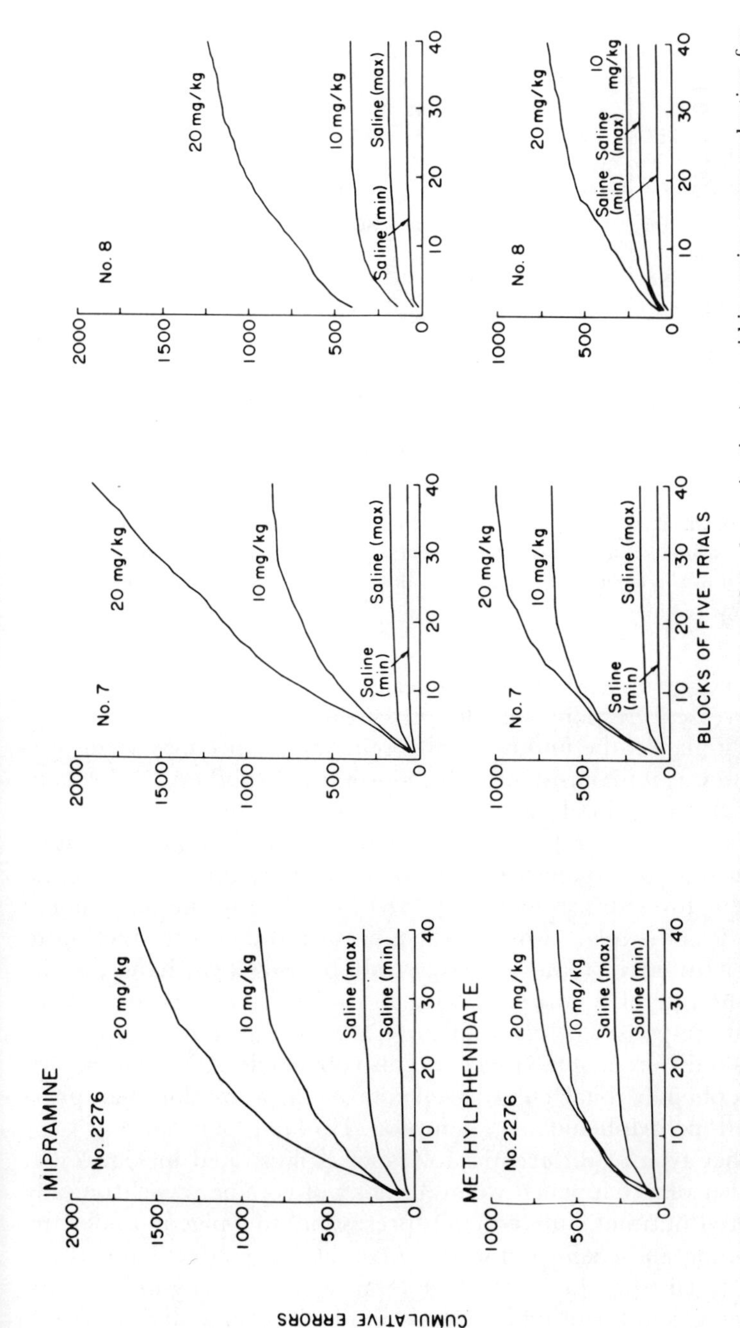

Figure 28. Effects of the higher doses of imipramine and methylphenidate (first determinations) on within-session error reduction for three pigeons (2276, 7, and 8) under the chain-learning condition. The saline (min) and saline (max) sessions were the sessions with the minimum and maximum total errors of all the saline sessions. [From Thompson (1976).]

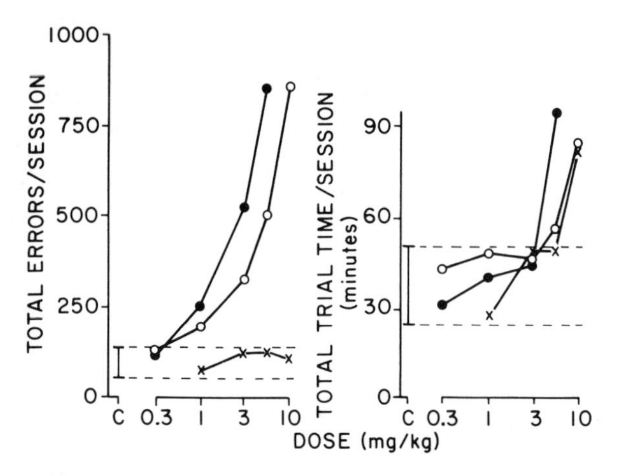

Figure 29. Dose effects of *d*-amphetamine (●), cocaine (○), and fenfluramine (×) on total errors and total trial time for a pigeon under the chain-learning condition. The brackets and dashed horizontal lines indicate the control (C) ranges (based on 26 saline sessions). Only the first of two determinations for each dose is shown; the second determinations yielded similar results.

at 20 mg/kg, errors), whereas no tolerance developed to the drug-induced increase in responses made during time-out.

At first glance, the finding of differential tolerance may seem puzzling. However, it is consistent with the working hypothesis of Schuster *et al.* (1966): "behavioral tolerance will develop in those aspects of the organism's behavioral repertoire where the action of the drug is such that it disrupts the organism's behavior in meeting the environmental requirement for reinforcements" (p. 181). Applied to the imipramine data, this would explain why tolerance was more likely to develop to the drug-induced increase in errors and pausing (which necessarily reduced the rate of reinforcement) than to the drug-induced increase in time-out responses (which had no effect on the rate of reinforcement). Such differential tolerance was also obtained in a similar experiment with phenobarbital, chlordiazepoxide, chlorpromazine, *d*-amphetamine, and methylphenidate (Thompson, 1974a).

Another type of differential tolerance is illustrated in Figure 31, which shows what happened when 3 mg/kg of cocaine was chronically administered (intramuscularly 5 min presession) to a pigeon under the chain-learning and chain-performance conditions. Under the learning condition (weak stimulus control), tolerance to the drug-induced increase in errors and pausing developed gradually over a 30-day period, whereas under the performance condition (strong stimulus control), these effects had disappeared by the tenth day. This finding is signifi-

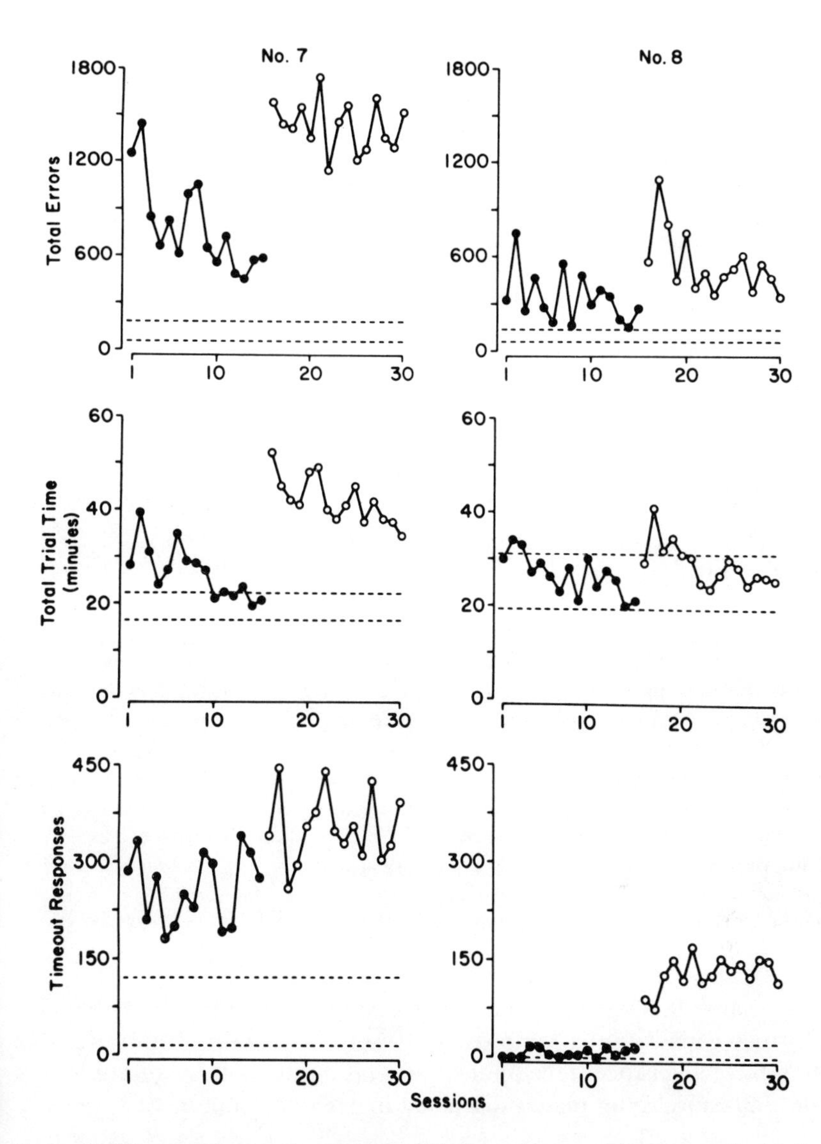

Figure 30. Effects of chronically administered imipramine on total errors, total trial time, and time-out responses for two pigeons (7 and 8) under the chain-learning condition. The dashed horizontal lines indicate the ranges for 10 saline sessions that preceded the chronic drug regimen. ●, 10 mg/kg; ○, 20 mg/kg.

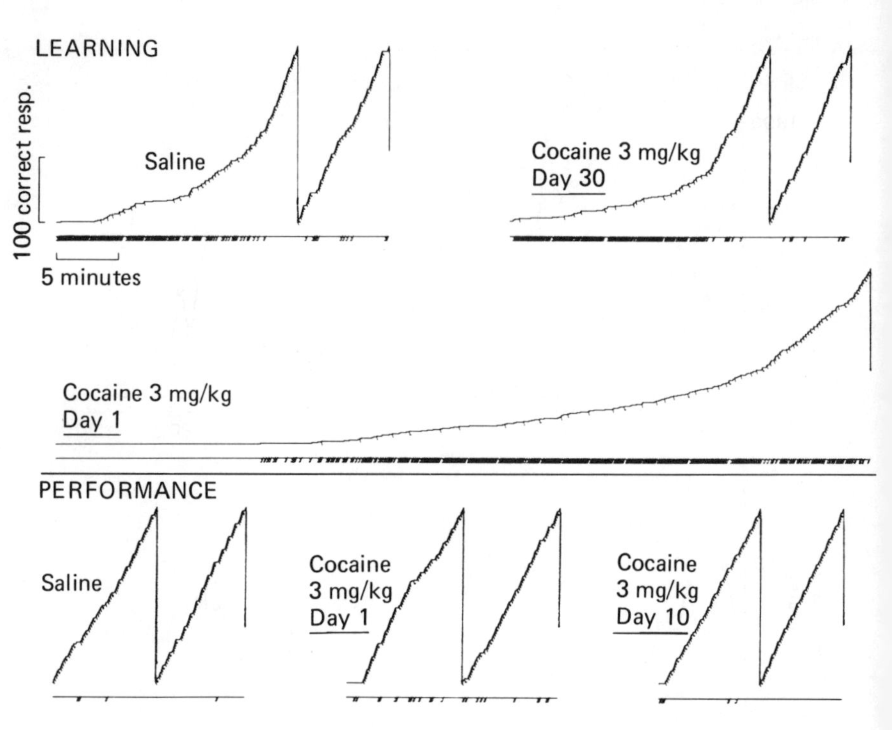

Figure 31. Development of behavioral tolerance to cocaine (3 mg/kg/day) in a pigeon under the chain-learning and chain-performance conditions. The drug was tested first under the performance condition and then under the learning condition. Before each chronic drug regimen began, the base line was stabilized (20–30 days) and then saline was administered (10 days). The cumulative records are from a representative saline session and the first and last drug sessions under each condition. The first two excursions of the response pen in each session are shown, except for day 1 under the learning condition, where only the first excursion is shown. Errors are indicated by the event pen below each record. For other recording details, see the legend for Figure 24.

cant because it represents one of the first demonstrations of behavioral tolerance with cocaine. Perhaps even more important, it indicates that the rate of tolerance development can be modulated by stimulus control. Behavioral tolerance is discussed in greater detail in Chapter 8.

4. Summary and Conclusions

The present chapter has shown that drug effects on operant behavior under stimulus control are determined by both pharmacological and behavioral variables. The pharmacological variables include the type of drug, the dose, and the history of drug administration (acute vs. chronic). The behavioral variables include the history of S^{Δ} responding, the predrug response rate, the type and degree of stimulus control established, the difference between the discriminative stimuli, the schedule of reinforcement, and whether the baseline involves learning or performance. Our current knowledge of how these variables interact is summarized below.

In the S^D–S^{Δ} studies reviewed, S^D responding was either unaffected or was generally decreased in a dose-related manner by a variety of drugs (e.g., pentobarbital, chlorpromazine, amphetamine). A decrease in S^D responding per se is not usually interpreted as a disruption of stimulus control since it could represent nothing more than a general depressant effect of the drug. The more critical indication of disrupted stimulus control is an increase in S^{Δ} responding. In general, drug-induced increases in S^{Δ} responding were not obtained if the predrug S^{Δ} rate was virtually zero, a sign of strong stimulus control. Such increases were found, however, if there was a certain minimum tendency to respond in S^{Δ} prior to drug administration. It was concluded that a history of S^{Δ} responding is a necessary but not a sufficient condition for obtaining this type of drug effect.

It has been shown that the differential responding that occurs in the presence of different discriminative stimuli in multiple fixed-ratio fixed-interval schedules can be reduced by a number of drugs. Such an effect (e.g., intrusions of fixed-ratio-like responding during the fixed-interval component) may represent a weakening of stimulus control. There have been two lines of experimental support for this interpretation, both involving chlorpromazine: (1) the drug effect was mimicked by changing to a mixed fixed-ratio fixed-interval schedule and (2) the drug effect disappeared when the fixed-ratio component was removed. An alternative interpretation is that the reduction in differential responding may simply represent a rate-dependent drug effect. It has been shown, for example, that amphetamine tends to decrease high rates of responding while increasing low rates, regardless of whether the responding is controlled by a multiple schedule or is studied in isolation. The difficulty in ruling out a rate-dependent interpretation is perhaps the major problem in using multiple schedules to study drug effects on stimulus control. A more recent approach involving multiple schedules is the modulation of drug effects by stimulus control. Comparisons of multiple vs. mixed schedules and of multiple-schedule components with and without added stimuli have shown that, in general, behavior under strong stimulus control is less readily disrupted by drug administration than behavior not under such control.

In S^D–S^D two-key procedures, each S^D also serves as an S^{Δ}. The drugs studied with this type of procedure have generally decreased accuracy (percent correct), regardless of whether the total response output increased (e.g., with pentobarbital and alcohol) or decreased (e.g., with large doses of chlorpromazine). The impaired accuracy obtained with scopolamine and LSD was associated with an increased tendency to respond on one key. The extent to which a drug effect reflects a change in "perceptual sensitivity" and/or "response bias" (key preference) can readily be determined through a signal detection type of analysis. This relatively new parametric approach provides a direction for future research that is likely to prove fruitful.

Drug studies using discrimination procedures involving response chains have yielded results that are consistent with those obtained using multiple schedules or related procedures. For example, comparisons of performance vs. acquisition of four-response chains and of FCN performance with and without an added S^D have shown that behavior under strong external stimulus control is generally less readily disrupted by drug administration than behavior under weak or "internal" stimulus control. There have also been several unexpected findings with certain drugs in certain situations involving chained responding. First, chained-schedule performance and the acquisition of response chains (i.e., behavior under external stimulus control) was more readily affected by drugs (e.g., chlorpromazine) than tandem-schedule performance and the acquisition of tandem response sequences (i.e., behavior under "internal" stimulus control). Second, at doses that decreased overall response rate, haloperidol had relatively little effect on FCN switching performance, and fenfluramine had no effect on chain-learning accuracy. Third, pentobarbital impaired accuracy to a greater extent in matching to sample than in oddity, even though the predrug accuracies were high in both tasks. Fourth, in delayed matching procedures, strychnine and chlordiazepoxide increased accuracy or the "limit of delay." Finally, under conditions of repeated acquisition and performance of response chains, behavioral tolerance developed to cocaine, and the rate of tolerance development was modulated by stimulus control. Not only should the findings above be replicated, but also other drugs should be tested in the same stimulus-control situations, and the same drugs should be tested in other stimulus-control situations. This would determine some of the pharmacological and behavioral "boundary conditions" for the findings.

Acknowledgment

Preparation of this chapter and some of the author's research reported therein were supported by U.S. Public Health Service grant

DA 01528. My thanks go to my wife, Annette, for her constructive criticism of the chapter, and to Ms. Gretchen Schultze, whose expert secretarial skills greatly facilitated its preparation.

5. References

Angle, H. V., 1973, Role of chlorpromazine in maintaining timing behavior in chronic schizophrenics, *Psychopharmacologia* **28:**185–194.

Berryman, R., Jarvik, M. E., and Nevin, J. A., 1962, Effects of pentobarbital, lysergic acid diethylamide, and chlorpromazine on matching behavior in the pigeon, *Psychopharmacologia 3:*60–65.

Blough, D. S., 1956, Technique for studying the effects of drugs on discrimination in the pigeon, *Ann. N.Y. Acad. Sci.* **65:**334–344.

Blough, D. S., 1966, The study of animal sensory processes by operant methods, *in: Operant Behavior: Areas of Research and Application* (W. K. Honig, ed.), pp. 345–379, Appleton-Century-Crofts, New York.

Boren, J. J., 1963, Repeated acquisition of new behavioral chains, *Amer. Psychol.* **17:**421 (abstract).

Byrd, L. D., 1974, Modification of the effects of chlorpromazine on behavior in the chimpanzee, *J. Pharmacol. Exp. Ther.* **189:**24–32.

Catania, A. C. (ed.), 1968, *Contemporary Research in Operant Behavior,* Scott, Foresman, Glenview, Ill.

Clark, F. C., and Steele, B. J., 1966, Effects of *d*-amphetamine on performance under a multiple schedule in the rat, *Psychopharmacologia* **9:**157–169.

Cook, L., and Davidson, A. B., 1968, Effects of yeast RNA and other pharmacological agents on acquisition, retention, and performance in animals, *in: Psychopharmacology: A Review of Progress, 1957–1967* (D. H. Efron, ed.), pp. 931–946, Government Printing Office, Washington, D.C.

Cook, L., and Kelleher, R. T., 1962, Drug effects on the behavior of animals, *Ann. N.Y. Acad. Sci.* **96:**315–335.

Dews, P. B., 1955, Studies on behavior. II. The effects of pentobarbital, methamphetamine, and scopolamine on performances in pigeons involving discriminations, *J. Pharmacol. Exp. Ther.* **115:**380–389.

Dews, P. B., 1958, Analysis of effects of psychopharmacological agents in behavioral terms, *Fed. Proc.* **17:**1024–1030.

Dews, P. B., 1963, Behavioral effects of drugs, *in: Conflict and Creativity* (S. M. Farber and R. H. L. Wilson, eds.), pp. 138–153, McGraw-Hill, New York.

Dykstra, L. A., and Appel, J. B., 1974, Effects of LSD on auditory perception: a signal detection analysis, *Psychopharmacologia* **34:**289–307.

Essman, W. B., 1971, Drug effects and learning and memory processes, *Advan. Pharmacol. Chemother.* **9:**241–330.

Fry, W., Kelleher, R. T., and Cook, L., 1960, A mathematical index of performance on fixed-interval schedules of reinforcement, *J. Exp. Anal. Behav.* **3:**193–199.

Green, D. M., and Swets, J. A., 1966, *Signal Detection Theory and Psychophysics,* Wiley, New York.

Harlow, H. F., 1949, The formation of learning sets, *Psychol. Rev.* **56:**51–65.

Hearst, E., 1959, Effects of scopolamine on discriminated responding in the rat, *J. Pharmacol. Exp. Ther.* **126:**349–358.

Hearst, E., 1964, Drug effects on stimulus generalization gradients in the monkey, *Psychopharmacologia* **6:**57–70.

Herrnstein, R. J., 1966, Superstition: a corollary of the principles of operant conditioning, *in: Operant Behavior: Areas of Research and Application* (W. K. Honig, ed.), pp. 33–51, Appleton-Century-Crofts, New York.

Jarvik, M. E., 1972, Effects of chemical and physical treatments on learning and memory, *Ann. Rev. Psychol.* **23:**457–486.

Kelleher, R. T., 1965, Operant conditioning, *in: Behavior of Nonhuman Primates* (A. M. Schrier, H. F. Harlow, and F. Stollnitz, eds.), Vol. 1, pp. 211–247, Academic Press, New York.

Kelleher, R. T., and Gollub, L. R., 1962, A review of positive conditioned reinforcement, *J. Exp. Anal. Behav.* **5:**543–597.

Kelleher, R. T., and Morse, W. H., 1964, Escape behavior and punished behavior, *Fed. Proc.* **23:**808–817.

Kelleher, R. T., and Morse, W. H., 1968, Determinants of the specificity of behavioral effects of drugs, *Ergeb. Physiol. Biol. Chem. Exp. Pharmakol.* **60:**1–56.

Keller, F. S., and Schoenfeld, W. N., 1950, *Principles of Psychology,* Appleton-Century-Crofts, New York.

Kimble, G. A., 1967, The definition of learning and some useful distinctions, *in: Foundations of Conditioning and Learning* (G. A. Kimble, ed.), pp. 82–99, Appleton-Century-Crofts, New York.

Laties, V. G., 1972, The modification of drug effects on behavior by external discriminative stimuli, *J. Pharmacol. Exp. Ther.* **183:**1–13.

Laties, V. G., and Weiss, B., 1966, Influence of drugs on behavior controlled by internal and external stimuli, *J. Pharmacol. Exp. Ther.* **152:**388–396.

Leander, J. D., 1975, Rate-dependent effects of drugs. II. Effects of some major tranquilizers on multiple fixed-ratio, fixed-interval schedule performance, *J. Pharmacol. Exp. Ther.* **193:**689–700.

Leander, J. D., and McMillan, D. E., 1974, Rate-dependent effects of drugs. I. Comparisons of *d*-amphetamine, pentobarbital, and chlorpromazine on multiple and mixed schedules, *J. Pharmacol. Exp. Ther.* **188:**726–739.

McGaugh, J. L., and Petrinovich, L. F., 1965, Effects of drugs on learning and memory, *Int. Rev. Neurobiol.* **8:**139–196.

Morse, W. H., 1955, An analysis of responding in the presence of a stimulus correlated with periods of non-reinforcement. Doctoral dissertation, Harvard University.

Nevin, J. A., 1973, Stimulus control, *in: The Study of Behavior* (J. A. Nevin, ed.), 115–152, Scott, Foresman, Glenview, Ill.

Nevin, J. A., and Liebold, K., 1966, Stimulus control of matching and oddity in a pigeon, *Psychon. Sci.* **5:** 351–352.

Nigro, M. R., Fraser, W. R., and Wade, E. A., 1967, Effects of chlorpromazine on a brightness discrimination in the rat, *Percept. Mot. Skills* **24:**739–745.

Sanger, D. J., and Blackman, D. E., 1976, Rate-dependent effects of drugs: a review of the literature, *Pharmacol. Biochem. Behav.* **4:**73–83.

Scheckel, C. L., 1963, The effect of chlorpromazine (Thorazine) and chlordiazepoxide (Librium) on delayed matching responses in the *Macaca mulatta.* Doctoral dissertation, Fordham University.

Scheckel, C. L., Boff, E., Dahlen, P., and Smart, T., 1968, Behavioral effects in monkeys of racemates of two biologically active marijuana constituents, *Science* **160:**1467–1469.

Schuster, C. R., Dockens, W. S., and Woods, J. H., 1966, Behavioral variables affecting the development of amphetamine tolerance, *Psychopharmacologia* **9:**170–182.

Sidman, M., 1960, *Tactics of Scientific Research,* Basic Books, New York.

Siegel, R. K., 1969, Effects of cannabis sativa and lysergic acid diethylamide on a visual discrimination task in pigeons, *Psychopharmacologia* **15:**1–8.

Skinner, B. F., 1938, *The Behavior of Organisms,* Appleton-Century-Crofts, New York.

Terrace, H. S., 1963, Errorless discrimination learning in the pigeon: effects of chlorpromazine and imipramine, *Science* **140:**318–319.

Terrace, H. S., 1966, Stimulus control, *in: Operant Behavior: Areas of Research and Application* (W. K. Honig, ed.), pp. 271–344, Appleton-Century-Crofts, New York.

Thomas, J. R., 1966, Differential effects of two phenothiazines on chain and tandem performance, *J. Pharmacol. Exp. Ther.* **152:**354–361.

Thompson, D. M., 1973, Repeated acquisition as a behavioral baseline for studying drug effects, *J. Pharmacol. Exp. Ther.* **184:**506–514.

Thompson, D. M., 1974a, Repeated acquisition of behavioral chains under chronic drug conditions, *J. Pharmacol. Exp. Ther.* **188:**700–713.

Thompson, D. M., 1974b, Repeated acquisition of response sequences: effects of *d*-amphetamine and chlorpromazine, *Pharmacol. Biochem. Behav.* **2:**741–746.

Thompson, D. M., 1975, Repeated acquisition of response sequences: stimulus control and drugs, *J. Exp. Anal. Behav.* **23:**429–436.

Thompson, D. M., 1976, Repeated acquisition of behavioral chains: effects of methylphenidate and imipramine, *Pharmacol. Biochem. Behav.* **4:**671–677.

Thompson, D. M., and Corr., P. B., 1974, Behavioral parameters of drug action: signalled and response-independent reinforcement, *J. Exp. Anal. Behav.* **21:**151–158.

Verhave, T., 1959, The effect of secobarbital on a multiple schedule in the monkey, *J. Exp. Anal. Behav.* **2:**117–120.

Waller, M. B., 1961, Effects of chronically administered chlorpromazine on multiple-schedule performance, *J. Exp. Anal. Behav.* **4:**351–359.

Weiss, B., and Laties, V. G., 1964, Drug effects on the temporal patterning of behavior, *Fed. Proc.* **23:**801–807.

Wilder, J., 1967, *Stimulus and Response: The Law of Initial Value,* Wright, Bristol, England.

Wiltz, R. A., Boren, J. J., Moerschbaecher, J. M., Creed, T. L., and Schrot, J. F., 1974, Generalization gradients and combined-stimulus control after equal training with two related stimuli. II. Effects of "errorless" training. III. Effects of chlorpromazine, *Psychol. Rec.* **24:**449–468.

Woods, J. H., and Tessel, R. E., 1974, Fenfluramine: amphetamine congener that fails to maintain drug-taking behavior in the rhesus monkey, *Science* **185:**1067–1069.

Drug-Induced Stimulus Control 4

J. C. Winter

1. Introduction

1.1. Scope

It is the purpose of this chapter to review selected aspects of the phenomenon of drug-induced stimulus control. Emphasis will be upon the experimental methods which have been employed to demonstrate drug-induced stimulus control and the interpretation of data generated by those methods. Specific examples have been chosen from the literature for purposes of illustration, but no attempt has been made to provide a comprehensive listing of drugs whose stimulus properties have been evaluated. It is hoped that the present review and discussion will be useful to those contemplating or just beginning a study of drug-induced stimulus control, as well as to the more experienced investigator who shares the author's fascination with the subject.

1.2. Terminology

1.2.1. State-Dependent Learning

Girden and Culler (1937) observed that dogs trained to emit a leg flexion escape response in the presence of curare failed to do so in the absence of curare and vice versa. They referred to this phenomenon as dissociation of learning. Subsequent investigators, following the lead of

---

J. C. Winter • Department of Pharmacology and Therapeutics, School of Medicine, State University of New York at Buffalo, Buffalo, New York 14214

Overton (1964), have used the terms "dissociation of learning" and "state-dependent learning" interchangeably, the latter phrase drawing attention to a drug state as the crucial independent variable in the dissociation phenomenon. The classic design for the evaluation of state-dependent learning is that described by Grossman and Miller (1961) and shown in Table I. The design employs four groups of subjects, two of which are trained and tested under the same conditions (I.1, placebo–placebo; II.2, drug–drug) and two of which are trained in one condition and tested in the other (I.2, placebo–drug; II.1, drug–placebo). Poorer test performance in groups I.2 and II.1 as compared with groups I.1 and II.2, respectively, is taken as evidence for state-dependent learning.

The experiments reported by Berger and Stein (1969) are a clear example of the application of the Grossman–Miller design (or as it is more commonly termed, the 2 × 2 design) to the question of whether scopolamine, an antagonist of acetylcholine, causes state-dependent learning. Rats were placed in a chamber in which a drinking tube containing sweetened milk was present and were trained to a criterion of 100 licks of the tube in 50 sec or less. Then, in a single session with the tube removed, the rats were placed in the chamber and electric shock was delivered to their feet for 1 sec. Seven days later, the subjects were placed in the chamber with the tube present and the time required to emit 100 licks was recorded. This procedure for training and testing was applied to four groups of rats as indicated in Table I, and the results are shown in Figure 1. The group trained with scopolamine and tested with saline (group II.1 of Table I) did indeed perform more poorly than the group trained and tested with scopolamine (II.2); that is, in terms of suppression of drinking, they acted as if they had received no prior training. In contrast, the performance of rats trained with saline was unaffected by testing in the presence of scopolamine. State-dependent learning observed in going from state A to state B, in

Table I. Experimental Design for Assessment of State-Dependent Learning

Training	Testing
I. Placebo	1. Placebo
	2. Drug
II. Drug	1. Placebo
	2. Drug

Source: After Grossman and Miller (1961).

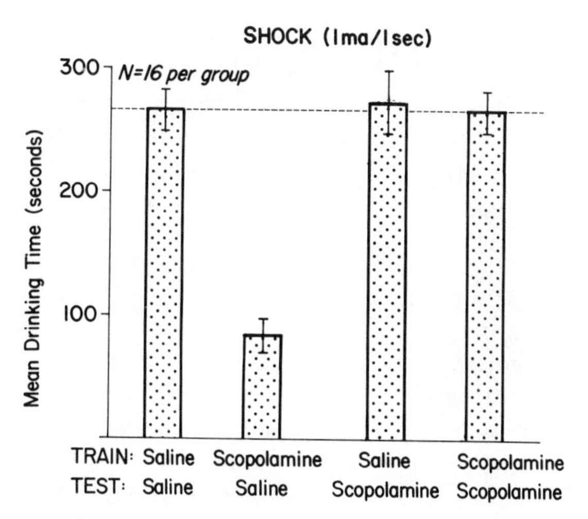

Figure 1. Evaluation of state-dependent learning with a 2 × 2 design. Ordinate: mean drinking time in seconds. Abscissa: respective training and test conditions. [Redrawn from Berger and Stein (1969).]

the present instance, from scopolamine to saline, but not from state B to state A is not uncommon (e.g., Barnhart and Abbott, 1967) and has been termed "asymmetrical dissociation" (Overton, 1968a). The crucial feature of the state-dependent learning design is that all training, however abbreviated or extensive, takes place under the same pharmacologic conditions, that is, in the same "state."

1.2.2. Drug-Induced Stimulus Control

In a study by Conger (1951) it was observed that food consumption that had been suppressed by the delivery of electric shock ("approach–avoidance conflict") was reinstated following the injection of ethanol. In an attempt to rationalize his results in terms of "approach and avoidance response tendencies," Conger quantified these tendencies using a strength-of-pull technique (Brown, 1948) and found that the avoidance tendency in rats trained without ethanol was significantly diminished when tested in the presence of ethanol. Identical experiments which measured the approach tendency revealed no comparable effect. Applying the criteria of the state-dependent learning design described above, we may consider these latter experiments to be separate state-dependent learning experiments in which only one-half of the design is completed, that is, placebo–placebo (I.1) and placebo–drug (I.2), with a significant effect being observed only when avoidance was the dependent variable. Conger did not complete the design. Instead, he reasoned that the results in the avoidance trials might be due to "a change in the stimulus situation." In setting out to test this hypothesis, Conger had as a "subsidiary purpose . . . to determine whether animals can establish a reliable discrimination based on the presence or absence of inebriation." In these experiments, following the injection of either saline or ethanol, the subjects were permitted to traverse a straight alley, at the end of which was a food platform. In some sessions, contact with the food caused the delivery of electric shock. For group 1, injection of saline was paired with the availability of food and injection of ethanol with food plus shock. For group 2, the pairings were reversed. An approach response was defined as movement to the food platform within 10 sec; an avoidance response as failure to move to the food platform within 60 sec. In a series of test trials following several weeks of training, discriminated responding was observed, that is, the approach response predominated following injection of saline in group 1 and ethanol in group 2; the avoidance response predominated following ethanol in group 1 and saline in group 2.

Examples of discriminated responding are found throughout nature and have long been the subject of experimental investigation (e.g., Lashley, 1912; Yerkes, 1907). Operant behavior which is reinforced only in the presence of a specified stimulus may come to occur with greater frequency in the presence of the stimulus than in its absence. In such a situation, the behavior is said to be under the control of the stimulus, which is then termed a discriminative stimulus. Conger's observation that behavior which is differentially reinforced following the injection of ethanol comes to occur with greater frequency in the presence of ethanol than in its absence demonstrates that the pharmacological effects of ethanol can function as a discriminative stimulus. In an extensive discussion of discrimination, Terrace (1966) has suggested the term "stimulus control" to refer "to the extent to which the value of an antecedent stimulus determines the probability of occurrence of a conditioned response. [Stimulus control] is measured as a change in response probability that results from a change in stimulus value." Those instances in which stimulus control is observed and the antecedent stimulus results from administration of a drug will in this chapter be referred to as drug-induced stimulus control. It must be acknowledged that the application of terms derived from nonpharmacological experiments to the effects of drugs exposes us to the risk that we will in turn apply, perhaps uncritically, concepts and conclusions drawn from the study of classical sensory stimuli. This risk seems well worth taking in view of the alternative course, which is to create a new terminology without reference to previous nonpharmacological experience.

1.2.3. State-Dependent Learning vs. Drug-Induced Stimulus Control

Possible relationships between the phenomena of state-dependent learning and drug-induced stimulus control are readily apparent. Indeed, each has at times been invoked to explain the other (e.g., Belleville, 1964; Overton, 1966) and reports in which the terminology appropriate to the two paradigms are freely mixed are not uncommon. As might be expected, this ambivalence has contributed to difficulties in communication of experimental observations. For example, in a paper entitled "Cue Value of Dexamethasone for Fear-Motivated Behavior," Pappas and Gray (1971) employed the state-dependent learning paradigm, while a report by Stewart *et al.* (1967), which dealt with drug-induced stimulus control, was entitled "State-Dependent Learning Produced with Steroids."

Any arbitrary attempt to define the terms "state-dependent learning" and "drug-induced stimulus control" may appear authoritarian and will conflict with specific instances of past usage. Nonetheless, it seems essential to adopt a nomenclature which cleanly separates the methods and experimental designs used to facilitate observation of pharmacological effects from hypothetical pharmacological mechanisms which might be responsible for those effects. In the present chapter, "state-dependent learning" will refer to the *observation* of a decrement in performance of a task learned in the presence of one pharmacological state when that task is tested in the presence of another state. (It should be noted that the complete absence of drugs from an organism is here considered to be a pharmacological state.) "Drug-induced stimulus control" will refer to the *observation* that the probability of occurrence of a conditioned operant is altered following differential reinforcement in the presence of two pharmacological states. These definitions of state-dependent learning and drug-induced stimulus control carry with them no implicit assumptions regarding mechanisms of learning, pharmacological receptors, sensory systems, or any of the other factors which may ultimately provide a sound theoretical basis for our behavioral observations. Catania's words (1971) are appropriate: "Discriminative control involves a behavioral relationship, a relationship between environmental events and responses; once this relationship is established, its behavioral status is not altered by demonstrating the involvement of a particular part of the anatomy."

2. Methods for the Demonstration of Drug-Induced Stimulus Control

2.1. Introduction

This section will consider those experimental methods which commonly have been employed to demonstrate the presence of drug-induced stimulus control. In the present instance, the initial separation of methods is according to whether drug-induced stimulus control is manifested by (1) emission of one of two different responses or (2) by differing rates of emission of a common response. Others might choose to divide methods according to the nature of the reinforcer employed or on the basis of specific schedules of reinforcement or according to any one of several other parameters. Schemes of classification readily present themselves and arguments, both theoretical and empirical, can be offered in support of each. However, because of our nearly complete ignorance of the role which a particular experimental method plays in the demonstration of drug-induced stimulus control, the ultimate choice is almost wholly arbitrary.

2.2. Response Choice

2.2.1. T-Maze

A number of T-maze designs have been presented in the literature and a representative device is shown in Figure 2. The influence which specific physical dimensions may have upon drug-induced stimulus control has not explicitly been explored, but results with a variety of designs appear to be in general agreement. Nearly all investigators conduct multiple training trials on a single day but, in recognition of the fact that the delivery of a punisher or reinforcer on the first trial of a session can itself function as a discriminative stimulus, only first-trial performance is used to determine the presence of drug-induced stimulus control and results of the remaining trials are not analyzed. However, it should be noted that Overton (1975) has found ketamine, a clinically useful anesthetic agent with a spectrum of activity distinctly different from either barbiturates or inert gas anesthetics (Garfield *et al.*, 1972; Little *et al.*, 1972; Hejja and Galloon, 1975), to produce significantly greater disruption of performance by rats in training trials subsequent to the first trial than does pentobarbital. Thus, routine analysis of performance throughout all training sessions seems more desirable than consideration of first-trial performance alone.

2.2.1a. Negative Reinforcers. A stimulus whose termination increases

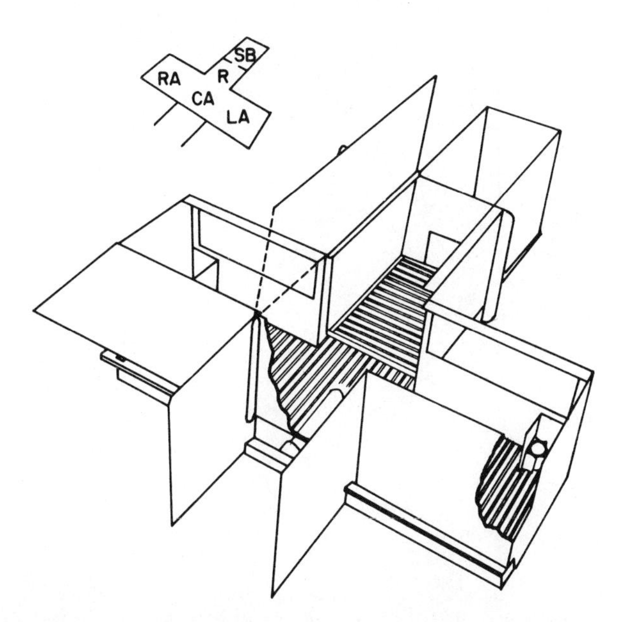

Figure 2. T-maze design in which responses may be punished with electric shock or reinforced with food or water. SB: start box; R: runway; CA: choice area; RA: right arm; LA: left arm. [From Schechter and Rosecrans (1971a); © 1971 Pergamon Press Ltd.]

the probability of occurrence of the operant that preceded that termination is called a negative reinforcer. In an experiment described by Overton (1966), rats were injected with saline or drug and a short time later dropped onto the starting point of the apparatus. With the exception of one goal box, the grid floor of the maze is electrified throughout and the subject is free to move in the maze until the shock-free goal box is reached. In this instance, electric shock delivered to the rat is a negative reinforcer and the operant which terminates it is termed an escape response. In Overton's experiments, the shock-free goal box ("the correct response") is determined by the pharmacological treatment which precedes each session, i.e., the shock-free area, whether left or right, is always paired with the same treatment, saline or drug, which in turn alternates each day. Results obtained using saline and sodium pentobarbital are shown in Figure 3 and indicate the ease with which some classes of drugs produce stimulus control. Weiss and Heller (1969) have questioned the wisdom of the use of a single alternation of treatments because of the possibility that alternation learning (Franchina and Kaiser, 1971) rather than drug-induced stimulus control is responsible for observed changes in response probability. While single alternation learning has been said to be a nonsignificant factor in drug-

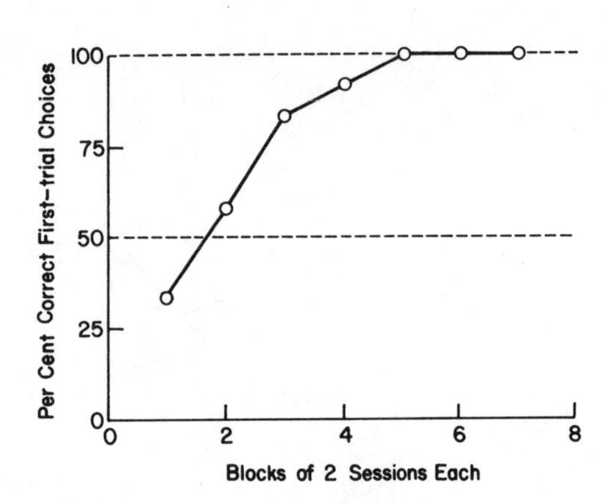

Figure 3. Stimulus control by sodium pentobarbital (20 mg/kg) and saline in a shock-escape T-maze task. Ordinate: percentage of all rats tested which performed correctly on the first trial of a daily session. Abscissa: successive pairs of sessions. [Redrawn from Overton (1966).]

induced stimulus control (Overton, 1974), many investigators have chosen to use a more complex order of presentation, the most common being a double-alternation sequence. Whatever sequence is chosen, it is prudent to test the influence of unknown variables in drug-induced stimulus control. This may efficiently be accomplished by periodic reversal in a single session of the drug-choice pairings (Winter, 1974a). If behavior remains appropriate for the conditions as previously trained, i.e., inappropriate for the reversed pairing, we may be confident that drug effects are indeed the major factor responsible for the observed stimulus control.

As an alternative to electric shock, Järbe and Henriksson (1973, 1974; Henriksson and Järbe, 1972) have used the escape response occurring in a water-filled T-maze for the study of tetrahydrocannabinols. Their results are in general agreement with those obtained with several other methods for demonstrating drug-induced stimulus control but, as is generally the case, no directly comparative studies have been reported. In view of the rather widespread use of shock escape for the study of drug-induced stimulus control and the extensive literature regarding avoidance behavior, that is, behavior which prevents or delays the occurrence of an aversive stimulus (Cook and Catania, 1964), it is surprising that only a few investigators have employed avoidance responses.

2.2.1b. Positive Reinforcers. A stimulus which is presented following the emission of an operant and which increases the future probability of occurrence of that operant is called a positive reinforcer. In contrast to a negative reinforcer such as electric shock, positive reinforcers rarely produce behaviorally disruptive unconditioned responses. Thus, Barry *et al.* (1965), to avoid "painful electric shock," trained rats with ethanol (1200 mg/kg) versus saline in a T-maze task with food as a positive reinforcer. They found that only four of eight rats exhibited stimulus control after 48 days of double alternation training, and they attributed this relative lack of efficacy to persistent position preferences.

2.2.1c. Positive Reinforcer plus Punisher. Reinforcers, both positive and negative, have been defined above as events which increase the probability of occurrence of operants which precede them. A punisher may be defined in an analogous manner as an event whose occurrence following an operant decreases the probability of emission of that operant in the future. Training in a T-maze with a negative reinforcer employs passive correction; that is, incorrect responses are "corrected" by the continuing presence of the negative reinforcer. This procedure has worked well enough with electric shock as the negative reinforcer but, if the report by Barry *et al.* (1965) may be taken as representative of other, unpublished reports, it has been less than fully satisfactory with a positive reinforcer. In their studies of nicotine-induced stimulus control, Schechter and Rosecrans (1971a, 1972) combined the use of a positive reinforcer (food) and a punisher (electric shock) in the T-maze shown in Figure 2; that is, choice of the correct arm was followed by access to food while inappropriate choices resulted in the delivery of the punisher. Data which would permit a determination of the efficacy in establishing drug-induced stimulus control of T-maze training with a negative reinforcer as compared with a positive reinforcer plus punisher are not presently available. However, a similar question will arise below in the discussion of tasks in which response emission is the dependent variable.

2.2.2. Two-Lever Choice

In recent years many investigators have chosen to employ a procedure in which drug-induced stimulus control is manifest by choice of an appropriate lever rather than of one arm of a T-maze. In their initial report of a two-lever choice task for the study of drug-induced stimulus control, Kubena and Barry (1969) argued that by choice of an appropriate schedule of reinforcement, ". . . the test can be extended to require a substantial number of lever presses, thus providing a more deliberate choice by the animal and a wider range of quantitative variation in the choice response." The opportunity to superimpose a variety of schedules of reinforcement upon a choice task has obvious appeal for many workers schooled in the Skinnerian tradition. Indeed, in experiments reported by Harris and Balster (1968), rats were trained with amphetamine and saline in a two-lever choice task in which different schedules of reinforcement were in effect on the two levers. However, the virtues of this rather complex approach were not convincingly demonstrated, and subsequent workers have employed the same schedule on both levers. In this regard it is unfortunate that so few schedules have as yet been employed, and no reports have appeared in which schedule variables have been systematically varied. This obviously presents a rich area for future investigation. In common with the T-maze, lever-choice procedures may employ punishers and reinforcers of various types, and these will be discussed briefly.

2.2.2a. Negative Reinforcers. Although extensive use has been made of shock escape in the T-maze and the germinal experiments by Cook *et al.* (1960) employed a leg flexion avoidance-escape task, it was not until very recently that two-lever avoidance escape was applied to the study of drug-induced stimulus control (Shannon and Holtzman, 1976). In a relatively complex discrete trial procedure, rats were trained to avoid electric shock by sequential emission of an observing response and an appropriate choice response on one of two additional levers.

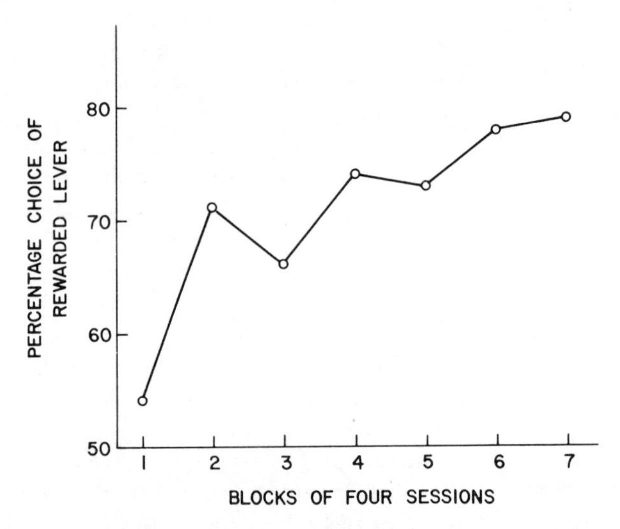

Figure 4. Stimulus control by ethanol (1200 mg/kg) and saline in a positively reinforced two-lever choice task. Ordinate: percentage of all rats tested which chose the appropriate lever. Abscissa: successive blocks of four sessions each. [From Kubena and Barry (1969); reproduced by permission of the copyright owner.].

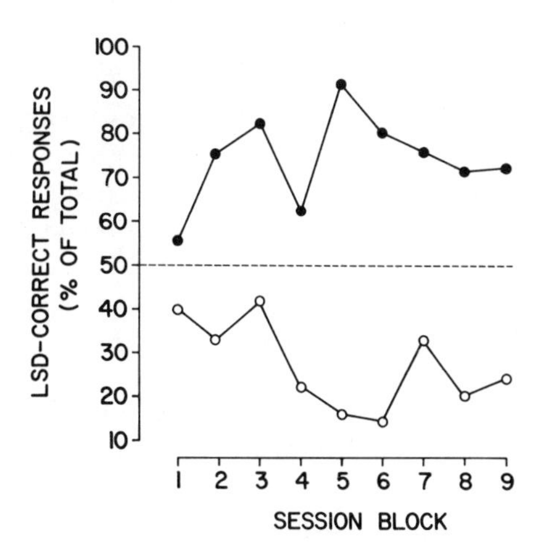

Figure 5. Stimulus control by LSD (tartrate, 120 mg/kg) and saline in a two-lever choice task. Ordinate: number of responses on the LSD-correct lever in the first 5 min of a session, expressed as a percentage of total responses. Abscissa: successive blocks of four sessions each. [From Hirschhorn and Winter (1971).]

2.2.2b. Positive Reinforcers. In the experiments of Kubena and Barry (1969), rats were treated with ethanol or saline and then presented with two levers. A variable-interval schedule of positive reinforcement was in effect on the lever appropriate for the preceding drug and no responses were reinforced on the other. Drug-induced stimulus control was rapidly apparent and results were expressed as a mean of correct percentages in four sessions equally divided between ethanol and saline (Figure 4). Subsequent investigators have usually chosen to express their results separately in terms of the drug-appropriate and saline-appropriate levers, as shown in Figure 5.

2.2.2c. Positive Reinforcer plus Punisher. A variation of the Kubena and Barry procedure described in the preceding paragraph was employed by Morrison and Stephenson (1969) in their studies of nicotine-induced stimulus control. They trained rats in a two-lever choice task in which appropriate responses were reinforced with water on a continuous reinforcement schedule and inappropriate responses were punished by the delivery of electric shock on a similar schedule. It is apparent that the delivery of reinforcers or punishers on a continuous basis (i.e., for each response which is emitted) does not provide the advantage envisaged by Kubena and Barry (1969) of extended testing and a "more deliberate choice" by the subject. The writer is unaware of any use, subsequent to that of Morrison and Stephenson, of punishers in a two-lever choice task.

2.3. Response Emission

As an alternative to tasks in which stimulus control is manifest by the appropriate choice of one of two responses, e.g., left or right turn in a T-maze, left or right lever-press response, some investigators have chosen to demonstrate drug-induced stimulus control on the basis of the emission of a single response. The use of the terms "approach" and "avoidance" appears necessary for efficient description of such procedures. It is, however, equally desirable that the varied implications of approach, avoidance, and related expressions such as "conflictual learning" and "experimental neurosis" not be permitted to distort the description or application of experimental procedures.

2.3.1. Approach–Avoidance

The protocol employed by Conger (1951), in which rats were permitted to move to the end of a straight alley and were reinforced or punished according to what pharmacological treatment had been given, illustrates the use of a single-response task to demonstrate drug-induced stimulus control. In what they termed a "conflict" procedure, Kubena and Barry (1969) substituted a lever-press response and defined approach and avoidance in terms of that response. Rats were trained in 5-min sessions on a fixed-ratio 5 schedule of positive reinforcement in the presence of either ethanol or saline in a balanced design. When the pharmacologic treatments were reversed for each subject, electric shock was delivered after every five responses. The treatments and their associated contingencies were presented "with equal frequency in a varied sequence." Approach was defined as the completion of at least five responses during a 5-min period. Representative data are given in Figure 6. In effect, performance on a fixed-ratio schedule of reinforcement or punishment is expressed as an all-or-none response (i.e., approach or avoidance). In their recent discussion of procedures applicable to drug-induced stimulus control, Colpaert *et al.* (1976) provide arguments for the initial expression of data, whether obtained using a response emission or a response choice task, on a nominal basis (i.e., approach–avoidance, correct–incorrect, and so forth). A critique of their arguments will be presented below.

2.3.2. Response Rate

In their discussion of the conflict procedure described above, Kubena and Barry (1969) noted that "the measure of performance did not provide quantitative variation in strength of the approach or avoidance

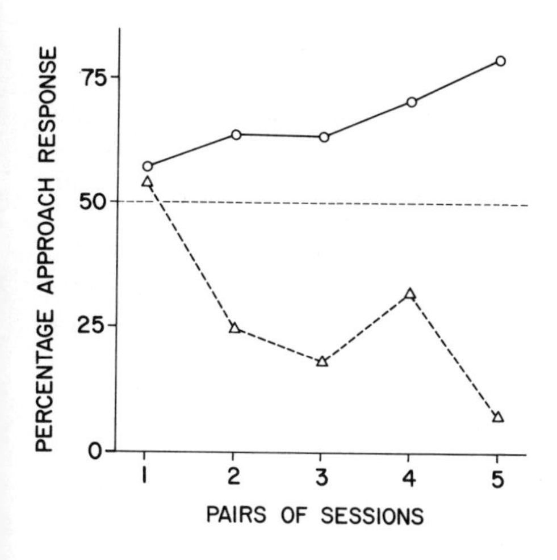

Figure 6. Stimulus control by ethanol (1200 mg/kg; circles) and saline (triangles) in a single-lever response emission task. Ordinate: percentage of all rats tested which emitted five or more responses during a session. Abscissa: successive pairs of sessions. [From Kubena and Barry (1969); reproduced by permission of the copyright owner.]

response." This feature of the procedure, which arises as a consequence of the use of a nominal scale of measurement and which some may regard as an asset, is readily altered by substitution of an interval scale of measurement. For example, Winter (1973) trained rats in a balanced design with mescaline and saline. For an individual subject, responses following one treatment were reinforced on a variable-interval 32-sec schedule of reinforcement, and following the other treatment, responses had no programmed consequence. Tests for the presence of drug-induced stimulus control consisted of 5-min sessions in which no responses were reinforced. In the initial applications of this procedure (Winter, 1973, 1974a,b, 1975a,b), a punishment contingency was also employed; that is, inappropriate responses were punished by the delivery of electric shock on the same schedule as was in effect for the reinforcer. This is analogous to the use of a positive reinforcer plus punisher in a T-maze or two-lever choice task except that only one of the two possible contingencies is in effect on a given day. The rationale for the use of punishment as a "correction" for inappropriate responses is that discrimination learning may be facilitated. However, more recent experience in the author's laboratory (Winter, 1975b, 1976 unpublished) suggests that the use of punishment in a single-lever response-rate task introduces behavioral and technical complications.

2.4. Comment

Even a brief outline of the methods which have been employed to study drug-induced stimulus control leaves the reader uncertain of his ability to make general statements regarding the stimulus properties of a given drug from data obtained with but a single procedure. The situation is made still more complex by the absence of any unifying theoretical concept of the nature of drug-induced stimulus control. Some have lamented the present absence of methodological and theoretical uniformity; the present writer does not. It is true that matters of interpretation and interlaboratory verification would be simplified if all were to employ the same task, reinforcer, schedule, and protocol. Indeed, the sometimes extravagant claims made upon introduction of a new procedure or a variation of an old procedure may result from a desire to have all other workers adopt a uniform approach to the study of drug-induced stimulus control. But if, as seems highly probable, the pharmacological effects which serve as the basis for drug-induced stimulus control are both complex and dose-dependent, the simplification which would attend the adoption of common procedure would come at too high a price. First, the record shows that conclusions drawn with respect to a single drug from data obtained with different procedures have been remarkably compatible. Second, if contradictory results are obtained, we are immediately directed to an examination of pharmacological and behavioral variables which might explain the disparate results. In this process, new facets of drug-induced stimulus control will be discovered which would have remained hidden should a uniform approach have been taken. These remarks are not a defense of inadequate experimental design and analysis or failure to consider all relevant confounding variables. The point intended is that the royal road to an understanding of drug-induced stimulus control is not before us. There may thus be merit in following several of the sometimes rough and rutted paths available to us in the hope that they will someday join to become that road.

3. Interpretations of Drug-Induced Stimulus Control

3.1. Dimensions

3.1.1. Efficacy and Potency

Lord Kelvin is reported to have said that "When you cannot express it in numbers, your knowledge is meagre and unsatisfactory." Even a cursory examination of the literature reveals frequent use of terms such as "stronger discriminability," "strength of response control," and "strong discriminable effects." In a widely cited review, Overton (1971) lists 42 drugs tested for "discriminative control" (usually in a shock-escape T-maze task) and categorizes them in terms of strong, moderate, or weak control. Can we "express it in numbers"? The answer is quite obviously yes, and, indeed, it is Overton who has contributed most of the data which make a preliminary quantitative assessment possible.

It was previously noted that creation of new jargon to describe drug-induced stimulus control is undesirable if established terms are appropriate. The most common quantification of dose–effect curves rests firmly upon certain assumptions regarding the interaction between a drug and its receptor. No comparable theory is available for quantitative treatment of dose–effect curves when the effect is drug-induced stimulus control. Nonetheless, the concepts of efficacy and potency, although they are derived from consideration of drug–receptor interactions, seem applicable to the quantification of drug-induced stimulus control. Certain of Overton's data are shown in Figures 7 and 8 and will be used for illustrative purposes. Efficacy may be defined as the ability to bring about a specified effect and we might wish to classify drugs according to their ability, or lack of it, to induce stimulus control. Such a classification seems hardly worthwhile in that (1) it would be a nominal rather than a quantitative system and (2) it is an experimental impossibility to prove that a drug cannot induce stimulus control. Thus, it is not efficacy as defined in its simplest sense which is of interest but, instead, efficacy as measured in terms of maximum possible effects. For a strip of muscle suspended in a bath we might measure the maximum degree of shortening; for drug-induced stimulus control the most obvious variable is the rate at which stimulus control is established.

In Figure 7, the logarithm of the number of sessions required to reach a criterion of 8 of 10 correct first-choice responses is plotted versus log dose; hence, the maximum rate occurs at minimum sessions to criterion. [Those who feel more comfortable with curves which rise to a maximum may wish to plot the reciprocal of log (sessions to criterion)]. As the dose of a drug is increased, a minimum value for sessions to criterion will be reached and the curve will then begin to rise again as the dose is increased still further (see data for atropine, Figure 8). For purposes of the present discussion, the highest dose of each of the three drugs shown in Figure 7 will be assumed to produce the minimum possible number of sessions to criterion. Thus, the relative efficacies are in the order pentobarbital > ethanol > scopolamine, and the numerical values of minimum sessions to criterion provide comparative measurements on an interval scale. A quantitative assessment would be further enhanced by the estimation of variability of the data and application of standard statistical tests.

Potency, the quantity of drug required to produce a specified ef-

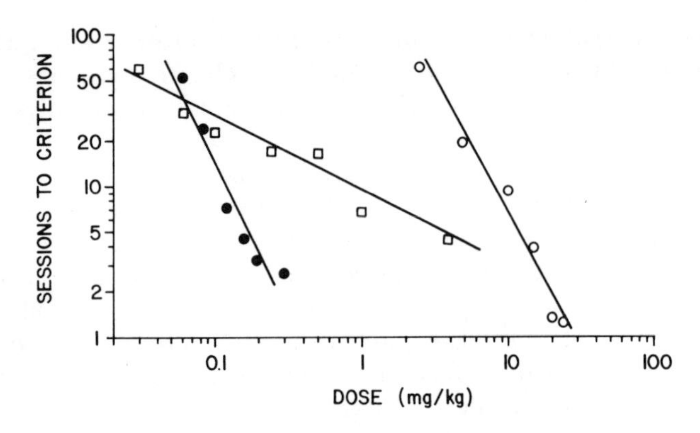

Figure 7. Number of training sessions required to establish stimulus control as a function of dose for ethanol (filled circles), scopolamine hydrobromide (open squares), and sodium pentobarbital (open circles). Ordinate: number of sessions prior to the beginning of criterion performance expressed on a log scale. Abscissa: dose in mg/kg expressed on a log scale (doses for ethanol are multiplied by 10^{-4}). [Redrawn from Overton (1974).]

fect, is readily determined from plots of the kind shown in Figures 7 and 8. However, with the exception of two drugs for which the curves are identical except for their position on the abscissa, we must specify the number of sessions to criterion at which potencies were determined. For example, atropine and pentobarbital (Figure 8) are roughly equipotent at values between 10 and 60 but, for less than four sessions to criterion, the drugs are not comparable with respect to potency because of the lesser efficacy of atropine. In addition, it must be recognized that both efficacy and potency may be influenced by the particular experimental methods which are employed. For example, chlorpromazine was found to be ineffective in inducing stimulus control at a dose of 5 mg/kg in rats in a T-maze shock-escape task (Overton, 1966) but others were successful with doses of 1–4 mg/kg in rats when alternative methods were employed (Stewart, 1962; Barry *et al.,* 1974).

3.1.2. Compound Stimuli (Composite Stimuli, Complex Stimuli)

In the preceding section, a dose–effect relationship was discussed in which the dependent variable is the rate of achievement of stimulus control. A second and more common kind of dose–effect relationship is obtained in subjects in whom drug-induced stimulus control is already established at a given dose of the drug and tests are then conducted with a variety of doses of the same drug or of another agent. An implicit assumption in many discussions of such dose–effect relationships is that a given dose produces a specific stimulus. Higher or lower doses simply increase or decrease the intensity of that stimulus in a fashion analogous to increasing the intensity of a light or tone without alteration in frequency. This assumption is, on the one hand, pharmacologically naive and, on the other, likely to cause the neglect of potentially helpful knowledge regarding compound stimuli. If, instead, we assume that every drug produces a number of different effects of potential significance to drug-induced stimulus control and that this number varies with dose, then an extensive literature dealing with compound stimuli becomes relevant to drug-induced stimulus control.

Two examples will suffice. The first is the work by Lashley (1938, 1942), which indicates that the relative importance of the individual components of a compound stimulus may show interanimal variation. For the interested reader, Terrace (1966) provides an extended discussion. Of perhaps greater significance to those who would derive general statements regarding the stimulus properties of a drug from data obtained with a specific task are those experiments which suggest that the relative importance of the individual components of a compound stimulus is influenced by the nature of the reinforcer which is em-

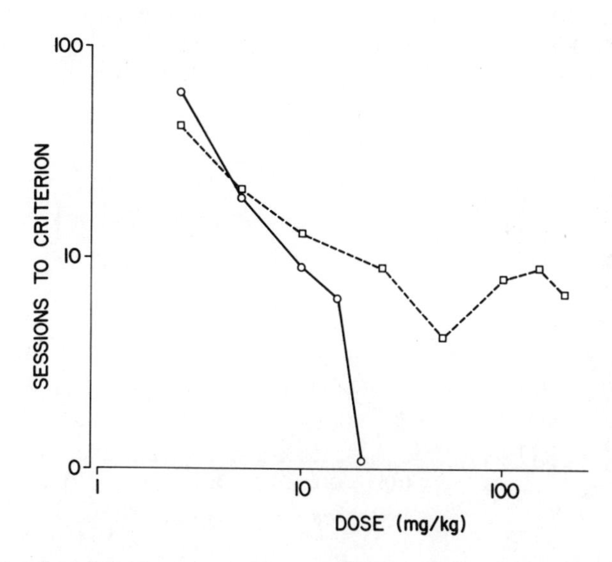

Figure 8. Number of sessions required to establish stimulus control in a T-maze shock-escape task as a function of dose of sodium pentobarbital (circles) and atropine sulfate (squares). Ordinate: number of sessions prior to the beginning of criterion performance expressed on a log scale. Abscissa: dose in mg/kg expressed on a log scale. [Redrawn from Overton (1971)]

ployed. LoLordo and Furrow (1976) found that for pigeons trained in the presence of a compound stimulus (tone plus light) to avoid shock or to obtain grain, the light controlled much more responding in the appetitive tests than did the tone while in the avoidance tests, the tone controlled more responding than did the light. If a drug produces compound stimuli, as is almost certainly the case particularly over a range of doses, we should expect to observe complex interactions among drug, dose, and discriminative task. The present absence of clear-cut examples of such drug–dose–task interactions may be but a reflection of the almost total neglect of this area of investigation.

3.2. Analysis of Data

3.2.1. Dose–Effect Relationships

Two types of dose–effect relationships have been discussed above: (1) those in which the effect (i.e., the dependent variable) is the number of sessions which elapse before a predetermined criterion for stimulus control is reached and (2) those in which the dependent variable is a measure of the appropriateness of responding with varying doses of a drug in subjects in which drug-induced stimulus control is already well established. Only dose–effect relationships of the latter type will be elaborated upon in this section.

In the initial report from the writer's laboratory concerning the

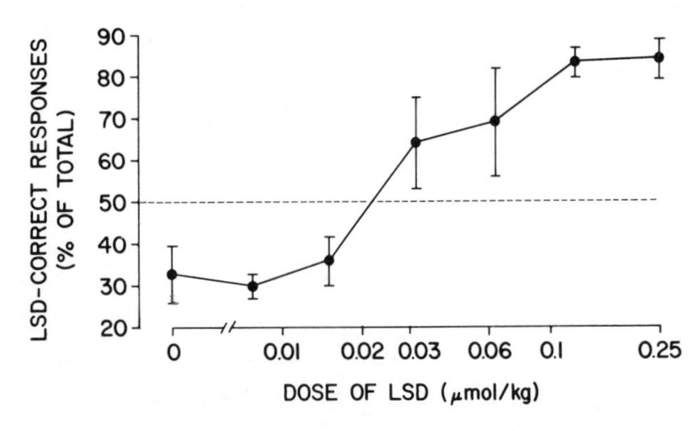

Figure 9. Dose-effect relationship for LSD in rats trained with LSD (0.25 μmol/kg) and saline in a two-lever choice task. Ordinate: number of responses on the LSD-correct lever in the first 5 min of a session, expressed as a percentage of total responses. Abscissa: dose of LSD in μmol/kg expressed on a log scale. [From Hirschhorn and Winter (1971).]

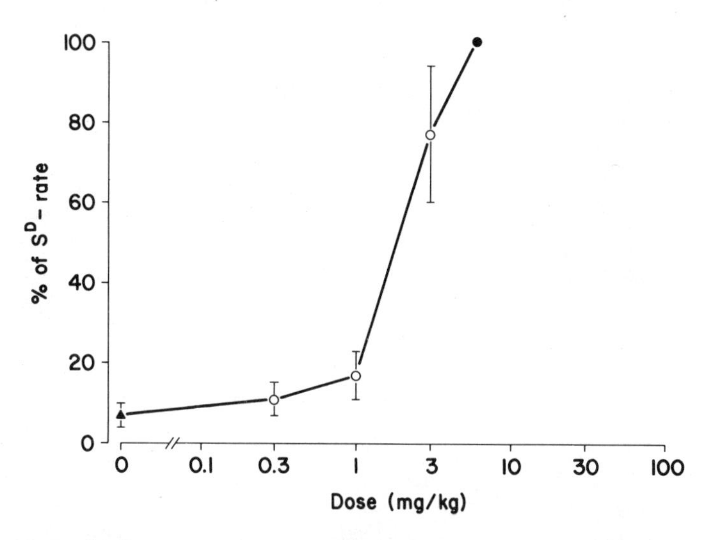

Figure 10. Dose–effect relationship for morphine in rats trained to discriminate the effects of morphine sulfate (6 mg/kg, circles, S^D) and saline (triangles, S^Δ) in a single-lever response emission task. Ordinate: mean rate of responding expressed as a percentage of the rate in sessions following the training dose of morphine. Abscissa: dose of morphine sulfate in mg/kg expressed on a log scale. [Redrawn from Winter (1975b).]

stimulus properties of hallucinogens (Hirschhorn and Winter, 1971), it was stated that "if discriminated responding is a consequence of the pharmacologic effects of a drug, then the dose of the drug and the degree of discrimination should vary concomitantly, i.e., one should observe a typical dose–effect relationship." Figure 9 shows data from a two-lever choice task and Figure 10 for the S^D-condition of a single-lever response-rate task. The relationship between dose and effect is entirely as expected; as dose increases toward the training dose, responding becomes more appropriate for the training condition. It should be noted that the training dose is a very significant factor in determining both the shape of the curve and its position on the dose axis; that is, a family of curves will be generated, each corresponding to a particular training dose. This fact has long been recognized and is perhaps best illustrated in the study by Greenberg *et al.* (1975). Rats were initially trained with lysergic acid diethylamide (LSD; 80 μg/kg) versus saline and a dose–effect relationship was determined. The same subjects were retrained with LSD at a dose of 10 μg/kg. The results are shown in Figure 11 and clearly support the general statement that the dose–effect relationship is significantly influenced by the training history of the subjects.

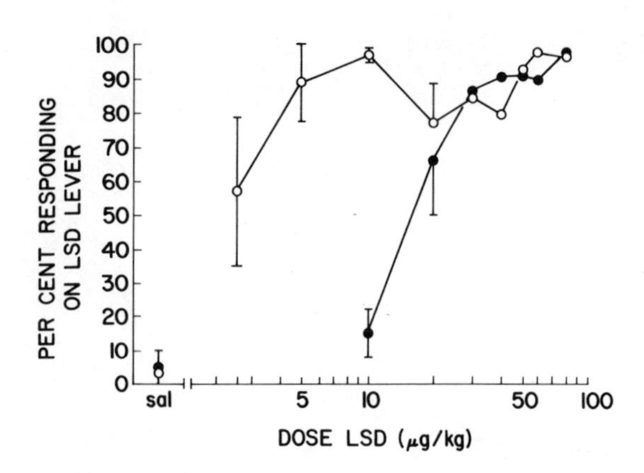

Figure 11. Dose–effect relationships for LSD in rats trained in a two-lever choice task first with 80 μg/kg (closed circles) and then with 10 μg/kg (open circles). Ordinate: number of responses on the LSD-correct lever expressed as a percentage of total responses. Abscissa: dose of LSD in μg/kg expressed on a log scale. [From Greenberg *et al.* (1975).]

3.2.2. Cross Tests

We may conduct sessions in which previously trained subjects are treated with a range of doses of a variety of pharmacological agents just as intermediate doses of the training drug are used to establish a dose–effect relationship. Such sessions have been referred to as "transfer tests," a term derived from the early literature on state-dependent learning in which a performance decrement such as that shown in Figure 1 was said to arise because of a failure of learning to "transfer" to a novel pharmacologic condition. Alternatively and by analogy with traditional psychophysics, the phrase "test of generalization" has been applied. The writer's preference is to refer to such sessions simply as cross tests. Just as "cross tolerance" refers to a pharmacological observation whose origin may involve one or more of a variety of factors, the term "cross test" is descriptive of an experimental procedure whose results may be interpreted in a variety of ways, none of which is implied by the procedure per se. The use of a neutral term has certain advantages. For example, a cross test cannot be "overinclusive" (Overton, 1974). Overinclusiveness refers to the observation that cross tests may "yield results suggesting that drugs are similar when in fact they differ." This is reminiscent of Barsa's argument that double-blind clinical trials must be invalid because they sometimes yield results at odds with preconceived notions about psychoactive drugs (Barsa, 1963).

The conduct of cross tests may differ somewhat depending upon the task which has been employed during training. For positively motivated tasks, responses are usually not reinforced and, as a consequence, these cross tests have sometimes been called "extinction tests. The rationale is that minimal disturbance of the previously trained discrimination will be produced by a cross test in which responses have no programmed consequence. Alternatively, all responses may be reinforced during cross tests, as is typically the case in shock-motivated escape tasks and as has been recently reported by Colpaert *et al.* (1976) using a food-motivated lever-choice procedure. A direct comparison of possible interactions of the two types of cross tests with the maintenance of drug-induced stimulus control has not been reported.

3.2.2a. Intermeditate Results. When subjects previously trained with saline versus a specified dose of a drug are tested with intermediate doses of that drug, it is expected that intermediate degrees of drug-appropriate responding will occur and relationships of the kind shown in Figures 9 and 10 will emerge. In contrast with the ready acceptance of intermediate results as a part of a dose–effect relationship, similar data derived from cross tests with a pharmacologic agent different from the training drug have often been (1) ignored, (2) dismissed as "chance responding" (ignoring the fact that random responding occurs under neither training condition), or (3) ascribed to a defect inherent in the test procedure.

A few investigators have eliminated intermediate results by fiat; for example, "drug Y was considered to substitute for drug X if at least 90% of choices were correct" (i.e., appropriate for drug X). Anything less than 90% correct is regarded simply as failure to substitute, despite the fact that the saline training condition might yield no more than 10% drug-appropriate responding. Colpaert *et al.* (1976) regard the elimination of intermediate results as a desirable feature of any cross test. These investigators achieve that end by regarding the chosen lever in a two-lever choice task as the one on which 10 responses are first emitted. A still simpler method, whether using a T-maze or a two-lever choice task, is to record only the first response. However, it is obvious that the specification of an all-or-none response, hence by definition not intermediate, simply postpones the observation of intermediate results until intra-animal or group means are determined. Dose–effect and cross-test relationships derived from data obtained from tasks in which no intermediate results are possible in a given test seem to differ not at all from curves generated by response-rate tasks in which intermediate rates of responding are possible during each cross test. Rather than devising procedures in which intermediate results are obscured or artificially eliminated, we may wish to direct our attention to interpretation and verification of such results.

3.2.2b. Saline-Appropriate Responding. A discussion of saline-appropriate responding in cross tests may reasonably begin with a consideration of the dose–effect relationship for a drug, X. Subjects trained with dose A of X versus saline will invariably respond, when treated with some lower dose, B, in a fashion appropriate for the saline condition. Indeed, our curve is not complete until the null-effect dose is determined. Likewise, there exists a dose of any other drug, Y, which when cross-tested in subjects trained with X will yield results indistinguishable from those of saline. As the dose of Y is increased, one of three things will happen: (1) the curve will rise until a dose of Y is reached which mimics the training dose of X (i.e., X and Y are interchangeable); (2) the curve will rise until the effect differs from both training conditions (intermediate results) but then, at still higher doses, falls back toward saline-appropriate responding; (3) at all doses tested (the absolute upper limit being the lethal dose) responding remains appropriate for the saline condition. Were we to consider drug-induced stimulus control in the absence of any experimental evidence, we might conclude that (3) is an unlikely outcome on the grounds that, however X and Y might differ in terms of their stimulus effects, each would differ to a greater extent from saline. It may well be that the increasing number of reports of intermediate results with drugs which differ markedly from the training drug in terms of the rest of their pharmacologic actions may reflect what Overton (1974) has called "a rather general normal versus abnormal discrimination." On the other hand, a large number of studies have yielded outcome (3), that is, saline-appropriate responding across a range of doses of Y. A few of these studies may be dismissed on the grounds that no evidence was provided that the range of doses of Y included ones which were discriminable from saline. The majority, however, employed doses of Y known to be discriminable from saline (for representative data, see Winter, 1975a,b) yet responding remained appropriate for the saline condition. Such observations suggest that the pharmacological effects which serve as the basis for stimulus control are quite specific and also that intermediate results are indicative of a similarity in stimulus properties rather than a reflection of some inadequacy of the cross test.

3.2.2c. Third-State Hypothesis. The observation that saline-appropriate responding may occur despite the presence of a drug in a concentration adequate, under other circumstances, to exert stimulus control, has led to a speculation called the third-state hypothesis: an animal trained with drug X versus saline will respond in a fashion appropriate for the saline condition when presented with drug-induced stimuli which resemble neither those of drug X nor those of saline (Frey and Winter, 1977). This hypothesis adequately explains, for example, the observation that rats trained with ethanol versus saline continue to yield saline-appropriate responding when cross-tested with doses of morphine known to exert stimulus control when paired with saline (Winter, 1975b).

Verification of the third-state hypothesis will require additional experimental evidence but, on purely theoretical grounds, it is of present relevance in the interpretation of experiments in which an attempt is made to antagonize the stimulus effects of drugs. In a typical test of antagonism, subjects are trained with drug X versus saline and combinations of X and Z, a purported antagonist of X, are then cross-tested. Responding appropriate for the saline condition following X plus Z is interpreted as blockade of the stimulus effects of X by Z. However, the third-state hypothesis offers an alternative interpretation: saline-appropriate responding results, not from direct pharmacological antagonism, but from a third stimulus state produced by the combination of X and Z.

The probability of the presence of such a third state is predictable and its actual presence is readily tested. For example, it is improbable that antagonism of the stimulus properties of morphine by naloxone (Rosecrans *et al.,* 1973; Winter, 1975b; Shannon and Holtzman, 1976) is due to a third state because (1) a direct antagonistic action of naloxone on morphine receptors has been demonstrated in a number of other pharmacologic systems, (2) antagonistically effective doses of naloxone when given alone appear to produce few significant stimuli in man or animals, and (3) the actions of naloxone appear to be specific for the stimulus effects of opiates such as morphine; stimulus control by neither pentobarbital (Rosecrans *et al.,* 1973) nor ethanol (Winter, 1975b) is altered by naloxone. However, other examples may be chosen in which the probability of a more complex interaction among agonist, antagonist, and stimulus effects is considerably greater.

It has been found that amphetamine-induced stimulus control is significantly reduced by presumed antagonists of dopamine such as pimozide (Ho and Huang, 1975) and haloperidol (Schechter and Cook, 1975). As a result, it has been concluded by some that the stimulus properties of amphetamine are mediated by the release and subsequent pharmacological effects of dopamine. This interpretation is simple, plausible, and quite possibly correct. However, we should note that the dose of haloperidol most effective in antagonizing amphetamine's stimulus effects (0.5 mg/kg, i.p., 90 min before testing; Schechter and Cook, 1975) is itself likely to produce stimulus effects. Colpaert *et al.*

(1976) observed stimulus control with saline and haloperidol at a dose of 0.02 mg/kg (sc) given 30 min before training. In a recent investigation by Järbe and Johansson (1976), it was found that stimulus control by Ditran (1.6 mg/kg) was blocked by physostigmine (0.5 or 1.0 mg/kg). Nonetheless, a reliable discrimination was demonstrable after training other groups with Ditran (1.6 mg/kg) plus physostigmine (0.5 or 1.0 mg/kg) versus saline. The foregoing, and other examples which might be offered, urge caution in the interpretation of studies of the antagonism of drug-induced stimulus control.

3.3. Origin and Nature of Drug-Induced Stimuli

3.3.1. Sites of Action

Quite early in the study of drug-induced stimulus control, the notion became firmly established that stimulus control can be brought about only by drugs which act directly upon the brain. Indeed, the results of the majority of those experiments designed to distinguish the role of central and peripheral sites of action have favored this idea. Nonetheless, compelling reasons exist for the modification, if not the outright rejection, of the postulate that a direct action upon the central nervous system is a necessary prerequisite for drug-induced stimulus control. It is well established that a wide variety of pharmacological agents may act upon peripheral receptors to produce a significant input to the central nervous system. (A convincing, personal, demonstration of this fact has been provided to anyone every stung by a bee.) Thus, on purely logical grounds, drug-induced peripheral stimuli should be adequate to establish drug-induced stimulus control. More important, a limited yet significant amount of experimental evidence favors this view. In the previously cited study by Cook *et al.* (1960), the emission of a conditioned avoidance response was controlled by intravenous injection of epinephrine, norepinephrine, and acetylcholine, drugs which do not have general access to the central nervous system following peripheral administration. In a more recent study, Colpaert *et al.* (1975) found that isopropamide, a peripherally acting cholinergic antagonist, was effective in controlling responding in a positively reinforced, two-lever choice task.

When taken as a whole, the data presently available suggest that drug-induced peripheral stimuli can indeed acquire stimulus control. However, for drugs able to freely enter the brain tissue from the blood, it is probable that the most significant elements of stimulus control arise directly in the central nervous system. The latter conclusion does not diminish the need to clearly establish the role which peripheral effects play in drug-induced stimulus control. A limited, yet informative, approach to this problem has been taken by those who have trained animals following intraperitoneal injection and have then cross-tested with lower doses of the same agent injected into the cerebral ventricles (Schechter, 1973; Browne *et al.,* 1974). Although chemical determinations have not been reported, it is reasonable in these experiments to assume that insignificant quantities of drug reach the peripheral circulation following intraventricular injection and that the observation of stimulus control after small doses given via the ventricles is indicative of a central locus of action. An analogous experiment in which subjects are trained with an agent presumed to act in the periphery and then cross-tested with the drug given intraventricularly has not been reported.

3.3.2. Sensory Pathways

The sensory functions of the nervous system permit a remarkable diversity of stimuli to interact with the brain. In seeking an explanation for drug-induced stimulus control, a plausible hypothesis is that drugs alter the function of one or more sensory systems. Thus, the discriminative stimulus produced by a drug would arise either by direct stimulation of sensory receptors or by modification of ongoing activity in those areas of the nervous system which subserve vision, audition, olfaction, pain, or any of the visceral or somatic sensations. Virtually no progress has been made in determining the role of sensory pathways in drug-induced stimulus control and a series of factors may be cited by way of explanation. (1) The immense experimental difficulties to be encountered in testing this hypothesis are immediately apparent and have surely daunted more than one investigator. (2) A limited but highly influential series of experiments by Overton (1964, 1968b) yielded essentially negative results. (3) It appears that no investigators with the requisite skills and training in neurophysiology, physiological psychology, or neuropharmacology have been attracted to the study of drug-induced stimulus control.

4. Epilogue

Drug-induced stimulus control provides a nearly perfect example of the joys as well as the sorrows of the marriage of convenience between psychology and pharmacology. In drug-induced stimulus control we have no less than a learning process mediated by pharmacological effects. Adequate investigation of the phenomenon will strain the knowledge, intuition, and technical skills of even the most broadly trained psychologist or pharmacologist. The preceding sections have outlined in the barest fashion those factors which require our immediate attention if orderly progress is to be made toward an understanding of this complex and varied phenomenon.

ACKNOWLEDGMENTS

Experimental work from this laboratory was supported in part by grant 15406 from the National Institute of Mental Health and by a grant from the Research Institute on Alcoholism, New York State Department of Mental Hygiene. I thank Ms. Susan Regan, Mrs. Dennis W. Opala, and Ms. Linda Chavez for their help in the preparation of this chapter. I am indebted to Dr. LeRoy G. Frey for many helpful discussions.

This chapter is dedicated to Douglas Shepard Riggs, M.D., Professor of Pharmacology and Therapeutics, School of Medicine, State University of New York at Buffalo, in the year of his retirement.

5. References

Barnhart, S. S., and Abbott, D. W., 1967, Dissociation of learning and memprobamate, *Psychol. Rep.* **20:**520–522.

Barry H., III, Koepfer, E., and Lutch, J., 1965, Learning to discriminate between alcohol and nondrug condition, *Psychol. Rep.* **16:**1072.

Barry, H., Steenberg, M. L., Manina, A. A., and Buckley, J. P., 1974, Effects of chlorpormazine and three metabolites on behavioral responses in rats, *Psychopharmacologia* **34:**351–360.

Barsa, J., 1963, The fallacy of the double blind, *Amer. J. Psychiat.* **119:**1174–1175.

Belleville, R. E., 1964, Control of behavior by drug-produced internal stimuli, *Psychopharmacologia* **5:**95–105.

Berger, B. D., and Stein, L., 1969, An analysis of learning deficits produced by scopolamine, *Psychopharmacologia* **14:**271–283.

Brown, J. S., 1948, Gradients of approach and avoidance responses and their relation to level of motivation, *J. Comp. Physiol. Psychol.* **41:**450–465.

Browne, R. G., Harris, R. T., and Ho, B. T., 1974, Stimulus properties of mescaline and N-methylated derivatives: difference in peripheral and direct central administration, *Psychopharmacologia* **39:**43–56.

Catania, A. C., 1971, Discriminative stimulus functions of drugs: interpretations, *in: Stimulus Properties of Drugs* (T. Thompson and R. Pickens, eds.), pp. 149–155, Appleton-Century-Crofts, New York.

Colpaert, F. C., Niemegeers, C. J. E., and Janssen, P. A. J., 1975, Differential response control by isopropamide: a peripherally induced discriminative cue, *J. Pharmacol.* **34:**381–384.

Colpaert, F. C., Niemegeers, C. J. E., and Janssen, P. A. J., 1976, Theoretical and meth-

odological considerations on drug discrimination learning, *Psychopharmacologia* **46:**169–177.
Conger, J. J., 1951, The effects of alcohol on conflict behavior in the albino rat, *Quart. J. Stud. Alc.* **12:**1–29.
Cook, L., and Catania, A. C., 1964, Effects of drugs on avoidance and escape behavior, *Fed. Proc.* **23:**818–835.
Cook, L., Davidson, A., Davis, D. J., and Kelleher, R. T., 1960, Epinephrine, norepinephrine, and acetylcholine as conditioned stimuli for avoidance behavior, *Science* **131:**990–991.
Franchina, J. J., and Kaiser, P., 1971, Acquisition, transfer, and reacquisition of single-alternation responding in the rat, *J. Comp. Physiol. Psychol.* **76:**256–261.
Frey, L. G., and Winter, J. C., 1977, Current trends in the study of drugs as discriminative stimuli, *in: Drug Discrimination and State Dependent Learning* (D. Chute, B. T. Ho, and D. W. Richards, eds.), pp. 35–45, Academic Press, New York.
Garfield, J. M., Garfield, F. B., Stone, J. G., Hopkins, D., and Johns, L. A., 1972, A comparison of psychologic responses to ketamine and thiopental–nitrous oxide–halothane anesthesia, *Anesthesiology* **36:**329–338.
Girden, E., and Culler, E. A., 1937, Conditioned responses in curarized striate muscle in dogs, *J. Comp. Psychol.* **23:**261–274.
Greenberg, I., Kuhn, D. M., and Appel, J. B., 1975, Behaviorally induced sensitivity to the discriminable properties of LSD, *Psychopharmacologia* **43:**229–232.
Grossman, S. P., and Miller, N. E., 1961, Control for stimulus-change in the evaluation of alcohol and chlorpromazine as fear-reducing drugs, *Psychopharmacologia* **2:**342–351.
Harris, R. T., and Balster, R. L., 1968, Discriminative control by dl-amphetamine and saline of lever choice and response patterning, *Psychon. Sci.* **10:**105–106.
Hejja, P., and Galloon, S., 1975, A consideration of ketamine dreams, *Can. Anaesth. Soc. J.* **22:**100–105.
Henriksson, B. G., and Järbe, T., 1972, Δ^9-tetrahydrocannabinol used as discriminative stimulus for rats in position learning in a T-shaped water maze, *Psychon. Sci.* **27:**25–26.
Hirschhorn, I. D., and Winter, J. C., 1971, Mescaline and lysergic acid diethylamide (LSD) as discriminative stimuli, *Psychopharmacologia* **22:**64–71.
Ho, B. T., and Huang, J. T., 1975, Role of dopamine in *d*-amphetamine-induced discriminative responding, *Pharmacol. Biochem. Behav.* **3:**1085–1092.
Järbe, T. U. C., and Henriksson, B. G., 1973, State-dependent learning with tetrahydrocannabinols and other drugs, *Ciencia Cult.* (*Sao Paulo*) **25:**752.
Järbe, T. U. C., and Henriksson, B. G., 1974, Discriminative response control produced with hashish, tetrahydrocannabinols (Δ^8-THC and Δ^9THC), and other drugs, *Psychopharmacologia* **40:**1–16.
Järbe, T. U. C., and Johansson, J. O., 1976, Drug discrimination in rats: effects of mixtures of Ditran and cholinesterase inhibitors, *Pharmacol. Biochem. Behav.* **4:**151–157.
Kubena, R. K., and Barry, H., III, 1969, Two procedures for training differential responses in alcohol and nondrug conditions, *J. Pharm. Sci.* **58:**99–101.
Lashley, K. S., 1912, Visual discrimination of size and form in the albino rat, *J. Anim. Behav.* **2:**310–331.
Lashley, K. S., 1938, The mechanism of vision. XV. Preliminary studies of the rat's capacity for detail vision, *J. Gen. Psychol.* **18:**123–293.
Lashley, K. S., 1942, An examination of the continuity theory as applied to discriminative learning, *J. Gen. Psychol.* **26:**241–265.
Little, B., Chang, T., Chucot, L., Dill, W. A., Enrile, L. L., Glazko, A. J., Jassani, M., Kretchmer, H., and Sweet, A. Y., 1972, Study of ketamine as an obstetric anesthetic agent, *Amer. J. Obstet. Gynecol.* **113:**247–260.

LoLordo, V. M., and Furrow, D. R., 1976, Control by the auditory or the visual element of a compound discriminative stimulus: effects of feedback, *J. Exp. Anal. Behav.* **25:**251–256.

Morrison, C. F., and Stephenson, J. A., 1969, Nicotine injections as the conditioned stimulus in discrimination learning, *Psychopharmacologia* **15:**351–360.

Overton, D. A., 1964, State-dependent or "dissociated" learning produced with pentobarbital, *J. Comp. Physiol. Psychol.* **57:**3–12.

Overton, D. A., 1966, State-dependent learning produced by depressant and atropine-like drugs, *Psychopharmacologia* **10:**6–31.

Overton, D. A., 1968a, Dissociated learning in drug states (state-dependent learning), *in: Psychopharmacology, A Review of Progress, 1957–1967* (D. H. Efron, J. O. Cole, J. Levine, and R. Wittenborn, eds.), Public Health Service Publ. 1836, pp. 918–930, Government Printing Office, Washington, D. C.

Overton, D. A., 1968b, Visual cues and shock sensitivity in the control of T-maze choice by drug conditions, *J. Comp. Physiol. Psychol.* **66:**216–219.

Overton, D. A., 1971, Discriminative control of behavior by drug states, *in: Stimulus Properties of Drugs* (T. Thompson and R. Pickens, eds.), pp. 87–110, Appleton-Century-Croft, New York.

Overton, D. A., 1974, Experimental methods for the study of state-dependent learning, *Fed. Proc.* **33:**1800–1813.

Overton, D. A., 1975, A comparison of the discriminable CNS effects of ketamine, phencyclidine, and pentobarbital, *Arch. Int. Pharmacodyn.* **215:**180–189.

Pappas, B. A., and Gray, P., 1971, Cue value of dexamethasone for fear-motivated behavior, *Physiol. Behav.* **6:**127–130.

Rosecrans, J. A., Goodloe, M. H., Bennett, G. J., and Hirschhorn, I. D., 1973, Morphine as a discriminative cue: effects of amine depletors and naloxone, *Eur. J. Pharmacol.* **21:**252–256.

Schechter, M. D., 1973, Transfer of state-dependent control of discriminative behavior between subcutaneously and intraventricularly administered nicotine and saline, *Psychopharmacologia* **32:**327–335.

Schechter, M. D., and Cook, P. G., 1975, Dopaminergic mediation of the interoceptive cue produced by *d*-amphetamine in rats, *Psychopharmacologia* **42:**185–193.

Schechter, M. D., and Rosecrans, J. A., 1971a, CNS effect of nicotine as the discriminative stimulus for the rat in a T-maze, *Life Sci.* **10:**821–832.

Schechter, M. D., and Rosecrans, J. A., 1971b, Behavioral evidence for two types of cholinergic receptors in the CNS, *Eur. J. Pharmacol.* **15:**375–378.

Schechter, M. D., and Rosecrans, J. A., 1972, Nicotine as a discriminative cue in rats: inability of related drugs to produce a nicotine-like cueing effect, *Psychopharmacologia* **27:**379–387.

Shannon, H. E., and Holtzman, S. G., 1976, Evaluation of the discriminative effects of morphine in the rat, *J. Pharmacol. Exp. Ther.* **198:**54–65.

Stewart, J., 1962, Differential responses based on the physiological consequences of pharmacological agents, *Psychopharmacologia* **3:**132–138.

Stewart, J., Drebs, W. H., and Kaczender, E., 1967, State-dependent learning produced with steroids, *Nature* **216:**1223–1224.

Terrace, H. S., 1966, Stimulus control, *in: Operant Behavior: Areas of Research and Application* (W. K. Honig, ed.), pp. 271–344. Appleton-Century-Crofts, New York.

Weiss, B., and Heller, A., 1969, Methodological problems in evaluating the role of cholinergic mechanisms in behavior, *Fed. Proc.* **28:135**–146.

Winter, J. C., 1973, A comparison of the stimulus properties of mescaline and 2, 3, 4-trimethoxyphenylethylamine, *J. Pharmacol. Exp. Ther.* **185:**101–107.

Winter, J. C., 1974a, Hallucinogens as discriminative stimuli, *Fed. Proc.* **33:**1825–1832.
Winter, J. C., 1974b, The effects of 3, 4-dimethoxyphenylethylamine in rats trained with mescaline as a discriminative stimulus, *J.Pharmacol. Exp. Ther.* **189:**741–747.
Winter, J. C., 1975a, The effects of 2.5-dimethoxy-4-methylamphetamine (DOM), 2.5-dimethoxy-4-ethylamphetamine (DOET), *d*-amphetamine, and cocaine in rats trained with mescaline as a discriminative stimulus, *Psychopharmacologia* **44:**29–32.
Winter, J. C., 1975b, The stimulus properties of morphine and ethanol, *Psychopharmacologia* **44:**209–214.
Yerkes, R. M., 1907, *The Dancing Mouse,* Macmillan, New York.

The Effects of Drugs on Adjunctive Behavior

5

D. J. Sanger and D. E. Blackman

1. Operant and Adjunctive Behavior

1.1. Introduction

Most experimental studies of the effects of reinforcement schedules focus their attention on only one aspect of the subject's behavioral repertoire. A pattern of behavior is selected which is readily recorded by the experimenter and which is convenient to the subject, such as pressing a lever for rats or pecking a key for pigeons. These acts are not defined in terms of their topography: a rat is normally free to press a lever in any way, with either forepaw, with both paws, or with the nose. Instead, the acts are defined operationally. Thus, any behavior which results in the closure of a microswitch attached to a lever is termed an *operant response.* Responses thus defined provide the functional units of behavior whose frequency of occurrence may then be related to events (reinforcers) which follow them. The occurrence of any other aspects of the subject's behavior which do not affect the frequency of reinforcement, such as grooming or moving about in the experimental space, are not usually recorded in any systematic manner. Despite the experimenter's ignorance of such features of the subject's behavior, orderly effects of schedules of reinforcement on defined operant responses are usually obtained in such studies, and they provide sensitive base lines for the study of the effects of drugs on behavior, as is demonstrated in other chapters of this book.

D. J. Sanger and D. E. Blackman • Department of Psychology, University College, Cardiff CF1 1XL, Wales, U.K.

Although they may not normally be recorded, patterns of behavior other than defined operants do, however, occur when reinforcers are delivered intermittently, sometimes with an intensity which is striking, even puzzling. Some of this behavior has been termed by Falk (1971) *adjunctive.* In the first part of this chapter we briefly consider the kinds of adjunctive behavior which may develop in a systematic way, and we outline some of the explanations which have been suggested to account for their occurrence. Earlier, and more detailed, reviews of these matters may be found in Falk (1971) and Hawkins *et al.* (1972). We then review the effects of drugs on adjunctive behavior for the first time. We hope thereby to evaluate in this chapter the role which the study of adjunctive behavior can play in the general analysis of the behavioral effects of drugs.

1.2. Examples of Adjunctive Behavior

The prototype of Falk's adjunctive behavior is to be found in schedule-induced polydipsia, a phenomenon first reported by Falk himself (1961a) and of which the potential significance in the experimental analysis of behavior was also first discussed by Falk (e.g., 1964, 1971). He found that rats which had been deprived of food but *not* of water and which were exposed to a simple variable-interval schedule of food reinforcement began to ingest excessive amounts of water from a drinking tube which was mounted in the test chamber. In sessions which lasted for rather more than 3 hours, Falk's rats drank an average of 92 ml of water, compared with their preexperimental *daily* intake of only 27 ml. Falk was much impressed by the apparent absurdity of this excessive drinking: rats whose energy resources were depleted by food deprivation were choosing to squander these by taking in large quantities of superfluous water at room temperature and heating it to body temperature, only to excrete it as urine. Moreover, the rats had not been deprived of water, and drinking was not specified as a required operant response for reinforcement. The surprising nature of this behavior is further emphasized by the findings that it may be sustained at such an intensity that its occurrence leads to a lower overall frequency of food reinforcement (Falk, 1961b) or that it may occur when access is allowed to hypertonic NaCl (Falk, 1964, 1966) or ethanol solutions (e.g., Falk *et al.*, 1972). This latter finding has led to an interest in the use of schedule-induced polydipsia as a method of obtaining the self-administration of drugs in animals, and this research is reviewed separately by Gilbert in Chapter 6.

Schedule-induced polydipsia has now been extensively studied. Figure 1 shows a typical record of such drinking engendered by a

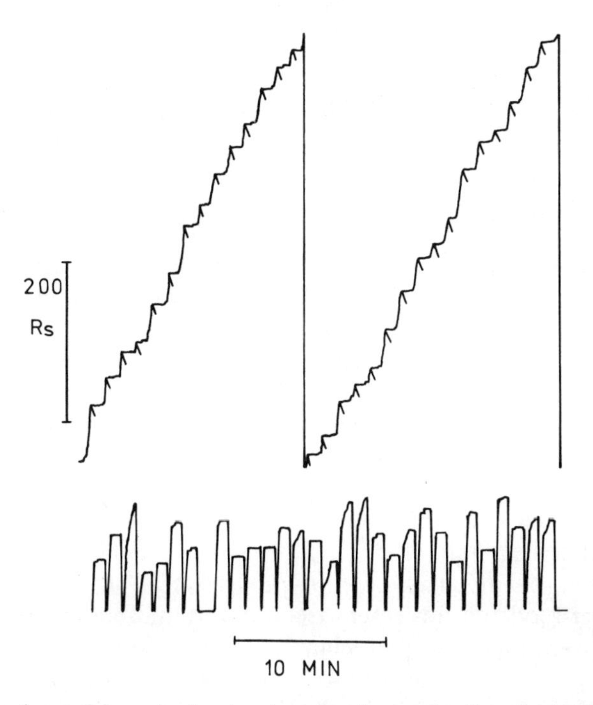

Figure 1. Sections of records showing bar pressing and adjunctive licking of a rat maintained on a fixed-interval 1-min schedule of food reinforcement. The top record shows cumulative bar presses, the delivery of each food pellet being indicated by a deflection of the pen. The lower record shows licking. After delivery of each food pellet this pen was reset, and it can be seen that licking was characterized by a rapid burst after consumption of each pellet.

fixed-interval 60-sec schedule of food reinforcement. Each lick by a rat at a water spout stepped the lower response pen cumulatively, and it was reset by the delivery of food reinforcement. Lever presses (the designated operants in this study) were recorded separately and are indicated by the top record. It can be seen that the rat characteristically engaged in a sustained bout of licking after the delivery of food (in fact, after the 45-mg pellet of food had been eaten). After an average of about 100 licks at the spout, a pause is observed, and this is followed by a series of lever presses until the next reinforcer is delivered, whereupon the sequence is repeated.

Strictly speaking, Figure 1 is not in itself evidence for *polydipsic* drinking, since there is no indication given of the amount of water drunk either during the experimental session or in control conditions, and so there is no evidence of excessive drinking. It could be argued, however, that the licking which is displayed in Figure 1 is excessive in that it occurs with substantial vigor, although it is not a requirement for the delivery of a reinforcer. The term "schedule-induced-licking" is therefore more appropriate in this case, and this term or (when the dependent variable is amount of liquid drunk) schedule-induced drinking is also appropriate in many of the studies which have followed Falk's pioneering observations.

The determinants of schedule-induced licking when animals are exposed to schedules of food reinforcement are now well understood. The amount of such licking is a positive function of the severity of prior food deprivation (Falk, 1969) and is also positively related to the amount of food delivered intermittently (Bond, 1973; Hawkins *et al.*, 1972; Rosenblith, 1970). The amount of licking is further determined by the intermittency between successive presentations of food: licking and drinking increase as the interval between pellet delivery increases to approximately 3 minutes but declines as this interval increases further (Bond, 1973; Falk, 1966; Hawkins *et al.*, 1972). Although schedule-induced licking has been demonstrated with many different schedules of food reinforcement (see reviews by Bond, 1974, and Falk, 1971), a programmed dependency between an operant response and the delivery of food is not, in fact, a necessary condition for such licking to occur. Thus, licking develops in an analogous way when food pellets are delivered intermittently but completely independently of an animal's behavior, as in fixed-time or variable-time schedules (e.g., Bond, 1973; Burks, 1970; Falk, 1961b; Hawkins *et al.*, 1972).

Although schedule-induced drinking at a water spout has been studied most extensively, Falk (1971) has suggested that there are other topographical patterns of behavior which may be generated in similar ways when reinforcers are scheduled to occur intermittently. If no water spout is available, patterns of licking at a stream of air (Mendelson and Chillag, 1970) or nitrogen (Taylor and Lester, 1969) may develop in rats, and Villareal (1967) reported that food-deprived rhesus monkeys began to ingest wood shavings, but only when food pellets were delivered intermittently. There is also some evidence that rats may develop patterns of schedule-induced wheel running during schedules of intermittent food or water delivery (King, 1974a; King and Sides, 1975; Levitsky and Collier, 1968; Segal, 1969). However, the results of other reports indicate that such running may not be closely comparable with the drinking which develops under similar conditions (Skinner and Morse, 1957; Staddon and Ayres, 1975).

It has also been reported that animals will exhibit vigorous patterns of attack behavior directed toward other animals or to surrogates after a food reinforcer has been delivered. With pigeons such behavior has been observed during fixed-ratio (Cherek and Pickens, 1970; Cohen and Looney, 1973; Gentry, 1968), fixed-interval (Cherek *et al.*, 1973), differential reinforcement of low rate (Knutson and Kleinknecht, 1970) and fixed-time (Dove, 1976; Flory, 1969) schedules, and during extinction components of multiple schedules (Azrin *et al.*, 1966; Knutson, 1970). The biting of a hose made available during performance on fixed-ratio schedules has also been reported in monkeys (Hutchinson *et al.*, 1968), although similar patterns of schedule-induced attack in rats have proved to be more difficult to demonstrate (Gentry and Schaeffer, 1969; Hymowitz, 1971; Knutson and Schrader, 1975). A further behavioral phenomenon which has been well studied takes the form of attacking other animals or even inanimate objects immediately after an electric shock has been delivered, a phenomenon which has sometimes been termed pain-elicited aggression (Ulrich *et al.*, 1965) but which is more objectively described as a shock-induced pattern of behavior (Ulrich and Craine, 1964).

Falk has suggested (1971) that there are similarities between all these patterns of behavior and schedule-induced polydipsia, in that they all appear to be the side effects of schedules of intermittent reinforcement. When it has been possible for them to occur, and when they have been recorded, all have been demonstrated to be exhibited systematically and with striking intensity, and yet none of them affects the frequency of reinforcement. Falk goes on to note some similarities between the controlling variables of schedule-induced licking and the less comprehensively researched other patterns of behavior induced by schedules of reinforcement, and he concludes that they may be said to form a separate class of behavior which he terms "adjunctive behavior." In this way, Falk adds to the functional classes of elicited and emitted behavior (respondents and operants) a further class: "behavior maintained at high probability by stimuli whose reinforcing properties in the situation are derived primarily as a function of schedule parameters governing the availability of another class of reinforcers" (1971, p. 586). To take the best-rehearsed example of such a behavior, that of schedule-induced polydipsia, Falk is here suggesting that the liquid which the animal drinks has become a reinforcing stimulus, and thus sustains licking and drinking despite the lack of the normal deprivational conditions which are required to make the liquid a reinforcer. This reinforcing effect is derived from the fact that another reinforcer (food) which has derived its effect from a conventional history of prior deprivation is being delivered according to an intermittent schedule.

Falk has been influential in directing our attention to the fact that operant responses which are defined operationally and to which reinforcement is related are not necessarily the only patterns of behavior which may be generated systematically in experimental situations. The patterns of behavior which we have considered in this section are all strictly irrelevant to the exigencies of a schedule of reinforcement and yet all may be an important component of the subject's behavioral repertoire determined by that schedule. These often-disregarded patterns of behavior may therefore provide an important further object of study in behavioral pharmacology. However, if Falk is justified in postulating the need for a further category of behavior to accommodate the examples we have discussed, the need for an analysis of the effects of drugs on this behavior becomes more pressing. Such an analysis may, in turn, contribute to our understanding of the need for a further behavioral class, in that comparisons will become possible between the effects of drugs on these behaviors and on typical operants which have been more extensively studied. But first, what are the nonpharmacological arguments that these patterns of behavior cannot be accommodated in conventional categories?

1.3. Interpretations of Schedule-Induced Behavior

In reviewing the argument for invoking a class of adjunctive behavior, we are forced to direct our attention almost exclusively to the specific example of schedule-induced licking and water consumption. The suggestion that such behavior cannot be interpreted within the traditional categories of behavior provides the paradigm case for Falk's adjunctive behavior. The argument that there are other examples of adjunctive behavior depends largely on general similarities which may be observed between these and schedule-induced licking in limited situations. This section is therefore addressed almost exclusively to the question of explaining schedule-induced licking.

There has been no shortage of explanatory accounts of schedule-induced licking (see Falk, 1971). One suggestion has been that the unusual amount of drinking results simply from the unusual circumstances of providing pellets of food intermittently: it is as if the animal is exposed to many small meals, each of which is sufficient to prompt an approximation to normal food-associated drinking. Such an effect might be mediated by local factors such as dryness of the mouth engendered by eating each "mini-meal." Falk (1971) has dismissed this interpretation, largely on the grounds that schedule-induced licking occurs even after reinforcement in the form of liquid food (Falk, 1967; see also Hawkins *et al.*, 1972). More recent experiments may also be cited against this interpretation. For example, Gilbert (1974) showed that rats which were deprived of the opportunity to drink immediately after food reinforcement nevertheless exhibited large numbers of licks when the water spout was made available only later in the interreinforcement interval. Indeed, when the rats were allowed limited periods of access to the water spout at different points in the interreinforcement interval, the greatest numbers of licks were not observed in the immediate postreinforcement period, as this interpretation would suggest. A further difficulty for the food-associated drinking hypothesis is provided by reports that large numbers of licks may be induced in the periods immediately after nonnutritive events such as conditioned reinforcers. For example, Corfield-Sumner *et al.* (1977) exposed rats to a second-order schedule in which fixed intervals ended at random and with equal probability with either food reinforcement or a brief stimulus (which was never paired with food). Large numbers of licks occurred after each brief stimulus, although it should be added that even more licks occurred after each presentation of food reinforcer. Similar poststimulus drinking has been reported by Rosenblith (1970) and Porter and Kenshalo (1974), although other studies have failed to obtain such an effect (Allen *et al.,* 1975; Porter *et al.,* 1975), and these findings suggest that the ingestion of food *per se* is not a necessary condition for schedule-induced licking to occur. However, the fact that the amount of licking varies as a function of the size and constituency of the food reinforcer indicates that food-related or oral effects may be implicated (Falk, 1971).

Schedule-induced polydipsia cannot be fully understood then merely in terms of food-associated drinking. This conclusion is supported by findings which suggest that polydipsia is not the result of physiological, systemic, or metabolic effects prompted by the relatively unusual feeding situations which induce the behavior. For example, Stricker and Adair (1966) examined blood samples of rats which exhibited schedule-induced polydipsia, and found dilution and overhydration of the body fluids and tissues: and yet the animals continued to drink. Similarly, while it is known that loading water directly into the stomachs of *water-deprived* rats just before they are allowed access to water leads to a reduction in the regulatory water intake (Stricker, 1966), Falk (1969) has demonstrated that such gastric loading has little effect on drinking induced by intermittent food reinforcement. Furthermore, a suggestion (Chapman and Richardson, 1974) that gastric loading inhibits the *development* of schedule-induced polydipsia has been challenged by a recent study which produced little evidence for such inhibition (Cope *et al*., 1976). It seems, then, that an explanation is called for not in terms of physiological or metabolic mechanisms but in terms of *behavioral* mechanisms which may be prompted by the experimental situations of which the behavior has been shown to be a function: hence Falk's use of the term "psychogenic" in discussion of schedule-induced polydipsia (e.g., 1969).

Behavioral mechanisms which have been considered in this context include the possibility that schedule-induced licking is the result of known processes which affect respondent or operant behavior. In the former case, it might be suggested that the licking is an *elicited* behavior, an unconditioned response elicited by the ingestion of food. Here again, however, this cannot be a complete explanation of schedule-induced licking, since drinking occurs at relatively low levels when animals are first exposed to the intermittent feeding conditions; the drinking increases to asymptotic levels over a number of experimental sessions (e.g., Hawkins *et al.*, 1972). The sensitivity of schedule-induced licking to motivational variables and to the scheduling of the events which might be thought of as unconditioned stimuli is a further problem. Nor is it possible readily to interpret the gradual development of drinking to its characteristic high levels as a process of classical conditioning which is built on the foundations of a smaller unconditioned response originally elicited by the intermittent food delivery, since one is at a loss to construct an appropriate Pavlovian paradigm in which both conditioned and unconditioned stimuli are identified.

The possibility that schedule-induced licking is controlled by operant conditioning processes which are well understood in other contexts is a little more difficult to discount. Here, as in so many contexts which have given rise to problems of interpretation in the operant laboratory, the concept of adventitious reinforcement or superstitious behavior has been invoked. Clark (1962) and Stein (1964), for example, suggested that high levels of drinking might develop because of chance correlations between this behavior and the delivery of a reinforcer for which the animal is appropriately motivated. One can see that the longer an animal licks after a reinforcer on a variable-interval schedule, the greater is the probability that the next reinforcer will be obtained by the next specified operant response to be emitted, thus leading to the strengthening of this entire sequence of behavior. Such an interpretation can, of course, be readily extended to any time-based schedule of reinforcement, including those in which no operant response is formally specified, such as variable-time and fixed-time schedules. However, putting aside difficulties with the concept of superstition (Staddon and Simmelhag, 1971), there are several problems for such an account. The first is provided by the finding that in most experiments in which access to water is allowed continuously schedule-induced licking is typically a postpellet phenomenon, occurring in the period immediately after the ingestion of the food reinforcer rather than just prior to the delivery of a subsequent reinforcer as this interpretation might expect (see, for example, Figure 1). Similarly, schedule-induced licking has been shown to develop on fixed-ratio schedules of reinforcement (e.g., Carlisle, 1971) which by their very nature and that of the operant behavior which they engender reduce the possibility of any direct contingency between licking and food reinforcement of the sort that might be envisaged with time-based schedules.

The traditional way to minimize adventitious reinforcement effects in operant conditioning experiments is to introduce a delay between the occurrence of the behavior in question and the delivery of reinforcement, thereby eliminating chance correlations between the two events (e.g., Zeiler, 1970). It has been found, however, that introducing delays in reinforcement whenever licks occur has little or no effect on established schedule-induced licking (Falk, 1964; Hitzig, 1968). The resistance of established licking to disruption by delays of reinforcement has been used by Falk (1969) as evidence that this behavior is not sensitive to control by environmental factors which may modify the frequency with which conventional operant responses are emitted. This view, added to the oddness of the excessive nature of schedule-induced drinking on which we have already commented, has led to a latent view that there is some unusual kind of inevitability about this behavior in the appropriate setting conditions. However, this is not always the case. For example, it has been reported that established schedule-induced licking can be readily and specifically reduced in frequency by lick-contingent shocks or periods of time out from the schedule of reinforcement delivery (punishment procedure—Bond *et al.*, 1973; Flory and Lickfett, 1974; Galantowicz and King, 1975), although there have also been reports of enhanced licking when shocks are very low in intensity (Galantowicz and King, 1975; King, 1975). Other studies (Bond and Blackman, 1975; Bond *et al.*, 1973; Freed *et al.*, 1974; Hymowitz, 1976; Hymowitz and Freed, 1974) have shown that licking may also be attenuated by presentation of noncontingent electric shocks. For example, Bond *et al.* (1973) found that schedule-induced licking was suppressed during a stimulus which signaled the delivery of occasional slight but unavoidable shocks (the conditioned suppression procedure which some have used as a model of anxiety—see Blackman, 1977). In these experiments, schedule-induced licking in fact appeared to be more sensitive to control by punishment and conditioned suppression procedures than was the operant response which led to reinforcement. In a later study, Bond and Blackman (1975) exposed rats to a fixed-time schedule of food pellet delivery and showed that the suppression of schedule-induced licking during a signal associated with unavoidable shock could take two forms; with very slight shocks, the reduction in licking was due to a decrease in the number of licks after each reinforcer, the percentage of reinforcers followed by licks being unchanged. With a higher shock intensity, however, both the proportion of reinforcers followed by a lick and the number of licks in a bout of drinking were lower during the signaled periods than in the control periods. These results are illustrated in Figure 2.

It seems from the research above, then, that even though schedule-induced licking and conventional operant responding may be *initiated* by different conditions, both patterns of behavior may show similar changes with respect to variations in reinforcement rate (Bond, 1973) and to response suppression procedures such as punishment and conditioned suppression. These findings may be taken to imply that two types of behavior are *maintained* by similar factors. The resistance of schedule-induced licking to suppression by lick-dependent delays in reinforcement remains an anomaly. However, it may be noted that such a procedure will inhibit the *development* of schedule-induced drinking (Hawkins *et al.*, 1972), and the failure to disrupt well-established polydipsia (e.g., Falk, 1961b) may be due to the fact that there is no discrete or signaled stimulus associated with the delay.

We may see then that the nature of schedule-induced behavior is still a matter for theoretical debate. Falk's suggestion that the behavior should be designated as a class, that of adjunctive behavior, has some

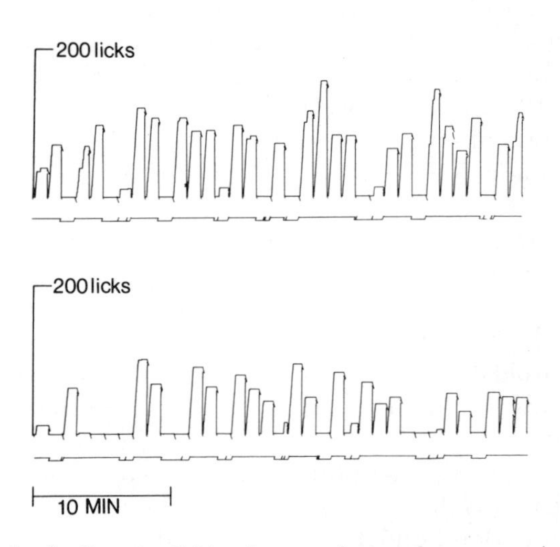

Figure 2. Records of adjunctive licking in a rat during the presentation of a stimulus associated with electric shock of either low (top record) or high (lower record) intensity. Stimulus presentations are shown by the deflections of the event pen and shock presentations are shown by brief deflections of both pens. [From Bond (1974).]

merit, although the case depends unduly at present on the systematic study of only one example of such behavior, and it may also appear to have been somewhat overstated in the light of more recent research. A particularly interesting aspect of Falk's discussions, however, is to be found in the analogy he has drawn (e.g., Falk, 1971) between adjunctive behavior observed in the operant laboratory and the displacement activities which have long been studied by ethologists in other contexts. Tinbergen (1952) defined displacement activity as "an activity belonging to the executive motor pattern of an instinct other than the instinct motivated." An often-cited empirical example of this somewhat dynamically expressed generalization is to be found in the short burst of preening behavior which a duck may suddenly interpose in a sequence of courtship behavior. Falk suggests that with both adjunctive behavior and displacement activity, the interruption of a consummatory behavior in an intensely motivated animal produces the occurrence of another pattern of behavior.

It is interesting that Falk would describe the occurrence of adjunctive behavior as "induced" while the ethologists would describe the occurrence of displacement activity as "released." In both cases, the word is intended to convey a relationship between an environmental event and behavior which is less bound than the eliciting relationship between antecedent stimulus and respondent yet perhaps more bound than is the relationship between a discriminative stimulus and the operant behavior which is emitted at various rates in its presence. McFarland (1966) suggests that displacement activities are "the by-product of a mechanism which enables animals to break away from a specific course of action when progress in that course of action comes to a standstill" (p. 231). Such a standstill results, for example, if the releasing stimulus appropriate to the next species-specific response in a consummatory sequence is for some reason not presented. Such a condition might be said to "thwart" the further consummatory behavior appropriate to the instinct. It is but a step to suggest that adjunctive behavior arises in conditions in which the reduction of a motivational state is thwarted.

How might it be said that the delivery of food which is appropriate to a motivational state set up by prior deprivation induces licking and drinking by thwarting that state? An answer to this obvious question is to be found in the *intermittency* of reinforcement, which we have seen to be such an important determinant of schedule-induced polydipsia. Although the delivery of a reinforcer is appropriate to the state resulting from food deprivation, that reinforcer is usually limited to a small pellet and it also signals (to varying extents depending on the nature of the schedule) a period when the probability of further reinforcement is temporarily at a very low or even zero level. The latter is particularly the case, of course, with such schedules as fixed-interval, fixed-time, and fixed-ratio.

Several experimental findings may readily be discussed within the context of this description of schedule-induced behavior. We have already emphasized that the behavior should normally be regarded as a *post*reinforcement effect as would seem to be required by this account. The finding that licking is induced by a nonconsumable brief stimulus or conditioned reinforcer in a second-order schedule (Corfield-Sumner *et al.*, 1977) is also compatible with this account, since the brief stimulus in this experiment had similar signaling properties to food in relation to the future probability of food reinforcement. In fact, the discriminative properties of these two events were identical, and the finding that there was less licking immediately after the conditioned reinforcer than after food suggests that the idea of a thwarting of a motivational state is not a complete explanation for the occurrence of schedule-induced licking.

Another interesting finding in the context of thwarting is that of Segal and Holloway (1963). They exposed rats to a schedule which differentially reinforced low rates of operant responding by delivering a food pellet only after a response which occurred at least 30 sec since the previous response (DRL 30 sec). A water spout was continously available to the rats. It was found that food reinforcement induced the licking behavior since shown to be typical of so many intermittent schedules. However, the rats in this study also licked after premature operant responses which were not followed by reinforcement. Although this was interpreted by Segal and Holloway in terms of the adventitious reinforcement by the schedule of sequences of timing behavior of which licking formed an important part, such behavior might also be predicted by an account of licking as being induced by thwarting, since each operant response, whether followed by food reinforcement or not, set back the possibility of further food reinforcement by 30 sec. Finally, it should perhaps be noted that an account of adjunctive behavior in terms of the thwarting of a motivational state may seem to some particularly apposite in the context of such behavior as the schedule-induced aggression reported by Azrin *et al.* (1966) to occur at times of low reinforcement probability.

Falk (e.g., 1971) seems to come close to arguing that the idea of motivational thwarting, with its analogy to explanations of displacement activity, is an appropriate "psychogenic" explanation for adjunctive behavior, although it should be noted that his definition of this class of behavior, which was discussed earlier, does not make this a defining characteristic. The motivational and emotional overtones of the concept of thwarting serve to make contact with other discussions of schedule-induced behavior which should be briefly considered. For example, Segal and Oden (1965) discussed the possibility that schedule-induced polydipsia is attributable in part to emotional substrates of behavior which may be set up by conditions of food deprivation and intermittent delivery of food. Thus schedule-induced licking might serve as some form of "emotional pacification." The emotional state may serve to energize the most probable pattern of behavior in any situation; immediately after ingestion of food, of course, drinking has a high probability of occurrence, and so schedule-induced licking may be generated in this way. King (1974b) found that giving rats electric shocks before the daily presentation of a schedule of intermittent reinforcement led to an increase in the amount of schedule-induced polydipsia, an effect which he interprets as being due to an enhancing effect of the shocks on the emotional substrate of drinking. Similarly, Segal and Oden (1969) found that rats showed an increase in schedule-induced licking when foot shocks followed the delivery of food reinforcers. However, in other experiments an *attenuation* of schedule-induced behavior has been reported as a function of shocks delivered independently of behavior (e.g., Bond and Blackman, 1975; Hymowitz, 1976; Hymowitz and Freed, 1974). There remains a need for further experimental analysis of schedule-induced behavior in order to evaluate these motivational/emotional accounts. Of course, investigations of the effects of drugs which are thought to affect motivational or emotional systems would prove very useful in this context, and a number of experiments are discussed later in this chapter which are relevant to this debate.

Experiments with drugs are also relevant to a suggestion (Denny and Ratner, 1970; Kissileff, 1973) that schedule-induced drinking is the result of frustrative nonreward engendered by the intermittency of reinforcement. Such frustration has been thought of as a motivating force which enhances the vigor of the immediately following behavior (Amsel, 1962), and since it is drinking which follows the ingestion of the reinforcer, it is this pattern of behavior which is said to be increased in vigor as a result of the frustrative effects of intermittent reinforcement. Thomka and Rosellini (1975) have obtained some experimental evidence apparently supporting an association between schedule-induced drinking and frustration, although Falk (1973) has pointed to the deficiencies in such an approach.

Before drawing this section to a conclusion, an important paper by Staddon (1977) should be considered. His discussion develops from an earlier and influential paper by Staddon and Simmelhag (1971), and centers on the notion that behavior in a conventional operant conditioning situation may contain important sequential characteristics which we must attempt to understand if we are to understand any single aspect of behavior. A schedule, such as a fixed-time schedule, which periodically presents a reinforcer may lead to sequences of behavior which Staddon puts into three groups. Some patterns of behavior emerge in the presence of stimuli which are associated with an event such as food. This behavior Staddon calls *terminal responses,* and examples of such behavior are to be found in their most obvious form in the research on sign-tracking behavior in pigeons (see, for example, Hearst and Jenkins, 1974). Thus, a localized stimulus which is associated with the delivery of food prompts pigeons to orient toward or peck that stimulus in a systematic way, although such behavior is in no sense a requirement for the delivery of food. In conventional schedules of reinforcement in which food is made *dependent* on the occurrence of a specified operant response, the occurrence of this behavior may be influenced by the processes which engender terminal responses in the absence of a formal specification of an operant. At times when such events as food are unlikely to be delivered, other patterns of behavior may emerge. These Staddon terms *interim activities,* and the patterns of schedule-induced or adjunctive behavior on which we have largely concentrated in this chapter are clear examples of such activities. Finally, other patterns of behavior which may emerge Staddon terms *facultative.* In the interval between successive presentations of food, Staddon suggests that interim, facultative, and terminal activities compete for expression in the animal's behavior at any given moment, and he thus emphasizes his view that the observed behavioral repertoire is the outcome of the interactions of these dispositions. Staddon goes on to suggest that interim, facultative, and terminal activities reflect underlying states or "moods" of the behaving animal. It is an interesting question within this analysis to ask, therefore, whether the "thirst" which might be said to prompt the interim drinking which is typical of schedule-induced polydipsia is similar to the "thirst" which might prompt terminal activities in other situations (such as the lever pressing of water-deprived rats, which is reinforced by presentation of water). Again, we shall see later in this chapter that pharmacological investigations may be highly relevant to our attempts to answer this question.

Staddon concludes his discussion by considering what is known about the temporal aspects of the interactions among interim, facultative, and terminal activities. He argues that the "laws" of operant behavior which have emerged from conventional experiments which have recorded only defined operants (terminal responses) are not a property of an isolated class of behavior but "emergent properties of a set of variations among induced states and their associated behaviors." Each kind of behavior may be induced by the schedule to which an animal is exposed, and each is controlled by factors such as environmental or temporal stimuli. Any environmental change (such as the administration of a drug) which affects the terminal or instrumental response, for example, does so both directly and indirectly through its effects on other (interim or facultative) activities which may be causally related to the terminal activity. The extension of this argument to one which urges an analysis of the effects of drugs on interim (or adjunctive) behavior in this context is of obvious and immediate impact.

1.4. Importance of Adjunctive Behavior in Behavioral Pharmacology

We are now in a position to summarize the first three introductory sections of this chapter, in which we have attempted to suggest why adjunctive behavior may prove to be of value in the behavioral analysis of the effects of drugs. In many experimental situations there arise patterns of behavior which are often not measured and which seem to arise as a function of a schedule of reinforcement, although they are not specified as a requirement for a reinforcer to be delivered. Such behavior may nevertheless occur with great vigor, the most thoroughly researched example being provided by schedule-induced licking at water shown by animals which have been deprived of food and whose operant behavior is reinforced by the intermittent presentation of food. Falk (e.g., 1971) has aruged that this behavior is one example of a larger class which he has termed "adjunctive." The necessity for such a class of behavior, which Falk sees as analogous to displacement activities, is found in the difficulty in accounting fully for its occurrence within existing principles of respondent or operant behavior. However, Falk's argument is a subject of theoretical debate, and other more limited suggestions have been made that behavior such as schedule-induced licking is the outcome of motivational or emotional states whose genesis can be understood in more traditional terms. Furthermore, Staddon (1977) places Falk's adjunctive behavior into a broader context in which it is seen as interim behavior which is in a constant state of interaction with other behavioral dispositions which are a function of schedules of reinforcement.

An interest in the effects of drugs on what Falk termed "adjunctive behavior" may be justified on several grounds. First, if the argument is to be considered that a new category is required in behavioral analysis to supplement those of respondent and operant behavior, it is important to ask whether the effects of drugs on adjunctive behavior conform to the general principles which have emerged in studies of other behavior. More specifically, is it possible to find any general analogies to rate-dependent drug effects on operant behavior (Chapter 1), of exteroceptive stimulus control as a parameter in behavioral pharmacology (Chapter 3), or of tolerance to repeated administration of drugs (Chapter 8)? In turn, if it is not possible to adduce such general similarities, this may strengthen the argument for conceptualizing these behaviors separately.

Another interesting question which pharmacological research may seek to answer concerns the extent to which the actions of drugs on patterns of adjunctive behavior are similar to, or different from, the effects of the same drugs on behavior which is topographically similar but which is generated and maintained by other means. It is possible, for instance, to induce animals to consume water by means of a period of water deprivation as well as by several other techniques. If, as Staddon (1977) has suggested, adjunctive drinking is induced by a state of thirst, then it might seem reasonable to ask whether the effects of a drug on adjunctive drinking are similar to its effects on deprivation-induced drinking, since it is sometimes assumed that drugs act on motivational or emotional states hypothesized to underlay behavior. Similarly, attack behavior has sometimes been considered to be produced by an aggressive drive. Such behavior can be induced by a number of experimental manipulations, including schedules of food or shock delivery, and comparisons of the effects of drugs on aggression induced by different means are thus of considerable interest. Although assumptions concerning the actions of drugs on states underlying behavior have not proved fruitful thus far in behavioral pharmacology (see Chapters 1 and 2), it will clearly be useful to make comparisons between the actions of drugs on patterns of behavior induced by schedules of reinforcement and by other means.

There is also a strong argument that the effects of drugs on behavior such as schedule-induced licking should be assessed simply because such behavior can provide a striking component of an animal's total behavioral repertoire in an experimental situation (regardless of how the behavior is to be interpreted). It is here, perhaps, that Staddon's paper (1977) is most relevant. He argues that there is a need for an analysis of the interactions among what he terms interim, facultative, and terminal activities. The study of the effects of drugs may be particularly useful in helping us to appreciate the as yet poorly formulated details of these interactions.

Thus, the studies which are reviewed in the remainder of this chapter may provide an important addition to the study of the effects of drugs on operant behavior which forms the bulk of behavioral pharmacology at present. It may add both to our understanding of the behavioral effects of drugs in general and also to our experimental analysis of behavior itself.

2. Drugs and Adjunctive Behavior

2.1. Effects of Amphetamines

Amphetamines are drugs which have been shown to exert a wide variety of actions on the behavior of laboratory animals. Not surprisingly, several studies have been concerned with the effects of members of this group of drugs on adjunctive drinking. It seems that this behavior can be markedly disrupted by administration of these agents.

Falk (1964) trained rats to lever-press for food reinforcement on a variable-interval 1-min schedule with water tubes available. When adjunctive drinking had developed, the effects of a dose of 0.5 mg/kg of methamphetamine were investigated. Drinking was found to be abolished by drug administration, although there was little effect on rates of lever pressing. Although only one dose of methamphetamine was used in this study, the results suggested that adjunctive drinking might be particularly sensitive to disruption by amphetamine administration, a view which seems to have been confirmed by much, though not all, of the more recently published research.

A number of studies have made use of differential reinforcement of low rate schedules in this context. Such schedules require that subjects emit responses a certain minimum time apart in order for reinforcers to be obtained. When efficient responding has developed, there are relatively long periods of time during which no responding occurs, and high rates of drinking will occur during these times if water is available. Segal and her colleagues (Segal and Oden, 1968; Segal and Deadwyler, 1964) found that *dl*-amphetamine in doses of 1.5 and 2.0 mg/kg decreased adjunctive drinking in rats maintained on such schedules while increasing the rate of operant behavior. Similar effects were found both when the operant response was lever pressing and when it was licking at a water tube.

More recently, Smith and Clark (1975) have described the results of a systematic and detailed study concerned with the effects of several drugs on drinking and wheel running displayed by rats which were maintained on a multiple differential reinforcement of low rate schedule of lever pressing for food reinforcement. The rats were placed in running wheels in which water tubes, levers, and food cups were available. The animals pressed the levers on a multiple schedule which had three differential reinforcement of low rate components of 10, 20, and 60 sec, and bar presses, licking, and wheel running were recorded. It was found that the rate and efficiency of bar pressing and the rate of licking were inversely related to the differential reinforcement of low rate parameter while no consistent relationships between rate of wheel running and the schedule value were observed (Smith and Clark, 1974). Figure 3 shows that a wide range of doses of *d*-amphetamine disrupted all three behaviors. Lever pressing was generally increased at lower doses and decreased by higher doses (although there were some differences between the different schedule components), while licking was either decreased or unaffected by this drug. Wheel running was increased at some doses and decreased by others, but these effects were not consistent across animals.

The results of this study showed, in general, that the actions of *d*-amphetamine, and indeed of the other drugs studied (see later sections), on licking and wheel running were variable both within and between subjects. This, the authors concluded, was probably related to the possibility that the licking and wheel running observed in their study was more "loosely" controlled than the lever pressing, which was generally affected in a more consistent manner by drug administration. However, this view probably does not apply to other studies which have made use of different procedures to maintain adjunctive behavior and in which less variable effects of amphetamines have been found.

Several studies have thus shown that licking induced by food reinforcement on differential reinforcement of low rate schedules is markedly depressed by administration of amphetamines. However, these experiments can be criticized on the grounds that the effects of the drugs on licking may be an indirect result of their effects on rates of operant responding. In these and other studies, amphetamines have been shown to produce large increases in rates of differential reinforcement of low rate responding, and this results in decreases in the frequency of reinforcement. Since adjunctive drinking is a function of reinforcement frequency (Hawkins *et al.*, 1972), a predictable consequence of a reduction in the frequency of food presentations would be a decrease in drinking.

Several studies, however, have maintained operant responding on other schedules, and in most of these experiments adjunctive drinking has also been found to be attenuated by adminstration of amphetamines. Falk's (1964) study, in which a variable-interval schedule was used, has already been mentioned, and a number of other experiments have made use of fixed-interval schedules (McKearney, 1973; Wayner *et al.*, 1973a; Wuttke and Innis, 1972). Wayner *et al.* (1973a) found that in two rats adjunctive drinking was markedly attenuated at doses of *d*-amphetamine which concurrently increased lever pressing (0.5–2.0

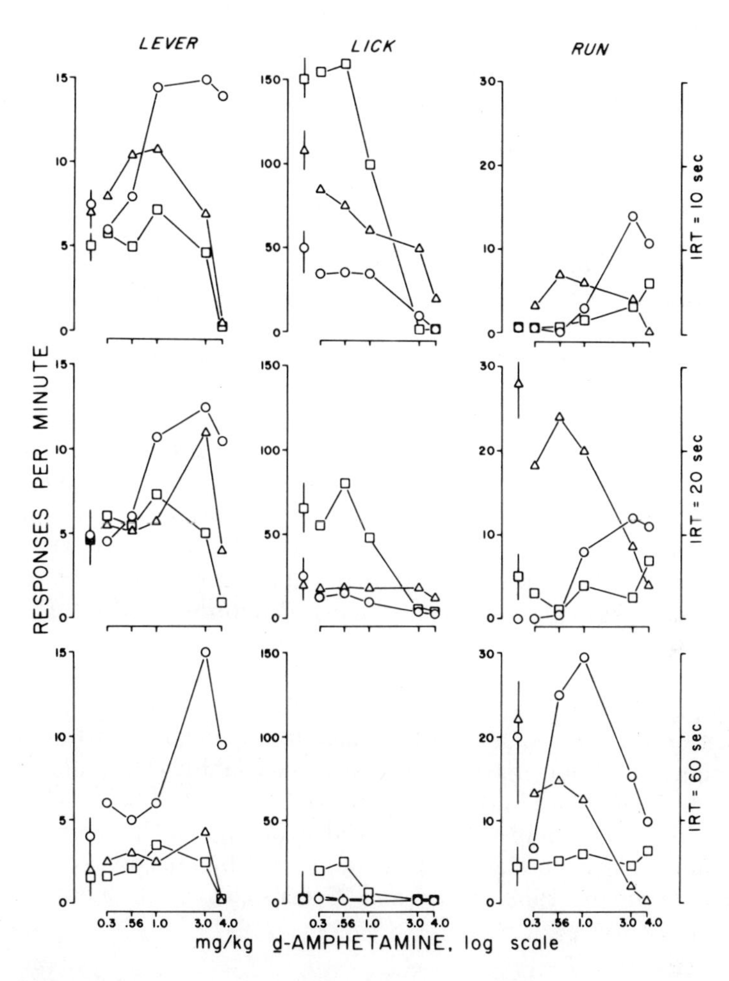

Figure 3. Dose–response curves showing the effects of *d*-amphetamine on mean rates of bar pressing, licking, and wheel running at each of the three schedule parameters of the multiple DRL 10-DRL 20-DRL 60 schedule. Circles show effects for rat 1, triangles for rat 2, and squares for rat 3. Unconnected points with vertical lines show the mean and range of five saline control sessions. [From Smith and Clark (1975); © 1975 by the Society for the Experimental Analysis of Behavior.]

mg/kg). At lower doses, however (0.05, 0.25 mg/kg), there was some indication that adjunctive drinking was facilitated in one animal. Wuttke and Innis (1972) made use of a complex second-order fixed-interval schedule to induce adjunctive drinking in rats and again it was found that *d*-amphetamine reduced adjunctive licking at doses which increased rates of lever pressing. Similar effects have been reported by Byrd (1973), who studied the actions of the same drug on the key pressing and the drinking of two chimpanzees maintained on a multiple fixed-interval fixed-ratio schedule, and it has also been shown that drinking induced by a fixed-time procedure is attenuated by administration of amphetamines (Segal *et al.*, 1965).

Adjunctive drinking has therefore generally been shown to be attenuated in these studies at doses which do not exert rate-decreasing effects on operant behavior. However, a careful experiment described by McKearney (1973) provides an exception to this generalization. Three rats were maintained on a fixed-interval 3-min schedule of food reinforcement for which the operant response was licking a water spout. This procedure generated biphasic patterns of licking: shortly after reinforcement a burst of licking occurred (presumed to be adjunctive in nature), but then more moderate rates were observed (operant behavior) until the next reinforcer was delivered. This operant licking was typical of fixed interval behavior. Several doses of methamphetamine were administered to the rats, and while the lowest dose (0.03 mg/kg) increased the rate of operant licking, this licking was decreased in a dose-related manner by the higher doses. However, the drug had very little effect on adjunctive licking except at the highest dose (1.7 mg/kg), which exerted a marked depressant effect. This effect is illustrated in Figure 4.

In spite of McKearney's results, a number of studies have shown that adjunctive drinking is attenuated by the administration of amphetamine, and it is reasonable at this stage to ask whether such an effect represents an action of these drugs on mechanisms of water intake. When rats are allowed access to water only at certain, relatively short, periods daily, the deprivation-induced drinking which occurs during these times has been shown to be attenuated by injections of amphetamines (Epstein, 1959; Glick and Greenstein, 1973; Knowler and

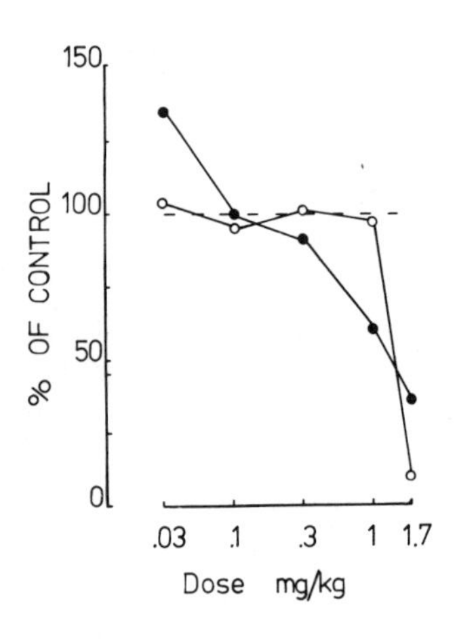

Figure 4. Dose–response curves showing the effects of methamphetamine on schedule-induced (open circles) and operant (filled circles) licking in rats maintained on a fixed-interval 3-min schedule. Each point is the mean change from control values in nine rats. [Drawn from data in McKearney (1973).]

Ukena, 1973; Mogenson, 1968; Teitelbaum and Derks, 1958). Drinking induced by injections of sodium chloride solution is also blocked by these drugs (Andersson and Larsson, 1956; DeWied, 1966). On the other hand, water intake in nondeprived rats is apparently not reduced by amphetamines (Houser, 1970; Soulairac, 1969). Glick and Muller (1971) have, in fact, reported that the food-associated drinking of rats deprived of food but not of water is facilitated by a low dose of *d*-amphetamine (0.05 mg/kg). This effect may correspond to the facilitation of adjunctive drinking reported by Wayner *et al.* (1973a) after a similarly low dose. However, in the latter experiment, the effect was small and was observed in only one animal.

It has also been shown that when drinking is maintained by an operant schedule, it may be facilitated by amphetamines. As described above, McKearney (1973) found an increase in the *operant* licking of rats after a low dose of methamphetamine. Wuttke (1970) has described similar increases in the schedule-controlled drinking of monkeys after low doses of *d*-amphetamine. Teitelbaum and Derks (1958) maintained the licking of rats by a shock-avoidance procedure and observed very large increases in lick rates after administration of *dl*-amphetamine. In this experiment, however, it seems likely that the stereotyped movements induced by the relatively high doses used (Randrup and Munkvad, 1974) may have at least contributed to the drug effect.

It is thus clear that the actions of amphetamines on drinking depend critically upon the circumstances under which the drinking occurs. This is not to say, of course, that the effects of these drugs on adjunctive drinking may not be similar to, or even related to, their actions on drinking induced by water deprivation or some other procedures. However, before any conclusions can be reached concerning relationships between the effects of amphetamines on adjunctive drinking and their effects on thirst mechanisms, it is necessary that experiments in which direct comparisons between adjunctive and other forms of drinking are made should be carried out. As yet, it seems that there have been no experiments in which the effects of amphetamines on adjunctive drinking have been directly compared, either in individual animals, or against appropriate controls, with drinking induced by other experimental procedures.

Attempts have been made to relate the effects of amphetamines on adjunctive drinking to the rate-dependent actions of these drugs. It is now well established that while amphetamines increase low rates of operant responding, similar doses have little effect on, or even decrease, higher response rates (Dews, 1958; Kelleher and Morse, 1968; Sanger and Blackman, 1976a). Since adjunctive licking is a pattern of behavior which generally occurs at a very high rate, it might be predicted that this behavior would be quite sensitive to rate-decreasing effects of amphetamines. The results of several of the experiments described in this section would seem to be consistent with this view, but experimenters who have explicitly analyzed their data with the possibility of rate dependence in mind have generally not been able to provide clear demonstrations of such effects.

McKearney (1973) recorded rates of licking during successive 18-sec segments of the fixed-interval 3-min schedule described previously, a technique similar to those often used to analyze rate-dependent drug effects on other responses (e.g., Leander and McMillan, 1974). Although this provided a range of rates of both operant and adjunctive licking, the effects of methamphetamine on these rates were not clearly dependent upon their control values.

The data obtained by Smith and Clark (1975) would also appear to be amenable to a rate-dependent analysis, since different overall rates of licking and wheel running were observed in the three components of the multiple differential reinforcement of low rate schedule used in their experiment. The highest rates of licking, which occurred in the differential reinforcement of low rate component having the shortest interresponse time requirement, were, in general, reduced to a greater extent than the lower rates which occurred in the components with longer interresponse time requirements. However, no consistent increases in rates of licking were observed even when this behavior was emitted at very low rates under control conditions. Smith and Clark concluded that their results did not demonstrate systematic rate-dependent effects of *d*-amphetamine.

Thus, the actions of amphetamines on adjunctive behavior have not yet been shown to depend upon control rates of responding. However, it can be argued that such a rate-dependent analysis cannot be appropriately applied to the consumatory (as opposed to operant) licking of rats. Rate dependence can be considered in terms of interresponse times, short interresponse times being lengthened by doses of amphetamines which concurrently shorten long interresponse times (Dews, 1958). Such an effect, of course, requires that the response under consideration can occur under control conditions with a wide range of interresponse times. Until recently, however, it was assumed that rats licked at a constant rate, and that this behavior was under the control of a neural "on–off" mechanism (Corbit and Luschei, 1969). Recently, Cone and her associates have questioned this assumption of invariance of lick rates (Cone, 1974), and have presented data showing that rates of licking are affected by a number of factors, including time of day (Cone and Cone, 1973), deprivation conditions (Cone *et al.*, 1975), and age (Wells and Cone, 1975). For the present discussion, however, the importance of these data lies in the fact that the variations in lick rates observed in these experiments (approximately 5–7.5 licks/sec) were relatively small. It therefore still seems reasonable to conclude that the consummatory licking of rats occurs either at a high rate or not at all (i.e., interresponse times are either very short or very long). If this is the case, then clearly discussion of drug effects on adjunctive licking in terms of rate dependence is not particularly meaningful since drug-induced changes in overall rates of licking could probably be due only to changes in *durations* of bursts of licking and not to effects on interresponse times within lick bursts.

Clearly, more systematic studies are required of the actions of amphetamines on adjunctive drinking in a variety of experimental situations, and these should also be related to studies involving drinking induced by other procedures. It would also seem desirable that other patterns of behavior which might also bc adjunctive in nature should be included in such experimental analyses. For example, it might be asked whether amphetamines would increase rates of adjunctive wheel running, since they stimulate locomotor activity in many other situations, or whether wheel running would be depressed in situations where adjunctive drinking is attenuated by these drugs. As yet, the only study which has attempted to investigate this problem (Smith and Clark, 1975) has not produced results clearly favoring either possibility.

2.2. Effects of Anxiolytics

Drugs used clinically for their anxiolytic properties (mainly benzodiazepines and barbiturates) have a variety of actions on the behavior of laboratory animals, and it has been demonstrated recently that adjunctive drinking is a pattern of behavior which is sensitive to their effects. Falk (1964) and Segal *et al.* (1965) found that pentobarbital in doses of 2 or 3 mg/kg depressed levels of adjunctive drinking in rats. In the former experiment the rats were required to press a bar for food on a variable-interval schedule and while this behavior was said to be relatively little affected by administration of pentobarbital the post-pellet drinking which occurred under control conditions was abolished by the drug. Similarly, Segal and her colleagues (Segal *et al.*, 1965) maintained that pentobarbital reduced levels of adjunctive licking, although in this experiment the decrease was quite small. More recently, Wuttke and Innis (1972), using the complex second-order schedule mentioned earlier, have also reported that a range of doses of pentobarbital (1–10 mg/kg) reduced levels of adjunctive licking in two rats. Bond (1974), however, using a fixed-time procedure, found that certain doses (10, 40 mg/kg) of another barbiturate, phenobarbital, slightly increased levels of adjunctive licking in rats, although with a higher dose (70 mg/kg) licking was decreased. It remains to be seen whether this facilitation of drinking is due to the particular procedure used in Bond's experiment or is related to the particular drug whose action he chose to investigate.

There thus appears only to have been one report of a reliable barbiturate-induced facilitation of adjunctive drinking. However, there are several recent reports of facilitated drinking following the administration of other anxiolytic drugs. Barrett and Weinberg (1975) trained squirrel monkeys to press a lever for food pellets on a fixed-interval 3-min schedule. Water bottles were also available and the monkeys were found to consume an average volume of 125 ml of water during a 150-min session while their usual home-cage water consumption during 21 hr was of the order of 30 ml. A range of doses of chlordiazepoxide was found to increase rates of lever pressing, an action often observed with this drug, and certain doses also increased the volume of fluid consumed during a session. Quite substantial increases in water intake were observed at some doses.

In another experiment from the same laboratory, Bacotti and Barrett (1976) maintained the bar-pressing behavior of four rats on a multiple fixed-ratio 80 fixed-interval 2-min schedule in which the component changed after each food pellet delivery. Water bottles were available and adjunctive licking developed, licking being more pronounced after the fixed-ratio reinforcer than after the fixed-interval reinforcer in three animals, while the converse was true for the fourth rat. Administration of chlordiazepoxide was again found to increase the volumes of water consumed during a session, but it was also found that the extent to which adjuctive licking was facilitated depended upon the schedule component in which licking occurred (Figure 5). The effects of the drug also varied between animals, but the authors of this report related the effect of the drug to the control rates of licking. Low control rates were apparently facilitated to a relatively greater extent by the drug than were higher rates. However, as discussed in the previous section, it is not clear whether such a rate-dependent analysis is appropriate for consumatory licking in rats.

McKearney (1973), however, also stressed the importance of control rate of licking in his experiment concerned with the action of drugs on adjunctive licking. In this study, the procedure of which has been described in the preceding section, chlordiazepoxide was found to facilitate *operant* licking maintained by a fixed-interval 3-min schedule but not to increase levels of adjunctive licking in the same rats (Figure 6). Since operant licking normally occurred at a much lower rate than

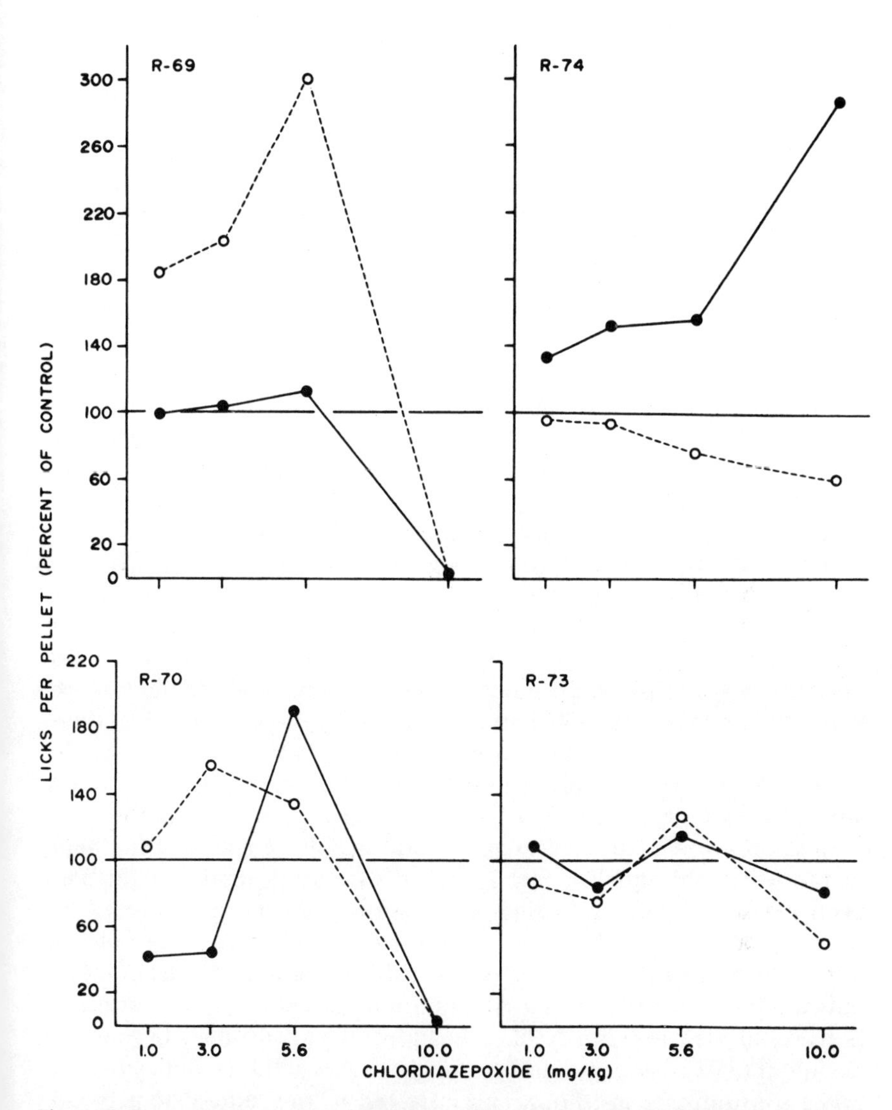

Figure 5. Dose–response curves showing the effects of chlordiazepoxide on rates of adjunctive licking in each of four individual rats maintained on a multiple schedule. The horizontal line at 100% indicates control performance. Open circles represent licks per pellet under a fixed-interval 2-min schedule component, and filled circles show licks per pellet under a fixed-ratio 80 component. [From Bacotti and Barrett (1976).]

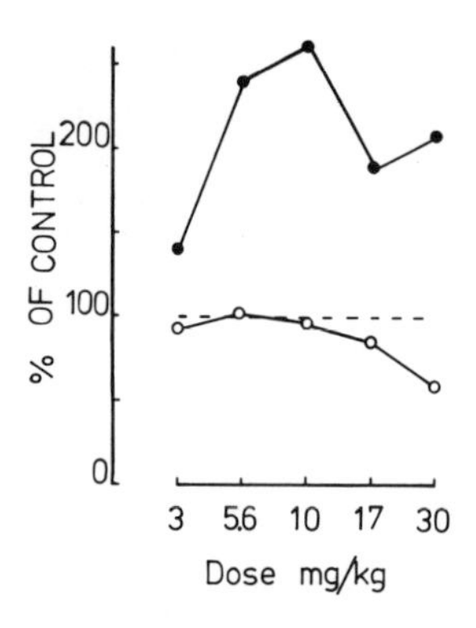

Figure 6. Dose–response curves showing the effects of chlordiazepoxide on schedule-induced (open circles) and operant (filled circles) licking in rats maintained by a fixed-interval 3-min schedule. Each point is the mean change from control values in nine rats. [Drawn from data in McKearney (1973).]

adjunctive licking, McKearney suggested that this result might be an example of rate dependence, lower rates of responding being relatively more sensitive to chlordiazepoxide-induced increases. However, the results of this experiment nevertheless appear a little inconsistent with other published research, since no facilitation of adjunctive licking was observed at any dose of chlordiazepoxide.

This apparently anomalous result, together with the atypical effects of methamphetamine observed in this experiment (see preceding section), may be related to a number of procedural matters which distinguish McKearney's experiment from the others described in this section. Perhaps the most obvious difference lies in the fact that topographically the operant behavior and the adjunctive behavior were the same in McKearney's study, and this may have prevented in some way any facilitation of adjunctive licking from being observed. Another possibility, however, is that chlordiazepoxide may have changed the manner in which the rats licked the tube so that water intake might have been facilitated without being accompanied by an increase in the number of adjunctive licks recorded. Clearly, McKearney was not able to present volumes of water consumed during adjunctive licking since only a single water tube was used and thus measures of water consumption would also necessarily have included that consumed by operant licking. There is some evidence, however, that adjunctive licking and water consumption are not always affected to the same extent by administration of anxiolytic drugs.

Sanger and Blackman (1976b) maintained adjunctive drinking in four rats during daily 1-hr sessions in which food pellets were delivered at 1-min intervals. When steady base lines of drinking had developed, the effects were studied of diazepam, which like chlordiazepoxide is a benzodiazepine, and of ripazepam, which has many pharmacological properties in common with chlordiazepoxide (Poschel *et al.*, 1974). Low doses of both drugs were found to produce small but reliable increases in the volumes of water consumed while the numbers of licks were not increased to the same extent. This effect is shown for diazepam in Figure 7, in which both measures are expressed as percentages of base-line values. While there are reports that under some conditions chlordiazepoxide can increase levels of adjunctive licking (Bacotti and Barrett, 1976; Sanger and Blackman, 1975), the results of this experiment nevertheless indicate that measures of both licking and water intake should be taken wherever possible, since drugs may affect the two measures differently. This difference presumably indicates that the drugs changed the way the rats licked the water spouts. Clearly, experiments including more sophisticated analyses of the patterns of adjunctive licking which occur after administration of anxiolytic drugs are required to cast light on this problem.

The studies described thus far in this section show that the benzodiazepines can produce reliable increases in adjunctive water drink-

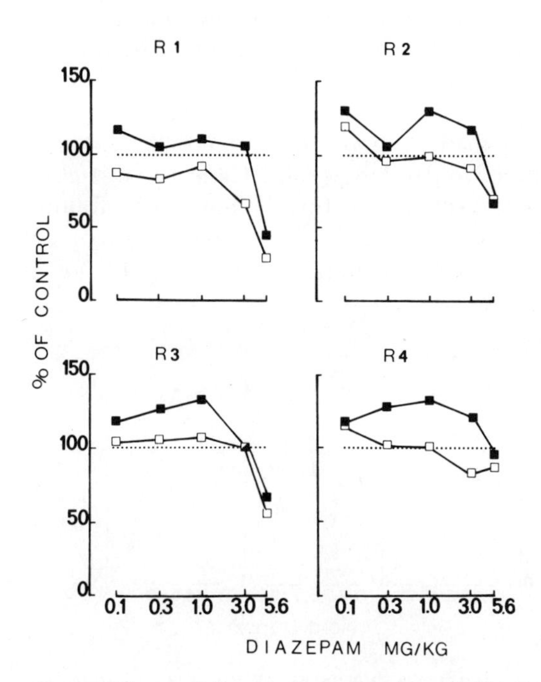

Figure 7. Effects of several doses of diazepam on adjunctive drinking in four individual rats maintained on a fixed-time 1-min schedule of food pellet delivery. Data are the percentage of control values for the volume of water consumed (filled squares) and for the number of licks (open squares) during a session. [Modified from Sanger and Blackman (1976b).].

ing in both rats and primates. Adjunctive drinking can be used to induce animals to ingest solutions of other fluids (Gilbert, Chapter 6), and such drinking has also been found to be facilitated by chlordiazepoxide. Barrett and Weinberg (1975) found that the adjunctive self-administration of ethanol in two monkeys was increased by chlordiazepoxide. Figure 8 shows the actions of this drug on adjunctive drinking of a solution of *d*-amphetamine in four rats, and again low doses of chlordiazepoxide increased the volumes of fluid consumed while higher doses decreased drinking.

Thus, benzodiazepines facilitate adjunctive drinking, although it is not clear whether similar effects can be reliably seen with barbiturates. Ethanol, a drug which is also sometimes classed as an anxiolytic and has been shown to exert effects similar to those of benzodiazepines and barbiturates in some experimental situations (e.g., Cook and Davidson, 1973), appears only to depress adjunctive drinking, however (Gilbert, 1973).

As with the amphetamines, it is reasonable to ask whether the actions of anxiolytic drugs on adjunctive drinking are related to effects on mechanisms of water intake. Under some circumstances, barbiturate administration can produce large increases in the deprivation-induced water intake of rats (Schmidt, 1969). However, when direct comparisons have been made between the effects of pentobarbital on home-cage and adjunctive drinking (Falk, 1964; Segal *et al.*, 1965), doses of the drug which facilitate the former have been found to depress the latter. On the other hand, it seems that doses of chlordiazepoxide which increase levels of adjunctive drinking do not always facilitate

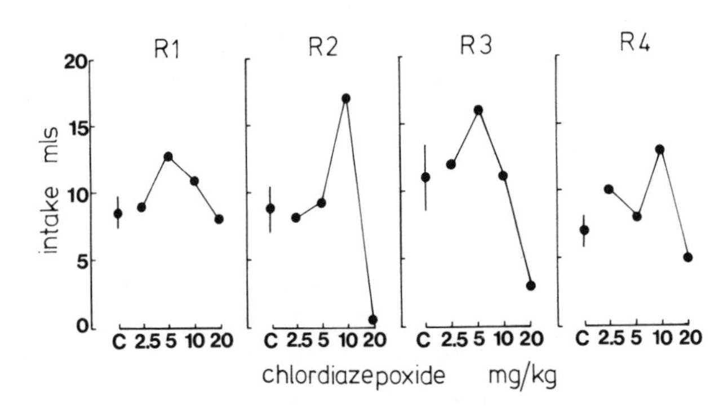

Figure 8. Dose–response curves showing the effects of chlordiazepoxide on the adjunctive drinking of a solution of *d*-amphetamine sulfate in water (0.01 mg/ml) in four individual rats. Drinking was induced by a fixed-time 1-min procedure. Each point shows the fluid intake during a 60-min session after injection of a dose of chlordiazepoxide. The points at C show the means plus or minus the standard deviations of fluid intakes on control sessions.

drinking induced by other means. There have been reports that chlordiazepoxide can increase the levels of water intake of rats deprived of water (Knowler and Ukena, 1973; Maickel and Maloney, 1973), although such an effect was not observed by Falk and Burnidge (1970). Bacotti and Barrett (1976) included a condition in their experiment during which rats were given the same number of food pellets in their home cages as they had normally earned during their daily sessions in the operant test chambers. The four rats which served as subjects in this experiment drank small quantities of water under this condition, and this drinking was not consistently facilitated by a dose of chlordiazepoxide (5.6 mg/kg), which had been found to produce quite substantial increases in adjunctive drinking in three of the four animals.

Anxiolytic drugs are sometimes considered to act on emotional or motivational states such as fear or anxiety which are hypothesized to underlie certain patterns of behavior. Since such emotional states have also been invoked in attempts to explain adjunctive behavior, it is instructive to consider the actions of these drugs on adjunctive drinking in the light of such views. It has been mentioned earlier that Falk's (1971) view that adjunctive behaviors occur under conditions where other behaviors are "thwarted" has been interpreted by some as an indication that adjunctive behavior is a manifestation of a state of frustration. It has also been suggested recently by Gray (1977), in a scholarly and wide-ranging review, that the actions of anxiolytic drugs can be related generally to effects on frustration, since these drugs are said to exert marked effects on behavior in situations involving nonreward or punishment. These two hypotheses, taken together, lead, of course, to the prediction that anxiolytic drugs should exert a profound and selective depressant action on adjunctive behavior. At least in the case of adjunctive drinking, the evidence certainly does not support this prediction, suggesting either that, as Falk (1973) has maintained, it is not useful to consider adjunctive behavior in terms of frustration, or, conversely, that anxiolytic drugs do not exert specific actions on the behavioral consequences of frustration.

Benzodiazepines are thus able to modify patterns of adjunctive drinking induced under a variety of circumstances and have generally been found to increase drinking. As with amphetamines, however, it is not clear whether other examples of adjunctive behavior would be affected in similar ways by these drugs. In the experiment carried out by Smith and Clark (1975), described earlier, in which drinking and wheel running were measured during bar pressing maintained by a multiple differential reinforcement of low rate schedule, chlordiazepoxide was not found to facilitate wheel running. Indeed, the rats with the higher rates of running showed a decrease in the frequency of this behavior at doses which had little effect on either licking or lever pressing. Unfortunately, little can be concluded from this result, however, since the drug effects on both licking and running were quite variable and licking was only facilitated by one dose of chlordiazpoxide in one animal.

It would be of considerable interest to determine whether chlordiazepoxide and other anxiolytic drugs would facilitate other behaviors which might occur in the place of adjunctive drinking. One of the earliest claims made for the benzodiazepines was that they exerted a pronounced and specific taming effect on the aggressive behavior of members of several species (Randall *et al.*, 1960). Such depressant effects on attack and fighting behaviors have been reported by experimenters using several procedures, including the shock-induced fighting technique described earlier (Christmas and Maxwell, 1970; Quenzer *et al.*, 1974). Manning and Elsmore (1972), however, found that chlordiazepoxide only reduced the frequency of shock-induced fighting at relatively high doses. As yet, the actions of anxiolytic drugs on attack induced by schedules of positive reinforcement appear not to have been studied, although Moore *et al.* (1976) have recently described an experiment concerned with the attack behavior of pigeons during the extinction components of a multiple schedule (multiple continuous reinforcement extinction). In this experiment two pigeons pecked vigorously at a mirror at the start of each extinction component, and a dose of chlordiazepoxide (5 mg/kg) was found to reduce this attack behavior without affecting rates of key pecking.

Clearly, there is considerable scope for studies of the effects of anxiolytic drugs on patterns of schedule-induced attack, and the results of such studies could profitably be compared with what is known about the effects of these drugs on adjunctive drinking and on aggressive behavior induced by other means. Care will be needed, however, in the interpretation of the results of such studies, since it is already known that the actions of anxiolytic drugs on aggressive behavior are dependent upon a variety of variables, including the dose and the experimental procedure used (DiMascio, 1973; Hoffmeister and Wuttke, 1969; Miczek, 1974).

2.3. Effects of Anticholinergic Drugs and the Central Control of Adjunctive Behavior

2.3.1. Anticholinergics and Drinking

The actions of drugs with anticholinergic properties on adjunctive drinking are of particular interest because the effects of these agents on other forms of drinking have been well studied. Both atropine and scopolamine, injected either systemically or intracranially, have been found to reduce drinking induced by a variety of procedures. These include water deprivation (Dissinger and Carr, 1971; Gerald and Maickel, 1969; Khavari and Russell, 1969; Stein, 1963), injection of sodium chloride solution (Block and Fisher, 1970; DeWied, 1966), and central injection of carbachol and other substances (Grossman, 1969).

These findings, together with the observation that acetylcholine and other cholinergic substances can induce drinking in rats (Grossman, 1960), led to the suggestion that, at least in rats, drinking may be under the control of central cholinergic neurons (Fisher and Coury, 1962; Grossman, 1969; Stein and Seifter, 1962). However, studies in which the effects of anticholinergic agents on drinking induced by different procedures have been compared have found that the effects of these drugs are, to some extent, dependent upon the methods used to induce drinking. It has been shown that doses of atropine which completely block carbachol-induced drinking have much smaller effects on drinking induced by deprivation or injection of sodium chloride or angiotensin (Blass and Chapman, 1971; Block and Fisher, 1970; Fitzsimons and Setler, 1971). Adams (1973) has also shown that doses of atropine which reduce water intake in water-deprived rats do not have a similar effect on the lower intakes of nondeprived animals, and Soulairac (1969) has reported that chronic administration of a dose of atropine may greatly increase the home-cage water intake of rats. Such results have led to the suggestion that several neural systems may be involved in the central control of water intake (Fisher, 1969).

Also confronting any attempts to explain the actions of anticholinergic drugs on drinking is the problem of the relative importance of central and peripheral mechanisms in their actions. Stein (1963) reported that while atropine and scopolamine markedly reduced levels of deprivation-induced drinking in rats, the quaternary derivatives of these drugs (atropine and scopolamine methyl nitrate), which are believed to penetrate to the brain in much smaller quantities, were considerably less effective. Some other researchers have obtained similar results (Adams, 1973; Houser, 1970), but others have found that the quaternary compounds are also effective in reducing levels of drinking (Gerald and Maickel, 1969; Khavari and Russell, 1969).

The mechanisms by which anticholinergic agents affect drinking are therefore far from being clearly known, although it has been well established that drinking induced by a variety of procedures is attenuated by these drugs. Adjunctive drinking has also been found to be blocked by the administration of anticholinergics.

Burks and Fisher (1970) induced adjunctive drinking in rats with a fixed-time 1-min procedure and found that drinking was reduced by several doses of atropine sulfate (3, 6, 9 mg/kg) and that methyl atropine had similar effects but was slightly less potent. Similar effects of scopolamine have also been reported by Sanger (1976) using a similar intermittent feeding procedure (Figure 9). In this experiment it was found that a dose of physostigmine, an anticholinesterase agent, did not consistently modify the action of scopolamine.

The use of fixed-time schedules in both these experiments rather than fixed-interval schedules with a specified operant is open to the problem that the drugs may have affected consumption of the food pellets. Anticholinergics are known to attenuate eating (Stein, 1963; Whitehouse *et al.*, 1964) and, of course, failure to eat intermittently delivered pellets would be expected to disrupt adjunctive drinking. Both Burks and Fisher, and Sanger, reported that all pellets were consumed, except at the highest doses of atropine and scopolamine, thus suggesting that, at the lower doses at least, the drugs were exerting direct actions on adjunctive drinking. Nevertheless, it would clearly be of great interest to know whether these drugs would exert similar effects on adjunctive behavior during schedules of response-dependent food delivery at doses which did not markedly disrupt the operant behavior.

As in the case of deprivation-induced drinking, the relative importance of central and peripheral actions of anticholinergics in determining their effects on adjunctive drinking is far from clear. As mentioned above, Burks and Fisher (1970) found that methyl atropine was slightly less active than atropine in attenuating adjunctive drinking, although it nevertheless produced large decreases in water intake. These researchers preferred to emphasize central actions of atropine, and the

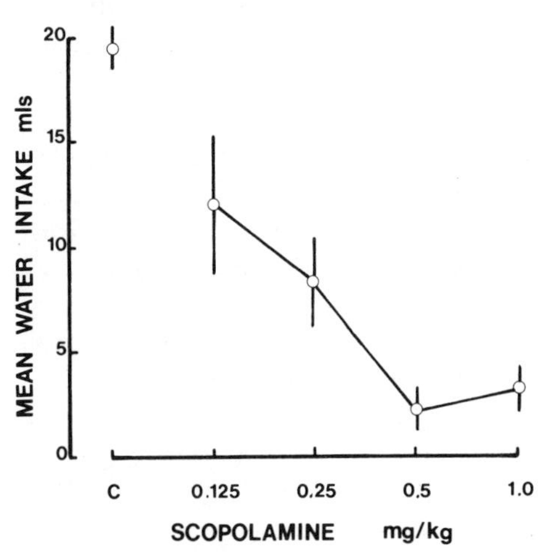

Figure 9. Dose–response curves showing the effects of scopolamine on adjunctive drinking. Nine rats were maintained on a fixed-time 1-min procedure, and each point shows the mean plus or minus the standard error of water intakes after a dose of scopolamine. The point at C shows the mean plus or minus the standard error of control sessions. [Modified from Sanger (1976).].

evidence presented in the next section certainly suggests that central effects of anticholinergics may attenuate adjunctive drinking. However, the effectiveness of methyl atropine in this experiment suggests that peripheral actions of anticholinergic drugs may also interfere with adjunctive drinking. One possibility is that actions on the salivary glands are involved, since both atropine and scopolamine are known to inhibit the flow of saliva. However, Keehn and Nagai (1969) and Keehn (1972) showed that trihexyphenidyl, a substance with anticholinergic properties but which was said to exert only mild effects on the secretion of saliva, also attenuated adjunctive drinking, although it apparently did not affect home-cage water consumption. Murphy and Brown (1975) have also reported that surgical desalivation of rats prevents neither the development nor the maintenance of adjunctive drinking.

2.3.2. Central Control of Adjunctive Drinking

Systemic administration of anticholinergic drugs can thus exert marked attenuating effects on adjunctive drinking, effects which are generally similar to the actions of these drugs on other forms of drinking. It has also been demonstrated by Carlisle (1973) that injections of atropine or methyl atropine into either the lateral hypothalamus or the lateral preoptic area of rats reduces adjunctive water consumption during performance on a food-reinforced variable-interval schedule. This result, together with the evidence that cholinergic mechanisms in the hypothalamus are involved in the control of water intake, leads to the possibility that this area of the brain may play an important role in the central control of adjunctive behavior. In fact, Wayner (1970, 1974) has developed an interesting and wide-ranging theory concerned with the involvement of the lateral hypothalamus in the control of adjunctive behavior, and it would seem appropriate to discuss the theory briefly at this point.

The basis of the theory is the apparent similarity between adjunctive behavior and behavior which can be elicited by electrical stimulation of the lateral hypothalamus (stimulus-bound behavior). Such electrical stimulation frequently elicits eating in rats, but other behaviors such as drinking and gnawing may also be induced (Wise, 1974). It seems that the particular pattern of behavior which emerges may depend upon aspects of the environment in which the subject is tested (Valenstein *et al.*, 1970). It is possible that the hypothalamus contains neural circuits specific for different patterns of behavior: eating circuit, drinking circuit, and so on, and that these circuits, being anatomically adjacent, could be activated by stimulation at the same or similar electrode sites. In contrast to this view, however, Wayner (1970) has suggested that the lateral hypothalamus may instead contain a nonspecific motor pathway which controls "general motor excitability." He has further postulated that intermittent reinforcement gives rise to activity in the lateral hypothalamus and that this manifests itself as adjunctive behavior, the particular behavior depending upon the environment.

As yet there appears to be relatively little empirical evidence directly relevant to this theoretical view of the physiological basis of adjunctive behavior. The attenuation of adjunctive drinking produced by anticholinergic drugs can be considered to be consistent with this theory, since they also block drinking induced by chemical and electrical stimulation of the hypothalamus. Also consistent are the reports that lesions of the hypothalamus attenuate adjunctive drinking (Falk, 1964; Kulkosky *et al.*, 1975). Wayner has suggested that a specific prediction from his theory is that electrical stimulation of the hypothalamus (which as well as inducing stimulus-bound behavior can be used as a reinforcer for operant responding) would serve in place of intermittent food delivery for inducing adjunctive drinking. Wayner *et al.* (1973b) maintained that they were able to demonstrate such an effect but only in one of four animals. Even in this animal, however, the drinking which occurred when fixed-interval lever pressing was maintained by electrical stimulation of the lateral hypothalamus was considerably less than drinking during a similar schedule of food reinforcement. Atrens (1973) has also reported excessive eating and drinking in rats whose responding was maintained on either fixed-interval or variable-interval schedules of electrical stimulation of the hypothalamus. These behaviors, however, differed from drinking induced by intermittent food delivery, since they showed a marked decline after a few sessions even though rates of bar pressing were reported to remain relatively stable. More recently, Cohen and Mendelson (1974) have described a well-designed study in which the lever pressing of five rats was maintained by variable-interval schedules for which either food or stimulation of the lateral hypothalamus was the reinforcing stimulus. Although all five animals developed postfood drinking, such drinking did not occur after the electrical stimulation.

Thus, at present, the experimental evidence does not appear to provide unequivocal support for a relationship between the lateral hypothalamus and adjunctive behavior as proposed by Wayner (1970, 1974). Quite apart from the empirical data, however, it is possible to question the assumptions on which the theory is based. The first major assumption is that the lateral hypothalamus is the site of a common motor pathway rather than neural circuits involved in the control of specific consumatory and other behaviors. Although there is certainly evidence that such specific circuits may not exist at this site (e.g., Valenstein *et al.*, 1970; Stricker, 1976), Wise (1974) has argued persuasively, in a major review of the relevant data, that patterns of stimulus-bound behavior are not produced by "non-specific motor excitation."

Second, the theory assumes, after Falk (1971), that adjunctive behavior can take a variety of forms, depending upon aspects of the environment in which the subject is tested. However, as noted before, evidence for the generality of adjunctive behavior is relatively sparse (Staddon, 1977). Thus, at present, support for an association between the lateral hypothalamus and adjunctive behavior, at least in the way suggested by Wayner, would appear to be far from strong. However, the theory is certainly ingenious in bringing together several areas of behavioral research and should serve to stimulate further research on the physiological basis of adjunctive behavior.

2.3.3. *Anticholinergic Drugs and Prandial Drinking*

It is of interest to compare the studies described in the preceding sections, in which anticholinergic drugs have been shown to attenuate adjunctive and other forms of drinking, with experiments which have made use of atropine to *induce* prandial drinking in rats. Prandial drinking is a pattern of food-associated drinking shown by desalivate rats consisting of frequent small drinks (Kissileff, 1969). Chapman and Epstein (1970) have shown that rats given small doses of atropine (0.25–1.0 mg/kg) also develop prandial drinking, and these researchers have suggested that adjunctive drinking may be a related form of behavior. If this is the case, however, it would seem difficult to explain why atropine should produce such marked decreases in adjunctive drinking, although it should be pointed out that the doses used by Burks and Fisher (1970) were considerably larger than those used by Chapman and Epstein to induce prandial drinking.

Rats require several sessions of atropine administration before prandial drinking develops (Chapman and Epstein, 1970) and it is, therefore, of interest to know what the effects of repeated administration of anticholinergic drugs on adjunctive drinking would be. Figure 10 shows data from an experiment which investigated this question. In this experiment four experimentally naive rats were allowed to develop adjunctive drinking on a fixed-time 1-min schedule and were subsequently given 10 daily injections of a dose of scopolamine (1.0 mg/kg) which had previously been found to markedly reduce drinking (Sanger, 1976). As expected, the drug initially suppressed levels of water intake, but over the 10 successive sessions of drug administration, this effect gradually declined. Although this effect could indicate the development of pharmacological tolerance to the action of scopola-

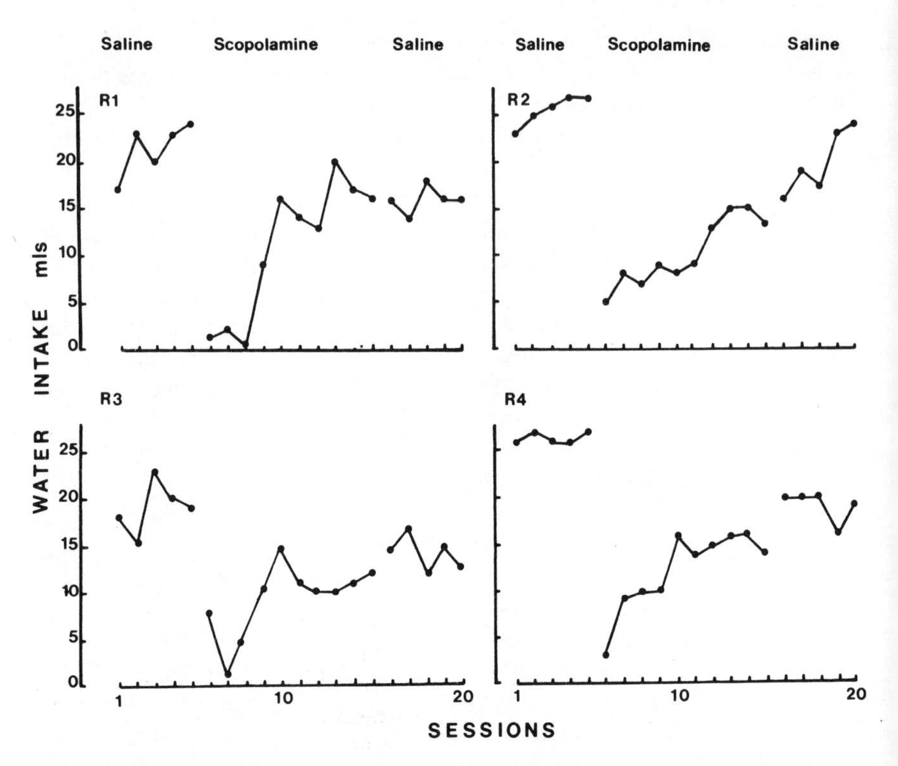

Figure 10. Effects of daily administration of scopolamine on adjunctive drinking in four individual rats. Before sessions 1–5 and 16–20, each animal was injected with physiological saline, while before sessions 6–15, each rat received an injection of scopalamine hydrobromide at a dose of 1 mg/kg.

mine, another possibility is that the dry mouth induced by the drug caused the rats to develop a second pattern of postpellet drinking. Perhaps consistent with this interpretation is the observation, shown in Figure 10, that when daily drug administration was discontinued, drinking did not immediately return to predrug levels.

It may therefore be possible to reconcile the results of research concerned with the effects of anticholinergics on adjunctive and prandial drinking. It is clear, however, that the actions of these drugs on drinking are influenced by a variety of variables, including the dose, the number of drug administrations, and the circumstances in which drinking is occurring. In the particular context of adjunctive drinking, further studies of long-term administration of these drugs, perhaps at relatively low doses, could be of special interest.

2.4. Effects of Other Drugs

The majority of the published research concerned with the effects of drugs on adjunctive behavior has involved drugs from the categories discussed in the preceding sections of this chapter. However, there have been a few studies concerned with other drugs, and these will be described in this section.

2.4.1. Neuroleptics

Smith and Clark (1975), in the experiment involving a multiple differential reinforcement of low rate schedule described earlier, studied the effects of several doses of chlorpromazine (0.25–2.0 mg/kg) on lever pressing, licking, and wheel running. Rates of lever pressing were consistently reduced by higher doses of this drug, but it had more variable effects on licking and wheel running. In two of the three rats, higher doses reduced rates of licking, but in the third animal the highest dose actually increased lick rates.

Bond (1974) found that doses of chlorpromazine of 2 and 3 mg/kg decreased water intake in rats during intermittent food delivery. Buxton (personal communication, 1976) has obtained similar results, but has also found that lower doses actually produce small increases in drinking. This result is interesting in view of the possibility that low doses of some phenothiazines may share some of the behavioral properties of anxiolytic drugs. Byrd (1974) found a reduction of drinking in two chimpanzees maintained on a schedule of food reinforcement. In this experiment the subjects were trained to obtain food by pressing a key on a schedule with alternating fixed-interval and fixed-ratio components, these components being separated by 1-min periods of time out from the schedule. Water was continuously available to the chimpanzees, and they were observed to drink frequently during the fixed-interval component, to a lesser extent during the time-out periods, and rarely during the fixed-ratio component. Chlorpromazine increased fixed-interval response rates at lower doses (0.1, 0.3 mg/kg) and reduced all response rates at the higher doses (1, 3 mg/kg). Water intake was unaffected by the lower doses but was markedly reduced by the doses which also reduced operant responding.

It is interesting to compare this result with that obtained in an earlier experiment by Byrd (1973), in which the effects of *d*-amphetamine on similar patterns of behavior in chimpanzees were investigated. In his experiment, *d*-amphetamine produced a dose-related decrease in water intake, while lower doses increased and higher doses decreased rates of key pressing. Taken together, these two experiments demonstrate that drugs can differentially affect operant responding and adjunctive drinking. Low does of *d*-amphetamine (which increased operant response rates) decreased water intake, while low doses of chlorpromazine also increased operant response rates but had no effect on drinking.

Haloperidol is a pharmacological agent with properties similar to those of chlorpromazine, and Keehn and his colleagues (Keehn *et al.*, 1976) have studied the actions of this drug on adjunctive drinking in rats. The animals were trained to lever-press for food reinforcement on a fixed-interval schedule with water available. Haloperidol was administered by the rather unconventional technique of adulterating the food pellets with the drug, and it was found that drinking was attenuated both when the drugged pellets were obtained during the sessions and when they were given before sessions. Since haloperidol was said to have been shown to interfere with drinking associated with angiotensin (Fitzsimons, 1972), the authors of this report suggested that the attenuation of adjunctive drinking may also have been due to interference with the "renin–angiotensin hormone system." However, there would seem to be little evidence for such a view, since no attempt was made to study angiotensin-induced drinking under similar experimental conditions. A more likely explanation would seem to be that haloperidol exerted a general depressant action as suggested by the reduced rates of operant lever pressing.

2.4.2. Tetrahydrocannabinol (THC)

Wayner and his colleagues (Wayner *et al.*, 1973b) have investigated the actions of Δ^9-THC on adjunctive drinking in relation to the proposed relationship between adjunctive behavior and the lateral hypothalamus, (Wayner, 1970; see earlier section). It was suggested by these workers that small doses of THC might act on the lateral hypothalamus to give rise to what they described as a nonspecific enhancement of excitability of the central nervous system. This would lead, it was hypothesized, to a facilitation of adjunctive behavior.

This hypothesis was put to the test in several rats in which adjunctive drinking developed on a fixed-interval schedule of food reinforcement. However, THC was administered during a part of the experiment when the animals had been returned to their free-feeding body weights and were thus displaying relatively low levels of lever pressing and drinking in the experimental chambers. Small doses of THC were found slightly to increase rates of lever pressing and licking, a result which was held to be consistent with a specific action of this drug on adjunctive behavior. However, the results of this experiment appeared to be rather variable, and since no attempt was apparently made to study the effects of THC on established adjunctive drinking, conclusions about specific effects on adjunctive behavior seem premature.

A more systematic investigation of the actions of Δ^9-THC on adjunctive behavior has been carried out by Cherek and his associates (Cherek *et al.*, 1972; Cherek and Thompson, 1973), who studied the effects of this drug on schedule-induced attack behavior in pigeons. In these experiments, the key pecking of pigeons was maintained on a response-initiated fixed-interval schedule (Cherek *et al.*, 1973). Also available was a transparent walled chamber containing a target pigeon. The experimenters noted consistent patterns of attacking the chamber containing the second bird or pecking at a second, target key which provided access to the chamber, generally shortly after food reinforcement. Several doses of THC (0.125–1.0 mg/kg) were found to produce dose-related decreases in pecking on both the fixed-interval and target keys and of attacking the chamber containing the target bird. However, even when response rates on the fixed-interval and target keys were equated by adding a differential reinforcement of low rate contingency to the fixed-interval schedule, the drug produced greater decreases in responses on the target key.

The authors of these reports pointed out that the effects of THC could represent either a specific action on adjunctive behavior or a specific effect on aggression, and they considered that the latter possibility was more likely. However, Abel (1975) has pointed out that the effects of THC depend upon the procedure used to induce aggressive behavior. For example, Manning and Elsmore (1972), using a shock-induced fighting procedure with rats, found that Δ^9-THC over a wide range of doses had no effect on fighting. It is also not possible to say whether the effects of THC observed by Cherek *et al.* (1972, 1973) are related to actions on adjunctive behavior in general, since no studies have looked at effects of this drug on other forms of adjunctive behavior maintained by a similar procedure. Clearly, there is scope for considerably more systematic research concerned with the actions of THC on adjunctive behavior.

3. Conclusions

In the preceding sections of this chapter, we have attempted to describe the patterns of behavior which Falk (1971) has called "adjunctive," and we have mentioned some of the many variables which have been shown to be important in the development and maintenance of such behavior. We have also described in some detail much of the pharmacological research which has been carried out with examples of this behavior. It has already been pointed out that studies concerned with the actions of drugs on adjunctive behavior may prove to be of considerable importance in behavioral pharmacology. They may help to indicate the extent to which general principles of drug action derived from studies of operant behavior can be extended to behavior maintained by other means. They may also provide a greater understanding of the nature of adjunctive behavior. We are now in a position to consider the extent to which these aims have been achieved, and how far the general questions asked in the earlier sections of the chapter have been answered by the published research. It will have become apparent that the majority of the pharmacological studies which have been published to date have been concerned with adjunctive drinking. This is understandable, since a great deal more is known about drinking than about other patterns of behavior which may also be adjunctive. Indeed, although Falk (1971) has argued persuasively that the concept of a general class of adjunctive behavior is a useful one, relatively little is known about the degree of similarity between patterns of adjunctive drinking and other behavior such as wheel running and attack which have been reported to occur under generally similar conditions.

As described earlier, Staddon (1977) has found it convenient to place such behaviors in several categories. Pharmacological research may be particularly valuable here, since studies of the effects of a drug on a number of adjunctive behaviors may help to define the similarities or difference between these behaviors. However, such comparisons cannot yet be made. Although a good deal is known of the effects of some drugs (e.g., amphetamines and chlordiazepoxide) on adjunctive drinking, the actions of these agents on other examples of adjunctive behavior have yet to be thoroughly investigated. In contrast, the experiments of Cherek and his colleagues (Cherek *et al.*, 1972; Cherek and Thompson, 1973) have established the actions of THC on schedule-induced attack in pigeons, but little is known of the effects of this drug on adjunctive drinking.

The research described in this chapter shows quite clearly that adjunctive behavior, particularly schedule-induced drinking, may be very sensitive to the effects of many drugs. It is also clear that such drug effects may be quite different from the actions of the drugs on concurrently occurring patterns of operant behavior. For instance, *d*-amphetamine may increase rates of operant responding while decreasing the amount of adjunctive drinking (Wayner *et al.*, 1973a). However, it is not clear at present to what extent the effects of drugs on adjunctive behavior are governed by the same principles governing drug action on operant behavior. It is well established that the actions of amphetamines on operant behavior are rate-dependent, but it is not clear whether it would be possible for these drugs to affect adjunctive licking in a rate-dependent way. Schedule-induced attack, however, may not be under the same physiological constraints as is the licking of rats, and thus it may be possible to manipulate rates of attack behavior and compare the effects of drugs on these rates with their effects on similar rates of operant responding. As has been described earlier, Cherek and Thompson (1973) found that THC exerted a greater depressant effect on key pecking that produced access to a chamber containing a second pigeon than on similar rates of pecking maintained by food. Such procedures could usefully be applied to studies of other drugs.

Many other questions concerning similarities between the actions of drugs on operant and adjunctive behavior must also remain unanswered for the present. It is for future research to determine, for instance, the extent to which adjunctive behavior can be brought under the control of exteroceptive stimuli and whether such stimulus control can affect the actions of drugs. Another interesting question, which might be raised, is whether anxiolytic drugs can attenuate the effects of punishment procedures on adjunctive behavior as they do with operant behavior.

Since much of the pharmacological research involving adjunctive behavior has been concerned with the effects of drugs on drinking, there has been considerable emphasis placed, in the present chapter, on comparisons between drug effects on drinking induced by various procedures. There are certainly some similarities between the actions of drugs on adjunctive and other forms of drinking; for instance, amphetamines and anticholinergics have been shown to attenuate adjunctive, deprivation-induced, and other forms of drinking. However, it is also clear that the degree to which drinking is attenuated depends on the circumstances under which the behavior occurs. Most of the comparisons made in this chapter have necessarily involved consideration of different experiments in which many other factors, as well as the particular form of drinking, may differ. As an example of the type of experiment which greatly facilitates such comparisons, we may consider a study by Singer and his associates (Singer *et al.*, 1975).

The purpose of this experiment was to study the effects of norepinephrine applied to the lateral hypothalamus on adjunctive and other types of drinking. Rats were first reduced in body weight by restricting access to food but not water. They were then given daily sessions during which they were fed food pellets in a bowl with water available. A high dose of norepinephrine (648×10^{-4}M) was found to attenuate the food-associated drinking which occurred in this condition. In the second stage of the experiment, food pellets were obtained by the rats on a fixed-interval schedule, and the adjunctive drinking which developed was unaffected by any dose of norepinephrine. Finally, the rats were returned to free feeding and the effects of norepinephrine on home-cage water intake were measured and found to be nonexistent. Interpretation of the results of this experiment is a little difficult, since only one dose of norepinephrine had any effect, and the lack of effect in the second and third stages of the experiment could conceivably have been due to the development of tolerance. However, the importance of this study lies in its design, which involved the investigation of the actions of a drug on patterns of drinking under three sets of conditions in the same animals. It is to be hoped that other studies will be carried out in the near future, in which animals will be subjected to a number of experimental conditions and the effects of drugs on drinking in these different conditions studied.

We must conclude this chapter, then, by looking to the future. There remains a pressing need for systematic investigations of the effects of drugs on adjunctive behavior. In particular, more attention should be paid to patterns of adjunctive or interim behavior other than schedule-induced licking. In general, schedule-induced behavior provides a challenge to traditional principles in the experimental analysis of behavior. We believe that behavioral pharmacologists still have much to gain by focusing more of their attention on these often overlooked but potentially important effects of intermittent reinforcement.

Acknowledgment

This chapter was prepared while both authors were at the Department of Psychology at the University of Birmingham. D. J. Sanger was supported by an I.C.I. Research Fellowship.

4. References

Abel, E. L., 1975, Cannabis and aggression in animals, *Behav. Biol.* **14:**1–20.

Adams, P. M., 1973, The effects of cholinolytic drugs and cholinesterase blockade on deprivation based activity and appetitive behavior, *Neuropharmacology* **12:**825–833.

Allen, J. D., Porter, J. H., and Arazie, R., 1975, Schedule-induced drinking as a function of percentage reinforcement, *J. Exp. Anal. Behav.* **23:**223–232.

Amsel, A., 1962, Frustrative non-reward in partial reinforcement and discrimination learning; some recent history and a theoretical extension, *Psychol. Rev.* **69:**306–328.

Andersson, B., and Larsson, S., 1956, Water and food intake and the inhibitory effect of amphetamine on drinking and eating before and after "prefrontal lobotomy" in dogs, *Acta. Physiol. Scand.* **38:**22–30.

Atrens, D. M., 1973, Schedule-induced polydipsia and polyphagia in non-deprived rats reinforced by intracranial stimulation, *Learn. Motiv.* **4:**320–326.

Azrin, N. H., Hutchinson, R. R., and Hake, D. F., 1966, Extinction-induced aggression, *J. Exp. Anal. Behav.* **9:**191–204.

Bacotti, A. V., and Barrett, J. E., 1976, Effect of chlordiazepoxide on schedule-controlled responding and schedule-induced drinking, *Pharmacol. Biochem. Behav.* **4:**299–304.

Barrett, J. E., and Weinberg, E. S., 1975, Effects of chlordiazepoxide on schedule-induced water and alcohol consumption in the squirrel monkey, *Psychopharmacologia* **40:**319–328.

Blackman, D. E., 1977, Interactions between classical and operant conditioning, *in: Handbook of Operant Behavior* (W. K. Honig and J. E. R. Staddon, eds.), pp. 340–363, Prentice-Hall, Englewood Cliffs, N.J.

Blass, E. M., and Chapman, H. W., 1971, An evaluation of the contribution of cholinergic mechanisms to thirst, *Physiol. Behav.* **7:**679–686.

Block, M. L., and Fisher, A. E., 1970, Anticholinergic central blockade of salt-aroused and deprivation-induced drinking, *Physiol. Behav.* **5:**525–527.

Bond, N. W., 1973, Schedule-induced polydipsia as a function of the consummatory rate, *Psychol. Rec.* **23:**377–382.

Bond, N. W., 1974, Some comparisons of operant behaviour and schedule-induced polydipsia; unpublished doctoral dissertation, University of Nottingham.

Bond, N. W., and Blackman, D. E., 1975, Conditioned suppression of schedule-induced polydipsia in rats, *Psychol. Rep.* **37:**63–68.

Bond, N. W., Blackman, D. E., and Scruton, P., 1973, Suppression of operant behavior and schedule-induced licking in rats, *J. Exp. Anal. Behav.* **20:**375–383.

Burks, C. D., 1970, Schedule-induced polydipsia: are response-dependent schedules a limiting condition? *J. Exp. Anal. Behav.* **13:**351–358.

Burks, C. D., and Fisher, A. E., 1970, Anticholinergic blockade of schedule-induced polydipsia, *Physiol. Behav.* **5:**635–640.

Byrd, L. D., 1973, Effects of *d*-amphetamine on schedule-controlled key pressing and drinking in the chimpanzee, *J. Pharmacol. Exp. Ther.* **185:**633–641.

Byrd, L. D., 1974, Modification of the effects of chlorpromazine on behavior in the chimpanzee, *J. Pharmacol. Exp. Ther.* **189:**24–32.

Carlisle, H. J., 1971, Fixed-ratio polydipsia: thermal effects of drinking, pausing, and responding, *J. Comp. Physiol. Psychol.* **75:**10–22.

Carlisle, H. J., 1973, Schedule-induced polydipsia: blockade by intrahypothalamic atropine, *Physiol. Behav.* **11:**139–143.

Chapman, H. W., and Epstein, A. N., 1970, Prandial drinking induced by atropine, *Physiol. Behav.* **5:**549–554.

Chapman, H. W., and Richardson, H. M., 1974, The role of systemic hydration in the acquisition of schedule-induced polydipsia by rats, *Behav. Biol.* **12:**501–508.

Cherek, D. R., and Pickens, R., 1970, Schedule-induced aggression as a function of fixed-ratio value, *J. Exp. Anal. Behav.* **14:**309–311.

Cherek, D. R., and Thompson, T., 1973, Effects of Δ^1-tetrahydrocannabinol on schedule-induced aggression in pigeons, *Pharmacol. Biochem. Behav.* **1:**493–500.

Cherek, D. R., Thompson, T., and Heistad, G. T., 1972, Effects of Δ^1-tetrahydrocannabinol and food deprivation level on responding maintained by the opportunity to attack, *Physiol. Behav.* **9:**795–800.

Cherek, D. R., Thompson, T., and Heistad, G. T., 1973, Responding maintained by the opportunity to attack during an interval food reinforcement schedule, *J. Exp. Anal. Behav.* **19:**113–124.

Christmas, A. J., and Maxwell, D. R., 1970, A comparison of the effects of some benzodiazepines and other drugs on aggressive and exploratory behaviour in mice and rats, *Neuropharmacology* **9:**17–29.

Clark, F. C., 1962, Some observations on the adventitious reinforcement of drinking under food reinforcement, *J. Exp. Anal. Behav.* **5:**61–63.

Cohen, I. L., and Mendelson, J., 1974, Schedule-induced drinking with food, but not ICS, reinforcement, *Behav. Biol.* **12:**21–29.

Cohen, P. S., and Looney, T. A., 1973, Schedule-induced mirror responding in the pigeon, *J. Exp. Anal. Behav.* **19:**395–408.

Cone, A. L., and Cone, D. M., 1973, Variability in the burst lick rates of albino rats as a function of sex, time of day, and exposure to the test situation, *Bull. Psychon. Soc.* **2:**283–284.

Cone, A. L., Wells, R., Goodson, L., and Cone, D. M., 1975, Changing lick rate of rats by manipulating deprivation and type of solution, *Psychol. Rec.* **25:**343–347.

Cone, D. M., 1974, Do mammals lick at a constant rate? A critical review of the literature, *Psychol. Rec.* **24:**353–364.

Cook, L., and Davidson, A. B., 1973, Effects of behaviorally active drugs in a conflict–punishment procedure in rats, *in: The Benzodiazepines* (S. Garattini, E. Mussini, and L. O. Randall, eds.), pp. 327–345, Raven Press, New York.

Cope, C. L., Sanger, D. J., and Blackman, D. E., 1976, Intragastric water and the acquisition of schedule-induced drinking, *Behav. Biol.* **17:**267–270.

Corbit, J. D., and Luschei, E. S., 1969, Invariance of the rat's rate of drinking, *J. Comp. Physiol. Psychol.* **69:**119–125.

Corfield-Sumner, P. K., Blackman, D. E., and Stainer, G., 1977, Polydipsia induced in rats by second-order schedules, *J. Exp. Anal. Behav.* **27:**265–273.

Denny, M. R., and Ratner, S. G., 1970, *Comparative Psychology,* Dorsey, Homewood, Ill.

DeWied, D., 1966, Effect of autonomic blocking agents and structurally related substances on the "salt arousal of drinking," *Physiol. Behav.* **1:**193–197.

Dews, P. B., 1958, Analysis of the effects of pharmacological agents in behavioral terms, *Fed. Proc.* **17:**1024–1030.

DiMascio, A., 1973, The effects of benzodiazepines on aggression: reduced or increased? *Psychopharmacologia* **39:**95–102.

Dissinger, M. L., and Carr, W. J., 1971, Effects of tertiary vs. quaternary scopolamine on water and air drinking in rats, *Psychon. Sci.* **25:**17–18.

Dove, L. D., 1976, Relation between level of food deprivation and rate of schedule-induced attack, *J. Exp. Anal. Behav.* **25:**63–68.

Epstein, A. N., 1959, Suppression of eating and drinking by amphetamine and other drugs in normal and hyperphagic rats, *J. Comp. Physiol. Psychol.* **52:**37–45.

Falk, J. L., 1961a, Production of polydipsia in normal rats by an intermittent food schedule, *Science* **133:**195–196.

Falk, J. L., 1961b, The behavioral regulation of water–electrolyte balance, *in: Nebraska Symposium on Motivation* (M. R. Jones, ed.), pp. 1–33, University of Nebraska Press, Lincoln, Neb.

Falk, J. L., 1964, Studies on schedule-induced polydipsia, *in: Thirst: First International Symposium on Thirst in the Regulation of Body Water* (M. J. Wayner, ed.), pp. 95–113, Pergamon Press, New York.

Falk, J. L., 1966, Analysis of water and NaCl solution acceptance by schedule-induced polydipsia, *J. Exp. Anal. Behav.* **9:**111–118.

Falk, J. L., 1967, Control of schedule-induced polydipsia: type, size, and spacing of meals, *J. Exp. Anal. Behav.* **10:**199–206.

Falk, J. L., 1969, Conditions producing psychogenic polydipsia in animals, *Ann. N.Y. Acad. Sci.* **157:**569–589.

Falk, J. L., 1971, The nature and determinants of adjunctive behavior, *Physiol. Behav.* **6:**577–588.

Falk, J. L., 1973, Invited comment, *in: The Neurospsychology of Thirst* (A. N. Epstein, H. R. Kissileff, and E. Stellar, eds.), pp. 225–228, V. H. Winston, Washington, D.C.

Falk, J. L., and Burnidge, G. K., 1970, Fluid intake and punishment attenuating drugs, *Physiol. Behav.* **5:**199–202.

Falk, J. L., Samson, H. H., and Winger, G., 1972, Behavioral maintenance of high concentrations of blood ethanol and physical dependence in the rat, *Science* **177:**811–813.

Fisher, A. E., 1969, The role of limbic structures in the central regulation of feeding and drinking behavior, *Ann. N.Y. Acad. Sci.* **157:**894–901.

Fisher, A. E., and Coury, J. N., 1962, Cholinergic tracing of a central neural circuit underlying the thirst drive, *Science* **138:**691–693.

Fitzsimons, J. T., 1972, Thirst, *Physiol. Rev.* **52:**468–561.

Fitzsimons, J. T., and Setler, P. E., 1971, Catecholaminergic mechanisms in angiotensin-induced drinking, *J. Physiol. (London)* **218:**43–44.

Flory, R. K., 1969, Attack behavior as a function of minimum inter-food interval, *J. Exp. Anal. Behav.* **12:**825–828.

Flory, R. K., and Lickfett, G. G., 1974, Effects of lick-contingent timeout on schedule-induced polydipsia, *J. Exp. Anal. Behav.* **21:**45–55.

Freed, E. X., Hymowitz, N., and Fazzaro, J. A., 1974, Effects of response-independent electric shock on schedule-induced alcohol and water intake, *Psychol. Rep.* **34:**63–71.

Galantowicz, E. P., and King, G. D., 1975, The effect of three levels of lick-contingent footshock on schedule-induced polydipsia, *Bull. Psychon. Soc.* **5:**113–116.

Gentry, W. D., 1968, Fixed-ratio schedule-induced aggression, *J. Exp. Anal. Behav.* **11:**813–817.

Gentry, W. D., and Schaeffer, R. W., 1969, The effect of FR response requirement on aggressive behavior in rats, *Psychon. Sci.* **14:**236–238.

Gerald, M. C., and Maickel, R. P., 1969, Evidence for peripheral cholinergic components of thirst-induced water consumption, *Int. J. Neuropharmacol.* **8:**337–346.

Gilbert, R. M., 1973, Effects of ethanol on adjunctive drinking and bar pressing under various schedules of food reinforcement, *Bull. Psychon. Soc.* **1:**161–164.

Gilbert, R. M., 1974, Ubiquity of schedule-induced polydipsia, *J. Exp. Anal. Behav.* **21:**277–284.

Glick, S. D., and Greenstein, S., 1973, Pharmacological inhibition of eating, drinking, and prandial drinking, *Behav. Biol.* **8:**55–61.

Glick, S. D., and Muller, R. U., 1971, Paradoxical effects of low doses of *d*-amphetamine in rats, *Psychopharmacologia* **22:**396–402.

Gray, J. A., 1977, Drug effects on fear and frustration: possible limbic site of action of minor tranquilizers, *in: Handbook of Psychopharmacology* (L. L. Iversen, S. D. Iversen, and S. H. Snyder, eds.), Vol. 8, pp. 433–530, Plenum Press, New York.

Grossman, S. P., 1960, Eating or drinking elicited by direct adrenergic or cholinergic stimulation of hypothalamus, *Science* **132:**301–302.

Grossman, S. P., 1969, A neuropharmacological analysis of hypothalamic and extrahypothalamic mechanisms concerned with the regulation of food and water intake, *Ann. N.Y. Acad. Sci.* **157:**902–912.

Hawkins, T. D., Schrot, J. F., Githens, S. H., and Everett, P. B., 1972, Schedule-induced polydipsia: an analysis of water and alcohol ingestion, *in: Schedule Effects: Drugs, Drinking and Aggression* (R. M. Gilbert and J. D. Keehn, eds.), pp. 95–128, University of Toronto Press, Toronto.

Hearst, E., and Jenkins, H. M., 1974, *Sign-Tracking: The Stimulus–Reinforcer Relation and Directed Action,* Psychonomic Society, Austin, Texas.

Hitzig, E. W., 1968, Schedule-induced polydipsia: a reinforcement analysis; unpublished doctoral dissertation, Florida State University, cited by Hawkins et al., 1972.
Hoffmeister, F., and Wuttke, W., 1969, On the actions of psychotropic drugs on the attack and aggressive–defensive behaviour of mice and cats, *in: Aggressive Behaviour* (S. Garattini and E. B. Sigg, eds.), pp. 273–280, Excerpta Medica Foundation, Amsterdam.
Houser, V. P., 1970, The effects of adrenergic and cholinergic agents upon eating and drinking in deprived rats, *Psychon. Sci.* **20:**153–155.
Hutchinson, R. R., Azrin, N. H., and Hunt, G. M., 1968, Attack produced by intermittent reinforcement of a concurrent operant response, *J. Exp. Anal. Behav.* **11:**489–495.
Hymowitz, N., 1971, Schedule-induced polydipsia and aggression in rats, *Psychon. Sci.* **23:**226–228.
Hymowitz, N., 1976, Effects of electric-shock delivery on schedule-induced water intake: delay of shock, shock intensity, and body-weight loss, *J. Exp. Anal. Behav.* **26:**269–280.
Hymowitz, N., and Freed, E. X., 1974, Effects of response-dependent and independent electric shock on schedule-induced polydipsia, *J. Exp. Anal. Behav.* **22:**207–213.
Keehn, J. D., 1972, Effects of trihexyphenidyl on schedule-induced alcohol drinking by rats, *Psychon. Sci.* **29:**20–22.
Keehn, J. D., and Nagai, M., 1969, Attenuation of schedule-induced polydipsia by trihexyphenidyl, *Psychon. Sci.* **15:**61–62.
Keehn, J. D., Coulson, G. E., and Klieb, J., 1976, Effects of haloperidol on schedule-induced polydipsia, *J. Exp. Anal. Behav.* **25:**105–112.
Kelleher, R. T., and Morse, W. H., 1968, Determinants of the specificity of behavioral effects of drugs, *Ergeb. Physiol. Biol. Chem. Exp. Pharmakol.* **60:**1–56.
Khavari, K. A., and Russell, R. W., 1969, Depression of drinking by tertiary and quaternary cholinolytic drugs, *Physiol. Behav.* **4:**461–463.
King, G. D., 1974a, Wheel running in the rat induced by a fixed-time presentation of water, *Anim. Learn. Behav.* **2:**325–328.
King, G. D., 1974b, The enhancement of schedule-induced polydipsia by preschedule noncontingent shock, *Bull. Psychon. Soc.* **3:**46–48.
King. G. D., 1975, The enhancement of schedule-induced polydipsia by FR-20 and FR-80 lick-contingent shock, *Bull. Psychon. Soc.* **6:**542–544.
King, G. D., and Sides, J. P., 1975, Punishment of schedule-induced wheel running, *Bull. Psychon. Soc.* **5:**323–324.
Kissileff, H. R., 1969, Food-associated drinking in the rat, *J. Comp. Physiol. Psychol.* **67:**284–300.
Kissileff, H. R., 1973, Nonhomeostatic controls of drinking, *in: The Neuropsychology of Thirst* (A. N. Epstein, H. R. Kissileff, and E. Stellar, eds), pp. 163–198, V. H. Winston, Washington, D.C.
Knowler, W. C., and Ukena, T. E., 1973, The effects of chlorpromazine, pentobarbital, chlordiazepoxide, and *d*-amphetamine on rates of licking in the rat, *J. Pharmacol. Exp. Ther.* **184:**385–397.
Knutson, J. F., 1970, Aggression during the fixed-ratio and extinction components of a multiple schedule of reinforcement, *J. Exp. Anal. Behav.* **13:**221–231.
Knutson, J. F., and Kleinknecht, R. A., 1970, Attack during differential reinforcement of low rate of responding, *Psychon. Sci.* **19:**289–290.
Knutson, J. F., and Schrader, S. P., 1975, A concurrent assessment of schedule-induced aggression and schedule-induced polydipsia in the rat, *Anim. Learn. Behav.* **3:**16–20.
Kulkosky, P. J., Moe, K. E., Woods, S. C., and Riley, A. L., 1975, Effect of ventromedial hypothalamic lesions on schedule-induced polydipsia, *Physiol. Psychol.* **3:**172–174.
Leander, J. D., and McMillan, D. E., 1974, Rate dependent effects of drugs. I. Compari-

son of d-amphetamine, pentobarbital and chlorpromazine on multiple and mixed schedules. *J. Pharmacol. Exp. Ther.* **188:**726–739.

Levitsky, D., and Collier, G., 1968, Schedule-induced wheel running, *Physiol. Behav.* **3:**571–573.

Maickel, R. P., and Maloney, G. J., 1973, Effects of various depressant drugs on deprivation-induced water consumption, *Neuropharmacology* **12:**777–782.

Manning, F. T., and Elsmore, T. F., 1972, Shock-elicited fighting and delta-9-tetrahydrocannabinol, *Psychopharmacologia* **25:**218–228.

McFarland, D. J., 1966, On the causal and functional significance of displacement activities, *Z. Tierpsychol.* **23:**217–235.

McKearney, J. W., 1973, Effects of methamphetamine and chlordiazepoxide on schedule controlled and adjunctive licking in the rat, *Psychopharmacologia* **30:**375–384.

Mendelson, J., and Chillag, D., 1970, Schedule-induced air licking in rats, *Physiol. Behav.* **5:**535–537.

Miczek, K. A., 1974, Intraspecies aggression in rats: effects of *d*-amphetamine and chlordiazepoxide, *Psychopharmacologia* **39:**275–301.

Mogenson, G. J., 1968, Effects of amphetamine on self-stimulation and induced drinking, *Physiol. Behav.* **3:**133–136.

Moore, M. S., Tychsen, R. L., and Thompson, D. M., 1976, Extinction-induced mirror responding as a baseline for studying drug effects on aggression, *Pharmacol. Biochem. Behav.* **4:**99–102.

Murphy, L. R., and Brown, T. S., 1975, Effects of desalivation on schedule-induced polydipsia in the rat, *J. Exp. Psychol. Anim. Behav. Proc.* **104:**309–317.

Porter, J. H., and Kenshalo, D. R., 1974, Schedule-induced drinking following ommission of reinforcement in the rhesus monkey, *Physiol. Behav.* **12:**1075–1077.

Porter, J. H., Arazie, R., Holbrook, J. W., Cheek, M. S., and Allen, J. D., 1975, Effects of variable and fixed second-order schedules on schedule-induced polydipsia in the rat, *Physiol. Behav.* **14:**143–149.

Poschel, B. P. H., McCarthy, D. A., Chen, G., and Ensor, C. R., 1974, Pyrazapon (Cl-683): a new antianxiety agent, *Psychopharmacologia* **35:**257–271.

Quenzer, L. F., Feldman, R. S., and Moore, J. W., 1974, Toward a mechanism of the anti-aggression effects of chlordiazepoxide in rats, *Psychopharmacologia* **34:**81–94.

Randall, L. O., Schallek, W., Heise, G. A., Keith, E. F., and Bagdon, R. E., 1960, The psychosedative properties of methaminodiazepoxide, *J. Pharmacol. Exp. Ther.* **129:**163–171.

Randrup, A., and Munkvad, I., 1974, Pharmacology and physiology of stereotyped behaviour, *J. Psychiat. Res.* **11:**1–10.

Rosenblith, J. Z., 1970, Polydipsia induced in the rat by a second-order schedule, *J. Exp. Anal. Behav.* **14:**139–144.

Sanger, D. J., 1976, Scopolamine and adjunctive drinking in rats, *Psychopharmacology* **48:**307–309.

Sanger, D. J., and Blackman, D. E., 1975, The effects of chlordiazepoxide on the development of adjunctive drinking in rats, *Quart. J. Exp. Psychol.* **27:**499–505.

Sanger, D. J., and Blackman, D. E., 1976a, Rate-dependent effects of drugs: a review of the literature, *Pharmacol. Biochem. Behav.* **4:**73–83.

Sanger, D. J., and Blackman, D. E., 1976b, Effects of diazepam and ripazepam on two measures of adjunctive drinking in rats, *Pharmacol. Biochem. Behav.* **5:**139–142.

Schmidt, H., 1969, Alterations of central thirst mechanisms by drugs, *Ann. N.Y. Acad. Sci.* **157:**962–976.

Segal, E. F., 1969, The interaction of psychogenic polydipsia with wheel running in rats, *Psychon. Sci.* **14:**141–142.

Segal, E. F., and Deadwyler, S. A., 1964, Amphetamine differentially affects temporally spaced bar pressing and collateral water drinking, *Psychon. Sci.* **1:**349–350.

Segal, E. F., and Holloway, S. M., 1963, Timing behavior in rats with water drinking as a mediator, *Science* **140:**888–889.

Segal, E. F., and Oden, D. L., 1965, Determinants of polydipsia in rats: a reply to Stein: I. Emptying the water bottle, *Psychon. Sci.* **2:**201–202.

Segal, E. F., and Oden, D. L., 1968, Concurrent facilitation of food reinforced, spaced licking, and depression of schedule-induced polydipsic drinking by amphetamine, *Psychon. Sci.* **10:**155–156.

Segal, E. F., and Oden, D. L., 1969, Effects of drinkometer current and of foot shock on psychogenic polydipsia, *Psychon. Sci.* **14:**13–15.

Segal, E. F., Oden, D. L., and Deadwyler, S. A., 1965, Determinants of polydipsia. V: Effects of amphetamine and pentobarbital, *Psychon. Sci.* **3:**33–34.

Singer, G., Armstrong, S., and Wayner, M. J., 1975, Effects of norepinephrine applied to the lateral hypothalamus on schedule-induced polydipsia, *Pharmacol. Biochem. Behav.* **3:**869–872.

Skinner, B. F., and Morse, W. H., 1957, Concurrent activity under fixed-interval reinforcement, *J. Comp. Physiol. Psychol.* **50:**279–281.

Smith, J. B., and Clark, F. C., 1974, Intercurrent and reinforced behavior under multiple spaced-responding schedules, *J. Exp. Anal. Behav.* **21:**445–454.

Smith, J. B., and Clark, F. C., 1975, Effects of *d*-amphetamine, chlorpromazine, and chlordiazepoxide on intercurrent behavior during spaced-responding schedules, *J. Exp. Anal. Behav.* **24:**241–248.

Soulairac, A., 1969, The adrenergic and cholinergic control of food and water intake, *Ann. N.Y. Acad. Sci.* **157:**934–961.

Staddon, J. E. R., 1977, Schedule-induced behavior, *in: Handbook of Operant Behavior* (W. L. Honig and J. E. R. Staddon, eds.), pp. 125–152, Prentice-Hall, Englewood Cliffs, N.J.

Staddon, J. E. R., and Ayres, S. L., 1975, Sequential and temporal properties of behavior induced by a schedule of periodic food delivery, *Behaviour* **54:**26–49.

Staddon, J. E. R., and Simmelhag, V. L., 1971, The "superstition" experiment: a re-examination of its implications for the principles of adaptive behavior, *Psychol. Rev.* **78:**3–43.

Stein, L., 1963, Anticholinergic drugs and the central control of thirst, *Science* **139:**46–48.

Stein, L., 1964, Excessive drinking in the rat: superstition or thirst? *J. Comp. Physiol. Psychol.* **58:**237–242.

Stein, L., and Seifter, J., 1962, Muscarinic synapses in the hypothalamus, *Amer. J. Physiol.* **202:**751–756.

Stricker, E. M., 1966, Extra-cellular fluid volume and thirst, *Amer. J. Physiol.* **211:**232–238.

Stricker, E. M., 1976, Drinking by rats after lateral hypothalamic lesions: a new look at the lateral hypothalamus, *J. Comp. Physiol. Psychol.* **90:**127–143.

Stricker, E. M., and Adair, E. R., 1966, Body fluid balance, taste, and post-prandial factors in schedule-induced polydipsia, *J. Comp. Physiol. Psychol.* **62:**449–454.

Taylor, D. B., and Lester, D., 1969, Schedule-induced nitrogen "drinking" in the rat, *Psychon. Sci.* **15:**17–18.

Teitelbaum, P., and Derks, P., 1958, The effects of amphetamine on forced drinking in the rat, *J. Comp. Physiol. Psychol.* **51:**801–810.

Thomka, M. L., and Rosellini, R. A., 1975, Frustration and the production of schedule-induced polydipsia, *Anim. Learn. Behav.* **3:**380–384.

Tinbergen, N., 1952, "Derived" activities: their causation, biological significance, origin, and emancipation during evolution, *Quart. Rev. Biol.* **27:**1–32.

Ulrich, R. E., and Craine, W. H., 1964, Behavior: persistence of shock-induced aggression, *Science* **143:**971–973.

Ulrich, R. E., Hutchinson, R. R., and Azrin, N. H., 1965, Pain-elicited aggression, *Psychol. Rec.* **15:**111–126.

Valenstein, E. S., Cox, V. C., and Kakolewski, J. W., 1970, Re-examination of the role of the hypothalamus in motivation, *Psychol. Rev.* **77:**16–31.

Villareal, J. E., 1967, Schedule-induced pica; paper read at meeting of the Eastern Psychological Association, Boston, cited by Falk, 1971.

Wayner, M. J., 1970, Motor-control functions of the lateral hypothalamus and adjunctive behavior, *Physiol. Behav.* **5:**1319–1325.

Wayner, M. J., 1974, Specificity of behavioral regulation, *Physiol. Behav.* **12:**851–869.

Wayner, M. J., Greenberg, I., and Trowbridge, J., 1973a, Effects of *d*-amphetamine on schedule-induced polydipsia, *Pharmacol. Biochem. Behav.* **1:**109–111.

Wayner, M. J., Greenberg, I., Fraley, S., and Fisher, S., 1973b, Effects of Δ^9-tetrahydrocannabinol and ethyl alcohol on adjunctive behavior and the lateral hypothalamus, *Physiol. Behav.* **10:**109–132.

Wells, R. N. and Cone, A. L., 1975, Changes in burst lick rate of albino rats as functions of age, sex, and drinking experience, *Bull. Psychon. Soc.* **6:**605–607.

Whitehouse, J. M., Lloyd, A. J., and Fifer, S. A., 1964, Comparative effects of atropine and methylatripine on maze acquisition and eating, *J. Comp. Physiol. Psychol.* **58:**475–476.

Wise, R. A., 1974, Lateral hypothalamic electrical stimulation: does it make animals "hungry," *Brain Res.* **67:**187–209.

Wuttke, W., 1970, The effects of *d*-amphetamine on schedule-controlled water licking in the squirrel monkey, *Psychopharmacologia* **17:**70–82.

Wuttke, W., and Innis, N. K., 1972, Drug effects upon behavior induced by second-order schedules of reinforcement: the relevance of ethological analyses, *in: Schedule Effects: Drugs, Drinking, and Aggression* (R. M. Gilbert and J. D. Keehn, eds.), pp. 129–147, University of Toronto Press, Toronto.

Zeiler, M. D., 1970, Other behavior: consequences of reinforcing not responding, *J. Psychol.* **74:**149–155.

Schedule-Induced Self-Administration of Drugs 6

R. M. Gilbert

1. Introduction

Adjunctive behavior appears at first sight to be a notable exception to the general rule that behavior is determined by its consequences. The various induced behaviors mentioned in Chapter 5 occur without any obvious advantage to the behaving organism. Indeed, there have been repeated observations that adjunctive behavior can reduce the frequency of delivery of the spaced reinforcers (e.g., Falk, 1961; Gilbert, 1974a), providing, on the face of it, a considerable disadvantage to the organism. At a more local level, however, the principle of reinforcement is not violated. Falk (1966) demonstrated that rats will work for the opportunity to engage in schedule-induced excessive drinking. Thus, adjunctive behavior may be thought of as happening because certain operations (e.g., spaced feeding) make reinforcers of certain stimuli (e.g., water) when they would not otherwise be reinforcers. Adjunctive behavior, considered in this way, does not necessarily violate the useful principle that behavior is determined by its consequences. One puzzle with adjunctive behavior is the relatively indiscriminate nature of the inducing operation. The inducing operation seems to cast its spell on whatever stimuli happen to be available. Although it is perhaps helpful to think of schedule induction as an increased reinforcing effectiveness of certain available stimuli, it is also difficult to avoid the conclusion that it is behavior that is induced, rather than a reinforcing property, that the inducing environment exaggerates behavior that is already appropriate to that environment. Behavior, too,

R. M. Gilbert • Addiction Research Foundation, Toronto, Canada

however, can be viewed as a reinforcer, as Premack (1972) proposed: accordingly, reinforcement operations of the kind demonstrated by Falk (1966) arise because access to high-rate behavior—drinking in this case—is itself a reinforcer. Recognizing reinforcement operations within adjunctive behavior does not explain the phenomenon or its essential unadaptiveness. Lack of knowledge of the mechanism of schedule-induced behavior should nevertheless not detract from appreciation of its conspicuous feature: it is behavior that occurs at a high rate without obvious consequence and advantage to the organism.

Frequently, the stimuli available in experimental situations have been drugs. In fact, Lester's (1961) demonstration of schedule-induced alcohol intoxication in the rat was the second reported study of adjunctive behavior. Since then, in addition to many studies of adjunctive consumption of ethanol solutions, there have been studies of schedule-induced excessive intake of solutions of other drugs. While also considering consumption of these other drugs, the focus here will be upon schedule-induced ethanol drinking, for three reasons. The first is that almost all of the work on schedule-induced drug consumption has involved ethanol rather than other drugs. The second is that most studies of schedule-induced behavior have examined drinking, rather than the many other behaviors that can be induced by spaced reinforcement. Third, of the drugs whose consumption causes concern in North America, in Europe, and in many other parts of the world, ethanol is conspicuous among those that are taken orally.

2. Schedule-Induced Ethanol Consumption

2.1. Lester's Original Observations

Lester (1961) observed ethanol consumption and its effects in nine rats, each bar-pressing for food on a schedule that provided one 45-mg pellet every 55 sec, on the average. Under these conditions rats drank an hourly average of 9.9 g of a 5.6% ethanol solution per 3-hr session, which may be compared with the rate of approximately 3.0 g of ethanol solution per hour that Lester described as nonpolydipsic consumption, and with the average rate of water consumption of 29.2 ml/hr found by Falk (1961), both under similar conditions.

These two findings of Lester—that (1) ethanol polydipsia can be induced by spaced feeding, but (2) generally not to the extent of water polydipsia—have been substantiated by subsequent research, as has his observation that schedule-induced consumption of ethanol can be so excessive as to cause intoxication (e.g., Senter and Sinclair, 1967).

Three other findings by Lester have been contradicted:

1. He reported that schedule-induced ethanol consumption did not occur when the food pellets were presented noncontingently (i.e., independently of the animal's behavior). Many studies have since shown that noncontingent presentation can induce excessive ethanol consumption (e.g., Everett and King, 1970; Falk *et al.,* 1972; Freed, 1972; Gilbert, 1974b,c; Hawkins *et al.*, 1972; Lester and Freed, 1972a; Meisch and Thompson, 1974a; Ogata *et al.*, 1972a,b).

2. Lester found that ethanol polydipsia did not occur when bar pressing was reinforced according to a fixed-interval 55-sec schedule of reinforcement, under which a pellet was delivered for the first bar press that occurred more than 55 sec since the previous pellet delivery. Much subsequent work has involved the successful induction of ethanol polydipsia by fixed-interval schedules (e.g., Freed, 1971a; Freed and Lester, 1970; Freed *et al.*, 1970; Holman and Myers, 1968; Woods and Winger, 1971).

3. Lester also reported that ethanol polydipsia did not occur if ethanol was introduced once the animal had become adapted to the variable-interval schedule. This finding has not been clearly contradicted with respect to ethanol polydipsia. However, Meisch and Thompson (1971, 1972) trained rats to work for food on a 1-min variable-interval schedule before making water available. Water polydipsia developed rapidly when it became possible. Hymowitz *et al.* (1970) made a similar finding with respect to a fixed-interval 50-sec schedule. Presumably, because of the general similarity of ethanol and water polydipsia, ethanol drinking would have developed to excess under the same conditions. However, the possibility of a difference here between water and ethanol might be further explored.

2.2. Differences between Schedule-Induced Ethanol Polydipsia and Schedule-Induced Water Polydipsia

The minimum conditions for schedule-induced water polydipsia appear to be that water is available, and that reinforcing events are occurring at intervals averaging between about 30 sec and 4 min, optimally about 90 sec. These conditions seem also to obtain for ethanol polydipsia, although there are insufficient data to be sure of the effective range of interreinforcement times. Although there is similarity in the general features of ethanol and water polydipsias (see Figure 1), certain differences have been reported. They are noted below.

1. *Ethanol polydipsia is generally less than water polydipsia.* Although in a majority of studies of schedule-induced ethanol consumption, water polydipsia was induced before ethanol was introduced, few studies

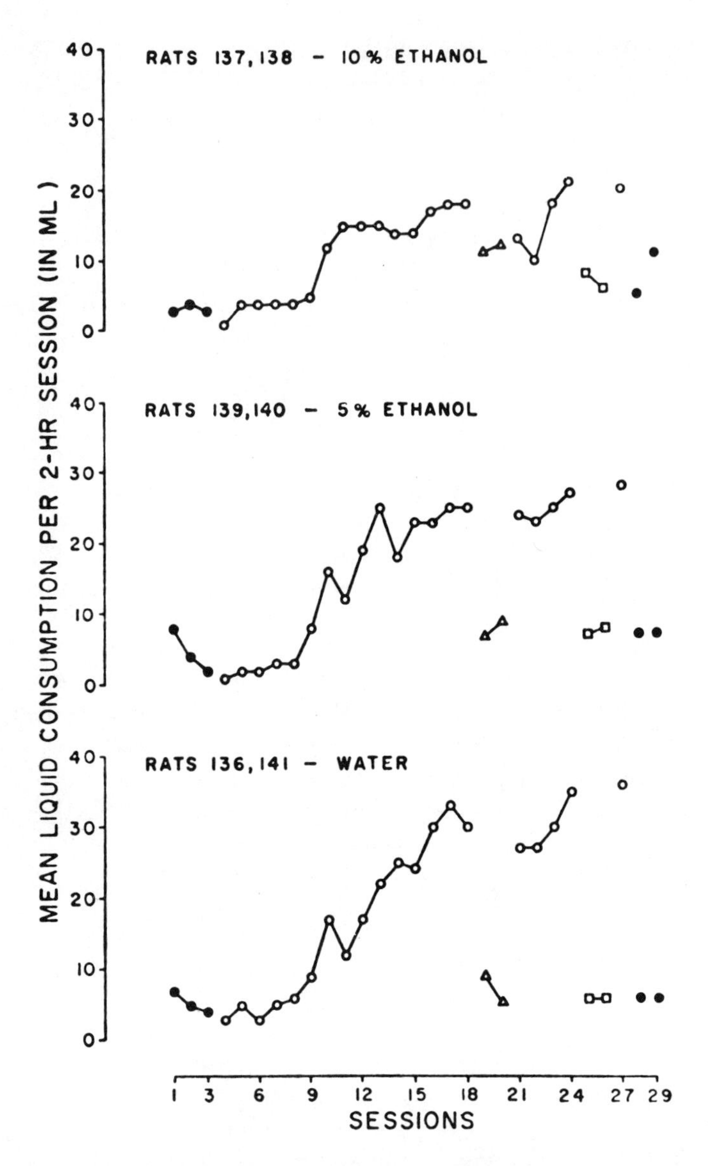

Figure 1. Consumption of the indicated fluids during daily sessions by the three pairs of rats studied by Gilbert (1974b). Water was the available fluid for all rats during sessions 1–3, 28, and 29 (filled circles), when all 120 pellets were available at the session start. Open circles indicate that 45-mg pellets were presented at 60-sec intervals throughout the 2-hr sessions; triangles indicate that all 120 pellets were again presented at the session start; squares indicate that no pellets were presented throughout the 2-hr session. The figure shows (1) that polydipsia, both ethanol and water, takes some sessions to develop; (2) that ethanol polydipsia is less than water polydipsia, according to the concentration; and (3) that water polydipsia ceases in the absence of the intermittent pellet presentation, but ethanol polydipsia continues, again according to the ethanol concentration.

allow acceptable comparison of water and ethanol intakes. Those that do allow comparison have either repeatedly reversed water and ethanol solution as the available fluid (e.g., Meisch and Thompson, 1972; Githens *et al.,* 1973) or used control animals that had access only to water (e.g., Gilbert, 1974b,c). The degree of polydipsia has been found to decline with increasing concentration of the ethanol solutions (see Figure 1), although Meisch and Thompson (1972) and Githens *et al.* (1973) reported that the actual quantity of ethanol consumed increased with concentration. Meisch and Thompson also noted that ethanol solution consumption was generally *above* water control levels during the first 10 min of each ethanol session and that the lower session totals reflected within-session decrements in ethanol consumption, decrements that were most substantial in the case of the highest concentration used (32%, w/v).

2. *Ethanol polydipsia disappears within a 2-hr session, but water polydipsia persists.* Freed *et al.* (1970), Gilbert (1974c), and Colotla and Keehn (1975) have also reported that ethanol polydipsia declined during extended sessions when compared with water polydipsia. Githens *et al.* (1973) reported a similar decline when ethanol polydipsia was induced by a differential reinforcement of low rate schedule under which a bar press was reinforced by a food pellet only if it followed the preceding bar press by at least 20 sec. Freed and Lester (1970) also demonstrated that schedule-induced consumption of an acetone solution declined during sessions. Acetone and ethanol have similar pharmacological properties, according to Freed and Lester, and thus it is possible that the within-session decline is a pharmacological effect (i.e., an effect late in the session of the drug ingested early in the session). This possibility is supported by the observation that intraperitoneally administered ethanol causes a much greater decrement in schedule-induced behavior than in behavior that is explicitly maintained by a reinforcement schedule (Gilbert, 1973). An alternative reason for the within-session decline in ethanol and acetone consumption might be the aversive taste of the two fluids. However, I have found in unpublished experiments that polydipsia for even more unpalatable caffeine solution does not decline during extended sessions.

3. *Ethanol consumption declines less than water consumption when intermittent reinforcement ceases.* This effect was first noted by Freed *et al.* (1970), and has been confirmed by Freed and Lester (1970), Freed (1972), and Gilbert (1974b,c)—see Figure 1. Furthermore, Meisch and Thompson (1971) reported that ethanol consumption that had been elevated by schedule induction remained elevated for 4 months after intermittent feeding had ceased. Lester and Freed (1972a) have argued that ethanol drinking persists only because the animals remain hungry and because ethanol is a food. If this were the

case, food satiation would remove the continuing ethanol polydipsia. Meisch and Thompson (1971) reported that food satiation did indeed result in a decline in intake, but that in time ethanol drinking returned to 70% of its previous level. They concuded that "ethanol drinking during food extinction is neither transient nor solely a function of food deprivation." The question of the persistence of ethanol drinking will be returned to in the discussion of the suitability of schedule-induced ethanol consumption in the rat as a model of human alcoholism.

4. *Contingent or noncontingent electric shock may reduce water polydipsia more than ethanol polydipsia.* Freed (1971a) reported that interpolating brief punishment periods had the effect of reducing water polydipsia but not ethanol polydipsia. Freed *et al.* (1974) presented response-independent electric shock and likewise observed a decrease in schedule-induced consumption of water but not ethanol. Freed (1974) observed a similar decrease in water but not ethanol consumption when unpredictable noncontingent shock was presented during a regular polydipsia procedure that involved a choice between ethanol and water. These are the only studies of this kind that involved both ethanol and water polydipsia. Because some of the reported effects upon water consumption differ from those of other studies (e.g., Segal and Oden, 1969; Bond *et al.*, 1973; King, 1974; see Chapter 5), and because of uncertainties regarding procedure and interpretation of results, claims of a difference between ethanol and water polydipsia in these reports should be regarded with caution until further data are available.

2.3. Schedule-Induction as a Means of Generating Excessive Ethanol Consumption

2.3.1. Intoxication

Most authors that have reported schedule-induced ethanol consumption have been concerned merely to secure excessive ethanol intake rather than to examine the special characteristics of adjunctive ethanol polydipsia. The point of Lester's (1961) original paper was that the schedule-induced polydipsia technique provided a means of causing ethanol intoxication in rats. Since then other methods have been developed (e.g., Freund, 1973; see Woods and Winger, 1971 for a review), but the schedule-induction technique remains popular. The technique has generated signs of intoxication in mice (Ogata *et al.*, 1972a,b), in rats (Falk *et al.*, 1972), and in rhesus monkeys (Woods and Winger, 1971). [It has also been used, when applied chronically to rats, to induce tolerance to the intoxicating effect of acute doses of ethanol

(Samson and Falk, 1974b).] Blood alcohol levels in excess of 200 mg/ml were reported in each case. One notable exception to the reports of intoxication is the study by Mello and Mendelson (1971), whose rhesus monkeys drank more bourbon than usual when food was delivered intermittently, but not to the extent of intoxication. Mello and Mendelson's technique had an unusual feature. Food delivery was contingent upon drinking from a second bottle. Reinforcers are known to have a local inhibitory effect upon the behavior they reinforce (Catania, 1973), and thus it is plausible to suggest that bourbon drinking by Mello and Mendelson's monkeys was suppressed by food delivery, at least relative to what would have occurred if drinking had not been explicitly reinforced. Thus their failure to obtain intoxication or to observe high blood alcohol levels might possibly be related to the peculiarities of their procedure.

Some authors have been concerned to induce a high level of ethanol consumption in order to study effects of the drug other than intoxication. For example, Freed (1968, 1971b) used the schedule-induction technique to examine the effects of ethanol upon behavior in a conflict situation. Other authors have used the technique to provide a base line of excessive ethanol drinking, against which to examine the effects of procedures that might reduce ethanol consumption. Thus Keehn (1972), stimulated by reports that anticholinergic drugs reduce drinking, explored the effects of trihexyphenidyl on rat ethanol consumption that had been induced to excess by spaced feeding. The drug did indeed attenuate ethanol consumption, results that led Mottin (1973) to suggest that anticholinergics might be used in alcoholism therapy to eliminate excessive intake of alcohol.

2.3.2. Physical Dependence on Ethanol

Three reports published in 1972 described withdrawal signs in rodents consequent upon cessation of a regimen of excessive ethanol consumption induced by spaced feeding. In one (Hawkins *et al.*, 1972), the withdrawal state occurred fortuitously, and it is difficult to evaluate the determining conditions. In two others (Ogata *et al.*, 1972a; Falk *et al.*, 1972) withdrawal signs were evident in mice and rats, respectively, following termination of a procedure that involved spaced feeding during multiple daily sessions. Falk *et al.*, in particular, fed rats one 45-mg food pellet every 2 min during 1-hr feeding periods that were separated by 3-hr intervals. After an adaptation phase during which water or a low concentration of ethanol was the available fluid, each of eight rats had 5% (w/v) ethanol available continuously over a period of 3 months. Mean daily intake of ethanol by the eight rats was 13.1 g/kg.

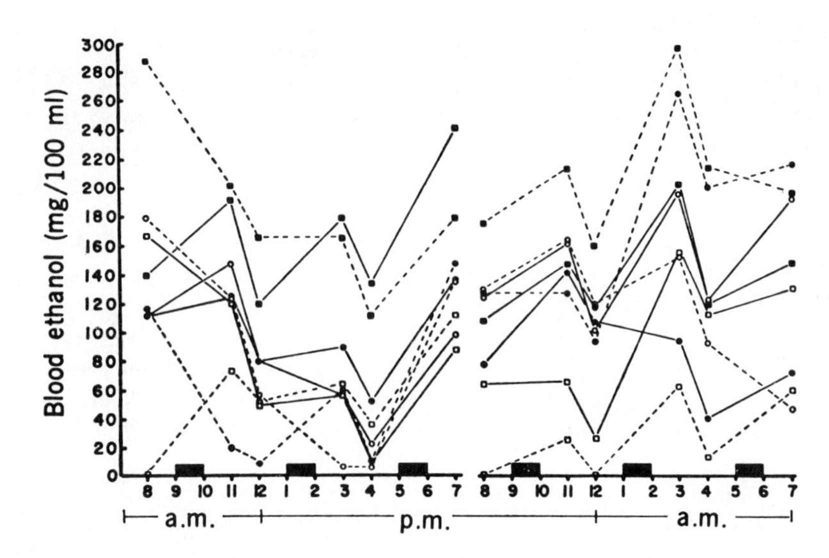

Figure 2. Blood-alcohol levels of rats studied by Falk *et al.* (1972). Rats received one 45-mg food pellet every 2 min during the six 1-hr food delivery periods (▬). Rat 1 (○—○), 2 (○---○), 3 (●—●), 4 (●---●), 5 (□—□), 6 (□---□), 7 (■—■), 8 (■---■). This procedure appears to be capable of producing a continuously high blood-alcohol level, which, some authors believe, is a necessary condition for the occurrence of physical dependence.

Blood-alcohol levels are illustrated in Figure 2. Four of the rats were observed for withdrawal signs after removal from the test cages. All four animals became hyperactive within 4 hr after the previous feeding period. Two convulsed and died when keys were shaken nearby. The third showed "all the preconvulsive symptoms" but did not convulse on key shaking, perhaps because key shaking was delayed in this case until 15 hr after withdrawal of ethanol: Hunter *et al.* (1975) reported a rapid decline in susceptibility to audiogenic seizure during withdrawal in certain of their rats, although most were susceptible at 15 hr; the data of Majchrowicz (1975) also suggest that susceptibility would usually be evident 15 hr postwithdrawal. The fourth of Falk *et al.*'s rats was similar to the third except that no attempt was made to produce an audiogenic seizure. The authors reported that normal rats of the same strain could not be induced to convulse by key shaking, even after extensive exposure to a water polydipsia condition (Falk *et al.*, 1973a,b). Audiogenic seizure during withdrawal is very often considered to be a sign of physical dependence on ethanol in the rat (Hunter *et al.,* 1975; Majchrowicz, 1975). Falk and Samson (1975) "regarded the production of a full tonic-clonic convulsion after withdrawal of ethanol as proof of physical dependence."

Subsequently, Samson and Falk (1974a,b,c, 1975) conducted a

number of studies that exploited or varied the basic paradigm of chronic exposure to a daily regimen of many spaced-feeding sessions. This work has been reviewed recently by Falk and Samson (1975). None of the four studies has provided exact replication of the Falk *et al.* (1972) study. One (Samson and Falk, 1974c) involved a similar procedure except that 0.25% saccharin was added to the 5% ethanol solution, raising mean schedule-induced ethanol intake from 13.1 to 15.1 g/kg/day. All three tested rats evidenced audiogenic seizures some hours after replacement of the saccharin–ethanol solution by water. None of 14 animals drinking the same solution in home cages seized or showed other signs of an abstinence syndrome when ethanol was withdrawn: their mean ethanol intake was 11.7 g/kg/day. The two animals in the Falk *et al.* (1972) study, and the three saccharin-drinking animals in the Samson and Falk (1974c) study are the only animals in this series that have manifested audiogenic seizures during withdrawal testing after a chronic regime of schedule-induced ethanol polydipsia (i.e., five of six tested animals have convulsed).

Several other studies have involved similar procedures. One (Heintzelman *et al.*, 1976) attempted a close replication of the original Falk *et al.* (1972) study. The seven surviving animals were drinking a mean 11.7 g/kg/day ethanol as a 5% solution during the last 10 days of the 3-month exposure to a 1-hr polydipsia session every 4 hr. No seizures occurred when keys were shaken some hours after withdrawal. Three of the seven animals showed some hyperactivity. The discrepancies between the results of the two studies are discussed by Falk *et al.* (1976).

In another study (Gilbert, 1977) four animals were examined for withdrawal signs after exposure to a chronic procedure similar to that of Falk *et al.* (1972), differences being that exposure to the highest ethanol concentrations was for a briefer period—15 days rather than 3 months—and that a 12-hr darkness–light cycle obtained, rather than the constant illumination of the studies by Falk and his associates. Following the work of Geller (1971), the second difference might have been expected to produce higher ethanol consumption than in the Falk *et al.* (1972) study. In fact, mean consumption was lower, at 10.6 g/kg/day. Just one of the four animals convulsed during withdrawal testing. It was the rat that was drinking the highest ethanol dose, 13.3 g/kg/day. The nonseizing animals were all drinking less than 12 g/kg/day. In another study (McMillan *et al.*, 1974) audiogenic seizures were reported after as few as 8 days of schedule-induced polydipsia sessions occurring at 2-hr intervals. Information was not given about the number of rats tested or the amounts ingested, except that they were more than 10 g/kg/day.

Samson and Falk (1975) also tested for audiogenic seizures after chronic ethanol drinking that involved twice-daily 1-hr polydipsia sessions, beginning at 9 A.M. and 9 P.M. for seven animals and at 5 A.M. and 9 P.M. for the other seven. No seizures were observed, nor were any observed in a group of four rats in the Gilbert (1977) study that experienced one 6-hr polydipsia session each day, beginning at 8 P.M. Samson and Falk (1975) argued from their data that more frequent ethanol exposure is required for physical dependence than two 1-hr sessions, however separated. A more significant feature of the data may have been the low ethanol intake by both groups; means were less than 9 g/kg/day. Moreover, no animal receiving a daily 6-hr session in the Gilbert (1977) study drank more than 12 g/kg/day. Thus, it appears that one of the conditions for inducing physical dependence using the spaced feeding procedure may be the ingestion of something in excess of 12 g/kg/day. Questions such as the role of the distribution of individual sessions within the day cannot be resolved by comparison of rats drinking different amounts of ethanol solution, and the conclusion of Samson and Falk (1975) that "the development of physical dependence on ethanol requires more than an episodic peaking of the blood ethanol level once or twice a day" seems premature.

Indeed, what may have been a form of physical dependence on ethanol has been demonstrated after once-daily intubation by Gibbins *et al.* (1971), Le Blanc *et al.* (1975), and Gilbert (1976a). The first two studies involved low ethanol doses—7.1 and 2.2 g/kg/day—and assessment of withdrawal in terms of startle-threshold and open-field behavior, respectively. In both cases there was what might be described as heightened emotionality after ethanol was no longer administered. The effects may not have been indicative of "true" physical dependence, in the sense that the emotionality could have been merely a compensatory response to ethanol's depressant effect, a response evoked by environmental features predictive of ethanol intubation, and which was not counteracted when ethanol was predicted but not administered. "True" dependence, if considered as compensation, is usually thought of as a somewhat permanent state of physiological adaptation that is induced by the relatively continuous presence of the drug, and that subsides when the drug is absent, but sufficiently slowly to produce a temporary disequilibrium that is the basis of a withdrawal syndrome (Goldstein, 1976). The alternative view—that dependence is the existence of environmentally evoked compensatory responses to drug administration—has much support in the work of Siegel (e.g., 1975) on the situation specificity of tolerance to morphine analgesia. Such a view does not restrict the development of physical dependence on a drug to any particular temporal distribution of the daily dose. It holds only that withdrawal signs will appear when drug administration is expected and does not occur. The third study mentioned at the beginning of this paragraph (Gilbert, 1976a) attempted to address the question of dose division and physical dependence directly by administering a fixed daily dose divided in different ways for different groups of rats. Animals receiving what was effectively one 10 g/kg intubation each day were much more likely to display audiogenic seizures on withdrawal than those receiving 2.5 g/kg at 6-hr intervals. They were also much more debilitated by the ethanol adminstration regime. The debilitation may have made them seizure-prone (see review by Munn, 1950), a state that could, paradoxically, have been masked by daily adminstration of ethanol (Yanai and Ginsburg, 1975) and not revealed until ethanol was withdrawn. Seizure proneness caused by ethanol toxicity, but also masked by ethanol, could have been the basis of much of the work in which audiogenic seizures during withdrawal provided the main index of physical dependence on alcohol, including the Falk *et al.* (1972) and the Samson and Falk (1974c) studies. Clearly, as long as there is cause for uncertainty regarding the nature of physical dependence and the validity of withdrawal signs, evaluation of the schedule-induced polydipsia technique as a means of generating excessive ethanol intake should rely on as wide a range of measures of ethanol-induced and ethanol-withdrawal-induced change as can be devised.

In addition to seizure susceptibility, Falk and his associates have employed two other kinds of measure of the effects of chronic ethanol overdrinking induced by multiple daily spaced-feeding sessions. One involved a fine motor discrimination (Samson and Falk, 1974b). Rats drinking as little as 7.8 g/kg/day under the previously described schedule-induction procedure showed marked dyskinesia on ethanol withdrawal. Performance during ethanol ingestion, even as much as 14 g/kg/day, was similar to performance prior to the introduction of ethanol, and marked tolerance to the effects of acute doses was evident. The other measure employed was alteration of preference for ethanol, a feature regarded by some (e.g., Deutsch, 1973) as an essential component of ethanol dependence. Samson and Falk (1974a) reported that rats exposed to multiple-session spaced-feeding procedure for 3 months preferred a 5.0% ethanol solution to dextrose solutions having concentrations up to and including 3.0% (experiment 1—see Figure 3), whereas rats receiving an equivalent amount of food presented in a single daily ration preferred the 5.0% ethanol over detrose concentrations only up to 1.4% (experiment 4). Samson and Falk concluded that, for the spaced-feeding group but not the single-ration group, "prior ethanol overdrinking resulting in physical dependence shifted the dextrose–ethanol preference function to ethanol at comparatively high competing dextrose concentrations" (1974a, pp. 375–376). It is impor-

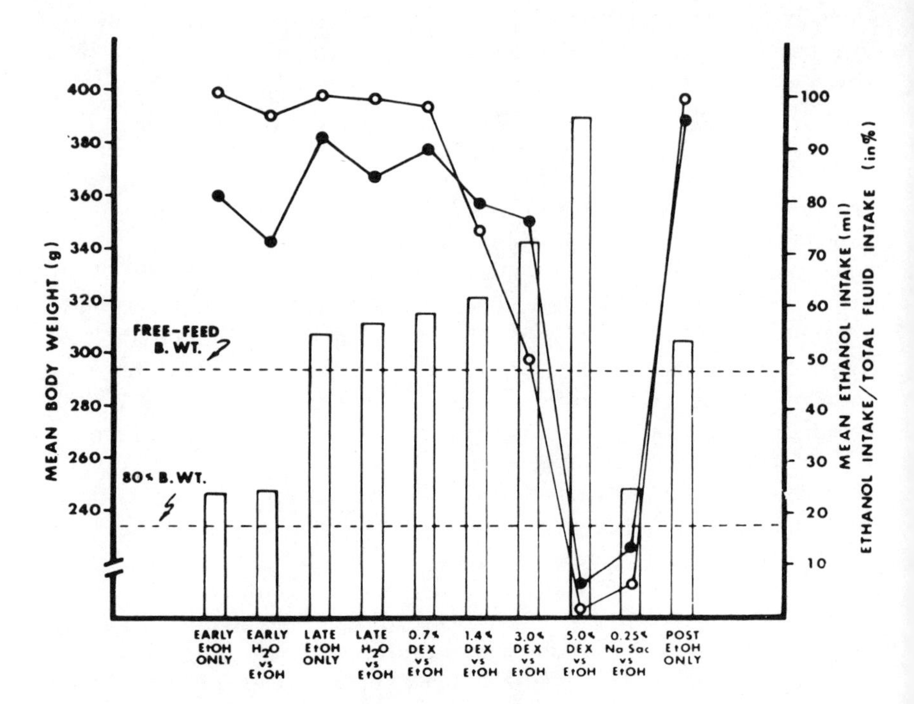

Figure 3. Mean alcohol intake by the eight rats studied by Samson and Falk (1974c: experiment 1). Rats could be "weaned" from alcohol by providing a dextrose solution as an alternative, but only when the dextrose concentration was higher than 3%. Note the large and sometimes fatal decline in body weight (□) when saccharin was substituted for dextrose. EtOH intake, ml (●—●); EtOH intake/total fluid intake × 100 (○—○). © The Williams and Wilkins Co., Baltimore.

tant to stress that the spaced-feeding group had been drinking more ethanol on the average than the comparable rats in the single-ration group during most of the prior exposure to ethanol: at the end of the main ethanol exposure phase, the respective mean intakes were 11.8 and 7.8 g/kg/day. In this case it can be argued that the preference function shifted in one group and not the other, because of the greater ethanol drinking experience of the group manifesting the shift, rather than because the animals in only one of the two groups were physically dependent. The argument that the difference was a simple matter of degree of exposure to ethanol seems contradicted by the results from yet another group of animals used by Samson and Falk (1974a). They were maintained under a single-ration regimen, were drinking 11.7 g/kg/day at the end of the main ethanol exposure phase, and yet did not show a shift in preference testing. However, this single-ration group is not strictly comparable to the spaced-feeding group. Its body weight was kept about 10% lower by restricted feeding, a procedure that in itself might be expected to have a dramatic impact on palatability, by making preferred fluids more palatable (Jacobs and Sharma, 1969; Gilbert, 1972). The lack of a preference shift toward the ethanol solution could have been a consequence of this reduced weight.

An interesting final stage of the Samson and Falk (1974a) study involved all three of the groups tested for a shift in preference. When given a choice between the 5% ethanol solution and a highly palatable but nonnutritious 0.25% saccharin solution, all animals much preferred the saccharin (see Figure 3). Very little ethanol was drunk and body weights in some cases declined to a point where general health was compromised, even though sufficient calories for the maintenance of health could have been gained from the ethanol solution. This result emphasizes the importance of palatability in the control of fluid choice, a point that will be returned to shortly.

2.3.3. Induction of Ethanol Reinforcement

Some authors (e.g., Meisch and Thompson, 1974a; Meisch *et al.*, 1975) have used the term dependence to refer merely to the fact that an organism self-administers a drug. In this sense drug dependence exists whenever a drug is a reinforcer. Although contrary to common use (because it does not seem to allow for the "need" or "craving" aspects of what is usually regarded as drug dependence), this view has a most useful consequence. It suggests that reinforcement is the key feature of a drug when its consumption and dependence or addiction (Collier, 1972) liability are being considered. It seems that most drugs are initially nonreinforcing. Indeed, there are many demonstrations that the first exposure to reinforcing doses of drugs may be punishing (e.g., Cappell *et al.*, 1973). Thus, procedures that make drugs into reinforcers have special importance. Orally consumed ethanol is generally a less effective reinforcer than water, possibly on account of its aversive orosensory properties. However, even merely a few hours of schedule-induced ethanol polydipsia has been shown to be sufficient to establish ethanol as a reinforcer (Meisch and Thompson, 1974b). Other research has shown that, following schedule induction, rats will work more for ethanol solutions up to a concentration of 32% (w/v) than for water (Meisch and Thompson, 1971). Meisch (1975) has stressed, however, that schedule-induced polydipsia may be no more effective than other procedures that induce drinking of ethanol solutions.

3. Determinants of Schedule-Induced Ethanol Polydipsia

The determinants of schedule-induced ethanol polydipsia are probably in large part identical to the determinants of water polydipsia. For fuller discussion of the determinants of schedule-induced water polydipsia, the reader is referred to other sources (e.g., Falk, 1972; Segal, 1972; Staddon, 1977). This section is concerned first with three properties of ethanol that may have a bearing on the occurrence of schedule-induced ethanol polydipsia—its calorific value, its pharmacological effects, and its taste—and second with situations in which more than one adjunctive behavior is possible.

3.1 Ethanol's Calorific Value

Ethanol differs from most other drugs in that it has significant food value in the usual dose range. Calorimetrically, it provides 7.1 kcal/g, and normally the same yield occurs when it is consumed (Mayer, 1970), although, in humans at least, there is a little evidence that the yield is lower (Lieber, 1975). A rat drinking 30 ml of 5% ethanol per 2-hr session (typical values when ethanol consumption is schedule-induced) gains 10.7 kcal at the rate of 7.1 kcal/g. The 120 Noyes pellets that would be delivered during the same session yield 23.2 kcal (5.4 at 4.3 kcal/g). The Teklad diet that might be fed after the session to maintain body weights at 80% of its normal value would provide a further 23.4 cal (9 g at 2.6 kcal/g). Thus, the schedule-induced alcohol consumption provides a significant proportion of the daily energy intake, and a much greater proportion of the calories obtained during the experimental session.

The arguments that ethanol's food value is responsible for its consumption come both from these considerations (Deutsch, 1973) and from data concerning differences between ethanol polydipsia and polydipsia involving other fluids (Freed and Lester, 1970; Lester and Freed, 1972a; Freed, 1974). The difference emphasized by these authors is the relative persistence of ethanol polydipsia after cessation of food pellet presentation, when compared with polydipsia involving water or an equi-intoxicating solution of acetone or water. The difference beteen ethanol and water occurs even when food is massed at the beginning of the session rather than omitted (Gilbert, 1974b), thus removing any objection that the difference arises solely because of the absence of food.

It is plausible to argue that consumpton of ethanol solutions persists because of its higher caloric yield, although this has not yet been put to a direct test. One way of assessing the role of calorific value in the relative persistence of ethanol drinking following cessation of intermittency of reinforcer presentation would be to examine the effect of cessation on the drinking of solutions isocaloric with ethanol but without pharmacological effect. If degree of persistence were found to be a function of calorific value, independently of type of solution, this would be strong evidence for a calorific basis for the persistence of ethanol consumption. Other relevant evidence could come from situations in which the reinforcement intermittency does not involve food restriction, such as the use of intermittent intracranial stimulation (as by Atrens, 1973) and intermittent unlocking of a running wheel (Singer *et al.*, 1974), both of which have induced water polydipsia. Whatever the basis for the relative persistence of ethanol polydipsia, it does not follow that the same factors are responsible for its development and maintenance. As already indicated, water and ethanol polydipsia develop in much the same way. If caloric yield were the only important factor, water polydipsia would never occur.

It seems very evident that ethanol polydipsia, like water polydipsia, occurs because reinforcers are occurring intermittently. A few studies have employed satisfactory controls that illustrate this point beyond question (e.g., Falk *et al.*, 1972). Perhaps the most satisfying demonstration would involve induction of ethanol and water polydipsia in sated animals by spaced presentation of reinforcers unrelated to food. The fact that removal of spaced feeding does cause a decline in ethanol polydipsia (e.g., Freed and Lester, 1970), even if not to low water levels, also argues for the contribution of schedule induction. Quite possibly ethanol polydipsia is generated and maintained initially by spaced reinforcers, but eventually by a combination of causes, including calories and spaced reinforcers, and perhaps also the pharmacological properties of ethanol.

3.2. Ethanol's Pharmacological Effect

The only evidence of implication of a pharmacological effect of ethanol in schedule-induced ethanol polydipsia is the within-session decline in ethanol consumption that was discussed earlier. It is likely that ethanol's pharmacology is such as to reduce intake during a schedule-induction procedure. This does not remove the possibility that ethanol consumption during schedule induction is maintained in part by its pharmacological consequences or their by-products, positive or negative. Clearly behavior can be maintaind by ethanol reinforcement, although it is more reasonable to attribute the reinforcing property to pharmacology when an intravenous route is used (Woods *et al.*, 1971) than when the ethanol is self-administered orally (Meisch and Thompson, 1974a,b), especially when, in the former case, there is no food deprivation.

3.3. Taste

The only remaining source of reinforcement of ethanol drinking seems to be the taste of ethanol. However, this is generally regarded as aversive (Myers, 1966), and it seems implausible that ethanol should be drunk on account of its taste. Taste could enter into the determination of ethanol drinking in two ways. It could be the aversive taste that prevents initially excessive ethanol consumption. Schedule-induction forces adaptation to the aversive taste, which then allows other determinants to appear when spaced reinforcement ceases. Taste could also be a factor in the development of ethanol reinforcement. It could come to signal the reinforcing consequences of ingestion, thus assuming conditioning reinforcing properties (Meisch and Thompson, 1974a). In the absence of suitable evidence, it might be presumed that the taste of ethanol itself is not ordinarily an important factor in the induction of drinking low and moderate concentrations of ethanol by spaced-feeding procedures. The taste of the ethanol-containing fluid, or of other available fluids, can have a profound effect on the amount of ethanol that is consumed, which was indicated earlier in the discussion of one of Samson and Falk's (1974a) studies, and which will be returned to in the next section.

3.4. Polydipsia under Conditions of Choice

Drinking seems to occur in preference to other behavior, in that other induced behaviors are rarely reported when a fluid is available. This view is supported by the results of a study in which an explicit choice of potentially excessive behaviors was made available (Segal, 1969). In Segal's study, four rats could run or drink water between spaced pellet presentations. Three developed a drink–run pattern. The fourth rat rarely ran, although when it ran it ran before drinking. A basic drink–run pattern has also been reported by Staddon and Ayres (1975).

Several reports have been concerned with the nature of the polydipsia that occurs when a choice between fluids is available. Lester and Freed (1972a) gave rats a choice between 5.6% ethanol and water, and reported briefly that the ratio of fluids drunk remained unchanged over an interpellet interval range of 15–150 sec. However, they did not report quantities, and we do not know if more ethanol solution was consumed than water. Freed (1974) gave rats choices between pairs of 5.6% ethanol, 5.6% acetone (equi-intoxicating), 6.05% butanediol (isocaloric) and water, while pellets were being delivered at 50-sec intervals. Generally speaking, the preference hierarchy was butanediol (most preferred), ethanol, water, acetone. Keehn and Coulson (1975) reported that three of four animals drank hardly any of 7.2% ethanol during 12 daily spaced-feeding sessions when water was also available and when both fluids were available in home cages. Satisfactory controls were not employed and it is not possible to analyze further this interesting demonstration of what might have been inhibition of development of schedule-induced ethanol polydipsia.

In our own laboratory we have found the preference hierarchy between 5% ethanol and water to be very labile in some animals under conditions of schedule induction (Gilbert, 1976c). It can be affected by the relative positions of the tubes, and it is subject to inexplicable long-term drifts, with ethanol being preferred for many days and then water being preferred for many days, but with polydipsia with respect to one, the other, or both fluids occurring throughout (see Figure 4). One clear feature is that preference for ethanol can be stabilized by the addition of 0.2% saccharin to the ethanol solution. With a choice between ethanol–saccharin solution and water, water consumption falls to near zero. This is a provocative finding, especially when it is considered that alcohol is very frequently drunk in sweetened form—as wines, which may contain as much as 20% sucrose, but probably average about 5%, and as spirits, which, even if they already contain sugar, are generally mixed with generous portions of beverages that comprise about 10% sucrose. The equally provocative, complementary finding—that ethanol consumption declines markedly in the face of a highly palatable alternative fluid (Samson and Falk, 1974a)—has been discussed already, a further illustration is given in Figure 5. Together these findings indicate that palatability is a very important, perhaps the most important, determiner of choice between an ethanol-containing and another fluid under conditions of spaced feeding. Moreover, spaced-feeding procedures appear to interact with sweetness in single-fluid situations to produce an especially high liquid consumption. Samson and Falk (1974c) showed that addition of saccharin to an ethanol solution during the multiple daily session procedure increased daily consumption, whereas the addition of saccharin to the ethanol solution drunk by other animals living in home cages had no effect on consumption. Keehn *et al.* (1970) had made a similar observation, but on the effect of adding saccharin to water in experimental sessions.

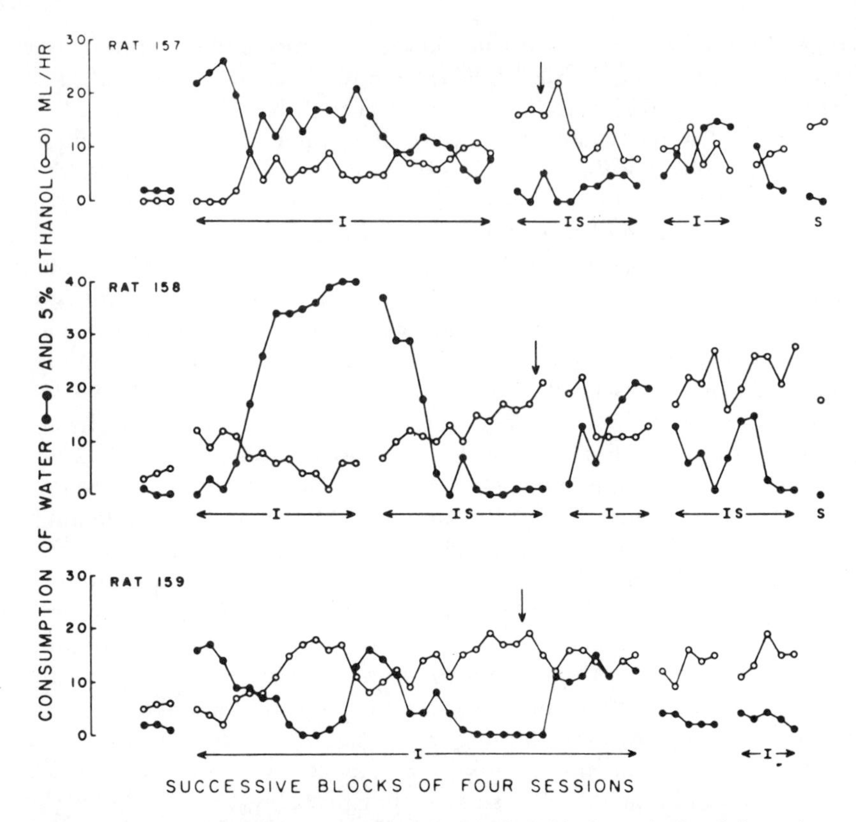

Figure 4. Consumption of water and 5% alcohol by individual rats during daily sessions. Food pellets were delivered at 1-min intervals during some sessions (I), and massed at the beginning of the session in others. Saccharin was added to the alcohol in some sessions (S). Session length was reduced from 2 hr to 1 hr at the vertical arrow. From Gilbert (1976c). Reprinted by permission; copyright by Journal of Studies on Alcohol, Inc., New Brunswick, N.J. 08903.

3.5. Loss of Control by the Inducing Schedule

In their regrettably brief report, McMillan *et al.* (1974) noted that the multiple-daily-session spaced-feeding procedure lost control of alcohol drinking: ". . . the drinking pattern became characterized by long bursts of drinking during which pellets were not eaten, by occasional pellet deliveries not followed by drinking, and by consumption of alcohol during the 2 hour periods in which no pellets were delivered." Substantial ethanol drinking continued, nonetheless, perhaps for some of the same reasons that ethanol drinking continues when food presentation ceases, or ceases to be intermittent. Falk and his colleagues do not mention such loss of control by the inducing schedule. Perhaps they did not look for it. None of their reports provides relevant evidence.

Two kinds of evidence on loss of control have come from an experiment in which drinking of 5% ethanol under regimens of 6 1-hr and one 6-hr spaced-feeding sessions each day (Gilbert, 1977). Animals in the former group continued to confine most of their drinking to sessions as the ethanol concentration was increased, although the percentage drunk during the 3-hr intervals between sessions increased in a concentration-related manner: it was 23% when the concentration was 6.25%. Animals having one 6-hr session each day drank more than half their daily intake of 6.25% ethanol during the 18-hr interval between sessions. Thus, in both groups, but to differing degrees, ethanol drinking came under the control of events happening between rather than during the spaced-feeding sessions. More compelling as an indication of loss of control by the spaced-feeding procedure was the observation

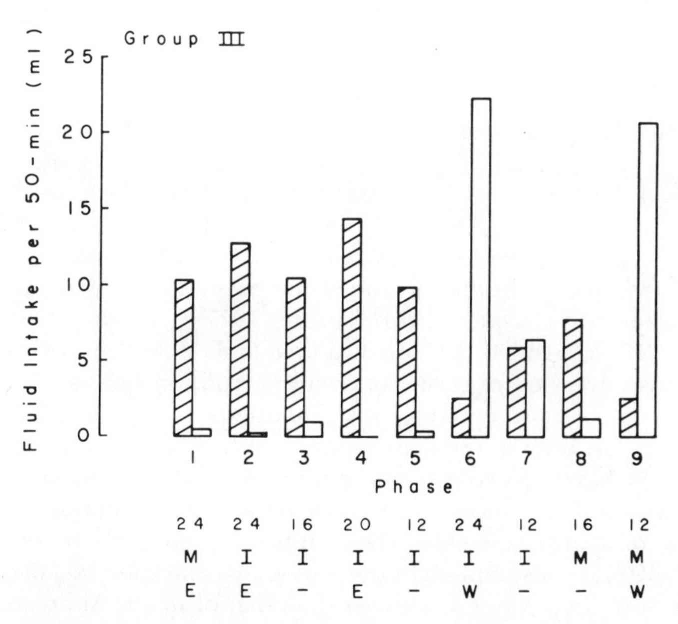

Figure 5. Mean consumption of 5% alcohol (hatched bars) and water by three rats during the last four sessions of each of the nine indicated phases. The three rows below the abscissa show the number of sessions in each phase, whether the 50 pellets per session were presented at the beginning of the session (M) or at 1-min intervals (I), and when 0.2% saccharin was added to alcohol (E) or water (W). A certain amount of lability is evident (e.g., phases 5 and 7), but it is nevertheless clear that the most dramatic changes in alcohol consumption were achieved by providing a more palatable alternative.

that substitution of water for 6.25 % ethanol after some weeks of exposure to ethanol drinking under the procedure produced what appeared to be a permanent loss of polydipsia. Initial water intake levels were not regained. Daily fluid consumption was similar to what might have been expected if each day's ration of food pellets had been presented all together. This loss occurred only in the group having 6 1-hr sessions per day. Polydipsic water drinking was quickly recovered in the other group. The loss of control could have been the result of the withdrawal experience in the group having 6 1-hr sessions, an experience possibly not shared by the other group. More plausibly, the spaced-feeding schedule lost control while ethanol was being drunk, something that did not happen to the group having one 6-hr session daily, because animals in this group did not drink much of the ethanol solution while food was being presented. If, indeed, there are intrinsic features in the schedule-induced consumption of ethanol that cause the spaced-feeding procedure to lose control over ethanol drinking, the utility of the procedure as a model of chronic ethanol abuse may be in jeopardy, as will be discussed in a later section.

4. Schedule-Induced Consumption of Drugs Other Than Ethanol

Spaced-feeding procedures have been used to induce drinking of solutions of narcotic analgesics (Jacquet, 1975; Leander *et al.*, 1975a,b; McMillan and Leander, 1976; Stretch *et al.*, 1974; Thompson *et al.* 1971), barbiturates (Kodluboy and Thompson, 1971; Meisch, 1969), chlordiazepoxide (Jacquet, 1975; Sanger, 1977a), and amphetamines (Jacquet, 1975; Sanger, 1977b). Leander and McMillan (1975) have provided an overview of their work with narcotic analgesics.

In general, consumption of drug solutions during spaced-feeding procedures has been lower than water consumption, but has exceeded what would have occurred if the solution had been available without the spaced-feeding procedure. In this respect, consumption of these solutions of drugs resembles consumption of ethanol. In one case (Sanger, 1977a) consumption of the lowest concentration of a drug (0.1 mg/ml chlordiazepoxide) was higher than that of water. Although fluid consumption generally decreased with increasing concentration, drug consumption increased, again in a manner similar to ethanol. Where spaced feeding was contingent upon bar pressing or some other behavior, changes in the rate of food-reinforced behavior were sometimes reported, consisting of an increase (Leander *et al.*, 1975b) and a decrease (Stretch *et al.*, 1974) in rate when morphine was being ingested, and an increase (Kodluboy and Thompson, 1971) and a decrease (Meisch, 1969) in rate when a barbiturate solution was being consumed—the differences could have been related to the differences in drug, reinforcement schedule, and dose between the various studies. The changes in base-line rate were most likely a pharmacological effect, although it is possible that palatability-induced changes in drinking rate could have affected the rate of food-reinforced behavior.

Palatability might also have been a factor in some of the changes in liquid intake that occurred when the drugs were introduced, but it is likely, too, that pharmacological factors played a part. The effects of drugs on schedule-induced behavior are discussed more thoroughly in Chapter 5. One feature should be mentioned further here, however. It is the frequent reporting of loss of control by the inducing schedule over the drinking of drug solutions. This has been most clearly evident in the work by McMillan, Leander, and associates on the schedule-induced consumption of narcotic analgesics. Leander *et al.* (1975b) found that during chronic exposure to 4-hr daily sessions in which pellets were delivered at close to 90-sec intervals, drinking episodes increased in length but became less frequent, their occurrence eventually bearing little relation to the usual postpellet ingestion pattern found in spaced-feeding procedures.

As in the earlier-discussed case of ethanol, the loss of control by the inducing schedule could have occurred because the chronic exposure to morphine or methadone had induced physical dependence on the drug, which in turn was determining the pattern of drinking within sessions. An acute pharmacological effect can be ruled out because acute morphine ingestion did not produce loss of control (Leander *et al.*, 1975b).

Evidence of physical dependence was also provided in these studies by injecting a narcotic antagonist. Naloxone precipitated characteristic withdrawal signs in rats that had been ingesting morphine during daily 4-hr spaced-feeding sessions for 130 days (Leander *et al.*, 1975b). The time of naloxone administration was not specified, and thus the possible paradox implied in the occurrence of physical dependence after what were effectively once-daily morphine administrations cannot be further discussed. In another study in the series, excessive drinking of a saline solution of etonitazene, a potent opiate-like drug, was induced by spaced feeding sessions occurring four times per day (McMillan and Leander, 1976). Naloxone temporarily suppressed drinking of this drug solution in chronically exposed rats but had little effect on the drinking of a saline solution by rats not given etonitazene. If the rats had been "in need" of etonitazene, the effect of administering an opiate antagonist might more reasonably have been to increase drinking of the drug solution, in order to compensate for antagonistic effect, in the same way as nalorphine increases responding for intravenously administered morphine (Goldberg *et al.*, 1971). More compelling evidence of dependence—or, rather, the induced reinforcing property of the drug—was provided in the McMillan and Leander study by the observation that etonitazene added to saline made it more preferable to water under conditions in which water was usually preferred to saline. Occasional opiate abstinence signs were also observed in these rats, on days when little etonitazene drinking occurred. However, it is puzzling that they do not seem to have been as severe as in another study by these authors in which withdrawal signs were observed after 12 days of consumption of an etonitazene solution, without the benefit of the spaced-feeding procedure, at much lower levels of intake, that is, 0.5 rather than 2.5 mg/kg/day (McMillan *et al.*, 1976). As in the case of ethanol, the ability of the schedule-induction procedure to produce physical dependence on psychotropic drugs is clearly in need of further elaboration.

5. An Animal Model of Human Alcoholism

Human alcoholism is variously defined, without consensus as to whether emphasis should be placed upon physical dependence, behavioral disruption, amount of consumption, or damage to health (de Lint and Schmidt, 1976). Although few would disagree that physical dependence implies alcoholism, there is little agreement as to what constitutes dependence, and rather more as to the possibility of alcoholism without dependence. The trend seems to be toward the kind of behavioral definition of an alcoholic proposed by Trice (1970): "any individual whose repeated or continued use of alcohol interferes with the efficient performance of his work." It is difficult to translate such a definition into requirements of an animal model. This section consists of brief evaluations of the different kinds of animal models of alcoholism that have been developed, with emphasis on the induction of alcohol drinking by spaced-feeding procedures.

5.1. Forced Consumption of Ethanol

Generally speaking, preparations that have been presented as animal models of alcoholism have merely produced physical dependence upon ethanol. Dependence in rhesus monkeys, beagle dogs, and rats has been achieved by intragastric intubation (Ellis and Pick, 1973; Hunter *et al.*, 1975; Majchrowicz, 1975), in mice by inhalation (Goldstein, 1973), and in rhesus monkeys, miniature swine, and mice by diet adulteration (Pieper and Skeen, 1972; Tumbleson *et al.*, 1973). Each procedure was successful in that apparently unequivocal withdrawal signs occurred when ethanol was no longer available. However, in each case ethanol consumption was essentially unavoidable. Such preparations are extremely useful when the prime object of research is to examine the pathological consequences of ethanol dependence rather than to discover a possible basis for the development and maintenance of alcoholism in humans.

5.2. Intravenous and Intragastric Self-Administration

Where ethanol-seeking behavior is of concern, it is important that an animal model incorporate "voluntary" self-administration of the drug. One method of achieving self-administration that causes ethanol dependence is to allow an animal to deliver an ethanol solution directly into its bloodstream (Woods *et al.*, 1971; Smith *et al.*, 1975a). A similar method involves intragastric administration of ethanol or other drugs (Marfaign-Jallat *et al.*, 1974; Smith *et al.*, 1975b). It has been used to demonstrate reinforcement by drug self-administration but not physical dependence. Such a model approximates more closely to the elective feature of human alcoholism. The rhesus monkeys of Woods and his colleagues could abstain from pushing on the lever that caused the ethanol to flow in the permanently indwelling intravenous catheter without suffering consequences other than those related to ethanol. Furthermore, their monkeys exhibited behavior patterns that resemble those of some human alcoholics: in particular, there were instances of spontaneous cessation of ethanol self-administration with consequent self-induced signs of withdrawal. However, intravenous and intragastric self-administration, although useful in investigating the reinforcing properties of ethanol, are deficient as a basis for an animal model of human alcoholism for at least three reasons:

1. Human ethanol consumption is invariably by the oral route, a route that provides feedback relations between ethanol-seeking behavior and the effects of ethanol that are possibly quite different from those provided by the intravenous or the intragastric route. (It can be argued, however, that because animals cannot easily bridge the 10–40 min intervals that occur between the oral consumption of ethanol and its effects on the central nervous system, the intravenous route, which gives rise to practically instantaneous effects, is a better basis for an animal model.)

2. It might be important to consider ethanol drinking as part of the general drinking pattern of the organism. Preliminary analysis of

the Addiction Research Foundation's Ontario Drinking Survey suggests that heavy alcohol drinkers also drink more than average amounts of other fluids, although the proportion of fluid consumed as alcohol increases with alcohol consumption. A different kind of evidence comes from a study by Marlatt *et al.* (1973). When requested to drink what was reported to be vodka and tonic or tonic alone, a group of alcoholics drank much more of either fluid than a group of social drinkers. The groups differed especially with regard to mean sip size, although even the social drinkers took larger-than-normal sips when they thought they were drinking vodka. Sip size has been found to be a major distinguishing factor in other studies of alcoholic drinking behavior (Sobell *et al.*, 1972; Williams and Brown, 1974). If alcoholism is determined even in part by factors that determine the drinking of other fluids, then an animal model should allow both that these factors can determine alcohol intake and that the relation between different kinds of drinking can be examined. Neither is possible with intravenous or intragastric administration of ethanol.

3. A third reason for the intravenous model's deficiency is that it is difficult to incorporate an extrinsic reinforcement aspect. There is considerable evidence that some ethanol consumption in humans is maintained by consequences quite unrelated to those that result directly from ethanol consumption (Giffen, 1966). However, extrinsic reinforcement of ethanol drinking alone does not seem to provide a satisfactory model. Intoxication in rats has been achieved by reinforcing ethanol consumption by food presentation (Keehn, 1969), but dependence under these conditions has not been demonstrated. One reason that explicit reinforcement of ethanol drinking in animals has not been more thoroughly investigated as a potential model may be the somewhat unfair comparison by Mello and Mendelson (1971) of reinforced and schedule-induced drinking, which favored the latter. A vivid example of explicit reinforcement of alcohol drinking in humans, in this case by the drinker's colleagues, was described recently by Trice (1975), who noted that "liquor cabinets" often emerge around company presidents, encouraging the "top guy" to drink so that he is unable to exert control over immediate subordinates.

5.3. Schedule-Induced Ethanol Consumption

Although degree of consumption in itself is not a sufficient basis for distinguishing alcoholics from other alcohol users, there can be little question that, in general, people with alcohol problems drink more alcohol than those without, and, moreover, that the likelihood of suffering an alcohol-related disease, such as liver cirrhosis, increases with amount consumed (de Lint, 1976; Lelbach, 1974). Where the toxicology of ethanol is the focus, almost any means of getting the drug into the animal, be it intubation, inhalation, intravenous infusion, or intraperitoneal injection, is useful. If we are to use an animal model to understand how it is that some people drink a lot of alcohol, a prime characteristic of the model should be the excessive drinking of an ethanol solution.

The spaced-feeding procedure is one that induces a lot of ethanol drinking. It has often been proposed as a model of alcohol abuse (e.g., Falk and Samson, 1975; Falk *et al.*, 1972; Gilbert, 1975, 1976b; Gilbert and Keehn, 1972). In the first detailed exposition of the animal model, Falk *et al.* (1972) noted that their multiple daily session, spaced-feeding procedure provided a satisfactory animal model in that: (1) chronic and excessive oral ethanol self-administration occurred to the extent that high blood-ethanol levels were maintained, (2) separate sources of ethanol and other food were available so that it was possible to estimate the role of nutritional factors in the consumption of the ethanol, and (3) ethanol consumption was not maintained by explicitly programmed reinforcing events. Falk *et al.* claimed, with justification, that their animals satisfied these criteria, and they effectively countered a criticism by Deutsch that the excessive drinking might have arisen from "simple malnutrition" (Deutsch, 1973; Falk *et al.*, 1973b).

Lester and Freed (e.g., 1972a,b) have claimed that a model based on schedule-induced polydipsia is invalid because the ethanol is being consumed for its calories, whereas humans drink alcohol for its pharmacological effect. The possible role of nutrition in schedule-induced ethanol polydipsia was discussed in an earlier section, where the importance of spaced reinforcement was emphasized. Acceptance of that argument means that the question of nutrition becomes irrelevant. Whether or not this kind of model is invalid because schedule-induced ethanol drinking is not maintained by its pharmacological consequences is another matter. Lester and Freed's assertion implies two things: (1) that pharmacological effects are important determinants of human ethanol-drinking behavior, and (2) that schedule-induced ethanol consumption is not maintained by pharmacological variables.

Regarding the first implication, there is considerable evidence that nonpharmacological factors play an important role in both the initiation and the maintenance of drug abuse, including the abuse of alcohol. In the course of a brief review of some of this evidence I have argued elsewhere, indeed, that the pharmacological effects of drugs may not have very much to do with excessive drug use, and that it may be as wise to search for the causes of drug abuse among the causes of all kinds of excessive behavior as it is to focus upon the peculiarly pharmacological aspects of the drug-taking situation (Gilbert, 1975, 1976b). Since arguing that view, I have become impressed by certain lines of evidence that point to a joint role for pharmacological and environmental variables. Most important is the work of Siegel (1975), who has demonstrated that stimuli that predict drug administration come to evoke a compensatory response. Thus, the injection routine will evoke hyperalgesia if the analgesic morphine is usually administered. The drug effect and the evoked compensatory effect may cancel each other out to provide what is known as pharmacological tolerance, according to Siegel. The compensatory effect may also form the basis of physical dependence; not necessarily the kind that arises from continuous presence of the drug in the body, but sufficient to produce a "withdrawal" reaction when the drug is predicted but not administered (i.e., the compensation occurs without the drug effect). Thus, any stimulus associated with a drug might produce a withdrawal effect, *even if withdrawal has never before been experienced.* Stimuli-predicting drugs may thus come to evoke drug seeking that is reinforced by escape or avoidance of the withdrawal reaction that the stimuli evoke. In this respect it is fascinating to note that craving for alcoholic beverages, as measured by a Desire to Drink Scale, was found in hospitalized abstinent alcoholics to be low when alcohol was unavailable, to be high when alcohol was available for 16 days, and to fall again when alcohol was withdrawn, although not so rapidly as blood-alcohol levels fell (Gross *et al.*, 1977). Craving, in line with the above analysis, is the subjective experience of the compensatory response elicited by stimuli that reliably predict drug administration. This new-found enthusiasm for pharmacology should not be misinterpreted. I still believe the earlier analysis to be valid (Gilbert, 1975, 1976b), that the important questions to ask of an alcoholic are, in this order: (1) Why does he or she behave to excess? (2) Why is alcohol drinking the excessive behavior? Consideration of pharmacological factors such as conditioned compensatory responses may be of more help in answering the less important second question than in discovering the cause to excess. Regarding even abuse of narcotics, which is often thought to be entirely a pharmacological matter, it is instructive to note the summary of Freedman and Senay (1973) on the subject, in the course of a discussion of methadone maintenance therapy for heroin addiction:

> The bulk of evidence, we believe, indicates that addiction is a disorder profoundly reinforced in its *initiation* by social-psychological as well as pharmacological factors. "Friends" group together and supply each other to be different, "cool" and daring. Addiction is then sustained by social and psychological factors in which the reinforcing value of narcotic drugs plays an important, but not an essential, role. Whether tranquilizing and antianxiety

> drug effects are contributory motives in sustaining addiction is as yet unclear; but we do know that euphorigenic effects decrease and in some instances disappear entirely as the dependence grows older. We do not think that physical dependence itself is sufficient to generate the profoundly self-destructive behaviors characteristic of the modal pattern of narcotics addiction with which the public is most concerned (p. 155).

Freedman and Senay concluded, nonetheless, that treatment programs that substitute one narcotic for another are generally more successful than those that do not.

Contrary to Lester and Freed's assertion, Falk and Samson (1975) have argued that schedule-induced ethanol consumption may be maintained in part by the pharmacological consequences of ethanol ingestion. They claim that the effect of the "generator schedule" is to exaggerate the reinforcing efficacy of a marginal reinforcing agent such as a weak ethanol solution. The reinforcement may be initially pharmacological, or may become pharmacological if physical dependence develops. The generator schedule is also required to maintain the excessive ethanol consumption, according to Falk and Samson, which continues until the schedule is changed or until an alternative, stronger reinforcer is available. The authors also note the possibility of synergism between the generator schedule and other potential determinants of excessive drinking, as in the case of the very high level of consumption that occurred when saccharin was added to the ethanol solution being consumed under a spaced-feeding regimen (Samson and Falk, 1974c).

Another criticism of the schedule-induction model made by Deutsch (1973) and also by Heintzelman *et al.* (1976) was that excessive ethanol consumption does not persist once the spaced-feeding regimen is terminated. The evidence, as reviewed above, is that ethanol drinking does tend to persist more than water drinking, but not usually to the extent found when the spaced-feeding regimen is in effect. This criticism presupposes that excessive alcohol use in humans does persist in full degree when environmentally inducing conditions are removed. There is a certain amount of evidence that it does not. Some comes from the Addiction Research Foundation's Bon Accord project, a residential, work-oriented program located 60 miles from Toronto, where skid-row alcoholics engage in what can reasonably be called moderate social drinking, maintaining voluntary abstinence on most days, with only occasional flights into frank intoxication (Oki, 1977).

A more substantial criticism of the model rests on evidence that the spaced-feeding procedure loses control of ethanol consumption during prolonged treatment (Gilbert, 1977; McMillan *et al.*, 1974). If such loss of control is an inevitable feature of chronic application of the procedure, it can be argued that schedule-induction fails as a model of the factors that maintain excessive drinking in humans. It could continue, nevertheless, as a model of how excessive drinking develops. Even if reason were found for excluding the schedule-induction procedure as a model of any of the environmental factors that determine drinking, the drinking of large amounts of ethanol by animals under a spaced-feeding regimen would still provide a useful preparation for the study of many of the features of the human alcohol-drinking situation. Already, the discovery that palatability is of extraordinary importance in the determination of ethanol drinking or its inhibition under the spaced-feeding procedure has drawn attention to the fact that much human alcohol drinking involves sweet solutions of the drug (Samson and Falk, 1974a; Gilbert, 1976c).

A for-the-moment, final criticism of the schedule-induction model is that humans do not usually do their alcohol drinking while receiving small portions of their daily food ration at 90-sec intervals, and, therefore, excessive drinking in animals that is induced by spaced feeding cannot be very relevant to the human condition. Falk and Samson (1975) have countered this objection by noting that spaced presentation of other reinforcers has induced excessive behavior in animals and humans, noting particularly a study by Kachanoff *et al.* (1973) in which polydipsia, excessive pacing, and various bizarre acts were induced in schizophrenic patients by intermittent availability of pennies for pulling a cord. Falk and Samson argued that ". . . certain environmental contexts in which people live may constitute appropriate schedules for generating inordinate amounts of excessive behavior. While some of these behaviors may be as inconsequential as scratching, talking, or gesticulating, others may have more serious consequences, such as smoking, drinking alcoholic beverages, or self-administering drugs." Further evidence on the applicability of the schedule-induction procedure to humans has come from a study by Wallace *et al.* (1975), who observed large increases in the rates of emission of various kinds of behavior in university students during intermittent access to an experimentally controlled pinball-machine simulator. Such demonstrations are a necessary prelude to conviction that schedule induction is a feature of human excessive behavior. If the current speculation about the importance of schedule induction in the etiology and maintenance of human excessive behavior is to be taken seriously, an attempt must be made to identify, at least at an intuitive level, the conditions of everyday life that can induce excessive behavior. One approach might be to explore the possibly relevant, common features of the interactions between behavior and environments of people who engage in conspicuous excessive behavior, and to compare them with the interactions of people who do not appear to behave excessively, and also to compare situations in which overbehavers overbehave with those in which they do not. If the speculation is to be elevated to the status of a hypothesis, the comparisons should reveal different patterns of reinforcement between overbehavers and normals, or between overbehaving and nonoverbehaving situations. The environments of overbehavers should correspond to the conditions for inducing excessive behavior, especially when they are behaving excessively. The environments of normal people should not.

6. Summary

Excessive consumption of water can be induced in rats and other animals by feeding small portions of a reduced daily food ration at intervals on the order of 90 sec. The phenomenon is known as schedule-induced polydipsia. The drinking of large amounts of solutions of ethanol and other drugs can also be induced in this way, amounts being larger than with any other procedure that has been investigated. Palatability of the ingested fluid is possibly the most important determinant of how much of a fluid is drunk under a schedule-induction procedure, and of which fluid is selected when more than one is available. Signs of physical dependence on ingested drugs have been demonstrated when the solution is withdrawn after exposure for many days to sessions of schedule induction that occur at frequent intervals throughout each day. The inducing schedule appears to lose control over the ingestion of drugs during chronic treatment of the kind that produces physical dependence. This loss of control argues against the use of schedule induction of excessive drug consumption in animals as a model for the maintenance of human drug abuse. The animal model may nevertheless be useful in understanding the etiology of drug abuse. It is certainly useful as a preparation that features the main behavioral characteristic of alcoholism—the inordinate consumption of solutions of ethanol.

Acknowledgments

This chapter has had a checkered history. Its origin lies in a presentation entitled "Schedule-Induced Phenomena: Drug Taking as Excessive Behaviour," made at the Annual Meeting of the Canadian Psychological Association, Windsor, Ontario, in June, 1974, as part of a symposium on *Behavioural Models of Drug Dependence.* The symposium proceedings were to have been published as a book of the same title, and a chapter based on my presentation, and having the same title, was sometimes cited accordingly. That book did not materialize and I am grateful to the editors of this volume for the invitation to update the earlier work, and thereby rescue it from oblivion. I am grateful, too, to H. D. Cappell and J. D. Keehn for their helpful comments on a draft of the original chapter, and to Marilyn Schwieder for her continuing assistance in the laboratory.

7. References

Atrens, D. M., 1973, Schedule-induced polydipsia and polyphagia in non-deprived rats reinforced by intracranial stimulation, *Learn. Motiv.* **4:**320–326.

Bond, N. W., Blackman, D. E., and Scruton, P., 1973, Suppression of operant behavior and schedule-induced licking in rats, *J. Exp. Anal. Behav.* **20:**375–383.

Cappell, H., LeBlanc, A. E., and Endrenyi, L., 1973, Aversive conditioning by psychoactive drugs: effects of morphine, alcohol, and chloridiazepoxide, *Psychopharmacologia* **29:**239–246.

Catania, A. C., 1973, Self-inhibiting effects of reinforcement, *J. Exp. Anal. Behav.* **19:**517–526.

Collier, H. O. J., 1972, The experimental analysis of drug dependence, *Endeavour* **31:**123–129.

Colotla, V. A., and Keehn, J. D., 1975, Effects of reinforcer-pellet composition on schedule-induced polydipsia with alcohol, water, and saccharin, *Psychol. Rec.* **25:**91–98.

de Lint, J., 1976, Epidemiological aspects of alcoholism, *Int. J. Mental Health* **5:**29–51.

de Lint, J., and Schmidt, W., 1976, Alcoholism and mortality, *in: The Biology of Alcoholism* (B. Kissin and H. Begleiter, eds.), Vol. 4, pp. 275–305, Plenum Press, New York.

Deutsch, J. A., 1973, Behavioral maintenance of high concentrations of blood ethanol and physical dependence in the rat, *Science* **180:**880.

Ellis, F. W., and Pick, J. R., 1973, Animal models of ethanol dependency, *Ann. N.Y. Acad. Sci.* **215:**215–217.

Everett, P. B., and King, R. A., 1970, Schedule-induced alcohol ingestion, *Psychon. Sci.* **18:**278–279.

Falk, J. L., 1961, Production of polydipsia in normal rats by an intermittent food schedule, *Science* **133:**195–196.

Falk, J. L., 1966, The motivational properties of schedule-induced behavior, *J. Exp. Anal. Behav.* **9:**19–25.

Falk, J. L., 1972, The nature and determinants of adjunctive behaviour, *in: Schedule Effects: Drugs, Drinking and Aggression* (R. M. Gilbert and J. D. Keehn, eds.), pp. 148–173, University of Toronto Press, Toronto.

Falk, J. L., and Samson, H. H., 1975, Schedule-induced physical dependence on ethanol, *Pharmacol. Rev.* **27:**449–464.

Falk, J. L., Samson, H. H., and Winger, G., 1972, Behavioral maintenance of high concentrations of blood ethanol and physical dependence in the rat, *Science* **177:**811–813.

Falk, J. L., Samson, H. H., and Tang, M., 1973a, Chronic ingestion techniques for the production of physical dependence on ethanol, *in: Alcohol Intoxication and Withdrawal: Experimental Studies I* (M. M. Gross, ed.), pp. 197–211, Plenum Press, New York.

Falk, J. L., Samson, H. H., and Winger, G., 1973b, Behavioral maintenance of high concentrations of blood ethanol and physical dependence in the rat, *Science* **180:**881.

Falk, J. L., Samson, H. H., and Winger, G., 1976, Polydipsia-induced alcohol dependency in rats, *Science* **192:**492.

Freed, E. X., 1968, Effect of self-intoxication upon approach–avoidance conflict in the rat, *Quart. J. Stud. Alc.* **29:**323–329.

Freed, E. X., 1971a, Effects of conflict upon schedule-induced consumption of water and alcohol, *Psychol. Rep.* **29:**115–118.

Freed, E. X., 1971b, Alcohol and conflict: role of drug-dependent learning in the rat, *Quart. J. Stud. Alc.* **32:**13–28.

Freed, E. X., 1972, Alcohol polydipsia in the rat as a function of caloric need, *Quart. J. Stud. Alc.* **33:**504–507.

Freed, E. X., 1974, Fluid self-selection by rats given choices under schedule-induced polydipsia, *Quart. J. Stud. Alc.* **35:**1035–1043.

Freed, E. X., and Lester, D., 1970, Schedule-induced consumption of ethanol: calories or chemotherapy? *Physiol. Behav.* **5:**555–560.

Freed, E. X., Carpenter, J. A., and Hymowitz, N., 1970, Acquisition and extinction of schedule-induced polydipsic consumption of alcohol and water, *Psychol. Rep.* **26:**915–922.

Freed, E. X., Hymowitz, N., and Fazzaro, J., 1974, Effects of response-independent electric shock on schedule-induced alcohol and water intake, *Psychol. Rep.* **34:**63–71.

Freedman, D. X., and Senay, E. C., 1973, Methadone treatment of heroin addiction, *Ann. Rev. Med.* **24:**153–164.

Freund, G., 1973, Alcohol, barbiturate, and bromide withdrawal syndromes in mice, *Ann. N.Y. Acad. Sci.* **215:**224–234.

Geller, I., 1971, Ethanol preference as a function of photoperiod, *Science* **173:**456–458.

Gibbins, R. J., Kalant, H., Le Blanc, A. E., and Clark, J. W., 1971, Effects of chronic administration of alcohol on startle thresholds in rats, *Psychopharmacologia* **19:**95–104.

Giffen, P. J., 1966, The revolving door: a functional interpretation, *Can. Rev. Sociol. Anthropol.* **3:**154–166.

Gilbert, R. M., 1972, Persistence of palatability-induced polydipsia, *Psychon. Sci.* **29:**55–58.

Gilbert, R. M., 1973, Effects of ethanol on adjunctive drinking and bar-pressing under various schedules of reinforcement, *Bull. Psychon. Soc.* **1:**161–164.

Gilbert, R. M., 1974a, Ubiquity of schedule-induced polydipsia, *J. Exp. Anal. Behav.* **21:**277–284.

Gilbert, R. M., 1974b, Schedule-induced ethanol polydipsia in rats with restricted fluid availability, *Psychopharmacologia* **38:**151–157.

Gilbert, R. M., 1974c, Schedule-induced ethanol polydipsia, *in: Aportaciones al Análisis de la Conducta* (J. E. Díaz, E. Ribes, and S. Gomar, eds.), pp. 136–155, Trillas, Mexico, D.F.

Gilbert, R. M., 1975, Drug abuse as excessive behavior, *Addictions* **22:**52–72.

Gilbert, R. M., 1976a, Dose-division and debility in the production of ethanol withdrawal signs, Substudy No. 753, Addiction Research Foundation, Toronto.

Gilbert, R. M., 1976b, L'abus des drogues, indice d'un comportement excessif, *Toxicomanies* **9:**7–23.

Gilbert, R. M., 1976c, Shifts in the water and alcohol solution intake by rats under conditions of schedule-induction, *J. Stud. Alc.* **37:**940–949.

Gilbert, R. M., 1977, Chronic alcohol drinking and subsequent withdrawal in rats exposed to different diurnal distributions of schedule-induction sessions, *in: Alcohol Intoxication and Withdrawal: Experimental Studies IIIb* (M. M. Gross, ed.), pp. 503–522, Plenum Press, New York.

Gilbert, R. M., and Keehn, J. D., ed., 1972, *Schedule Effects: Drugs, Drinking, and Aggression,* pp. ix–xii, University of Toronto Press, Toronto.

Githens, S. H., Hawkins, T. D., and Schrot, J., 1973, DRL schedule-induced alcohol ingestion, *Physiol. Psychol.* **1:**397–400.

Goldberg, S. R., Woods, J. H., and Schuster, C. R., 1971, Nalorphine-induced changes in morphine self-administration in rhesus monkeys, *J. Pharmacol. Exp. Ther.* **176:**464–471.

Goldstein, D. B., 1973, Quantitative study of alcohol withdrawal signs in mice, *Ann. N.Y. Acad. Sci.* **215:**218–223.

Goldstein, D. B., 1976, Pharmacological aspects of physical dependence on ethanol, *Life Sci.* **18:**553–562.

Gross, M. M., Kierzenbaum, H., Lee, Y., Lewis, E., and Downes, M. 1977, Appetite for alcohol during human alcoholization and withdrawal, paper presented at the Third Biennal International Interdisciplinary Symposium of the Biomedical Alcohol Research Section, International Council on Alcohol and the Addictions, Lausanne, June 1976.

Hawkins, T. D., Schrot, J. F., Githens, S. H., and Everett, P. B., 1972, Schedule-induced polydipsia: an analysis of water and alcohol ingestion, *in: Schedule Effects: Drugs, Drinking, and Aggression* (R. M. Gilbert and J. D. Keehn, eds.), pp. 95–128, University of Toronto Press, Toronto.

Heintzelman, M. E., Best, J., and Senter, R. J., 1976, Polydipsia-induced alcohol dependency in rats: a reexamination, *Science* **191:**482–483.

Holman, R. B., and Myers, R. D., 1968, Ethanol consumption under conditions of psychogenic polydipsia, *Physiol. Behav.* **3:**369–371.

Hunter, B. E., Riley, J. N., and Walker, D. W., 1975, Ethanol dependence in the rat: a parametric analysis, *Pharmacol. Biochem. Behav.* **3:**619–629.

Hymowitz, N., Freed, E. X., and Lester, D., 1970, The independence of bar-pressing and schedule-induced drinking, *Psychon. Sci.* **20:**45–46.

Jacobs, H. L., and Sharma, K. N., 1969, Taste vs. calories: sensory and metabolic signals in the control of food intake, *Ann. N.Y. Acad. Sci.* **157:**1084–1125.

Jacquet, Y. F., 1975, Schedule-induced drug ingestion: differences due to type of drug; paper given to the Eastern Psychological Association.

Kachanoff, R., Leveille, R., McLelland, J. P., and Wayner, M. J., 1973, Schedule induced behavior in humans, *Physiol. Behav.* **11:**395–398.

Keehn, J. D., 1969, "Voluntary" consumption of alcohol by rats, *Quart. J. Stud. Alc.* **30:**320–329.

Keehn, J. D., 1972, Effects of trihexyphenidyl on schedule-induced alcohol drinking by rats, *Psychon. Sci.* **29:**20–22.

Keehn, J. D., and Coulson, G. E., 1975, Schedule-induced choice of water versus alcohol, *Psychol. Rec.* **25:**325–328.

Keehn, J. D., Colotla, V. A., and Beaton, J. M., 1970, Palatability as a factor in the duration and pattern of schedule-induced drinking, *Psychol. Rec.* **20:**433–442.

King, G. D., 1974, The enhancement of schedule-induced polydipsia by preschedule non-contingent shock, *Bull. Psychon. Soc.* **3:**46–48.

Kodluboy, D. W., and Thompson, T., 1971, Adjunctive self-administration of barbiturate solutions, *Proceedings of the 79th Annual Convention of the American Psychological Association,* pp. 749–750.

Leander, J. D., and McMillan, D. E., 1975, Schedule-induced narcotic ingestion, *Pharmacol. Rev.* **27:**475–487.

Leander, J. D., McMillan, D. E., and Harris, L. S., 1975a, Effects of narcotic agonists and antagonists on schedule-induced water and morphine ingestion, *J. Pharmacol. Exp. Ther.* **195:**271–278.

Leander, J. D., McMillan, D. E., and Harris, L. S., 1975b, Schedule-induced oral narcotic self-administration: acute and chronic effects, *J. Pharmacol. Exp. Ther.* **195:**279–287.

Le Blanc, A. E., Gibbins, R. J., and Kalant, H., 1975, Generalization of behaviorally augmented tolerance to ethanol, and its relation to physical dependence, *Psychopharmacologia* **44:**241–246.

Lelbach, W. K., 1974, Organic pathology related to volume and pattern of alcohol use, *in: Research Advances in Alcohol and Drug Problems* (R. J. Gibbins, Y. Israel, H. Kalant, R. E. Popham, W. Schmidt, and R. G. Smart, eds.), Vol. 1, pp. 93–198, Wiley, New York.

Lester, D., 1961, Self-maintenance of intoxication in the rat, *Quart. J. Stud. Alc.* **22:**223–231.

Lester, D., and Freed, E. X., 1972a, The rat views alcohol—nutrition or nirvana? *in: Biological Aspects of Alcohol Consumption* (O. Forsander and K. Eriksson, eds.), pp. 51–57, Finnish Foundation for Alcohol Studies, Helsinki.

Lester, D., and Freed, E. X., 1972b, A rat model of alcoholism? *Ann. N.Y. Acad. Sci.* **197:**54–59.

Lieber, C. S., 1975, Alcohol and malnutrition in the pathogenesis of liver disease, *J. Amer. Med. Ass.* **233:**1077–1082.

Majchrowicz, E., 1975, Induction of physical dependence upon ethanol and the associated behavioral changes in rats, *Psychopharmacologia* **43:**245–254.

Marfaing-Jallat, P., Pruvost, M., and Le Magnen, J., 1974, La consommation d'éthanol par auto-administration intragastrique chez le rat, *J. Physiol.* (*Paris*) **68:**81–95.

Marlatt, G. A., Demming, B., and Reid, J. B., 1973, Loss of control drinking in alcoholics, *J. Abnorm. Psychol.* **81:**233–241.

Mayer, J., 1970, Alcohol as calories, *Postgrad. Med.* **47:**281–282.

McMillan, D. E., and Leander, J. D., 1976, Schedule-induced oral self administration of etonitazene, *Pharmacol. Biochem. Behav.* **4:**137–141.

McMillan, D. E., Leander, J. D., and Ellis, F. W., 1974, Consumption of ethanol and water under schedule-induced polydipsia (SIP), *Pharmacologist* **16:**637.

McMillan, D. E., Leander, J. D., Wilson, T. W., Wallace, S. C., Fix, T., Redding, S., and Turk, R. T., 1976, Oral ingestion of narcotic analgesics by rats, *J. Pharmacol. Exp. Ther.* **196:**269–279.

Meisch, R. A., 1969, Self-administration of pentobarbital by means of schedule-induced polydipsia, *Psychon. Sci.* **16:**16–17.

Meisch, R. A., 1975, The function of schedule-induced polydipsia in establishing ethanol as a positive reinforcer, *Pharmacol. Rev.* **27:**465–473.

Meisch, R. A., and Thompson, T., 1971, Ethanol intake in the absence of concurrent food reinforcement, *Psychopharmacologia* **22:**72–79.

Meisch, R. A., and Thompson, T., 1972, Ethanol intake during schedule-induced polydipsia, *Physiol. Behav.* **8:**471–475.

Meisch, R. A., and Thompson, T., 1974a, Ethanol as a reinforcer: an operant analysis of ethanol dependence *in: Drug Addiction,* Vol. 3, *Neurobiology and Influences on Behavior* (J. M. Singh and H. Lal, eds.), pp. 117–133, Symposia Specialists, Miami.

Meisch, R. A., and Thompson, T., 1974b, Rapid establishment of ethanol as a reinforcer for rats *Psychopharmacologia* **37:**311–321.

Meisch, R. A., Henningfield, J. E., and Thompson, T., 1975, Establishment of ethanol as a reinforcer for rhesus monkeys via the oral route: initial results, *in: Alcohol Intoxication and Withdrawal: Experimental Studies II* (M. M. Gross, ed.), pp. 323–342, Plenum Press, New York.

Mello, N. K., and Mendelson, J. H., 1971, Evaluation of a polydipsia technique to induce alcohol consumption in monkeys, *Physiol. Behav.* **7:**827–836.

Mottin, J. L., 1973, Drug-induced attenuation of alcohol consumption: review and evaluation of claimed, potential, or current therapies, *Quart. J. Stud. Alc.* **34:**444–472.

Munn, N., 1950, *Handbook of Psychological Research on the Rat,* Houghton Mifflin, Boston.

Myers, R. D., 1966, Voluntary alcohol consumption in animals: peripheral and intracerebral factors, *Psychosomat. Med.* **28:**484–497.

Ogata, H., Ogata, F., Mendelson, J. H., and Mello, N. K., 1972a, Evaluation of a technique to induce alcohol dependence and tolerance in the mouse by the use of schedule-induced polydipsia, *Jap. J. Stud. Alc.* **7**:27–35.

Ogata, H., Ogata, F., Mendelson, J. H., and Mello, N. K., 1972b, A comparison of techniques to induce alcohol dependence and tolerance in the mouse, *J. Pharmacol. Exp. Ther.* **180**:216–230.

Oki, G., 1977 (in press), Alcohol use by Skid Row alcoholics. I. Drinking at Bon Accord, *J. Stud. Alc.*

Pieper, W. A., and Skeen, M. J., 1972, Induction of physical dependence on ethanol in rhesus monkeys using an oral acceptance technique, *Life Sci.* **11**:989–997.

Premack, D., 1972, The effect of extinction on the preference relations between the instrumental and contingent events, *in Reinforcement: Behavioral Analyses* (R. M. Gilbert and J. R. Millenson, eds.), pp. 51–65, Academic Press, New York.

Samson, H. H., and Falk, J. L., 1974a, Alteration of fluid preference in ethanol-dependent animals, *J. Pharmacol. Exp. Ther.* **190**:365–376.

Samson, H. H., and Falk, J. L., 1974b, Ethanol and discriminative motor control: effects on normal and dependent animals, *Pharmacol. Biochem. Behav.* **2**:791–801.

Samson, H. H., and Falk, J. L., 1974c, Schedule-induced ethanol polydipsia: enhancement by saccharin, *Pharmacol. Biochem. Behav.* **2**:835–838.

Samson, H. H., and Falk, J. L., 1975, Pattern of daily blood ethanol elevation and the development of physical dependence, *Pharmacol. Biochem. Behav.* **3**:1119–1123.

Sanger, D. J., 1977a, Schedule-induced drinking of chlordiazepoxide solutions by rats, *Pharmacol. Biochem. Behav.* **7**:1–6.

Sanger, D. J., 1977b, *d*-Amphetamine and adjunctive drinking in rats, *Psychopharmacology* **54**:273–276.

Segal, E. F., 1969, The interaction of psychogenic polydipsia with wheel running in rats, *Psychon. Sci.* **14**:141–144.

Segal, E. F., 1972, Induction and the provenance of operants, *in: Reinforcement: Behavioral Analyses* (R. M. Gilbert and J. R. Millenson, eds.), pp. 1–34, Academic Press, New York.

Segal, E. F., and Oden, D. L., 1969, Effects of drinkometer current and foot shock on psychogenic polydipsia, *Psychon. Sci.* **14**:13–15.

Senter, R. J., and Sinclair, J. D., 1967, Self-maintenance of intoxication in the rat: a modified replication, *Psychon. Sci.* **9**:291–292.

Siegel, S., 1975, Evidence from rats that morphine tolerance is a learned response, *J. Comp. Physiol. Psychol.* **89**:498–506.

Singer, G., Wayner, M. J., Stein, J., Cimino, K., and King, K., 1974, Adjunctive behavior induced by wheel running, *Physiol. Behav.* **12**:493–495.

Smith, S. G., Werner, T. E., and Davis, W. M., 1975a, Intravenous drug self-administration in rats: substitution of ethyl alcohol for morphine, *Psychol. Rec.* **25**:17–20.

Smith, S. G., Werner, T. E., and Davis, W. M., 1975b, Technique for intragastric delivery of solutions: application for self-administration of morphine and alcohol by rats, *Physiol. Psychol.* **3**:220–224.

Sobell, M. B., Schaeffer, H. H., and Mills, K. C., 1972, Differences in baseline drinking behavior between alcoholics and normal drinkers, *Behav. Res. Ther.* **10**:257–267.

Staddon, J. E. R., 1977, Schedule-induced behavior, *in: Handbook of Operant Behavior* (W. K. Honig and J. E. R. Staddon, eds.), pp. 125–152, Prentice-Hall, Englewood Cliffs, N.J.

Staddon, J. E. R., and Ayres, S. L., 1975, Sequential and temporal properties of behavior induced by a schedule of periodic food delivery, *Behaviour* **54**:26–49.

Stretch, R., Gerber, G. J., and Lane, E. B., 1974, Oral intake of morphine during schedule-induced polydipsia, paper given at the annual meeting of the Canadian Psychological Association, Windsor, Ontario.

Thompson, T., Bigelow, G., and Pickens, R., 1971, Environmental variables influencing drug self-administration, *in: Stimulus Properties of Drugs* (T. Thompson and R. Pickens, eds.), pp. 193–207, Appleton-Century-Crofts, New York.

Trice, H. M., 1970, The alcoholic employee and his supervisor: a general management problem, *in Alcohol and Alcoholism* (R. E. Popham, ed.), pp. 338–345, University of Toronto Press, Toronto.

Trice, H. M., 1975, Presentation at the 1st Canadian Conference on Occupational Alcoholism and Drug Abuse, Ottawa.

Tumbleson, M. E., Dexter, J. D., Hutcheson, D. P., and Middleton, C. C., 1973, Miniature swine as models for human alcoholism, *J. Anim. Sci.* **27**:227.

Wallace, M., Singer, G., Wayner, M. J., and Cook, P., 1975, Adjunctive behavior in humans during game playing, *Physiol. Behav.* **14**:651–654.

Williams, R. J., and Brown, R. A., 1974, Differences in baseline drinking behaviour between New Zealand alcoholics and normal drinkers, *Behav. Res. Ther.* **12**:287–294.

Woods, J. H., and Winger, G., 1971, A critique of methods of inducing ethanol self-intoxication in animals, *in: Recent Advances in the Study of Alcoholism* (N. K. Mello and J. H. Mendelson, eds.), pp. 413–416, Government Printing Office, Washington, D.C.

Woods, J. H., Ikomi, F., and Winger, G., 1971, The reinforcing property of ethanol, *in: The Biological Aspects of Alcohol* (M. K. Roach, W. M. McIsaac, and P. J. Creaven, eds.), pp. 371–388, University of Texas Press, Austin.

Yanai, J., and Ginsburg, B. E., 1975, Suppressant effects of alcohol on audiogenic seizures, *Epilepsia* **16**:491–496.

Drugs as Reinforcers 7

Chris E. Johanson

1. Introduction

Historically, the basis for the interest in demonstrating that drugs could serve as reinforcers for operant behavior of laboratory animals was the development of an animal model of human drug abuse. The relevance of data from animal studies to the human problem of drug abuse was based upon the validity of two assumptions: (1) drugs that are reinforcers in infrahuman organisms can serve the same function in man, and (2) humans and animals are comparable in their sensitivity to the effects, including the toxic ones, of the self-administered drug. As more data have been accumulated, these assumptions have been increasingly validated.

The advantages of any animal model need almost no elucidation. The range of experimental manipulations ethically possible with animals allows experiments to be done which would be impossible using human subjects. In addition, using animals in the study of the behavioral aspects of drug abuse forces investigators to divest themselves of psychological preconceptions and be less prone to use vaguely defined personality or character disorders as an explanation of drug self-administration.

The research literature concerned with drugs as reinforcers has rapidly grown in both quantity and scope over the past few years. This rapid expansion of the field makes a comprehensive review of the important issues and literature a prohibitive task. There have been, however, several previous reviews which complement this chapter (Schuster and Thompson, 1969; Schuster and Johanson, 1974; Goldberg, 1976).

Chris E. Johanson • Department of Psychiatry, Pritzker School of Medicine, The University of Chicago, Chicago, Illinois 60637

Many areas not covered completely in this paper are discussed in greater detail in these reviews.

A large proportion of drug self-administration studies emphasizes the pharmacological properties of drugs. For instance, laboratory procedures using animals self-administering drugs have been utilized to evaluate the possibility of developing immunological or pharmacological treatments to aid in the rehabilitation of drug abusers. Bonese *et al.* (1974) used rhesus monkeys trained to self-administer heroin to investigate the feasibility of developing immunization procedures which would block the reinforcing actions of heroin. Although it was found possible to immunize monkeys against the pharmacological actions of heroin, the toxicity of the treatment precluded its application to man. Of importance in the present context, however, is the fact that this evaluation was possible using an animal model of drug abuse.

Self-administration procedures have also been used to study the neurochemical mediation of drug reinforcement. In a study by Ryder *et al.* (1977), animals self-administering methamphetamine were treated chronically with α-methylparatyrosine, which blocks the synthesis of dopamine and norepinephrine, in order to elucidate the role of these neurotransmitters in mediating the reinforcing effects of psychomotor stimulant drugs. Drug self-administration procedures can also be used to study the interaction between drugs. Several investigators (Wilson and Schuster, 1972; Johanson *et al.*, 1976a) have shown that certain doses of a phenothiazine, such as chlorpromazine or perphenazine, increased the rate of self-administration of cocaine. Higher doses decreased its rate of self-administration. On the basis of these studies, it has been postulated that phenothiazines can antagonize the reinforcing properties of cocaine.

As can be seen, these studies of drugs as reinforcers emphasize the nature of the drug as the controlling consequence. Other studies, however, have emphasized the study of the contingency relationship between the behavior and the drug reinforcer. By viewing drugs as reinforcers, it is possible to profit from previous studies of the dynamic variables affecting the rate, pattern, and persistence of behavior maintained by food and water. Research to date has made it increasingly obvious that responding maintained by drugs is similar to responding maintained by any stimulus event (Morse, 1975; Kelleher and Goldberg, 1975). The illicit use of drugs is a behavioral problem and the factors which affect it are the same as those which modify all behavior. Persistent drug-seeking behavior is analogous to the persistent behaviors maintained by certain schedules of food reinforcement. Behaviors which are viewed as abnormal are controlled by the same variables which control the incidence of normal behaviors. Therefore, an animal model of drug abuse can best be included within the general area of understanding the control of behavior.

In the present review, the development of the area of drugs used as reinforcers will be traced, showing the gradual shift in emphasis from pharmacological to behavioral considerations. In addition, a variety of the variables which modify responding maintained by drugs will be discussed. In all these studies, it is the nature of the contingencies governing the relationship between responding and drug reinforcement which are emphasized. The next section of this paper will describe an application of the behavioral research which emphasizes differences between drugs. However, this application owes its usefulness to the appreciation of the fact that drugs function as reinforcers in exactly the same manner as other reinforcers. In the final section, studies involving human drug self-administration will be described.

2. Establishment of Drugs as Reinforcers

Initially, there were two principal problems that deterred the development of an animal model of drug abuse. The first of these was the design of a methodology for delivering the drug. Although drugs can be delivered via a variety of routes, including oral, inhalation, intracerebral, intraperitoneal, intramuscular, and intravenous, the latter route seemed the most desirable. Since drugs of high abuse liability such as heroin and cocaine are administered principally by this route (alcohol is an exception), the use of an intravenous route has more face validity than others. Techniques for the intravenous delivery of drugs were originally described for rats by Weeks (1962, 1964) and Davis (1966), and for rhesus monkeys by Yanagita *et al.* (1965) and Wilson (1970). Such systems have several fundamental aspects: (1) the chronic implantation of a venous catheter into the organism to allow immediate delivery of a drug; (2) a restraining device which allows the organism relatively unrestricted movement within the experimental space, yet still protects the catheter; and (3) an automatic programming system for the delivery of drug, contingent upon some response by the animal.

There are a variety of different designs that have been developed as modifications of these early systems. A description of one of these is adequate to demonstrate the general principles. In a system used at the University of Chicago for rhesus monkeys (Schuster and Johanson, 1974), each animal is fitted with a tubular steel harness which is connected to the wall of a cubicle by a metal spring. This harness and spring arm allow the animal to move freely. The catheter, after exiting the animal, runs through the metal spring to an infusion pump controlled by electronic equipment. As a result, it is possible to deliver a drug instantaneously into a vein without disturbing the animal. Originally, catheters were implanted in either the right or left internal jugular vein and were threaded subcutaneously to an exit point in the midback area of the animal. However, as experiments became more complex, there was a demand for preparations that could be maintained for longer durations. Such demands not only resulted in the development of modifications of the basic system but, in addition, encouraged the sequential use of other veins (e.g., femorals and external jugulars) for catheterization. As a result of all these improvements, it is now possible for investigators with minimal surgical, medical, or electronic skills to deliver intravenous drugs as reinforcers almost as easily as they deliver food reinforcers.

The second problem which prevented the development of a systematic research effort was conceptual. Early theories of drug abuse viewed drug taking as a pathological behavior developed because of psychodynamic or sociological aberrations in the history of the abuser (Chein *et al.*, 1964; Hill *et al.*, 1960). Such personality disorders would be difficult to study using animals unless extraordinary assumptions were made and there were many who believed that the development of an animal model of drug abuse was foolish if not impossible (Lindesmith, 1937). On the other hand, human drug taking could be viewed within the conceptual framework of behavior analysis. The fundamental principle underlying behavior analysis (operant conditioning) is that certain aspects of behavior are controlled by their consequences. Behavior controlled by its consequences is termed operant behavior, and the controlling consequence for the operant behavior is defined as a reinforcer. Within this framework, drugs are viewed as reinforcers capable of controlling behavior in the same manner as conventional reinforcers. One of the major advantages of such an analysis is that it enables the experimenter to utilize a wide range of data derived from the analysis of behavior maintained by these other reinforcers. This, plus a technology for delivering the drug, was a major breakthrough in the development of an animal model of drug abuse.

The first drug studied using both the techniques of delivering drugs intravenously via a catheter and the principles of behavior analysis was morphine. However, it was assumed that morphine and morphinelike drugs, such as heroin, since they produced physical dependence, derived their reinforcing properties at least in part from their ability to alleviate the withdrawal syndrome, as well as from their euphoric effects. Therefore, in the original studies, animals were made physically dependent on morphine prior to any opportunity for self-administration of the drug. Weeks (1962) found that physically dependent rats would regularly press a lever when the response was followed by a 10 mg/kg injection of morphine. In a second study, Weeks and Collins (1964) found that lowering the dose of morphine increased the rate of responding but decreased overall intake. One of the first studies using rhesus monkeys which were dependent on morphine was done by Thompson and Schuster (1964). In this study, monkeys were reinforced with an intravenous injection of morphine following the completion of a chained fixed-interval 2-min fixed-ratio 25 response requirement. The details of this experiment will be discussed in a subsequent section.

The results of early studies, while demonstrating some of the possibilities of using the methodology for the study of drugs as reinforcers, did not establish whether morphine or any drug would be self-administered in the absence of physical dependence. Most humans who become opiate addicts have not been treated with the drug to establish prior physical dependence. In addition, other drugs, such as cocaine, which are also abused by humans, do not produce physical dependence. It was essential, therefore, for the validation of the self-administration animal model to demonstrate that morphine could act as a reinforcer in the absence of physical dependence.

In fact, a variety of studies have suggested that physical dependence is not a necessary condition for morphine to serve as a positive reinforcer. Deneau *et al.* (1969) demonstrated that it was not essential for rhesus monkeys to be made physically dependent on morphine for them to self-administer the drug. Similarly, Schuster (1970) found that over a 30-day period, originally naive monkeys steadily increased their self-administration of 1.0 mg/kg/injection of morphine. However, in both studies, rates of responding for morphine during the first 6–10 days were not greater than base-line rates of responding for saline, yet were high enough at the doses used to produce physical dependence after that period of time. Therefore, it still was not clear whether morphine was a positive reinforcer in the absence of physical dependence. Since the development of physical dependence on morphine is dose-related, Woods and Schuster (1968) studied responding maintained by intravenous morphine across a wide range of doses, including ones too low to produce dependence. Monkeys were trained to respond under a variable-interval 2.5-min schedule of reinforcement during a 1-hr period every 6 hrs. Food was available under the same schedule for a 1-hr period immediately preceding the four drug periods. Doses of morphine, which ranged from 0.01 to 1.0 mg/kg, were tested for 15 days with saline replacing the morphine for at least 10 days between each dose. As dose was increased, response rates first increased and then decreased. The lowest dose of 0.01 mg/kg maintained responding at higher response rates than saline and therefore was a positive reinforcer despite the fact that this dose did not produce physical dependence even after the 15 days of exposure. Higher doses, on the other hand, did produce dependence, as evidenced by the disruption in responding maintained by food and the observation of signs of withdrawal when saline was substituted. Rates of responding during extinction (i.e., saline substitution), though, were higher in animals whose responding had been reinforced with higher doses of morphine and as a consequence were physically dependent. On the basis of these studies, it was concluded that (1) morphine can serve as a positive reinforcer independently of its ability to terminate the withdrawal syndrome, and (2) the reinforcing properties of morphine are enhanced if animals are physically dependent (Schuster, 1970; Woods and Schuster, 1971).

Other investigators showed that a variety of drugs such as cocaine (Deneau *et al.,* 1969; Pickens and Thompson, 1968; Woods and Schuster, 1968) and amphetamine (Deneau *et al.,* 1969) were also capable of functioning as positive reinforcers. However, it was quickly discovered that one of the problems of using drugs as reinforcers is that, in addition to having reinforcing properties, drugs possess other pharmacological properties which alter responding. Responding maintained by a drug is influenced not only by its reinforcing actions but also by its other pharmacological properties. As shown in Figure 1, a drug which is a positive reinforcer will increase responding leading to its delivery. This effect is dependent on the contingency relationship. The drug, however, also has direct effects on responding regardless of the event maintaining it. In fact, these effects have been the primary concern of the field of behavioral pharmacology (see the other chapters). Drugs

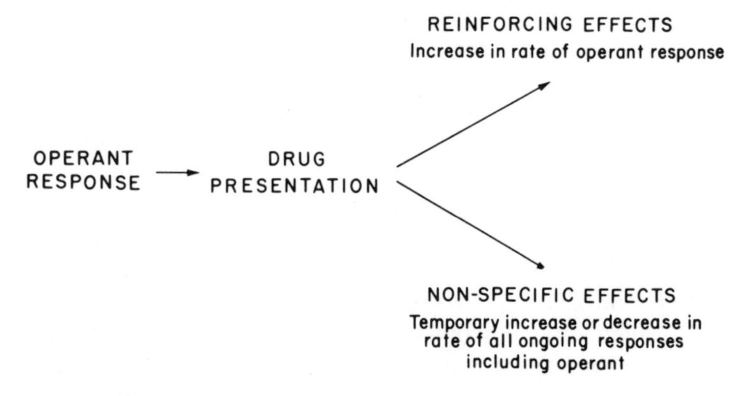

Figure 1. Two types of effects that drug delivery contingent on an operant response can exert. [From Johanson and Schuster (1977b).]

can either increase or decrease responding, depending on the environmental situation. Most important, these direct effects are not dependent on the contingency relationship between responding and drug delivery. It is well known, for instance, that drugs such as cocaine and the amphetamines given noncontingently increase many kinds of motor activity in a dose-dependent fashion. It could be questioned, therefore, whether these drugs were increasing rates of responding because of their reinforcing effects or whether the rate increases were elicited by the drugs. As a result, in early studies purporting to show that these drugs were positive reinforcers, investigators were forced to use extraordinary controls in each and every study. For instance, in a study by Pickens and Thompson (1968), many manipulations, such as reversing the operative lever in the middle of the session, were made to demonstrate that cocaine maintained responding rather than merely directly produced it.

A second problem encountered in the early studies was that rates of responding maintained by drugs under many schedules were extremely low relative to other reinforcers (Kelleher, 1975). Unless the dose of the drug is selected carefully, rates of responding will often be below rates of responding maintained by saline. These low rates initially caused many behavioral researchers to question whether drugs were, in fact, positive reinforcers. So, although some investigators were encouraged by the results of these early studies, the real significance of the findings was not appreciated by the general scientific community of behavioral researchers until the degree of control over responding maintained by drugs was increased by using more optimal experimental parameters (Morse, 1975).

One of the most important variables influencing responding maintained by any stimulus event is the schedule of presentation (Ferster and Skinner, 1957). As the literature in behavioral pharmacology has demonstrated, the schedule under which responding is maintained can be more important in determining how a variety of variables influence responding than the nature of the maintaining event itself (Kelleher and Morse, 1968). It has also been found that schedule of reinforcement is an extremely important variable in influencing responding maintained by drugs (Kelleher, 1975). By using optimal schedules and parameters, responding maintained by drugs has been brought under extremely high levels of control. More important, however, such responding has been shown to be similar in pattern and frequency to that maintained by other reinforcing events, such as food. It was unfortunate that early studies of drug self-administration used schedules and session lengths which resulted in high rates of drug intake. The low rates of responding engendered under these conditions obscured the remarkable similarity between drugs and other reinforcers. The discovery of this similarity has broadened the relevance of this research, since its findings are not only important for understanding the behavioral mechanisms of drug abuse but also for understanding the control of behavior in general.

In this section, studies of schedule-controlled responding maintained by drugs will be reviewed, and the pattern and rates of responding compared to those maintained by other positive reinforcers. As shown by these studies, the ability of drugs to control high rates of responding under a variety of experimental conditions is the most adequate demonstration that drugs can function as reinforcers and has contributed most significantly to progress in the field.

2.1. Fixed-Ratio Schedules

In fixed-ratio schedules of drug delivery, animals must emit a set number of responses in order to receive an injection of the drug. Several studies have shown that responding can be maintained under such schedules by a variety of drugs across a wide range of parameters (Goldberg and Kelleher, 1976; Balster and Schuster, 1973b; Pickens and Thompson, 1968; Hoffmeister and Schlichting, 1972). In addition, such schedule-controlled responding has been found with a variety of species, including rats (Weeks and Collins, 1964; Pickens and Thompson, 1968), dogs (Jones and Prada, 1973), rhesus monkeys (Wilson *et al.,* 1971; Downs and Woods, 1974), squirrel monkeys (Goldberg, 1973a), and baboons (Griffiths *et al.*, 1975a; Griffiths *et al.*, 1976c). Figure 2 (top panel) shows an example of responding maintained by cocaine injections under a fixed-ratio 10 schedule in rhesus monkeys (Johanson, 1976). The pattern of responding, typical of performances maintained by other events (Ferster and Skinner, 1957), is characterized by an initial pause followed by a high terminal rate of responding.

While responding under ratio schedules has been maintained by most drugs, Goldberg *et al.* (1971a) observed that pentobarbital maintained about the same rates of responding as cocaine only under a fixed-ratio 1 schedule of drug delivery. Under a fixed-ratio 10 schedule, the rates of responding maintained by cocaine were increased relative to the fixed-ratio 1 schedule, whereas the rates maintained by pentobarbital were unaffected, which resulted in a decrease in frequency of reinforcement. While these results suggest that barbiturates are not as effective as cocaine in maintaining characteristic fixed-ratio performances, additional research is needed with this class of drugs. In fact, other investigators have not always found significant differences be-

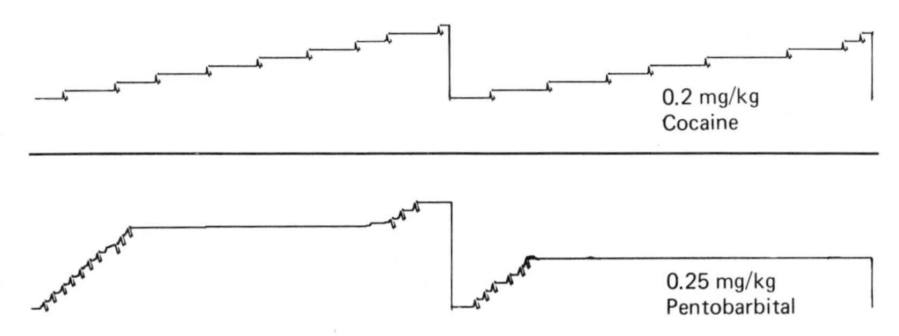

Figure 2. Representative cumulative response records of fixed-ratio 10 performance maintained by 0.2 mg/kg cocaine (top panel) and 0.25 mg/kg pentobarbital (bottom panel) in a rhesus monkey. Ordinate: cumulative responses. Abscissa: time. Each downward deflection of the response pen indicates the delivery of a 10-sec infusion. The response pen resets every 30 min.

tween pentobarbital and cocaine. As shown in Figure 2 (bottom panel), the rate of responding maintained by 0.25 mg/kg pentobarbital was similar to the rate maintained by 0.2 mg/kg cocaine under a fixed-ratio 10 schedule (Johanson, 1976). Despite differences in the overall distribution of the injections, for both drugs, the delivery of each reinforcer was followed by an initial pause in responding, which, in turn, was followed by a high terminal rate.

Although the pattern of ratio responding maintained by drugs is similar to that maintained by other events, the rates of responding typically found in drug self-administration studies have been low compared to rates maintained by food (Kelleher, 1975). In many studies, however, rates are higher at the beginning of the session (Downs and Woods, 1974). This generally low or decreasing rate is most likely due to the direct actions of the drug, which decrease responding. Since increased responding in ratio schedules results in increased rates of drug intake, the problem is particularly striking under this schedule. Several techniques have been used to avoid these effects while still using ratio schedules. Goldberg and Kelleher (1976), for instance, limited the number of available injections each session and, as well, imposed a time-out between injections. As seen in Figure 3, these modifications resulted in much higher rates of responding compared to those found by other investigators. Similar results have been found in other studies using the same techniques (Downs and Woods, 1974; Woods and Schuster, 1968). However, it is important to note that these modifications have simply decreased the length of the pause following the de-

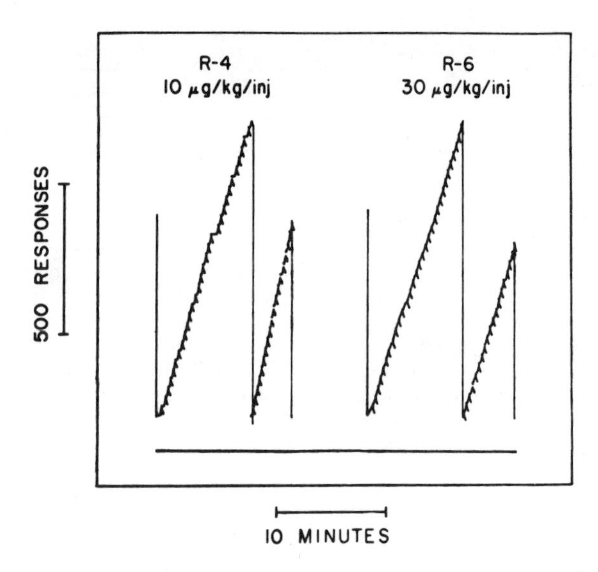

Figure 3. Characteristic performances of rhesus monkeys (R-4 and R-6) under 30-response fixed-ratio schedules of intravenous cocaine injections. Ordinate: Cumulative responses. Abscissa: time. The recording pen reset to the base line whenever 1100 responses had accumulated and at the end of each experimental session. Short diagonal strokes on the records indicate cocaine hydrochloride injections; the recorder stopped during the 1-min time-out period after each injection. Note the brief initial period of pausing followed by an abrupt change to a high rate of responding in each fixed-ratio segment. [From Goldberg and Kelleher (1976); © 1976 by the Society for the Experimental Analysis of Behavior.]

livery of the reinforcer. Even in studies with low overall rates of responding, the dynamic characteristics of responding maintained under ratio schedules are present.

The most powerful demonstrations of the similarity of responding maintained by drug delivery and food presentation are provided by studies which use both reinforcers to maintain responding under identical conditions. In a study by Goldberg (1973a), responding was maintained by food presentation in one group of squirrel monkeys and by cocaine injections in a second group, both under fixed-ratio schedules of reinforcement. Sessions lasted only 100 minutes, and each drug delivery or food presentation was followed by a 1-min time-out. The maximal rates of responding maintained by the different events were similar, as were the effects of varying the amounts of food presented and drug injected. Unlike many studies which vary the magnitude of food presentation, this study varied the amount of food delivered after the ratio was completed over an extremely large range. When the amount was relatively large, rates of responding decreased to relatively low levels similar to drug-maintained responding. In another study designed to directly compare responding maintained by drugs and food, Woods *et al.* (1975) maintained responding under a multiple fixed-ratio 30 schedule of codeine delivery and food presentation. Although sessions were also relatively short and time-outs were programmed after each delivery of a reinforcer, rates of responding maintained by food were over twice as high as rates of responding maintained by drug. Both events, however, maintained similar patterns of responding. Unlike the Goldberg (1973a) study, animals responded for drug and food within the same experimental session. If the cumulative effects of the codeine, as is often claimed, simply decrease all ongoing responding regardless of the event maintaining it, it is surprising that food-maintained rates were not lower. These results suggest that the cumulative intake of codeine had a specific effect in decreasing responding maintained by codeine injections rather than a generalized effect on responding.

2.2. Fixed-Interval Schedules

As was previously pointed out, under ratio schedules, rates of responding and rates of reinforcement vary together. In interval schedules, the first response emitted after a specified period of time results in the delivery of a reinforcer. Other responses have no programmed consequences but are simply recorded. The characteristic pattern of responding generated by this type of schedule consists of an initial pause followed by a gradually accelerating rate (Ferster and Skinner, 1957). Although there is some evidence to the contrary (Branch and Gollub, 1974), the pattern is usually described as a scallop. An important feature of interval schedules is that rates of responding can change considerably over a large range without affecting rate of reinforcement. In drug studies, this means that the number of drug injections can be held constant despite changes in responding. Unless responding drops to extremely low rates, the interinjection interval is determined by the schedule parameter.

One of the first studies using an interval schedule of drug delivery was done by Balster and Schuster (1973a). They used a fixed-interval 9-min schedule with a 3-min limited hold with responding maintained by both cocaine injections and food delivery. (A limited-hold contingency sets an upper limit to the period of time for which a reinforcer remains available after the schedule first sets it up.) In addition, there was a 15-min time-out following the delivery of each reinforcer. Figure 4 shows representative cumulative response records from this study. As

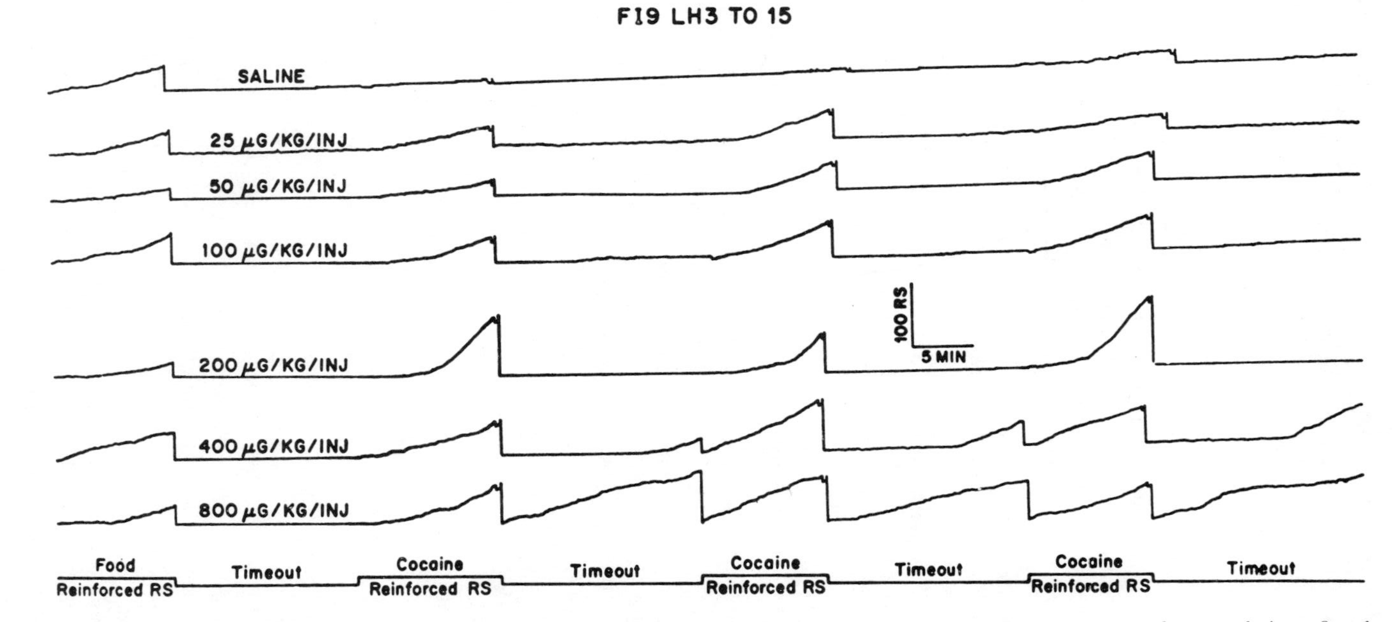

Figure 4. Portions of the cumulative records for the last day at each test dose for animal A019. The pen reset at the completion of each fixed-interval or limited-hold and also after each time-out. [From Balster and Schuster (1973a); © 1973 by the Society for the Experimental Analysis of Behavior.]

can be seen, the pattern of responding maintained by cocaine was similar to that maintained by food. Similar results were found in a study by Goldberg and Kelleher (1976) using a fixed-interval 5-min schedule maintained by cocaine injections.

Despite some of the obvious advantages of using interval schedules, in addition to their wide use with food-maintained responding, almost no studies have been done with this schedule with drugs besides cocaine. However, as seen in Figure 5, Johanson (1976) has demonstrated that characteristic responding can be maintained by 0.2 mg/kg pentobarbital under a fixed-interval 5-min schedule. While considerably more research is needed, these results taken as a whole further demonstrate the reinforcing properties of drugs as well as their similarity to other reinforcers in controlling responding.

2.3. Complex Schedules

Although single schedules can be combined in a variety of ways, a majority of the studies using drugs as reinforcers have utilized combinations of fixed-interval and fixed-ratio schedules. In a two-member chained schedule, in the presence of one discriminative stimulus (S^D), responding produces a second S^D and responding in its presence results in the delivery of a reinforcer. The schedule of reinforcement in effect in the presence of each S^D is a single schedule, such as a fixed-interval. One of the first studies showing that drugs could function as reinforcers in rhesus monkeys used a chained fixed-interval 2-min fixed-ratio 25 schedule of morphine delivery in effect once every 6 hr (Thompson and Schuster, 1964). In the presence of a green light, the first response after 2 min turned on a tone and completion of a fixed-

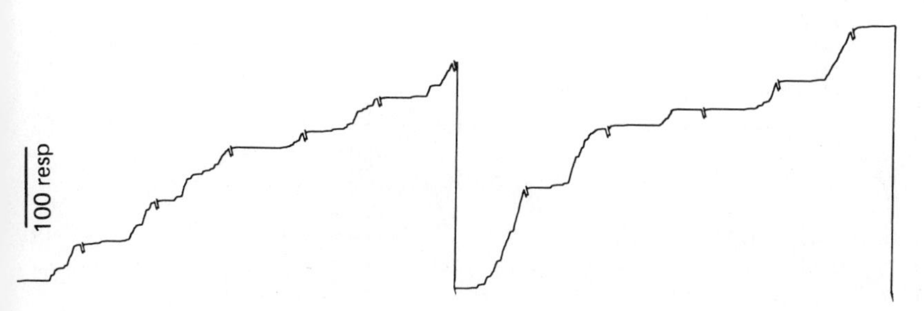

Figure 5. Representative cumulative response record of fixed-interval 5-min performance maintained by 0.2 mg/kg pentobarbital in a rhesus monkey. Ordinate: cumulative responses. Abscissa: time. Each downward deflection of the response pen indicates the delivery of a 10-sec infusion. The response pen resets every 30 min.

ratio 25 in the presence of this tone resulted in the delivery of morphine. Responding in the presence of the green light and tone were typical of interval and ratio performance, respectively, thus showing that drugs can maintain responding under chained schedules. This same study showed that such a schedule is sensitive to a variety of manipulations such as drug deprivation.

Fixed-interval and fixed-ratio schedules can also be combined in a multiple schedule of drug delivery. As in a chained schedule, a multiple schedule consists of two or more schedules which alternate in some manner, each associated with a different discriminative stimulus. However, in a multiple schedule, a drug injection is delivered following the completion of each schedule requirement. Goldberg and Kelleher (1976) have shown that responding can be maintained by injections of cocaine under a multiple fixed-ratio 10 fixed-interval 5-min schedule.

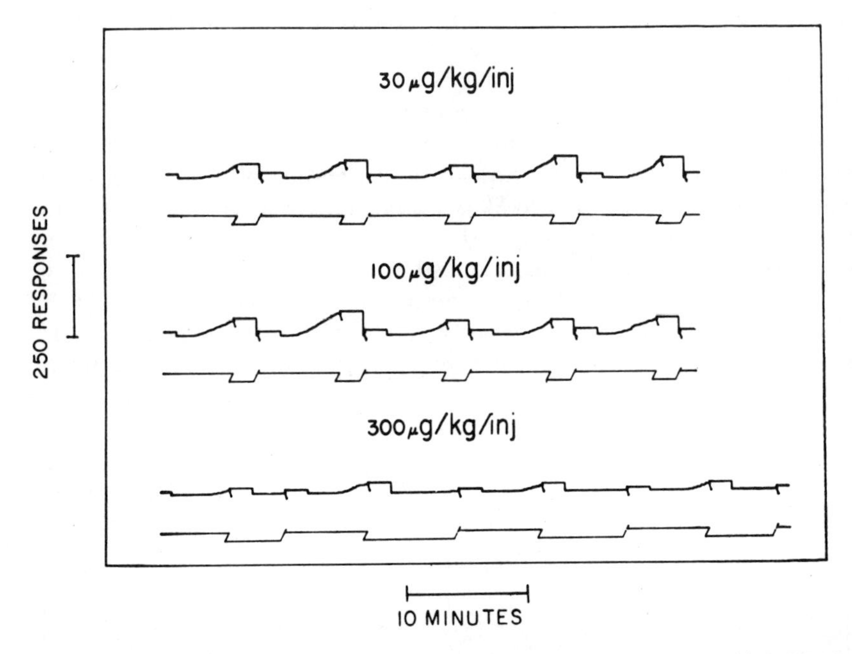

Figure 6. Representative performances of a rhesus monkey (R-4) under a multiple FR 10 FI 5-min schedule at various doses of cocaine. Ordinate: cumulative responses. Abscissa: time. Short diagonal strokes on the cumulative record indicate cocaine injections. The recording pen reset to the base line at the end of the 100-sec time-out period following each injection. The event pen remained offset during the time-out period after each fixed-interval component and during the next fixed-ratio component. Note the decrease in fixed-ratio responding at 300 µg/kg injection. [From Goldberg and Kelleher (1976); © 1976 by the Society for the Experimental Analysis of Behavior.]

As has been shown in other areas of behavioral pharmacology, this multiple schedule can be extremely useful for studying the effects of drugs, since several rates and patterns of responding are generated in the same animal during a single experimental session (Figure 6). While responding is maintained by injections of cocaine under this schedule, research demonstrating its usefulness in studying the effects of a variety of other variables has just begun (Goldberg and Kelleher, 1976).

A third schedule which combines single schedules is a second-order schedule. In this type of schedule, responding specified by one particular schedule is treated as a unitary response that is itself reinforced by another schedule (Kelleher, 1966). In many studies, the responding, which is treated as a unitary response, is followed by the presentation of a brief stimulus previously paired with the delivery of the reinforcer. Goldberg (1973a,b) using squirrel monkeys, studied responding maintained by cocaine and *d*-amphetamine as well as food under a fixed-ratio schedule of stimulus presentation (2-sec yellow light), which itself was maintained under a fixed-interval schedule of drug or food delivery. This schedule was designated a second-order FI 5-min (FR 30:S). As seen in Figure 7, this schedule maintained extremely high rates of responding and ratiolike performance when cocaine was used. In addition, responding maintained by food was virtually identical in both pattern and rate (Goldberg, 1973a). Additional studies using second-order schedules have shown that responding can be maintained by both cocaine and morphine even when only a single injection is delivered at the end of a 60-min session (Goldberg and Morse, 1973; Goldberg, 1975; Kelleher, 1975; Goldberg *et al.,* 1975). This is true for both fixed-ratio performance maintained under a fixed-interval schedule (FI[FR]) as well as fixed-interval performance maintained under a fixed-ratio schedule (FR[FI]) (Kelleher, 1975). With both these types of schedules, characteristic patterns of responding are seen and rates are relatively high.

In the complex schedules discussed above, only a single schedule was in effect at any one time. In a concurrent schedule, however, two or more schedules operate simultaneously but independently. For a variety of experimental reasons, a concurrent variable-interval variable-interval schedule has been used extensively in studies where responding is controlled by food. Iglauer and Woods (1974) used a concurrent variable-interval 1-min variable-interval 1-min schedule of cocaine delivery with each injection separated by a 5-min time-out and found most aspects of responding similar to that maintained by food.

Although most studies of drugs as reinforcers still use ratio schedules, enough results are now available with other schedules to indicate that drugs are capable of controlling responding in much the same way

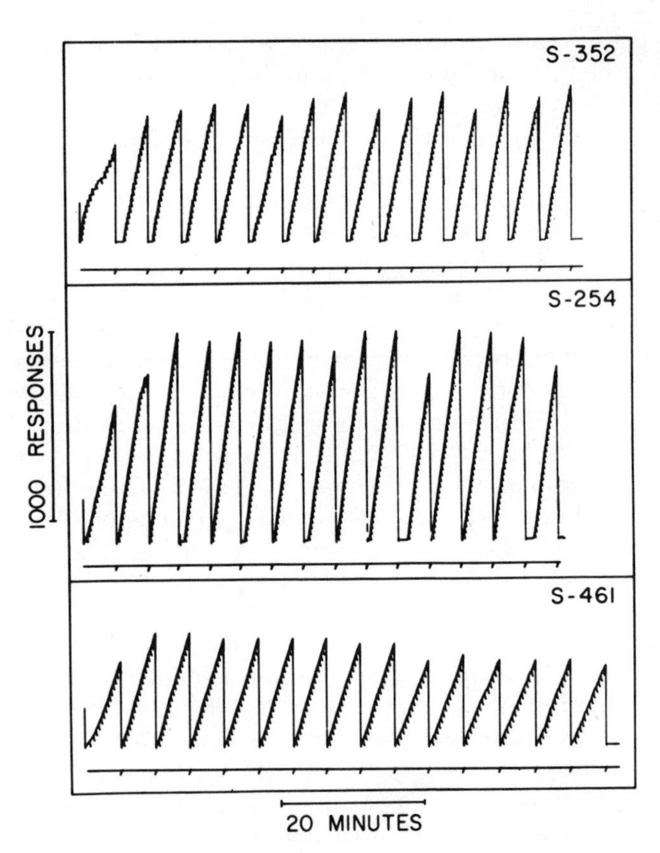

Figure 7. High rates of responding maintained in three squirrel monkeys (S-352, S-254, and S-461) under a second-order schedule in which the first 30-response fixed-ratio component completed after 5-min produced an intravenous injection of cocaine. Ordinate: cumulative responses. Abscissa: time. Short diagonal strokes on the cumulative records indicate 2-sec presentations of a yellow light at the completion of each fixed-ratio component. Diagonal strokes on the event record and the resetting of the recording pen indicate intravenous injections of 100 μg of cocaine hydrochloride per kilogram. After each injection there was a 1-min time-out period. The recorder was stopped during presentations of the yellow light and during time-out periods. [From Goldberg (1973b).]

as other events. As with these other events, the major determinant of responding is the schedule of presentation. Responding maintained by drugs under fixed-ratio, fixed-interval, and complex schedules is remarkably similar to responding maintained by events such as food under the same schedule. On the other hand, responding maintained by the same event differs considerably depending on how it is scheduled. Therefore, as more and more evidence has accumulated, there has been a gradual shift from viewing drugs as unique, to viewing them as just one example of an event which can control responding. While the study of drugs as reinforcers grew mainly out of an interest in developing an animal model of drug abuse, this similarity in responding has generated wider interest.

3. Type of Drug

Before the similarity between drug-maintained responding and responding controlled by any stimulus event was fully appreciated, drug self-administration studies concentrated on determining which drugs could function as reinforcers, and stressed the differences between these drugs, particularly in terms of pattern of intake. Most of these studies used low-valued fixed-ratio schedules (e.g., FR 1 and FR 10) and were concerned not with demonstrating that large repertoires of behavior could be brought under control, but with testing as many different compounds as possible from a wide variety of drug classes. While from a behavioral viewpoint this research may seem simplistic, it is impressive how many drugs do serve as reinforcers despite diverse pharmacological actions. Perhaps the failure of investigators to find common physiological or biochemical effects with all these drugs helped shift the emphasis of the research from the pharmacological properties of these drugs to their behavioral properties.

Several studies (Pickens, 1968; Pickens and Harris, 1968; Pickens *et al.*, 1967; Pickens and Thompson, 1968) have shown that intravenous cocaine and the amphetamines can maintain behavior in rats. Deneau *et al.* (1969), Yanagita *et al.* (1969), Yanagita *et al.* (1970), and Woods and Schuster (1968) showed that these drugs also could function as reinforcers in rhesus monkeys given both unlimited and limited daily access. A more extensive study of a wide variety of amphetaminelike psychomotor stimulant drugs was done by Wilson *et al.* (1971). They found that cocaine, methylphenidate, phenmetrazine, pipradrol, and SPA all maintained responding during daily 4-hr sessions. Balster and Schuster (1973b) showed that *d*-amphetamine, *l*-amphetamine, and methamphetamine were positive reinforcers under limited access conditions. In a study by Johanson *et al.* (1976a), many of these same drugs were tested under conditions of unlimited access under a fixed-ratio 1 schedule for a period of 30 days. All drugs tested maintained responding, but few animals survived access to cocaine, *d*-amphetamine, and methamphetamine. Figure 8 shows the results from four animals given access to 0.05 mg/kg of *d*-amphetamine. Two of these animals died after 2 or 3 days, during which time food intake was suppressed. The

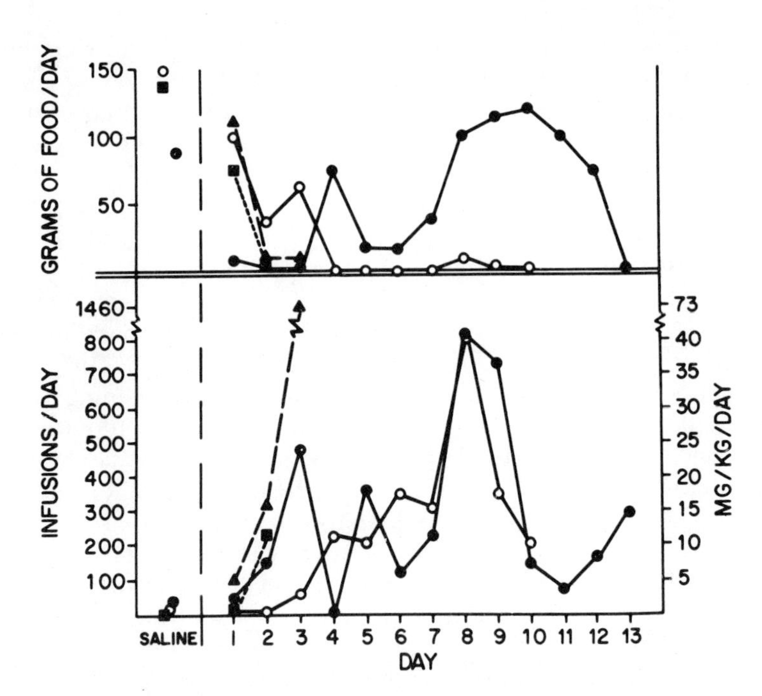

Figure 8. Number of infusions and drug intake (bottom panel) and food intake (top panel) on each day of access to 0.05 mg/kg/infusion *d*-amphetamine sulfate for monkeys 4004 (●—●), 4032 (■---■), A010 (▲---▲), and 3140 (○—○). Mean number of saline infusions and mean food intake for the 3 days prior to drug access are shown to the left of both panels for three of the monkeys. [From Johanson *et al.* (1976a).]

other two animals survived for a longer period, although they also died after self-administering large quantities of drug. Their day-to-day intake fluctuated considerably during this period, which seems to be a pattern characteristic of psychomotor stimulant intake (Deneau *et al.*, 1969). This pattern was even more pronounced for diethylpropion because animals lived for longer periods and in some cases survived the entire 30-day period. The erratic pattern of intake is even more obvious if intake is viewed over a 48-hr period, as shown in Figure 9. Under conditions of limited access (3–4 hr/day), on the other hand, responding maintained by psychomotor stimulants is stable from day to day (Wilson *et al.*, 1971; Balster and Schuster, 1973b). The stability of intake is particularly striking with cocaine since it is self-administered at regular intervals even within a session (see Figure 2).

A second class of drugs which has been studied extensively is the opiates. As previously discussed, morphine was one of the first drugs studied for its ability to maintain responding, and only later were drugs

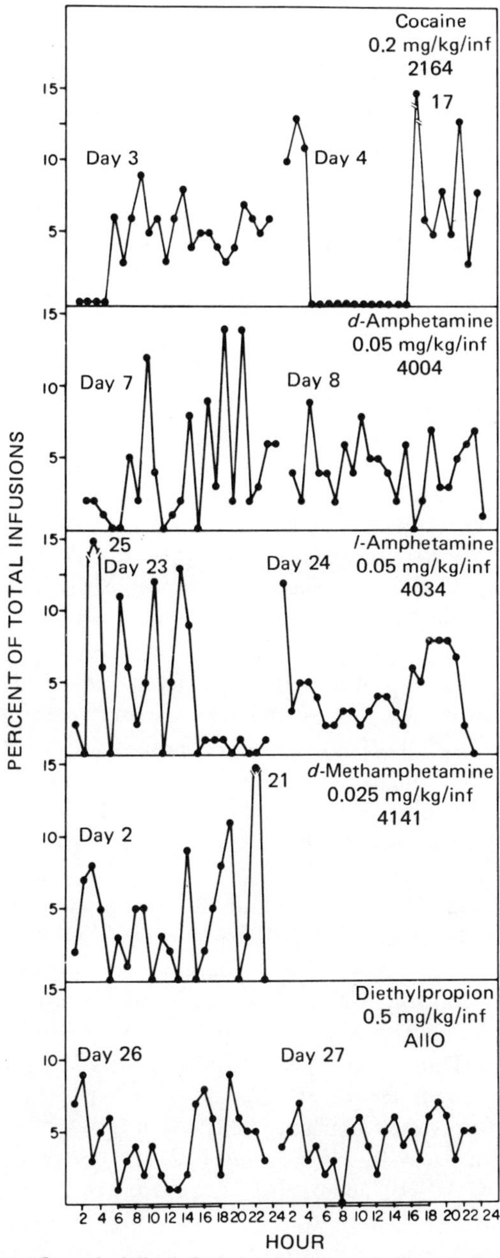

Figure 9. Percent of total daily infusions during each hour of access to cocaine, *d*-amphetamine, *l*-amphetamine, *d*-methamphetamine, and diethylpropion on two consecutive days. Night hours are indicated by the black bar on the abscissa. [From Johanson *et al.* (1976a).]

besides morphine tested. Examples include methadone, codeine, heroin, propoxyphene, pentazocine, and propiram (Balster *et al.*, 1971; Hoffmeister and Schlichting, 1972; Moreton *et al.*, 1976; Killian *et al.*, 1977). In most respects, the pattern and characteristics of intake for all these drugs are similar to morphine, despite differences in potencies. Under unlimited access conditions, morphine is self-administered initially at irregular intervals with fewer injections occurring at night (Deneau *et al.*, 1969). As animals become more physically dependent, overall rates of intake increase, injections occur at more regular intervals, and the diurnal cycle is more pronounced (Schuster, 1970; Deneau *et al.*, 1969). If availability is limited, opiates are self-administered in bursts, primarily at the beginning of the session (Killian *et al.*, 1977).

Early studies of barbiturate self-administration were conducted under conditions of stress (e.g., unavoidable electric shock) since it was felt this class of drugs would only be taken to alleviate anxiety (Davis and Miller, 1963; Davis *et al.*, 1968). However, Goldberg *et al.* (1971a) demonstrated that pentobarbital was also self-administered under conditions similar to those for cocaine, although they pointed out that this drug was not as effective as cocaine in maintaining responding under ratio schedules above a fixed-ratio 1. Winger *et al.* (1975) showed that other barbiturates—barbital, amobarbital, thiopental, and methohexital—all maintained responding under a fixed-ratio 1 schedule. Other studies have also shown this to be true for secobarbital (Findley *et al.*, 1972; Griffiths *et al.*, 1975a). Most of these studies were conducted under conditions of limited access, so the role of physical dependence in altering levels of responding has not been evaluated. There is every reason to believe, however, that the results will be similar to those found with the opiates.

The list of drugs capable of maintaining responding seems endless (see Schuster and Johanson, 1974, for a more complete list). In general, drugs which are abused by man are self-administered by animals (Schuster and Johanson, 1974). However, this has only been found to be limitedly true for the hallucinogens. Phencyclidine, which is taken by man for its LSD-like effects, is self-administered readily by monkeys (Balster *et al.*, 1973). However, this drug also possesses other pharmacological properties which may be more important for maintaining responding. In a study by Harris *et al.* (1974), rhesus monkeys did not self-administer Δ^9-THC even after programmed injections. When a cocaine solution was added to the THC, this combination was self-administered. However, when the cocaine was removed, responding again declined. Pickens *et al.* (1973), on the other hand, were able to get monkeys to self-administer Δ^9-THC after experience with phencyclidine self-administration. Other psychotomimetics, such as mescaline, do not seem to maintain responding in animals (Deneau *et al.*, 1969), although it remains to be seen whether this is due to a failure to adequately manipulate certain experimental parameters such as route of administration and interinjection time.

Despite the fact that the stimulants, opiates, barbiturates, and a variety of other drugs are strikingly similar in their ability to maintain responding, their differences should not be overlooked. For instance, the amount of morphine self-administered increases daily over a 30-day period as tolerance develops (Schuster, 1970), whereas cocaine intake remains stable over extended periods (Balster and Schuster, 1973b). In addition, during limited access conditions, responding maintained by cocaine occurs at regular intervals. Other drugs, such as pentobarbital, however, are self-administered in bursts separated by long pauses (see Figure 2). If care is not taken in terms of the scheduling of injections, these differences can obscure the overwhelming similarities between drugs capable of maintaining responding and complicate the analysis (Kelleher, 1975).

It should also be pointed out that many drugs, such as nalorphine and imipramine, do not maintain responding (Hoffmeister and Schlichting, 1972; Hoffmeister and Goldberg, 1973). One class of drugs which is particularly striking in this regard is the phenothiazines (Hoffmeister and Goldberg, 1973; Johanson *et al.*, 1976b). The ability of these drugs to maintain responding resulting in an injection being postponed (avoidance) or terminated (escape) will be discussed in a following section.

4. Magnitude of Reinforcement

The effects of varying magnitude of reinforcement on responding have been studied in a variety of situations with food or intracranial stimulation. Magnitude of dose has also been one of the primary manipulations made in drug self-administration studies, since pharmacological research has stressed the necessity of generating dose–response functions. Since the dose of a drug can be precisely and accurately varied when delivered intravenously, drugs are ideal for studying the relationship between responding and reinforcer magnitude totally from a behavioral point of view.

Although there are small differences among drugs in terms of the shape of the dose–response function, the schedule of drug delivery is the major variable determining how changes in drug dose will affect responding. As previously described, responding is maintained by drugs under a variety of different schedules. Of major interest in many studies of drug-maintained responding is the finding that the pattern of responding is remarkably similar to responding maintained by other stimulus events. Such similarities were stressed in the previous section of this review. Of equal interest, however, is how other variables, such as the dose of the drug, affect the schedule-controlled responding. The most extensive research on the effects of varying magnitude of reinforcement on the rate and pattern of schedule-controlled behavior has used drugs to maintain responding. In fact, in most drug self-administration studies, as many as 5–6 doses are used, which is considerably more than in studies where responding is maintained by food.

When responding is maintained under a ratio schedule of drug delivery, there is an inverse relationship between responding and the dose of the drug. This can be seen in Figure 10, which shows the mean number of injections self-administered by rhesus monkeys responding for *d*-amphetamine, *l*-amphetamine, or methamphetamine under a fixed-ratio 10 schedule (Balster and Schuster, 1973b). As dose increased, rate of responding decreased; at the highest doses tested, responding was often below rates of responding maintained by saline injections. Similar dose–response functions have been found in other studies with stimulants (Wilson *et al.,* 1971), opiates (Hoffmeister and Schlicting, 1972), and barbiturates (Winger *et al.,* 1975). Some studies, however, have characterized the relationship between responding and dose as having an inverted U-shape with responding initially increasing as dose is increased and finally decreasing as dose is raised even further. The failure to find this sort of relationship in the other studies may have been due to not testing low enough doses. In a study by Johanson and Schuster (1977a), there was an inverted U-shaped function relating responding, maintained by diethylpropion under a fixed-ratio 10 schedule, and dose which was varied across an extremely large range (0.01–3.0 mg/kg). Even in this study, however, the major portion of the dose–response curve showed that responding decreased as dose was increased.

Although ratio schedules are useful in determining whether a drug can simply maintain responding, there are difficulties using any schedule where increased responding leads to increased drug intake as discussed above in relation to Figure 1. The problem with ratio schedules is that as rate of responding increases, drug effects cumulate, and eventually the direct effects of the drug become a more important determinant of further responding than the reinforcing effects.

To avoid this problem, the effects of varying drug dose have been studied using schedules where rate of responding only minimally influences rate of drug delivery or using schedules which limit drug intake by the use of time-outs or other schedule parameters. In a study by

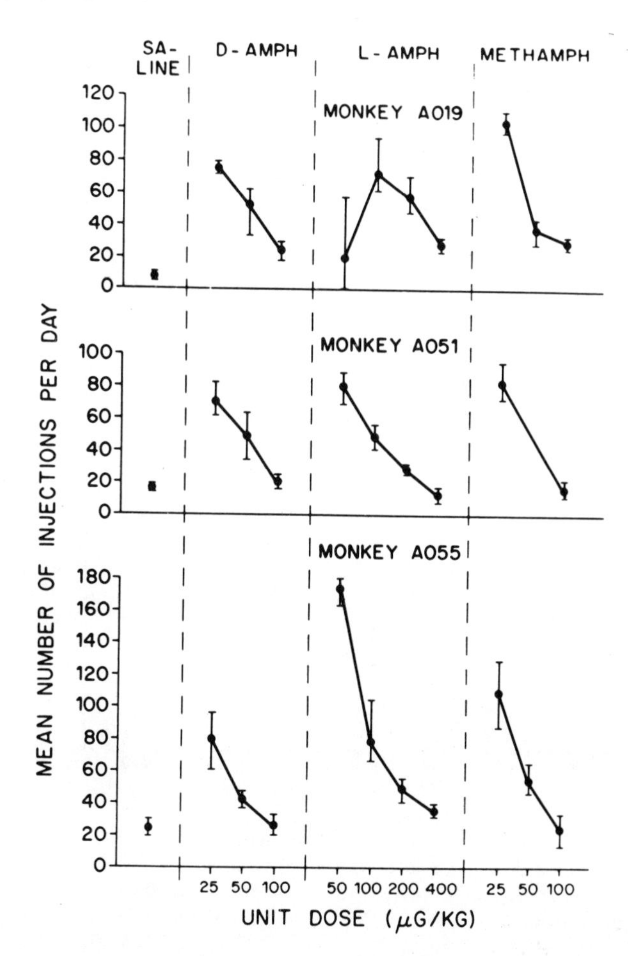

Figure 10. Mean number of injections per day for *d*-amphetamine, *l*-amphetamine, and methamphetamine at the various doses tested. The vertical bars indicate the range. Saline control levels are also shown. [From Balster and Schuster (1973b).]

Balster and Schuster (1973a), both of these techniques were utilized. In their study, responding was maintained by various doses of cocaine (0.025–0.8 mg/kg) under a 9-min fixed-interval schedule of drug delivery. Food was also available under the same schedule (see Figure 4). Not only did changes in rate of responding maintained by drug have little effect on frequency of reinforcement due to the schedule contingencies, but, in addition, the investigators scheduled a 15-min time-out between the delivery of each reinforcer. Figure 11 shows that as dose increased, rate of responding also increased. In two of the animals,

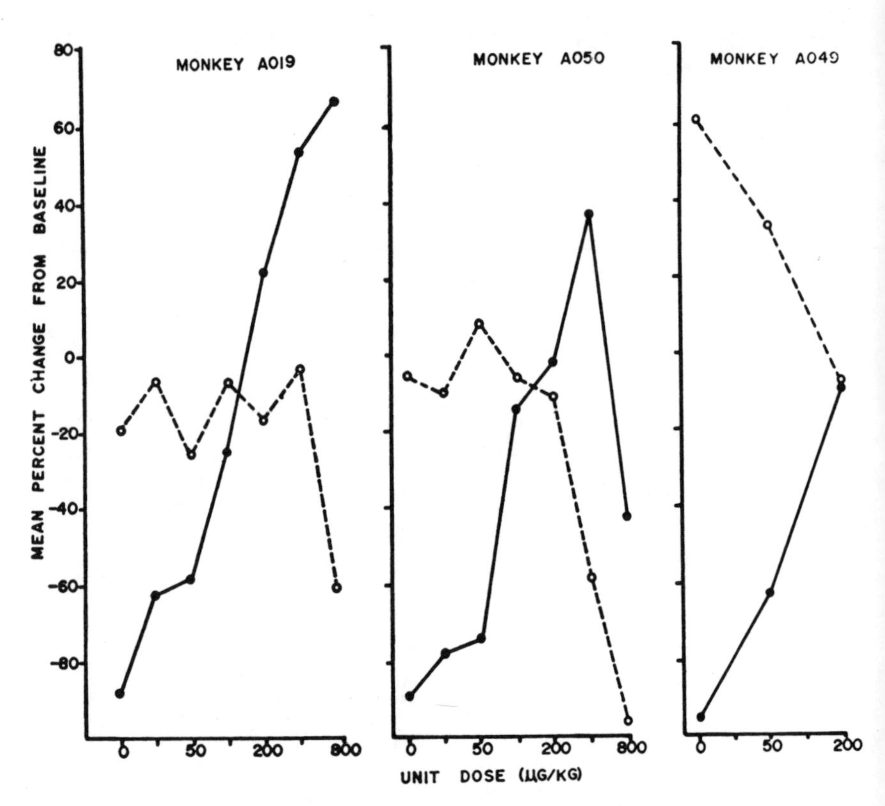

Figure 11. Change in fixed-interval response rate for food (○) and cocaine (●) reinforcement as a function of dose per reinforcement of cocaine for three animals. Values represent the mean percent change in response rate for the last three sessions at each unit dose from the 3 days of base-line dose (200 μg/kg/inj) just preceding it. [From Balster and Schuster (1973a); © 1973 by the Society for the Experimental Analysis of Behavior.]

food-maintained responding was relatively unaffected except at the higher doses. Although these results could have been due to the use of the fixed-interval schedule, other studies using fixed-interval schedules of cocaine delivery seem to indicate that the relatively long time between injections (9 min plus the 15-min time-out period) was the most important variable determining the shape of the dose–response function. For instance, Dougherty and Pickens (1973) found that rate of responding maintained by rats under a fixed-interval schedule of cocaine delivery decreased as dose increased. Although Goldberg and Kelleher (1976) also imposed a time-out between drug injections, they found that rate of responding decreased as dose of cocaine was increased above 0.05 mg/kg. However, in their study the size of the fixed-interval was 5 min and the time-out duration was only 1 min, so that the time between injections was much less compared to the Balster and Schuster (1973a) study. Therefore, it seems that by imposing relatively large time-outs between injections, the shape of the dose–response curves can be drastically altered. One of the problems of this solution is that by simply using time-outs in this manner, very little responding is generated. Certain schedules, however, effectively limit drug intake by separating injections but at the same time generate a great deal of responding during the periods between injections. One such schedule is the second-order schedule used originally by Goldberg (1973a,b), described in a previous section. Goldberg (1973a) compared rates of responding maintained by cocaine under both a fixed-ratio and second-order schedule. He found that compared to responding generated by a single fixed-ratio schedule, maximal rates maintained by the FI 5-min (FR 20:S) schedule of cocaine delivery were no higher, although a wider range of cocaine doses maintained rates above saline levels. Similar results, however, were not found by Johanson (1976). As seen in Figure 12, although rates of responding maintained by injections of cocaine under a second-order schedule were generally higher than under the single fixed-interval 5-min schedule, the shape of the dose–response functions was similar; responding initially increased as dose increased but then rapidly declined as dose was further increased. While it is clear that second-order schedules can generate high rates of responding and exert powerful control over responding, the behavioral effects of the drug not related to reinforcement are still a major determinant of responding. Since these effects are directly related to dose, a comparison of the reinforcing properties of different doses is confounded.

Several other procedures have been used to compare different doses of drug, as well as different drugs, in terms of their ability to maintain responding in the absence of any confounding influence (Iglauer and Woods, 1974; Iglauer *et al.*, 1975; Johanson, 1975; Johanson and Schuster, 1975; Findley *et al.*, 1972; Griffiths *et al.*, 1975a; Griffiths *et al.*, 1976c). One of these, described in a previous section, involves a concurrent variable-interval schedule of cocaine injections in rhesus monkeys (Iglauer and Woods, 1974). In this study, relative reinforcing efficacy was evaluated by comparing relative response frequencies. A standard dose of cocaine was available under a variable-interval 1-min schedule on one of two levers; the dose available under an identical schedule on the second lever (variable-dose lever) was varied to include both higher and lower doses of cocaine. In all cases, injections were followed by a 5-min time-out. As shown in Figure 13, the proportion of responses which occurred on the variable-dose lever increased as the

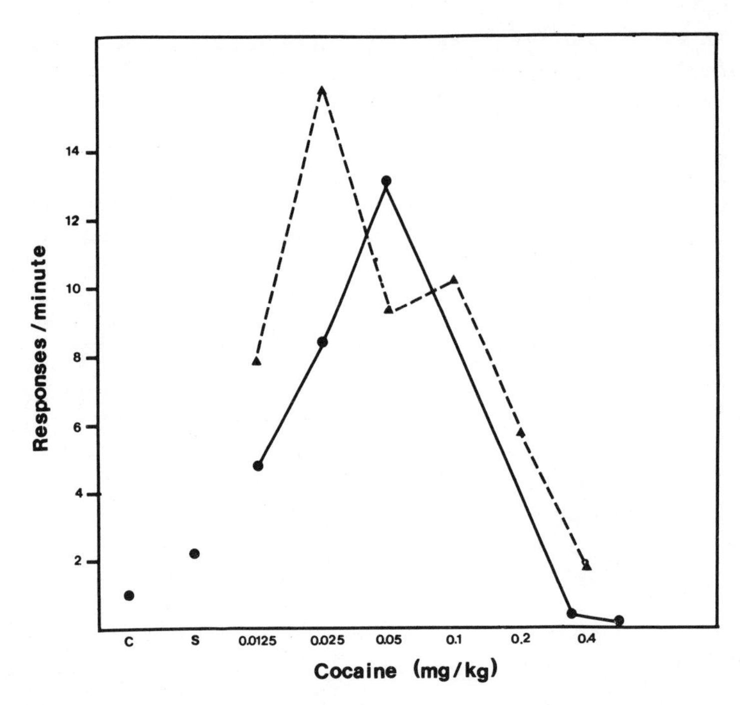

Figure 12. Dose–response functions relating responses per minute as a function of dose of cocaine for two different schedules of reinforcement in a single rhesus monkey. The closed circles are the function for a fixed-interval 5-min schedule of drug delivery and the triangles are for a second-order fixed-interval 5-min schedule of fixed-ratio 10 components. Control value (C) for the fixed-interval schedule indicates when no pump or stimulus change occurred contingent upon responding, while the saline (S) control indicates when saline rather than cocaine was delivered following the completion of the response requirement.

dose available on that lever increased; in all cases, the larger of two doses presented for comparison was preferred. However, in many comparisons, responding occurred exclusively (e.g., Willis in Figure 13) on the lever scheduled to deliver the highest dose. Therefore, it was impossible to compare two doses of drug, each of which had been directly compared to the standard dose. In order to compare these additional doses, direct comparisons would be necessary. Except for exclusive preferences, these data are similar to those where responding is maintained under a concurrent schedule of food delivery (Catania, 1963). More important, however, in the present context, is the demonstration of a direct function relating dose and preference. While this study did not totally avoid the influence of rate-decreasing effects on responding which contributed to the incidence of exclusive preferences

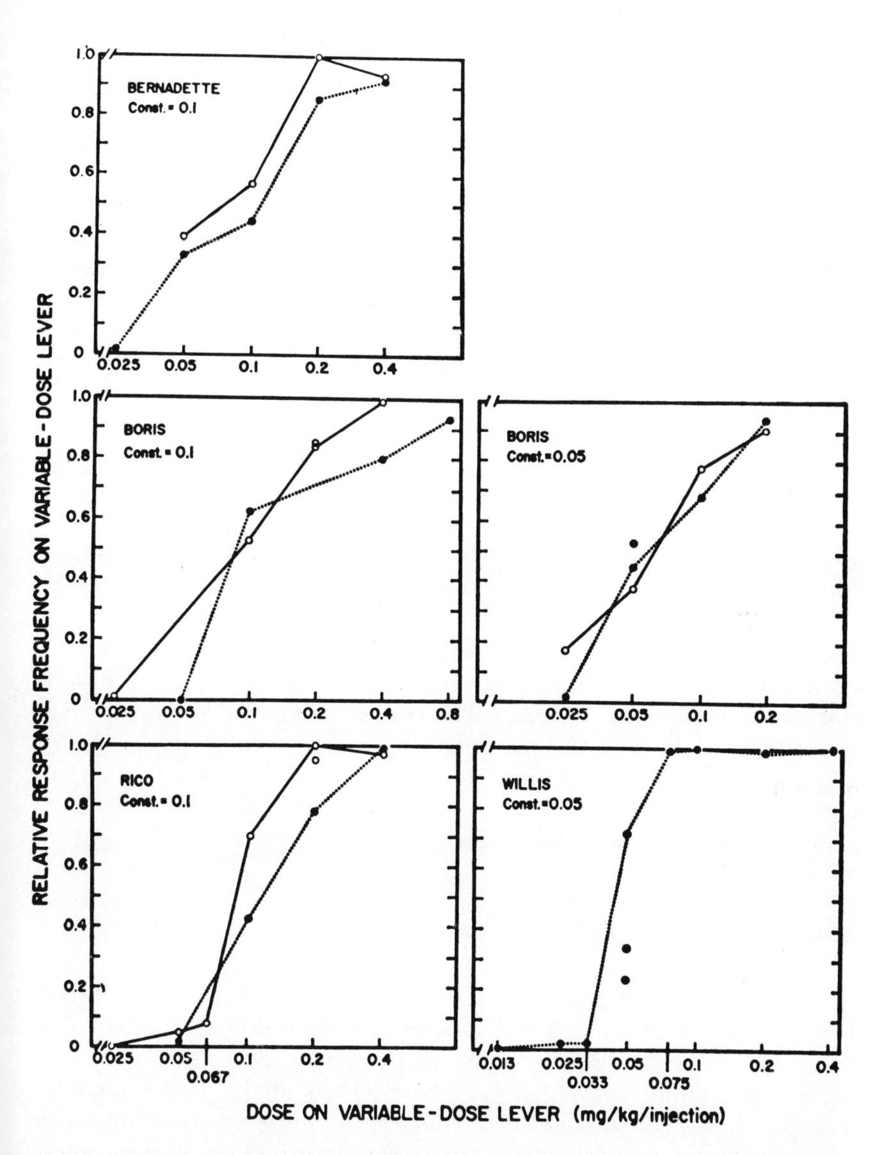

Figure 13. Relative response frequency on the variable-dose lever as a function of dose on this lever, first experiment. Doses are logarithmically spaced. The constant dose is indicated on each graph under the monkey's name. With repeated determinations in a sequence, only the first is joined on the line. ●, Determinations in first sequence; ○, determinations in second sequence. [From Iglauer and Woods (1974); © 1974 by the Society for the Experimental Analysis of Behavior.]

(Iglauer *et al.*, 1975), it did show that higher doses were more reinforcing than lower doses.

Another method designed to compare reinforcing properties involves the use of discrete choice trials. In a study by Johanson and Schuster (1975), rhesus monkeys were given an opportunity to choose between two drug solutions. The number of trials during which one option rather than the other one was selected was counted and used as the measure of reinforcing efficacy. Injections were followed by a 15-min time-out period. As in the Iglauer and Woods (1974) study, higher doses of cocaine were preferred to lower doses (Figure 14). Additional studies compared high and low doses of other psychomotor stimulants and found similar results (Johanson and Schuster, 1975; Johanson, 1975).

There are several important characteristics of both the choice and concurrent schedules which make them ideal for studying the effects of varying magnitude of reinforcement on responding. First, as in many other studies, injections are followed by time-out periods. This allows time for the rate-modifying effects to dissipate and as well limits intake. More important, however, is the use of measures which are not influenced by rate as well as the concurrent evaluation of the reinforcing properties of both drug solutions. For instance, in the choice paradigm, both options are available at the same time. The rate of responding is not used as a measure of reinforcing efficacy; a count is simply made of which lever is selected. If a previous injection suppresses responding, it will most likely suppress it equally on both levers. Since it does not matter how fast or slow an option is selected, but only that it is selected, the nonspecific drug effects do not influence the results.

5. Satiation and Deprivation

Responding maintained by food, water, and sex has been shown to vary as a function of satiation as well as deprivation (Skinner, 1938; Ferster and Skinner, 1957). These two variables, as well, can alter responding maintained by drug injections. Most of the studies demonstrating their effects have used opiates, and more specifically morphine, to maintain responding. However, the principles derived apply to other drug classes as well.

Drug satiation can be accomplished by pretreating animals who are self-administering a particular drug with graded amounts of the agent used as the reinforcer. Thompson and Schuster (1964) pretreated physically dependent monkeys with 2, 4, or 6 mg/kg of morphine 45 min before periods when the animals were scheduled to self-administer

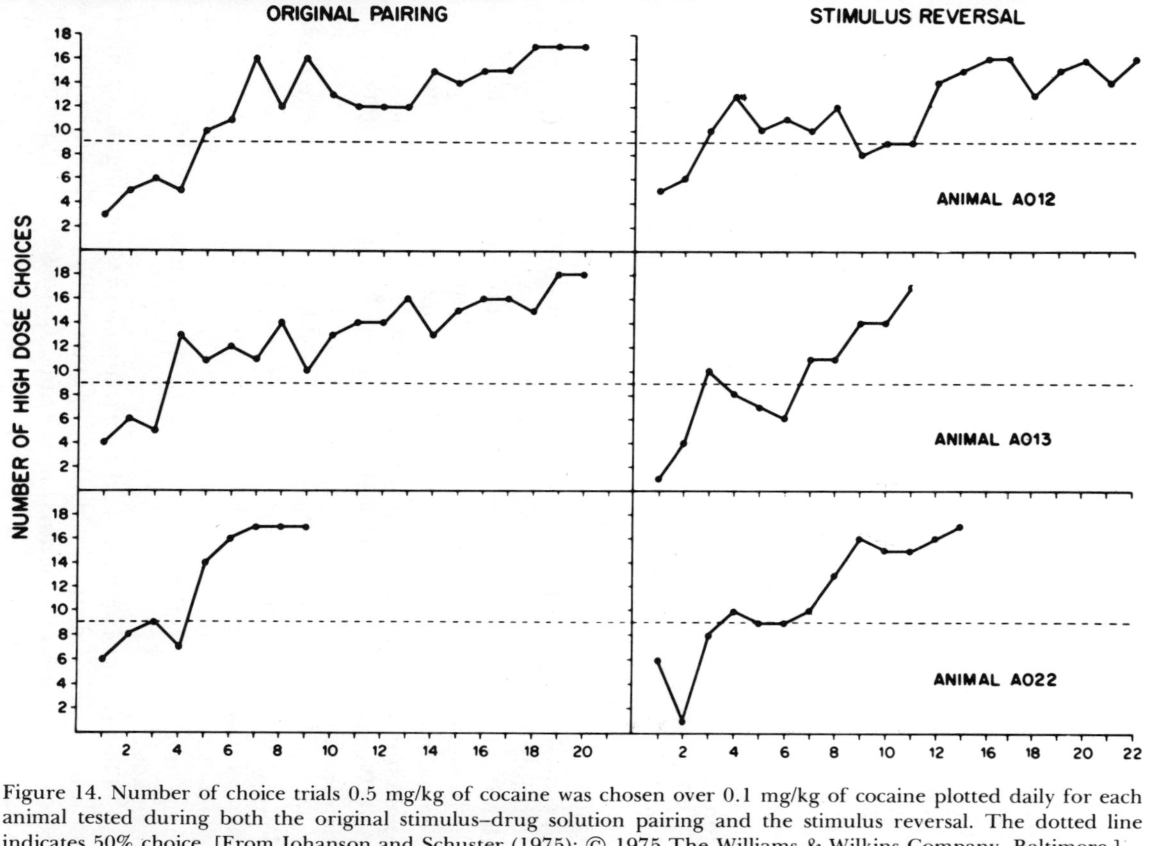

Figure 14. Number of choice trials 0.5 mg/kg of cocaine was chosen over 0.1 mg/kg of cocaine plotted daily for each animal tested during both the original stimulus–drug solution pairing and the stimulus reversal. The dotted line indicates 50% choice. [From Johanson and Schuster (1975); © 1975 The Williams & Wilkins Company, Baltimore.]

morphine. Responding for morphine was maintained under a chained fixed-interval 2-min fixed-ratio 25 schedule of reinforcement. The investigators found that the length of time required to complete the fixed-ratio 25 component of the schedule varied directly with the pretreatment dose. Thompson (1968) found that responding maintained by morphine could be decreased by pretreating animals with methadone. Using a different opiate to alter responding maintained by morphine points out one of the possible uses of this type of research. As in drug discrimination (Chapter 4) and cross-tolerance (Chapter 8) studies, it may be possible to determine whether different drugs share certain properties, both pharmacological and behavioral, with another drug. For instance, although Weeks and Collins (1964) found that etonitazene, codeine, and meperidine pretreatment decreased the rate of responding maintained by morphine, dexoxadrol and dextromethorphan did not. Such studies may be useful in designing drug treatment programs similar to methadone maintenance (Schuster and Johanson, 1973), which utilize the principles of drug substitution.

The effects of opiate deprivation in physically dependent animals are the opposite of those of satiation. In the same study described above, Thompson and Schuster (1964) found that increasing the deprivation of the monkeys responding for morphine from 6 to 24 hr produced a marked increase in the rate of responding on the chained schedule. One of the advantages of using opiates to study deprivation is that it can also be produced by the administration of opiate antagonists, such as naloxone or nalorphine. Using the latter antagonist, these investigators found comparable increases in morphine-maintained responding as found with deprivation produced by time. Weeks (1962) and Weeks and Collins (1964) also reported that administration of nalorphine to rats self-administering morphine produced increases in response rate on a ratio schedule comparable with that observed following morphine deprivation. Although Goldberg *et al.* (1971c) reported that this action of nalorphine was dose-dependent, at low doses (0.03–0.3 mg/kg) they also found that nalorphine caused an increase in morphine-reinforced lever pressing by physically dependent rhesus monkeys.

The effects of satiation and deprivation on responding maintained by other types of drugs are virtually unknown. Pilot studies in our laboratory have shown that varying the time between 3-hr experimental sessions from 1 to 45 hr has no effect on responding maintained by 0.2 mg/kg cocaine under a fixed-ratio 10 or fixed-interval 5-min schedule of drug delivery. These results are not surprising given the short duration of action of cocaine and its inability to produce physical dependence. In addition, similar results were found with 0.5 mg/kg or 1.0

mg/kg pentobarbital in nondependent animals. So while the effects of deprivation and satiation on responding maintained by morphine in physically dependent animals are similar to their effects on food-maintained responding, additional research is necessary to establish the generality of these results.

In all these studies of drug satiation and deprivation, rate of responding has been used as the dependent variable. As explained in the previous section, response rate may not be a suitable measure in some drug studies. Griffiths *et al.* (1975b), therefore, evaluated the effects of naloxone and methadone on responding maintained by heroin injections in a choice situation. Baboons were given eight daily choices between a heroin injection and the delivery of food pellets. Under baseline conditions, heroin was chosen between 1 and 3 times daily. Naloxone increased and methadone decreased the number of heroin choices. The authors persuasively argue that these systematic changes in choice cannot be attributed to changes in stimulus control, general response suppression, or the interaction of the drug with rate and pattern of responding, since all these variables would have equally affected responding for both options. Instead, the data indicate that these drugs altered the reinforcing properties of heroin injections.

6. Conditioned Drug Effects

The ability of the antagonists to alter responding maintained by opiates is undoubtedly related to their ability to produce signs of opiate withdrawal. By associating the injections of antagonists with various environmental stimuli, these stimuli themselves can alter drug-maintained responding. The possibility of conditioning drug effects was originally demonstrated by Irwin and Seevers (1956). Using monkeys dependent on methadone, keto-bemidone, or racemorphan, which had repeatedly experienced nalorphine-induced withdrawal, they showed that an injection of saline elicited aspects of the withdrawal syndrome even after the animals had been drug-free for 1–2 months. They interpreted these results as indicating that through classical or Pavlovian conditioning, the injection procedure itself (the CS) had acquired the ability to elicit the withdrawal response because of its temporal association with nalorphine (the UCS). Wikler and Pescor (1967) found that rats showed certain signs of opiate withdrawal when they were put in cages where they had previously been deprived of morphine and allowed to undergo withdrawal. Placing the animals in these cages continued to elicit such signs for 1–5 months following the termination of morphine treatment.

Goldberg and Schuster (1967), using a conditioned emotional response (CER) procedure, have provided the most elegant demonstration that stimuli can be effective in producing withdrawal-like effects when associated with injections of nalorphine. Nalorphine (a UCS), when given to morphine-dependent monkeys responding for food under a fixed-ratio 10 schedule, caused a disruption in responding. When a tone was repeatedly presented 5 min before and after such an injection, it alone became capable of suppressing food-reinforced responding. As shown in Figure 15, the tone plus an injection of saline originally had no effect on responding. Nalorphine, on the other hand, suppressed this responding for the entire session. After the tone had been paired several times with the injection of nalorphine, it suppressed responding in the 5-min period before nalorphine was given. In addition, presentation of the tone plus an injection of saline were also capable of suppressing responding for as long as 40 days. Other withdrawal signs, such as bradycardia, emesis, and salivation, were also conditioned by this procedure. Surprisingly, however, this did not occur in all animals, nor was it true of all signs of withdrawal. In a follow-up study, Goldberg and Schuster (1970), using the same experimental procedure, also found that stimuli could elicit signs of withdrawal even in animals who were no longer dependent on morphine. As in the first experiment, a stimulus, this time a red light, paired with nalorphine injections suppressed responding maintained on the fixed-ratio 10 schedule of food delivery during the 5 min before the nalorphine injection. Morphine injections were then discontinued for 30 days and the animals underwent withdrawal. When the animals were returned to the experimental situation and responding was again maintained by food, the red light and injections of saline disrupted responding. After continued presentation of the light and saline, the conditioned response finally extinguished. However, the effects were rapidly reconditioned, despite the fact that the animals had been drug-free for at least 2 months.

Of more relevance to the study of drug-seeking behavior is a demonstration that responding maintained by morphine can be altered by stimuli associated with injections of opiate antagonists. In a study by Goldberg *et al.* (1969), which directly addressed this question, a light was presented for 10 min before and 30 min after an intravenous injection of either saline or 0.1 mg/kg of nalorphine. The saline originally had no effect on responding, whereas nalorphine increased it. With repeated pairings of the light and the injection of nalorphine, saline injections also resulted in large increases in responding, although the effect decreased rapidly. Therefore, not only can withdrawal signs and the effects of nalorphine on responding maintained by food be condi-

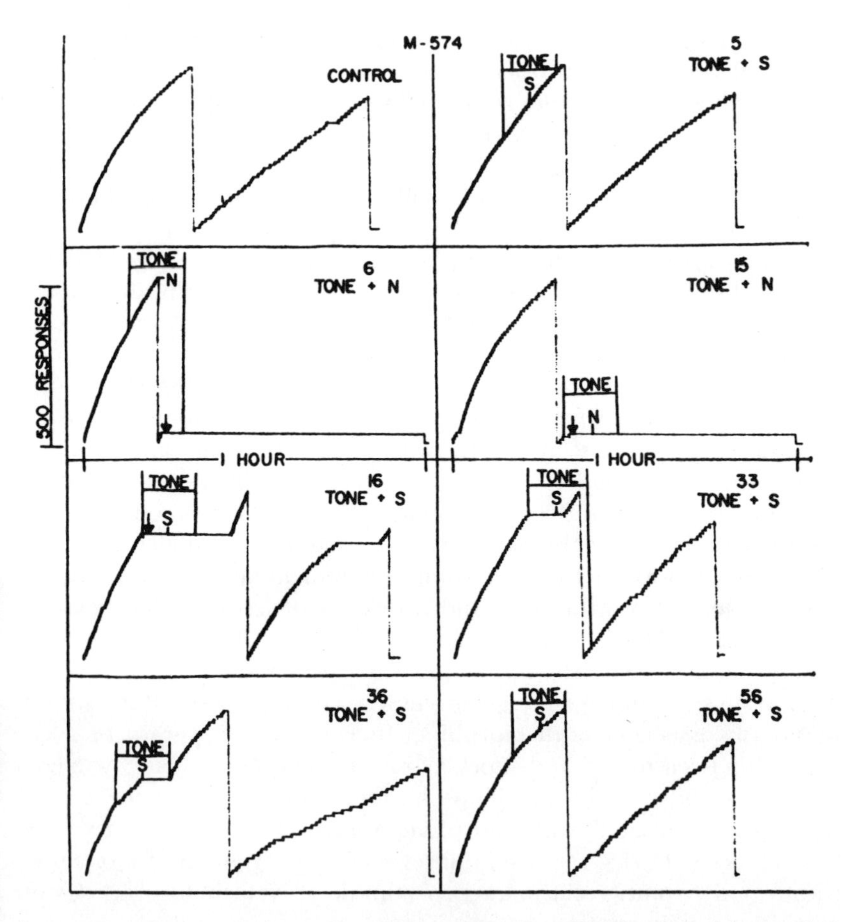

Figure 15. Cumulative response curves from M574. Each segment shown is a complete FR 10 food-component record extracted from a 2-hr session. A control session before tone-injection pairings is shown first; 5 was a session establishing tone and saline injection as neutral stimuli; 6 was the first conditioning session; 15 was the tenth conditioning session; 16 was the first extinction session, 33 the eighteenth, 36 the twenty-first, and 56 the forty-first extinction session. S, saline; N, nalorphine. Arrows indicate observation of emesis and excessive salivation. [From Goldberg and Schuster (1967); © 1967 by the Society for the Experimental Analysis of Behavior.]

tioned but more importantly in the present context, the effect of nalorphine on responding maintained by morphine can also be conditioned so that the presentation of an environmental stimulus alone can result in an increase in morphine-reinforced responding.

Conditioned drug effects are not unique to stimulus events paired with opiate antagonists. Stimuli associated with the administration of an opiate can also acquire the ability to elicit some of its actions. The first report of a conditioned opiate effect was that of Collins and Tatum (1925). These investigators accidentally discovered an interesting conditioned effect in the process of studying the effects of daily injections of morphine on the dog. They found that after seven or eight injections, salivation and emesis, originally seen only after morphine administration, began to occur when the experimenter merely entered the room in which the dogs were housed. Subsequently, Kleitman and Crisler (1927) confirmed these findings and systematically studied the conditioning and extinction of salivation with morphine as the unconditioned stimulus.

Thompson and Schuster (1964) also investigated the ability of a stimulus paired with morphine injections to alleviate some of the behavioral disruptions seen during withdrawal. In addition to self-administering morphine on a chained fixed-interval fixed-ratio schedule, the animals in their study also responded under stimulus control at different periods during the day to receive food and avoid electric shock. When the opportunity to self-administer morphine was removed, the animals went into withdrawal and showed a progressive deterioration in responding. However, allowing the animals to self-administer one injection of morphine returned responding to base-line levels. In addition, when the animals were given saline accompanied by all the stimuli previously associated with morphine, there was a temporary recovery of the food-reinforced and shock-avoidance behaviors. Thus the alleviation of withdrawal by morphine became conditioned to the stimuli previously associated with morphine reinforcement. More recently, Roffman *et al.* (1973) reported the reversal or prevention of morphine-withdrawal hypothermia in rats by stimuli previously associated with morphine administration.

Not only can stimuli paired with the administration of an opiate alleviate withdrawal symptoms in animals who are physically dependent on morphine, but these same stimuli can maintain responding previously followed by drug injections. One of the first demonstrations of this effect was in a study by Schuster and Woods (1968). They showed that a light previously paired with morphine injections was able to maintain high response rates in extinction even after an interpolated 20-day period of drug abstinence (Figure 16). Thus the conditioned reinforcing effect was independent of the organism's state of physical dependence.

In recent years, the ability of stimuli to maintain responding when paired with drug injections has been demonstrated more clearly in experiments using second-order schedules of drug delivery. Although more evidence is needed to establish clearly the importance of the asso-

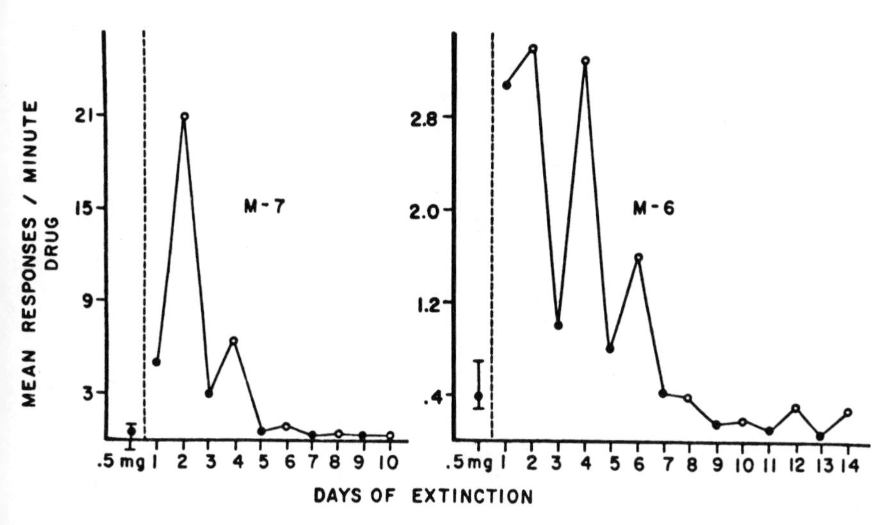

Figure 16. Mean response rates for monkeys M-6 and M-7 under a variable-interval schedule of drug injection. The far-left point shows the mean and the brackets the range of daily response rates during the final 5 days when responses intermittently resulted in presentation of a red light and intravenous injection of morphine. Points to the right of the dashed line show response rates on subsequent days when morphine injections were discontinued (extinction). On alternating days of extinction, responses either intermittently produced the red light and a saline injection under the variable-interval schedule (open symbols: RL + S), or had no specified consequences (closed symbols: no RL or S). Note the difference in scale for the ordinates with the two monkeys. [From Schuster and Woods (1968); reproduced by courtesy of Marcel Dekker, Inc.]

ciation between the stimulus and the drug injection (Kelleher and Goldberg, 1975), the results to date seem to indicate that these stimuli are capable of maintaining large amounts of responding over extended periods of time. Goldberg (1973a) found rates of responding maintained by cocaine and *d*-amphetamine as well as food to be relatively high under a second-order fixed-interval schedule of ratio components. Every tenth response resulted in the illumination of a red light; the first ratio completed after 5 min had elapsed resulted in the illumination of this light as well as an injection of cocaine. Not only were the rates of responding relatively high but, in addition, the patterns of responding controlled by the presentation of the light were similar to those described previously under first-order fixed-ratio schedules. Similar results have been found with other types of second-order schedules. For instance, Kelleher (1975) described a study where the completion of each 5-min fixed-interval component produced a 2-sec yellow light; the completion of the tenth such component produced both the light and 10 rapidly pulsed injections of cocaine. He found that the light maintained characteristic patterns of fixed-interval responding throughout the session. Other studies have shown that responding maintained by drugs such as morphine and methohexital can also be generated at high rates under similar second-order schedules even in situations where only a single drug injection is administered at the end of the session (Kelleher, 1975). While research using this approach has just begun, it is obvious that stimuli paired with drug injections can exert powerful control over drug self-administration.

These findings are extremely important in understanding factors which maintain continued drug acquisition and use in humans. The chain of behaviors, which often totally occupies the drug taker, involves obtaining money, purchasing the drug, preparing it, and only after a long period of time actually taking it and experiencing its effects. With drugs such as heroin, these effects are minimal given the poor quality of available drug. All parts of this ritual, however, have stimulus properties which can be conditioned because they are associated, at least intermittently, with the primary reinforcing actions of the drug. Since the ability to control behavior by conditioned reinforcers is not dependent upon the presence of physical dependence, it may survive detoxification periods in hospitals or prisons and contribute to relapse, as originally suggested by Wikler (1955). Although there are a few studies which have tested this possibility directly in humans (O'Brien, 1975), additional studies are necessary to demonstrate the relevance of conditioned drug effects in maintaining drug use or more importantly in contributing to drug use after a period of successful abstinence.

7. Drugs as Negative Reinforcers

As pointed out in a previous section, many drugs, such as the narcotic antagonists and the phenothiazines, are not capable of maintaining responding leading to their delivery. It is difficult using such procedures to determine whether these drugs have no reinforcing properties, like saline, or are acting as punishers in decreasing responding. More powerful techniques for demonstrating the aversive properties of drugs are ones where responding either postpones (avoidance) or terminates (escape) an injection (Holz and Gill, 1975). It should be pointed out that avoidance studies, where animals respond to turn off a stimulus which had been paired with a drug injection, also demonstrate the ability to condition the effects of drugs in a different context (Goldberg, 1975). More important, these studies of drugs as negative reinforcers extend the range of situations where drugs have been shown to function like other stimulus events, since responding maintained by drug avoidance or escape is virtually identical to that maintained by shock avoidance or escape (Morse and Kelleher, 1966; Holz and Gill, 1975; McKearney, 1975).

The studies of drugs as negative reinforcers have used a variety of experimental paradigms and have examined several drugs, although the class of drugs that has been investigated most extensively is the narcotic antagonists. One of the earliest studies was by Goldberg *et al.* (1971b), who showed that rhesus monkeys physically dependent on morphine would respond either to terminate a stimulus which was paired with the injections of nalorphine and naloxone or to terminate the injection of the antagonist itself. In one experiment, monkeys were made physically dependent on morphine by administering 3 mg/kg of this drug once every 4 hrs. During experimental sessions, a green light was present and a 10-sec injection of 0.01 mg/kg of nalorphine was delivered every 30 sec. Each lever-press response terminated the green light and the associated injections for a 60-sec time-out period during which injections never occurred and responses had no programmed consequences. Under these conditions responding was well maintained; substituting saline for the nalorphine injection resulted in a decrease in responding to about 40% of previous levels. Responding could be immediately restored to previous high rates, however, by replacing injections of saline with injections of either nalorphine or naloxone. These findings demonstrated that behavior can be maintained in morphine-dependent animals by the termination of a stimulus associated with nalorphine or naloxone injections. In another study (Goldberg *et al.*, 1972), similar results were found with pentazocine and propiram in dependent monkeys. However, in nondependent monkeys, that is, monkeys who had no experimental history of opiate dependence, these same drugs did not maintain responding leading to termination of a stimulus associated with their injection. On the other hand, Hoffmeister and Wuttke (1973) demonstrated that nalorphine would maintain avoidance–escape responding in drug-naive animals but naloxone would not. Naloxone has been shown to maintain escape responding if higher doses than are found effective in dependent animals are used. Downs and Woods (1975a) found that naloxone infusion rates above 0.1 mg/kg/min can generate and maintain escape responding in nondependent monkeys. These investigators used a naloxone-escape procedure in the nondependent monkeys that was essentially the same as that used with dependent animals, and comparable escape responding was maintained at infusion rates which were roughly 1000 times greater than in morphine-dependent animals. For both groups of animals, response rates were maximal at some dose and decreased as this dose was either increased or decreased.

Downs and Woods (1975a,b) have used a variety of schedules to further demonstrate the similarity between responding maintained by avoidance or escape from naloxone and electric shock. In their original study, naloxone was continually infused throughout the entire session and responding resulted in a 1-min time-out during which the infusion was terminated. Initially, a single response on the lever terminated the infusion, but this requirement was gradully raised to a fixed-ratio 20 or 30. As seen in Figure 17, there was an inverted U-shaped function relating response rate to dose. Pretreating the animals with morphine decreased the escape responding in a dose-dependent fashion. In another study, a stimulus was on for 30 sec before a 10-sec infusion of naloxone began. Responding under a fixed-ratio 30 schedule resulted in the termination of the stimulus (avoidance) or, if the infusion had begun, it terminated the infusion itself (escape). With this avoidance-escape procedure, changes in the dose or infusion rate of naloxone had little effect on rate of responding, perhaps because the animals had very little chance to come in contact with the injection itself (Figure 18).

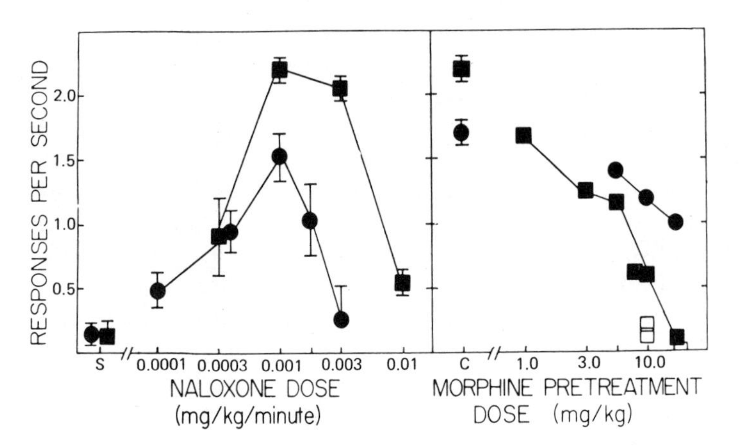

Figure 17. Left panel: response rate as a function of naloxone dose (mg/kg/min) or saline in each of two monkeys under the FR 20 escape procedure. Each point represents the mean of the last three of up to seven sessions at each dose averaged over all replications. Vertical lines indicate ± one standard error. Right panel: response rate in the FR 20 naloxone escape procedure (0.001 mg/kg/min) as a function of morphine pretreatment dose. The points at C show the mean ± one standard error of the last three naloxone escape sessions before beginning morphine pretreatment. Each morphine dose point represents one determination. A replication at 10.0 mg/kg is slightly offset from the first determination. Filled square, 672; filled circle, 673; open symbols for 672 represent morphine pretreatments when saline was substituted for naloxone. [From Downs and Woods (1975a); © 1975 by the Society for the Experimental Analysis of Behavior.]

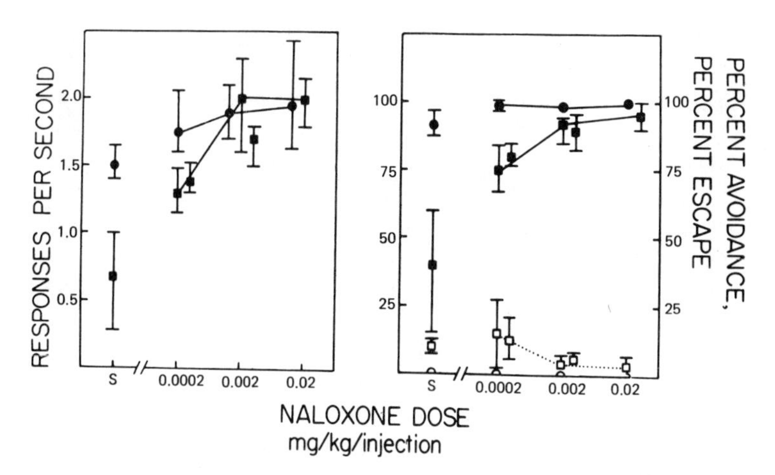

Figure 18. Left panel: response rate as a function of naloxone dose or saline in the FR 30 avoidance-escape procedure in each of two monkeys. Each point represents the mean of the last 5 of 20 sessions at each dose. One exception is the point at S for 672, which represents the mean of five sessions only. Vertical lines indicate the range about each mean. Replications are offset from original determinations. Circle, 643; square, 672. Right panel: percent avoidance (solid symbols) and percent escape (open symbols) means and ranges corresponding to response-rate data shown in left panel. [From Downs and Woods (1975a); © 1975 by the Society for the Experimental Analysis of Behavior.]

As Goldberg (1976) points out, the greater sensitivity of the escape procedure to changes in dose may make it ideal for comparing different drugs.

Responding which results in escape from naloxone can also be maintained by a variety of other schedules much as responding which results in escape from electric shock (Morse and Kelleher, 1966). Although rates of responding on a fixed-interval 5-min schedule of escape were maintained at levels above operant, they were relatively low when compared to responding maintained by electric shock escape. These rates increased, however, when the schedule was changed to a second-order schedule. In this schedule, the completion of five responses resulted in the brief illumination of a stimulus associated with time-out from drug injection. The first ratio completed after 5 min had passed resulted in the escape from the naloxone injection. In addition, changing the dose of the naloxone had effects similar to that described above for the fixed-ratio escape procedure.

While it seems obvious that narcotic antagonists can function to maintain responding in much the same manner as electric shock, recent studies have begun to show that this is true for other drugs as well, particularly drugs which have been unable to maintain responding leading to their delivery. In a study by Kandel and Schuster (1977), rhesus monkeys responded to escape infusions of perphenazine, a phenothiazine. Hoffmeister and Wuttke (1973), using an avoidance-escape procedure similar to that previously described, found that animals would respond to avoid or terminate a stimulus associated with injections of LSD, STP, and chlorpromazine. Responding was not maintained, however, by the termination of a stimulus associated with injections of either imipramine or pentobarbital. The effects of these same drugs were also assessed on responding maintained by electric shock avoidance, and the investigators found that their ability to function as negative reinforcers was independent of the influence the drug exerted on shock avoidance responding (i.e., nonspecific effects).

The results of studies using drugs as negative reinforcers extend the range of conditions under which drugs have been found to be similar to other reinforcing events. Just as many drugs are similar to food in terms of their ability to function as positive reinforcers, other drugs are similar to electric shock in terms of their ability to function as negative reinforcers. There is no doubt that the properties of a stimulus including a drug are determined to a great extent by its context. Under certain conditions, for instance, responding can be maintained by the presentation of electric shock (Byrd, 1969; McKearney, 1968, 1969). This is true, as well, for nalorphine (Goldberg *et al.*, 1971b) and naloxone (Woods *et al.*, 1975). In the latter study, the avoidance–escape procedure as described above was used. The avoidance–escape requirement was eliminated and the time-out following the completion of each fixed-ratio 30 was reduced to 1.5 sec. The completion of every tenth fixed-ratio 30 component resulted in an injection of naloxone. In early sessions response rates under this second-order schedule were well maintained but decreased when saline was substituted for the naloxone. However, over extended sessions of response-contingent naloxone injections, responding was not maintained. While these results suggest that narcotic antagonists can maintain responding in a manner analogous to responding maintained by electric shock, there are pharmacological differences among drugs which influence the probability that they will function under most experimental situations as either a positive or negative reinforcer. The pharmacological differences may have important therapeutic implications.

8. Punishment

Responding maintained by both injections of drugs or avoidance–escape of drugs resembles responding maintained by other events. This similarity between drugs and other reinforcers enables researchers to utilize the vast literature of behavior analysis to understand how this behavior is controlled. Although there is increasing evidence that variables which affect behavior in other contexts have effects on drug-maintained responding, it is still necessary to extend this generality to include a range of additional manipulations.

The effects of punishment on behavior have been studied extensively. Punishment is defined as a reduction in the probability of a response as a consequence of the presentation of a stimulus contingent on the response (Azrin and Holz, 1966). The effects of concurrent punishment on behavior are of particular interest when responding is maintained by drugs. First, if the effects of punishment on drug-maintained responding are similar to its effects on other behaviors across a wide range of experimental paradigms, it increases the generality of the assumption that drugs are not unique as reinforcers. Second, it would be interesting to compare the effects of drugs on punished responding maintained by other events to a situation where the same drugs are used to maintain the behavior being punished. Certain drugs, such as the barbiturates, attenuate the suppressant effects of punishment, whereas other drugs, such as the amphetamines, do not (Geller and Seifter, 1960; see Chapter 2). It would be interesting to determine whether these differential effects generalize to a situation where the drugs function as reinforcers. One might predict that under similar conditions, responding maintained by a barbiturate would be more difficult to suppress with punishment than responding maintained by amphetamine. The effects of punishing drug-reinforced responding are also interesting because of practical considerations as part of an animal model of drug abuse. Punishment has been used as a principal means of controlling drug taking in humans. The making and continual remaking of laws has been almost a preoccupation of many governments in regulating drug use. Prevention and treatment have only recently been added to incarceration as a means of decreasing the use of illicit drugs. Despite this fact, systematic research on the effects of punishment on drug taking is almost totally lacking.

One of the few studies in this area was done by Grove and Schuster (1974), who compared the ability of extinction and punishment to suppress responding maintained by cocaine injections in rhesus monkeys. Punishment was accomplished by delivering a brief electric shock ranging from 1 to 8 mA at the onset of an injection. Responding was maintained under a multiple schedule shown in Table I. During each 3-hr session of base-line conditions, the two fixed-ratio 1 components of the multiple schedule alternated, and 0.1 mg/kg cocaine was delivered for each response. When responding during one component no longer produced an injection (extinction), responding decreased in

Table I. Explanation of the Component Schedule Conditions Used in the Control (Multiple Base-Line), Extinction, and Punishment Conditions[a]

Stimulus conditions		Reinforcement schedule conditions		
Discriminative stimulus	Signaled components	Multiple base line	Multiple extinction	Multiple punishment
S^D1	1, 3, 5	FR-1: drug	FR-1: drug	FR-1: drug
S^D2	2, 4, 6	FR-1: drug	Ext	FR-1: shock + drug

[a] Across all conditions S^D1 signaled FR-1 access to drug in the first, third, and fifth half-hours of each session; S^D2 signaled FR-1 drug on control sessions or extinction or shock in treatment conditions. See the text for details.
Source: Grove and Schuster (1974).

most animals. Next, sessions in which responses were punished during one component of the multiple schedule by the delivery of electric shock alternated with base-line conditions. Responding maintained by both 0.1 and 0.2 mg/kg cocaine decreased as a function of the intensity of the shock. As seen in Figure 19, the degree of suppression expressed as a percent of control rates was surprisingly the same for the two doses. Increasing the magnitude of reinforcement did not seem to attenuate the effects of punishment, as might be expected if one assumes that higher doses have greater reinforcing efficacy. This finding, however, is difficult to interpret since the base-line rates of responding maintained by the different doses of cocaine were not the same. Since a ratio schedule was used, the rates maintained by the higher dose were lower. Therefore, a decrease in responding with this dose as a result of punishment which is similar in terms of percentage to the decrease seen with the lower dose actually represents a smaller absolute change in number of injections.

In a study by Johanson (1975, 1977), the problem of using rate as a dependent variable was obviated by using a choice procedure similar to that described previously (Johanson and Schuster, 1975). Rhesus monkeys were given a choice between two alternatives of intravenous cocaine. These alternatives were initially equal in dose but in subsequent comparisons, they differed in magnitude. Electric shock was delivered at the onset of the delivery of one of the alternatives. When the two doses were equal, the nonshocked alternative was chosen. For some animals, the nonshocked alternative was preferred even when the shocked alternative was a higher dose. These results are similar to the results of studies where responding was maintained by the delivery of food (Azrin *et al.*, 1965) and further extend the notion that drugs, or at least cocaine injections, are functionally similar to other positive reinforcers in their effects on responding in a punishment situation. The study goes even further, however, in delineating the effects of punishment when its avoidance involves choosing an alternative positive reinforcer of a lower magnitude. In this same study, all animals eventually preferred the shocked alternative when dose was further increased, although the increase in dose required to alter the effects of punishment varied between animals. Nevertheless, it seems that these effects can be attenuated by increasing magnitude of reinforcement. This further shows that higher doses of a drug are more efficacious as reinforcers since responding maintained by them, at least in a choice situation, is harder to suppress.

Clearly, research on the effects of punishment on drug-maintained responding has just begun. Nevertheless, these few studies seem to indicate that as in other schedule-controlled situations, responding maintained by drugs is remarkably similar to responding maintained by other events. However, since drugs administered noncontingently have differential effects on punished responding maintained by other events,

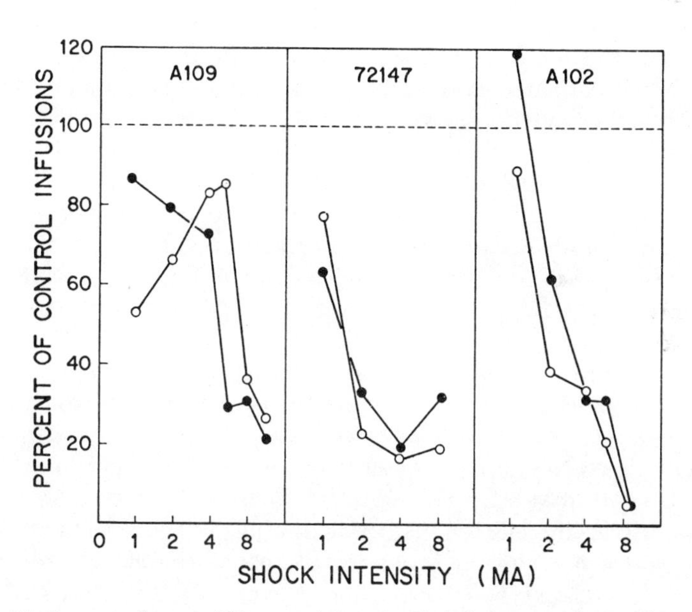

Figure 19. Percent of mean S^D2 control (nonshock) infusion rate across the averaged S^D2 infusion rate over each replication of a shock intensity. Plotted for both high (200 μg/kg) (●—●) and low (100 μg/kg) (○—○) unit dose. The reference (100%) infusion rate was determined as the mean of S^D2 infusions during multiple base-line control conditions. [From Grove and Schuster (1974).]

the generality of this notion awaits further research, particularly involving responding maintained by drugs from different pharmacological classes.

9. An Application of Drug Self-Administration Techniques: The Preclinical Assessment of the Abuse Liability of New Compounds

It has been the general theme of this review that although the investigation of drugs as reinforcers was originally viewed entirely within the context of developing an animal model of drug abuse, the finding that responding maintained by drugs is similar to responding maintained by other stimulus events has shifted attention to broader issues of the control of behavior as reviewed above. This discovery that drugs are like other reinforcers has enabled researchers to view drug-seeking behavior within the context of behavior analysis. Variables found significant in controlling other types of behavior as well affect drug seeking in a similar way. While drugs possess some unique properties, their pharmacological properties are relatively unimportant. As discovered in behavioral pharmacological research and emphasized in this review, the nature of the ongoing behavior is by far the major determinant of responding maintained by drugs. It is important to continue to demonstrate the similarity between responding maintained by drugs and that maintained by other reinforcers, by doing experiments such as those described in the section on punishment. However, there is little justification in developing a separate animal model of drug abuse to simply evaluate variables which affect drug self-administration, since they are most likely the same variables which control responding maintained by any event.

Nevertheless, there is an application of drug self-administration studies where the pharmacology of the drug is important; this area is the preclinical assessment of the abuse liability of new compounds. While research in this area borrows heavily from general behavioral research, there are some unique aspects of the application which require a separate description.

The use of animals for the prediction of the abuse liability of new compounds began with the screening of analgesics for physical dependence of the opiate type (Deneau and Seevers, 1962; Villarreal, 1972). In this simple procedure, rhesus monkeys were initially made physically dependent on morphine. When a new compound was tested, it was merely substituted for morphine and observations for signs of withdrawal were made. The same preparation could be used to determine whether the compound was an opiate antagonist as well. The elegance of this screening procedure was due to its simplicity and efficiency. Many compounds over a wide range of doses could quickly be assessed for abuse liability at a relatively low cost. This rapid and economical procedure undoubtedly helped to make pharmaceutical houses willing to submit their compounds for testing and led to the Food and Drug Administration of the United States government adopting this as mandatory for analgesic testing. Subsequently, procedures which directly determine the dependence-producing properties of drugs have been included in the testing of new analgesic compounds to improve the specificity of the screening program. These procedures have proved so useful over the years that the general concept of using animals for the preclinical assessment of analgesics is well accepted. However, the usefulness of this approach for preventing the development of drugs with high abuse liability is predicated on the assumption that the chronic intake of all drugs of abuse results in the development of physical dependence and that all drugs which produce physical dependence are abused.

In 1932, the amphetamines were introduced into the medical pharmacopaeia as decongestants and, in addition, as a replacement for ephedrine in the treatment of bronchial asthma. Although they were relatively ineffective in this latter regard, their impressive central nervous system stimulant effects soon became obvious and led eventually to their use in the treatment of obesity, hyperkinesis, and narcolepsy. Only over the last 10–15 years have clinicians generally recognized the abuse liability of the amphetamines and related compounds (Angrist and Gershon, 1969; Kramer *et al.,* 1967). Because of this potential abuse, there have been increasing efforts on the part of the pharmaceutical industry to develop new psychomotor stimulant drugs with lower abuse potential than those currently available. This search is analogous to the attempts to find an analgesic compound which does not produce physical dependence. The methodology used with analgesics is not applicable, since the chronic administration of psychomotor stimulant drugs does not result in physical dependence (Tatum and Seevers, 1929). However, there is little question that with the psychomotor stimulants a state is developed in certain individual of psychological dependence which is characterized by the repeated use of this class of drugs.

This repeated use in humans may be analogous to responding maintained by drugs in animals. Evidence for the validity of this analogy is rapidly accumulating. As previously reviewed, animals self-administer the same drugs which humans use for nonmedical purposes; these include psychomotor stimulants, opiates, barbiturates, and alcohol (Schuster and Thompson, 1969; Schuster and Johanson, 1974). In addition, the pattern of intake of these drugs in experimental animals is very similar to the pattern of their illicit use by man. Stimulants, for instance, are taken in cycles with days of high intake alternating with days of low intake (see Figure 8; Deneau *et al.*, 1969; Johanson *et al.*, 1976a). This pattern is reminiscent of that reported for humans (Kramer *et al.*, 1967). Finally, the physiological and behavioral consequences of the repeated self-administration of drugs is similar from animal to man (Fischman and Schuster, 1975). Therefore, if animals self-administer some drug, it is highly probable that humans will abuse it.

This fact is of little importance for drugs currently available, since their abuse liability is more accurately assessed by determining the actual incidence of illegal use. However, as new compounds are developed for whatever therapeutic reason, it might be possible to determine their abuse potential before they are marketed. It might also be possible to develop new therapeutic agents which have lower abuse potential than drugs currently used for the same purpose. For example, pharmaceutical companies are eagerly trying to develop new psychomotor stimulant drugs of lower abuse potential than the amphetamines. If they are successful, the production of psychomotor stimulant drugs with high abuse potential could be sharply curtailed, thus reducing the quantities available for rediversion into the illicit market. If animal studies are valid predictors, it should be possible to evaluate new stimulant compounds for their dependence potential during their preclinical testing. Although it is true that some drugs appear to lack positive reinforcing properties (e.g., chlorpromazine, fenfluramine), it is unlikely that the psychomotor stimulants can be replaced in all their applications with drugs completely devoid of positive reinforcing properties. A more realistic goal is to find drugs with significantly less dependence potential than those currently available. The problem then is to develop procedures to determine first whether a drug is capable of serving as a positive reinforcer, and, if so, to be able to measure its relative reinforcing efficacy. In operant terms, this is comparable to assessing the strength of a positive reinforcer (Hodos, 1961).

A variety of self-administration procedures are presently considered useful for the preclinical assessment of the abuse liability of new compounds (Brady *et al.*, 1975; Brady and Griffiths, 1977; Griffiths *et al.*, 1975a; Griffiths *et al.*, 1976c). In fact, a review of these procedures has recently been published (Thompson and Unna, 1977) as a report of a meeting entitled, "Testing for Dependence Liability of Stimulants and Depressants in Animals and Man" sponsored by the Committee on Problems of Drug Dependence (NAS–NRC) and various agencies of the U.S. government (NIDA, FDA, and DEA). Rather than reviewing

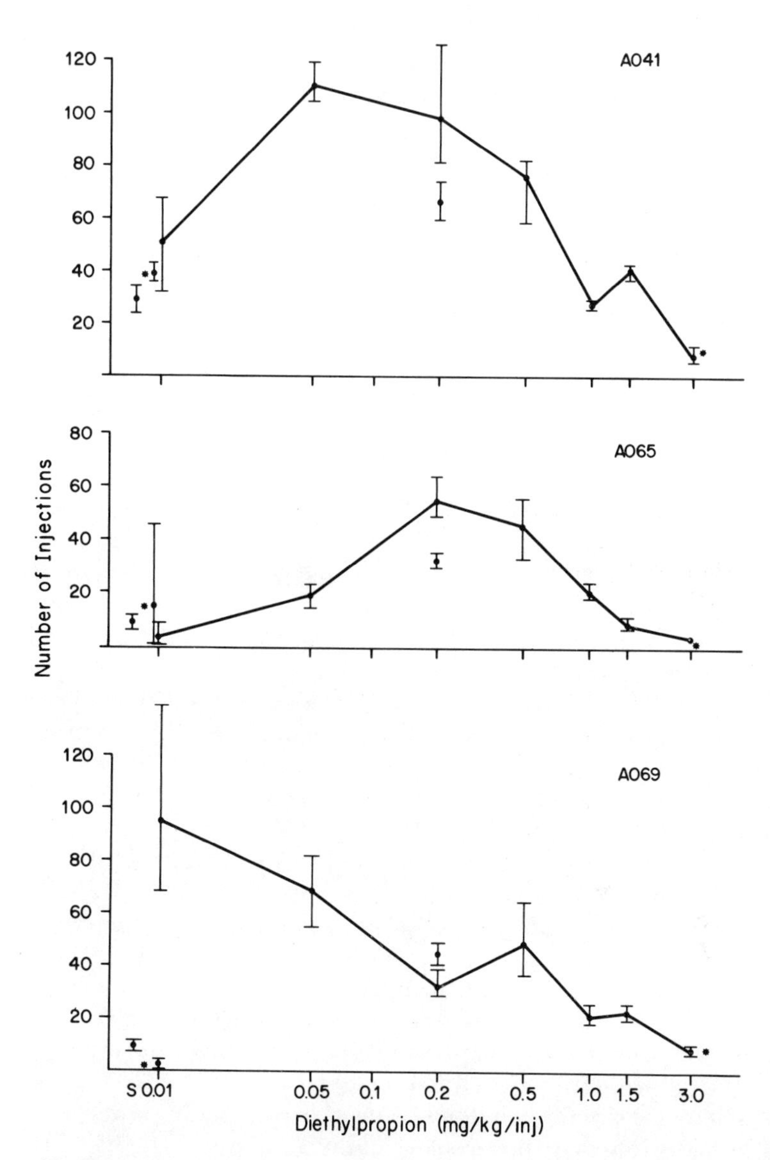

Figure 20. Dose–response functions showing the mean number of injections self-administered at different doses of diethylpropion for three animals in the substitution procedure. These means are derived from data obtained on the last three sessions at each dose. Means for saline and 0.2 mg/kg cocaine are also shown. Brackets indicate range. [From Johanson and Schuster (1977a).]

the enormous literature in this area, it may be more useful to demonstrate, at least in part, how a single drug was tested in order to illustrate the general approach. The example is a psychomotor stimulant drug, diethylpropion. It should be pointed out that in testing a drug, several procedures, including ones where responding is not maintained by drugs, must be used to thoroughly assess any drug. However, only the most important ones will be discussed in this review. For a more complete description, see Johanson and Schuster (1977b).

By and large, the majority of the studies which demonstrate that psychomotor stimulants, opiates, barbiturates, and alcohol can function as positive reinforcers have utilized some modification of a substitution procedure (Schuster and Johanson, 1974). Animals equipped with intravenous catheters are initially trained to respond for drugs such as cocaine or pentobarbital (base-line drug), usually on a fixed-ratio schedule of injection. After responding becomes stable, a test compound is substituted. Responding may be maintained by the test compound or decline to minimal levels. By alternating the base-line drug and different doses of the test compound, a dose–response function can be quickly obtained. Using a variation of this procedure, diethylpropion has been tested (Johanson, 1975; Johanson and Schuster, 1977a). Figure 20 shows that, in general, responding maintained by diethylpropion initially increased as dose was increased and then decreased as dose was further increased. These data demonstrate that like other psychomotor stimulant drugs, diethylpropion can act as a positive reinforcer. In addition, the shape of the dose–response curve was similar to those generated with other stimulants (Wilson *et al.*, 1971; Balster and Schuster, 1973b).

Although substitution procedures of this type are useful in determining whether a drug possesses any positive reinforcing properties, it is inadequate for assessing these properties relative to other drugs. As has been explained in the section on magnitude of reinforcement, responding maintained by a drug under schedules where intake is not limited (and increases in responding lead to increases in intake) is influenced not only by its reinforcing actions but by its other pharmacological properties as well (see Figure 1).

There are several schedules of drug presentation, however, which can be used to avoid the problem outlined above. The choice procedure (Johanson and Schuster, 1975) described in a previous section is useful for assessing more clearly the relative reinforcing efficacy of different drugs. This procedure was therefore used to compare diethylpropion to cocaine. It was found that in almost all comparisons, cocaine was preferred regardless of the dose of either drug (Johanson and Schuster, 1977a,b). This is in contrast to the results from comparisons

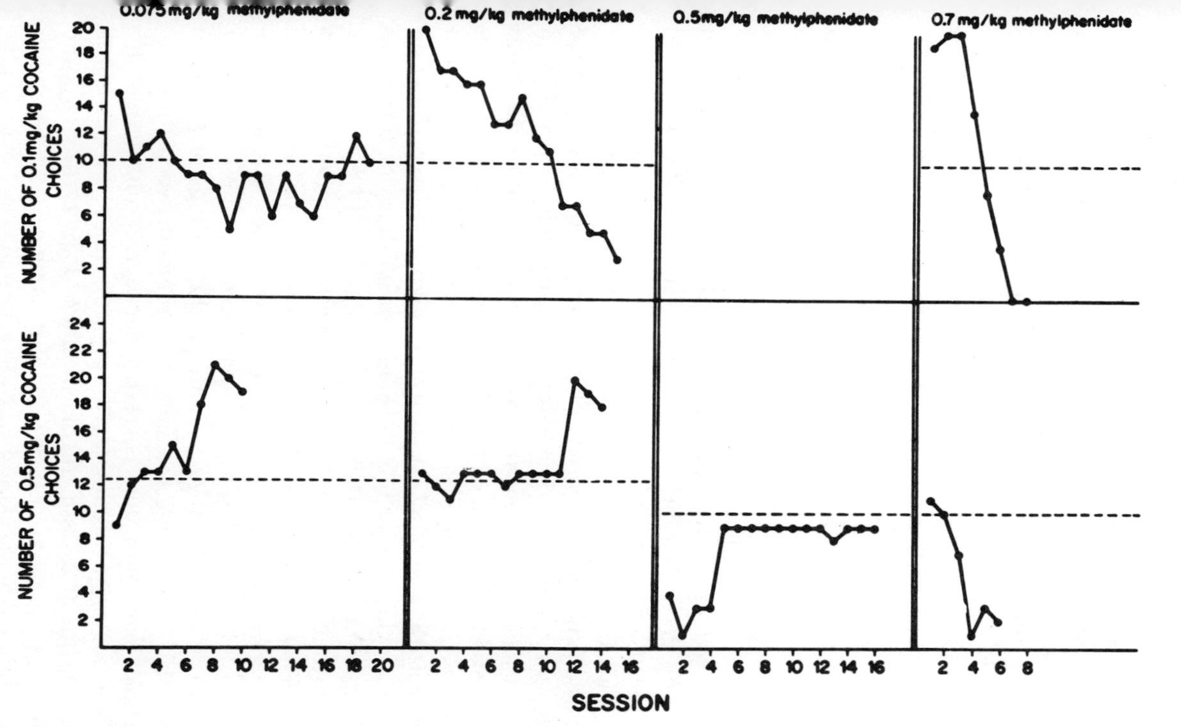

Figure 21. Number of choice trials 0.1 mg/kg of cocaine (top row) or 0.5 mg/kg of cocaine (bottom row) was chosen over different doses of methylphenidate plotted daily for each comparison for A022. The dotted lines indicate 50% choice. The comparisons shown here were made in the following order, although other comparisons were interspersed, as indicated by an asterisk (*): (1) 0.2 mg/kg of methylphenidate vs. 0.5 mg/kg of cocaine; (2) 0.075 mg/kg of methylphenidate vs. 0.5 mg/kg of cocaine*; (3) 0.5 mg/kg of methylphenidate vs. 0.5 mg/kg of cocaine*; (4) 0.7 mg/kg of methylphenidate vs. 0.1 mg/kg of cocaine*; (5) 0.2 mg/kg of methylphenidate vs. 0.1 mg/kg of cocaine*; (6) 0.7 mg/kg of methylphenidate vs. 0.5 mg/kg of cocaine; and (7) 0.075 mg/kg of methylphenidate vs. 0.1 mg/kg of cocaine. [From Johanson and Schuster (1975); © 1975 The Williams & Wilkins Company, Baltimore.]

between cocaine and methylphenidate, where dose appeared to be the major determinant of preference (Figure 21). Interestingly, the results from both the substitution and choice studies conform well to the reported relative incidence of abuse of these two drugs. Despite the fact that diethylpropion is similar in its profile of pharmacological actions to cocaine and the amphetamines (Jonsson, 1969) and has been available on the market for over 15 years, there is little evidence for nonmedical use, except when more preferred stimulant drugs are unavailable (Jasinski *et al.,* 1974).

The choice procedure is not the only procedure useful for comparing the relative reinforcing properties of different drugs (Thompson and Unna, 1977). Second-order and concurrent schedules may also be useful, but to date they have been applied to this problem only to a limited extent. A fourth procedure which has been used extensively to compare drugs, including diethylpropion, is the progressive ratio schedule. In this schedule, responding is maintained by a drug under a ratio schedule. After responding is well established, the number of responses required for each reinforcement is systematically increased until responding declines to below some criterion rate. The ratio value which leads to this criterion reduction is called the breaking point. Several studies with other positive reinforcers have shown that breaking point varies as a function of a variety of variables, including magnitude of reinforcement (Hodos, 1961; Keesey and Goldstein, 1968; Hodos and Kalman, 1963). This same procedure has been used with drugs maintaining responding. Yanagita (1973) showed that breaking point was a direct function of the dose of cocaine. Similar results were not obtained by Griffiths *et al.* (1975a); as seen in Figure 22, they found instead that the breaking point was the same for all doses of cocaine as well as methylphenidate, although the breaking point of the latter drug was lower than that of cocaine. In a subsequent study, however, Griffiths *et al.* (1976c) examined doses of cocaine below 0.4 mg/kg, and found that breaking point did vary directly with dose. In that same study, it was found that all doses of diethylpropion had generally lower breaking points than cocaine, which confirms the findings of Johanson and Schuster (1977a) showing the same difference between these two drugs in a choice paradigm. This correspondence in results despite differences in species and procedures gives great promise to their usefulness in the preclinical assessment of the abuse liability of new compounds. Although researchers interested in this type of animal model are well aware that drug-seeking behavior is largely a behavioral phenomenon, there are pharmacological differences between drugs which increase the probability of one agent being abused rather than another, all other conditions being equal. The development of an animal model

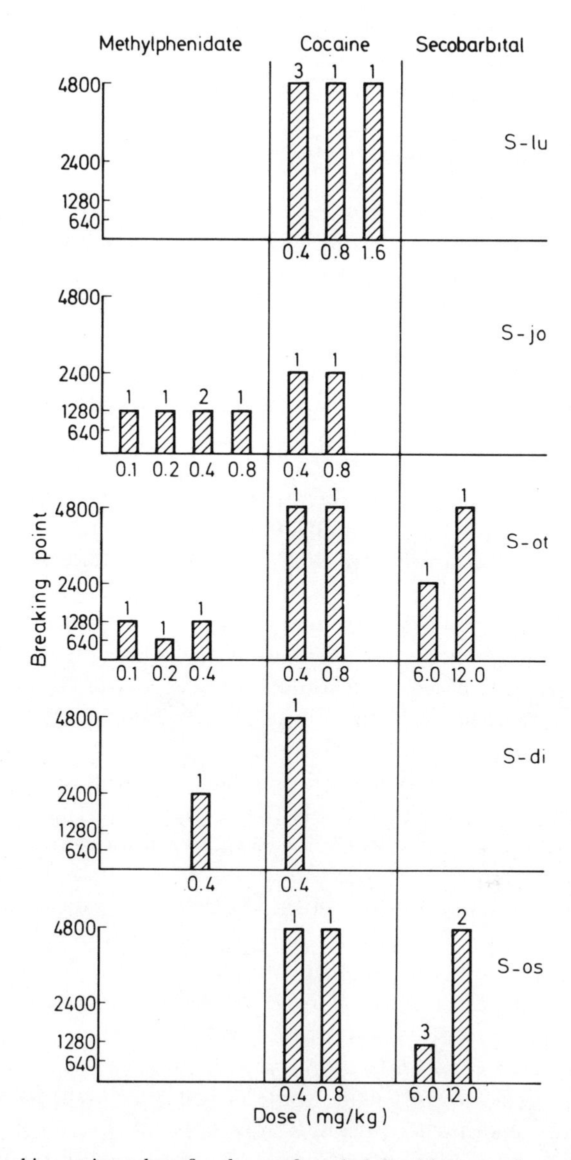

Figure 22. Breaking-point values for doses of methylphenidate, cocaine, and secobarbital in five subjects. Each bar represents breaking point obtained at indicated dose of drug. Numeral above bar indicates the number of determinations at the dose. In all cases, multiple determinations resulted in identical breaking-point values. Absence of bar indicates subject was not exposed to that condition. [From Griffiths *et al.* (1975a).]

designed to avoid the marketing of compounds with extremely high probabilities is certainly an important application for drug self-administration research.

10. Human Self-Administration Studies

In studying drugs as reinforcers as a model of drug abuse, the validity of the assumption that the variables which modify self-administration in animals are the same for man is of essential importance. While a great deal of research indicates that animals self-administer the same drugs that humans abuse, evidence supporting this relationship is difficult to obtain because of the problem of acquiring reliable human data. Although there are numerous reports giving estimates of the relative incidence of abuse of various drugs, these estimates are at best approximations, since they are based either upon the amount of drugs confiscated by law enforcement agencies or upon retrospective reports of use by individuals who in many instances do not really know what drugs they are purchasing. Another approach to determine the abuse potential of drugs has been to use subjective judgments of subjects who have used a variety of psychoactive drugs; these subjects are given a drug and then asked whether they like it and whether it resembles any drug they have ever abused. In some instances, mood scales purporting to measure a drug's ability to produce euphoria are used, on the assumption that a drug's euphorogenic properties are the basis of its abuse. However, there are no studies which show that euphoria in man and self-administration in animals are equivalent. It seems obvious, then, that the best way to determine whether humans and animals self-administer the same drugs, and the variables which control this behavior, is to extend the methodology of drug self-administration to humans and conduct systematic research similar to that done with animals. With human subjects, however, it is not always possible to use exactly the same methodologies as those employed with animals. Bigelow *et al.* (1975a) have pointed out some of the problems, such as subject interaction, shifts in base line, and subject withdrawal, which necessitate procedural changes. However, while some changes are necessary, and ethical considerations must constantly be kept in mind, it should be possible to do enough studies to determine the validity of an animal model.

One of the first drugs studied with humans was ethanol. In early studies, however, oral administration was programmed so that measuring pattern and rate of intake was impossible, since it was specified by the experiment (Mendelson and Mello, 1966). In more recent studies, ethanol has been made available to subjects by either simple request or the completion of some specified behavioral requirement. Although access has been restricted to only certain periods of the day in order to develop stable base lines of intake, over some range, rate of self-administration can vary. With unlimited access to ethanol, periods of high intake alternate in a random fashion with periods of low intake. Interestingly, this is also true in animal studies (Deneau *et al.,* 1969). Therefore, in order to develop a stable base line to allow the evaluations of the effects of manipulations on intake, it is necessary to restrict maximum intake in both animals and man.

In the first study of ethanol self-administration, only simple observations were made of the consequences of voluntary ethanol consumption. Griffiths *et al.* (1974a) showed that when subjects consume ethanol in a controlled laboratory setting, the incidence of social interactions increases. Volunteer subjects with a history of chronic alcoholism were admitted to a hospital ward and detoxified. Each day, either 12 1-oz drinks of 11.14 g of ethanol in 2 oz of orange juice or the orange juice alone was available. By making observations of the subject's behavior, an estimate of the incidence of social interactions was made. When ethanol was available on random or on successive days, the degree of social interactions were higher than on days when ethanol was not available. In all cases, when ethanol was available, subjects consumed the maximum amount. These results are in contrast to previous reports that alcoholics are social isolates (Mowrer and Mowrer, 1945; Zwerling and Rosenbaum, 1959). It may very well be, as the authors suggest, that humans consume alcohol in order to increase their social interactions. To test this possibility, Bigelow *et al.* (1974) required subjects to sit for 10 min in an isolation booth immediately following each drink of ethanol. As in the previous study, chronic alcoholics were admitted to a hospital ward and detoxified. Each day, 12–24 drinks were available upon request. When intake stabilized, the 10-min isolation requirement was imposed. In 7 of the 10 subjects, drinking declined to about 50% of base line. For 2 of the subjects not affected by this manipulation, the additional requirement that drinks be spaced by at least 1 hr also resulted in reduced drinking. Spaced drinking alone also decreased drinking, but not to the same extent as when both manipulations were made simultaneously. That the two manipulations together had an effect may indicate that ethanol drinking, like all drug self-administration, is controlled by more than one variable. In order to isolate relatively weak determinants of behavior, it is important to develop sensitive base-line procedures which will maximize the effects of the manipulation being tested. In this case, for instance, including the spaced drinking requirement as part of the base-line procedure made it possible to more completely characterize the role of contingent time-outs in controlling the incidence of ethanol drinking.

This same strategy was also used in the next study, which was designed to determine what aspect of the isolation used in the previous study controlled behavior (Griffiths *et al.,* 1974b). Using a procedure similar to that described above, chronic alcoholics were given access each day to 17 drinks separated by at least 40 min. When intake stabilized under base-line conditions, each drink was followed by a 40-min period of social but not physical isolation. In addition, the number of other available privileges (e.g., access to TV, reading materials, etc.) was varied. The results demonstrated that contingent time-out suppressed drinking as a direct function of the number of other available privileges. When no other restrictions were imposed, time-out had little effect on the drinking of most subjects. As privileges were restricted more and more, the effectiveness of the time-out increased. This again demonstrates the control of behavior by more than one variable.

In a final study, Griffiths *et al.* (1975c) used a somewhat different approach to determine the relationship between ethanol drinking by human subjects and social interactions. These subjects were given a choice between money and a period of social interactions every 20 min for a total of 12 times each day. On days when ethanol had been consumed, the choice of social interactions increased. This suggests that previously held views concerning the social behavior of chronic alcoholics have been inaccurate.

Similar studies of drug self-administration in humans have been done with sedatives. In a study by Griffiths *et al.* (1976a), subjects were required to ride an exercise bicycle to earn points, which could be exchanged for pentobarbital or diazepam given orally. By manipulating the minimum interingestion interval between administrations (i.e., requiring that intake be spaced), these investigators found that the intake of both drugs at a set dose decreased as the required interval increased. Similar results have been found with ethanol (Bigelow *et al.,* 1975a). In addition, increasing the dose of ethanol, diazepam, or pentobarbital increased intake. In another study (Bigelow *et al.,* 1975b), intake was found to be an inverse function of cost per administration. It should be pointed out that in all these studies using sedatives, subjects were required to complete a behavioral requirement (riding an exercise bicycle for a certain time) in order to receive drugs. Hopefully, future studies will continue this practice of using response requirements for the delivery of drug (schedule of reinforcement) so that comparisons between human and animal studies can be facilitated.

Despite its prevalent use in man, few studies have investigated the variables which contribute to tobacco smoking. Lucchesi *et al.* (1967)

showed that the intravenous infusion of nicotine decreased the number of cigarettes consumed by human volunteers compared to the number consumed when saline alone was infused. This indicates that the nicotine in tobacco contributes significantly to its self-administration. Griffiths *et al.* (1976b), using procedures similar to their other studies, investigated the effects of ethanol on the rate of tobacco self-administration. Across a wide range of experimental conditions, ethanol was found to increase tobacco consumption during a 6-hr experimental session. Control studies were performed which showed that smoking was not an adjunct of either ethanol drinking or social interactions, and that ethanol did not alter the amount of each cigarette consumed or the number of puffs per cigarette. The authors postulated several possible mechanisms to explain why ethanol increases cigarette consumption. It is possible, for instance, that ethanol is a nonspecific behavioral stimulant, increasing the rates of many behaviors, including smoking. It has been demonstrated, for instance, that under conditions of ethanol administration similar to the present study, ethanol increases the rate of social interactions in alcoholics (Griffiths *et al.,* 1974a). In addition, ethanol might selectively interact with the reinforcing properties of cigarettes as an antagonist, or tobacco itself might alter the objective and subjective effects of ethanol. Regardless of the mechanism, however, it can only be elucidated by a rigorous experimental analysis involving the systematic manipulations of environmental variables.

Another drug tested in the self-administration paradigm is marijuana, a substance alleged to produce an "amotivational syndrome" in humans (National Commission on Marijuana and Drug Abuse, 1972). Not only are there several conflicting reports of this (e.g., Marcus *et al.*, 1974) but motivational changes must be inferred from behavioral changes. Few studies have attempted to do this by actually measuring changes in behavior as a consequence of marijuana smoking. In a study by Mendelson *et al.* (1976), both heavy and casual marijuana users were required to press a button on a fixed-interval 1-sec schedule to earn a point. Each 1-g marijuana cigarette (containing 1.8–2.3% THC) cost 1800 points, which could be accumulated by 30 min of sustained work. Points not used to purchase cigarettes could be converted to money at the rate of 3600 points per $1.00. Both groups of subjects maintained high rates of responding throughout the 21-day period of marijuana access and purchased between 2 and 3 cigarettes per day (casual group) or between 4.3 and 6 cigarettes per day (heavy group). In most cases, point earnings exceeded the number used for cigarettes, so subjects also accumulated money during this period. In addition, subjects worked most during periods of maximal marijuana use. Although there was some correlation between the number of cigarettes smoked on one day and the work output on the following day, earnings were still in excess of the amount used for cigarette purchasing. These results certainly do not support the contention that marijuana produces an "amotivational syndrome" if rate of responding for points is used as a measure of motivation. While additional studies are clearly necessary, this research demonstrates the importance of systematic self-administration research in determining the functional consequences of marijuana use. It adds data to the body of human self-administration literature in a situation comparable to that used with animals to determine both behavioral mechanisms of action as well as the consequences of chronic drug use.

Several studies have also been done using opiates. In one series done by Schuster and his colleagues, an attempt was made to rank codeine, methadone, and pentazocine, given orally, in terms of their reinforcing properties. Such studies are essential for validating animal studies designed to assess the abuse potential of drugs preclinically (see previous section). All three drugs given intravenously maintain responding in rhesus monkeys which are not physically dependent on opiates; however, in dependent monkeys, pentazocine is a negative reinforcer, whereas the other two drugs will still maintain responding (Schuster, 1975; Goldberg *et al.,* 1972). In the first study in humans (Schuster, 1975), subjects who were former heroin addicts were detoxified and admitted to a hospital ward. A drug capsule was available every 4 hr on request from the nursing staff. For group 1, the drug was a placebo; for group 2, the available drug was 50 mg of codeine; and for group 3, it was 50 mg of pentazocine. Table II shows that both codeine and pentazocine were requested almost maximally across a 4-day period, whereas the placebo was not.

In a second study (Schuster *et al.*, 1971), out-patient heroin addicts on the waiting list for enrollment in the State of Illinois Drug Abuse Rehabilitation Program were used. Each day, these subjects could re-

Table II. Average Number of Medication Requests for Placebo, Codeine (50 mg), and Pentazocine (50 mg) in Hospitalized Exheroin Users

	Days			
Medication group	1	2	3	4
Placebo ($n = 6$)	5.0	3.5	1.8	1.5
Codeine ($n = 6$)	5.3	5.0	4.6	5.3
Pentazocine ($n = 5$)	5.6	4.8	5.2	5.0

Source: Schuster (1975); © 1975 The Williams & Wilkins Company, Baltimore.

Table III. Frequency of Clinic Attendance (in Percentage) for Subjects Receiving Codeine (400 mg), Methadone (40 mg), Pentazocine (400 mg), or Placebo

	Days									
	With monetary reinforcement					Without monetary reinforcement				
Drug group	1	2	3	4	5	6	7	8	9	10
Codeine ($n = 23$)	100	78	74	70	57	61	52	44	48	35
Methadone ($n = 19$)	100	84	63	58	68	47	21	37	32	32
Pentazocine ($n = 23$)	100	65	44	48	39	22	18	22	18	13
Placebo ($n = 23$)	100	61	57	53	49	26	22	26	13	18

Source: Schuster (1975); © 1975 The Williams and Wilkins Company, Baltimore.

port to the clinic and, after completing a minimal behavioral requirement which required about 1 hr of their time, received capsules of codeine (group 1), methadone (group 2), pentazocine (group 3), or placebo (group 4). During the first 5 days of the experiment, subjects received a payment ($2) to cover their traveling expenses. However, on the last 5 days, no money was given. Table III shows the frequency of subjects who returned to the clinic over the 10-day period. While all groups had a high attrition rate, only the codeine and methadone groups, and not the pentazocine group, had higher return rates than the placebo group under both monetary and nonmonetary conditions. There are several explanations to account for the different results obtained with pentazocine in these two experiments. Since the response requirements in the first experiment were minimal, it may be that pentazocine is a weak reinforcer that does not maintain responding when the requirements are increased, in much the same way that methylphenidate has a lower breaking point than cocaine in progressive ratio experiments (Griffiths *et al.*, 1975a). On the other hand, it is highly likely that subjects in the second experiment were still physically dependent on opiates. Pentazocine is not a positive reinforcer in animals who are physically dependent on opiates, but instead is a negative reinforcer. Although it is impossible to determine which of these possibilities is correct, these studies are exciting first steps in determining whether animal and human self-administration is controlled in a similar manner.

The search for this similarity has been extended to studies of opiate agonist–antagonist interactions using the intravenous administration of heroin. Meyer *et al.* (1976) showed that when heroin was available following the completion of a certain number of button presses, most subjects self-administered maximum amounts over a 10-day period of access. However, when a narcotic antagonist was given (blockade) over a second 10-day period of heroin access, few injections of heroin were taken. This study was designed to determine whether treatment with a narcotic antagonist will result in the extinction of heroin self-administration (Wikler, 1974). Unfortunately, however, extinction requires that behavior that is no longer being reinforced actually be emitted. When animals are exposed to extinction, responding typically shows an initial increase and then declines to low levels. Similar results have been found in studies where rhesus monkeys self-administering heroin were pretreated with naloxone over a 10-day period (Killian *et al.,* 1977). At some dose of naloxone, responding initially increased but then declined. That these results were not found with humans may illustrate one of the problems of using this species. The subjects in the Meyer *et al.* study were informed when they were being blocked by an antagonist. Unlike animals, they were aware of the effects of narcotic antagonists and did not need to "experience" the blockade to appreciate its effects. While this speculation needs verifying, there is no question that instructional control, whether intended or not, can contribute significantly to the outcome of experiments involving human self-administration.

11. Summary

Research involving drugs as reinforcers has increased considerably in both volume and scope over the last 10 years. The methodology for delivering intravenous drugs to experimental animals originally evolved as part of an effort to develop an animal model of drug abuse. As such, it represented a major shift in emphasis concerning an understanding of the variables which contribute to human drug abuse. Viewing drug abuse as a problem of primarily sociological and psychiatric etiology did not provide enough information for the development of successful prevention and treatment programs. A research methodology which allowed animal laboratory investigators to manipulate a wide variety of variables in a controlled situation offered great promise for determining some of the factors which contribute to persistent drug use. In addition, the use of a well-developed technology, behavior analysis, provided researchers with a framework within which they could perform parametric studies.

The investigation of drugs as reinforcers in the study of human drug abuse has pointed up the importance of both pharmacological and behavioral variables. One factor often overlooked by clinicians was the drug itself. Early self-administration research showed that drugs such as the opiates, psychomotor stimulants, barbiturates, and alcohol all maintained responding in animals. Other drugs, such as the narcotic antagonists and phenothiazines, did not. It seemed, then, that the same drugs humans abused were self-administered by animals. In addition, the pattern and consequences of chronic intake were similar in animals and man. Treatment possibilities based upon the pharmacology of a drug could therefore be tested in animals. In fact, much self-administration research is aimed at elucidating the pharmacological and biochemical mechanisms of action of psychotropic drugs (e.g., Goldberg *et al.*, 1971c; Ryder *et al.*, 1977). Further, as more and more research accumulated, it became obvious that responding maintained by drugs was remarkably similar to responding maintained by other stimulus events, such as food, water, and intracranial stimulation. In early studies using low-valued fixed-ratio schedules, this similarity had been obscured by the low rates of responding generated by those conditions. Using schedules which generated a great deal of responding but which limited intake emphasized the similarity between drugs and other positive reinforcers. Responding maintained by drugs under ratio, interval, chained, multiple, second-order, and concurrent schedules was shown to be similar in both rate and pattern to responding maintained by other events under similar conditions. Changes in magnitude of reinforcement (dose) produced predictable changes in behavior. Also, responding for drugs can be modified by conditions of deprivation and punishment. The effects of drugs, like the effects of food, can be classically conditioned. And finally, certain drugs were capable of functioning as negative reinforcers so that animals responded to avoid or escape their infusion. The similarities are abundant, and it is generally agreed that drugs can be classified as one category of reinforcers.

Despite the temptation to subsume the study of drugs as reinforcers under the general study of behavioral control, there are at least two areas where using only drugs as reinforcers are justified. The first of these involves the preclinical evaluation of the abuse potential of new compounds. Since the correlation between the drugs which animals self-administer and humans abuse is so high, it should be possible to develop a battery of animal procedures to determine whether a compound is capable of functioning as a positive or negative reinforcer under a variety of experimental conditions. It goes without saying that the reinforcing properties alone should not determine whether or not a compound should be marketed; its therapeutic efficacy, as well as other toxic side effects, must also enter into any decision. However, a knowledge of the abuse potential of a new drug is certainly valuable information.

The second area involves human self-administration in a controlled laboratory setting. There are many variables, such as social interactions, which contribute to the continued use of drugs by humans. These variables are difficult or perhaps less efficient to study using animals. This research is quite new, and few studies have been conducted. These have yielded interesting data, however, which show promise in adding to our understanding of the problems involved in human drug abuse.

ACKNOWLEDGMENT

The preparation of this chapter was supported by U.S. Public Health Service grants DA-00047 and DA-00250.

12. References

Angrist, B. M., and Gershon, S., 1969, Amphetamine abuse in New York City—1966–1968, *Seminars Psychiat.* **1:**195–207.

Azrin, N. H., and Holz, W. C., 1966, Punishment, *in: Operant Behavior: Areas of Research and Application* (W. K. Honig, ed.), pp. 380–447, Appleton-Century-Crofts, New York.

Azrin, N. H., Hake, D. F., Holz, W. C., and Hutchinson, R. R., 1965, Motivational aspects of escape from punishment, *J. Exp. Anal. Behav.* **8:**31–44.

Balster, R. L., and Schuster, C. R., 1973a, Fixed-interval schedule of cocaine reinforcement: effect of dose and infusion duration, *J. Exp. Anal. Behav.* **20:**119–129.

Balster, R. L., and Schuster, C. R., 1973b, A comparison of *d*-amphetamine, *l*-amphetamine, and methamphetamine self-administration in rhesus monkeys, *Pharmacol. Biochem. Behav.* **1:**67–71.

Balster, R. L., Schuster, C. R., and Wilson, M. C., 1971, The substitution of opiate analgesics in monkeys maintained on cocaine self-administration; paper presented at the 33rd Annual Meeting of the Committee on Problems of Drug Dependence, NAS-NRC.

Balster, R. L., Johanson, C. E., Harris, R. T., and Schuster, C. R., 1973, Phencyclidine self-administration in the rhesus monkey, *Pharmacol. Biochem. Behav.* **1:**167–173.

Bigelow, G., Liebson, I., and Griffiths, R. R., 1974, Alcoholic drinking: suppression by a brief time-out procedure, *Behav. Res. Ther.* **12:**107–115.

Bigelow, G., Griffiths, R. R., and Liebson, I., 1975a, Experimental models for the modification of human drug self-administration: methodological developments in the study of ethanol self-administration by alcoholics, *Fed. Proc.* **34:**1785–1792.

Bigelow, G., Griffiths, R. R., and Liebson, I., 1975b, Experimental human drug self-administration. Methodology and application to the study of sedative abuse, *Pharmacol. Rev.* **27:**523–531.

Bonese, K. F., Wainer, B. H., Fitch, F. W., Rothberg, R. M., and Schuster, C. R., 1974, Changes in heroin self-administration by a rhesus monkey after morphine immunisation, *Nature* **252:**708–710.

Brady, J. V., and Griffiths, R. R., 1977, Drug-maintained performance and the analysis of stimulant reinforcing effects, *in: Cocaine and Other Stimulants* (E. Ellinwood and M. Kilbey, eds.), pp. 599–613, Plenum Press, New York.

Brady, J. V., Griffiths, R. R., and Winger, G., 1975, Drug-maintained performance procedures and the evaluation of sedative hypnotic dependency potential, *in: Hypnotics: Methods of Development and Evaluation* (F. Kagan, T. Harwood, K. Rickels, A. Rudzik, and H. Sorer, eds.), pp. 221–235, Spectrum, Jamaica, N.Y.

Branch, M. N., and Gollub, L. R., 1974, A detailed analysis of the effects of *d*-amphetamine on behavior under fixed-interval schedules, *J. Exp. Anal. Behav.* **21:**519–539.

Byrd, L. D., 1969, Responding in the cat maintained under response-independent electric shock and response-produced electric shock, *J. Exp. Anal. Behav.* **12:**1–10.

Catania, A. C., 1963, Concurrent performances: a baseline for the study of reinforcement magnitude, *J. Exp. Anal. Behav.* **6:**299–300.

Chein, I., Gerard, D. L., Lee, R. S., and Rosenfeld, E., 1964, *The Road to H,* Basic Books, New York.

Collins, K. H., and Tatum, A. L., 1925, A conditioned reflex established by chronic morphine poisoning, *Amer. J. Physiol.* **74:**15–20.

Davis, J. D., 1966, A method for chronic intravenous infusion in freely moving rats, *J. Exp. Anal. Behav.* **9:**385.

Davis, J. D., and Miller, N. E., 1963, Fear and pain: their effect on self-injection of amobarbital sodium by rats, *Science* **141:**1286–1287.

Davis, J. D., Lulenski, G. C., and Miller, N. E., 1968, Comparative studies of barbiturate self-administration, *Int. J. Addict.* **3:**207–214.

Deneau, G. A., and Seevers, M. H., 1962, Evaluation of morphine-like physical dependence in the rhesus monkey (macaca mulatta). *Bull. Drug Addict. Narcotics* (addendum 2).

Deneau, G. A., Yanagita, T., and Seevers, M. H., 1969, Self-administration of psychoactive substances by the monkey. A measure of psychological dependence, *Psychopharmacologia* **16:**30–48.

Dougherty, J., and Pickens, R., 1973, Fixed-interval schedules of intravenous cocaine presentation in rats, *J. Exp. Anal. Behav.* **20:**111–118.

Downs, D. A., and Woods, J. H., 1974, Codeine- and cocaine-reinforced responding in rhesus monkeys: effects of dose on response rates under a fixed-ratio schedule, *J. Pharmacol. Exp. Ther.* **191:**179–188.

Downs, D. A., and Woods, J. H., 1975a, Fixed-ratio escape and avoidance-escape from naloxone in morphine-dependent monkeys: effects of naloxone dose and morphine pretreatment, *J. Exp. Anal. Behav.* **23:**415–427.

Downs, D. A., and Woods, J. H., 1975b, Naloxone as a negative reinforcer in rhesus monkeys: effects of dose, schedule, and narcotic regimen, *Pharmacol. Rev.* **27:**397–406.

Ferster, C. B., and Skinner, B. F., 1957, *Schedules of Reinforcement,* Appleton-Century-Crofts, New York.

Findley, J. P., Robinson, W. W., and Peregrino, L., 1972, Addiction to secobarbital and chlordiazepoxide in the rhesus monkey by means of a self-infusion preference procedure, *Psychopharmacologia* **26:**93–114.

Fischman, M. W., and Schuster, C. R., 1975, Behavioral, biochemical, and morphological effects of methamphetamine in the rhesus monkey, *in: Behavioral Toxicology* (B. Weiss and V. Laties, eds.), pp. 375–394, Plenum Press, New York.

Geller, I., and Seifter, J., 1960, The effects of meprobamate, barbiturates, *d*-amphetamine, and promazine on experimentally induced conflict in the rat, *Psychopharmacologia* **1:**482–492.

Goldberg, S. R., 1973a, Comparable behavior maintained under fixed-ratio and second-order schedules of food presentation, cocaine injection, or *d*-amphetamine injection in the squirrel monkey, *J. Pharmacol. Exp. Ther.* **186:**18–30.

Goldberg, S. R., 1973b, Control of behavior by stimuli associated with drug injections, *in: Psychic Dependence* (L. Goldberg and F. Hoffmeister, eds.), pp. 106–109, Springer-Verlag, Berlin.

Goldberg, S. R., 1975, Stimuli associated with drug injections as events that control behavior, *Pharmacol. Rev.* **27:**325–339.

Goldberg, S. R., 1976, The behavioral analysis of drug addiction, *in: Behavioral Pharmacology* (S. D. Glick and J. Goldfarb, eds.), pp. 283–316, C. V. Mosby, St. Louis.

Goldberg, S. R., and Kelleher, R. T., 1976, Behavior controlled by scheduled injections of cocaine in squirrel and rhesus monkeys, *J. Exp. Anal. Behav.* **25:**93–104.

Goldberg, S. R., and Morse, W. H., 1973, Behavior maintained by intramuscular injections of morphine or cocaine in the rhesus monkey, *Pharmacologist* **15:**236.

Goldberg, S. R., and Schuster, C. R., 1967, Conditioned suppression by a stimulus associated with nalorphine in morphine-dependent monkeys, *J. Exp. Anal. Behav.* **10:**235–242.

Goldberg, S. R., and Schuster, C. R., 1970, Conditioned nalorphine-induced abstinence changes: persistence in post-dependent monkeys, *J. Exp. Anal. Behav.* **14:**33–46.

Goldberg, S. R., Woods, J. H., and Schuster, C. R., 1969, Morphine: conditioned increases in self-administration in rhesus monkeys, *Science* **166:**1306–1307.

Goldberg, S. R., Hoffmeister, F., Schlichting, U. U., and Wuttke, W., 1971a, A comparison of pentobarbital and cocaine self-administration in rhesus monkeys: effects of dose and fixed-ratio parameter, *J. Pharmacol. Exp. Ther.* **179:**277–283.

Goldberg, S. R., Hoffmeister, F., Schlichting, U. U., and Wuttke, W., 1971b, Aversive properties of nalophine and naloxone in morphine-dependent rhesus monkeys, *J. Pharmacol. Exp. Ther.* **179:**268–276.

Goldberg, S. R., Woods, J. H., and Schuster, C. R., 1971c, Nalorphine-induced changes in morphine self-administration in rhesus monkeys, *J. Pharmacol. Exp. Ther.* **176:**464–471.

Goldberg, S. R., Hoffmeister, F., and Schlichting, U. U., 1972, Morphine antagonists: modification of behavioral effects by morphine dependence, *in: Drug Addiction*, Vol. 1, *Experimental Pharmacology* (J. M. Singh, L. Miller, and H. Lal, eds.), pp. 31–48, Futura, Mount Kisco, N.Y.

Goldberg, S. R., Kelleher, R. T., and Morse, W. H., 1975, Second-order schedules of drug injection, *Fed. Proc.* **34:**1771–1776.

Goodman, L. S., and Gilman, A., 1975, *The Pharmacological Basis of Therapeutics,* Macmillan, New York.

Griffiths, R. R., Bigelow, G., and Liebson, I., 1974a, Assessment of effects of ethanol self-administration on social interactions in alcoholics, *Psychopharmacologia* **38:**105–110.

Griffiths, R. R., Bigelow, G., and Liebson, I., 1974b, Suppression of ethanol self-administration by alcoholics by contingent time-out from social interactions, *Behav. Res. Ther.* **12:**327–334.

Griffiths, R. R., Findley, J. D., Brady, J. V., Dolan-Gutcher, K., and Robinson, W. W., 1975a, Comparison of progressive-ratio performance maintained by cocaine, methylphenidate, and secobarbital, *Psychopharmacologia* **43:**81–83.

Griffiths, R. R., Wurster, R. M., and Brady, J. V., 1975b, Discrete-trial choice procedure: effects of naloxone and methadone on choice between food and heroin, *Pharmacol. Rev.* **27:**357–365.

Griffiths, R. R., Bigelow, G., and Liebson, I., 1975c, Effect of ethanol self-administration on choice behavior: money vs. socializing, *Pharmacol. Biochem. Behav.* **3:**443–446.

Griffiths, R. R., Bigelow, G., and Liebson, I., 1976a, Human sedative self-administration: effects of interingestion interval and dose, *J. Pharmacol. Exp. Ther.* **197:**488–494.

Griffiths, R. R., Bigelow, G., and Liebson, I., 1976b, Facilitation of human tobacco self-administration by ethanol: a behavioral analysis, *J. Exp. Anal. Behav.* **25:**279–292.

Griffiths, R. R., Snell, J. D., and Brady, J. V., 1976c, Progressive-ratio performance in baboons and the assessment of the abuse liability of drugs: comparison of fenfluramine, chlorphentermine, diethylpropion, and cocaine; paper presented at the 38th Annual Meeting of the Committee on Problems of Drug Dependence, NAS-NRC.

Grove, R. N., and Schuster, C. R., 1974, Suppression of cocaine self-administration by extinction and punishment, *Pharmacol. Biochem. Behav.* **2:**199–208.

Harris, R. T., Waters, W., and McLendon, D., 1974, Evaluation of reinforcing capability of delta-9-tetrahydrocannabinol in rhesus monkeys, *Psychopharmacologia* **37:**23–29.

Hill, H. E., Haertzen, C. A., and Glaser, R., 1960, Personality characteristics of narcotic addicts as indicated by the MMPI, *J. Gen. Psychol.* **62:**127–139.

Hodos, W., 1961, Progressive ratio as a measure of reward strength, *Science* **134:**943.

Hodos, W., and Kalman, J., 1963, Effects of increment size and reinforcer volume on progressive-ratio performance, *J. Exp. Anal. Behav.* **6:**387.

Hoffmeister, F., and Goldberg, S. R., 1973, A comparison of chlorpromazine, imipramine, morphine, and *d*-amphetamine self-administration in cocaine-dependent rhesus monkeys, *J. Pharmacol. Exp. Ther.* **187:**8–14.

Hoffmeister, F., and Schlichting, U. U., 1972, Reinforcing properties of some opiates and opioids in rhesus monkeys with histories of cocaine and codeine self-administration, *Psychopharmacologia* **23:**55–74.

Hoffmeister, F., and Wuttke, W., 1973, Negative reinforcing properties of morphine-antagonists in naive rhesus monkeys, *Psychopharmacologia* **33:**247–258.

Holz, W. C., and Gill, C., 1975, Drug injections as negative reinforcers, *Pharmacol. Rev.* **27:**437–446.

Iglauer, C., and Woods, J. H., 1974, Concurrent performances: reinforcement by different doses of intravenous cocaine in rhesus monkeys, *J. Exp. Anal. Behav.* **22:**179–196.

Iglauer, C., Llewellyn, M. E., and Woods, J. H., 1975, Concurrent schedules of cocaine injection in rhesus monkeys: dose variations under independent and nonindependent variable-interval procedures, *Pharmacol. Rev.* **27:**367–383.

Irwin, S., and Seevers, M. H., 1956, Altered response to drug in the post-addict *Macaca mulatta*, *J. Pharmacol. Exp. Ther.* **116:**31–32.

Jasinski, D. R., Nutt, J. G., and Griffith, J. D., 1974, Effects of diethylpropion and *d*-amphetamine after subcutaneous and oral administration, *Clin. Pharmacol. Ther.* **16:**645–652.

Johanson, C. E., 1975, Pharmacological and environmental variables affecting drug preference in rhesus monkeys, *Pharmacol. Rev.* **27:**343–355.

Johanson, C. E., 1976, Unpublished observations.

Johanson, C. E., 1977, The effects of electric shock on responding maintained by cocaine injections in a choice procedure in the rhesus monkey, *Psychopharmacology* **53:**277.

Johanson, C. E., and Schuster, C. R., 1975, A choice procedure for drug reinforcers: cocaine and methylphenidate in the rhesus monkey, *J. Pharmacol. Exp. Ther.* **193:**676–688.

Johanson, C. E., and Schuster, C. R., 1977a, A comparison of cocaine and diethylpropion under two different schedules of drug presentation, *in: Cocaine and Other Stimulants* (E. H. Ellinwood and M. M. Kilbey, eds.), pp. 545–570, Plenum Press, New York.

Johanson, C. E., and Schuster, C. R., 1977b (in press), Procedures for the preclinical assessment of the abuse potential of psychotropic drugs in animals, *in: Predicting Dependence Liability of Stimulant and Depressant Drugs* (T. Thompson and K. Unna, eds.), University Park Press, Baltimore.

Johanson, C. E., Balster, R. L., and Bonese, K., 1976a, Self-administration of psychomotor stimulant drugs: the effects of unlimited access, *Pharmacol. Biochem. Behav.* **4:**45–51.

Johanson, C. E., Kandel, D. A., and Bonese, K., 1976b, The effects of perphenazine on self-administration behavior, *Pharmacol. Biochem. Behav.* **4:**427–433.

Jones, B. E., and Prada, J. A., 1973, Relapse to morphine use in dog, *Psychopharmacologia* **30:**1–12.

Jonsson, C. O., 1969, Behavioral studies of diethylpropion in man, *in: Abuse of Central Stimulants* (F. Sjoquist and M. Tottie, eds.), pp. 71–80, Raven Press, New York.

Kandel, D. A., and Schuster, C. R., 1977, An investigation of nalorphine and perphenazine as negative reinforcers in an escape paradigm, *Pharmacol. Biochem. Behav.* **6:**61–71.

Keesey, R. E., and Goldstein, M. D., 1968, Use of progressive fixed-ratio procedures in the assessment of intracranial reinforcement, *J. Exp. Anal. Behav.* **11:**293.

Kelleher, R. T., 1966, Conditioned reinforcement in second-order schedules, *J. Exp. Anal. Behav.* **9:**475–485.

Kelleher, R. T., 1975, Characteristics of behavior controlled by scheduled injections of drugs, *Pharmacol. Rev.* **27:**307–323.

Kelleher, R. T., and Goldberg, S. R., 1975, Control of drug-taking behavior by schedules of reinforcement, *Pharmacol. Rev.* **27:**291–299.

Kelleher, R. T., and Morse, W. H., 1968, Determinants of the specificity of behavioral effects of drugs, *Ergeb. Physiol. Biol. Chem. Exp. Pharmakol.* **60:**1–56.

Killian, A. T., Bonese, K., and Schuster, C. R., 1977, The effects of naloxone on behavior maintained by cocaine and heroin injections in the rhesus monkey; manuscript submitted to *Pharmacol. Biochem. Behav.*

Kleitman, M., and Crisler, G., 1927, A quantitative study of a salivary conditioned reflex, *Amer. J. Physiol.* **79:**571–614.

Kramer, J. C., Fischman, V. S., and Littlefield, D. C., 1967, Amphetamine abuse, *J. Amer. Med. Ass.* **201:**305–309.

Lindesmith, A. R., 1937, The nature of opiate addiction. Unpublished doctoral dissertation. The University of Chicago.

Lucchesi, B. R., Schuster, C. R., and Emley, G. S., 1967, The role of nicotine as a determinant of cigarette smoking frequency in man with observations of certain cardiovascular effects associated with the tobacco alkaloid, *Clin. Pharmacol. Ther.* **8:**789–796.

Marcus, A. M., Kolonoff, H., and Low, M., 1974, Psychiatric status of the marihuana user, *Can. Psychiat. Ass. J.* **19:**31–39.

McKearney, J. W., 1968, Maintenance of responding under a fixed-interval schedule of electric shock presentation, *Science* **160:**1249–1251.

McKearney, J. W., 1969, Fixed-interval schedules of electric shock presentation: extinction and recovery of performance under different shock intensities and fixed-interval durations, *J. Exp. Anal. Behav.* **12:**301–313.

McKearney, J. W., 1975, Drug effects and the environmental control of behavior, *Pharmacol. Rev.* **27:**429–436.

Mendelson, J. H., and Mello, N. K., 1966, Experimental analysis of drinking behavior of chronic alcoholics, *Ann. N.Y. Acad. Sci.* **133:**828–845.

Mendelson, J. H., Kuehnle, J. C., Greenberg, I., and Mello, N. K., 1976, Operant acquisition of marihuana in man, *J. Pharmacol. Exp. Ther.* **198:**42–53.

Meyer, R. E., Mirin, S. M., Altman, J. L., and McNamee, H. B., 1976, A behavioral paradigm for the evaluation of narcotic antagonists, *Arch. Gen. Psychiat.* **33:**371–377.

Moreton, J. E., Roehrs, R., and Khazan, N., 1976, Drug self-administration and sleep-awake activity in rats dependent on morphine, methadone, or 1-alpha-acetylmethadol, *Psychopharmacology* **47:**237–241.

Morse, W. H., 1975, Introduction: the control of behavior by consequent drug injections, *Pharmacol. Rev.* **27:**301–305.

Morse, W. H., and Kelleher, R. T., 1966, Schedules using noxious stimuli. I. Multiple fixed-ratio and fixed-interval termination of schedule complexes, *J. Exp. Anal. Behav.* **9:**267–290.

Mowrer, H. R., and Mowrer, E. R., 1945, Ecological and familial factors associated with inebriety, *Quart. J. Stud. Alc.* **6:**36–44.

National Commission on Marijuana and Drug Abuse, 1972, *Biological Effects of Marijuana,* Vol. 1, Chap. II, Appendix, pp. 15–67, Government Printing Office, Washington, D.C.

O'Brien, C. P., 1975, Experimental analysis of conditioning factors in human narcotic addiction, *Pharmacol. Rev.* **27:**533–543.

Pickens, R., 1968, Self-administration of stimulants by rats, *Int. J. Addict.* **3:**215–221.

Pickens, R., and Harris, W. C., 1968, Self-administration of *d*-amphetamine by rats, *Psychopharmacologia* **12:**158–163.

Pickens, R., and Thompson, T., 1968, Cocaine-reinforced behavior in rats, *J. Pharmacol. Exp. Ther.* **161:**122–129.

Pickens, R., Meisch, R. A., and McGuire, L., 1967, Methamphetamine reinforcement in rats, *Psychon. Sci.* **8:**371–372.

Pickens, R., Thompson, R., and Muchow, D. C., 1973, Cannabis and phencyclidine self-administration by animals, *in: Psychic Dependence* (L. Goldberg and F. Hoffmeister, eds.), pp. 78–86, Springer-Verlag, Berlin.

Roffman, M., Reddy, C., and Lal, H., 1973, Control of morphine-withdrawal hypothermia by conditional stimuli, *Psychopharmacologia* **29:**197–201.

Ryder, J. A., Schuster, C. R., and Seiden, L. S., 1977, The effects of alpha-methyltyrosine on methamphetamine intake and brain catecholamine levels; manuscript submitted to *J. Pharmacol. Exp. Ther.*

Schuster, C. R., 1970, Psychological approaches to opiate dependence and self-administration by laboratory animals, *Fed. Proc.* **29**(1):2–5.

Schuster, C. R., 1975, Drugs as reinforcers in monkeys and man, *Pharmacol. Rev.* **27:**511–521.

Schuster, C. R., and Johanson, C. E., 1973, Behavioral analysis of opiate dependence, *in: Opiate Addiction: Origins and Treatment* (S. Fisher and A. M. Freedman, eds.), pp. 77–92, V. W. Winston, Washington, D.C.

Schuster, C. R., and Johanson, C. E., 1974, The use of animal models for the study of drug abuse, *in: Research Advances in Alcohol and Drug Problems* (R. J. Gibbins, Y. Israel, H. Kalant, R. E. Popham, W. Schmidt, and R. G. Smart, eds.), Vol. 1, pp. 1–31, Wiley, New York.

Schuster, C. R., and Thompson, T., 1969, Self-administration of and behavioral dependence on drugs, *Ann. Rev. Pharmacol.* **9:**483–502.

Schuster, C. R., and Woods, J. H., 1968, The conditioned reinforcing effects of stimuli associated with morphine reinforcement, *Int. J. Addictions* **3:**223–230.

Schuster, C. R., Smith, B. B., and Jaffe, J. H., 1971, Drug abuse in heroin users: an experimental study of self-administration of methadone, codeine, and pentazocine, *Arch. Gen. Psychiat.* **24:**359–362.

Skinner, B. F., 1938, *The Behavior of Organisms,* Appleton-Century-Crofts, New York.

Tatum, A. L., and Seevers, M. H., 1929, Experimental cocaine addiction, *J. Pharmacol. Exp. Ther.* **36:**401–410.

Thompson, T., 1968, Drugs as reinforcers: experimental addiction, *Int. J. Addict.* **3:**199–206.

Thompson, T., and Schuster, C. R., 1964, Morphine self-administration, food-reinforced and avoidance behaviors in rhesus monkeys, *Psychopharmacologia* **5:**87–94.

Thompson, T., and Unna, K., eds., 1977, *Predicting Dependence Liability of Stimulant and Depressant Drugs,* University Park Press, Baltimore.

Villarreal, J. E., 1972, The effects of morphine agonists and antagonists on morphine-dependent rhesus monkeys, *in: Agonist and Antagonist Actions of Narcotic Analgesic Drugs* (H. W. Kosterlitz, H. O. J. Collier, and J. E. Villarreal, eds.), pp. 73–94, Macmillan, London.

Weeks, J. R., 1962, Experimental morphine addiction: method for autonomic intravenous injections in unrestrained rats, *Science* **138:**143–144.

Weeks, J. R., 1964, Experimental narcotic addiction, *Sci. Amer.* **210**(3):46–52.

Weeks, J. R., and Collins, R. J., 1964, Factors affecting voluntary morphine intake in self-maintained addicted rats, *Psychopharmacologia* **6:**267–279.

Wikler, A., 1955, Rationale of the diagnosis and treatment of addictions, *Conn. State Med. J.* **19:**560–568.

Wikler, A., 1974, Requirements for extinction of relapse facilitating variables and for rehabilitation in a narcotic antagonist treatment program, *in: Narcotic Antagonists: Advances in Biochemical Pharmacology.* (M. A. Braude, L. S. Harris, E. L. May, J. P. Smith, and J. E. Villarreal, eds.), pp. 399–414, Raven Press, New York.

Wikler, A., and Pescor, F. T., 1967, Classical conditioning of a morphine abstinence phenomenon, reinforcement of opioid drinking behavior and "relapse" in morphine-addicted rats, *Psychopharmacologia* **10:**255–284.

Wilson, M. C., 1970, Variables which influence the reinforcing properties of cocaine in the rhesus monkey; unpublished doctoral dissertation, University of Michigan.

Wilson, M. C., and Schuster, C. R., 1972, The effects of chlorpromazine on psychomotor stimulant self-administration in the rhesus monkey, *Psychopharmacologia* **26:**115–126.

Wilson, M. C., Hitomi, M., and Schuster, C. R., 1971, Psychomotor stimulant self-administration as a function of dosage per injection in the rhesus monkey, *Psychopharmacologia* **22:**271–281.

Winger, G., Stitzer, M. L., and Woods, J. H., 1975, Barbiturate-reinforced responding in rhesus monkeys: comparisons of compounds with different durations of action, *J. Pharmacol. Exp. Ther.* **195:**505–515.

Woods, J. H., and Schuster, C. R., 1968, Reinforcement properties of morphine, cocaine, and SPA as a function of unit dose, *Int. J. Addict.* **3:**231–237.

Woods, J. H., and Schuster, C. R., 1971, Opiates as reinforcing stimuli, *in: Stimulus Properties of Drugs* (T. Thompson and R. Pickens, eds.), pp. 163–175, Appleton-Century-Crofts, New York.

Woods, J. H., Downs, D. A., and Carney, J., 1975, Behavioral functions of narcotic antagonists: response-drug contingencies, *Fed. Proc.* **34:**1777–1784.

Yanagita, T., 1973, An experimental framework for evaluation of dependence liability of various types of drugs in monkeys, *Bull. Narcotics* **1:**25–57.

Yanagita, T., Deneau, G. A., and Seevers, M. H., 1965, Evaluation of pharmacologic agents in the monkey by long-term intravenous self- or programmed administration, *Excerpta Med. Int. Congr. Ser.* **87:**453–457.

Yanagita, T., Ando, K., Takahashi, S., and Ishida, K., 1969, Self-administration of barbiturates, alcohol (intragastric), and CNS stimulants (intravenous) monkeys; paper presented at the 31st Annual Meeting of the Committee on Problems of Drug Dependence, NAS-NRC.

Yanagita, T., Ando, K., and Takahashi, S., 1970, A testing method for psychological dependence liability of drugs in monkeys; paper presented at the 32nd Annual Meeting of the Committee on Problems of Drug Dependence, NAS-NRS.

Zwerling, I., and Rosenbaum, M., 1959, Alcohol addiction and personality (nonpsychotic conditions), *in: American Handbook of Psychiatry* (S. Arieti, ed.), Chap. 31, Basic Books, New York.

Behavioral Tolerance 8

P. K. Corfield-Sumner and I. P. Stolerman

1. Introduction

Advances in the analysis of operant behavior, and of the effects thereon of acute doses of drugs, have been accompanied by relatively few studies of behavioral changes associated with chronic drug treatment. The time now seems ripe for a survey of progress in the study of tolerance to the behavioral effects of drugs, and an evaluation of the main principles which have guided investigations. No attempt will be made to list all the published reports in the field, or to assess evidence for the various physiological mechanisms through which behavioral tolerance may be mediated. For illustrative purposes, emphasis will be placed on opiate drugs, Δ^9-tetrahydrocannabinol (Δ^9-THC) and central nervous system stimulants (amphetamine and nicotine).

One of the most common consequences of repeatedly administering a drug is the development of tolerance. Thus, the usual pharmacological use of the term "tolerance" restricts it to mean a reduction in any given effect of a drug when the same dose is administered repeatedly, and to the need to give an increased dose to obtain the original effect. Researchers usually regard initial sensitivity to a drug and acquired tolerance as distinct problems, but it may be noted that this assumption may tend to discourage some possibly useful lines of research. It seems possible, at least in principle, that factors such as environmental manipulations which affect initial sensitivity may do so by mimicking neurochemical or other physiological effects of chronic drug treatment (Glick and Milloy, 1972). Such manipulations might therefore provide clues useful for elucidating mechanisms of tolerance.

P. K. Corfield-Sumner • Department of Psychology, University of Birmingham, Birmingham B15 2TT, England, U.K. **I. P. Stolerman** • MRC Neuropharmacology Unit, The Medical School, Birmingham B15 2TJ, England, U.K.

The reasons for studying the consequences of chronic drug administrations, of which tolerance is a prime example, seem to be threefold. First, by far the greatest number of applications of drugs in psychiatric states involve prolonged treatment. Very often, major therapeutic actions of drugs are not apparent after the initial doses, but may take a few weeks to develop (e.g., with antidepressants such as imipramine), whereas it is thought that tolerance may develop fairly quickly to certain side effects (e.g., sedation with some antischizophrenic and antianxiety drugs). A second important consequence of repeated drug administration may be the development of drug dependence, and very often this seems to be closely associated with (although not to be equated with) tolerance. Understanding the conditions in which tolerance develops may therefore provide information pertaining, albeit indirectly, to the development of dependence. Finally, the ways in which an organism adapts to the perturbations brought about by the prolonged administration of a drug should aid understanding of homeostatic processes, the natural regulatory mechanisms which maintain the constancy of the internal environment. Behavioral change can be a very powerful means for achieving this constancy. In this context the most illuminating drugs for study may not be those of the greatest importance in psychiatry or as addictive agents, but substances with relatively specific actions on particular chemical systems in the brain; the chronic effects of such agents should lend themselves more readily to meaningful physiological interpretations.

It is important not to confuse tolerance with drug dependence, which is variously defined as a behavioral change (briefly, a tendency to repeatedly self-administer a drug for which there is no recognized medical indication) or in terms of the consequences of not taking the drug (withdrawal syndromes). In neither type of definition is the presence of tolerance taken as diagnostic, although it has at times been included as an "optional extra" in the definition. Nevertheless, dependence defined in either way is very frequently accompanied by tolerance, and this seems to apply to all the major, generally recognized groups of dependence-producing drugs. This correlation is particularly marked in some animal experiments on opiate tolerance (e.g., Way *et al.*, 1969), where a strong relationship has been found between the change in the analgesic dose of morphine (tolerance) and the amount of jumping behavior induced by the withdrawal of morphine (dependence). Kalant *et al.* (1971) have reviewed many of the relevant studies with ethanol and barbiturate drugs. The correlations may imply a close similarity between some of the mechanisms of tolerance and dependence, but the exact nature of the relationships among tolerance, withdrawal syndromes, and drug-seeking behavior has yet to be established.

The article by Kalant *et al.* (1971) also contains a wealth of information on many aspects of tolerance not included in this chapter.

Since the study of tolerance began long before the development of precise methods for the control of behavior, it is hardly surprising that effort has been concentrated to a great extent on tolerance to changes in physiological functions due to drug action. In many cases where behavioral indices have been used, these have been crude by current standards, although useful information may nevertheless have been obtained. Studies of the effects of chronic drug treatment on well-understood behavioral base lines become worthwhile only after acute effects on these base lines have been well delineated, and it can be argued that only in very recent years has this become the case. However, persistence in the use of traditional methods is hardly a virtue after limitations on their validity have time and again been made evident. As an illustration of this point, the way in which tolerance to opiate drugs is often examined will be considered in more detail.

The most common procedures for demonstrating tolerance to drugs such as morphine, heroin, and methadone involve assessments of their effects on unconditioned reactions to painful stimuli. Typically, the presumably painful stimulation is applied to a convenient portion of a rodent (almost all parts of the animal have been used at one time or another) and a gross response such as struggling or squealing is scored by an observer. In the widely used "hot-plate test," the animal is placed on a heated surface and the time before it lifts, licks, or blows on its paws is recorded (D'Amour and Smith, 1941; Woolfe and MacDonald, 1944). Eddy *et al.* (1950) interpreted licking of the foot as "showing what appears to be conscious recognition of the discomfort."

Clearly, a more operational approach is necessary to deal with the problem of inferring changes in sensation from observations of behavior, and this cannot be achieved simply by relabeling the effect of the drug as antinociception, since this term still implies some form of interaction of drug effect with the presumably painful nature of the maintaining stimulus. In an operational analysis, a necessary step in this case seems to involve determining whether the drug effect is specific to the aversive property of the stimulus eliciting the observed response. This would entail testing the action of morphine on paw lifting (or blowing, or licking), elicited by an aversive stimulus such as heat, and comparing this with paw lifting occurring at a similar rate but maintained by a positively reinforcing stimulus. This does not seem to have been done, nor is it being seriously advocated as an experimental approach. A relevant consideration seems to be the finding that, in general, the nature of a reinforcer maintaining behavior is not a critical determinant of drug action, whereas it has been frequently reported that the way reinforcement is programmed to occur in relation to behavior can have a very great influence (see Chapter 1). As, therefore, it has not been established that the results from hot-plate tests (or from similar procedures) provide a suitable base line for assessing the drug–reinforcer interaction, a main reason for their widespread use seems to be based on a dubious assumption. There is also an element of subjectivity in scoring the response of the animal. However, it must be recognized that the tests have been empirically useful, since they can be carried out very quickly, thus enabling dose–response curves to drugs to be compared in animals subjected to different experimental procedures, such as pretreatment with enzyme inhibitors or neurotoxins. There seems to be a case for "trading off" some of this rapidity of assessment in return for a base line which is meaningful within the context of recent progress in the analysis of behavior.

It should be apparent from the preceding discussion that the validity of behavioral procedures for assessing drug tolerance rests largely on their validity as indicators of acute drug actions. In studies of acute actions, it is accepted that the discriminative stimuli controlling the behavior should be identified, that the schedule of reinforcement be specified, that response sensing be objective and quantifiable, and that unjustified assumptions and inferences about motivational and emotional changes should be avoided. All of this is equally applicable to procedures for studying the effects of prolonged administration of drugs. Attention must also be given to changes within the organism which might have a bearing on the interpretation of the results (e.g., Section 2.2). Tolerance may be associated with changes in several physiological functions, and it is clear that the mechanisms may be different depending on the type of drug and the amounts and frequency with which it is administered. These pharmacological factors are considered in more detail in Section 3, where the possible role of response topography is also discussed.

It is now appropriate to consider the special advantages, for chronic drug studies, of using well-defined patterns of behavior as base lines. The techniques of operant conditioning have become an important tool in investigations of the effects of acute drug administrations on behavior. Moreover, these techniques have led to major advances in our understanding of the effects of acutely administered drugs by showing that the base-line behavior maintained by a particular schedule of reinforcement may itself be a determinant of the drug effect, as well as being the means by which the drug effect is assessed. The advantages afforded by operant techniques apply at least as strongly to studies of chronic drug administrations, where the ability to maintain a stable base line in individual subjects over long periods of time may be especially valuable.

One of the early studies of tolerance to the effects of drugs on operant behavior utilized a multiple fixed-ratio 30 fixed-interval 5-min schedule of food reinforcement in pigeons (McMillan and Morse, 1967). In the presence of a distinctive keylight, the thirtieth key-peck resulted in 3-sec access to grain, whereas in the presence of a different keylight the first peck after 5 min resulted in access to grain. After responding stabilized, drugs were injected 30 min before sessions. From Figure 1 it can be seen that the first time bird 48 received 3 mg/kg of morphine, fixed-interval responding was almost eliminated and fixed-ratio responding was greatly reduced. When morphine was being injected daily, 3 mg/kg had little effect on the fixed-ratio rate and the fixed-interval rate had shown considerable recovery. In bird 5639, the first 3-mg/kg dose of morphine decreased the fixed-interval rate early in the session, but after daily drug administrations, the rate was increased well above control levels, an effect that had been previously observed in this bird only at lower doses. Thus tolerance developed to effects of morphine on both fixed-ratio and fixed-interval responding. However, Figure 1 also shows that the temporal patterning of fixed-interval responding did not recover fully in tolerant birds.

Other experiments suggest that the development of tolerance may be schedule-dependent, although the evidence for this is not as clear as that for the acute effects of drugs. The major work to investigate whether schedule variables influence tolerance development has occurred only in the last decade, and much of it has been guided by the ideas put forward by Schuster *et al.* (1966), who suggested that loss of reinforcement might play a significant role in the development of tolerance. It seems that this idea has received less rigorous experimental evaluation than it deserves, and the evidence now available to support it is reviewed in detail in Section 4.

Finally, the very limited number of studies concerning tolerance to the stimulus properties of drugs will be examined (Section 5). It is known that many drugs can influence operant behavior by serving as discriminative, reinforcing, or aversive stimuli, and can also function as unconditioned stimuli in classical conditioning experiments. Since most of the evidence that drugs can have stimulus properties, as defined above, has appeared fairly recently, it is not surprising that there is minimal information available about the possibility of tolerance development. This is likely to be an area of greater research activity in the future and a brief consideration of relevant work concludes this chapter.

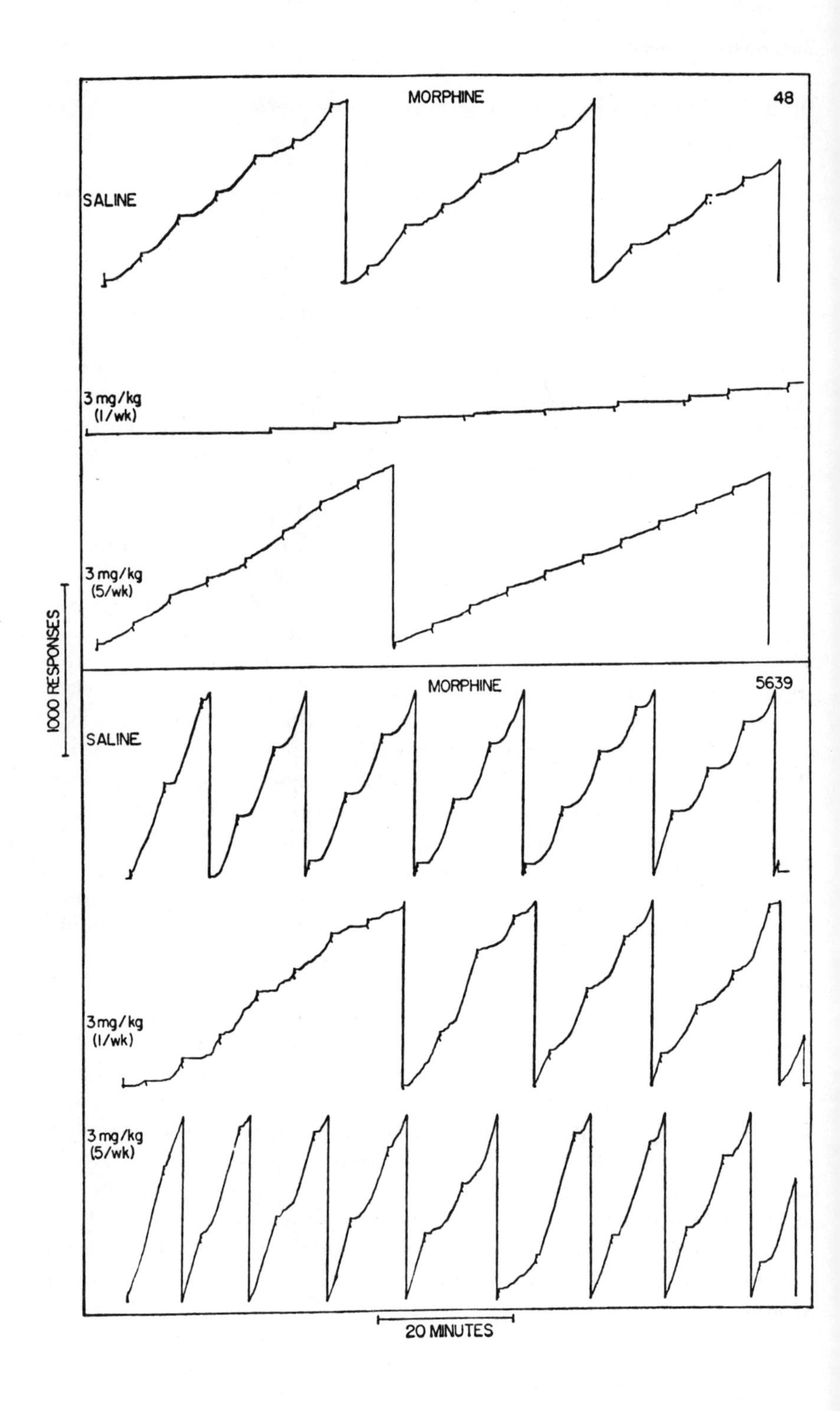
MORPHINE
48
SALINE
3 mg/kg
(1/wk)
3 mg/kg
(5/wk)
1000 RESPONSES
MORPHINE
5639
SALINE
3 mg/kg
(1/wk)
3 mg/kg
(5/wk)
20 MINUTES

2. Behavioral Tolerance in Perspective

2.1. Behavioral Tolerance

The traditional definitions of tolerance in terms of a reduced drug effect and a concomitant need to increase the dose upon chronic treatment have been given in Section 1. Over the last several years it has become increasingly popular to refer to metabolic tolerance, physiological tolerance, learned tolerance, and behavioral tolerance without making it clear whether these terms are thought to be reflections of basically different processes or merely a convenient shorthand way of providing some information about the experimental procedures used. It is argued here that far too many qualifying terms have been used to indicate different types or mechanisms of tolerance, when in reality all that has been shown, with certain exceptions, is that several different methods can be used to induce or assess tolerance.

Since this chapter is about behavioral tolerance, the status of this term is considered first, in comparison with "physiological tolerance." To the present writers, behavioral tolerance means simply that tolerance to a behavioral effect of a drug has been demonstrated. It does not carry any implication to the effect that the organismic changes mediating the tolerance are either similar to or different from those mediating tolerance assessed by changes in physiological systems: behavioral tolerance may be accompanied by changes in neurotransmitter availability; in the sensitivity of drug receptors; in the absorption, distribution, and metabolism of drugs; or in any other relevant mechanism. Further, because an environmental or behavioral factor may influence the development of tolerance, it does not follow that the tolerance is not mediated through physiological mechanisms. Some of the physiological systems which may be affected by drugs (e.g., functions of the autonomic nervous system) are now known to be susceptible to environmental manipulations, including classical and operant conditioning procedures. It seems therefore that there is no hard-and-fast line dividing behavioral from physiological tolerance, although the terms are undoubtedly useful as a shorthand way of conveying some, albeit limited, information about the experimental procedures.

Figure 1. Development of tolerance to the effects of 3 mg/kg of morphine on schedule-controlled performance in pigeons. Cumulative response records under multiple FR 30 FI 5 min, pigeons 48 and 5639. The records show the effect of saline, the initial effect of 3 mg/kg of morphine (1/week series) and of 3 mg/kg of morphine during the daily morphine series (5/week). [From McMillan and Morse (1967); © 1967 by The Williams & Wilkins Company, Baltimore.]

2.2. Metabolic Tolerance

Pharmacological studies of the mechanisms of tolerance have revealed that changes in the metabolism of a drug can occur when it is given repeatedly. Most often, these take the form of an increased effectiveness ("induction") of enzymes in the liver which are responsible for chemically inactivating the drug. The consequences are that either a greater amount of a drug dose may be inactivated before it ever reaches the brain, or the time is reduced over which an effective concentration of drug may be maintained in the brain. Tolerance may therefore be mediated through changes in the absorption, distribution, or metabolism of a drug within the organism; when these mechanisms are thought to be significant, the state is often called "metabolic" or "drug-disposition" tolerance, although it may be manifested behaviorally in a similar way to tolerance associated with a change in the sensitivity of target systems in the brain. Metabolic tolerance has a number of important implications for behavioral studies, and these are considered in turn.

First, it is agreed that the demonstration of behavioral tolerance is not sufficient to establish that an adaptive process has been brought into operation in the central nervous system. Such adaptation only becomes reasonably likely when it can be shown that the amounts of the drug or its active metabolites (if important) are similar in the brains of tolerant and nontolerant organisms. There are also implications with regard to the profile of activity of the drug; more efficient metabolism is likely to produce rather uniform tolerance to several different actions of the drug, whereas differential tolerance to various effects is more easily linked to changes in the sensitivity of different systems in the CNS. Levorphanol is an opiate drug with actions resembling those of morphine. Figure 2 shows that tolerance to the locomotor excitant action of levorphanol in mice cannot be fully accounted for by the small difference in the amounts of the drug estimated to be present in the brains of tolerant and nontolerant mice (Goldstein *et al.*, 1973). At a given administered dose of levorphanol (e.g., 20 mg/kg), the brain level declined progressively from about 1μg/g to about 0.3 μg/g after doses every 4 hr for 1 week. However, by varying the dose injected, it was shown that even at a given brain level (e.g., 1 μg/g), the amount of locomotor activity was very much less for tolerant than for nontolerant mice. Rather similar, small changes in the brain levels of methadone and morphine in tolerant rats have been found by Misra *et al.* (1973) and by Bullock *et al.* (1975). It is not surprising that tolerance to opiate drugs cannot be accounted for entirely in terms of metabolism, since it

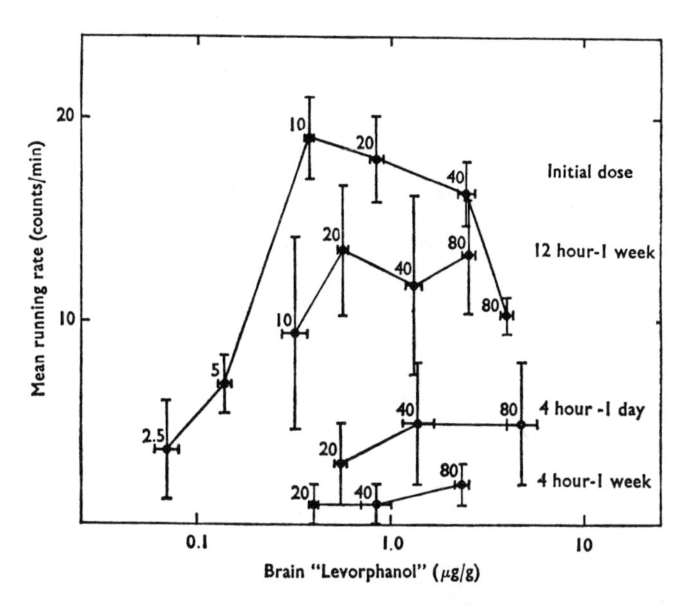

Figure 2. Relationship between brain radioactivity (apparent levorphanol) and running rate estimated in a photocell activity cage. The uppermost record represents nontolerant mice, the lower three curves are for mice maintained on 20 mg/kg doses of levorphanol at the intervals and for the durations shown. The vertical and horizontal bars show one standard error on each side of the means, and the number next to each point is the dose (mg/kg) of radio-labeled levorphanol given 30 min previously. [From Goldstein *et al.* (1973).]

is known that the different effects of these drugs can show very different degrees of tolerance (e.g., Seevers and Deneau, 1963).

Many barbiturate drugs can induce the enzymes responsible for their own inactivation, and this seems to account for a substantial degree (but not all) of the tolerance associated with large doses of these drugs (e.g., Remmer, 1969). On the other hand, tolerance to amphetamine does not seem associated with enzyme induction (Mitchard *et al.*, 1970; Sever *et al.*, 1973). Detailed accounts of the role of metabolic factors in tolerance to drugs have been given elsewhere (e.g., Kalant *et al.*, 1971).

The final implication of metabolic tolerance relates to its transfer to different drugs (i.e., cross-tolerance). Since liver enzymes are often concerned with the metabolism of more than one class of drug, there is a general tendency for a greater degree of cross-tolerance than is the case when a change in CNS sensitivity is primarily involved. It is even possible for drugs to induce enzymes which produce a much greater degree of tolerance to substances other than the inducing agent itself. Some environmental pollutants may have such effects and the implications are as yet hardly explored. For example, cigarette smoke has the capacity to induce liver enzymes (Beckett and Triggs, 1967), and Gritz and Jarvik (1977) have cited several studies reporting that cigarette smokers show a corresponding insensitivity to certain drugs. Other intriguing, recent findings suggest that liver enzyme activity can come under discriminative control by environmental stimuli, although the conditioning processes involved deserve further analysis (Roffman and Lal, 1974).

2.3. Learned Tolerance

Much has been written about the role of learning in the development of tolerance. References to "learned tolerance" have become more frequent, and it seems necessary to consider what this may mean and whether there is sufficient evidence to justify the application of the term.

Claims have been made that two distinct forms or mechanisms of tolerance exist, learned tolerance and physiological tolerance. Chen (1968) developed a procedure which was claimed to make such a distinction possible. Rats were trained to run in a circular runway for food reinforcement, and were then given injections of ethanol either shortly *before* or soon *after* the sessions in the runway. A test injection of ethanol was then given to all the rats shortly before a final runway session. The results showed that ethanol given before a session produced a marked decrement in the accuracy of a discriminative response when the rats had not previously received any ethanol. Clear tolerance to the decrement developed in the rats given ethanol *before* training, but tolerance was not seen in the rats which had previously received the ethanol *after* training. Chen concluded that "in order to explain this type of tolerance effect, physio-biochemical mechanisms are not sufficient." A dichotomy of physiological and behavioral mechanisms of tolerance was clearly implied but, it has been argued, not established (Kalant *et al.*, 1971; Kumar and Stolerman, 1977).

The procedure used by Chen, which for clarity we shall call the "before-and-after" technique, has been applied to a number of different drugs and behavioral responses. Carlton and Wolgin (1971) found tolerance to the anorexigenic action of *d*-amphetamine when the drug was administered prior to feeding tests, but not when the same number of injections were given after testing. Similar results were obtained with a differential reinforcement of low rate (DRL) schedule (Campbell and Seiden, 1973). Differential tolerance development to hexobarbital, chlorpromazine, and scopalamine has been found with variants of the before-and-after technique (Wahlström, 1968; Carro-Ciampi and Bignami, 1968).

More recently, Carder and Olson (1973) examined the effects of marijuana extracts on bar-pressing for food or water reinforcers in rats. The results of a before-and-after comparison were interpreted as evidence of a learning process in tolerance to marijuana, and Carder and Olson raised the possibility that this was a form of state-dependent learning. It was suggested that animals given marijuana before testing would have the opportunity to relearn the response under the changed stimulus conditions, and would thus show tolerance. A difficulty with this experiment is the lack of any clear evidence that tolerance developed at all, since the rate of responding of the "before" group remained essentially constant over the period of drug administration.

There are further grounds for questioning the experiments cited as evidence for a learning process in tolerance development, especially when the before-and-after technique is used. The original finding of Chen has been confirmed, but more extensive data shed doubt on his interpretation (LeBlanc *et al.*, 1973). It was found that the difference between before-and-after training administrations of ethanol was solely one of the rate at which tolerance developed; just as much tolerance developed with after-training ethanol if the experiment was carried on a little longer (Figure 3). Daily intubations of ethanol did not increase tolerance further in either case, suggesting that "behavioral" and "physiological" tolerance were not separate functions which could be combined to produce greater overall tolerance. Finally, and perhaps most important, rats made tolerant to ethanol in a treadmill test were also tolerant to its effect on a maze-running test, even though no transfer of learning was demonstrable between the tasks (LeBlanc *et al.*, 1975). Studies with Δ^9-THC also supported the view that behavioral variables influence principally the rate at which tolerance develops (Glick and Milloy, 1972).

A series of experiments on tolerance to the analgesic effect of morphine failed to reveal a role for learning in that instance, although certain procedural and apparatus factors did affect tolerance (Kayan *et al.*, 1973); these influences seem to contribute only to a small extent to the huge degree of tolerance which can develop to morphine. Some very ingenious experiments described by Siegel (1975) can be interpreted as evidence that morphine tolerance may be enhanced by learned compensatory, hyperalgesic responses elicited by the drug administration procedure. However, the postulated conditioned stimuli in these experiments were merely the cues present in the room to which the animals were moved when drugged. Evidence of stimulus control by

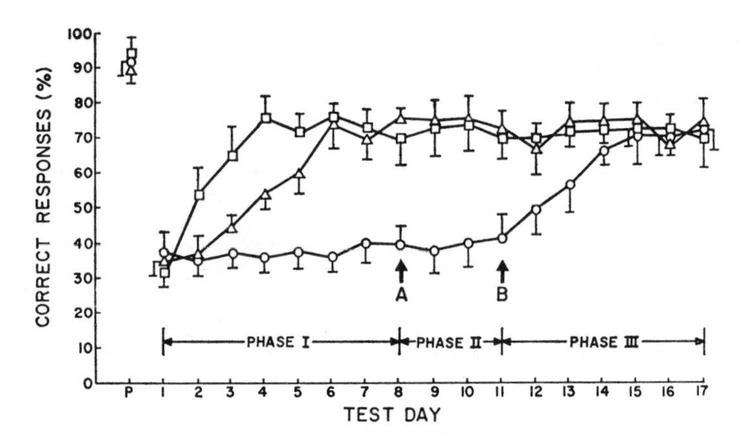

Figure 3. Comparisons of rates and levels of development of tolerance to ethanol in a circular maze test. The points at P indicate performance prior to any administrations of ethanol. The consecutively numbered test days were separated by three intervening treatment days. The circles indicate the control group which received alcohol on test days only, until phase III. The squares and triangles represent the "before" and "after" groups, respectively, which received ethanol on treatment *and* test days. Arrow A indicates the start of ethanol intubation in the before and after groups, and arrow B indicates the start of ethanol intubation in the control group. Vertical bars indicate the positive or negative half of the standard deviation at each point. [From LeBlanc *et al.* (1973).]

specific, identified environmental events would help to validate the hypothesis. The possibility also exists that the only influence of the environmental manipulations was on the rate at which tolerance developed, rather than on its nature.

In conclusion, it is questionable whether the before-and-after technique is able to provide evidence for different mechanisms of learned and physiological tolerance. It would seem that many factors must be excluded for such interpretations to be valid. First, it is necessary to consider whether the absorption, distribution, or metabolism of a drug is changed when it is administered before or after training. The metabolic state of an animal could vary depending on whether it was food- or water-deprived, as is often the case before training, or satiated and metabolizing nutrients after training. Negative reinforcement would not necessarily solve this problem, since changes associated with stress may occur. In addition, posttrial administrations of drugs are liable to induce behavioral changes due to factors such as retrograde amnesia or facilitation of performance, and possible reinforcing or aversive properties of the drugs. Finally, it must be emphasized that specific learned responses or coping behaviors under drugs have not yet been identified. At the present time, learning in relation to tolerance remains as a hypothetical intervening variable, inferred but not defined independently from the behavioral changes for which it purports to account. In this instance "learning" may be merely a synonym for unidentified neurophysiological or biochemical changes. In summary, it is proposed that two major criteria should be fulfilled if "learning" is to be established as a factor contributing to tolerance: (1) identification of a specific learned response or responses, and (2) exclusion of factors such as different metabolism of drugs as a function of test performance.

In view of all these practical complications and difficulties, it seems doubtful that it will be possible to establish a valid distinction between learned and physiological tolerance. Presumably, animals drugged in their home cages could acquire coping responses which might transfer to the test situation, thus rendering almost impossible a conclusive demonstration of exclusively "physiological" tolerance. Similarly, an organism with "learned" tolerance is almost bound to show physiological changes correlated with its test performance, thus rendering almost impossible a conclusive demonstration of exclusively "learned" tolerance. It does not seem necessary to postulate a different mechanism simply because a particular procedure increases the degree of tolerance or the rate at which it develops; the term "behavioral augmentation of tolerance" was proposed by Kalant *et al.* (1971), and it seems to be a more accurate description of the observed consequences of the experimental procedures.

2.4. Acute Tolerance

The amount of a drug administered can be an important factor determining the degree of tolerance (Section 3), and a related matter concerns the number of doses required to induce tolerance. In many instances, it has been assumed that repeated dosing is necessary, but sometimes a degree of tolerance has been reported to develop following only a single administration of a drug. Such "acute" tolerance is likely to be less marked than "chronic" tolerance and, accordingly, it is more difficult to demonstrate. Conditions need to be defined more precisely, and inadequate exploration over a wide range of values of dose and time factors can easily lead to falsely negative conclusions. This is illustrated by experiments on tolerance to morphine.

Kornetsky and Bain (1968) trained rats in a shock-attenuation procedure to assess the analgesic activity of morphine. In this test, the rats were trained to escape from a gradually increasing shock by rotating a paddle wheel through one quarter of a revolution. Paddle responses terminated shock for 15 sec, after which time shock came on again but at a lower intensity. If the animal failed to respond, the shock intensity was increased every 15 sec. Acute administration of morphine increased the amount of shock taken by the rats. However, the effect of the morphine was dependent on the previous drug history of the rats. At the very beginning of the experiment, half of the rats were injected with morphine once and were then returned to their home cages, whereas the remaining rats received a control injection of isotonic saline. When compared with the control animals, the morphine-pretreated animals showed tolerance to the drugs when they were tested with morphine in the shock-attenuation procedure; the longer the time between the initial dose and the test dose, the greater was the degree of tolerance. Little tolerance was apparent when the time interval was 24 hr, whereas tolerance was clearly apparent at 1–4 months. Other experiments have also shown that tolerance can develop after a single dose of morphine and that this can be quite a long-lasting phenomenon (e.g., Cochin and Kornetsky, 1964; Kayan and Mitchell, 1972; Huidobro and Huidobro, 1973). Acute tolerance to a number of drugs has been reported, and much of this evidence has been reviewed by Kalant *et al.* (1971). The time course and duration of single-dose effects varies greatly from drug to drug, and this may be illustrated by the following experiment on tolerance to nicotine. The short time course of acute behavioral tolerance to this drug may be contrasted with that for morphine.

In a series of experiments on acute and chronic tolerance to nicotine, the depressant effect of this drug on the spontaneous locomotor activity of rats was assessed in a Y-shaped runway (Stolerman *et al.*, 1973). In rats which had no previous history of exposure to the drug or the apparatus, nicotine reduced the numbers of entries into the arms of the runway and of rears onto the hind feet. However, after a single administration of nicotine, acute tolerance to the actions of a second dose developed with a definite time course, becoming maximal after 2 hr and largely wearing off after about 8 hr (Figure 4). The whole-brain levels of nicotine were estimated immediately after activity trials and were found to be 1.09 ± 0.09 μg/g (mean ± S.E., $n = 10$) for nontolerant rats and 1.18 ± 0.13 μg/g ($n = 9$) for acutely tolerant rats (Fischer *et al.*, 1973). In contrast with the short-lasting acute tolerance, chronic tolerance induced by repeated doses of nicotine (given three times daily for 8 days) was found to persist for at least 90 days after the end of regular treatment with the drug. The mean brain level of nicotine in chronically tolerant rats was 0.83 ± 0.08 μg/g ($n = 9$) as compared with 0.67 ± 0.10 μg/g ($n = 9$) in nontolerant controls. It appears, therefore, to be difficult to account for either acute or chronic tolerance to the depressant action of nicotine in terms of changes in the absorption or

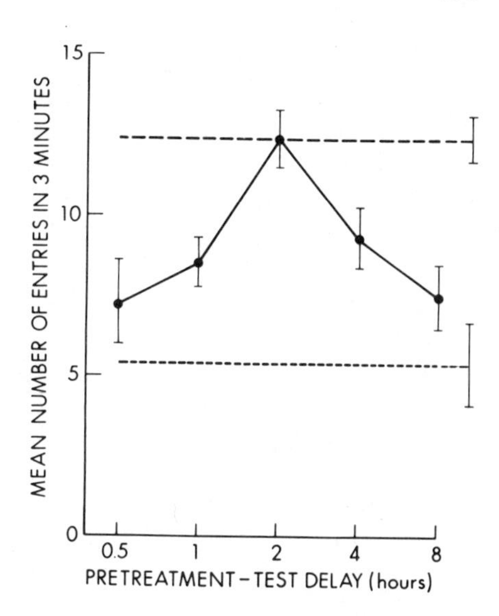

Figure 4. Time course of acute tolerance after a single injection of nicotine. Seven different groups of rats were used and each rat was tested once only ($n = 10$). Pretreatment with 1 mg/kg of nicotine 2 hr before test prevented the decrease in activity otherwise brought about by nicotine (1 mg/kg) injected 5 min before activity tests. The doses are those of nicotine tartrate, and the vertical bars indicate one standard error on each side of the mean. ---, saline only; -----, saline pretreatment, nicotine challenge; ●—●, nicotine pretreatment and challenge. [From Stolerman *et al.* (1973).]

metabolism of the drug. Tolerance to behavioral depression after the administration of nicotine has been reported in other experiments (e.g., Morrison and Stephenson, 1972; Keenan and Johnson, 1972; Domino and Lutz, 1973).

Thus, acute tolerance may be defined as that tolerance evident after a single dose of a drug, whereas chronic tolerance is regarded as that tolerance induced by repeated doses. No implication about possible similarities or differences between the mechanisms of acute and chronic tolerance need be implied by the use of these descriptive terms, but it may be noted that some characteristics of acute and chronic tolerance may differ, as was the case for nicotine. There is also evidence that acute tolerance can limit the effects of even the very first dose of a drug (Kalant *et al.*, 1971). The possibility that acute tolerance to a drug may occur, and especially that this may be a persistent effect, has important implications for the design of experiments on behavioral tolerance. There is a definite possibility that dose–response functions determined by several administrations of a drug to the same organism may be affected, and estimates of tolerance development may then be in error when the dose–response curve is redetermined after a period of chronic treatment. This problem may be particularly apparent with the benzodiazepine drugs, whose clinical antianxiety action seems to be correlated with an ability to disinhibit animal behavior which has been suppressed by punishment. The antipunishment effect is not very prominent when a benzodiazepine is given to a drug-naive rat, and it has been hypothesized that it may be masked by a general response rate-decreasing action. After several doses, it appears that tolerance develops to the rate-decreasing action, as assessed by recovery of the unpunished base line, and a very marked blockade of punishment suppression is then seen (Margules and Stein, 1968; Cook and Sepinwall, 1975; see Chapter 2). The rapidity with which these changes occur makes it almost impossible to determine a complete dose–response curve on a single rat without inducing some degree of tolerance. However, it must be emphasized that this case is an exception, if not an isolated one.

2.5. Cross Tolerance

In the experiments cited in the preceding paragraphs, the drugs used to induce and to test for tolerance were the same in any individual experiment. In practice, a question which arises very frequently is whether a history of exposure to one drug is likely to induce "cross tolerance" to another drug. As a general rule, it is thought that cross tolerance occurs to drugs in the same pharmacological class as the agent inducing the tolerance, but not to drugs in different classes. However, this assumption tends to inhibit experimenters from carrying out the necessary empirical tests. Certain exceptions to the rule have been known for some time (Section 2.2) and others have become apparent recently. A basic premise is that psychoactive drugs can be classified reliably, but this is not always easy. It is even conceivable that it would be empirically useful to employ the presence of cross tolerance as one rule for classification, rather than to use preconceived notions about classification as a rule for predicting cross tolerance.

A notable recent example of a failure to find cross tolerance where it might reasonably have been expected can be seen in the work of Tilson and Sparber (1973). Suitable doses of either *d*- or *l*-amphetamine increased response rates of rats on a fixed-interval schedule but decreased responding on a fixed-ratio schedule. Tolerance developed to both the rate-increasing and the rate-decreasing effects of both isomers, but there was virtually no evidence of cross-tolerance in either direction.

The conditioning of "flavor aversions" with psychoactive drugs has yielded surprising evidence for cross-tolerance between agents of different classes. Typically, a drug is administered to a rat shortly after the consumption of a distinctively flavored, but harmless, substance (Revusky and Garcia, 1970). Subsequently it is found that the rat will not consume the flavored material, but ingestion of other substances is normal. These findings are usually interpreted as evidence that the drug served as an aversive stimulus, with the flavor presumably acting as a discriminative stimulus signaling occasions when consummatory behavior would be punished by drug-induced "illness." As one might expect, chronic treatment with a number of drugs can considerably reduce their subsequent efficacy as conditioning agents in flavor-aversion experiments. This form of tolerance is considered further in Section 5; for the present purpose, attention is focused upon studies in which one drug was used for pretreatment and a different drug for conditioning.

In one such experiment, rats were allowed access to fluid for only 15 min each day, and on every third day a solution of saccharin was presented instead of the usual drinking water (Cappell *et al.,* 1975). Shortly after each presentation of saccharin, either amphetamine (1.0 mg/kg) or morphine (6.0 mg/kg) was injected (in different rats). In rats not previously exposed to drugs, the intakes of saccharin declined progressively over successive presentations, thus showing the conditioning of flavor aversions in the usual way. Other rats were pretreated for about 2 weeks with large doses of amphetamine (up to 20 mg/kg) or morphine (up to 40 mg/kg), and subsequently were tested for the development of aversions. Pretreatment with morphine prevented the development of flavor aversion to morphine, but not to amphetamine, which was in accordance with the usual ideas about drug classification and cross tolerance. However, pretreatment with amphetamine reduced flavor aversion not only to amphetamine, but also to morphine. Chlordiazepoxide, on the other hand, did not induce cross tolerance to either amphetamine or morphine. A further complication arises since Goudie and Thornton (1975) confirmed the tolerance to amphetamine, but were unable to show that there was cross tolerance to fenfluramine, a drug which is thought to be more closely related to amphetamine than is morphine. Furthermore, repeated doses of fenfluramine induced tolerance, and rats tolerant to fenfluramine were cross-tolerant to amphetamine. In other experiments, tolerance developed to the suppressant effects of amphetamine and fenfluramine on milk consumption, but there was no cross tolerance (Kandel *et al.,* 1975).

At present, speculations about the possible significance of these various demonstrations of cross tolerance must necessarily be limited by the paucity of data, as Goudie *et al.* (1976) have indicated. Misleading conclusions about the generality of the effects reported could easily be reached; there is little information available about the effects of varying size and frequency of the doses used to induce tolerance, or about the degree of tolerance as assessed by shifts of dose–response curves (Section 3.1). It has also been suggested frequently that pretreatment effects in flavor aversion experiments can be accounted for by learning processes rather than by tolerance, but how far these explanations are mutually incompatible remains debatable. Further investigations of cross tolerance seem desirable to determine how far the effects found are specific to the flavor-aversion studies, or whether they can be generalized to other effects of the drugs.

2.6. Sensitization (Reverse Tolerance)

As a rule, increases in the intensity of reactions to drugs (sensitization) have received less attention than decreases (tolerance), but a fairly substantial number of reports do exist and further study seems warranted. Different authors have referred to increased reactivity as reverse tolerance, intolerance, sensitization, or augmentation. These are descriptive terms which carry no implications about possible mechanisms, and "sensitization" is used here merely for convenience. "Augmentation" is perhaps best avoided to prevent confusion with "behaviorally augmented" tolerance. Much discussion has centered on sensitization to cannabis, but clear evidence to support the subjective impressions of users has not been presented. Many studies have established the ability of Δ^9-THC to induce tolerance, and some of these are discussed below (Section 4). However, most psychiatrists are agreed that 2–3 weeks are needed for the development of the therapeutic effects of many antidepressant drugs, and this phenomenon may be regarded as a possible example of sensitization. The development of psychosis when amphetamine is taken repeatedly and in large doses may also be associated with sensitization, and some of the relevant animal studies are considered next.

In a study of spontaneous motor activities in rats, Segal and Mandell (1974) reported evidence for sensitization to amphetamine. Locomotor activity was assessed by recordings from a special floor installed in the rats' home cages. Initially, *d*-amphetamine (1.0 mg/kg) increased the activity scores obtained during a 3-hr period. After 15 daily injections, the effect of the drug had become significantly greater than on the first day, and it was also observed that stereotyped sniffing and chewing movements became much more marked. Rather similar evidence for sensitization was also obtained with lower and higher doses of *d*-amphetamine, but more precise dose–response analyses are needed for the strength of the effects to be assessed. Klawans *et al.* (1975) have also reported sensitization after chronic treatment with relatively large doses of *d*-amphetamine. However, it is notable that clear tolerance can develop to the suppressant effects of similar doses of amphetamine on fixed-ratio responding (e.g., Brown, 1965; Tilson and Rech, 1973a) and in flavor-aversion experiments (e.g., Goudie and

Thornton, 1975). Thus, it seems unlikely that a progressive accumulation of the drug can account for the sensitization found by Segal and Mandell (1974). Sensitization to cocaine has been reported by Post and Kopanda (1976).

Sensitization reactions have also been found with large doses of barbital (Aston, 1973) and with narcotic drugs and their antagonists. The repeated administration of a narcotic such as morphine most frequently produces tolerance, but sensitization can be demonstrated with certain dose regimens and strains of mouse (Shuster *et al.*, 1975). The development of cross sensitization to narcotic antagonists has been reported more frequently, and this may be illustrated by studies of operant behavior in rhesus monkeys.

Nalorphine is a narcotic "partial agonist" and can therefore either mimic or block effects of morphine, depending on the circumstances. In monkeys with extensive exposure to a fixed-ratio 10 schedule of food reinforcement, but with no history of morphine administration, small doses of nalorphine (about 0.2 mg/kg) had no effect on responding (Goldberg, 1971). Larger doses (e.g., 3 mg/kg) suppressed responding. However, when the monkeys were, at the same time, receiving morphine several times daily, even small doses of nalorphine (about 0.2 mg/kg) suppressed responding. This effect, which could readily be conditioned to suitable environmental stimuli, was evidently mediated through the precipitation of the morphine withdrawal state by nalorphine acting as a morphine antagonist. An empirical description would emphasize that the repeated doses of morphine sensitized the monkeys to the rate-depressant action of nalorphine. It was also found that sensitization persisted for at least 3 months after the administration of morphine was terminated, although in such cases it was necessary to administer about 1 mg/kg of nalorphine to suppress responding on the fixed-ratio schedule. It is more difficult to account for this long-term effect in terms of antagonism of morphine, since it is unlikely that very much morphine remained in the monkeys for three months. The behavioral observations thus give a hint that there may be other, adaptive changes occurring in the nervous system, and these may possibly involve either the narcotic agonist action of nalorphine, or endogenous substances thought to act on the same receptor sites as morphine and its antagonists (e.g., Hughes *et al.*, 1975).

Evidence for sensitization to other drugs will not be considered in detail; it is argued merely that sensitization may be a fruitful area for future research. An emerging principle seems to be that at a given receptor site, repeated administrations of drugs which act as antagonists seem to increase sensitivity to agonists. This may be seen with antagonists of dopamine (e.g., haloperidol, chlorpromazine, and many other neuroleptics), in relation to directly or indirectly acting dopamine agonists, e.g., apomorphine and amphetamine, respectively (Tarsy and Baldessarini, 1974; Moore and Thornburg, 1975). On the other hand, chronic treatment with drugs acting directly or indirectly as agonists has also been examined and linked to changes in sensitivity to antagonists (e.g., Chippendale *et al.,* 1972; Beuthin *et al.,* 1972).

3. Pharmacological and Organismic Factors

In this section, the importance of certain pharmacological factors (e.g., the parameters of chronic dosing regimes) is considered in relation to tolerance. As in other areas of behavioral pharmacology, it is necessary to investigate the effects of a wide range of doses in order to be sure that results are not specific to one, arbitrary dose. With certain drugs, the time between successive doses must also be carefully controlled if tolerance is to be seen (Section 2.4), and the development of tolerance may be facilitated by continuous administration of a drug. Special techniques to achieve this have been developed, and some of these are outlined below. The age, sex, and strain of subjects can all be influential. For example, Nozaki *et al.* (1975) found that tolerance to the analgesic effect of morphine developed more slowly in older than in young rats. When morphine was injected every 1.5 hr, the analgesic effect declined to about one half of its initial value after 3–4 doses in rats aged about 4 weeks. In 12-week-old rats, 6 doses were required to elicit a similar degree of tolerance. In these experiments, analgesia was assessed from vocalization and retraction of the paws following footshock. Many pharmacological investigations have been concerned with possible changes within the organism which may mediate tolerance, for example the induction of enzymes which metabolize drugs (Section 2.2). Response topography is a rather different type of organismic factor, and very much less is known about its possible significance in tolerance development. It will be argued in Section 3.3 that the possible role of response variables may deserve greater attention than it has received to date.

3.1 Dose Level

It is difficult to quantify comparisons of tolerance assessed by different behavioral or physiological indices. Scaling problems preclude precise comparisons between changes of different patterns of behavior. For example, one cannot say that a doubling of a fixed-ratio response rate is equivalent to a doubling of spontaneous motor activity, or to any

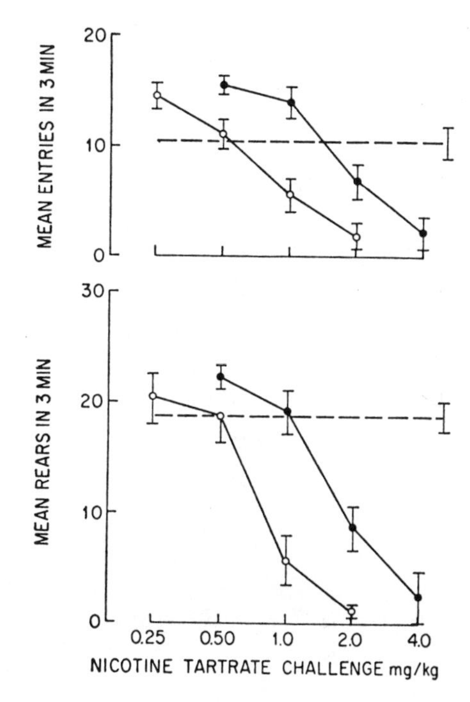

Figure 5. Acute tolerance elicited by a single pretreatment with nicotine (0.75 mg/kg 2 hr previously). Tolerance is shown by approximately parallel shifts of dose–response curves for the effects of nicotine on two measures of motor activity in rats ($n = 9$). ---, Saline only; ○—○, saline pretreatment, nicotine challenge; ●—●, nicotine pretreatment and challenge. The vertical bars indicate one standard error on each side of the mean. [From Stolerman *et al.* (1974).]

given change in an index of curvature calculated from performance on a fixed-interval schedule. It is also possible to fail to recognize tolerance altogether, if the acute dose–response curve is shallow or has reached an asymptote around the dose used. It has been argued that the most satisfactory method for quantifying the degree of tolerance is to determine how far a dose–response curve is shifted (Kalant *et al.,* 1971). Tolerance can then be expressed as the ratio of the doses of drug required to produce a given effect in tolerant and nontolerant subjects. The principle can be illustrated by experiments on tolerance to nicotine and morphine in rats.

In experimentally naive rats, a single administration of nicotine reduced locomotor activity in a dose-related manner (Figure 5). The larger the dose of nicotine, the lower the mean number of entries into the arms of the runway, or the number of rears onto the hind feet (Stolerman *et al.,* 1974). The dose–response curves were shifted to the right after a single pretreatment with nicotine; thus, acute tolerance had developed. A substantially increased dose of nicotine was required to produce a given degree of behavioral suppression in the acutely tolerant rats, as compared with the drug-naive rats. For example, the dose of nicotine which reduced the indices of activity by 50% was increased

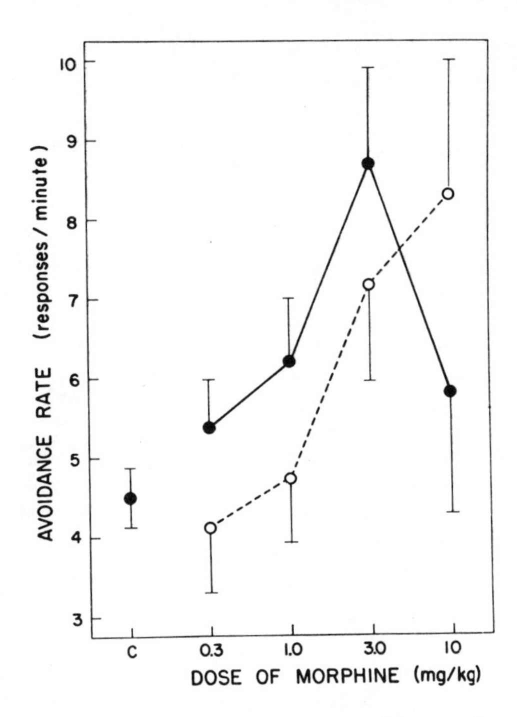

Figure 6. Dose-response curves of the effects of morphine on the rate of avoidance responding of nontolerant (filled circle) and morphine-tolerant (open circle) rats. The mean rate of responding in control sessions is indicated by the point at C. Each point represents the mean rate of responding for a complete 4-hr experimental session ($n = 6$). The vertical bars show one standard error on each side of the mean. [From Holtzman (1974).]

by a factor of about 2.4 for both entries and rears. For such comparisons to be meaningful, the dose–response curves must be parallel, as they were, for practical purposes, in these experiments. It may be noted that certain lower doses of nicotine had little effect in the nontolerant rats, but increased activity scores in tolerant animals. This could easily have been mistaken for sensitization (reverse tolerance) if an inadequate range of doses had been studied. A similar point may be made about the following experiments with morphine.

Holtzman (1974) determined dose–response curves for the rate-increasing effects of morphine on continuous avoidance responding in rats. Each lever press postponed the delivery of shock for 30 sec, whereas failure to respond for 15 sec after a shock resulted in delivery of a further shock. Moderate doses of morphine increased the response rate, but the largest dose disrupted the temporal patterning of responding, thus increasing the number of shocks delivered. Each dose of morphine was retested after 3 days of repeated morphine administration. It was then found that both the rate-increasing effects of the lower doses and the disruptive effect of the highest dose were attenuated. Tolerance was therefore shown by a shift of the dose–response curve to the right (Figure 6). Again, it may be noted that a very misleading conclusion could have been reached if testing had been confined to the highest dose only. The results show how schedule-controlled behavior can be utilized to demonstrate tolerance to a stimulant effect of the narcotic agonist morphine. Tolerance also developed to the effects of pentazocine, a narcotic partial agonist, and morphine-tolerant rats were cross-tolerant to pentazocine.

Since considerable time and effort are required to determine dose–response relations in nontolerant and tolerant subjects, the literature contains very incomplete information on the matter. The dose factors which have been reported vary widely for different drugs, and inevitably, they must be dependent on the dose regime used to induce tolerance. However, alcohol generally seems to be characterized by a low factor, typically about 1.5 (LeBlanc *et al.*, 1969), whereas a factor of several thousand has been reported for Δ^9-THC. Tolerant pigeons continued to respond for food reinforcement on a multiple fixed-ratio fixed-interval schedule after 1800 mg/kg of Δ^9-THC, whereas 0.3 mg/kg can decrease the rate of responding in nontolerant pigeons (Ford and McMillan, 1971). One report suggests that the factor for amphetamine may be about 4 (Hitzemann *et al.,* 1973).

3.2 Dose Frequency

Frequently repeated administrations of drugs have been thought to encourage the development of tolerance, and Seevers and Deneau (1963) went so far as to suggest that "continuous neuronal exposure" to a drug would provide optimal conditions. This seems to hold quite well for the opiate drugs, which had been most studied by 1963. For example, Goldstein and Sheehan (1969) studied the facilitation of locomotor activity produced in mice by a narcotic analgesic, levorphanol. The shorter the interval between successive doses, the more rapidly did tolerance develop. Thus, very marked tolerance developed when the drug was give every 8 hr, but virtually none when the drug was given every 48 hr (Figure 7). With morphine, a closely related compound, tolerance has been reported in rats with intervals of 3 weeks (Kayan and Mitchell, 1972), and even several months (Kornetsky and Bain, 1968). Precise comparisons between the degrees of tolerance in the various experiments are difficult without more complete dose–response

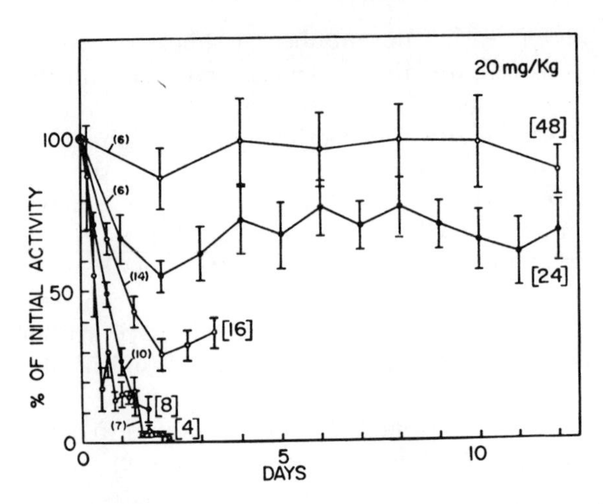

Figure 7. Effect of different injection intervals upon the development of tolerance to levorphanol (20 mg/kg) in mice housed three to a cage (one to a cage for the 4-hr interval). The number of cages is indicated in parentheses and the vertical bars indicate one standard error on each side of the mean. The intervals between injections (hr) are shown in brackets to the right of each curve. [From Goldstein and Sheehan (1969); © 1969 by The Williams & Wilkins Company, Baltimore.]

information, and it still appears that frequent or continuous administration may be most effective with the opiates. There is also some evidence that this applies to alcohol, barbiturates (Jaffe and Sharpless, 1965; Yanagita and Takahashi, 1970), and amphetamine (Hitzemann *et al.*, 1973). It seems that tolerance to a behaviorally depressant action of nicotine in rats is not necessarily linked to a high frequency of drug administration. Very much the same degree of tolerance developed when the same total dose of nicotine was given either three times a day for three days, or once every three days for 30 days (Stolerman *et al.*, 1974). Unfortunately, there is very little information available about the significance of dose frequency when tolerance is assessed with schedule-controlled behavior.

Changes in tolerance could be related to quite subtle aspects of the temporal parameters of drug administration, if the appropriate investigations were carried out. Studies on acute tolerance have been considered in Section 2.4, and there seems scope for much more work. For example, Turner (1971) measured the concentrations of nicotine in the blood of cats after intravenous infusions of the drug. When a given dose was administered as a series of small infusions (i.e., 4 μg/kg every 60 sec for 20 min), higher concentrations of nicotine were found than when the same total dose was infused continuously at 4 μg/kg/min. Whether this effect can be correlated with behavioral changes and tolerance is not known, but it is of interest in view of the intermittent way in which people inhale cigarette smoke.

The development of tolerance can sometimes be facilitated by administering a drug very frequently, but repeated administrations can cause harmful effects around the sites of injection, and the time and effort required can also become excessive. These problems can be minimized either by repeated infusions through implanted cannulae (e.g., Yanagita and Takahashi, 1970; Fischman and Schuster, 1974) or by various formulations designed to ensure the slow release of a drug over a prolonged period of time. The methods involving implanted cannulae have been the least used in studies of tolerance, although many of the technical problems have been solved for studies of drug self-administration (e.g., Deneau *et al.*, 1969). Most frequently, cannulae are implanted intravenously, and this route is advantageous because it avoids variations in the absorption of drugs. Techniques for intragastric self-administration might also be useful for studies of tolerance (e.g., Smith *et al.*, 1975; Gotestam, 1973); however, it would generally be preferable for drug administrations to be programmed by the experimenter, thus avoiding unwanted variations in dose frequency. The potential applicability of oral self-administration techniques is limited by uncontrolled variations in dose and dose frequency, unless drinking can be reliably controlled by such tactics as licking for extraneous reinforcement (e.g., food or shock avoidance) or by schedule-induced polydipsia (cf. Harris *et al.*, 1968; Falk *et al.*, 1972; see Chapter 6). However, methods involving slow-release formulations have been used most extensively when simple injections are unsatisfactory, and these are considered next.

The formulation which has been most used consists of a tablet which can be implanted subcutaneously in a rat or mouse. With this method, a high level of tolerance to morphine can be produced in mice in about 3 days, and large numbers of animals can be used because the surgery required is simple and quick (Way *et al.*, 1969). However, some pharmaceutical facility is necessary to produce the tablets, and it is not easy to reproduce precisely the characteristics of drug release across different batches of tablets. Furthermore, it would be very difficult to determine the exact daily dose received by an individual animal, although some estimate can be made by surgically removing the tablet residue and assaying the drug remaining in it. The short duration (i.e., a few days only) over which drug release is usually maintained also represents a severe limitation for studies of schedule-controlled behavior.

Up to the present, only tablets releasing morphine have been studied extensively, although the technique has been adapted for amphetamine (Hitzemann *et al.,* 1973) and pentobarbital (Ho, 1976).

Other workers have formulated emulsions which can be injected subcutaneously in the rat, and which then release morphine slowly over a period of about 2 days (Collier *et al.,* 1972). A single injection of an emulsion can produce tolerance. A shift of the dose–response curve has been reported, such that the dose of morphine has to be about double to produce a given degree of analgesia (Frederickson and Smits, 1973), suggesting only a moderate degree of tolerance.

Since the emulsions are viscous and possibly irritant, it is not clear that repeated injections are feasible. It is also very difficult to determine the doses absorbed since residues cannot be removed surgically, and the tissue samples required for assays of radio-labeled drugs would not often be obtainable. However, phenothiazine drugs are now used clinically in slow-release preparations for intramuscular injection, and the experimental use of these preparations could be explored.

Another method which has been used successfully with morphine involves implanting subcutaneously a small reservoir of the drug solution. The reservoir is constructed from siliconized rubber tubing and terminates in a semipermeable membrane through which the drug can diffuse outward. The contents of the reservoir can be replaced since polythene tubes can be brought from the reservoir through the skin of the rat (Goode, 1971). Similar reservoirs have also been used to induce tolerance to nicotine (Stolerman *et al.*, 1973). An advantage of the reservoir over other methods, such as tablets or emulsions, is the relative ease with which administration of a drug can be stopped. However, the washings from the reservoir must be analyzed to determine the doses actually administered, and it has not proved feasible to maintain an implanted rat for more than about 9 days. In general, slow-release formulations have certain disadvantages apart from those already mentioned. It is not known whether the mechanisms of tolerance are similar when drugs are administered in discrete doses or continuously, and the available information about continuous release is almost entirely restricted to rodents, whereas clinically, drugs are most often administered as discrete doses.

3.3 Response Topography

It is well known that the extent to which tolerance to a drug is seen may be dependent on how its potency is assessed. Different patterns of behavior may show different degrees of tolerance. However, such observations are not sufficient to isolate the role of the behavioral *response.* Factors associated with the schedule of reinforcement are generally considered to be much more important as determinants of the effects of drugs than the nature of the response or reinforcer (Chapter 1). However, in relatively few experiments has response topography been varied systematically, and its role may therefore be worthy of further study. For example, Lyon and Robbins (1975) have argued that the acute effects of amphetamine are very much dependent on response compatibility. They suggest that conditioned behavior will be facilitated when the response which it demands is compatible with unconditioned responses induced by the drug. In the case of amphetamine, this implies facilitation when the stereotype induced by the drug is compatible with the operant specified by a schedule of reinforcement. For example, amphetamine had different effects on bar-pressing and bar-holding responses when both were reinforced by the termination of shock, and this was related to a general tendency to initiate, but not to complete, responses after the administration of amphetamine (Lyon and Randrup, 1972). Until much more information is available about the possible importance of response variables in sensitivity to acute doses of drugs, it is probably premature to undertake extensive work with drugs given chronically. However, it is possible to speculate upon one way in which response topography might influence tolerance.

Seligman and Hager (1972) have argued that the acquisition of a conditioned response is very much dependent on the nature of the reinforcer (or punisher) with which it is paired: "The relative preparedness of an animal for learning about a contingency is defined by how degraded the input can be before that output rapidly occurs which means that learning has taken place." A "highly prepared" response may therefore be defined as one which conditions rapidly with a given reinforcer across a wide range of circumstances, notably those circumstances which tend to impair conditioning (e.g., delay of reinforcement). When defined empirically (if a little loosely) in this way, "prepared responses" seem to be correlated with those responses which the species normally emits as part of its total pattern of behavior in its natural environment. While recognizing that many aspects of the "preparedness" hypothesis remain controversial, it may be instructive to consider its possible relevance to behavioral tolerance, with amphetamine taken as an example.

As an illustration, consider the possible consequences of chronically administering a drug which initially reduces the rate of a "highly prepared" response. One might anticipate that such a response would develop resistance (tolerance) relatively rapidly to the degrading effect of the drug on performance. On the other hand, the development of tolerance might be retarded if the acute effects of the drug shifted responding toward another, more "highly prepared" pattern. This may be seen as an application in behavioral pharmacology of the ideas underlying the concept of "instinctive drift," the tendency of organisms to modulate their behavior toward more naturalistic responses when this modulation is not specified in the controlling schedule (Breland and Breland, 1961). In the context of tolerance, it is not proposed that "preparedness" is necessarily a universally important or critical factor; attention is merely being directed to a possibly relevant variable which may be added to those already identified (e.g., the schedule effects discussed in Section 4). The hypothesis seems eminently testable, since it would mainly require manipulations of response topography while other factors are held constant.

Some observations on tolerance to amphetamine seem consistent with a role for response topography, although the limited amount of relevant information makes assessment very difficult. Fairly rapid development of tolerance to the anorexigenic effect of amphetamine has been reported on many occasions (e.g., Herman *et al.*, 1971; Kandel *et al.*, 1975), and there can be little doubt that natural feeding behavior involves "highly prepared" responses. Stereotyped behaviors induced by amphetamine in rodents show little tolerance or even show sensitization (e.g., Segal and Mandell, 1974; Hitzemann *et al.*, 1973); this one might expect, since the drug shifts responding toward presumably "naturalistic" sniffing, licking, and gnawing when it induces stereotypy. On the other hand, bar-pressing operants can develop tolerance to amphetamine quite readily, although schedule effects clearly play a role here (e.g., Brown, 1965; Tilson and Sparber, 1973), and these are considered in much more detail in the next section. The absence of systematic studies which have isolated response topography makes any definite conclusion impossible at this time, but there does seem considerable scope for further work.

4. Environmental Factors: The Reinforcement Density Hypothesis

Rather than attempting to list all the possible environmental factors which may influence the development of tolerance, this section concentrates on the possible roles of reinforcing and aversive events. This limitation may be justified by the much greater amount of information which is available about their effects, as compared with other factors, such as temperature, lighting, and population density. It is now well established that factors associated with the schedule of reinforcement maintaining an animal's behavior are crucial determinants of the effects of acute drug administrations (see Chapter 1). More recently, it has been suggested that the effects of chronic drug administration may also be schedule-dependent. This may be illustrated by experiments on tolerance to Δ^9-THC in monkeys.

The base-line performance of a rhesus monkey responding on a multiple fixed-ratio 30 DRL 15-sec schedule of reinforcement is shown to the left of Figure 8 (Harris *et al.*, 1972). An initial injection of 2.0 mg/kg of Δ^9-THC produced almost complete suppression of responding in both the schedule components for about 8 hr (not shown). During the course of five daily injections, the duration of response suppression in the DRL component was progressively reduced to about 3 hr (i.e., partial tolerance developed). Once responding commenced in this component, it was faster than the original base line for about 30 min. However, responding in the fixed-ratio component did not recover within seven sessions (Figure 8, right). Further support for the suggestion that tolerance to the effect of THC may be schedule-dependent was provided by a second experiment. Rhesus monkeys trained on a discriminated avoidance schedule showed periods of postinjection response suppression similar to those observed in the previous experiment with an initial injection of the same dose of Δ^9-THC. Unlike the effects on DRL responding, complete tolerance (measured in terms of the time to begin responding) was observed after five daily injections. Thus, Harris *et al.* (1972) observed complete tolerance, partial tolerance, or no tolerance at all to behavioral effects of the same dose of the same drug, depending on the schedule of reinforcement.

This demonstration of schedule-dependent tolerance does not, of course, identify the crucial environmental variables which are responsible for the effects, since the different schedules generated different base-line response rates, different patterns of responding over time, different base-line reinforcement frequencies, and, presumably, different dose–response curves to acute administrations of THC. However, many reports which have been addressed to the question of schedule determinants of behavioral tolerance have strongly suggested that changes in reinforcement density produced by the initial behavioral effect of the drug may be a crucial determinant of whether or not behavioral tolerance will develop.

The possible importance of changes in reinforcement density as a determinant of tolerance was first clearly suggested by Schuster *et al.* (1966). In one experiment rats were trained to lever-press on a multiple DRL 30-sec fixed-interval 30-sec schedule. After base-line training and the determination of a dose–response curve for several acute administrations of *d*-amphetamine, the three rats were then injected with 1.0 mg/kg of *d*-amphetamine for 30 consecutive days. The main findings of this study are summarized in Table I, which shows the initial ef-

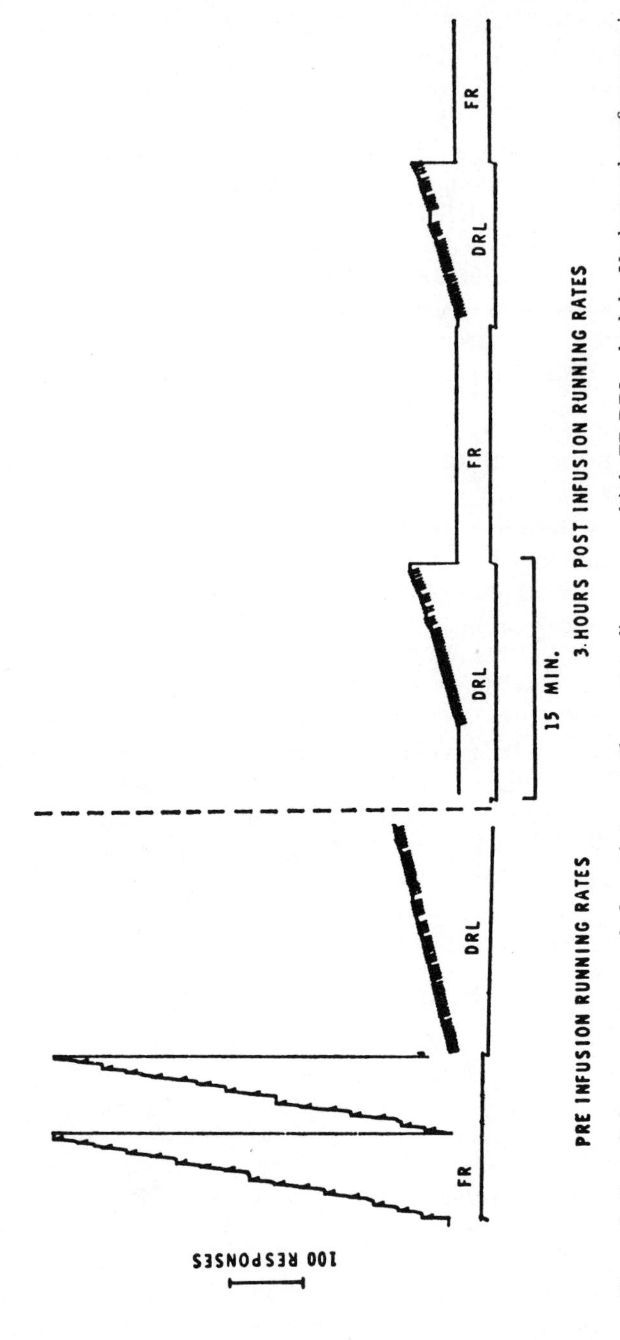

Figure 8. Cumulative response records for a rhesus monkey responding on a multiple FR DRL schedule. Undrugged performance is shown in the left segment. Initial doses of 2.0 mg/kg of Δ^9-THC completely suppressed responding in both components of the schedule. The right segment shows efficient performance in the DRL component after the development of tolerance, but continuing complete suppression of FR performance. [Modified from Harris *et al.* (1972).]

Table I. Pattern of Tolerance Development to Amphetamine in 3 Rats[a]

	Rat 2		Rat 4		Rat 5	
	FI	DRL	FI	DRL	FI	DRL
A: initial effect on response rate	Up	Up	Down	NC	NC	Up
B: initial effect on reinforcement density	NC	Down	Down	Down	NC	Down
C: tolerance to rate change	No	Yes	Yes	NA	NA	Yes

[a]Tolerance developed when the initial effect of the drug was to reduce the density of reinforcement. NC, no change; NA, not applicable (no initial effect).
Source: Schuster *et al.* (1966).

fect of the drug on overall response rate (A), the effect of any initial change in response rate on reinforcement density (B), and whether tolerance to any change in response rate was evident after 30 days (C). It can be seen that tolerance to a change in response rate developed whenever this change resulted in a decrease in reinforcement density. Tolerance development was independent of changes in response rate per se, since tolerance developed to both increases (in DRL) and decreases (in the fixed interval) as long as reinforcement density was reduced. Furthermore, tolerance did not develop when the drug-induced change in response rate did not affect reinforcement density (rat 2, fixed interval). It should be noted that Table I reveals that for rat 4 there was a reduction in reinforcement density in the DRL component, although there was no change in overall response rate. Data on the temporal distribution of responses revealed that this animal made more premature responses following the initial drug administrations but did not increase its overall reponse output. Consistent with the other findings summarized in Table I, tolerance developed to this disruption of response patterning, which reduced reinforcement density. Subsequent work has extended, and in part confirmed, these observations. For example, tolerance developed to the rate-depressant effect of amphetamine when it was administered to rats maintained on a fixed-ratio schedule, where it reduced the density of reinforcement; under generally similar conditions, tolerance did not develop to the overall rate-depressant effect on fixed-interval responding, where the drug did not affect reinforcement density (R. A. Harris, personal communication).

In a second experiment, Schuster *et al.* (1966) trained rats on a modified free-operant avoidance schedule in which electric shock was delivered every 30 sec unless a lever press was emitted, in which case the shock was avoided. After base-line training, *d*-amphetamine was administered for 35 consecutive days to four animals described as "poor" avoiders (i.e., those who failed to avoid many of the shocks). In all cases response rates were increased by the drug and hence the number of shocks decreased; tolerance did not develop in any rat over the 35 days of testing.

On the basis of their findings, Schuster *et al.* (1966) suggested that "Behavioral tolerance will develop in those aspects of the organism's behavioral repertoire where the action of the drug is such that it disrupts the organism's behavior in meeting the environmental requirement for reinforcements. Conversely, where the actions of the drug enhance, or do not affect the organism's behavior in meeting reinforcement requirements, we do not expect the development of behavioral tolerance." Gollub and Brady (1965) pointed out with reference to an earlier presentation of these findings ". . . . schedule-dependent tolerance indicates that tolerance may not be accounted for completely in terms of physiological processes alone, but rather that interactions between the drug-produced behavioral changes and consequences for reinforcement must be considered in the equation." It is important to note a further point made by Schuster *et al.*: "This hypothesis is not intended as a replacement for the classical physiological theories of drug tolerance. . . . Rather this hypothesis is put forth as an additional variable which may be operative in those behavioral situations where tolerance develops in a manner not predictable from the classical conceptions." To consider reinforcement density in the tolerance equation does not therefore exclude other environmental, or physiological, factors from also being considered.

Many studies have been able to implicate changes in reinforcement density as a determinant of tolerance to a variety of drugs. The next section will be a survey of studies which are consistent with the hypothesis, which will be referred to throughout simply as the *density hypothesis.* Although tolerance to the behavioral effects of a variety of drugs may be interpreted within the terms of the density hypothesis, most of the relevant research has been concerned with Δ^9-THC, and so many of the examples cited will deal with this drug.

4.1. Data Consistent with the Hypothesis

The density hypothesis may be invoked to account for some interesting findings of Davis and Borgen (1975). In this report four groups of rats were trained on a variable-interval 1-min schedule and then Δ^9-THC was injected repeatedly at a dose of 10 mg/kg, but with different intervals between successive doses. The initial effect of the drug was to reduce the response rates of all animals to near zero. Little tolerance developed with any of the groups by the end of the injection series. Response rates recovered only to 7–24% of the control values. With variable-interval schedules, of course, it is possible for a reduction in response rate to occur without greatly affecting reinforcement density. Although tolerance development, as indicated by response rate, was generally poor in this study, it is clear from the cumulative records that the partial tolerance which developed was sufficient to restore the density of reinforcement. Such data are entirely consistent with the density hypothesis, although the authors did not explore this possibility in their report and, unfortunately, quantitative data on reinforcement density were not presented. Although these findings are interesting with respect to the density hypothesis, it cannot be concluded that the changes in the density of reinforcement actually influenced tolerance.

Further support for the density hypothesis comes from the findings of Manning (1973). Three rhesus monkeys were trained on a DRL 60-sec schedule and then given one of six different doses of Δ^9-THC, ranging from 0.07 to 2.86 mg/kg, 3 hr before test sessions. The initial effect of each dose was to disrupt DRL performance; response rates increased, and there were more premature responses resulting in delivery of fewer reinforcers. However, it appeared that acute tolerance developed within a single session. Across subjects and over the range of doses studied, 68% of the total premature responses occurred in the first half of the sessions. These results therefore suggested that after the lower density of reinforcement at the start of the session, the animals adjusted their performance in order to meet the reinforcement requirements successfully. However, as Manning pointed out, these results could also be interpreted as simply being a reflection of the normal time course of the drug's action and independent of any drug-behavior interaction. Manning therefore conducted a second experiment, in which rhesus monkeys were tested on the DRL schedule 3 hr after drug administration on one occasion and 4 hr after drug administration on another. Only one dose of 0.75 mg/kg of Δ^9-THC was used in this experiment. If the tolerance he had apparently observed was simply due to the time course of the drug's action, then the animals tested after 4 hr should show "tolerance" as soon as they were exposed to the DRL schedule. In fact, the initial behavioral disruption and subsequent tolerance development within the session was very similar whether the animals were tested 3 or 4 hr after drug administration (Table II). There is also a possibility that an analogous effect was found by Janků (1964), who studied suppression of avoidance responding in a shuttle box after administration of chlorpromazine. The decrement in performance due to the drug was apparently much less after a 60-min

Table II. Efficiency of Performance of 3 Monkeys on a DRL Schedule 3 and 4 Hr after Ingestion of Δ^9-THC (0.75 mg/kg)[a]

		Reinforcements per response			
		3-hr delay		4-hr delay	
Subject		First hour	After 1 hr	First hour	After 1 hr
K681	Drug	0.61	0.79	0.51	0.72
	Placebo	0.94	0.91	0.98	0.94
H363	Drug	0.27	0.58	0.38	0.55
	Placebo	0.88	0.73	0.79	0.78
H090	Drug	0.75	0.83	0.65	0.87
	Placebo	0.98	0.93	0.92	0.93
Means:	Drug	0.54	0.73	0.57	0.71
	Placebo	0.93	0.86	0.90	0.88

[a]The results suggest the development of acute tolerance after the first hour of the drug sessions.
Source: Modified from Manning (1973).

exposure to the avoidance contingencies, as compared with the decrement after 60 min in the home cage. Manning (1973) pointed out that "It is clear that delaying the onset of behavioral testing until 4 hr after THC injection is considerably less effective as a method of eliminating errors than is allowing the monkey to interact with the contingencies of reinforcement for that extra hour." Manning incorporated his findings with the density hypothesis by noting that "Explanations of tolerance which emphasize absorption, distribution, metabolism, sensitivity of target tissue, or excretion all handle [the data of] the present experiment, only with extreme difficulty. However, they are entirely consistent with the learning hypothesis expressed here that a substantial proportion of tolerance to behavioral effects of THC is due to the general tendency of organisms to maximize reinforcement density." However, it is not clear why it should have apparently been necessary for the monkeys to "relearn" to respond on each occasion that they were drugged. Tolerance to disruptions of DRL performance induced by Δ^9-THC has also been observed by Sodetz (1972) and by Ferraro and Grisham (1972), who used chimpanzees as subjects.

Although Manning's experiments are important in that they implicate "experience with the schedule" while under the influence of Δ^9-THC as an important determinant of tolerance, they do not unequivocally isolate reinforcement density as the crucial controlling variable. For example, Manning's findings could equally be interpreted in terms of a more general "state-dependency" hypothesis (Kalant *et al.*, 1971; Sodetz, 1972). Such explanations are especially attractive when tolerance develops to the initial drug-induced disruption of behavior and then a further disruption of behavior is observed upon drug withdrawal. Sodetz (1972) relates his findings to the density hypothesis, but he also points out that one could equally conceive of ". . . both drug administration and withdrawal as simply altering the context in which the behavior has been established and maintained. Under such conditions an adjustment in performance consistent with the contingencies controlling behavior would occur, as would be predicted if the animals were run in a different chamber, or the manipulandum were changed. Each such change would produce a transient perturbation in performance followed by reacquisition and stabilization of schedule control of behavior. Recovery of such perturbations in performance can be attributed to the schedule control over behavior."

Ferraro and Grisham (1972) offer a similar state-dependency hypothesis for their data in terms of the animal making compensatory responses during chronic drug administration. However, they also note that such explanations ". . . do not help to isolate the variables that control the acquisition or performance of the presumed compensatory responses." This is the important point. Although the density and state-dependent hypotheses appear very similar, the density hypothesis goes further in predicting that any return to schedule-controlled performance in the drugged state will occur because the drug effect on behavior resulted in a detrimental change in reinforcement density, and that relearning in the drugged state will not occur if the drug-induced behavioral disruption does not reduce or increases reinforcement density. A state-dependency hypothesis would predict recovery of schedule control whatever the effect on reinforcement density. A crucial test of the density hypothesis therefore requires a demonstration of differential tolerance, which may be shown most clearly by different degrees of tolerance to a given dose of a drug, depending on whether its initial effect is to reduce the density of reinforcement during one schedule component, or to increase or not affect reinforcement density in another schedule component. Since the original study by Schuster *et al.* (1966), other reports of differential tolerance have appeared, and these are reviewed in the next section.

4.2. Direct Support from Differential Tolerance

Ferraro (1972) observed differential tolerance in rhesus monkeys to the effects of daily oral administrations of 2.0 mg/kg of Δ^9-THC after the animals had been stabilized on a variable-interval 45-sec schedule of reinforcement. The main findings of this study are presented in Figure 9. It can be seen that the initial dose of Δ^9-THC

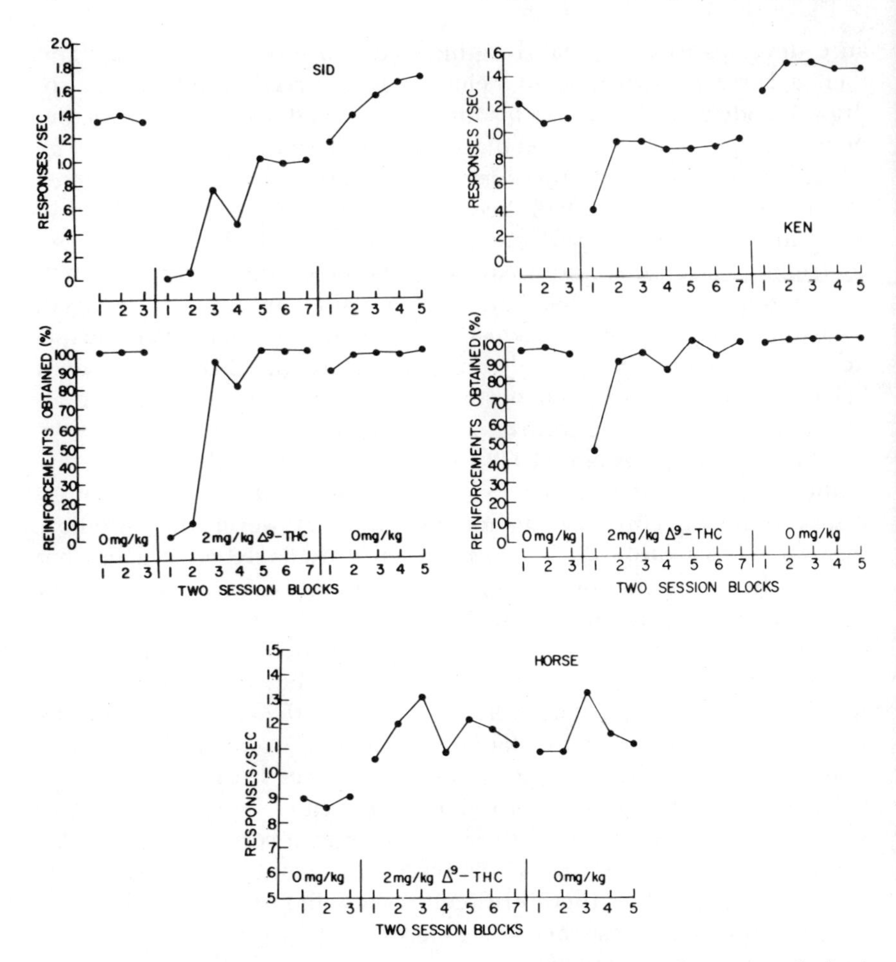

Figure 9. Mean VI response rates and percentages of available reinforcements obtained before, during, and after chronic administration of Δ^9-THC in three rhesus monkeys. It can be seen that tolerance to rate depression developed in Sid and Ken, and this was sufficient to restore the density of reinforcement to its predrug base line, whereas tolerance did not develop to the increased response rate in Horse. [Modified from Ferraro (1972).]

reduced the response rates of subjects Sid and Ken. With repeated administrations of the drug, the response rates increased but did not return to the predrug control levels. However, examination of the reinforcement frequencies obtained by these animals reveals that the increases in response rate were sufficient to achieve a similar percentage of reinforcement to that in control conditions. This finding is similar to that of Davis and Borgen (1975), but Ferraro's experiment offers stronger support for the density hypothesis, since the initial effect of Δ^9-THC administration with the third subject (Horse) produced an increase in response rate which did not affect reinforcement density, and tolerance did not develop with this animal. It can, of course, be argued that this experiment does not fully isolate reinforcement density as the controlling variable, since the failure to observe tolerance with the third animal might be because increases in response rate per se are not subject to tolerance with Δ^9-THC, and the fact that reinforcement density was unchanged by the effect of the drug on behavior might not be relevant. Although the role of this possible confounding variable cannot be isolated from this study, it should be noted that behavioral tolerance to the rate-enhancement effects of THC has been observed in rhesus monkeys (e.g., Manning, 1973).

Differential tolerance to Δ^9-THC has also been reported with behavior maintained by avoidance schedules. Pirch *et al.* (1972) have reported that Δ^9-THC disrupted the performance of rats which had good avoidance base lines but improved the performance of those rats with poor avoidance base lines. Tolerance developed only to the disruption of performance, which resulted in an increase in the density of electric shocks received. This report offers clear support for the density hypothesis and is in accord with the findings of Schuster *et al.* (1966) in which tolerance was not observed to the rate-enhancing effect of amphetamine on a continuous avoidance schedule. However, other experiments suggest that changes in shock density are not necessarily the major determinant of tolerance in such schedules.

Margules and Stein (1968) trained rats on a multiple schedule in which lever presses were reinforced on a variable-interval 2-min schedule in one component; in the other component every response was reinforced but also punished by the delivery of an electric shock. In base-line conditions, virtually complete suppression of responding was observed in the punished component, and responding was maintained at a steady rate in the unpunished component. The effects of oxazepam, a drug used clinically to relieve anxiety, were then studied. An initial injection of 20 mg/kg of oxazepam greatly suppressed responding in the unpunished component. With chronic dosing tolerance to this effect developed and, indeed, response rates continued to increase beyond the control values. In the punished component, however, the drug initially increased response rates, and tolerance did not develop to this effect. Thus, a drug-induced increase in response rate also increased shock density, and yet tolerance did not develop. This finding has been confirmed and extended by Cook and Sepinwall (1975).

Taken together, these results suggest that in schedules involving electric shock (avoidance or punishment contingencies), response-rate increases may not be very susceptible to tolerance, despite changes in shock density. However, it is important to note that interpretation is difficult because the response-rate increases in the experiments of Margules and Stein, and Cook and Sepinwall, were accompanied by increases in density of positive reinforcement as well as of shock. Combined avoidance and punishment schedules might clarify this situation. For example, with paced schedules (Blackman, 1972), drug-induced increases in response rate above the minimum required to meet the avoidance contingency could actually lead to an increased density of shock. In this way it should be possible to distinguish between changes in shock density and increases in response rate per se as determinants of tolerance.

It is clear that demonstrations of differential tolerance within individual animals offer stronger support for the density hypothesis since such studies more clearly indicate that physiological explanations of tolerance must take account of environmental influences. Differential tolerance within subjects has been observed by Fischman and Schuster (1974). Rhesus monkeys were trained on a fixed-ratio 10 schedule and then received 8 injections per day at 3-hr intervals of *d*-methamphetmine through chronically implanted intravenous catheters. Over the course of the study the doses per injection ranged from 0.0625 to 6.0 mg/kg. The smallest doses initially suppressed responding during the 2-hr sessions, but tolerance developed with chronic treatment. Doses were then increased, and when tolerance was observed, were increased again, and so on. Tolerance to the rate-suppressant effect of doses from 0.0625 to 1.0 mg/kg was observed. At doses greater than 1.0 mg/kg, no further suppressant effects were observed in tolerant monkeys. Although tolerance to all doses of the drug was observed, the animals still behaved in a highly abnormal fashion during the 22 hr outside the experimental session. They engaged in bizarre, repetitive, and exaggerated grooming behaviors, typical of amphetamine-induced stereotypy. Fischman and Schuster interpreted their findings in terms of the density hypothesis by pointing out that "Behavioral tolerance developed most rapidly to the effects of the drug which interfere with meeting reinforcement requirements. . . . On the other hand, behavior outside the experimental session was not under contingency control, and persisted in an abnormal fashion for a considerably longer period of time." Similarly, Harris *et al.* (1972) noted that although complete tolerance to Δ^9-THC developed on an avoidance schedule, the monkeys were still ". . . rendered stuporous to a degree which permitted handling of their heads. . . ." This effect has also been observed by Pieper and Skeen (1973) with chronic ethanol administration in rhesus monkeys. Tolerance developed to the initial effects of ethanol, which disrupted performance on a discrimination-reversal task and hence reduced the density of reinforcement, yet the animals still showed general tranquilization outside the experimental situation, which, for example, permitted easier handling of the animals for blood sampling.

Although the findings above are important for the density hypothesis, there are obviously problems, since sterotypy and tranquilization were not assessed systematically or quantified. However, both Schuster and Zimmerman (1961) and Thompson (1974) have been able to support these findings by experiments in which behavior not under contingency control was quantified. Schuster and Zimmerman investigated the effects of chronic injections of 0.75 or 1.5 mg/kg of *dl*-amphetamine on the performance of rats trained on a DRL 17.5-sec schedule. On alternate days the effect of the drug on spontaneous activity in an activity chamber was assessed. The drug initially increased response rates, disrupted temporal patterning on the DRL schedule, and increased general activity in the activity chamber. Tolerance developed to the effects of the drug on behavior controlled by the DRL schedule but did not develop to the increase in general activity which was not under contingency control. Similarly, Thompson (1974; see Chapter 3) trained pigeons on a complex task in which they were required to peck four keys in a certain order in order to obtain food. The task was either the same each day (performance condition), or was varied each day (learning condition). Incorrect responses were followed by a 5-sec period of time-out during which the keylights were extinguished and responding had no effect. This procedure was then used to investigate the effects of chronic administration of chlordiazepoxide, *d*-amphetamine, methylphenidate, phenobarbital, and chlorpromazine. In general, when the drugs increased the number of incorrect responses made by the animals, and hence reduced reinforcement density, behavioral tolerance was observed. However, when a drug increased the number of responses made in the time-out period, similar tolerance was not observed. Since time-out responding had no effect on reinforcement density, Thompson interpreted this within-subject differential tolerance in terms of the density hypothesis.

A powerful demonstration of differential tolerance within animals with parameters other than the extreme ones of behavior under contingency control compared with behavior which is not under contingency control comes from Manning (1976). Seven rats were trained on a continuous avoidance schedule in which shocks were delivered every 5 sec unless a response was emitted, in which case the shock was delayed for 20 sec. Then 3 hr prior to each experimental session, the rats were given intragastric intubations of 30 mg/kg of Δ^9-THC for between 10 and 45 sessions. The effects of the drug on overall response rates were variable between subjects and not statistically significant. However, changes in the temporal pattern of responding resulted in increases in shock density for three subjects (AV 3, AV 4, and AV 8), and tolerance developed to this effect. Another animal (AV 2) experienced a decrease in shock density with Δ^9-THC, and tolerance did not develop to this effect (Figure 10). This finding of between-subject differential tolerance depending upon the way in which the drug affected shock density was consistent with the density hypothesis and with previous reports of the effects of chronic drug administrations on behavior controlled by free-operant avoidance schedules. However, the effect of Δ^9-THC on the density of shocks received by the other three animals (AV 1, AV 5, and AV 7) are even more important for the density hypothesis. These three animals initially experienced an increase in shock density, and tolerance developed to this effect. However, shock density continued to fall below control values, and tolerance to this decrease did not develop even though subjects AV 5 and AV 1 were exposed to Δ^9-THC treatment for a considerable period. This finding of within-subject differential tolerance thus provides powerful support for the density hypothesis. Manning emphasized the importance of the density hypothesis by pointing out that "the transience of many of the THC-induced performance decrements may be viewed as a natural and adaptive response to a sudden decrease in reinforcement, a view which emphasizes the interaction of the organism and the external rather than internal environment."

Although the experiments cited so far offer much support for the density hypothesis for a variety of drugs, especially Δ^9-THC, it must be noted that reports have appeared in which behavioral tolerance has not developed even though the drug-induced behavioral change has resulted in a decrease in reinforcement density, and other reports have appeared in which tolerance has developed when the drug-induced behavioral change has not resulted in any change in reinforcement density. Some of these studies will be considered in the next section.

4.3. Exceptions

There have been several experiments where investigators have failed to observe tolerance, even though the initial effect of the drug on behavior resulted in a decrease in reinforcement density. For example, Minkowsky (1939) found that *dl*-amphetamine greatly increased the number of errors made by rats which were learning a maze for food, but no tolerance developed during 22 days of chronic drug treatment.

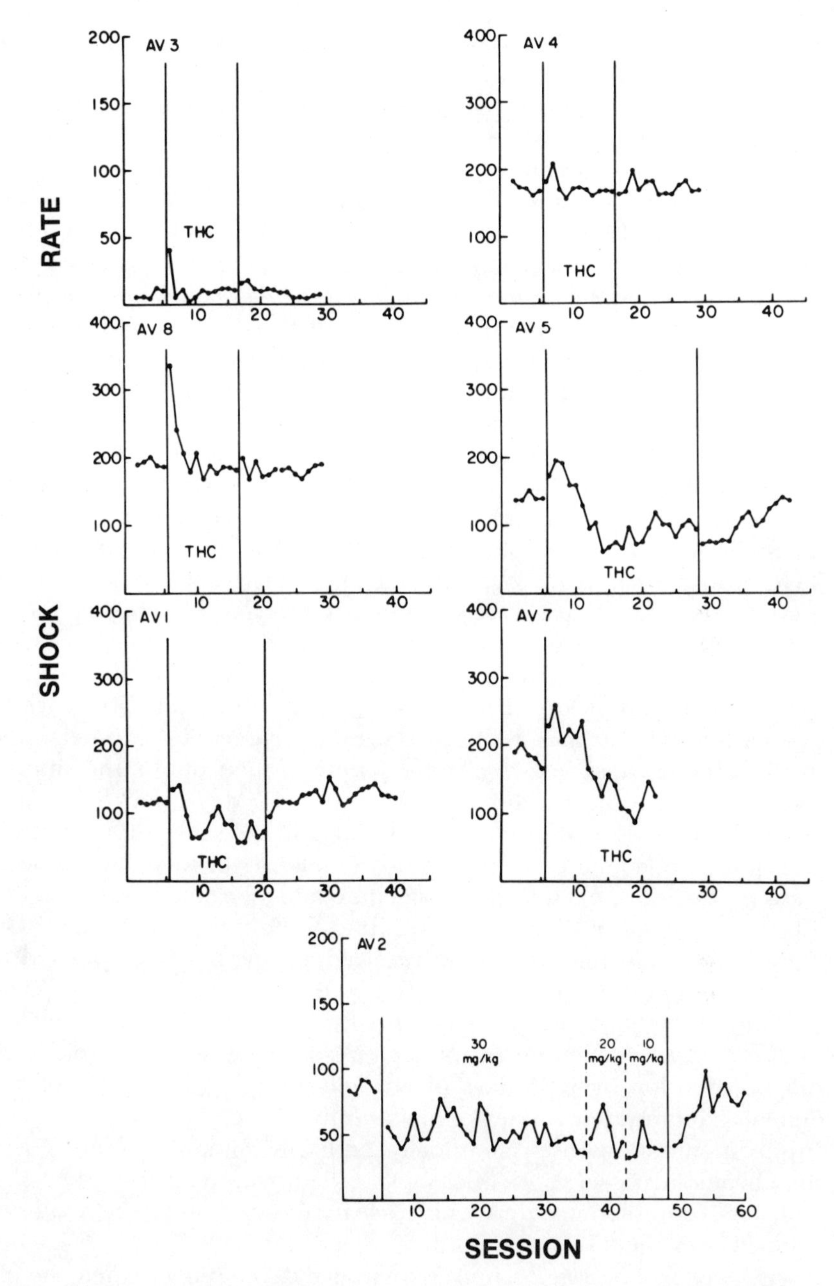

Figure 10. Total shocks received by seven rats on a continuous avoidance schedule before, during, and after chronic administration of Δ^9-THC (30 mg/kg except where noted). Tolerance developed when the initial doses of the drug increased the frequency of shocks. [From Manning (1976).]

Similarly, Mercier and Dessaigne (1959, cited in Kosman and Unna, 1968) found no tolerance to the suppressant effect of amphetamines on water-reinforced performance. Water-deprived rats were trained on a color-discrimination task in which they were presented with two tanks containing red and green water. Drinking of the red water resulted in an electric shock, and the animals eventually learned to drink only the green water. Different groups were then tested daily during a regime of chronic intraperitoneal administration of *dl*-amphetamine (10 mg/kg for 42 days), *d*-amphetamine (10 mg/kg for 54 days), and methamphetamine (5 mg/kg for 31 days). The effect of the drugs was to suppress responding, with the animals running back and forth without attempting to drink, and responding never recovered over the whole of the drug series.

In operant conditioning situations there have been several failures to observe tolerance to the rate-suppressant effects of drugs on fixed-ratio schedules, even though these resulted in a decrease in reinforcement density. One example is the study of Harris *et al.* (1972) with THC, which has already been discussed. Similarly, Brown (1965) observed tolerance to the rate-suppressant effect of 3.0 mg/kg of *d*-amphetamine in rats responding on a fixed-ratio 50 schedule but failed to observe tolerance to the suppressant effect of the same dose of this drug in a second group of rats in which the only major difference in procedure was that they received several injections of *d*-amphetamine in their home cages before chronic administration of *d*-amphetamine under the schedule conditions were begun. D'Mello and Stolerman (1975) have also failed to observe tolerance to the rate-suppressant effect of *d*-amphetamine on fixed-ratio responding in rats. The subjects were trained on a fixed-ratio 40 schedule and were then administered 1.0 or 1.5 mg/kg of *d*-amphetamine intraperitoneally for 25 days. On days 26–30 those rats which had received 1.0 mg/kg were switched to 1.5 mg/kg, and those given 1.5 mg/kg were switched to 1.0 mg/kg. The findings of this study are presented in Figure 11. It can be seen that 1.0 mg/kg of *d*-amphetamine suppressed responding and that tolerance did not develop over 25 days of chronic drugging. With two of the animals administered 1.5 mg/kg of *d*-amphetamine, there was a marked suppression of response rate initially, and only minimal tolerance over the chronic drug series can perhaps be detected. With the other animal, far from tolerance developing, clear sensitization to the drug developed over the 25 days of testing.

As well as failures to observe tolerance development when the effect of a drug has been to reduce reinforcement density, there is also evidence available of tolerance development even though the initial

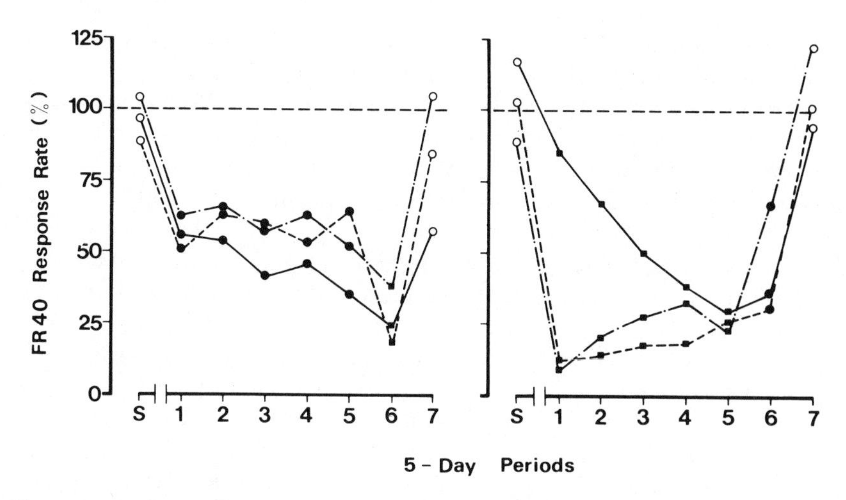

Figure 11. Performance of six rats on a FR 40 schedule of food reinforcement before, during, and after chronic administration of *d*-amphetamine. Response rates are expressed as percentages of preinjection rates. The points at *S* show responding when saline was injected i.p. immediately before a single session. Periods 1–7 show mean responding for each rat averaged over 5-day periods, with *d*-amphetamine or saline injected as indicated. Very little tolerance developed to the rate-depressant action of the drug; one rat yielded clear evidence of sensitization. ○—○, saline; ●—●, *d*-amphetamine 1.0 mg/kg; ■—■, *d*-amphetamine 1.5 mg/kg.

drug effect has not led to any changes in reinforcement density. For example, Tilson and Sparber (1973) trained rats on a fixed-interval 75-sec schedule of reinforcement and then administered 0.5 mg/kg of *l*-amphetamine. The initial effect of the drug was to increase overall rates, this increase largely being due to an increase in response rates in the final 45 sec of each interval. This change in performance had no effect on reinforcement density, and yet tolerance developed within 6–7 days of chronic drugging. A challenge dose of 0.16 mg/kg of *d*-amphetamine the day after tolerance development produced an increase in responding in the first 15 sec of the fixed interval and in the last 30 sec (i.e., no cross tolerance). Again, tolerance to these effects developed after 4–6 sessions. Similarly, Djahanguiri *et al.* (1966) presented cumulative records to show that in cats, 0.2 mg/kg of morphine increased fixed-interval responding and thus had no effect on reinforcement density, and yet chronic tolerance developed. Similar effects have also been observed on variable-interval schedules. Freedman *et al.* (1964) administered 195 μg/kg of LSD-25 to rats responding on a variable-interval 90-sec schedule. The initial effect was suppression of responding but only a very slight reduction in reinforcement density. However, tolerance developed within 9 days.

Other problems for the density hypothesis arise when tolerance develops to an extent which would not be predicted from the hypothesis. For example, Kosersky *et al.* (1974) trained pigeons on a variable-interval 3-min schedule and then injected 0.3 mg/kg of Δ^9-THC or the same dose of 11-OH-Δ^9-THC prior to each daily 2-hr session. With four pigeons, responding was completely suppressed for several days, but thereafter response rates gradually increased to reach predrug levels. This finding is inconsistent with those of Davis and Borgen (1975) and Ferraro (1972), since complete recovery of response rate on variable-interval schedules is not necessary for the animals to reach the predrug reinforcement levels. Findings such as those of Kosersky *et al.* (1974) thus suggest that the decreased reinforcement densities in the studies of Davis and Borgen, and of Ferraro, may not have been the variable controlling tolerance development.

Problems also arise for the density hypothesis when suppressed response rates recover, but independently of any recovery of reinforcement densities. This was observed by Elsmore (1976), who used a multiple schedule similar to that of Schuster *et al.* (1966). Rhesus monkeys were trained on a multiple fixed-interval 120-sec DRL 120-sec schedule. After base-line training, the animals received 1 mg/kg of Δ^9-THC each day at 0800 hr. The animals were then tested on the multiple schedule at 1000, 1600, 2200, and 0400 hr each day. In this paper Elsmore presented data from the session at 1000 hr (i.e., 2 hr after drug administration). As in the study by Schuster *et al.*, Elsmore observed an increase in responding in both components of the multiple schedule. Although response rates were quite variable from day to day, they remained generally elevated in the fixed-interval component over 40 days of chronic drug administration. However, DRL response rates returned to base line within 3–5 days. Taken at face value, these findings appear to offer strong support for the density hypothesis. However, data pertaining to daily reinforcement frequencies revealed that the return to base-line response rates in the DRL component was not correlated with a concomitant increase in reinforcement density and, indeed, reinforcement frequencies never returned to predrug control levels over the whole course of the experiment. As Elsmore pointed out, ". . . it would be difficult to account for the recovery in DRL response rate by the effect such recovery might have on reinforcement rate, since the time courses of the two effects are quite different." These findings of Elsmore are clearly problematical for the density hypothesis, and the situation becomes even more complex when one considers an alternative behavioral mechanism put forward by Elsmore as a possible explanation for his findings: "The increased DRL response rates produced a reduction in reinforcement frequency in only that component of the mutiple schedule. It is well-established that decreases in reinforcement frequency lead to corresponding reductions in response rate (Catania and Reynolds, 1968). Thus, the reduction in DRL response rate that appears to be tolerance to the drug effect may simply reflect a general weakening of the behavior in that component of the multiple schedule due to the reduction in reinforcement frequency under the DRL conditions."

It is clear from the findings reported in this section that caution must be exercised in ascribing tolerance development to changes in reinforcement density when other possible contributory factors have not been excluded from consideration. The studies which have found tolerance when there has been no effect on reinforcement density are clearly a problem for the density hypothesis, and if they are confirmed by further research, the density hypothesis will need revision in this light.

4.4. Assessment of the Density Hypothesis

The importance of the density hypothesis lies in its operational clarity and explicit predictions regarding the effects of repeated drug administrations. In this way it represents a clear advance over hypotheses of behavioral tolerance which simply emphasize general behavioral factors such as "learning" or "experience with the schedule" as important determinants of behvioral tolerance. The density hypothesis has been found to be applicable to a variety of drugs other than amphetamines, upon which it was based (although unfortunately too many of the exceptions are with amphetamines!). However, it is also clear that a decade of research has not yet firmly established the hypothesis as a general principle underlying behavioral tolerance, since there are some findings directly contradicting the hypothesis, and other observations which appear to support the hypothesis may be open to alternative interpretations.

In any experimental test of the density hypothesis, at least two conditions must be fulfilled: changes in the absorption, distribution, or metabolism of the drug must be ruled out; and changes in reinforcement density as the important behavioral variable must be demonstrated rather than inferred. Clearly, demonstrations of differential tolerance associated with changes in reinforcement density within individual animals can provide the most convincing evidence for the density hypothesis; however, such demonstrations of differential tolerance have either emerged fortuitously (Ferraro, 1972; Manning, 1976) or have used rather gross parameters of reinforcement density, as in the experiments which have compared the effects of chronic drug administration on behavior under contingency control with the effects of the drug on behavior which is not under contingency control. The technique of operant conditioning is a very powerful tool in the investigation of drug effects on behavior, yet it has not been fully exploited in the investigation of the reinforcement density hypothesis of behavioral tolerance. A more definitive assessment of the density hypothesis could be achieved by greater use of multiple schedules (e.g., Schuster *et al.*, 1966), yet such studies have been notable by their absence. By utilizing present knowledge of the effects of acute doses of drugs on schedule-controlled behavior, it should be possible to arrange multiple schedules so that a variety of changes in reinforcement density, both in direction and extent, were experienced by individual animals. In this way it would be possible to assess the limits to the density hypothesis, e.g., are all behavioral changes which result in a reduction in reinforcement density subject to tolerance, or only those changes which reduce reinforcement density by at least a certain amount? It is well established that the behavior of animals in traditional operant conditioning experiments may be precisely controlled by quite subtle changes in reinforcement density (e.g., Baum, 1973; Herrnstein and Hineline, 1966), yet it remains to be seen whether behavioral tolerance might also develop in a systematic manner as a function of similar subtle changes in reinforcement density.

More precise manipulations of reinforcement density rather than "all-or-none" changes are required in order, for example, to establish the point at which purely pharmacological determinants of tolerance such as dosage take over from behavioral determinants such as reinforcement density. For example, although the findings of Thompson (1974; see Chapter 3) may be interpreted in terms of the density hypothesis, he noted that tolerance development was also dependent upon drug dosage and on whether the animals were responding in the "learning" or "performance" condition. Thompson noted that ". . . under the learning condition at relatively large doses of *d*-amphetamine and methylphenidate, little or no tolerance developed to the error-increasing effect of these drugs, despite the fact that this effect necessarily reduced the rate of reinforcement." Similarly, Freedman *et al.* (1964) found that doses of 130 and 195 μg/kg of LSD-25 produced exactly the same reduction of response rate on fixed-ratio schedules, and hence the same reduction in reinforcement density, but tolerance developed only to the suppressant effect of 130 μg/kg. Further experiments are clearly needed in order to investigate the interactions between drug dosage and changes in reinforcement density as they influence the development of behavioral tolerance.

Although it has been suggested that multiple schedules offer an important means by which the density hypothesis can be assessed, care must be taken in the design of experiments if reinforcement density is to be clearly demonstrated as the important behavioral variable. With respect to the assessment of acute administrations of amphetamine, Sanger and Blackman (1976) have noted that with multiple schedules, apparent rate-dependent effects may be confounded by other factors inherent in the component schedules. These other factors include different base-line reinforcement densities and different temporal patterns of responding. Similarly, apparent reinforcement density effects in studies of chronic drug administrations may also be confounded by other schedule variables. For example, a return to base-line performance with chronic drug administration has frequently been observed on DRL schedules, but this phenomenon does not appear to be so robust with fixed-ratio schedules. It may thus be that certain schedules per se limit the development of behavioral tolerance independently of any changes in reinforcement density. With respect to fixed-ratio schedules, many studies have shown that such schedules are aversive in the sense that animals will make an alternative response in order to obtain a period of time-out from them (e.g., Appel, 1963; Azrin, 1961). Thus, it might be suggested that a drug which abolishes fixed-ratio responding serves a negative reinforcing function, and this factor could override the fact that at the same time the density of positive reinforcement has been reduced.

A further problem arises when attempts are made to compare the effects of drug-induced changes in reinforcement density between different schedules. If one conceives of tolerance development as relearning in the drugged state resulting from the animals adjusting their performance in order to receive an increased density of reinforcement, then certain schedules may inherently facilitate such relearning. This facilitating effect of the schedule may confound the effects of reinforcement density per se. For example, on an interval schedule a single response after a period of drug-induced suppression of responding will be successful in obtaining reinforcement. On the other hand, with ratio schedules, several responses must be emitted before the animal is reinforced. In this context it is interesting to note that in the multiple DRL fixed-ratio schedule of Harris *et al.* (1972), tolerance developed to the suppression of responding induced by Δ^9-THC in the DRL component but did not develop in the fixed-ratio component. Similarly, Freedman *et al.* (1964) observed tolerance to the suppressant effect of 195 μg/kg of LSD-25 on a variable-interval schedule, but a separate group of rats did not develop tolerance to the suppressant effect of the same dose of this drug on a fixed-ratio schedule.

Different base-line reinforcement densities obtained in different reinforcement schedules may also confound apparent density effects in tolerance development. For example, in the study of Harris *et al.* (1972) the density of reinforcement before drug administration appears to be greater in the DRL component than in the fixed-ratio component (Figure 8). The initial injection of Δ^9-THC resulted in a complete absence of reinforcement in both components, but the absolute loss of reinforcement appeared greater in the DRL component, and tolerance developed in this component only. It is clearly advisable to attempt to equate base-line reinforcement densities when attempting to assess the role of this factor in tolerance development.

It is clear from the preceding paragraphs that definitive tests of the density hypothesis are still required. The use of multiple schedules to demonstrate schedule dependency of tolerance is suggested, but care must be taken in the choice of component schedules to control for factors other than reinforcement density. One possible solution here is the use of "paced" reinforcement schedules (e.g., Blackman, 1972). For example, it is possible to train an animal on a multiple schedule with two variable-interval components. In one component the schedule is a conventional variable-interval schedule, while in the other component the same schedule is in operation with the additional requirement that reinforcements can only be obtained if the response to be reinforced is separated by no more than, e.g., 1 sec from the preceding response (i.e., a "paced" variable-interval schedule). Such a schedule tends to generate a generally high overall response rate. In this way it is possible to generate, in base-line conditions, patterns of responding in the components of a multiple schedule which are generally similar with respect to overall response rate, response patterning, and reinforcement density. However, if a drug is then given which reduces overall response rate in the two components, the animal will suffer a great reduction in reinforcement density in the paced component but will suffer no reduction or only a small reduction in the conventional variable-interval component. Since the only change has been a reduction of reinforcement density in the paced component, a demonstration of tolerance in this component but not in the conventional component would offer very powerful support for the density hypothesis since all other schedule factors would have been controlled. Similarly, it is possible to add a low pacing requirement so that responses must be spaced by at least a certain period in one component. A drug which reduced response rate might now increase the density of reinforcement in this component while having no effect in the other component. Using these means it should be possible to assess more clearly whether the direction of response-rate changes influences tolerance development independently of changes in reinforcement density. It might also be possible to encourage the development of sensitization to a drug by arranging for its initial effects to be associated with an increased density of reinforcement.

5. Tolerance to Stimulus Properties of Drugs

In the preceding sections, the effects of selected pharmacological, organismic, and environmental factors on the development of behavioral tolerance were discussed to illustrate points which may be of general significance. For example, it can be concluded that the appearance of tolerance is very dependent on the parameters of chronic dosing, and it is therefore necessary to study a suitably wide range of dose levels and frequencies. Furthermore, changes in the absorption, distribution, or metabolism of drugs can contribute to tolerance, and such effects need to be considered in studies of possible environmental influences. It may be noted that almost all of the work dealt with the response-rate-increasing or response-rate-decreasing effects of drugs, but this was not the result of deliberate selection. Much less information is available about the development of tolerance to the discriminative, reinforcing, or aversive properties of drugs, but it is being increasingly recognized that pharmacological influences on behavior frequently involve such "stimulus properties" of drugs.

The ability of a drug to serve as a discriminative stimulus is typically shown in studies of operant behavior by differential responding on one of two levers according to the administration of drug or saline, or by temporal patterning of responding appropriate for one of two schedules (see Chapter 4). Since animals trained on such tasks receive repeated drug doses, the fact that good discriminative control can be maintained indicates that complete tolerance does not develop. For example, Colpaert *et al.* (1975) have commented that over a period of 4–5 months, no tolerance was revealed to the discriminative property of fentanyl, a narcotic analgesic. However, most experiments in which drugs serve as discriminative stimuli are not intended to provide evidence for tolerance, and it would be very difficult to set up appropriate controls. The dose parameters typically used may also tend to minimize tolerance; injections of drugs are given on average every second day, and may be omitted altogether at weekends. The development of tolerance would probably be facilitated if the drugs were administered more frequently (Section 3.2). It also seems possible that an animal would appear not to be tolerant when in fact it was, since it would have been trained to discriminate between a drug-withdrawal state and a relatively normal condition. This issue is very difficult to resolve experimentally, since it would probably be necessary to develop a three-way discrimination among drugged, normal, and withdrawn states. Tolerance to the discriminative stimulus properties of several drugs has been reported, and an experiment with barbital is used as an illustration.

York and Winter (1975) trained two groups of rats to discriminate between barbital and saline. In the first group, barbital served as the positive discriminative stimulus (S^D) for responding on a fixed-ratio 8 schedule, whereas in the second group, barbital was the negative stimulus (S^Δ). Good stimulus control was established, suggesting that minimal tolerance had developed. Training was then stopped for a period, during which daily administrations of a large, hypnotic dose of barbital were given. Upon subsequent testing for stimulus control by the original, lower dose of barbital, it was found that a significant degree of tolerance had developed, but only in the group in which barbital served as S^Δ. Interruptions of training which were not accompanied by daily barbital doses did not disrupt subsequent discrimination performance in either group. Either this or similar procedures could be used to test for tolerance to a wider range of drugs. Tolerance to the discriminative stimulus properties of nicotine, morphine, and Δ^9-THC has also been reported (Schechter and Rosecrans, 1972; Hirchorn and Rosecrans, 1974).

The possibility that tolerance can develop to the reinforcing stimulus properties of drugs has received surprisingly little attention in view of the frequent comments of drug-dependent individuals to the effect that they need progressively larger doses to obtain a "high." Pretreatment with opiate drugs tends to facilitate the acquisition of opiate self-administration behavior (e.g., Weeks and Collins, 1964; Stolerman and Kumar, 1970); at first sight this might indicate sensitization to the reinforcing action, possibly mediated through the termination of the drug-withdrawal syndrome. Smith *et al.* (1976) have shown that such effects may be clearly related to the doses used for pretreatment. Interpretation of such results from simple fixed-ratio schedules is difficult, since there is an inverse relationship between response rate and dose per infusion, probably because large doses of morphine have rate-depressant effects (e.g., Kelleher and Goldberg, 1976). Increases in response rate on continuous reinforcement or fixed-ratio schedules of drug self-administration can therefore be interpreted as either sensitization of the reinforcing property of the drug or as tolerance to rate-depressant effects. Procedures which minimize confounding of reinforcement with rate changes have been described; typically, these limit the frequency of self-administered doses by suitable fixed-interval or second-order contingencies (Balster and Schuster, 1973; Goldberg, 1973), or use concurrent (choice) schedules (e.g., Iglauer *et al.,* 1976; see Chapter 7). Such techniques should facilitate attempts to quantify the reinforcing strengths of drug doses and thus may allow the possible development of tolerance or sensitization to be assessed more rigorously than has previously been possible.

Aversive properties of drugs have received much less study than their discriminative or reinforcing actions. With the techniques of operant conditioning, it has been possible to demonstrate aversive properties for a limited range of drugs, notably narcotic antagonists, LSD, and chlorpromazine (Hoffmeister and Wüttke, 1976), but it is not clear to what degree, if at all, tolerance can be developed. The conditioning of flavor aversions has yielded evidence for aversive actions of a wider range of compounds and for the development of tolerance. The main features of these experiments have been described earlier in connection with cross tolerance (section 2.5) and will not be repeated here. At the present time, it has not been established that such experiments demonstrate true punishing actions of drugs rather than conditioned suppression. In this respect the situation may be more like conditioned suppression of operant responding by stimuli paired with shock, rather than response-contingent punishment (Blackman, 1972). However, regardless of the ultimate interpretation, flavor aversions are notable for yielding clear evidence for the development of behavioral tolerance (e.g., Cappell *et al.*, 1975; Jacquet, 1973; Goudie and Thornton, 1975; Revusky and Taukulis, 1975). It remains to be determined whether the mechanisms of such tolerance are similar to those involved in tolerance to other effects of the drugs concerned.

In a number of experiments, it has been reported that environmental stimuli previously paired with drug administrations can elicit conditioned physiological or behavioral changes. In such experiments the drug serves as an unconditioned stimulus. For example, after repeated pairings with LSD, a 2-min presentation of a white light reduced responding by rats maintained on a variable-interval schedule of water reinforcement (Cameron and Appel, 1976). The authors noted that no tolerance to the unconditioned suppressive effect of the drug occurred, and it was not therefore possible to assess whether cross tolerance developed from unconditioned to conditioned drug effects, or whether the extinction of a conditioned drug reaction affected subsequent sensitivity to the unconditioned stimulus (drug). As a rule, it seems that investigations of unconditioned stimulus functions of drugs have not progressed to a stage where the problem of tolerance is significant. However, Tilson and Rech (1973b) have pointed out the possible importance of controlling for such conditioned reactions when assessing tolerance to other effects of drugs.

6. Conclusions

Behavioral tolerance has been demonstrated with many different drugs, but there are no good grounds for supposing that tolerance to behavioral effects of drugs is fundamentally different from tolerance to their physiological or biochemical actions. The importance of pharmacological factors is widely recognized and it cannot be emphasized too strongly that valid interpretations of the consequences of chronic drug treatments are dependent on adequate dose–response information relating to acute actions. Many of the studies with schedule-controlled behavior have not included as much manipulation of dose parameters as is desirable, although the considerable time and effort required should not be underestimated. Studies of the effects of the schedule of reinforcement and of other environmental factors on the development of tolerance have been appearing with increasing frequency. The reinforcement density hypothesis has guided much of this work, and its further, critical assessment offers considerable scope for the future. The possible role of response topography is almost entirely unknown, although some speculative suggestions have been made in this chapter. A combination of all the factors considered above suggests that tolerance is most likely to be seen when (1) a drug is administered frequently, (2) a range of doses is studied, (3) its initial effect results in a loss of reinforcement, and (4), more controversially, its initial effect is to suppress "highly prepared" responses. Determining how far these several factors act in additive, synergistic, or antagonistic ways provides a continuing challenge to behavioral pharmacologists.

ACKNOWLEDMENT

P. K. Corfield-Sumner's research was supported by the Mental Health Trust and Research Fund.

7. References

Appel, J. B., 1963, Aversive aspects of a schedule of positive reinforcement, *J. Exp. Anal. Behav.* **6**:423–428.

Aston, R., 1973, Mechanisms contributing to barbiturate intolerance in rats, *Brit. J. Pharmacol.* **49**:527–533.

Azrin, N. H., 1961, Timeout from positive reinforcement, *Science* **133:**382–383.

Balster, R. L., and Schuster, C. R., 1973, Fixed-interval schedule of cocaine reinforcement: effect of dose and infusion duration, *J. Exp. Anal. Behav.* **20:**119–129.

Baum, W. H., 1973, The correlation-based law of effect, *J. Exp. Anal. Behav.* **20:**137–153.

Beckett, A. H., and Triggs, E. J., 1967, Enzyme induction in man caused by smoking, *Nature* **216:**587.

Beuthin, F. C., Miya, T. S., Blake, D. E., and Bousquet, E. F., 1972, Enhanced sensitivity to noradrenergic agonists and tolerance development to α-methyltyrosine in the rat, *J. Pharmacol. Exp. Ther.* **181:**446–456.

Blackman, D. E., 1972, Conditioned anxiety and operant behavior, *in: Schedule Effects: Drugs, Drinking, and Aggression* (R. M. Gilbert and J. D. Keehn, eds.), pp. 26–49, University of Toronto Press, Toronto.

Breland, K., and Breland, M., 1961, The misbehavior of organisms, *Amer. Psychol.* **16:**681–684.

Brown, H., 1965, Drug-behavior interaction affecting development of tolerance to *d*-amphetamine as observed in fixed ratio behavior of rats, *Psychol. Rep.* **16:**917–921.

Bullock, P., Spanner, S., and Ansell, G. B., 1975, The distribution of ($Me^{-14}C$) morphine in rat brain after subcutaneous injection; paper presented at 5th International Meeting of the International Society for Neurochemistry, Barcelona, Spain. Abstracts, p. 551.

Cameron, O. G., and Appel, J. B., 1976, Drug-induced conditioned suppression: specificity due to drug employed as UCS, *Pharmacol. Biochem. Behav.* **4:**221–224.

Campbell, J. C., and Seiden, L. S., 1973, Performance influence on the development of tolerance to amphetamine, *Pharmacol. Biochem. Behav.* **1:**703–708.

Cappell, H., LeBlanc, A. E., and Herling, S., 1975, Modification of the punishing effects of psychoactive drugs in rats by previous drug experience, *J. Comp. Physiol. Psychol.* **89:**347–356.

Carder, B., and Olson, J., 1973, Learned behavioral tolerance to marihuana in rats, *Pharmacol. Biochem. Behav.* **1:**73–76.

Carlton, P. L., and Wolgin, D. L., 1971, Contingent tolerance to the anorexigenic effects of amphetamine, *Physiol. Behav.* **7:**221–223.

Carro-Ciampi, G., and Bignami, G., 1968, Effects of scopolamine on shuttle-box avoidance and go–no go discrimination: response–stimulus relationships, pretreatment baselines, and repeated exposure to drug, *Psychopharmacologia* **13:**89–105.

Catania, A. C., and Reynolds, G. S., 1968, A quantitative analysis of the responding maintained by interval schedules of reinforcement. *J. Exp. Anal. Behav.* **11:**327–383.

Chen, C., 1968, A study of the alcohol-tolerance effect and an introduction of a new behavioural technique, *Psychopharmacologia* **12:**433–440.

Chippendale, T. J., Zawolkow, G. A., Russell, R. W., and Overstreet, D. H., 1972, Tolerance to low acetylcholinesterase levels: modification of behavior without acute behavioral change, *Psychopharmacologia* **26:**127–139.

Cochin, J., and Kornetsky, C., 1964, Development and loss of tolerance to morphine in the rat after single and multiple injections, *J. Pharmacol. Exp. Ther.* **145:**1–10.

Collier, H. O. J., Francis, D. L., and Schneider, C., 1972, Modification of morphine withdrawal by drugs interacting with humoral mechanisms: some contradictions and their interpretation, *Nature* **237:**220–223.

Colpaert, F. C., Lal, H., Niemegeers, C. J. E., and Janssen, P. A. J., 1975, Investigations on drug produced and subjectively experienced discriminative stimuli. I. The fentanyl cue, a tool to investigate subjectively experienced narcotic drug actions, *Life Sci.* **16:**705–716.

Cook, L., and Sepinwall, J., 1975. Behavioral analysis of the effects and mechanisms of action of benzodiazepines, *in: Mechanism of Action of Benzodiazepines* (E. Costa and P. Greengard, eds.), pp. 1–27, Raven Press, New York.

D'Amour, F. E., and Smith, D. L., 1941, A method for assessing loss of pain sensation, *J. Pharmacol. Exp. Ther.* **72:**74–79.

Davis, W. M., and Borgen, L. A., 1975, Tolerance development to the effect of Δ^9-tetrahydrocannabinol on conditioned behaviour: role of treatment interval and influence of microsomal metabolism, *Arch. Int. Pharmacodyn.* **213:**97–112.

Deneau, G., Yanagita, T., and Seevers, M. H., 1969, Self-administration of psychoactive substances by the monkey. A measure of psychological dependence, *Psychopharmacologia* **16:**30–48.

Djahanguiri, B., Richelle, M., and Fontaine, O., 1966. Behavioral effects of a prolonged treatment with small doses of morphine in cats, *Psychopharmacologia* **9:**363–372.

D'Mello, G. D., and Stolerman, I. P., 1975, unpublished observations.

Domino, E. F., and Lutz, M. P., 1973, Tolerance to the effects of daily nicotine on rat bar pressing behavior for water reinforcement, *Pharmacol. Biochem. Behav.* **1:**445–448.

Eddy, N. B., Touchberry, C. F., and Lieberman, J. E., 1950, Synthetic analgesics. I. Methadone isomers and derivatives, *J. Pharmacol. Exp. Ther.* **98:**121–137.

Elsmore, T. F., 1976, The role of reinforcement loss in tolerance to chronic Δ^9-tetrahydrocannabinol effects on operant behavior of rhesus monkeys, *Pharmacol. Biochem. Behav.* **5:**123–128.

Falk, J. L., Samson, H. H., and Winger, G., 1972, Behavioral maintenance of high concentrations of blood ethanol and physical dependence in the rat, *Science* **177:**811–813.

Ferraro, D. P., 1972, Effects of Δ^9-*trans*-tetrahydrocannabinol on simple and complex learned behavior in animals, *in: Current Research in Marijuana* (M. F. Lewis, ed.), pp. 49–95, Academic Press, New York.

Ferraro, D. P., and Grisham, M. G., 1972, Tolerance to the behavioral effects of marihuana in chimpanzees, *Physiol. Behav.* **9:**49–54.

Fischer, J., Bunker, P., and Stolerman, I. P., 1973, unpublished results.

Fischman, M. W., and Schuster, C. R., 1974, Tolerance development to chronic methamphetamine intoxication in the rhesus monkey, *Pharmacol. Biochem. Behav.* **2:**503–508.

Ford, R. D., and McMillan, D. E., 1971, Behavioral tolerance and cross-tolerance to 1-Δ^8-tetrahydrocannabinol (Δ^8-THC) and 1-Δ^9-tetrahydrocannabinol (Δ^9-THC) in pigeons and rats, *Fed. Proc.* **30:**279.

Frederickson, R. C. A., and Smits, S. E., 1973, Time course of dependence and tolerance development in rats treated with "slow release" morphine suspensions, *Res. Commun. Chem. Pathol. Pharmacol.* **5:**867–870.

Freedman, D. X., Appel, J. B., Hartman, F. R., and Molliver, M. E., 1964, Tolerance to behavioral effects of LSD-25 in rat, *J. Pharmacol. Exp. Ther.* **143:**309–313.

Glick, S. D., and Milloy, S. M., 1972, Tolerance, state-dependency, and long-term behavioral effects of Δ^9-THC, *in: Current Research in Marijuana* (M. F. Lewis, ed.), pp. 1–24, Academic Press, New York.

Goldberg, S. R., 1971, Nalorphine: conditioning of drug effects on operant performance, *in: Stimulus Properties of Drugs* (T. Thompson and R. Pickens, eds.), pp. 51–72, Appleton-Century-Crofts, New York.

Goldberg, S. R., 1973, Comparable behavior maintained under fixed-ratio and second-order schedules of food presentation, cocaine injection, or *d*-amphetamine injection in the squirrel monkey, *J. Pharmacol. Exp. Ther.* **186:**18–30.

Goldstein, A., and Sheehan, P., 1969, Tolerance to opioid narcotics. I. Tolerance to the "running fit" caused by levorphanol in the mouse, *J. Pharmacol. Exp. Ther.* **169:**175–184.

Goldstein, A., Judson, B. A., and Sheehan, P., 1973, Cellular and metabolic tolerance to an opioid narcotic in mouse brain, *Brit. J. Pharmacol.* **47:**138–140.

Gollub, L. R., and Brady, J. V., 1965, Behavioral pharmacology, *Ann. Rev. Pharmacol.* **5:**235–262.

Goode, P. G., 1971, An implanted reservoir of morphine solution for rapid induction of physical dependence in rats, *Brit. J. Pharmacol.* **41:**558–566.

Gotestam, K. G., 1973, Intragastric self-administration of medazepam in rats, *Psychopharmacologia* **28:**87–94.

Goudie, A. J., and Thornton, E. W., 1975, Effects of drug experience on drug induced conditioned taste aversions: studies with amphetamine and fenfluramine, *Psychopharmacologia* **44:**77–82.

Goudie, A. J., Thornton, E. W., and Wheeler, T. J., 1976, Drug pretreatment effects in drug induced taste aversions; effects of dose and duration of pretreatment, *Pharmacol. Biochem. Behav.* **4:**629–633.

Gritz, E. R., and Jarvik, M. E., 1977, Nicotine and smoking, *in: Handbook of Psychopharmacology* (L. L. Iversen, S. D. Iversen, and S. H. Snyder, eds.), Vol. 11, pp. 425–464, Plenum Press, New York.

Harris, R. T., Claghorn, J. L., and Schoolar, J. C., 1968, Self-administration of minor tranquilizers as a function of conditioning, *Psychopharmacologia* **13:**81–88.

Harris, R. T., Waters, W., and McLendon, D., 1972, Behavioral effects in rhesus monkeys of repeated intravenous doses of Δ^9-tetrahydrocannabinol, *Psychopharmacologia* **26:**297–306.

Herman, Z. S., Trzeciak, H., Chrusciel, T. L., Kmieciak-Kolada, K., Drybanski, A., and Sokola, A., 1971, The influence of prolonged amphetamine treatment and amphetamine withdrawal on biogenic amine content and behavior in the rat, *Psychopharmacologia* **21:**74–81.

Herrnstein, R. S., and Hineline, P. N., 1966, Negative reinforcement as shock-frequency reduction, *J. Exp. Anal. Behav.* **9:**421–430.

Hirschorn, I. D., and Rosecrans, J. A., 1974, Morphine and Δ^9-tetrahydrocannabinol: tolerance to the stimulus effects, *Psychopharmacologia* **36:**243–253.

Hitzemann, R. J., Loh, H. H., Craves, F. B., and Domino, E. F., 1973, The use of *d*-amphetamine pellet implantation as a model for *d*-amphetamine tolerance in the mouse, *Psychopharmacologia* **30:**227–240.

Ho, I. K., 1976, Systematic assessment of tolerance to pentobarbital by pellet implantation. *J. Pharmacol. Exp. Ther.* **1976:**479–487.

Hoffmeister, F., and Wüttke, W., 1976, Psychotropic drugs as negative reinforcers, *Pharmacol. Rev.* **27:**419–428.

Holtzman, S. G., 1974, Tolerance to the stimulant effects of morphine and pentazocine on avoidance responding in the rat, *Psychopharmacologia* **39:**23–37.

Hughes, J., Smith, T., Morgan, B., and Fothergill, L., 1975, Purification and properties of enkephalin—the possible endogenous liquid for the morphine receptor, *Life Sci.* **16:**1753–1758.

Huidobro, J. P., and Huidobro, F., 1973, Acute morphine tolerance in new born and young rats, *Psychopharmacologia* **28:**27–34.

Iglauer, C., Llewellyn, M. E., and Woods, J. H., 1976, Concurrent schedules of cocaine injection in rhesus monkeys: dose variations under independent and nonindependent variable interval procedures, *Pharmacol. Rev.* **27:**367–383.

Jacquet, Y. F., 1973, Conditioned aversion during morphine maintenance in mice and rats, *Physiol. Behav.* **11:**527–541.

Jaffe, J. H., and Sharpless, S. K., 1965, The rapid development of physical dependence on barbiturates, *J. Pharmacol. Exp. Ther.* **150:**140–145.

Janků, I., 1964, The influence of delayed and immediate exposure to trials upon the effect of chlorpromazine on conditioned avoidance behaviour, *Psychopharmacologia* **6:**280–285.

Kalant, H., LeBlanc, A. E., and Gibbins, R. J., 1971, Tolerance to, and dependence on, some non-opiate psychotropic drugs, *Pharmacol. Rev.* **23:**135–191.

Kandel, D., Doyle, D., and Fischman, M. W., 1975, Tolerance and cross-tolerance to the effects of amphetamine, methamphetamine, and fenfluramine on milk consumption in the rat, *Pharmacol. Biochem. Behav.* **3:**705–707.

Kayan, S., and Mitchell, C. L., 1972, Studies on tolerance development to morphine: effect of the dose-interval on the development of single dose tolerance, *Arch. Int. Pharmacodyn.* **199:**407–414.

Kayan, S., Ferguson, R. K., and Mitchell, C. L., 1973, An investigation of pharmacologic and behavioral tolerance to morphine in rats, *J. Pharmacol. Exp. Ther.* **183:**300–306.

Keenan, A., and Johnson, F. N., 1972, Development of behavioural tolerance to nicotine in the rat, *Experientia* **28:**428–429.

Kelleher, R. T., and Goldberg, S. R., 1976, General introduction: control of drug-taking behavior by schedules of reinforcement, *Pharmacol. Rev.* **27:**291–299.

Klawans, H. L., Crosset, P., and Dana, N., 1975, Effect of chronic amphetamine exposure on stereotyped behavior: implications for pathogenesis of l-DOPA-induced dyskinesias, *in: Advances in Neurology* (D. Calne, T. N. Chase, and A. Barbeau, eds.), Vol. 9, pp. 105–112, Raven Press, New York.

Kornetsky, C., and Bain, G., 1968, Morphine: single-dose tolerance, *Science* **162:**1011–1012.

Kosersky, D. S., McMillan, D. E., and Harris, L. S., 1974, Δ^9-tetrahydrocannabinol and 11-hydroxy-Δ^9-tetrahydrocannabinol: behavioral effects and tolerance development, *J. Pharmacol. Exp. Ther.* **189:**61–65.

Kosman, M. E., and Unna, K. R., 1968, Effects of chronic administration of the amphetamines and other stimulants on behavior, *Clin. Pharmacol. Ther.* **9:**240–254.

Kumar, R., and Stolerman, I. P., 1977, Experimental and clinical aspects of drug dependence, *in: Handbook of Psychopharmacology* (L. L. Iversen, S. D. Iversen, and S. H. Snyder, eds.), Vol. 7, pp. 321–367, Plenum Press, New York.

LeBlanc, A. E., Kalant, H., Gibbins, R. J., and Berman, N. D., 1969, Acquisition and loss of tolerance to ethanol by the rat, *J. Pharmacol. Exp. Ther.* **168:**244–250.

LeBlanc, A. E., Gibbins, R. J., and Kalant, H., 1973, Behavioral augmentation of tolerance to ethanol in the rat, *Psychopharmacologia* **30:**117–122.

LeBlanc, A. E., Gibbins, R. J., and Kalant, H., 1975, Generalization of behaviorally augmented tolerance to ethanol and its relation to physical dependence, *Psychopharmacologia* **44:**241–246.

Lyon, M., and Randrup, A., 1972, The dose–response effect of amphetamine upon avoidance behavior in the rat seen as a function of increasing stereotypy, *Psychopharmacologia* **23:**334–347.

Lyon, M., and Robbins, T., 1975, The action of central nervous system stimulant drugs: a general theory concerning amphetamine effects, *in: Current Developments in Psychopharmacology* (W. Essman and L. Valzelli, eds.), Vol. 2, pp. 79–163, Spectrum, Jamaica, N.Y.

Manning, F. J., 1973, Acute tolerance to the effects of delta-9-tetrahydrocannabinol on spaced responding by monkeys, *Pharmacol. Biochem. Behav.* **1:**665–671.

Manning, F. J., 1976, Chronic delta-9-tetrahydrocannabinol. Transient and lasting effects on avoidance behavior, *Pharmacol. Biochem. Behav.* **4:**17–21.

Margules, D. L., and Stein, L., 1968, Increase of "antianxiety" activity and tolerance of behavioral depression during chronic administration of oxazepam, *Psychopharmacologia* **13:**74–80.

McMillan, D. E.., and Morse, W. H., 1967, Some effects of morphine and morphine antagonists on schedule-controlled behavior, *J. Pharmacol. Exp. Ther.* **157:**175–184.

Mercier, J., and Dessaigne, S., 1959, Détermination de l'accoutumance expérimentale par une méthode psycho-physiologique (III. Mémoire). Étude de quelques médicaments psychotoniques, *Ann. Pharm. Franc.* **17:**606–615.

Minkowsky, W. L., 1939, The effect of benzedrine sulphate upon learning, *J. Comp. Psychol.* **28:**349–360.

Misra, A. L., Mulé, S. J., Bloch, R., and Vadlamani, N. L., 1973, Physiological disposition and metabolism of levo-methadone-1-^{3}H in nontolerant and tolerant rats, *J. Pharmacol. Exp. Ther.* **185:**287–299.

Mitchard, M., Kumar, R., Salmon, J. A., and Shenoy, E. V. B., 1970, Plasma levels and excretion rates of amphetamine in a dexamphetamine tolerant man, *Exerpta Medica Int. Cong. Series* No. 220, 72–77.

Moore, K. E., and Thornburg, J. E., 1975, Drug-induced dopaminergic supersensitivity, *in: Advances in Neurology* (D. Calne, T. N. Chase, and A. Barbeau, eds.), Vol. 9, pp. 93–104, Raven Press, New York.

Morrison, C. F., and Stephenson, J. A., 1972, The occurrence of tolerance to a central depressant effect of nicotine, *Brit. J. Pharmacol.* **46:**151–156.

Nozaki, M., Akera, T., Lee, C. Y., and Brody, T. M., 1975, The effects of age on the development of tolerance to and physical dependence on morphine in rats, *J. Pharmacol. Exp. Ther.* **192:**506–512.

Pieper, W. A., and Skeen, M. J., 1973, Development of functional tolerance to ethanol in rhesus monkeys (*Macaca mulatta*), *Pharmacol. Biochem. Behav.* **1:**289–294.

Pirch, J. H., Osterholm, K. C., Barratt, E. S., and Cohn, R. A., 1972, Marijuana enhancement of shuttle-box avoidance performance in rats, *Proc. Soc. Exp. Biol. Med.* **141:**590–592.

Post, R. M., and Kopanda, R. T., 1976, Cocaine, kindling, and psychosis, *Amer. J. Psychiat.* **133:**627–634.

Remmer, H., 1969, Tolerance to barbiturates by increased breakdown, *in: Scientific Basis of Drug Dependence* (H. Steinberg, ed.), pp. 111–128, Churchill, London.

Revusky, S., and Garcia, J., 1970, Learned associations over long delays, *in: The Psychology of Learning and Motivation* (G. H. Bower, ed.), Vol. 4, pp. 1–84, Academic Press, New York.

Revusky, S., and Taukulis, M., 1975, Effects of alcohol and lithium habituation on the development of alcohol aversions through contingent lithium injection, *Behav. Res. Ther.* **13:**163–166.

Roffman, M., and Lal, H., 1974, Stimulus control of hexobarbital narcosis and metabolism in mice, *J. Pharmacol. Exp. Ther.* **191:**358–369.

Sanger, D. J., and Blackman, D. E., 1976, Rate-dependent effects of drugs: a review of the literature, *Pharmacol. Biochem. Behav.* **4:**73–83.

Schechter, M. D., and Rosecrans, J. A., 1972, Behavioral tolerance to an effect of nicotine in the rat, *Arch. Int. Pharmacodyn.* **195:**52–56.

Schuster, C. R., and Zimmerman, J., 1961, Timing behavior during prolonged treatment with *dl*-amphetamine, *J. Exp. Anal. Behav.* **4:**327–330.

Schuster, C. R., Dockens, W. S., and Woods, J. H., 1966, Behavioral variables affecting the development of amphetamine tolerance, *Psychopharmacologia* **9:**170–182.

Seevers, M. H., and Deneau, G. A., 1963, Physiological aspects of tolerance and physical dependence, *in: Physiological Pharmacology* (W. S. Root and F. G. Hofmann, eds.), Vol. 1, pp. 565–640, Academic Press, London.

Segal, D. S., and Mandell, A. J., 1974, Long-term administration of *d*-amphetamine: progressive augmentation of motor activity and stereotypy, *Pharmacol. Biochem. Behav.* **2:**249–255.

Seligman, M. E. P., and Hager, J. L., 1972, *Biological Boundaries of Learning,* p. 4, Appleton-Century-Crofts, New York.

Sever, P. S., Caldwell, J., Dring, L. G., and Williams, R. T., 1973, The metabolism of amphetamine in dependent subjects, *Eur. J. Pharmacol.* **6:**177–180.

Shuster, L., Webster, G. W., and Yu, G., 1975, Increased running response to morphine in morphine-pretreated mice, *J. Pharmacol. Exp. Ther.* **192:**64–72.

Siegel, S., 1975, Evidence from rats that morphine tolerance is a learned response, *J. Comp. Physiol. Psychol.* **89:**498–506.

Smith, S. G., Werner, T. E., and Davis, W. M., 1975, Technique for intragastric delivery of solutions: application for self-administration of morphine and alcohol by rats, *Physiol. Psychol.* **3:**220–224.

Smith, S. G., Werner, T. E., and Davis, W. M., 1976, Effects of tolerance on intravenous morphine self-administration behavior, *Physiol. Psychol.* **4:**97–98.

Sodetz, F. J., 1972, Δ^9-Tetrahydrocannabinol: behavioral toxicity in laboratory animals, *in: Current Research in Marijuana* (M. F. Lewis, ed.), pp. 25–48, Academic Press, New York.

Stolerman, I. P., and Kumar, R., 1970, Preferences for morphine in rats: validation of an experimental model of dependence, *Psychopharmacologia* **17:**137–150.

Stolerman, I. P., Fink, R., and Jarvik, M. E., 1973, Acute and chronic tolerance to nicotine measured by activity in rats, *Psychopharmacologia* **30:**329–342.

Stolerman, I. P., Bunker, P., and Jarvik, M. E., 1974, Nicotine tolerance in rats: role of dose and dose interval, *Psychopharmacologia* **34:**317–324.

Tarsy, D., and Baldessarini, R. J., 1974, Behavioral supersensitivity to apomorphine following chronic treatment with drugs which interfere with the synaptic function of catecholamines, *Neuropharmacology* **13:**927–940.

Thompson, D. M., 1974, Repeated acquisition of behavioral chains under chronic drug conditions, *J. Pharmacol. Exp. Ther.* **188:**700–713.

Tilson, H. A., and Rech, R. H., 1973a, Prior drug experience and effects of amphetamine on schedule-controlled behavior, *Pharmacol. Biochem. Behav.* **1:**129–132.

Tilson, H. A., and Rech, R. H., 1973b, Conditioned drug effects and absence of tolerance to *d*-amphetamine induced motor activity, *Pharmacol. Biochem. Behav.* **1:**149–153.

Tilson, H. A., and Sparber, S. B., 1973, The effects of *d*- and *l*-amphetamine on fixed-interval and fixed-ratio behavior in tolerant and nontolerant rats, *J. Pharmacol. Exp. Ther.* **187:**372–379.

Turner, D. M., 1971, Metabolism of small multiple doses of (^{14}C)-nicotine in the cat, *Brit. J. Pharmacol.* **41:**521–529.

Wahlström, G., 1968, Differences in tolerance to hexobarbital (enhexymalum NFN) after barbital (diemalum NFN) pre-treatment during activity or rest, *Acta. Pharmacol. Toxicol.* **26:**92–104.

Way, E. L., Loh, H. H., and Shen, F.-H., 1969, Simultaneous quantitative assessment of morphine tolerance and physical dependence, *J. Pharmacol. Exp. Ther.* **167:**1–8.

Weeks, J. R., and Collins, R. J., 1964, Factors affecting voluntary morphine intake in self-maintained addicted rats, *Psychopharmacologia* **6:**267–279.

Woolfe, G., and MacDonald, A. D., 1944, The evaluation of the analgesic action of pethidine hydrochloride (Demerol), *J. Pharmacol. Exp. Ther.* **80:**300–307.

Yanagita, T., and Takahashi, S., 1970, Development of tolerance to and physical dependence on barbiturates in rhesus monkeys, *J. Pharmacol. Exp. Ther.* **172:**163–169.

York, J. L., and Winter, J. C., 1975, Assessment of tolerance to barbital by means of drug discrimination procedures, *Psychopharmacologia* **42:**283–287.

Behavioral Toxicology 9

Hugh L. Evans and Bernard Weiss

1. Introduction

1.1. What Is Toxicology?

Toxicology is the science of poisons, encompassing agents as diverse as environmental pollutants, drugs, venoms, food additives, and numerous other chemicals. Many of these substances have been known since antiquity. Traditional toxicology emphasized lethality or morphologic change. It played an important role as an adjunct to the legal profession, as well as in screening for undesirable effects of pharmaceutical and industrial products. The last few decades have witnessed an increasing number of uses for a growing number of chemicals, a development accompanied by an increased appreciation of their pervasiveness and frightening examples of their deleterious effects upon biologic systems. Thousands of potential new chemical products, moreover, are formulated annually.

Environmental chemicals pose a greater potential threat to health than do drugs, because large numbers of people may be exposed to chemicals that linger in the environment for many years. Forty years of use was required before the polychlorinated biphenyls (PCBs) were recognized as enduring environmental poisons. By that time, thousands of tons of these materials had been released into the ecosphere. Environmental agents are now suspected of being a leading cause of cancer. In the United Sates, this awareness led to the enactment of the

Hugh L. Evans and Bernard Weiss • Environmental Health Sciences Center, Department of Radiation Biology and Biophysics, School of Medicine and Dentistry, University of Rochester, Rochester, New York 14642. Dr. Evans' present address is: Institute of Environmental Medicine, New York University Medical Center, New York, New York 10016

1976 Toxic Substances Control Act, under which chemicals may require testing before coming to market. Some of these chemicals will act on the central nervous system, others may produce behavioral effects less directly. A major function of behavioral toxicology is the prediction and evaluation of such effects.

Behavioral toxicology exemplifies how society now is demanding answers to new kinds of questions, requiring new approaches in toxicology. Regulatory agencies are being asked to make decisions about environmental quality and health risks, guided only by overt morphologic and morbidity data. Few rigorous animal models are available to substantiate the kind of human symptoms and functional changes that occur with low-level exposures. It is here that behavioral studies in toxicology hold the greatest promise.

1.2. Origins of Behavioral Toxicology

Although the developments in toxicology described above provided the thrust for the recent emergence of behavioral toxicology, the new discipline's early characteristics and rapid growth drew upon the strengths of several more traditional disciplines. Among these are environmental medicine and industrial hygiene, long concerned with environmental contaminants (e.g., Hunter, 1975; Zenz, 1975). From this tradition comes an orientation toward clinical and field studies, characterized by an emphasis on brief and simple tests that sometimes involve behavioral measures (e.g., Neal *et al.*, 1941; Hunter *et al.*, 1940). Another facet of behavioral toxicology originated in neuropsychology, where behavioral techniques are employed to assess brain function and to determine the consequences of brain lesions (e.g., Lashley, 1929; Chow, 1967). We have drawn upon these two traditions in launching much of our own behavioral research in toxicology (Evans *et al.*, 1975; Wood *et al.*, 1973).

The deepest roots of behavioral toxicology lie in behavioral pharmacology, which exemplifies our own background and the antecedent area probably most familiar to readers of this chapter. Behavioral pharmacology, whose development parallels the proliferation of central nervous system drugs, provides the most refined and advanced techniques for experimental analyses of chemically modified behavior.

In defining its tasks, behavioral toxicology can profit from lessons learned in behavioral pharmacology. The experimental end point should be behavioral changes with sublethal doses. Unlike traditional toxicology, behavioral toxicology does not employ death or severe illness as the end point because severely intoxicated animals do not provide an interesting or useful behavioral preparation.

With selected examples reflecting the breadth of the literature from behavioral toxicology, we hope to provide an understanding of the similarities and differences between the two disciplines. We then examine some general principles and unsolved problems. Additional topics were reviewed recently from another perspective (Bignami, 1976).

2. Distinguishing Features of Behavioral Toxicology

As a starting point, it is useful to indicate some similarities between pharmacology and toxicology. Many advances in pharmacology have involved the identification of poisons such as tetrodotoxin (Blankenship, 1976). Current examples in behavioral pharmacology include 6-hydroxydopamine, apomorphine, and parachlorinated amphetamines. The value of these toxins lies in their ability to interfere with neurochemical processes as well as markedly to disrupt ongoing behavior (e.g., Schoenfeld and Uretsky, 1973; Harvey *et al.*, 1975).

Our interest in the behavioral and environmental variables influencing the effects of α-methyltyrosine was responsible, in part, for our early involvement in behavioral toxicology (Weiss and Laties, 1969; Evans, 1971a). Detailed behavioral tests revealed situations which determined whether α-methyltyrosine would function as an antagonist or as an agonist of the behavioral effects of methamphetamine (Evans *et al.*, 1973).

In these examples, behavioral toxicology blends into the framework of behavioral pharmacology. The most common distinction between the two disciplines arises from the type of compound studied (environmental contaminants versus drugs and neurochemical tools). The substances of concern in toxicology impose some new characteristics which provide important distinctions between behavioral toxicology and pharmacology. These are summarized below.

2.1. Qualitative Evaluation of Effects

Quantitative evaluation is essential in toxicology, as elsewhere. Toxicology also emphasizes qualitative evaluation. Western toxicologists make a qualitative distinction between a "change" and a "toxic effect" (i.e., a true impairment of some function). The distinction implies understanding of basic mechanisms of action, an important principle to be illustrated below. Basic researchers in behavioral pharmacology were seldom expected to make this discrimination. The contributions to this volume illustrate superbly that many drugs can change the rate or probability of some behavior, depending on the details of the test situation. Since changes in "spontaneous" locomotor activity or operant response rates are difficult to relate to any specific mechanisms, rate changes alone are unlikely to define a toxic effect in the sense of greatest concern in making health decisions. Measures such as these do play an important role, however, in toxicity screening, as discussed near the end of this chapter.

The distinction between a toxic effect and a possible adaptive change requires new experimental procedures. For example, new behavioral tests were required to measure and define tremor, a distinct toxic effect of mercury vapor, an industrial pollutant (Wood *et al.*, 1973). Similarly, further understanding of familiar psychoactive drugs requires greater specification of their effects, including toxic effects. New, unconventional techniques are required to demonstrate unambiguously such toxic effects as dyskinesias caused by neuroleptics or methamphetamine (Weiss, 1975; Fischman and Schuster, 1975; Eibergen and Carlson, 1975). Such movement disorders impose severe limits upon the extent and utility of chemotherapy in psychiatry. They are expecially vexing when they appear late in treatment, since by that time irreversible or at least remarkably persistent neurochemical changes may have occurred. So far, an applicable methodology for primate studies remains to be developed.

2.2. Role of Threshold Estimates

The importance of threshold determinations in toxicology is attributable to the nature of the background information used in setting exposure standards. The validity of extrapolations to lower "no-effect" doses is currently an important question (e.g., Dinman, 1972). Although the behavioral pharmacologist may focus upon "big effects," the behavioral toxicologist is charged with determining the least noticeable effects, a much more difficult challenge. Pharmacologists do not consider it a deficiency of rodent studies that the dose of amphetamine required to affect behavior is much larger, on a mg/kg basis, than the effective dose in humans, as long as rodent studies illuminate mechanisms of action. Toxicologists also welcome whatever the rat can reveal about toxic mechanisms because, once mechanisms are understood, extrapolations can be made to other animal species more rationally. The burden of extrapolation, however, falls more heavily and immediately on the toxicologist.

Toxicologists commonly employ large populations of animals to define a threshold dose as that which produces toxic signs in a small proportion, say 1–10%, of the population. Since it seldom will be practical to conduct behavioral tests with large populations, the behavioral toxicologist must explore alternative strategies in probing for thresholds. Two possibilities will be discussed later: employing chronic, rather than acute exposure, and manipulating fundamental behavioral variables that may modulate the behavioral effects of toxins. An additional possibility is to exploit unique characteristics of certain animal species, such as the visual and auditory capabilities of nonhuman primates and the gustatory sensitivity of the rat.

Primates seem to provide a more sensitive assay than rodents for threshold estimates with many neurotoxins (Evans *et al.*, 1975; Evans *et al.*, 1977; Hardman *et al.*, 1973). Three general factors could logically contribute to the primate's greater sensitivity. First, there are many instances in which large animals metabolize drugs more slowly than smaller animals (Burns, 1970). Second, the primate's brain represents a greater proportion of total body mass than the rodent's (Radinsky, 1975), and thus represents a larger reservoir for chemicals with an affinity for neurons. Third, the primate provides a more elaborate behavioral repertoire for study than the rodent. To some extent, the behavioral scientist has some control over this factor. Obviously, language facilitates the identification of subtle and subjective symptoms of mild intoxication in humans. We suspect that the astute behavioral scientist could arrange ways for animals to reveal equally subtle effects, in spite of the obvious language limitations. Perhaps the most progress has occurred in animal experiments evaluating sensory impairment, where several examples indicate that animals can be trained to report their sensory capabilities as precisely and reliably as humans (Stebbins, 1970; Stebbins and Coombs, 1975; Evans, 1977).

Another intriguing possibility for obtaining objective reports of mild intoxication can be found in the phenomenon labeled as conditioned aversion. In the prototype situation, a rat, whose preference for say, saccharin-flavored, rather than plain, tap water has been established, is allowed to drink saccharin while exposed to a toxin (Garcia *et al.*, 1974). A typical effect is a reduction in saccharin preference, presumably because toxic signs have become associated with the distinctive taste of saccharin.

The search for threshold or near-threshold doses introduces a new problem: weak and variable results. Apparent toxic effects may wax and wane before becoming clear (e.g., Berlin *et al.*, 1975) or may disappear when replication is attempted (e.g., Golter and Michaelson, 1975). Several approaches are available to remedy this problem. The most obvious is to determine the full dose–effect function. This provides the basis for deciding whether the weak effects, seen after the administration of a low dose, represent the logical extrapolation of the clear effects determined with higher doses.

Well-known reference compounds can be employed to calibrate the behavioral task and to demonstrate its reliability and specificity before beginning to assess a poorly understood toxin. For example, scopolamine was used to validate a visual discrimination test later employed with methylmercury (Evans, 1975; Evans *et al.*, 1975). Chlorpromazine provided a reference for the behavioral effects of carbon monoxide (Johnson *et al.*, 1975). The use of reference substances is discussed by Horváth and Frantík (1973) and by Laties (1973).

A common effect of near-threshold doses may be an increase in the variability of behavior. Squirrel monkeys exposed chronically to parathion showed no change in auditory threshold, but displayed increased variability in threshold estimates during the exposure (Reischl *et al.* 1975). In dealing with threshold effects, it may be advisable to examine each animal's data separately instead of combining results, because of individual differences in base-line or characteristic response to the toxin. Soviet toxicologists have recognized these differences, which they describe in terms of response typology (e.g., Medved *et al.*, 1964; Trakhtenberg, 1974).

2.3. Chronicity Factor

Central nervous system drugs tend to be metabolized rapidly so that their acute effects often can be studied within an hour's test. In contrast, many of the substances of interest in behavioral toxicology are characterized by much slower uptake and elimination from the body. For example, methylmercury reaches its peak concentration in brain more than 5 days after administration. The half-time of elimination of heavy metals from the human body is measured in weeks, not hours. These facts account for both the vital importance of threshold determinations and the need for long-term studies of behavior. Daily exposure to small doses of a toxin, doses well below the threshold for producing any observable acute effect, may result in a gradual accumulation according to the well-known principles of pharmacokinetics. After a year, or a decade, concentrations of the toxin may reach critical levels in the target organs.

The chronicity factor incorporates a problem even more difficult than that of gradual accumulation, however. The best illustrations are found in the toxicity of carcinogens (Druckery, 1967). Even when a toxin is not accumulating in the body, the probability of toxic signs increases as a function of exposure duration, or the time for which the toxin is resident in the critical organ. Using behavioral changes as the end point, we have been accumulating evidence for a chronicity factor in the neurotoxicity of methylmercury (Evans *et al.*, 1977). For example, as seen in Figure 1, low concentrations of mercury in the blood induced impairment only after exposure had continued for several months (Evans *et al.*, 1975; Evans, 1977). It is clear that threshold estimates based upon acute or short-term exposure may be an order of magnitude higher than estimates based upon chronic, low-level exposures. Our work with haloperidol-induced dyskinesias provides another example (see below).

The chronicity factor is limited, in the case of carcinogens, only by the normal life expectancy of the organism (Druckery, 1967). It will be difficult to determine, for the many CNS toxins, if results with short-lived animals, such a rodents, can reveal the ultimate outcome of chronic exposure in long-lived animals such as primates. The interaction between toxins and other aspects of the aging process becomes important, therefore, (Weiss and Simon, 1975).

This interaction may be illustrated by Figures 2 and 3. The heavy line in Figure 2 represents the conclusions postulated by Kety (1956) after a review of the then-extant data on brain function and aging. Kety estimated that the brain suffers perhaps a 20% decline in functional capacity (as defined by the parameters of O_2 uptake, glucose consumption, and neuronal cell density) between early adulthood and old age. The lighter lines (Weiss and Simon, 1975) indicate the progress of functional decline assuming that the rates, say, of cell loss have been increased by exposure to a CNS toxin.

Figure 3 is a clearer extrapolation of the consequences. Even an additional decrement as minute (and undetectable) as 0.1% per year is significant when compounded over 40-year period. The relationships shown in the graphs suggest how at chronological age 65, the brain of an exposed individual could resemble that of a "normal" 73-year-old.

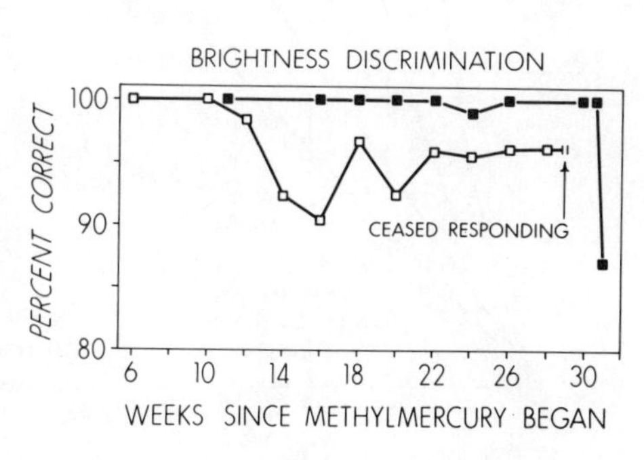

Figure 1. Selective impairment of sensitivity to stimuli of low luminance during a long-term exposure to methylmercury. Data are from the same monkey as is shown in Evans *et al.* (1975). Note the decline in detection of a dim light (open squares = $10^{-3.5}$ mLambert) after the tenth week of exposure, while detection of a bright light (filled squares) did not decline until after the thirtieth week of exposure. Blood mercury levels remained fairly constant after the fourth week.

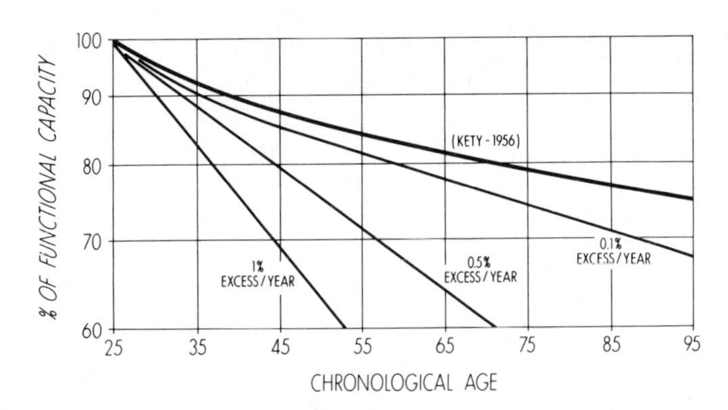

Figure 2. Extrapolations from function proposed by Kety (1956) to depict brain aging. Additional decrements in functional capacity of 0.1, 0.5, and 1% per year are shown. The base-line age is 25 years. [From Weiss and Simon (1975).]

Whether these consequences occur in nature, and whether they are significant for function is not determined, yet we do know that performance decrements occur with advancing age. Exposures to many environmental toxins may begin with conception, but not exert their most profound actions until later in the life span. Examples can be found in the work of Spyker (1975a,b).

Time-course determinations also assume special importance in behavioral toxicology because of the need for early-warning indicators of intoxication. Many CNS toxins, such as methylmercury, produce irre-

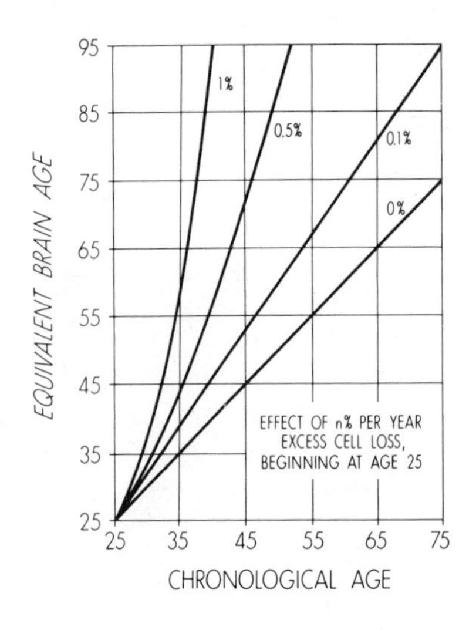

Figure 3. Equivalent brain age resulting from "normal" aging (0%) or from an accelerated cell loss of 0.1, 0.5, and 1% per year from age 25 to specified chronological age. [From Weiss and Simon (1975).]

versible impairment. Early recognition and remedial action is the only way to prevent the impairment from progressing to the more severe stages. Intoxications, in their earliest stages in humans, are heralded by the appearance of clinically covert, often vague, and subjective psychological symptoms; if they could be defined and precisely measured, steps could be taken to halt the possible progression to more severe and irreversible damage.

For the preceding reasons, behavioral toxicology needs to consider time–effect functions in addition to the traditional dose–effect relationship. The long-term, repeated observation procedures of operant conditioning seem to be among the best suited to chronic studies.

2.4. Complications Associated with Chronic Studies

Chronic studies present new problems seldom encountered in behavioral pharmacology. We will indicate several problems likely to occur in behavioral studies and refer the reader to the review of additional general considerations (Barnes and Denz, 1954).

The method of administration of a toxin may be harmful if repeated over a prolonged period of time. For example, our laboratory found no acute effects of oral administration of the vehicle used to prepare the methylmercury solution; however, the same vehicle preparation produced clear effects in some birds after chronic administration. This probably reflected a cumulative gastrointestinal irritation. Separating local from CNS effects has created problems elsewhere in behavioral toxicology (e.g., Snowdon, 1973; Evans *et al.*, 1975).

How should one report the dose in chronic exposures? Although the daily amount administered to each animal must be reported, some other datum may permit a more intelligible analysis of the results. The sum of the daily doses may relate poorly to chronic effects or to results from acute studies. Blood or brain concentrations of the toxin may more adequately reflect the complex processes of accumulation, metabolism and elimination which determine the "effective dose" at the target organ.

A cogent example is provided by Bushnell *et al.* (1977), who employed a daily mg/kg dose which produced blood lead concentrations which overshot target levels by two-to threefold margins. Adjusting the daily dose allowed blood levels to decline to the target range over a 6-week period. Since the exposure continued for 1 year, the mean of the weekly blood concentrations was close to the intended target. But is the mean of the severely skewed distribution of weekly blood concentrations a good index of "dose"? The critical fact may be the *peak* blood concentration rather than the *average* concentration.

What should be done about growth, that is, increases in body weight? Should the amount administered be increased so as to maintain a constant mg/kg proportion, or a constant relation to body surface area, or should it remain the same, since the target organ, the brain, is probably no longer increasing in mass or cell number throughout adulthood? Since effects of acute exposure can vary with age (e.g., Lin *et al.*, 1975; Benke and Murphy, 1975; Harbison, 1975; Lu *et al.*, 1965), effects may also vary as chronic exposure proceeds through different stages of the life span.

A further feature of chronicity that demands consideration is the transformation of the response that may occur with time. Base-line behavior may drift, particularly in long-term studies with repeated measurement (e.g., Cumming and Schoenfeld, 1958). This base-line drift can complicate the interpretation of behavioral results, particularly if an insufficient number of control animals are tested concurrently with the experimental animals (for further examples, see Evans *et al.*, 1975). Moreover, changes in sensitivity to the toxin may result from repeated or extended exposure. The initial effect may fade after prolonged exposure because of decreased sensitivity (tolerance, e.g., Bignami *et al.*, 1975). Increased sensitivity (anaphylaxis) or even more complex transformations, qualitative in nature, may occur.

The movement disorders produced by major tranquilizers such as haloperidol provide an immediate example from behavioral pharmacology. Early in therapy, many patients display signs that closely resemble Parkinsonism. These fade either spontaneously with continued treatment, or after reduction in dose. The tardive or persistent dyskinesias erupt after a prolonged treatment period, usually years. They seem virtually irreversible and may exacerbate upon reduction of dose or even upon cessation of therapy (e.g., Crane, 1968).

An attempt with a cebus monkey (*C. albifrons*) to reproduce such a syndrome in a laboratory primate provides a cogent example of the chronicity problem (Weiss, 1975). For the first 6 months of treatment (0.5 mg/kg/day of haloperidol, given in fruit juice), the typical pattern of response was sedation, deepest at 2–4 hr after dosing. After about 180 days of this treatment, episodes of violent movement occurred regularly following each dose. The monkey flung herself about the cage, crashing into the walls, sometimes somersaulting, sometimes gripping the perch while her legs thrust rhythmically back and forth in a pumping motion. This pattern continued until haloperidol administration ceased, 6 months later.

Such a qualitative transformation in response after prolonged treatment sharply exemplifies the danger, and perhaps the futility, of extrapolating from acute to chronic effects. Unfortunately, many of the questions posed by toxicology and environmental health are framed in a chronic context.

Another problem with long-term experiments is that they provide infrequent feedback (reinforcement) for the experimenter. This increases the risk that such studies will be neglected on a day-to-day basis, with small errors multiplied when extended over a long time. A recent example is the bungled studies of FD&C Red No. 2 (Boffey, 1976).

2.5. Multidisciplinary Features

Screening techniques in behavioral toxicology, as in behavioral pharmacology, can be empirical and purely phenomenological. Any treatment that causes "illness" is likely to disrupt the coordinated functioning of the nervous systems, and thus be reflected in a behavioral change. But to progress beyond the screening stage, we need to identify mechanisms both at the behavioral and biological levels of analysis. Extrapolation required to establish generality to other species, notably humans, is facilitated if the behavioral results are presented in a broader context, accompanied by pathology, tissue, and blood chemical determinations (e.g., Garman *et al.*, 1975; Evans *et al.*, 1977).

Chemical determinations assume great importance in chronic studies, where the most informative index of exposure may not be cumulative dose, but the peak concentration in the blood, the concentration of a metabolite, or another index of body burden.

Substances of interest in behavioral toxicology may be administered by routes of exposure seldom employed with CNS drugs: inhalation or ingestion of substances added to food or water may require collaboration with specialists in inhalation-chamber design, respiratory physiologists, nutritionists, and representatives from still other fields novel to behavioral pharmacology.

3. Behavioral Toxicology in the Soviet Union

Behavioral toxicology has occupied a central position in environmental health studies in the USSR for much longer than in Western countries. Part of the reason is the immense influence of Sechenov and Pavlov on Soviet physiology. Soviet programs in toxicology were likely to reflect their emphasis on the nervous system as the key system in physiology. In contrast, Western toxicologists seldom had contact with behavior because behavioral evaluations flowed in the currents of psychology.

Soviet authors contributed much to the notion that behavioral methods can be more sensitive to subtle effects of toxins than other traditional toxicologic end points. This conclusion occurs in reviews by Medved *et al.* (1964); Trakhtenberg (1974); Fitzpatrick (1974); and Pavelenko (1975). Unfortunately, few of the primary Russian research reports are available in English. Those described in the reviews and working documents seldom contain the details of methods and results to which Western scientists are accustomed. Scarcity of detail, coupled with the unfamiliar vocabulary, presents a formidable barrier to the rigorous appraisal of Soviet behavioral toxicology.

Methods for testing CNS toxicity described by Pavelenko (1975) seem similar to those employed elsewhere. Simple tests of unconditioned responses constitute the initial screening stage. Tests of conditioned reflexes involving defense (shock), alimentary (food), and the induction processes (acquisition or learning) occur later. One of the more advanced approaches is the "functional stress test," which uses CNS drugs as well as behavioral stress manipulations as probes for latent (subthreshold) effects. These stress manipulations are suggestive of those we describe below in terms of strength of stimulus and schedule control of behavior.

Both Medved *et al.* (1964) and Trakhtenberg (1974) offer conclusions which resemble our conclusion that behavior under control of a "weak" stimulus is more easily disrupted by toxic challenges than behavior under control of a "strong" stimulus (see below; Laties, 1975; Evans, 1975).

Medved *et al.* (1964) also cite the selective sensitivity of "freshly produced" conditioned reflexes. This most likely corresponds with the concept, in our vocabulary, of the selective sensitivity of behavior under weak schedule control, particularly newly acquired behavior, which may be especially sensitive to brain lesions (Ohrbach and Fantz, 1958) as well as to drugs (e.g., McGaugh and Petrinovich, 1965).

Trakhtenberg cites some startling findings, apparently not published in the archival scientific literature, which indicate a disruption of "higher nervous activity" by concentrations of mercury vapor 1/10 of the threshold limit value (the concentration above which adverse effects appear prevalent in Western countries). These disruptions accompany brain mercury concentrations that are approximately 1/10 of the brain concentration usually associated with mercury intoxication (Berlin *et al.*, 1969; Evans *et al.*, 1977). This illustrates an important distinction between the Soviets, who consider any change in physiological variables to be a toxic effect, and Western toxicologists, who distinguish between adaptive and deleterious changes.

The importance placed on results from individual organisms is indicated by sample data showing that 1.0 mg/kg of the pesticide mercaptophos produced a behavioral change in cats of "the unbalanced type," while cats of the "balanced type" were unaffected (Medved *et al.*, 1964). However, these feline personality types are not further defined, and both types of cats appear to have similar preexposure behavioral base lines. These authors conclude that, at least for pesticides, the earliest change in higher nervous activity "is an increase in the process of internal inhibition (differentiation and extinction)" and that tests of conditioned reflexes have resulted in Soviet tolerance limits for pesticides that are below those of the United States.

A representative behavioral experiment in English translation is that of Grigor'cv (1955). It employed a color discrimination, based upon a simple appetitive response in rats, to assess toxic effects of gasoline vapors. The responses consisted of running across a cage to a feeder in the presence of the stimulus signaling availability of food (S^D) or to refrain from running in the presence of the stimulus signaling nonavailability of food (S^Δ). Initially, a red light was the S^D and a white light the S^Δ. After rats learned the red–white discrimination, running to the red light was extinguished (no longer reinforced with food). When the rats no longer ran to either light, the original conditions were reversed so the white light now was the S^D and the red light the S^Δ. Rats with this experimental history were exposed to gasoline vapor. Low concentrations (0.25 mg/liter) caused "a slight increase in the latent period of response and of the reaction time." We interpret that to mean that the rats were slower to turn toward the feeder upon the appearance of the S^D, and also were slower to run to the food and to begin eating in the presence of the S^D. With higher concentrations of vapor (0.5 mg/liter), in additon to the preceding phenomena, "differentiation inhibition made its appearance." We interpret this to mean that the rats responded slowly to both S^D and S^Δ where they had responded slowly only to S^Δ under control conditions.

4. Substances of Current Interest

4.1. Mercury

We recently reviewed the behavioral effects of the various mercurial compounds (Evans *et al.*, 1975). The two substances of greatest interest are mercury vapor and methylmercury, because of their greater effectiveness in penetrating the central nervous system.

Methylmercury continues to stimulate the most behavioral research. Recent developments include evidence of important species differences in neurotoxicity, demonstrating the primate's greater prevalence of sensory impairment and the relationship of this finding to pharmacokinetic mechanisms (Evans, 1977; Evans *et al.*, 1977; Berthoud *et al.*, 1976). Methylmercury provides a clear example of the rodent's limitations as an experimental model for estimating human toxicity in terms of the profile of behavioral signs, effective dose, and the chronicity factor. Manipulations of visual discrimination parameters indicate that in the primate, methylmercury exerts a selective, irreversible damage to visual cortex, expressed as reduced sensitivity to dim stimuli (Evans *et al.*, 1975; Berlin *et al.*, 1975; Garman *et al.*, 1975). These visual studies are discussed more fully below, in considering strength of controlling stimuli as a modulator of behavioral toxicity. Advanced behavioral techniques, particularly when coupled with chronic exposure, are reducing the methylmercury dose that can be shown effective in animals (e.g., Evans, 1977; Evans *et al.*, 1977).

4.2. Lead

Lead has long been known to produce behavioral and neural signs of toxicity. Benjamin Franklin at one time became intrigued by lead poisoning (Franklin, 1786). In the last few years, lead has reemerged as a topic of lively interest. Renewed interest stems, in part, from demonstrations that young mammals appear more susceptible to lead's neurotoxic actions. Young organisms absorb a greater percentage of lead, and accumulate more of it in soft tissue and less in bone; furthermore, the developing brain appears to be more susceptible to lead than the mature brain (National Academy of Sciences, 1972; Lin-Fu, 1973).

Animal research has pursued the suggestion that mild lead intoxication causes hyperactivity and mental impairment in children (David *et al.*, 1972, 1976; Lin-Fu, 1973). Animal data are definitely needed; firm evidence of behavioral impairment in humans exposed to low blood levels of lead (40 μg%) has eluded numerous efforts, partly because of the limitations of current clinical tests with young children (Barocas and Weiss, 1974), and confounding variables such as socioeconomic status, cultural background, and health and nutritional status, which tend to covary with blood lead concentration (Klein *et al.*, 1974; Zielhuis, 1975).

Most experiments on lead-induced impairment of learning have employed discrete-trial discriminations with rats that require a locomotor response. Early negative results with simple, two-choice spatial discrimination learning suggest a limited utility of that situation, since treated rats showed clear effects in other tests: a reduction in the rate of previously trained bar pressing (Avery *et al.*, 1974), or noticeable impairment of swimming ability, and even death (Brown *et al.*, 1971). A multiple-choice spatial discrimination maze likewise failed to reveal effects of lead in doses sufficient to produce overt toxic signs and sometimes death in rats exposed as weanlings or as adults (Snowdon, 1973). The latter suggested that age may be an important determinant, since the same discrimination test revealed increased errors in rats nursed by lead-treated mothers. However, the number of trials required to reach the learning criterion was not affected. The increased number of errors was not accompanied by an increased running time, so that an increase in running speed, although unreported, probably occurred. However, it is difficult to determine whether the results reflect different doses received at different ages or a true critical period for lead intoxication.

Positive findings are yielded by more recent studies of the acquisition of two-choice visual discrimination following prenatal or neonatal exposures. Carson *et al.* (1974) identified difficulty of a visual discrimination, reflected by the number of trials required for control animals to learn the discrimination, as a determinant of degree of learning impairment. The subjects were lambs, tested following prenatal lead exposure.

Brown's report (1975) of a critical period in the rat for lead-induced learning impairment is especially provocative because the maximal blood lead concentrations fell below those reported for animal experiments, and even below estimated "no-effect" concentrations for children (Zielhuis, 1975). As adults, acquisition of a brightness discrimination was retarded in rats exposed neonatally to lead, whether through the mother's milk or by direct injection. Those exposed during days 1–10 after birth were affected by the lowest doses; those exposed on days 11–21 showed a similar impairment only if their mothers received four times the dose that was effective during 1–10 days of age. No evidence of overt effects on growth, development, or activity level was found.

A similar discriminative deficit, labeled a "learning deficit," was inferred when lead-exposed rats ran on a lower proportion of trials in a two-way shuttle box, even in the presence of shock (Sobotka *et al.*, 1975). Although no overt signs of toxicity were observed, most psychologists would be reluctant to accept these results as evidence of impaired learning until many of the nonselective variables long known to influence shuttle-box acquisition are ruled out (e.g., Ray and Barrett, 1975).

A discrete-trial shock escape–avoidance, employing a bar-press response, was also used by Sobotka *et al.* (1975). The test employed both spatial and brightness cues. Although the lead-treated rats learned the original discrimination as rapidly as the controls, the lead group may have been unable to reverse the discrimination, as suggested by the increased rate of responding by lead-treated rats on the previously reinforced lever following reversal. Although this interesting finding merits further investigation, several ambiguities prevent a clear interpretation. First, the "reversal" procedure changed the spatial cue but retained the original visual brightness cue. This departure from conventional reversal procedures makes it difficult to ascertain whether the reversal is critical for the effect, and which discriminative variable was more important. More importantly, this analysis illustrates ambiguities in using response *rate* to assess learning of a discrete-trial discrimination, especially because rate and stimulus discrimination appear to be independent factors (Dinsmoor, 1951). Sobotka *et al.* (1975) appear to have pooled discriminative responses with "surplus" responses made between trials when responding had no consequences. It is difficult to interpret this aggregate response rate in terms of discrimination learning, particularly since both control and lead-treated rats made more surplus responses under the reversal situation. The conclusions were rendered even more puzzling when another laboratory reported effects opposite those of Sobotka *et al.*: a lead-induced impairment of initial discriminative learning but no effect upon subsequent reversals (Driscoll and Stegner, 1976).

Offspring of lead-exposed rats were slower than controls in acquiring a T-maze brightness discrimination and slower in a swimming test which required no discrimination (Brady *et al.,* 1975). A unique feature of this experiment was the inclusion of a group of rats whose only lead-exposed parent was the father. Since these offspring showed impairment identical to that shown by those whose mother or both parents were exposed, the results suggest an additional, indirect effect of lead upon behavior. These recent experiments with lead, plus those of Spyker with methylmercury (Spyker, 1975a,b), indicate lasting behavioral deficits that can be measured long after the blood and body concentrations of the metals have returned to normal.

Understanding of lead's effects upon learned behavior is not keeping pace with the accelerating number of publications. One of the most recent offers another permutation of previous findings. Pre- and neonatal exposure to lead produced inferior acquisition of a brightness discrimination and superior acquisition of shuttle avoidance, but had no effects upon discrimination reversal or activity levels (Driscoll and Stegner, 1976). A systematic investigation of both dose and behavioral parameters is needed to determine reliability and generality of these findings.

A dynamic transition state such as learning is one of the most difficult behavioral phenomena to identify and to quantify. Progress in defining subtle consequences of early exposure to lead requires the segregation of performance variables from "learning and memory." The maze and shuttle-box techniques, so popular in this field, can be influenced by many effects of lead that have no bearing upon "learning," for example, neuromuscular impairment (Silbergeld *et al.*, 1974), hyperactivity, and nutritional deficits reported to accompany early exposure to lead (Silbergeld and Goldberg, 1973, 1974, 1975; Michaelson and Sauerhoff, 1974; Golter and Michaelson, 1975) and sensory impairment (Carson *et al.*, 1974; Bushnell *et al.*, 1977), in addition to the multitude of changes encompassed by the term "motivation." Since reduced nutrition and growth restriction can affect a variety of learning scores as well as activity levels (Smart *et al.*, 1973) these variables require greater attention by behavioral toxicologists.

The above-mentioned reports of hyperactivity as a consequence of early exposure to lead have generated considerable interest, but have not yet been consistently replicated (Michaelson and Bornshein, personal communication). Effects upon activity may appear to be inconsistent because there has been little effort to identify and manipulate variables that influence the behavior of animals in activity cages. Motor activity can be studied and manipulated much like conditioned behavior (e.g., Evans, 1971a,b). A limitation of motor activity measures, well known to behavioral pharmacologists, is their lack of specificity. Inhalation of marijuana smoke (Luthra *et al.*, 1976), or carbon monoxide (Culver and Norton, 1976), or intracisternal injection of 6-hydroxydopamine (Shaywitz *et al.*, 1976) all produce hyperactivity, much like that reported following lead exposure. Furthermore, activity levels are influenced by environmental variables, including the amount of ambient light and noise (Sheffield and Campbell, 1954). Thus, hyperactivity in animals seems no more definitive than the subjective complaints described in surveys of humans.

It is difficult to relate the Western literature to Soviet studies of lead. The latter have involved chronic exposure. Representative behavioral findings are summarized by the National Academy of Sciences (1972).

4.3. Carbon Monoxide

Carbon monoxide (CO) occupies a unique position in behavioral toxicology. It is one of the few substances for which a behavioral result contributed to the exposure standards for environmental health in the United States; and it is a toxin for which a substantial portion of the experimental work has involved human subjects (Beard and Grandstaff, 1975; O'Hanlon, 1975; Stewart *et al.*, 1975; Teichner, 1975). The prominence of its central nervous system actions, coupled with the critical situations in which excessive exposure might occur, as in operating internal combustion engines, induced a great deal of CO research. The result is a voluminous, confusing literature.

A thorough review of the behavioral effects of CO revealed several recurrent problems in this area (National Academy of Sciences, 1977). The most striking was the preoccupation of recent researchers to match or exceed the landmark report of a decrement in time estimation or vigilance with concentrations of CO as low as 50 ppm (Beard and Wertheim, 1967). Frequently, the results were ambiguous because of inadequate behavioral expertise in arranging the methodological controls essential for complete replication. Another common problem has been the failure to demonstrate sensitivity and reliability of new tests; this could have been accomplished by showing clear results with higher doses of CO or by employing reference compounds. Another problem has been the inconsistent specification of the critical exposure parameter. Blood carboxyhemoglobin seems to provide a better biologic index of CO exposure than concentration in the air, but smokers and nonsmokers show marked differences in base lines, suggesting a tolerance phenomenon as a further complication. Since blood carboxy-hemoglobin is influenced by exposure duration as well as by CO concentrations, the reader is burdened with attempting to translate from one index to another in comparing experiments.

Johnson *et al.* (1975) used an animal approximation of the paradigm used with humans by Beard and Wertheim (1967). Even moderately high concentrations of CO (600 ppm) had no effect upon the monkey's time-estimation performance. The reference drug, chlorpromazine, also was effective only in fairly large doses. These results, plus those from studies with alcohol (Laties and Weiss, 1962), suggest that "timing" performance is not very sensitive to doses below those producing overt signs of toxicity.

Recent operant experiments with animals illustrate the value of first determining the effects of higher CO concentrations before seeking the more subtle effects of lower concentrations (Ator *et al.*, 1976; Merigan and McIntire, 1976), and the usefulness of familiar central nervous system drugs as probes to reveal otherwise unapparent effects (McMillan and Miller, 1974). Although these studies broke no new ground in terms of threshold concentrations, the systematic exploration of mechanisms influencing CO's actions can help improve the understanding and sensitivity of future tests. Behavioral research relating hypoxia and CO exposure has been reviewed recently (Annau, 1975).

4.4. Pesticides

The agricultural benefits formerly provided by chlorinated hydrocarbons (e.g., DDT) are now based upon organophosphorus compounds. Unfortunately, the change has not reduced the human health risk, at least in terms of behavioral and neurological toxicity, particularly among agricultural workers (Hunter, 1975; Wadia *et al.*, 1974). The toxic effects of organophosphates arise from their disruption of cholinergic mechanisms. Ironically, the organophosphates are structurally and pharmacologically related to a drug of clinical utility in the treatment of myasthenia gravis and glaucoma: diisopropylflurophosphonate (DFP), which also has been used as a research tool (Weiss and Heller, 1969; Russell *et al.*, 1975; Bignami *et al.*, 1975). During acute exposure to compounds of this type, behavioral change correlates well with indices of cholinesterase inhibition, but during prolonged exposure correlation is poor because of the differential degree of tolerance shown by the two variables (Clark, 1971; Reiter *et al.*, 1973; Russell *et al.*, 1975; Bignami *et al.*, 1975).

Too often the human clinical findings with pesticides are either obvious effects such as an inability to sit up, or vague, such as "emotional lability." We will not discuss further the human clinical studies; they are reviewed by Clark (1971) and by Hunter (1975). Animal experiments should continue to provide estimates of threshold limits as well as ideas about new classes of mild symptoms. Interest in this field has focused upon behavioral effects which might reflect specific CNS impairment in addition to more obvious peripheral, somatic signs of intoxication.

The potent organophosphate Arman was reported to produce parallel decrements in avoidance behavior and in brain cholinesterase activity in fish (Rosic and Lomax, 1974). The behavioral task required swimming through an unusual shuttle tank motivated by a mechanical device that dropped into the water and hit the fish if it failed to respond promptly. The limited results provide no indication as to whether the effect was a general reduction in swimming or a more specific decrement in the avoidance behavior. Additional work, from Eastern European laboratories, showing the effects of pesticides upon conditioned reflex behavior, is reviewed by Medved *et al.* (1964) and has been described briefly above.

Clark (1971) reviews additional studies, with rats, of shuttlebox and maze running. Here, the most consistent finding has been an increased number of trials required to extinguish the response. Many of the studies suffer from an overgeneralization of results, particularly since a prolongation of extinction is difficult to assess in qualitative terms of toxicity and because the phenomenon has not been related to any of the effects reported in humans.

The more familiar operant reinforcement schedules have been employed by Mertens and his associates in a series of studies of the pesticide Mevinphos. This compound reduced the response rates of gerbils, previously trained on variable-interval, fixed-ratio, or differential reinforcement of low rate schedules, but only at doses accompanied by overt toxic signs (Mertens *et al.*, 1975). Because lower doses reduced variable-interval response rates of pigeons without producing overt signs of toxicity (Mertens *et al.*, 1976), the authors concluded that the variable-interval schedule was more sensitive to Mevinphos than the other schedules. We suspect that the differential sensitivity is related to species rather than the schedule, since the rodent is known to be less sensitive to several anticholinergic drugs than the pigeon (Laties, 1972) or the primate (Evans, 1975).

Parathion, another organophosphorous pesticide, has been studied in several behavioral tests of sensory function with monkeys. The mean absolute auditory threshold was unchanged during a prolonged exposure, but the standard deviation of the threshold scores increased (Reischl *et al.*, 1975). Weak and variable results such as these may be real, and representative of threshold phenomenon. But should these results be considered a toxic effect in the context of health decisions? Interpretation of these results is unnecessarily complicated because of the use of two markedly different kinds of response to indicate the two choices in the discrimination. The monkey was required to press a lever when a tone was presented and to do nothing when it was not. Suppose that parathion changed the probability of occurrence of many behaviors, including lever pressing, a reasonable assumption from substantial experience with CNS drugs (see reviews by Sanger and Blackman, 1976; Kelleher and Morse, 1968). Such a change in response probability would, with the present method, change the proportion of trials on which the monkey does nothing (i.e., indicates "I don't hear anything"). Such a result would not necessarily reflect altered auditory sensitivity; a change in motivation could be an equally likely explanation. Forcing the monkey to actively select one of two levers, to indicate the presence or absence of the stimulus, would have permitted the calculation of the percentage of correct discriminations independently of changes in response probability. Then, no default choice need be inferred from a withheld response. This approach has been illustrated with methylmercury and with anticholinergic drugs (Evans, 1975; Evans *et al.*, 1975).

Acute doses of parathion abolished two-choice visual discrimination responding in macaques (Reiter *et al.*, 1975). Complete recovery usually required several days. Several factors suggest that visual processes probably were not involved in these results. Rather, the effect typifies that of other organophosphorus compounds, which increase the incidence of pauses (i.e., periods of no responding) which intrude into otherwise-normal streams of behavior (e.g., Mertens *et al.*, 1975). First, parathion reduced response probability without markedly changing the accuracy of discrimination. Second, several variants of the discrimination problem, each with different stimulus patterns, revealed no differential effect related to stimulus complexity or task difficulty, two factors that should bear some relationship to degree of sensory impairment, as will be discussed below. Third, the abolition of responding was accompanied by marked, nonvisual, toxic signs. Fourth, two reference drugs, scopolamine and methylscopolamine, both produced an abrupt cessation of responding similar to parathion. Involvement of the eye or the brain would be indicated by a marked difference in the effectiveness of the two drugs (for further discussion and examples, see Evans, 1975). Furthermore, scopolamine did not antagonize the effect of parathion, as would be predicted by the conventional neurochemical hypothesis. Additional failures of central anticholinergic drugs to show the predicted antagonism of organophosphates indicate the limitations of current neurochemical explanations of the behavioral effects.

Age at time of exposure has been a variable of interest to investigators of pesticide toxicity (Benke and Murphy, 1975; Harbison, 1975; Lu *et al.*, 1965). It is clear that the age of maximum susceptibility is not the same for all compounds. Thus, age is another variable that must be investigated, rather than trusted to either precedent or intuition.

4.5. Volatile Anesthetics and Solvents

This broad area contains some of the earliest work in behavioral toxicology with animals. Because of the great diversity of experimental agents and of behavioral techniques, we can offer only a sample of the findings. A solvent, trichlorethylene, has been studied extensively in rats. Conclusions vary with the behavioral tests. Following chronic exposure, a decrement in swimming performance was a more consistent finding than were changes in activity or maze learning (Battig and Grandjean, 1963). In contrast, a decline in activity was the main finding of Silverman and Williams (1975), who observed no selective changes in any of several categories of social behavior. Representative studies with carbon disulfide are described below (Levine, 1976; Goldberg *et al.*, 1964).

Many of these agents may function as reinforcers, when made available to primates in the drug self-administration paradigm (Yanagita *et al.*, 1970). The possibility of active, as well as passive, exposure increases the risk posed by these agents. Questions of voluntary exposure are particularly well suited to the behavioral scientist. Studies from our laboratory indicate that squirrel monkeys will button-press for toluene, a solvent (Weiss *et al.*, 1977), and for nitrous oxide, an anesthetic (Wood *et al.*, 1977). Studies of passive exposure to nitrous oxide have revealed effects upon analgesia and mental tasks in humans (Parkhouse *et al.*, 1960) and impaired visual discrimination in macaque monkeys (Jarvik and Adler, 1961). Early exposure to another anesthetic, halothane, produced later learning deficits and brain malformations in rats (Quimby *et al.*, 1974).

5. Factors That Modulate the Behavioral Effects of Toxins

Certain variables and basic behavioral mechanisms are emerging as important factors in behavioral toxicology. Some of them have already proved to be important in behavioral pharmacology. Manipulation and study of these variables can improve the basis for identifying underlying neuromechanisms and help to extrapolate animal results to humans. In both cases, parametric manipulation of important controlling variables will help separate inconsistencies from the strong generalities in the findings. Too many studies in behavioral toxicology have been purely descriptive, with neither an attack on underlying mechanisms nor a clear extrapolation to human health questions, a flaw shared by much of behavioral pharmacology. It is difficult to extract a general principle or an important conclusion from descriptions of "the effects of substance X upon the response rate under schedule Y in animal species Z." A third rationale recommends the examination of specific mechanisms of action: the toxicologist's need to assess threshold doses, as described above. A study of basic mechanisms is compatible with the search for the threshold dose. In fact, the evidence reviewed below indicates that understanding of the basic mechanisms will ultimately improve a behavioral test's sensitivity to low doses.

5.1. Diurnal Rhythms

Diurnal rhythms are fluctuations that follow the normal daily changes in illumination. If they cycle with a regular 24-hr frequency, they can be designated circadian rhythms. Many physiologic and pharmacologic mechanisms display diurnal cycles. It is not surprising that the effects of drugs and toxins may covary with the time of administration relative to the light–dark cycle (Reinberg and Halberg, 1971). Determinations of diurnal rhythms in toxicity may indicate time of increased risk and may provide clues about neural mechanisms involved in the behavioral results (e.g., Moore, 1973). Rats' mortality was considerably greater if a single dose of *d*-amphetamine was administered during the dark part of the day than if administered during the light (Scheving *et al.*, 1968). Amphetamine's toxic effect and the operant response-rate increasing effect may share a common mechanism, since both reveal a similar diurnal rhythm; drug effects on locomotor activity do not show this rhythm (Evans *et al.*, 1973).

5.2. Degree of Schedule Control

This concept emerged early in the modern era of behavioral pharmacology (e.g., Dews, 1956; Morse and Herrnstein, 1956). It accounts for the long-lasting interest in the multiple fixed-interval fixed-ratio reinforcement schedule, a frequently used procedure. Substantial evidence indicates that responding under the fixed-interval component is more responsive to drugs and a variety of chemicals than is responding under the alternate fixed-ratio component. A large number of additional studies employ one or more varieties of the reinforcement schedules explored so diligently by Ferster and Skinner (1957). These studies all involved repeated observation of individual animals that had been trained to perform prior to the administration of the experimental drug or chemical. Together, these procedures provide extremely stable behavioral base lines that are indispensable when one is concerned with threshold effects that necessarily are quite small.

Pigeons, while intoxicated with an acute dose of pentobarbital, showed a greater disruption of the rate and pattern of responding under the fixed-interval component than under the fixed-ratio component (Morse and Herrnstein, 1956). A similar selective effect is shown by a wide variety of central nervous system drugs (see other chapters in this volume). The consistency of this finding apparently reflects the fact that the fixed-interval schedule permits great variety of responding, with only the terminal response at the interval's end crucial for obtaining the reinforcement; in contrast, the ratio schedule counts each response, with a change in response rate causing a proportional change in the rate of reinforcement delivery. Computers have enabled a dissection of the constituent parts of ratio performance, identification of differential sensitivity to drugs of the components, and further characterization of the causes of the robust nature of ratio performance (Weiss and Gott, 1972; Evans *et al.*, 1975).

The multiple fixed-interval fixed-ratio schedule probably was first used in toxicology to examine the progressive consequences of mercury vapor exposure in pigeons (Armstrong *et al.*, 1963). Daily exposure to a rather high concentration of mercury vapor resulted in a gradual decline in the daily mean response rates. Unlike the effect of pentobarbital described above, this effect was largely the result of pausing that occurred with increasing frequency under both schedule components as exposure continued. The important point here is that even with the high concentration, these behavioral changes occurred several weeks prior to the appearance of overt toxic signs. When the changes in operant behavior became large, the pigeons were sacrificed for histopathologic study. There were no microscopically detectable lesions and, had this been a new chemical, the histopathological studies alone would have warranted the conclusion that the chemical was safe to pigeons at these concentrations.

Further assessment of much lower mercury vapor concentrations (at the threshold limit value) caused the authors of the study to conclude that the lower concentration had no effect upon multiple fixed-interval fixed-ratio performance (Beliles *et al.*, 1967). It has recently been pointed out that these results may have been confounded by a major procedural problem, base-line drift (see Figure 2 in Evans *et al.*, 1975). Since the one control bird showed a steady increase in fixed-interval curvature during the experiment, the observation that the mercury-treated birds remained at their preexposure curvature values may have indicated a real, but subtle, selective effect upon fixed-interval performance without any changes in the fixed-ratio performance.

A standard multiple fixed-interval fixed-ratio preparation was used in the Rochester laboratories to assess one of the most venerable toxins, carbon disulfide (CS_2). Its toxic properties, documented for over a century, converge on the central nervous system, leading to numerous psychologic disturbances and overt neurologic dysfunctions. There are few published reports (e.g., Goldberg *et al.*, 1964) upon which to base a comprehensive behavioral interpretation of the effects of CS_2. After having inhaled CS_2 for 4 hr (642 ppm), pigeons showed a selective decline in fixed-interval response rate; fixed-ratio performance tended to remain intact until exposures that virtually eliminated fixed-interval responding (Levine, 1976).

Generality for the importance of the degree of schedule control can be found beyond operant methods. DFP-treated rats were slower than controls in learning to run through a maze, if the only consequence of errors was a slight delay in completion of the maze (Richardson and Glow, 1967). However, learning was not affected if aversive stimuli were contingent upon errors. In reviewing Soviet studies of pesticides, Medved *et al.* (1964) conclude that "freshly produced" conditioned responses are especially revealing of subtle effects, compared with highly overtrained responses which, we assume, would have come under greater control of the schedule of experimental events.

Experiments with the differential reinforcement of low rate schedule illustrate another way in which schedule control of behavior, and the resulting base-line performance, must be considered carefully in interpreting behavioral effects of toxins. Levine (1976) required pigeons to space key pecks at intervals of at least 20 sec in order to obtain food. Under control conditions, the pigeon typically responds too frequently and only a small percentage of the interresponse times are sufficiently long to meet the criterion for reinforcement. As indicated above, exposure to CS_2 reduces average response rate. With the differential reinforcement of low rate base line, CS_2 reduced response rate and allowed the pigeons to obtain many more reinforcers than under control conditions. Mevinphos, an insecticide, had a similar effect upon differential reinforcement of low rate responding in gerbils (Mertens *et al.*, 1975). In both experiments, the differential reinforcement of low rate schedule presents a paradox to those attempting a qualitative assessment of changes in behavior in terms of toxicity: the "toxin" resulted in "improved" performance, as evidenced by an elevated frequency of reinforcement while under the influence of the toxin.

5.3. Discriminative Stimuli

Manipulations of the strength of discriminative stimuli revealed subtle visual impairment as the earliest signs of methylmercury intoxication in primates (Evans *et al.*, 1975; Berlin *et al.*, 1975). A visual discrimination test, devised in the present authors' laboratories, was planned to facilitate the distinction between sensory and nonsensory effects. We tried to make the discrimination procedure more informative than the customary two-choice paradigm by requiring the animals to choose from among three discriminative stimuli. This expanded the range of scores between perfect (100%) and chance (33% correct with three choices, but 50% correct with two choices). Similarly, the three response choices provide an expanded base line for identifying nonsensory factors such as response position bias (Evans, 1975). A quantal index of strength of the controlling stimuli was achieved by varying the luminance of the stimuli in steps, instead of in an all-or-none fashion as was customary in previous drug studies. The resultant psychometric functions can be used to estimate the strength of the stimulus control of behavior and relate this to a quantal property of the stimulus (Evans, 1975, 1977).

Visual discrimination under the control of weak stimuli (low luminance) was more vulnerable to disruption by toxins than similar discriminative behavior controlled by strong stimuli (high luminance). Figure 1 provides an illustration from our work with methylmercury. Impairment of discrimination with low luminance stimuli was the first sign to emerge during chronic methylmercury exposure (Evans *et al.*, 1975; Evans, 1977), in agreement with findings reported at the same time by Berlin *et al.*, (1975). Generality for the conclusion was obtained in acute studies with anticholinergic drugs as reference compounds (Evans, 1975). Discriminative accuracy with weak controlling stimuli was impaired by a dose of scopolamine one-fourth of that required to slightly impair accuracy with strong stimuli.

The utility of parametric determinations of stimulus strength is also illustrated in a preliminary report of a selective decrement in visual discrimination. Lead-exposed monkeys, which had been considered "normal" after showing no deficits under high illumination, showed a deficit when later tested under low illumination (Bushnell *et al.*, 1977). This effect of inorganic lead resembles that of methylmercury described above.

Strengthening stimulus control in an operant task with pigeons may improve performance degraded by methylmercury (Laties, 1975). Manipulating stimulus control showed that the toxic effect involved stimulus, rather than motor, mechanisms, since the pigeons' response patterns returned to base line following the addition of a strong discriminative stimulus. The effect of increasing stimulus strength thus resembles the effect of increasing schedule control, as illustrated above.

The evidence described above indicates two benefits in manipulating stimulus strength. First, it increases the sensitivity of the test to low doses and to early, otherwise covert effects in chronic exposure. Reviewers of Soviet toxicology have come to a similar conclusion (Medved *et al.*, 1964; Trakhtenberg, 1974). Second, manipulations of stimulus strength facilitate conclusions about specific sensory mechanisms, with nonsensory factors considered separately. For example, selective effects related to luminance argue against an influence of memory, motivation, or motor coordination, since none of these factors could account for the consistent differences related to the brightness of the stimuli (e.g., Evans, 1975).

5.4. Stimulus Complexity

Thus far, we have focused on the strength or intensity of stimuli as a predisposing factor in determining sensitivity to toxins. It may be profitable to consider other stimulus attributes, such as complexity and similarity of the discriminative stimuli, as additional predisposing factors. Together, strength and complexity of stimuli seem to account for much of what might be referred to as the "difficulty" of sensory tasks. Difficulty could be related to the rate of reinforcement under control conditions, that is, the percent of correct choices. Analyzed in this way, a two-choice visual size discrimination was more difficult and more vulnerable to lead exposure than were easier form discriminations (Carson *et al.*, 1974). Likewise, impairment of visual discrimination by DFP was generally correlated with difficulty, as defined by the number of errors made by the control group (Richardson and Glow, 1967).

Current work with methylmercury and visual discrimination is accumulating additional evidence. When stimulus strength (luminance) is held constant, discrimination of relatively complex stimuli (three stimuli of equal area but different shape) seems more vulnerable to disruption than discrimination of less complex stimuli (selection of the brightest of three stimuli without regard to shape). Our monkeys are tested equally often on both discrimination tasks. Psychophysical data from normal monkeys and humans, as well as from monkeys exposed to methylmercury, suggest an interesting interaction between strength and complexity of the stimuli. More evidence is found in studies of drug-induced sensory impairment reviewed by Laties (1975).

Rats showed impaired visual pattern discriminations after exposure to tellurium, although a simple brightness discrimination was not impaired (Dru *et al.*, 1972). Alcohol selectively impaired detection of both auditory (Moskowitz and DePry, 1968) and visual (Moskowitz and Sharma, 1973) stimuli only when the task complexity was increased. Replication of this work is described by Xintaras and Johnson (1976). However, seemingly analogous manipulations of task complexity did not increase the disruption of timing performance by alcohol (Laties and Weiss, 1962). Obviously, "task complexity" should be defined in more specific terms.

Behavioral toxicologists should consider these and other variables influencing task difficulty as of basic importance as well as of practical utility. Task difficulty may be a determinant of the behavioral effects of toxins as it has long been recognized as a determinant of impairment following brain lesions. Performance of a very easy task is refractory to lesions that are sufficient to eliminate performance of very difficult tasks (Lashley, 1929; Chow, 1967). Most psychologists are familiar with Lashley's efforts to identify behavioral impairment associated with removal of large areas of the rat's brain; he found that as much as one half of the brain could be removed without altering the rat's ability to solve some mazes. This work, summarized in Figure 4, illustrates that

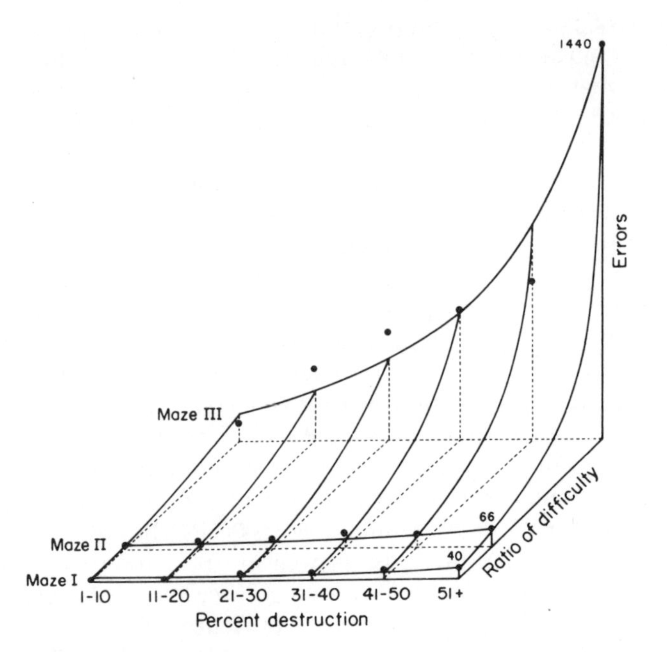

Figure 4. Importance of task difficulty in revealing impaired maze learning induced by brain lesions. Effects of moderate amounts of brain damage are revealed only by the most difficult task (maze III). Vast areas of the rat brain can be destroyed without greatly changing performance on easier tasks (mazes I and II). [From Lashley (1929).]

performance decrement is a joint function of task difficulty and the amount of brain damage, a 50-year-old fundamental principle that should be of utility to the fledgling discipline of behavioral toxicology.

6. Future Developments

The relatively brief history of behavioral toxicology, at least in the West, makes this chapter more a discussion of promise than of performance. Behavioral variables are destined for a key role, however, in environmental health, where adverse effects are increasingly defined in terms of subtle, long-term effects. Potential roles for behavioral studies can be illustrated by some recent, perhaps controversial issues.

6.1. Food Additives

Many natural constituents of food are toxic (Weiss *et al.*, 1975). They range from carcinogens, such as the aflatoxins found in peanuts, to the relative of LSD, the ergot alkaloids, often detected in grain and recently hypothesized to underlie the aberrant behavior that led to the Salem witch trials (Caporeal, 1976). The immense number of naturally occurring toxins represent a formidable challenge to contemporary food-processing technology. The dimensions of the challenge expand virtually beyond limit when exogenous chemicals are added to the list of potential toxins.

Behavioral evaluations of food additives became a sensitive issue with the claims by Feingold (1975) that a variety of natural and synthetic food consitutents, such as colors and flavors, may be responsible for a significant proportion of the population of so-called hyperactive children. Although detailed experimental data are still rare (see, for example, Connors *et al.,* 1976), the Feingold hypothesis is supported by many clinical observations.

The Feingold hypothesis underscored the rather narrow focus of toxicity testing, which does not routinely include functional and behavioral observations. As we indicated above, standard toxicity tests rely primarily upon lethality, longevity, and pathological findings from laboratory animals. It seems possible that microgram quantities of food additives could induce significant behavioral effects without leaving pathological traces, as do LSD and other drugs, for example. Documentation of effects such as these will provide an enduring role for behavioral toxicology.

6.2. Behavioral Teratology

Teratology traditionally has been the study of structural deformities induced by prenatal events or conditions. Only since the recent thalidomide episode has teratologic testing become an accepted routine in drug screening. Environmental agents such as the herbicide 2,4,5-T (agent orange) also are being implicated for their teratogenic potential.

A newer aspect of teratology, focused on function instead of structure, is now achieving prominence. Postnatal functional defects induced by prenatal exposures may range from aberrations expressed as metabolic disorders to deficits revealed mainly as behavioral abnormalities—hence the term, "behavioral teratology."

Werboff (1970) helped demonstrate the importance of prenatal chemical exposures by showing that the offspring of pregnant rats treated with CNS drugs performed differently on a variety of tests. Additional behavioral consequences of pre- and early postnatal exposure to CNS drugs have been reviewed by Bignami (1976). It was Spyker's work with methylmercury, however, that propelled behavioral teratology into a key role in environmental health concerns (Spyker,

1975a,b). By showing not only that prenatal exposures could induce subtle behavioral signs, but that these signs might not even be detectable until advanced age, she made it virtually impossible to ignore the place of both longitudinal and behavioral assessments in evaluations of toxicity. Such issues confront the experimenter not only with all the problems discussed previously under "chronicity," but with the challenge of designing tests optimally suited to the different stages of the life span.

6.3. Evaluations in the Natural Environment

Much of the information for exposure standards, as well as clues to unrecognized toxic potential, derives from epidemiologic research. As imprecise as such research may seem to the laboratory scientist, it is indispensable. Extrapolation from laboratory animals to human population is destined to remain an imperfect art, and no one would be prepared to disavow the contribution extracted from studies of humans *in vivo,* so to speak.

Behavioral science permits a greatly expanded scope for such studies. The kinds of subjective and objective measures that behavioral scientists are experienced in acquiring could be a vital supplement to the morbidity and mortality data that commonly constitute the epidemiologist's primary criteria.

The important task of assessing humans in their natural environment might profitably adopt the technology of applied behavioral analysis, which include methods for assessment in environments outside the laboratory (e.g., Fordyce, 1976). Barocas and Weiss (1974) indicated the relevance of this approach to provide the information demanded by the controversy over what constitutes a toxic body burden of lead. Techniques of applied behavioral analysis also could contribute to quantifying the alleged behavioral disruptions of certain food additives (see above), and to defining effects of atmospheric irritants such as photochemical smog in greater detail than the rate of absenteeism from school (Weiss, 1975).

6.4. Premarket Screening

It was observed in the Introduction that legislation such as the Toxic Substances Control Act would make more, perhaps all, new chemicals subject to mandatory premarket testing for adverse health effects. At least for some classes of substances, behavioral tests will provide either the prime or ancillary data for determination of health risk.

As in screening for therapeutic agents, some strategy has to be evolved to avert the hopeless situation of many parallel and expensive assays. One such strategy is to adopt a sequential scheme that proceeds through a series of increasingly specific, sensitive determinations, guided by the results of preceding, more general tests.

Figure 5 is a flow chart representing such a strategy for behavioral evaluation. After the traditional lethal doses are determined, screening for biologic effects usually begins with relatively simple assays capable

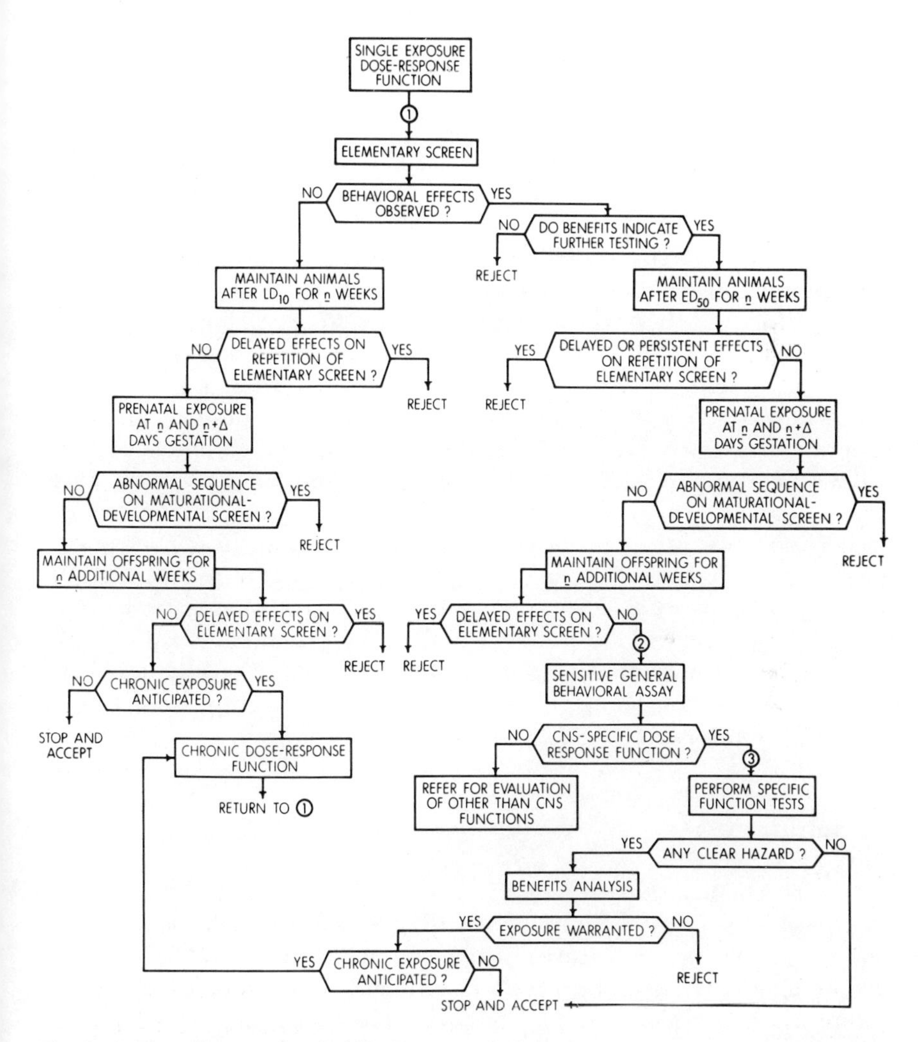

Figure 5. Flow diagram for decision sequence in behavioral toxicologic evaluation. For additional discussion, see National Academy of Sciences (1975).

of reflecting a broad range of impairments, including those related to CNS function. An indispensible step for toxicologic assessment is to determine whether delayed actions occur. Many toxic effects are first seen days or weeks after exposure; in the absence of immediate effects, the user could assume that the product is safe until exposure has continued to the point of severe risk. Developmental criteria serve a similar purpose, because of factors discussed under behavioral teratology.

Once CNS activity is discerned or suspected, either the substance is rejected because the risks exceed predicted benefits, or it is examined further if it appears to offer sufficient economic advantages or has the potential to displace an even more toxic agent. Branch points for such decisions are inserted at each successive step, of course.

CNS assessments focus on more specific mechanisms as they proceed from measurements of open-field behavior and motor activity to learned behaviors, such as shock escape and avoidance, to schedule-controlled operant behavior. The latter are useful for establishing dose–effect functions to guide more specific determinations of sensory impairment, disruptions of fine motor control, and other performances that reflect the efficacy of a circumscribed system. A similar hierarchy of testing can be observed in Soviet toxicology (Pavelenko, 1975).

Few novel agents will proceed in this idealized sequence, partly due to expense, partly due to the intrusion of other questions and considerations. No scheme now devised can possess enough inherent flexibility to encompass all conceivable variations. Still, such a scheme illustrates one of the most significant problems to confront behavioral toxicology: how is it possible to devise situations of sufficient sensitivity to detect adverse effects at low exposure levels, yet still permit them to be employed easily and inexpensively? The scope of this problem is quickly apprehended by asking whether methylmercury would have been denied a manufacturing license on the basis of conventional rodent screening tests alone. These issues are discussed at greater length in the National Academy of Sciences Report of 1975.

7. Summary

This chapter explored the origins of behavioral toxicology and compared this new discipline with its predecessor, behavioral pharmacology. Distinctive features of behavioral toxicology are its concern for qualitative evaluation, threshold estimates, and chronic exposures. These characteristics require a multidisciplinary approach. Substances of current interest in behavioral toxicology are mercury, lead, carbon monoxide, pesticides, and volatile agents. Behavioral toxicology appears to be playing a more influential role in the Soviet Union, although few detailed research reports are available.

The recent enactment of the Toxic Substances Control Act will increase the demand for behavioral assessment of potential toxicity. A protocol for premarket screening has been suggested, and we have emphasized the continuing importance of basic studies aimed at mechanisms of action. Fundamental variables such as diurnal rhythms, degree of schedule control, discriminative stimuli, and stimulus complexity modulate the behavioral effects of toxins; systematic manipulation of variables such as these will improve the sensitivity and reliability of behavioral tests. Future developments are likely to concern food additives, behavioral teratology, and procedures for behavioral evaluation in the natural environment.

ACKNOWLEDGMENTS

Supported in part by grants ES-01247 and ES-01248 from the U.S. National Institute of Environmental Health Sciences, MH-11752 from the National Institute of Mental Health, and by a contract with the U.S. Energy Research and Development Administration at the University of Rochester (Report UR-3490-1029).

8. References

Annau, Z., 1975, The comparative effects of hypoxic and carbon monoxide hypoxia on behavior, *in: Behavioral Toxicology* (B. Weiss and V. G. Laties, eds.), pp. 105–126, Plenum Press, New York.

Armstrong, R. D., Leach, L. J., Belluscio, P. R., Maynard, E. A., Hodge, H. C., and Scott, J. R., 1963, Behavioral changes in the pigeon following inhalation of mercury vapor, *Am. Ind. Hyg. Ass. J.* **24:**366–375.

Ator, N. A., Merigan, W. H., and McIntire, R. W., 1976, The effects of brief exposures to carbon monoxide on temporally differentiated responding, *Environ. Res.* **12:**81–91.

Avery, D. D., Cross, H. A., and Schroeder, T., 1974, The effects of tetraethyl lead on behavior in the rat, *Pharmacol. Biochem. Behav.* **2:**473–479.

Barnes, J. M., and Denz, F. A., 1954, Experimental methods used in determining chronic toxicity, *Pharmacol. Rev.* **6:**191–242.

Barocas, R., and Weiss, B., 1974, Behavioral assessment of lead intoxication in children, *Environ. Health Perspect.* **7:**47–52.

Battig, K., and Grandjean, E., 1963, Chronic effects of trichloroethylene on rat behavior, *Arch. Environ. Health.* **7:**694–699.

Beard, R. R., and Grandstaff, N. W., 1975, Carbon monoxide and human functions, *in: Behavioral Toxicology* (B. Weiss and V. G. Laties, eds.), pp. 1–25, Plenum Press, New York.

Beard, R. R., and Wertheim, G. A., 1967, Behavioral impairment associated with small doses of carbon monoxide, *Amer. J. Public Health.* **57:**2012–2022.

Beliles, R. P., Clark, R. S., Belluscio, P. R., Yuile, C. L., and Leach, L. J., 1967, Behavioral

effects in pigeons exposed to mercury vapor at a concentration of 0.1 mg/M^3, *Am. Ind. Hyg. Ass. J.* **28:**482–484.
Benke, G. M., and Murphy, S. D., 1975, The influence of age on the toxicity and metabolism of methylparathion and parathion in male and female rats, *Toxicol. Appl. Pharmacol.* **31:**254–269.
Berlin, M. J., Fazackerly, J., and Nordberg, G., 1969, The uptake of mercury in the brains of mammals exposed to mercury vapor and to mercuric salts, *Arch. Environ. Health* **18:**719–729.
Berlin, M., Grant, C. A., Hellberg, J., Hellstrom, J., and Schutz, A., 1975, Neurotoxicity of methylmercury in squirrel monkeys, *Arch. Environ. Health* **30:**340–348.
Berthoud, H. R., Garman, R. H., and Weiss, B., 1976, Food intake, body weight, and brain histopathology in mice following chronic methylmercury treatment, *Toxicol. Appl. Pharmacol.* **36:**19–30.
Bignami, G., 1976, Behavioral pharmacology and toxicology, *Ann. Rev. Pharmacol. Toxicol.* **16:**329–366.
Bignami, G., Rosic., N., Michalek, H., Milosevic, M., and Gatti, G. L., 1975, Behavioral toxicity of anticholinesterase agents: methodological, neurochemical, and neuropsychological aspects, *in: Behavioral Toxicology* (B. Weiss and V. G. Laties, eds.), pp. 155–210, Plenum Press, New York.
Blankenship, J. E., 1976, Tetrodotoxin: from poison to powerful tool, *Perspect. Biol. Med.* **19:**509–526.
Boffey, P. M., 1976, Color additives: botched experiment leads to banning of red dye No. 2, *Science* **191:**450–451.
Brady, K., Herrera, Y., and Zenick, H., 1975, The influence of parental lead exposure on subsequent learning ability of offspring, *Pharmacol. Biochem. Behav.* **3:**561–566.
Brown, D. R., 1975, Neonatal lead exposure in the rat: decreased learning as a function of age and blood lead concentrations, *Toxicol. Appl. Pharmacol.* **32:**628–637.
Brown, S., Dragann, N., and Vogel, W. H., 1971, Effects of lead acetate on learning and memory in rats, *Arch. Environ. Health.* **22:**370–372.
Burns, J. J., 1970, Species differences in drug metabolism and toxicological implications, *Proc. Eur. Soc. Study Drug Toxicity* **11:**9–13.
Bushnell, P. J., Bowman, R. E., Allen, J. R., and Marlar, R. J., 1977, Scotopic vision deficits in young monkeys exposed to lead, *Science* **196:**333–335.
Caporeal, L. R., 1976, Ergotism: the satan loosed in Salem? *Science* **192:**21–26.
Carson, T. L., Van Gelder, G. A., Karas, G. C., and Buck, W. B., 1974, Slowed learning in lambs prenatally exposed to lead, *Arch. Environ. Health.* **29:**154–156.
Chow, K. L., 1967, Effects of ablation, *in: The Neurosciences* (G. C. Quatron, T. Melnechuk, and F. D. Schmitt, eds.), pp. 705–713, Rockefeller University Press, New York.
Clark, G., 1971, Organophosphate insecticides and behavior, a review, *Aerospace Med.* **42:**735–740.
Connors, C. K., Goyette, C. H., Southwick, D. A., Lees, J. M., and Andrulonis, P. A., 1976, Food additives and hyperkinesis: a controlled double-blind experiment, *Pediatrics* **58:**154–166.
Crane, G. E., 1968, Tardive dyskinesia in patients treated with major neuroleptics: a review of the literature, *Amer. J. Psychiat.* **124:**41–48.
Culver, B., and Norton, S., 1976, Juvenile hyperactivity in rats after acute exposure to carbon monoxide, *Exp. Neurol.* **50:**80–98.
Cumming, W. W., and Schoenfeld, W. N., 1958, Some data on behavior reversibility in a steady state experiment, *J. Exp. Anal. Behav.* **1:**87–90.
David, O. J., Clark, J., and Voeller, K., 1972, Lead and hyperactivity, *Lancet* **2:**900–903.
David, O. J., Hoffman, S. P., Sverd, J., Clark, J., and Voeller, K., 1976, Lead and hy-

peractivity. Behavioral response to chelation: a pilot study, *Amer. J. Psychiat.* **133:**1155–1158.

Dews, P. B., 1956, Modification by drugs of performance on simple schedules of positive reinforcement, *Ann. N.Y. Acad. Sci.* **65:**268–281.

Dinman, B. D., 1972, "Non-concept" of "no-threshold": chemicals in the environment, *Science* **175:**495–497.

Dinsmoor, J. A., 1951, The effect of periodic reinforcement of bar-pressing in the presence of a discriminative stimulus, *J. Comp. Physiol. Psychol.* **44:**354–361.

Driscoll, J. W., and Stegner, S. E., 1976, Behavioral effects of chronic lead ingestion on laboratory rats, *Pharmacol. Biochem. Behav.* **4:**411–417.

Dru, D., Agnew, W. F., and Greene, E., 1972, Effects of tellurium ingestion on learning capacity of the rat, *Psychopharmacologia* **24:**508–515.

Druckery, H., 1967, Quantitative aspects of chemical carcinogenesis, *in: Potential Carcinogenic Hazards from Drugs* (*Evaluation of Risks*) (R. Truhart, ed.), UICC Monograph Series, pp. 60–78, Springer-Verlag, New York.

Eibergen, R. D., and Carlson, K. R., 1975, Dyskinesias elicited by methamphetamine: susceptibility of former methadone-consuming monkeys, *Science* **190:**588–590.

Evans, H. L., 1971a, Behavioral effects of methamphetamine and α-methyl-tyrosine in the rat, *J. Pharmacol. Exp. Ther.* **176:**244–254.

Evans, H. L., 1971b, Rats' activity: influence of light–dark cycle, food presentation, and deprivation, *Physiol. Behav.* **7:**455–459.

Evans, H. L., 1975, Scopolamine effects on visual discrimination: modifications related to stimulus control, *J. Pharmacol. Exp. Ther.* **195:**105–113.

Evans, H. L., 1977 (in press), Early methylmercury signs revealed in visual tests, *in: International Conference on Heavy Metals in the Environment* (1975), Proceedings, Vol. 3 (T. C. Hutchinson, ed.), University of Toronto Institute of Environmental Studies, Toronto.

Evans, H. L., Ghiselli, W. B., and Patton, R. A., 1973, Diurnal rhythm in behavioral effects of methamphetamine, *p*-chloromethamphetamine, and scopolamine, *J. Pharmacol. Exp. Ther.* **186:**10–17.

Evans, H. L., Laties, V. G., and Weiss, B., 1975, Behavioral effects of mercury and methylmercury, *Fed. Proc.* **34:**1858–1867.

Evans, H. L., Garman, R. H., and Weiss, B., 1977, Methylmercury: exposure duration and regional distribution as determinants of neurotoxicity in nonhuman primates, *Toxicol. Appl. Pharmacol.* **41:**15–33.

Feingold, B. F., 1975, *Why Is Your Child Hyperactive?* Random House, New York.

Ferster, C. B., and Skinner, B. F., 1957, *Schedules of Reinforcement,* Appleton-Century-Crofts, New York.

Fischman, M. W., and Schuster, C. R., 1975, Behavioral, biochemical, and morphological effects of methamphetamine in the rhesus monkey, *in: Behavioral Toxicology* (B. Weiss and V. G. Laties, eds.), pp. 375–395, Plenum Press, New York.

Fitzpatrick, W. H., 1974, Soviet Research in Pharmacology and Toxicology, 1963–1972, U. S. Department of Health, Education, and Welfare, Publ. NIH-75-696.

Fordyce, W. E., 1976, *Behavioral Methods for Chronic Pain and Illness,* C. V. Mosby, St. Louis.

Franklin, B., 1786, Reprint of letter to Benjamin Vaughan, *Med. Affairs* Sept. 1965: 26–27.

Garcia, J., Hankins, G., and Rusiniak, K., 1974, Behavioral regulation of milieu interne in man and rat, *Science* **185:**824–831.

Garman, R. H., Weiss, B., and Evans, H. L., 1975, Alkylmercurial encephalopathy in the monkey (*Saimiri sciureus* and *Macaca arctoides*), *Acta Neuropathol.* **32:**61–74.

Goldberg, M. E., Johnson, H. E., Possani, U. C., and Smyth, H. F., Jr., 1964, Behavioral response of rats during inhalation of tricholorethylene and carbon disulphide vapours, *Acta Pharmacol. Toxicol.* **21:**36–44.

Golter, M., and Michaelson, I. A., 1975, Growth, behavior, and brain catecholamines in lead-exposed neonatal rats: a reappraisal, *Science* **187:**359–361.

Grigor'ev, Z. E., 1955, Effect of volatile substances and of gases on the higher nervous activity of white rats in the course of inhalation exposure, *Farmakol. i Toksikol.* **18:**49–52.

Harbison, R. D., 1975, Comparative toxicity of some selected pesticides in neonatal and adult rats, *Toxicol. Appl. Pharmacol.* **32:**443–446.

Hardman, H. F., Haavik, C. O., and Seevers, M. H., 1973, Relationship of the structure of mescaline and seven analogs to toxicity and behavior in five species of laboratory animals, *Toxicol. Appl. Pharmacol.* **25:**299–309.

Harvey, J. A., McMaster, S. E., and Yunger, L. M., 1975, *p*-Chloramphetamine: selective neurotoxic action in brain, *Science* **187:**841–843.

Horváth, M., and Frantík, E., 1973, Quantitative interpretation of experimental toxicological data: the use of reference substances, *in: Adverse Effects of Environmental Chemicals and Psychotropic Drugs: Quantitative Interpretation of Functional Tests* (M. Horváth, ed.), Vol. 1, pp. 11–19, Elsevier, Amsterdam.

Hunter, D., 1975, *The Diseases of Occupations,* 5th ed., English Universities Press, London.

Hunter, D., Bomford, R. R., and Russell, D. S., 1940, Poisoning by methylmercury compounds, *Quart. J. Med.* **9:**193–213.

Jarvik, M. E., and Adler, M. W., 1961, Nature of efficiency decrement produced by nitrous oxide on monkeys in a visual discrimination and delayed response test, *J. Pharmacol. Exp. Ther.* **131:**108–114.

Johnson, B. L., Anger, W. K., Setzer, J. V., and Xintaras, C., 1975, The application of a computer-controlled time discrimination performance to problems in behavioral toxicology, *in: Behavioral Toxicology* (B. Weiss and V. G. Laties, eds.), pp. 129–151, Plenum Press, New York.

Kelleher, R. T., and Morse, W. H., 1968, Determinants of the specificity of behavioral effects of drugs, *Ergeb. Physiol. Biol. Chem. Exp. Pharmakol.* **60:**1–56.

Kety, S. S., 1956, Human cerebral blood flow and oxygen consumption as related to aging, *Res. Publ. Ass. Nervous Mental Dis.* **35:**31–45.

Klein, M. C., Sayre, J. W., and Kotok, D., 1974, Lead poisoning: current status of the problem facing pediatricians, *Amer. J. Dis. Children* **127:**805–807.

Lashley, K. S., 1929, *Brain Mechanisms and Intelligence,* University of Chicago Press, Chicago.

Laties, V. G., 1972, The modification of drug effects on behavior by external discriminative stimuli, *J. Pharmacol. Exp. Ther.* **183:**1–13.

Laties, V. G., 1973, On the use of reference substances in behavioral toxicology, *in: Adverse Effects of Environmental Chemicals and Psychotropic Drugs: Quantitative Interpretation of Functional Tests* (M. Horváth, ed.), Vol. 1, pp. 83–88, Elsevier, Amsterdam.

Laties, V. G., 1975, The role of discriminative stimuli in modulating drug action, *Fed. Proc.* **34:**1880–1888.

Laties, V. G., and Weiss, B., 1962, Effects of alcohol on timing behavior, *J. Comp. Physiol. Psychol.* **55:**85–91.

Levine, T., 1976, Effects of carbon disulfide and FLA-63 on operant behavior in pigeons, *J. Pharmacol. Exp. Ther.* **199:**669–678.

Lin, F. M., Malaiyandi, M., and Romero-Sierra, C., 1975, Toxicity of methylmercury: effects on different ages of rats, *Bull. Environ. Contam. Toxicol.* **14:**140–148.

Lin-Fu, J. S., 1973, Vulnerability of children to lead exposure and toxicity (two parts), *New Engl. J. Med.* **289:**1224–1233, 1289–1293.

Lu, F. C., Jessup, D. C., and Lavallee, A., 1965, Toxicity of pesticides in young versus adult rats, *Food Cosmet. Toxicol.* **3:**591–596.

Luthra, Y. K., Rosenkrantz, H., and Braude, M. C., 1976, Cerebral and cerebellar neurochemical changes and behavioral manifestations in rats chronically exposed to marijuana smoke, *Toxicol. Appl. Pharmacol.* **35:**455–465.

McGaugh, J. L., and Petrinovich, L. F., 1965, Effects of drugs on learning and memory, *Int. Rev. Neurobiol.* **8:**139–196.

McMillan, D. E., and Miller, A. T., Jr., 1974, Interactions between carbon monoxide and d-amphetamine or pentobarbital on schedule-controlled behavior, *Environ. Res.* **8:**53–63.

Medved, L. I., Spynu, E. I., and Kagan, I. S., 1964, The method of conditioned reflexes in toxicology and its application for determining the toxicity of small quantities of pesticides, *Residue Rev.* **6:**42–74.

Merigan, W. H., and McIntire, R. W., 1976, Effects of carbon monoxide on responding under a progressive ratio schedule in rats, *Physiol. Behav.* **16:**407–412.

Mertens, H. W., Steen, J., and Lewis, M. F., 1975, The effects of mevinphos on appetitive operant behavior in the gerbil, *Psychopharmacologia* **41:**47–52.

Mertens, H. W., Steen, J. A., and Lewis, M. F., 1976, Some behavioral effects of pesticides: the interaction of mevinophos and atropine in pigeons, *Aviat. Space Environ. Med.* **47:**137–141.

Michaelson, I. A., and Sauerhoff, M. W., 1974, An improved model of lead-induced brain disfunction in the suckling rat, *Toxicol. Appl. Pharmacol.* **28:**88–96.

Moore, M. C., 1973, Circadian rhythms of drug effectiveness and toxicity, *Clin. Pharmacol. Ther.* **14:**925–935.

Morse, W. H., and Herrnstein, R. J., 1956, Effects of drugs on characteristics of behavior maintained by complex schedules of intermittent positive reinforcement, *Ann. N.Y. Acad. Sci.* **65:**303–317.

Moskowitz, H., and DePry, D., 1968, The effect of alcohol upon auditory vigilance and divided attention tasks, *Quart. J. Stud. Alc.* **29:**54–63.

Moskowitz, H., and Sharma, S., 1973, Effect of alcohol on the visual autokinetic phenomenon, *Percept. Mot. Skills* **36:**801–802.

National Academy of Sciences, 1972, *Lead: Airborne Lead in Perspective,* National Academy of Sciences, Washington, D.C.

National Academy of Sciences, 1975, *Principles for Evaluating Chemicals in the Environment,* National Academy of Sciences, Washington, D.C.

National Academy of Sciences, 1977, *Carbon Monoxide,* National Academy of Sciences, Washington, D.C.

Neal, P. A., Flinn, R. H., Edwards, T. I., Reinhart, W. H., Hough, J. W., Dallavalle, J. M., Goldman, F. H., Armstrong, D. W., Gray, A. S., Coleman, A. L., and Postman, B. F., 1941, Mercurialism and its control in the felt-hat industry, *U.S. Public Health Bull.* 263.

O'Hanlon, J. F., 1975, Preliminary studies of the effects of carbon monoxide on vigilance in man, *in: Behavioral Toxicology* (B. Weiss and V. G. Laties, eds.), pp. 61–71, Plenum Press, New York.

Ohrbach, J., and Fantz, R. L., 1958, Differential effects of temporal neo-cortical resections on overtrained and non-overtrained visual habits in monkeys, *J. Comp. Physiol. Psychol.* **51:**126–129.

Parkhouse, J., Henrie, J. R., Duncan, G. M., and Rome, H. P., 1960, Nitrous oxide analgesia in relation to mental performance, *J. Pharmacol. Exp. Ther.* **128:**44–54.

Pavelenko, S. M., 1975, Methods for the study of the central nervous system in toxicological tests, *in: Methods Used in the U.S.S.R. for Establishing Biologically Safe Levels of Toxic Substances,* pp. 86–108, World Health Organization, Geneva.

Quimby, K. L., Aschkenase, L. J., Bowman, R. E., Katz, J. K., and Chang, L. W., 1974, Enduring learning deficits and cerebral synaptic malformation from exposure to 10 parts of halothane per million, *Science* **185:**625–627.

Radinsky, L., 1975, Primate brain evolution, *Amer. Scientist* **63:**656–663.

Ray, O. S., and Barrett, R. J., 1975, Behavioral, pharmacological, and biochemical analysis of genetic differences in rats, *Behav. Biol.* **15:**391–417.

Reinberg, A., and Halberg, F., 1971, Circadian chronopharmacology, *Ann. Rev. Pharmacol.* **11:**455–492.

Reischl, P., van Gelder, G. A., and Karas, G. G., 1975, Auditory detection behavior in parathion-treated squirrel monkeys, *Toxicol. Appl. Pharmacol.* **34:**88–101.

Reiter, L., Talens, G., and Woolley, D., 1973, Acute and subacute parathion treatment: effects on cholinesterase activities and learning in mice, *Toxicol. Appl. Pharmacol.* **25:**582–588.

Reiter, L., Talens, G., and Woolley, D., 1975, Parathion administration in the monkey: time course of inhibition and recovery of blood cholinesterases and visual discrimination performance, *Toxicol. Appl. Pharmacol.* **33:**1–13.

Richardson, A. J., and Glow, P. H., 1967, Discrimination behavior in rats with reduced cholinesterase activity, *J. Comp. Physiol. Psychol.* **63:**240–246.

Rosic, N., and Lomax, P., 1974, The toxic and behavioral effects of a cholinesterase inhibitor in fish (*Serranus scriba*), *Comp. Gen. Pharmacol.* **5:**187–189.

Russell, R. W., Overstreet, D. H., Cotman, C. W., Carson, V. G., Churchill, L., Dalglish, F. W., and Vasquez, B. J., 1975, Experimental tests of the hypotheses about neurochemical mechanisms underlying behavioral tolerance to the anticholinesterase, diisopropyl fluorophosphate, *J. Pharmacol. Exp. Ther.* **192:**73–85.

Sanger, D. J., and Blackman, D. E., 1976, Rate-dependent effects of drugs: a review of the literature, *Pharmacol. Biochem. Behav.* **4:**73–83.

Scheving, L. E., Vedral, D. F., and Pauly, J. E., 1968, Daily circadian rhythm in rats to *d*-amphetamine sulphate: effect of blinding and continuous illumination on the rhythm, *Nature* **219:**621–622.

Schoenfeld, R. I., and Uretsky, N. J., 1973, Enhancement by 6-hydroxydopamine of the effects of dopa upon the motor activity of rats, *J. Pharmacol. Exp. Ther.* **186:**616–624.

Shaywitz, B. A., Yager, R. D., and Klopper, J. H., 1976, Selective brain dopamine depletion in developing rats: an experimental model of minimal brain dysfunction, *Science* **191:**305–308.

Sheffield, F. D., and Campbell, B. A., 1954, The role of experience in the "spontaneous" activity of hungry rats, *J. Comp. Physiol. Psychol.* **47:**97–100.

Silbergeld, E. K., and Goldberg, A. M., 1973, A lead-induced behavioral disorder, *Life Sci.* **13:**1375–1383.

Silbergeld, E. K., and Goldberg, A. M., 1974, Lead-induced behavioral dysfunction: an animal model of hyperactivity, *Exp. Neurol.* **142:**46–157.

Silbergeld, E. K., and Goldberg, A. M., 1975, Pharmacological and neurochemical investigation of lead-induced hyperactivity, *Neuropharmacology* **14:**431–444.

Silbergeld, E. K., Fales, J. T., and Goldberg, A. M., 1974, The effects of inorganic lead on the neuromuscular junction, *Neuropharmacology* **13:**795–801.

Silverman, A. P., and Williams, H., 1975, Behaviour of rats exposed to trichloroethylene, *Brit. J. Ind. Med.* **32:**308–315.

Smart, J. L., Dobbing, J., Adlard, B. P. F., Lynch, A., and Sands, J., 1973, Vulnerability of developing brain: relative effects of growth restriction during the fetal and suckling periods on behavior and brain composition of adult rats, *J. Nutr.* **103:**1327–1338.

Snowdon, C. T., 1973, Learning deficits in lead-injected rats, *Pharmacol. Biochem. Behav.* **1:**599–603.

Sobotka, T. J., Brodie, R. E., and Cook, M. P., 1975, Psychophysiologic effects of early lead exposure, *Toxicology* **5:**175–191.

Spyker, J. M., 1975a, Behavioral teratology and toxicology, *in: Behavioral Toxicology* (B. Weiss and V. G. Laties, eds.), pp. 311–344, Plenum Press, New York.

Spyker, J. M., 1975b, Assessing the impact of low level chemicals on development: behavioral and latent effects, *Fed. Proc.* **34:**1835–1844.

Stebbins, W. C., ed., 1970, *Animal Psychophysics: The Design and Conduct of Sensory Experiments,* Appleton-Century-Crofts, New York.

Stebbins, W. C., and Coombs, S., 1975, Behavioral assessment of ototoxicity in nonhuman primates, *in: Behavioral Toxicology* (B. Weiss and V. G. Laties, eds.), pp. 401–428, Plenum Press, New York.

Stewart, R. D., Newton, P. E., Hosko, M. J., Peterson, J. E., and Mellender, J. W., 1975, The effect of carbon monoxide on time perception, manual coordination, inspection, and arithmetic, *in: Behavioral Toxicology* (B. Weiss and V. G. Laties, eds.), pp. 29–55, Plenum Press, New York.

Teichner, W. H., 1975, Carbon monoxide and human performance: a methodological exploration, *in: Behavioral Toxicology* (B. Weiss and V. G. Laties, eds.), pp. 77–102, Plenum Press, New York.

Trakhtenberg, I. M., 1974, *Chronic Effects of Mercury on Organisms* (English translation), Publ. (NIH) 74-473 of Department of Health, Education, and Welfare, Washington, D.C.

Wadia, R. S., Sadogopan, C., Amin, R. B., and Sardesai, H. V., 1974, Neurological manifestations of organophosphorous insecticide poisoning, *J. Neurol. Neurosurg. Psychiat.* **37:**841–847.

Weiss, B., 1975, Long-term behavioral consequences of exposure to drugs and pollutants, *in: Alcohol, Drugs, and Brain Damage* (J. G. Rankin, ed.), pp. 71–79, Alcoholism and Drug Addiction Research Foundation of Ontario, Toronto.

Weiss, B., and Gott, C. T., 1972, A microanalysis of drug effects on fixed-ratio performance in pigeons, *J. Pharmacol. Exp. Ther.* **180:**189–202.

Weiss, B., and Heller, A., 1969, Methodological problems in evaluating the role of cholinergic mechanisms in behavior, *Fed. Proc.* **28:**135–146.

Weiss, B., and Laties, V. G., 1969, Behavioral pharmacology and toxicology, *Ann Rev. Pharmacol.* **9:**297–326.

Weiss, B., and Simon, W., 1975, Quantitative perspectives on the long-term toxicity of methylmercury and similar poisons, *in: Behavioral Toxicology* (B. Weiss and V. G. Laties, eds.), pp. 429–438, Plenum Press, New York.

Weiss, B., Wood, R. W., and Macys, D. A., 1977 (in press), Behavioral toxicology of carbon disulfide and toluene. *Environ. Health Perspect.*

Werboff, J., 1970, Developmental psychopharmacology, *in: Principles of Psychopharmacology* (W. G. Clark and J. del Giudice, eds.) pp. 343–354, Academic Press, New York.

Wood, R. W., Weiss, A. B., and Weiss, B., 1973, Hand tremor induced by industrial exposure to inorganic mercury, *Arch. Environ. Health* **26:**249–252.

Wood, R. W., Grubman, J., and Weiss, B., 1977, Nitrous oxide self-administration by the squirrel monkey, *J. Pharmacol. Exp. Ther.* **202:**491–500.

Xintaras, C., and Johnson, B. L., 1976, Behavioral toxicology: early warning and worker safety and health, *Essays Toxicol.* **7:**155–201.

Yanagita, T., Takahashi, S., Ishida, K., and Funamoto, H., 1970, Voluntary inhalation of volatile anesthetics and organic solvents by monkeys, *Jap. J. Clin. Pharmacol.* **1:**13–16.

Zenz, C., 1975, *Occupational Medicine,* Year Book, Chicago.

Zielhuis, R. L., 1975, Dose–response relationships for inorganic lead, *Int. Arch. Occup. Health.* **35:**19–35.

Author Index

Boldface page numbers indicate a chapter in this volume.

Subject Index